THE FELIX CHRONICLES

FRESHMEN

BY R.T. LOWE

Cover design by Jenny Zemanek

Interior formatting by Amy Eye: The Eyes for Editing

ISBN-13: 978-1511958431

ISBN-10: 151195843X

For Mell

My sweetest friend.

PROLOGUE

(A.D. 336)

Chapter 1

THE WARNING

Hosius should have died on the day of his birth. Nature was to blame—even though it was his father who had tried to kill him. The unfortunate infant was never given a chance, as it was his father's right—his obligation—to expose the deformed child on the foothills to the north where the elements would remedy the mistake if the birds and wild dogs didn't do so first. Enraged at the sight of Hosius's writhing, crippled form, his father had snatched him from his mother's exhausted arms and dragged him out of the house by the wrist, his tiny feet staining the floor red with his mother's blood. But before his father could consummate the act of mercy, a strange thing happened. As they emerged into the bright midday sunshine, his father was struck dead. As for the newborn Hosius, he was found unharmed a short while later and returned to the comfort of his waiting mother.

His first brush with mortality had come even before his eyes fluttered open to take in the world around him. There had been many since, but it was always the first that he pondered at times like this, when the risk of death—*a violent, painful death*—awaited him within the hour.

Hosius calmed his thoughts, centering himself in the present as he struggled up the winding path to the castle. Soon, the north entrance, and the guards manning it, came into view. They pointed in his direction, and then came the laughter, rolling over him like thunder. Not even disinterested observers failed to notice Hosius's deformities; one leg was much shorter than the other, and his left arm ended at the elbow. No forearm, wrist, hand or fingers, and he didn't try to conceal it; his shirt was cut to the proper length and closed up with leather ties. He was also short and slight, not much larger than a boy of twelve or thirteen. He was able to walk without an aid, but his limp was severe, and to some people, like the guards, his awkward gait was cause for merriment. And barbs: "gimp" and "cripple" greeted him as he approached.

Hosius chuckled along stupidly with the bored guards, pretending to enjoy the same insults that had callused his ears as a child. When one of the heavily-armed brutes gave him a stiff shove, he toppled right over (necessary for the gaping onlookers to appreciate the full effect of the gag) and burst out in squalls of laughter as if he derived great joy from the man's stunted sense of humor. When they were done with him—after the usual jokes had run their tired course and they'd resorted to making light of his tattered clothes and his old man's tangled white beard—he heaped thanks on them for letting him enter the castle in the same way a slave thanks his master for not beating him when his master catches him eating scraps off the floor. But in the back of his mind, Hosius was planning for their next meeting. If he survived to see nightfall he would return. And when he did, he would pay the men his compliments in a much different manner. Hosius had never been the forgiving type.

The courtyard was chaotic, a place where sights, sounds and smells all came together to overwhelm the senses in an intoxicating (and slightly nauseating) rush. Hosius blended in with the sea of shuffling feet, allowing the waves of mayhem to wash over him. Merchants, money changers and peddlers of every good imaginable competed for the attention of soldiers, travelers, toilers from the countryside and haggard waifs uprooted by war and famine. Loud disgruntled animals—horses, fat-uddered goats, unshorn sheep, and chickens—huddled together in cramped enclosures in the shade of the towering stone walls.

He made his way to the west side of the ancient castle where the distant dull blue waters of Lake Iznik were visible in the distance and the sickly-sweet odor of animal dung mingling with flowering plants and cooking meats no longer permeated the air. The people gathered here were very different than those in the courtyard. Servants carrying wine and serving plates piled with savory herb breads and luscious figs dripping with honey scampered among clusters of finely dressed foreign dignitaries and lords great and small. The important people paid no attention to Hosius, although one held out an empty chalice at him and said something in an unfamiliar language that most likely meant "more wine."

The crowds thinned. The voices dimmed, and then faded away, and he was left alone with the cold stare of the lake and the punishing weight of a blazing sun. The heat was unbearable. Hosius could tolerate just about anything—even the flashing pain that streaked up and down his bad leg— but he wasn't immune to the conditions, and pinpricks of sweat clung to his olive skin like a swarm of blood-starved ticks as he arrived at an arched doorway carved out of a stone wall set well within the outer fortifications.

He stopped to catch his breath, and nearly gagged on the incense and perfumes saturating the air. It may have been tantalizing to some, but Hosius, whose tastes were simple (*unrefined* some might say), found it cloying and self-indulgent. His eyes scoured the room before him, assimilating everything in an instant. It was cavernous. And opulently appointed—*to frivolous excess*, Hosius would argue, if anyone sought his opinion on the matter. Mosaics, bold and bright, splashed across the floor. Vivid frescos and gold-framed paintings adorned the walls. On one side of the room, just off the entrance, a pair of marble busts, one of Venus, the other of Apollo, flanked a dining table and lounging couch. Eight square backless stools, each made of bronze, and ornamented with silver and gold leaf, surrounded the table. On top, a large hammered silver tray overflowed with fresh fruit. And in the back of the room, a giant marble bust of Emperor Constantine dominated the space from its perch atop a tall pedestal. Oil lamps—perfumed oil, which contributed to the throat-clenching muskiness—burned on stands that lined the walls, lighting the room.

He found the governor of Caesarea—the man he was looking for—standing beside the bust of Apollo embroiled in a heated discussion with six men wearing identical tunics, dusty brown and bejeweled. He was easy to spot. The governor—Eusebius—was a giant. And the men he was speaking with were cut from the same cloth: soft, pale and plump with an air of self-entitled contentment. That meant they could only be bureaucrats.

Bureaucrats.

It took some effort for Hosius to resist a smile because his chances of survival had just increased a hundredfold.

But Eusebius was no bureaucrat. His proportions were immense. A head taller than the next tallest man in the room, he was wide at the waist and shoulders and slightly hunchbacked, his features frighteningly hawk-like: a large hooked nose, leather-colored skin, and an Adam's apple the size of a child's fist. He wore an intricately decorated dark-blue tunic and an elaborate headdress that heightened the impression that he was an enormous bird of prey.

Hosius's arrival didn't elicit a reaction. He cleared his throat. Nothing. He did it again. This time louder, yet still no response from the governor, though one man—fat, purple-faced, and sweating through his tunic as he struggled to catch his breath—cast a haughty glance toward the doorway as if to say *go find someone else to throw you a moldy piece of bread, you filthy beggar!*

"*Lord* Eusebius," Hosius said, with emphasis on *Lord*, which the governor could construe as a show of respect, or sarcastic baiting. Hosius hoped for the latter.

Eusebius kept his eyes on the bureaucrats, his thin lips barely moving when he spoke. "Hosius. It's so good to see you." His clipped tone indicated otherwise. "I wasn't expecting to see you so soon. What brings you to Nicea?"

"A simple act of carelessness can sometimes have far-reaching consequences." Hosius entered the room, stepping past wine-filled amphorae stacked against the wall on either side of the doorway. The air inside was heavy and hot. No draft. "I've been told you misplaced something that belongs to the Emperor. A certain book."

Eusebius turned deliberately toward Hosius, then folded his arms across his thick chest. "Ahhhh... yes. About that..."

"Leave us!" Hosius demanded, tilting his head at the man still gasping for air; his tremendous girth (his neck was wreathed in rolls of fat that wriggled over his collar, pulling down on his chin and parting his lips) identified him as the highest ranking member of the governor's delegation.

The man's face reddened in sudden anger and he began to breathe even harder.

"Shall I summon the guards, my lord?" a man with hair cropped close to his skull asked the governor.

Eusebius didn't answer, his narrowed eyes unmoving.

"Now!" Hosius repeated. "Go to your sleeping quarters. You'll be reunited with the governor soon enough."

The fat man started for Hosius and said primly, "Guards won't be necessary. I'll dispose of this trespassing peasant myself." He settled his smug gaze on Hosius and added: "I'll teach you to respect your superiors, worm. In the presence of Eusebius, you bow your—"

"Shut up you imbecile!" Eusebius snapped at the man.

The man stopped, face pinched, his eyes trained on the floor.

The others stood there, their eyes darting uncertainly at one another, then at Eusebius, clearly expecting the governor to give the order to put Hosius in chains. But Eusebius only worked his jaw, grinding his teeth, looking as though he was suffering from a bout of severe constipation.

Hosius stifled a grin of amusement as he watched the bewildered men shifting their weight from one foot to the other, too afraid to look Eusebius in the eye. Finally, when he gave them no orders and none appeared forthcoming, they skulked toward the back of the room and shuffled past the bust of Constantine, disappearing through a doorway that led to the inner chambers.

His face deep crimson, Eusebius's hands slowly curled into fists and he lifted a foot as if to stamp it down hard, then he appeared to think better of it and eased the sole of his sandal onto the tiled floor. "How dare you! How dare you give orders to my men! *My* men! Don't you have anything better to do? Shouldn't you be... *dead?*"

Hosius thought this was quite funny, but he kept his face placid as he turned his back and studied a fresco depicting a scene from the Trojan War. The craftsmanship was excellent. He was simple, but no philistine. "Do you know who sent me?" He didn't intend it as a question.

"The mighty Constantine," Eusebius said in a dramatic voice, like an actor entertaining an audience in an outdoor theatre.

Hosius turned away from the fresco, surprised, but not stunned, by what he was hearing. "You're not actually mocking the Emperor... *are you?*"

"Why shouldn't I?" Eusebius's lips pressed together into a thin line. "His spies have obviously informed you of what happened to his precious *Manifesto*. We all know he grows more paranoid by the day. But to place spies in my Fortress is unconscionable. Perhaps you should remind the Emperor that I'm a master of one of the five Fortresses of the Order of Belus. If I find the spy—*and I will*—I'll feed her to my hounds." Sweat broke through his bushy eyebrows and he blinked hard, wiping at his forehead with the heel of his hand. "I'm sure it's a woman. They always make the best spies."

Hosius plucked a small empty amphora from off the floor and cradled it in the crook of his reed-like half arm, absently gazing at the familiar painting on it without really seeing it. "I was told that one of your Sourcerors was reading the book by candlelight, and that it got too close to the flame. I was also informed that she was drunk."

Eusebius raised his shoulders and let them drop heavily, his mouth twitching into a smirk.

Hosius paused, observing Eusebius from across the room. "So you don't deny it then?" He stroked his grizzled beard with a weathered hand. "Perhaps being a master of one of the five Fortresses you were aware that there are only five copies of *Constantine's Manifesto* in the entire realm. And you may have also heard it's rather important—that only Sourcerors initiated in the Order are permitted to know of its existence." Hosius was goading him, trying to get a reaction to determine if Eusebius was salvageable or not. "How did you allow that to happen?"

"Draft another copy for your Emperor." Eusebius cleared his throat and spat on the floor. "Isn't that what you and Constantine's other favorites do? The Emperor says he needs to piss, and you fight to see who can bring him the shiniest piss pot."

Hosius smiled, his eyes narrowing into slits. "Tell me—why do you harbor such hostility for the man who made you what you are? Constantine has always held you in the highest regard. He appointed you Governor of Caesarea. He gave you your own Fortress. And this... this is how you repay him? Do I need to remind you that Constantine could shatter every bone in your body with a thought?"

"Is that so?" Eusebius said skeptically, arching an eyebrow. "Then tell me why the governors have gathered here? It's no secret—despite what you may think. The Emperor's near death, and tomorrow we'll learn how he intends to administer his empire upon his passing. He's dying. And I have nothing to fear from a dying man."

"I see." Hosius paused. "Of course you must realize that one day your insolence will get you killed."

"Get *me* killed?" Eusebius snarled. "Enough! Enough with this nonsense! I know why you're here, and it has nothing to do with *Constantine's Manifesto* or any other book. Let me hear you say it! Say it!"

"You've broken your oath." Hosius's voice was calm. When he was a younger man, he would have allowed the anger inside him to flare up and consume him. But not now. Anger only clouded the mind, and he needed every bit of mental acuity if he was going to survive this day; one mistake, one wrong move, and Eusebius would snuff out his life in an instant. Then again, Hosius was a smart man—he had taken precautions. Eusebius, on the other hand...

"You called off the search for the boy," Hosius continued in the same wooden tone. "Every one of your Sourcerors is hiding in your Fortress instead of fulfilling their duty. Your insubordination is causing the Emperor to question your loyalty. He wants to know why, my dear governor, why?"

"They're weary," Eusebius said plainly.

"Weary?"

"Yes." Eusebius regarded him defiantly with his dark eyes. "My Sourcerors have grown weary of the quest."

"You can't be serious." Hosius laughed. "You think your ability to wield the Source will save you from the Drestian? Is that it? Because when he arrives, weariness will be the least of your problems."

"Perhaps."

"I think I know what this is all about," Hosius said pleasantly, twisting his neck to peek out through the doorway. Outside, all was silent except for the circling birds shrieking high overhead beneath thin ribbons of stagnant clouds. "You've become weak. Your position, your titles and all your political power have made you *soft*. You actually believe you're important—that you matter. You've forgotten your purpose. And now you're scared. You're scared to sacrifice the comforts you've grown accustomed to."

"Don't presume to tell *me* about sacrifice!" Eusebius bellowed, stepping away from the bust of Apollo and toward the center of the room. His movements were smooth and surprisingly graceful for a man his size. "Do you know how many years it's been since I passed the test and learned of the Source? I've squandered my life searching for this boy—this *Belus*." He spat out the word like a mouthful of wine that had spoiled and turned rancid. "My Sourcerors aren't stupid. They've lost faith that he'll ever be found. And I've come to realize that... that life is short. Time is the most precious of all gifts. And time is being wasted on this fruitless search."

"*Time?*" Hosius snorted. "Time is meaningless. We may have to wait a thousand years before the Belus is born. But the boy could be among us right now. And if he is"—he pointed at Eusebius—"it's your duty to find him."

Eusebius grunted, and his forehead, slick with moisture, creased with lines. "As if that were an easy task. Finding one boy." He shook his head and sniffed loudly, sneering. "It'd be easier to find a virgin in a brothel."

"Now you *must* be joking." Hosius threw his head back and laughed heartily. "You're telling me that finding one person in all the world is a difficult task? Were you expecting it to be as simple as asking your portly bureaucrats to finish off a herd of goats in one sitting? You are familiar with the concept of *duty*, are you not? It's your duty. It's my duty. It's the duty of the entire Order to find the boy born from a woman undefiled. *You know that.* If we don't, then all is lost. Only the boy can prevent the Drestian from fulfilling his destiny."

"So you say," Eusebius muttered dubiously. He dropped his arms and widened his stance as if he was preparing to get knocked off balance. His combative posture wasn't lost on Hosius. He slipped away from the dining table, giving him more space to operate. Then he cocked an ear toward the back of the room and listened, but he heard nothing. It wasn't time. Not yet. *Be patient*, he said to himself. *Be patient.*

"I shouldn't have to tell you that there are those who don't share Constantine's belief that the Order should be backing the boy," Eusebius went on. "They believe we're betting on the wrong chariot."

"The *Drestianites?*" Just saying the word caused Hosius immense discomfort. "They're fools who defy Constantine because they thirst for power."

"But what if they're right?" Beads of spittle were forming at the corners of Eusebius's wide mouth. "You know what The Warning says! They may be defying Constantine, but that doesn't make their interpretation of The Warning any less valid."

"Interpretation?" Hosius said incredulously, stepping closer, keeping his eyes on Eusebius's hands. "This isn't a matter of interpretation. I think you're forgetting the consequences of siding with the Drestian."

"I'm no Drestianite," Eusebius said, his voice rigid. "And I'm fully aware of the consequences. I'm simply telling you why some in the Order— including three of my own—have defected to join their ranks. They believe it's only the Wisps who have cause to fear him."

"*Wisps?*" Hosius asked, unfamiliar with the term.

"The Drestianites have taken to calling non-Sourcerors Wisps, presumably to account for their shorter life expectancy. I do not believe it's intended to be complimentary."

"Charming. But that doesn't explain why your Sourcerors are not searching for the boy."

"The Protectors," Eusebius said, his face darkening. "They blame us, you know, all Sourcerors, even the Drestianites, for damaging the Source. They don't believe it was man's iniquities and savagery that caused it. They think tha—"

"We Sourcerors have wounded the Source by tapping into it and using it for our own selfish devices." Hosius spoke rapidly, a habit derived from reporting to the Emperor, a man with little patience for long-winded dissertation. "They think that if they kill every last Sourceror, the Source will be healed and man will live in a state of blissful magnificence for all eternity in some lovely garden utopia. Yes, I'm familiar with the Protectors. They think we are demons birthed from some ancient evil abyss. But they are merely—what did you refer to them as?—*Wisps*. Are they not?"

"You're utterly misinformed. They may be Wisps, but they've killed two of my Sourcerors since our last meeting. They're no longer content to simply meddle in the Order's affairs. They've begun targeting all Sourcerors, regardless of their Fortress… or their abilities."

"That only demonstrates their recklessness," Hosius replied, a trace of anger creeping into his voice for the first time.

"You're still not getting it." Eusebius's jaw tightened in frustration. "You don't know what we're up against. If the Protectors stood in front of us and fought with honor, we'd have nothing to fear. But they're cunning, resourceful and completely immoral. Nothing's beneath these animals. They killed my people while they slept, strangling them with cords. Then they cut out their hearts. It's said they eat them like cannibals."

"And that frightens you?" Hosius said lightly, placing the amphora on the floor. "If the Emperor knew you were afraid of the Protectors he'd have your head."

"He can have it!" Eusebius growled and threw his hands up to his face. "You're boring me. The Warning bores me. The quest for the boy bores me. What's the point of all this? The world is changing. You must understand that searching for a boy born without a father wouldn't be viewed favorably in certain quarters. What would the church think if they discovered us? Constantine can't protect us when he's dead. We're already forced to operate in secret, and it will only get harder when he's gone." He went silent for a spell, a scornful look passing over his face. "You don't really expect us to find this boy... *do you?*"

"Excellent points, governor," Hosius said mockingly. He smiled, but his eyes remained guarded. "We should all just give up. Let's just pretend The Warning doesn't exist, shall we? You're hiding from reality because you fear... what? Excommunication? Exile? The Protectors? The Drestianites? For your own safety and that of your Sourcerors? You're a *coward*. The Emperor honors you, and what do you do? You cower in your Fortress like a frightened child scared of his own shadow."

With a pair of twisting veins rippling across his temples like half-coiled snakes Eusebius shouted with primal rage: "You've insulted me for the last time, you sanctimonious cripple!" He raised one arm to shoulder height, his long bony fingers pointing at Hosius.

"You should carefully consider the situation," Hosius remarked coolly, mirroring Eusebius's posture. "You're all alone. You brought none of your Sourcerors. That was a mistake. And here I was all these years thinking you were an intelligent man. Your whimpering, gluttonous bureaucrats can't help you."

"*A mistake?*" Eusebius snorted with laughter. "You disgust me! You've spent your pathetic life like a drooling dog, humping the Emperor's leg for a bit of bone. Your master can't protect you anymore, Hosius. Those days are over, old man. I think you've lived long enough."

Eusebius glanced quickly at the dining table. It was made of elm with a large round top, and like a tripod, three sturdy legs supported it. His retinue had finished their breakfast earlier, leaving behind a tumultuous collection of terracotta cups, bowls, water pitchers and oil vials for the servants to collect and carry back to the kitchens on the eastern edge of the courtyard. With a barely perceptible wave of his hand, every object on the table shot skyward and sliced through the air, hurtling toward Hosius like a flock of murderous birds.

Hosius stood his ground, his expression unchanged, heartbeat steady. As the terracotta swarm advanced to within arm's reach, every last piece came to an abrupt stop. It stopped, because Hosius *wanted* it to stop. This was easy. The Source flowed in Hosius's veins, allowing him to do things that normal people—Wisps—could not. With a thought, he scattered the dining implements in every direction, watching with a disappointed smile (*surely the governor could do better than that?*) as they exploded into shards and clay powder against the walls, floor and ceiling.

Eusebius flicked his wrist. The table and the lounging couch next to it lifted off the floor and shot across the room at blinding speed.

Hosius crouched for a split second, then jumped. They passed under him, torpedoing a large amphora, smashing it like an overripe grape. The furniture crashed against the wall, splintering a painting that depicted a nude girl frolicking in a vibrant green garden. The flames in the oil lamps flickered and shuddered, then went out in swirling plumes of white smoke. Hosius remained suspended high up in the air as the wine from the shattered amphora spread across the floor.

"Very impressive." Eusebius looked up at Hosius, his eyes filled with admiration. "It appears that I missed."

"That's very perceptive of you, governor. Perhaps you're not so dense after all."

"You're quite nimble for an old cripple," Eusebius hissed, his face red with anger, "but you can't go any higher than the ceiling." His hand twitched like he was swatting at a flying insect. The eight dining stools, heavy and made of solid bronze, sped toward Hosius like missiles.

When the projectiles were close enough for Hosius to reach out and touch, he froze them in place. Then he slowly descended from his lofty height, the stools still hovering near the ceiling. Once his feet touched the wine-puddled floor, he flicked his hand. Two of the stools flew sideways and smashed against a fresco of Alexander the Great on some ancient field of battle. The stools shattered and Alexander lost an eye and part of his head as the stone beneath the fresco crumbled to the floor, leaving a web-like divot in the wall. Another wave of Hosius's hand and four stools jetted toward the opposite wall where they smashed into a giant gilt-framed painting of Ulysses standing proudly in a boat full of his admiring men. He slung the last two directly at Eusebius. With a casual twitch of his index finger, Eusebius diverted their path to the back of the room; they landed with a loud clatter next to the bust of Constantine.

Silence returned to the room for a brief moment, then there was the faintest of sounds, not much more than a breath of wind too light to rustle the leaves of the smallest of saplings. It came from behind the back wall. Hosius heard it, but he had been listening for it. Eusebius heard nothing. Now confident that the individual pieces of his plan were coming together like a mosaic, Hosius grew even bolder, and leveled a stinging taunt at the governor: "You should strongly consider standing down before word gets out that you were bested by an old leg-humping cripple who has seen three hundred summers."

Eusebius smirked bitterly. "Stand down? I'm just getting started." With his palms facing, he drew his hands close together, then pulled them apart before they touched. And then he did it again. And again. As Hosius watched—more out of curiosity than anything else—something began to form in the space between Eusebius's hands. At first, it was just a flitter of wispy smoke. Slowly, it began to grow and take shape, the wafting streams of smoke forming into an orb-shaped cloud, black as death, and as large as a man's head. From some place deep within the thing's core, red lights flickered like fireflies, swirling and sparkling, then it ignited in scorching red flames.

By the time Hosius realized what he was looking at, it was too late.

Eusebius smiled with deep satisfaction, then he nodded, and it rocketed toward Hosius.

Streaming pulses of fire marked the object's path, illuminating the room in brilliant, intermittent flashes of orange light. Eusebius stood perfectly still and focused all his energy on stopping it. It gradually slowed, but continued to creep forward, eating up the space between them. Finally, when it was within inches of his outstretched hand, it stopped, the pulsating heat burning the tips of his fingers. An icy sweat trickled down his back as he flicked his wrist. In a sudden burst, it darted straight for the bust of Apollo.

"And the trouble with firestarters," Hosius observed, as the orb consumed the likeness of the pagan god, "is that firestarters lack control. You're as likely to kill yourself as your adversary." The marble bust melted, leaving nothing on the expertly-carved gold leaf pedestal but a pile of ash. With a wave of Hosius's hand it blistered across the room straight for Eusebius. Sparks and black smoke trailed in its wake.

Now it was Eusebius's turn to look nervous. He stared down the flaming ball, squinting hard as though he was gazing up at the sun. To Hosius's amusement, the governor began to scream in an unexpectedly high octave. The object slowed like it was moving through wine instead of air, bobbed up and down erratically, then crept along inch by inch before finally coming to a stop.

As it hovered in front of Eusebius spitting out fiery sparks, he made the same twitchy, clapping motion as before. The cloud grew smaller and fainter in color. The flames vanished and the inky blackness became a milky-gray as it shrank to the size of an apple. It lost its shape, turning amorphous and misty, and with a loud *clap*, it disappeared in a puff of white smoke.

"I'll show you control!" Eusebius growled, and pointed at the doorway. A host of amphorae stacked ten levels high and just as deep raised themselves off the floor and tore through the electrically charged air. As a fresco of Bacchus looked on (revealed for the first time by the clay swarm's departure), Hosius swatted them away, and smashed them against the wall to his left. Eusebius pointed again. As if invisible currents were directing them, another battery of amphorae, this one even more numerous, took flight. Hosius felt no sense of urgency as he blocked their path and tossed them aside to where the table and couch once stood. *Child's play.* Eusebius was getting careless. His anger was dictating his actions and fogging his senses.

It was almost time. And Eusebius was oblivious.

The governor jabbed a finger at the bust of Venus (already shorn off at the cheeks) and aimed it at Hosius's head. Half a room away from its intended target, Hosius flicked it away with a subtle gesture and crashed it against the fresco of Alexander the Great. This time, Alexander lost most of his torso and one wheel of his war chariot. *Eusebius should know better*, Hosius thought, surprised. *A few pounds of marble stood no chance of—*

The amphora throttling toward Hosius was huge. A storage vessel used to fill the smaller ones, the four sets of handles were not a decorative embellishment—tipping it into a pouring position and returning it to its base required eight servants. The speed at which it traveled seemed to warp the air around it, drawing in the flames from the oil lamps, dimming the room. He calmly assessed his situation: At its current speed, and given its size and weight, it would obliterate both him and the wall to his back.

This is more like it, governor.

Hosius didn't flinch. He fixed his gaze on the container and willed it to slow down, a task made easier by Eusebius's roiling emotions. It lurched to an abrupt stop and tottered back and forth like a tree in a stiff breeze, then it changed direction, seeking out its sender. Wine slopped out of the wide spout, dousing sharp-edged pieces of wood partly buried under drifts of crumbled stone and clay. He glanced up to see that Eusebius was having trouble with his headdress. It had fallen over his forehead at an angle and covered up one eye. He cursed and ripped it off his head, throwing it to the floor with a piercing howl. The vessel paused, and hovered there for a few moments, unmoving. It quivered, then the top leaned forward over the base, and it wobbled its way toward Hosius. But not for long. It stopped after a few feet and went back the way it came, turning in slow circles as it did so, wine cascading down the sides. It paused again, and reversed course, only to retrace its stuttering glide a second later. As another directional turnabout appeared inevitable, the handles at the top splintered and broke, falling to the floor along with the neck. The body began to form fissures along the surface. The fissures become cracks. The cracks widened.

All at once, unable to withstand the enormous pressure, the amphora exploded, rocking the room like an earthquake, the wine stored within it erupting in all directions. Before the dark liquid could shower the room, Hosius contained it, stopping it in midair, as if time stood still. He held it like that for a while, watching, soaking up the strange destructive beauty of the scene. Then he let it all go; thousands of terracotta shards along with the wine wafted down as gently as a wind-swept butterfly coming to rest in a dewy meadow. The wine spread across the floor, covering the mosaics like a river of blood.

"Enough!" Eusebius raged, lowering his arm to his side. "This is pointless! We'll destroy the castle before this is over."

"Then I suggest you obey the Emperor and fulfill your oath," Hosius replied stiffly.

Eusebius scratched the tip of his nose and surveyed what was left of the room. Only a fraction of the lamps were still burning, casting broken shadows across the floor. Lingering wisps of smoke curled up into the air from those that had gone dark. The bust of Constantine had survived the battle—but that was all. He straightened himself to impose the full scale of his height, then looked down on Hosius with his large avian eyes.

"I'm terribly sorry," he intoned, like a teacher lecturing a dimwitted pupil. "The Emperor can't possibly understand the Source. The Warning says *the Source yields two paths, but be careful where you tread, the will of the Source is not meant to be understood by men.* It couldn't be any clearer, yet the Emperor wastes our lives without a thought for the consequences. Without a shred of concern for the toll it's taking on all of us. You included—though you don't see it." He dragged a heavy hand through his mottled hair. "I'm tired of meddling in these affairs. The Source will have to manage without me. I'm done looking for a boy who will never be found. And if he ever turns up, the poor wretch will have to settle his dispute with the Drestian without my assistance."

Hosius nodded sagely, as if agreeing with the governor's sentiments. "I completely understand your... feelings. I really do. Unfortunately, you seem to have forgotten that the oath can't be rescinded." He went silent for a beat before adding conversationally, "I understand you've been blessed with a rather large family. You have, I believe, four daughters and a son?"

"What... what... I what?" Eusebius stammered, confused. At last, he gathered himself and corrected Hosius: "I have four daughters and *two* sons."

"*Two?*" Hosius paused, allowing Eusebius's heavy breathing to fill the silence until the timing was just right. "I'm afraid I have some rather unfortunate news regarding your family, Eusebius. The Emperor took the liberty of moving them to the royal residence in Constantinople until the meetings here have concluded. Regrettably, because of your arrogant refusal to honor the oath, the Emperor decided that your eldest son should be sacrificed as a lesson to you. I've been told that he died well. He didn't grovel or beg for his life. He accepted his fate. That should please you. But it's still a shame. I'm sure he would have made a fine Sourceror. Maybe even a master—*like his father.*"

Eusebius's face went pale, his eyes bulged. This was no bluff, and he knew the truth in Hosius's words. Without warning, he charged Hosius with his arms outstretched, his fingers bent like talons preparing to tear flesh.

Ka-whump! Ka-whump! Ka-whump! The sound of steel thumping against steel echoed throughout the room.

Eusebius froze in place.

From the corridor where the governor's delegation had departed emerged a detachment of Emperor Constantine's private guards dressed in full battle regalia. The flickering lights from the remaining lamps reflected off the polished steel of their swords and shields, casting shutters of shifting yellow light throughout the ruined room as they arrayed themselves behind Hosius.

Eusebius watched with his jaw slack, his arms still held out in front of his body. He blinked, and shook his head as if he was trying to clear his mind after waking from a deep slumber. Then he noticed that the soldiers hadn't come empty handed. Some of the guards—six of them—were carrying objects. And when he realized what those objects were, he let loose a terrible cry, a high-pitched wail filled with terror and revulsion.

The guards gripped the objects by the *hair* and tossed them at Eusebius's feet. He screamed as the blood spread across the floor and merged with the wine, forming pools around him. He looked down at the face of one of the men—the fat sweaty one, his cheeks no longer purple, but bone white in death. The face stared back at him, its eyes still open, the pink tongue lolling out of swollen blue lips.

"You... you have no right," Eusebius choked out. He had lost all color, his face a mask of terror. "How could you do this?"

"This is *your* fault, my dear governor. Not mine. Not the Emperor's." Hosius nodded at the captain of the guard and the soldiers began filing out of the room. Just as he was about to leave, he looked back at Eusebius, who was still staring blankly at the carnage surrounding him.

"One more thing, *Lord* Eusebius. If you choose to disobey Emperor Constantine again, you should know this: He'll mount your head on a pike and display it for all to see at the imperial palace in Constantinople. Vultures will strip away every piece of rotting flesh from your traitorous skull. And your family—they'll suffer the same fate as your eldest son. Every fucking one of them. *Now find the boy!*"

PART I

"COLLEGE"

(THE PRESENT DAY)

Chapter 2

IVY

Felix and Allison were in danger of being late for freshman orientation. Their dorm's RD, a spunky and very chatty sophomore named Fallon, had cornered them in the lobby and assaulted them with information about the illustrious history of Portland College. Among the unsolicited facts: it was the oldest college west of the Mississippi River; it had produced the current governor, Portland's mayor, and the last five senators; it was always included in the annual top ten ranking of the country's most beautiful campuses (fourth in this year's issue); and most everyone (even the three women who'd founded the school over 200 years ago) called it "PC." Felix had been staring off at the ninety-inch TV in the common room as Fallon droned on and on about the campus. He'd given her the occasional head nod to pretend like he was listening, but all he caught were a few stray words, like 'brick', 'cobblestone', 'arches', and 'ivy'.

"Do you believe her?" Allison asked him.

"Who?"

"Fallon."

"About what?" He had no idea what she was talking about.

"The *trees*," Allison said, exasperated. "Weren't you listening? She was saying they've never had to chop one down. Not even after that big storm."

"Oh," he muttered vaguely. "Okay." He hadn't been listening to that part, and even if he had, he wouldn't have cared enough to consider whether it was true or not. He gazed around. There was no disputing the fact that there were lots of trees. Some were big. Like the ones that edged both sides of the path they were hurrying along, their branches stretching high into the vibrant blue dome above them. Strong sunlight slanted down through the canopy and fell over the walkway and its aged worn stones. There were smaller trees too, the squat, spreading variety with their gorgeous red and purple leaves. He knew a few of their names—oak, maple, and fir came to mind—but he wasn't so sure about some of them and didn't care enough to see what Google had to say about it.

Allison changed the subject, apparently realizing he wasn't in the mood to discuss trees. "What do you think he's gonna say?" she asked.

"Who?"

"Taylor."

"Who the hell's that?" Felix had never heard of him.

"The President of PC, dummy. President Taylor."

"Oh. Okay."

They changed direction, getting onto a path that bordered a huge lawn everyone called The Yard. The grass was so green and pristine it reminded him of some of the golf courses he'd seen on TV. They were walking fast. Allison wasn't having any trouble with the pace. She was tall, her legs were long, and she ran every day, at least five miles. While Felix kept his eyes focused on his feet and any bodies that got within collision distance, Allison's eyes were skipping from Felix to the path and back again. And the second he began drifting off into his own private world, she seemed to sense it and her searching eyes flitted up to his face. It had been like this ever since her mom had dropped her off at the dorm this morning. He felt like she was probing him (or assessing whether he was on the verge of going postal) and it was starting to get on his nerves. He glanced over at her intending to tell her to quit looking at him, but when he saw what she was doing, all the irritation instantly melted away. Her long dark hair was twisted into a thick cord, resting on her chest over her left shoulder, and she was running her hands up and down it like she was climbing a rope. She only did this when she was severely stressed about something. And he knew what she was stressed about—*him*.

Her eyes narrowed and her brows drew together as if she was trying to tell him something she was too afraid to say out loud. There was something about her eyes that was impossible to ignore. It was the first thing he'd noticed when they met in a freshman geometry class in high school in a little town on the Oregon coast called Coos Bridge. They were such a surreal shade of green he remembered thinking she had to be wearing tinted contacts. She wasn't. They were just that green. But that was only part of it.

"You might want to remember his name," Allison suggested with a trace of sarcasm in her voice.

Felix grunted.

They walked for a spell. Felix said nothing. Allison hummed the lyrics to a song that sounded distantly familiar.

"Why do we even have to go to this stupid thing?" Felix complained as they maneuvered their way around a cluster of students parked in the middle of the path, diverting foot traffic to the grass on either side. "We're already late. That Fallon chick wouldn't shut the hell up."

"Because it's freshman orientation. And we're freshmen—remember? And that *Fallon chick* is our RD, so you better be nice to her. And I thought what she was saying was really interesting. PC's history is fascinating. A lot of strange stuff has gone on here. *Really strange stuff.*"

"Whatever."

"C'mon, Felix," she said, turning toward him as they slipped past another group of idlers. Worry lines creased her brow. Her forehead always tended to pucker with at least a few lines even when she was just hanging out and relaxed. But today, she didn't just look like she was worried, she *was* worried, worried about him. "Its not gonna be that bad. It's just orientation."

With a flat frozen expression on his face, he gazed down at the path and shrugged. He knew Allison was just trying to cheer him up, and he felt bad that she had to deal with him when he was like this. Felix was a train wreck—and he knew it. He could barely hold a conversation, and just being around people (excluding Allison) made him feel anxious and uncomfortable. But being alone was almost worse: with no one to distract him, he would start thinking about his life, and that wasn't a good thing because his life had recently swirled down a toilet into a bottomless pool of shit.

Allison was still watching him, and for a moment, he viewed himself through her eyes. Felix had learned to mask the noxious mixture of pain and anguish that consumed him every second of every day. Almost, that is. His eyes betrayed him. It was nothing obvious; they weren't puffy, watery or bloodshot. But it was there all the same, like a current flowing beneath a precarious sheen of river ice, and Allison zeroed in on it like a bat to a fluttering moth. She didn't see what everyone else saw: That he was tall with hair that turned from light brown to sandy blond during the summers, and pale blue eyes that drew lots of comparisons to Siberian huskies and chlorinated pools. All she saw was the distant hollow look in his eyes. He couldn't fool her. He didn't even try; there was no reason to.

"You meet your roommate?" she asked, her expression rigid.

"No. You?"

"Not yet." She paused, and chewed on her bottom lip as she searched for something else to talk about. The lulls in the conversation seemed to make her edgy. She looked up. "Check out this weather. Nice, huh?"

Felix almost laughed. She was right about the weather. Warm

afternoon sunlight drenched the campus. Light breeze. Perfect. *But seriously,* he thought, *the weather?* Allison was getting desperate. He felt sorry for her, which made him feel guilty, and that made him feel even worse about... everything.

"This'll probably be the only nice day all year." He gave her a tired smile, playing along. "You know it's gonna rain like every day for the next eight months. I just love Oregon."

She laughed, but it wasn't her usual laugh. That wasn't her fault—it was his. What he'd said wasn't that funny (obviously), but he appreciated what she was trying to do for him. Allison had a great laugh, but she was guarded around people she didn't know and she didn't share it with just anyone. By all accounts, Allison was intense, maybe even a little confrontational at times, and the word people often used to describe her was *fierce*. Felix wouldn't disagree—because it *was* fitting—but he would never try to sum up Allison with one word. It would be like describing her eyes as simply *pretty*.

She was still talking about the weather, but his attention had wandered to a milling crowd gathering at the entrance of a big brick and stone building in the distance—Rhodes Hall, the largest auditorium on campus. It looked like everyone was trying to file in at the same time and it had created a bottleneck.

Allison had followed his stare and was looking at the same thing. "Hey—I guess we're not gonna be late after all!" She smiled and let out an exaggerated "whew!" Then added: "Call me a loser if you want, but I was gonna die if we missed this thing."

Felix recoiled and sucked in a hissing breath of warm dry air. The word *die* (or *death*), along with *fire*, and sometimes even *burn*, caused this to happen. He was conscious of it, but awareness of the issue hadn't solved anything. His face tightened. The muscles on his jaw stood out like sinewy knots. A dark frown settled over his face.

Allison shrank back and held her breath, then looked up at him with wary eyes. Felix met her gaze. She blinked and quickly lowered her head as though a stranger had caught her staring on a public bus. He knew exactly what she was thinking—the pained expression was splashed across her face. He didn't want to think about it, but it was too late for that. His mind was in free fall and he was tumbling backward, sinking down inside himself, and there was no safety net to catch him.

A week after the *accident*—the word didn't come close to capturing the sheer horror of the event, but he didn't know what else to call it—Allison had found him just outside town holed up in a neon-signed motel that shared space with a pawn shop and an all-night liquor store. Allison had told him about the fire. She'd seen it. She'd been out for a predawn run and saw the smoke. She told him that it looked like a bomb had gone off. She told him that she'd thought he was dead. She told him how sorry she was. Her account of the fire—the fire that had killed his parents—was all he knew about it. He had no memory of the *accident*. On the morning of his eighteenth birthday, he awoke to find himself lying in his back yard with paramedics and firemen surrounding him. His house had burned to the ground (a gas leak was later identified as the likely cause), and he didn't remember a thing. An ambulance took him to Coos Bridge Memorial, and on the way, one of the paramedics had told him that his parents didn't make it out of the house. He reacted badly—he recalled someone shouting, "He's flipping out." Then they restrained him and gave him a sedative strong enough to incapacitate a horse.

Felix gave his head a stiff shake—as if haunting memories were erasable like the screen of an Etch-A-Sketch—and looked up from his flip flops, which he'd apparently been staring absently at for the last 200 yards. A good stretch of path behind him was a total blank. They were standing just outside Rhodes now where they'd joined their new classmates, two among hundreds jostling to get in. The crowd surged around them.

"This is gonna suck," he whispered to Allison as they squeezed their way through the doors into a darkened vestibule. The army of shuffling feet plowed forward. Eager, chattering voices filled the chamber. As he bodied his way along with the crowd, it occurred to him how excited everyone was. He didn't feel much excitement (none actually), but he understood what was going on: This was their first official function at PC. Once they entered the auditorium and took their seats, they would no longer be high school students. They were in college. An exciting prospect. But not for Felix.

"It'll be short and painless," Allison said to him. "C'mon, would I ever lie to you?"

Chapter 3

THE FACEMAN

"Angela?"

A voice. A blood chilling voice. The long twisting paths in Angela's mind led to a door that only opened at night when the frightening intangible things in her imagination became real. The voice was coming from the deepest recesses of her mind, from whatever dark realm lay hidden behind the door.

"Angela? Time to wake up. Oh Angela. Wakey wakey."

Her eyes fluttered, but failed. The smell of grease, rubber and dirt clung to her face like a mask. Her head was splitting with pain; it felt swollen. She was cold. Was it the air conditioning? Sometimes she forgot to turn it off and her bedroom became an icebox and her mom would freak out and yell at her for running up the electrical bill.

The voice from behind the door called out to her again, snaking its way through the heavy stupor clouding her mind. Then a vague vibrating sensation coursed through her. Someone was shaking her. By the leg? Or was it her foot? Her mom? Why? Was she late for school? What time was it? If she missed first period again, Mrs. Telfair told her to expect a call from the vice principal's office.

"Rise and shine, little missy," the voice said.

The sensation of being shaken grew steadier, more forceful. And it *was* her foot, she decided. The bottom of her foot. Someone was... *kicking her?* No. Not kicking her, but... prodding her. The hard square toe of a boot? She heard herself moan. It sounded funny, muffled. Her eyes snapped open—but the darkness remained. Confusion spilled over her in drowning waves. Was she blind? Did something happen to her? In her mind's eye, she saw an image of herself trapped below ground. Or was she trapped in some strange unreality? Trapped in a dream—behind the door. Then she felt something being pulled over her head, and a moment later, there was light. She blinked against the sudden brightness, squinting into the dirty golden cast of a late summer afternoon. Sunlight filtering in from above fell over her black yoga pants in a stripey pattern. She straightened her legs, then drew them up to her body and hugged them tight, cradling herself in a fetal position.

Where the hell am I?

"Oh wakey wakey, little girly."

That voice again. Where was it coming from?

She thought hard, and the effort made her brain hurt. The last thing she remembered was walking down the driveway before breakfast to get the mail. She was expecting—hoping—to get an early admissions acceptance letter from Vanderbilt. But there was just junk and some bills for her parents. She remembered flipping through an Old Navy catalogue and then... darkness. So what happened? What happ—

Abduction.

The word shattered her mind like a baseball crashing through a stained glass window. Her heart stopped beating and she went cold with fear. She screamed. Nothing came out. She tried again and gagged. Then she realized her mouth was open—pried open. Something was in it. Something had been stuffed in her mouth so deep it brushed against her tonsils. It tasted like sweat, sour milk, and lunch meat. The smell (and the taste) was starting to make her sick.

Then she saw it.

The thing hovering over her was mountainous. Its sheer bulk mystified her. It was too big to be a person. But her mind was playing tricks on her. Because it *looked* like a person; it had legs, arms, and... was that a head? But it was too gargantuan. It couldn't be human. It had to be something else. Didn't it?

"You hear that?" the monstrous thing said, and cupped a cinder block-sized hand to its ear. "That, my dear Angela, is the sound of a cargo train." The ground vibrated. She felt it in her legs and in her back, then the ground shook and swelled, jostling her like a trip down an unpaved country road in an old car. Shafts of sunlight streaming in through gaps in the walls caught the dust that swirled down from the ceiling and the little plumes that eddied up from the dirt floor.

She felt her eyes bulge in shock. It *was* a person. A man. Her disbelieving eyes drifted up to his face and cold fear flooded through her. *She knew who it was.* She sucked in a startled breath and gagged on the thing in her mouth. She coughed and choked and gasped for air. But each time she inhaled, it tickled the back of her throat, setting off another round of coughing, making her body tremor. Her vision shrank in on itself, starting at the edges. Everything went dark. She felt herself slipping into the blackness, then the voice—the chilling voice from behind the door—called her back to the light.

"The trains pass by here every five minutes this time of day," the man was explaining. He lifted his chin as if to indicate an area somewhere off in the distance and his head scraped against the ceiling, causing the corrugated-metal panels to shudder. He didn't seem to notice. He raised his voice a notch so she could hear him over the shriek of the train's whistle. "They're loud enough to mask almost anything. Anything could happen to you in here." He gestured around him, at what appeared to be the inside of a shed of some kind (four walls and a ceiling—all dilapidated, rusty, and streaked with stains). "And no one would hear a thing. You could scream. You could cry. You could bang on the walls. It won't matter. Nobody will hear a thing. Nobody. Does that frighten you?"

It did.

Her heart was racing so fast it thundered in her ears. Her brain felt soggy and useless, but some portion of it was sputtering into gear: It occurred to her that the train tracks were on the town's outskirts, a desolate area on the wrong side of the river—a place she'd always avoided. A place where bad things happened. She shivered and hugged her legs to her chest. She felt so cold. Partly from the fear, but she knew something else was at work. *Drugs?* Did he drug her? He must have. She was freezing, and Louisiana was in the midst of a brutal heat wave. She figured the air in the shed had to be molten at this time of day. But she was trembling like the emaciated greyhound she'd talked her parents into rescuing from the animal shelter just last week. She hadn't named him yet, still deciding between Gail and Peeta.

She steeled herself for a moment, then looked up, eyes wide, mouth open. The face staring back at her was inhuman. The head was far too big to be a head; it was the size of the beach ball she'd been keeping in the trunk of her car all summer. And his features were all wrong—distorted and... confusing. Parts of his face were *missing*: an ear, a chunk of nose, and one side of his upper lip. She couldn't stand to look at him anymore. So she closed her eyes and prayed that this was just a dream, just an awful, awful dream.

She waited. The ground was still. The whine of the train's whistle faded. She opened her eyes.

He was still there. Smiling. *This wasn't a dream.* She could feel the panic and fear bubbling up from her stomach, wrapping its icy fingers around her heart. Tears began to leak from the corners of her eyes, and before long her cheeks were slick and wet.

He stared down at her with a bemused expression on his terrible face. His dark eyes seemed to be dancing. She'd always imagined the eyes of a serial killer would be cold and lifeless, like the black soulless pits of a Great White Shark or some other brainless animal that acted on millions of years of evolutionary instinct. But the man's eyes were burning with *something*—pleasure?—excitement?—anticipation? And oddly, it reminded her of the way her friend Ashley had looked at her when she was crowned homecoming queen at the school assembly last fall.

Then he spoke: "I believe introductions are in order. I didn't get a chance before, because you were, well, unconscious. My name's Nick Blair, but I'm sure you know me by another name."

He waited for a response.

The rag in her mouth (if that's what it was) made it impossible to formulate words. Instead she wept as a little voice rang hollowly in her bewildered head: *This isn't happening. This isn't happening. This isn't*—

"Well nod if you've heard of the Faceman," he said, sounding disappointed.

She managed a quick nod as the tears streamed down her face. She started sobbing. She wanted to beg him to let her go, but she couldn't move her tongue and the words came out in choking, garbled spasms.

He leaned forward and his lips crept slowly back over his gums, revealing gold teeth filed to sharp points. He reached out with one hand, and Angela's eyes bulged as fingers the size of corn cobs stabbed at her face. She tried to lurch away from him, but his fingers were already in her mouth and she felt her lips straining wide at the corners. "We can't very well have a proper conversation like this," he said, and yanked out the rag all at once, a red bandanna crusted over with splotches of something that she hoped were just food stains. He stepped back, stuffing it into his pocket.

She flinched and banged up against the wall. The shed rattled and creaked. Her reactions were delayed, and her joints felt stiff. She dug her heels into the floor and pushed out, scrabbling to get away. But her muscles were frozen in terror and her legs felt dead. She was also backed up against a wall; a ridged panel was digging into the flesh between her shoulder blades. The panel was thin and unbraced and it bowed out limply, which allowed a finger of yellow light to seep in through a rift near the floor.

A grin stretched across his face as he looked down on her. "I know—

I'm not what most teenage girls consider a face man. I'm not exactly Bradley Cooper. But I think you know *why* I'm called the Faceman."

She said nothing. As her mind started to resolve itself to the fact that her alarm clock wouldn't be saving her, her throat began spasming in panic. Her heart pounded. She felt winded, like someone had punched her in the gut. A cold layer of sweat was starting to show through her T-shirt. The sour taste in her mouth lingered.

"Well?" he demanded.

She nodded.

"Was it the cop? I bet it was the cop." He shook his head, but he seemed pleased. "I knew that was a mistake. But I have a complicated relationship with the authorities. And that cop, well, he reminded me of this guy I knew from my military days who pissed me off one too many times so I—how do I put this delicately?—*I ripped his fucking head off."* He threw his head back and bellowed laughter. The sound rolled around the shed like a summer storm. Angela shrank back against the wall as the Faceman stared at his hands—hands that were without doubt big enough and strong enough to rip off a man's head.

Of course she knew why he was called the Faceman. Everyone did. For the past three years, a serial killer had terrorized the entire country, going from state to state, and from town to town, killing teenagers. But he didn't just kill them—he erased their faces. Six point blank rounds with a .44 magnum. Her parents, like millions of others across the country, wouldn't let her go out alone after dark (or out at all), and they insisted she carry pepper spray in her bag. Then at the end of last year, a cop had pulled over a van for speeding on a country road in the Midwest. The driver climbed out of the vehicle, pointed a gun at the officer's face, and blew his brains out the back of his head. Then he proceeded to shoot him five times in the face as he lay twitching on the side of the road. This was all caught on video from a camera mounted inside the patrol car. Every TV network in the country ran the censored footage on a loop (her parents wouldn't let her watch it), and every newspaper and magazine from coast to coast plastered the images of the shooter's face on their front pages. When the un-pixelated version hit YouTube, it racked up more views in one week than all of Beyonce's music videos combined and it crashed the website for five hours. The killer's trademark—one bullet to the head and five to the face—was unmistakable, but the country waited in breathless anticipation for the official announcement. The results from the ballistics tests confirmed what everyone was expecting: The gun that killed the cop was the same weapon used in the murders of at least fifty-seven teenagers. Two days later, the Faceman's identity—*the identity of the most prolific serial killer in U.S. history*—was released: His name was Nick Blair. He was thirty-three. A former Navy Seal. A decorated war hero.

"I didn't always look like this, you know." The Faceman smiled. Before Angela could consider what he was smiling about, he'd reached behind his waist and came away with a knife. She winced and jerked backward and her head cracked against the wall. This was no ordinary kitchen knife. Angela had never seen anything like it before; it was long (at least the length of his muscular, vein-bulging forearm), and she supposed it was a hunting knife, an instrument used to gut animals—*big* animals like elk and bear. He was still smiling as he pressed the flat side of the blade against his face. The tip rested on the side of his head. He was using it as a pointer, and what he was pointing at was so gross it was hard to look at: Where there should have been an ear, there was just a dark hole.

"This ugly crater here was once a nice piece of cartilage. Then some shrapnel blew it off. It was just like yours. Not as petite—of course. I've always been rather large for my age. At fifteen, I was big enough to bring down a bull with just these mitts of mine." He squeezed his hand into a bowling ball-sized fist. "That was the year my step daddy came at me with a pair of hedge clippers. They still haven't found his body." He doubled over in a deafening roar of laughter. Angela could feel the wall vibrating against her back.

"They should've asked the pigs what happened to him." A sly grin flickered on his face for an instant. "Anyway, I don't mean to digress. So what do you think of my chompers?" He peeled his lips back and jutted out his chin so that even the teeth in back were visible. "I once had my own. They were as white as an elephant's tusks. But a sniper in Afghanistan put a bullet through my cheek." His jaw tightened and he paused for a moment. "The bastard blew 'em out my mouth." The tip of the knife settled on a round, quarter-sized scar below his cheekbone. "That and some of my upper lip, which I've been told makes me look like a perpetual snarler. I strongly suspect that's the reason I'm finding it tough these days to maintain a proper social calendar." He laughed at that, but not as loudly as before, and it made Angela think it wasn't the first time he'd used that line. "And I always liked gold, so I thought why the hell not? Why shouldn't I treat myself? Life can't just be work, work, work, all the time, now can it?" He raised an eyebrow and added: "'But why the fangs?' you might be asking yourself. Is it because"—he let the word hang in the steamy, dust-moted air, his eyes trained on hers—"I eat my victims?" He gnashed his teeth together in a hard *click*, drawing blood that dribbled over his lower lip and down his chin in two unbroken lines.

Angela cringed and her hands involuntarily flew up to her face, then settled back down around her knees where she clasped them together. She was sobbing louder now, rocking herself, sucking in air in great shuddering gasps. Hysteria was beginning to set in despite her attempts to stay calm.

The Faceman shook his head in response to his own question. "I prefer ethnic food. And by that, I don't mean I eat minorities." He grinned broadly. "I did this"—he tapped the knife against his teeth—"because it looks badass and scares the shit out of people. And I have to confess"—he leaned in close as if he was disclosing a secret to a trusted friend—"I *love* scaring the shit out of people. Because without fear, where's the fun in all this?"

A train rumbled by and the Faceman paused to listen. "Don't you just love trains?" he asked cheerily after the rumbling had subsided to a faint, distant pulse.

She nodded. She wasn't exactly sure why, but the voice in her head was telling her that disagreeing with him could be fatal.

"And this was once a fine dignified nose, I'll have you know," he resumed, slowly tracing the tip of the knife over the arched side of his asymmetrical upper lip. "But then a bunch of terrorists in Pakistan went and broke it. But don't you worry. They got what was coming to them. Now that was a good time. And I got a medal of commendation for my efforts." He looked up at the ceiling and smiled at the memory. "Sorry, you'll have to forgive my vanity. This isn't about me—I realize that—but I am trying to explain something to you. You see—if that wasn't enough to spell the demise of my poor nose, I got into a little tussle with a boy of seventeen— the same age as you—and the little rascal tore most of it off with his bare hands." He grinned wickedly. "Now that boy had what it takes. *He passed the test.* The question is… will you?"

Angela knew she had to get a grip on herself, yet the fear was coiling around her like a living thing, leeching away her resolve and her ability to think. But she had to do something. So she swallowed down the dread and the terror, then drew in a deep breath and focused on one thing: getting out of here. *There had to be a way out.* The heroines in the books she liked to read always found a way out. They always survived. And she was clever and strong, just like the girls in those books. She just needed to think. This wasn't how her life was going to end. If her life was a story, then she was the heroine, and of one thing she was absolutely sure: *heroines don't die on page twenty*. And her story was still in the early chapters.

But the grotesque man towering over her was a giant. And he looked strong—strong enough to bench press a car. Even if he didn't have the knife, she didn't have any chance of overpowering him. She was one of the best athletes at her school—a starter on the basketball team and an all-league soccer player for the past two years. But the Faceman was *huge*. Big enough to squash her like a bug. *People can't be this big,* she thought. It was almost like he was unreal: The monster in a fairy tale that lives under a bridge terrorizing travelers until the heroine comes along to dispatch the horrible beast with a swift stroke of her shining sword. But no one was coming to her rescue; she would have to do it herself. She glanced all around, thinking. The shed was empty except for some cigarette butts and an orange candy wrapper sticking out of the dirt in the corner. There were no windows. The lone exit was a narrow cut-out on the far side—directly behind the Faceman. Rectangular lengths of light probed through wedges in the oxidized metal sheets, but they were far too narrow to squeeze through.

The Faceman was watching her, his eyes colorless and measuring. "As much as I'm enjoying our little chat, it's time to begin the test." He motioned with his hand. "Stand up. Up, up, up. C'mon now."

She wasn't sure if her legs were going to cooperate, but it didn't look like she had a choice. She braced her back against the wall, and using it for support, slowly pushed herself up. Her legs were shaking, and her feet felt cold, prickly and a little numb, but she kept her balance. She looked straight ahead and sucked in a panicked breath. Her head only reached up to the bottom of the Harley Davidson logo on the Faceman's shirt. He had to be at least eight feet tall. She felt like a toddler.

"You're an only child?" he asked.

She couldn't answer. Her vocal cords seemed paralyzed as she gaped at the hulking behemoth. His chest was three times as wide as a normal man's. *Where on earth does he get his clothes? You can't buy—*

The knife flashed out at her face, slicing through a flutter of sun caught dust. She jumped back and crashed into the aluminum panel. Better reflexes this time. Her legs felt less stiff, less like wooden boards. Not springy, but better than before. That was the good news. The bad news was the knife was so close to her face she could see the individual serrations etched into its polished surface.

"Angela, my dear, I will gut you like a rainbow trout if I have to. And"—a thin smile touched his face—"I'll enjoy it. But first things first. Answer the question."

She stared at the knife. It was long enough to cut her in half. "Yes," she said faintly.

He nodded. "I knew the answer already. I've done my diligence on you. But I do enjoy a little dialogue now and again and I was hoping you would answer so I could tell you that being an only child can be advantageous. It might help you."

Angela's brow wrinkled in confusion. She didn't understand how that could help her. The Faceman killed teenagers. And she knew the teenagers he killed were almost always only children. So why would it be a good thing to have no siblings?

"But please stop crying. Crying won't help. It never does. Okay?"

She brushed her hair back from her forehead. Then she wiped her eyes, but it didn't do much good; they were swimming with tears.

"Do you know why you're here?"

She shook her head.

"Would you like to guess?"

"I don't know!" she cried out. "Please let me go! Please! I'll give you anything, anything you want. I won't tell anyone. I swear."

"I would love to let you go," he said and he sounded sincere. "Honestly, I would. But whether you get to leave or not, is entirely up to you. It's not my decision. You just have to do one thing."

"*What?*" she choked out, the slightest glimmer of hope stirring inside her chest.

"You have to pass the test. Just like the boy who tore off my nose. If you pass, your life will be more amazing than you could possibly imagine. You, Angela, could be a Drestianite. And if you are, you'll stand by his side as the revolution spreads across the world. A higher purpose could be awaiting you, my dear."

"Just let me go!" she pleaded. "I don't know what you're talking about."

"Angela, Angela, Angela. I'll explain everything. I will. Trust me. Just as soon as you show me you're *special*. That's what this is all about. That's the question. Are you special?"

Special?

The Faceman was talking crazy now. She wondered how much longer it would be until he took out his gun (the gun she knew he had). She bent her knees for a second to test her legs. They still felt a little rubbery, but they were getting stronger. Being on her feet was helping with the circulation. She wasn't up for running a 10K, but she felt nimble enough to make a dash for it if she got the chance.

The Faceman was still talking about something, but she didn't catch it. He gave her a puzzled look, then used the knife to point at a half-submerged piece of kindling on the floor. It was between them (slightly closer to the Faceman) and a bit off to her left. It looked like it had once been a chair leg. Now it was splintered and decayed with amoeba-shaped patches of varnish still visible through the rot and dark grayish mold. "See that?" he asked.

She did.

"What? That?" She pointed at it, just to gauge the strength in her arm. It felt good, almost back to normal. Whatever he'd done to her—drugged her or chloroformed her or whatever—had worn off. Now she needed a plan. What would the heroines in her books do? *What would Katniss do?* she asked herself. Katniss would find a way out. She wouldn't let the story end here. Katniss wouldn't let herself die at the hands of some awful boy from another district. And neither would Angela. She tried to put herself in Katniss's place—*to channel her inner Katniss*—and an idea formed in her head. Angela's advantage on the Faceman was her quickness and agility. If she could distract him for just a second, she should be able to use those skills to get around him (or even dart between his legs) and escape out through the doorway to his back.

"Yes," the Faceman answered. "Make it move, and you pass the test— you get to live. Fail and… well, I think you get the idea."

"That's it?" Like a plank walker, she took a cautious, fumbling step forward.

"Stop!" he shouted.

She froze, cowering, waiting for the blade to plunge deep into her stomach. She ducked her head. Her hands went to her elbows and cupped them. The seconds ticked by. Sweat rolled down her back. Nothing. No blade. She was still on her feet. Still alive.

"Not like that, Angela. No. No. No." He waggled his forefinger back and forth like he was admonishing a child. "Make it move with your *mind.*" He placed both index fingers on his temples, and Angela thought he looked like a one-horned devil with the long blade poking up above his head. "Without touching it," he added.

This was her chance.

"With my mind?" She nodded at the wood scrap, hoping he would glance at it just long enough to get his attention off of her.

His eyes flickered over to it.

She rushed at the doorway in a sudden, explosive burst. She made it three steps and the Faceman's eyes were still on the wood. Her hand skimmed across the floor as she dipped her shoulder low and propelled herself forward, shooting for the space just beside his right knee. Another step. Her path now clear, the doorway flooded her vision with golden light, the world beyond the shed's gloom drawing near. Another step. The light grew larger, beckoning to her, the promise of freedom just a few yards away.

The light blinked out and she rammed into something hard, something as dense and immovable as a wall. She stutter-stepped backward, stunned. The wall was wearing a dark T-shirt with a red Harley Davidson insignia and faded camo pants tucked into black combat boots. With a deft lateral movement, the Faceman had planted himself between her and the exit. The little sidestep was quick and perfectly timed, as if they were dance partners moving in choreographed harmony. She shook the stars from her eyes and craned her neck to look up at his face.

The Faceman's eyes locked on hers and his lips peeled back from his wolf teeth in an indulgent, knowing smile. His horn had changed. It was still long and silver, but now it looked dull and flat at the tip. No, not a horn she realized, but a gun that he held next to his face, the barrel pointed at the ceiling.

"Angela, do I strike you as an amateur?" He tilted his head at the weapon. "This is a forty-four magnum. Do you have any idea what one bullet from this will do to your face?" She knew. A kid at school had shown her a picture on the Internet of one of the Faceman's victims. She'd slapped the kid. Then she threw up on his shoes.

She screamed as she tried to distance herself from him but in just a few steps, she was right back where she'd started, right up against the wall.

"In Louisiana, no one can hear you scream." He grinned his livid grin for a moment as though he was enjoying some private joke, then it dimmed. "That's not going to help. Didn't we go over this?"

As if on cue, a train's whistle sounded in the distance and the ground began to jitter beneath her feet.

"The test, Angela. *The test!* Let's resume, shall we? Show me what you've got."

She stared at him, beaten, confused and scared. She didn't know what to do. *She couldn't move things with her mind.* There was no way out. She was trapped.

"Angela!" he bellowed, turning her name into a threat.

"I don't... I don't understand." She looked at the chair leg. "I don't und—"

"It's simple. Move it with your mind. I don't require much. Just an inch—even a centimeter—will do. Just show me that you're a Sourceror. Then you can leave. We'll leave together. I'll buy you lunch. You like quesadillas? I'm in the mood for Mexican. Now do it."

Angela just stood there looking from the Faceman to the piece of wood and back again, trying to make sense out of the lunacy spewing from his twisted mouth.

He brought the barrel down slowly, leveling it at her forehead. "Do it!"

There was a heavy silence for a moment, then she screamed up at his face: "I can't move it with my mind! You know I can't! It's impossible." For the first time since Angela had discovered herself in the shed, her voice projected tenacity and strength. She sounded confident—believable. It was the voice she used when she'd had enough, when even her dad knew not to push her. But when she saw the Faceman's expression her heart plummeted. She'd made a mistake and she realized it immediately. She was trying to convince him of something that if true, meant death. His frightening face had turned even darker. The intact part of his upper lip curled back over his teeth. Then he frowned deeply, and an indescribable, glacial coldness passed over his eyes.

Angela had lived her life believing that bad things only happen to other people. She knew she would die—eventually—but not until she was 100, with kids and grandkids and great grandkids surrounding her in her warm loving bed. If she was on a plane that crashed—she would survive. If her ship sank at sea—she would survive. She would survive anything. But now, a sense of foreboding rose up from her stomach and lodged itself in her throat, and a thought, strange and surreal, gripped her mind: *I'm going to die.* She wasn't Katniss. She was just a girl. A girl who lived in the suburbs. A girl who went to school and liked music and books and movies and going to the mall with her friends. She was just an ordinary girl. A girl.

"—do you want my ugly mug to be the last thing you ever see?" he was asking her. "Your choice. Focus. You can do it." He lifted an eyebrow and said icily, "Or... can you?"

"I can't. Oh God. Oh God." She stared at his awful face, trembling with fear.

"Make it move, Angela!"

"How? I don't know... how... how can I—?"

"I'm going to count down from ten. If you haven't accomplished this task by the time I reach zero, I'm putting a bullet in your head. And I won't stop with just one. Think of your parents, Angela. Do you want mommy and daddy to see their beloved little girl with her brains spread across the county? No? Then I would encourage you to try a little harder."

"Oh God. No. I can't. I don't want to die. I—"

"Ten, nine, eight…"

"No! No!" she wailed, holding her hands out to him plaintively. "Don't. Please. Don't do this to me. Please."

"Seven, six, five, four…"

"Move," she said weakly, her eyes skirting to the piece of wood. She was bawling. It wasn't supposed to end like this. "Please move. Please. Move. Move. Move…"

It didn't budge.

"Three, two, one…"

Angela looked up at him, begging him with her hopeful teenage eyes. His eyes were cold and lifeless—the black soulless pits of a Great White Shark. It was the last thing she ever saw.

"Zero."

* * *

He squeezed the trigger. The gun went off with a deafening roar, shaking the foundation of the broken shell of a building. Angela's head jerked back and she collapsed to the dirt floor in a crumpled heap. Blood, bone and hair leaped high into the air and spattered the wall behind her in dripping clots.

Silence came crashing back.

Dust and gunsmoke stirred in the patches of sunlight.

He stepped over to her body and looked down at the mask of terror and confusion staring back at him. The public knew many things about him—but not everything. Most people thought he desecrated his victim's faces because he either hated himself (and the faces he removed were thus a reflection of his self-loathing) or that he was simply a savage with a bloodlust craving. It was neither of those things. Most serial killers take something from their victims. A token of some kind: jewelry, a lock of hair, a finger, clothing. The Faceman took something else. He found inimitable beauty in death. The beauty of Angela's face—her shoulder length auburn hair, light brown eyes, soft youthful skin tanned from the long hot summer—was enhanced a million times over because her entire life was etched into every single pore. It was all there—in the wondering eyes, the set of the mouth—an indelible imprint that said *everything that I am, and will ever be, is gone.* THAT WAS POWER.

But the Faceman was selfish. He wasn't going to share that beauty with anyone. It was his. He'd made her this way. He'd created it. No one else would ever see it. So he gazed down on her face for a long time (trains passed by twice), until he'd absorbed every last detail and locked it away in his mind. He closed his eyes for a moment and smiled. The deed was done. The mental picture was taken. He would carry it with him and treasure it, forever. He pointed the gun at Angela's face and pulled the trigger five times, eradicating it in a shower of blood.

He ducked out of the oppressive heat of the shed. Crisp afternoon sunshine and a gentle breeze greeted him as he approached a white cargo van parked next to a mountain of old tractor trailer tires. Stopping beside the van, he took a cell phone from his pocket, using the edge of his little finger to touch the screen which fit snugly within his palm. He waited patiently, watching a pair of geese making their way across a hazy blue sky.

"Yes," a voice on the other end answered.

"She failed," the Faceman said. "She was a Wisp."

"I'll let him know," the voice replied. "Tucson. A girl. Gabriela Conseco. Call when you arrive."

Chapter 4

ORIENTATION

Felix was right. Orientation sucked—though he probably couldn't get Allison to admit to it because she so badly wanted to like it. President Taylor turned out to be a total bore. His speech was tedious and punctuated with canned jokes he'd obviously been using forever. Just when it was becoming awkward and everyone in the enormous auditorium (maybe a third of the seats were in use) grew restless, Taylor murmured something that no one could hear and quickly exited the stage. A few kids clapped, but it sounded apologetic. Felix was slumped down in a theater-style seat next to Allison twenty or so rows back from the stage. He glanced over at her and tried to communicate '*I told you so*' with his eyes. Allison glared, then covered up her mouth to keep from bursting out in laughter.

The dean of students, Dr. Borakslovic, stepped up to the microphone next. Thin and reedy to the point of looking brittle, she spoke with such condescending assertiveness it was almost as if she was trying to challenge the freshman class to a fight. Felix didn't like her. Not at all. Twenty minutes later, Dr. Borakslovic seemed satisfied that she'd sufficiently bored everyone in attendance with the *fundamental importance* of complying with the school's code of conduct (which she actually compared at one point to the Constitution) and PC's zero-tolerance public intoxication policy. She paused for a moment and looked out at her audience with a contented glint in her eyes. Then she cleared her throat primly and broke into a big smile as she introduced the president of the Student Union—Grayson Bentley. Felix was more concerned with picking off a scab on the back of his hand without making it bleed than whatever Borakslovic was talking about, but he did hear her say something about Grayson being the first freshman ever elected president.

Grayson had already taken the stage and was waving at the crowd and engaging in a little back-and-forth with the kids in the front rows with the polished grace of a seasoned politician. He was tall and blond and dressed like he wanted people to think he worked on Wall Street. Allison elbowed Felix in the arm. "Yum," she purred.

"Who?" Felix said, rolling his eyes at her. "Borakslovic? Yeah, she's hot."

Allison smiled at Felix's dumb joke, but her eyes stayed fixed on the stage.

As Grayson approached the podium, Dr. Borakslovic's smile grew even wider, and she shouted excitedly into the microphone: "Grayson Bentley, everybody!" She started clapping (way too enthusiastically; Felix thought she might snap a wrist), then she gave the crowd an exasperated eye-bulging stare when she realized no one was joining in. Just about everyone stared back at her in blank-faced confusion, but a few overly-eager kids eventually returned the applause.

"Weird," Felix said to Allison and snickered. "You think they're dating? Like boyfriend and girlfriend?"

"You know who he is, don't you?" Allison's tone suggested that he should.

"Grayson Bentley."

"Smartass," she replied quietly. "*Bentley*. His dad's Dell Bentley. You know—the Governor of California."

"No shit!" Felix said, louder than he'd intended.

The kid sitting in the seat in front of him turned around and scowled darkly at him.

A sudden rage flashed over Felix. He leaned forward until his face was just inches from the kid's, who drew back, wide-eyed. "What?" Felix rasped softly. "This look like a church to you? You gotta problem?" The kid's head snapped back around in a hurry and he slouched down in his chair like he was trying to hide.

Shit, Felix thought regretfully, instantly feeling terrible.

Allison stared at him, her worried eyes traveling over his face. "You all right?"

He nodded, embarrassed. It wasn't like him to do something like that.

"Anyway," she said in a low voice, "that's why Grayson's the first freshman to be president. The administration kisses his ass and lets him run the school. He's only a sophomore now, so he's gonna be here for a while, so whatever you do, don't make enemies with him."

Felix shrugged. He wasn't planning to make enemies with anyone. Then again, the kid he'd growled at probably wouldn't want to hang out with him.

Grayson placed his hands on the podium and began speaking into the microphone without even a hint of nervousness. He oozed confidence, and clearly relished the opportunity to speak to such a large and captive audience. He made a few jokes (the quality of the cafeteria food got the brunt), and spoke about community involvement, philanthropy, and the importance of appreciating PC's academic traditions. Felix caught some of it. But mostly he was beating himself up for snapping at the poor kid in front of him who hadn't moved a muscle in ten minutes; maybe he figured Felix couldn't see him if he kept perfectly still.

"In conclusion," Grayson said, and Felix's ears perked up. Then Grayson raised one arm over his head, made a fist and shouted: "Once a Sturgeon, forever a Sturgeon!"

That got the biggest laugh of the day.

PC's mascot, the Sturgeon, was unquestionably the lamest school mascot in the entire country. And the unofficial school motto—*Once a Sturgeon, forever a Sturgeon*—was too ridiculous for anyone to take seriously. It reminded Felix of the *Monty Python* movies his dad made him watch to prove that his sense of humor was still, as his dad used to say, 'with it'.

And so ended freshman orientation.

Chapter 5

DIRK

"Heroin?" the man with the soft, sunburned face complained to Dirk. "If I'd known there was going to be heroin in the room I wouldn't have signed up for this. I definitely wouldn't have called the police."

"You signed up for this, David," Dirk told the man, "because I'm making you rich." David was Dirk's agent. David's agency had signed Dirk right out of high school and landed him the role—'Scab' in *Alien Armageddonator*—that launched his career. Now he was David's biggest client. By any measure, Dirk was enormously successful. Sprawling symbols of that success could be found in Maui, New York City, Italy, and in Malibu where Dirk was presently sitting with his agent beside the infinity pool at a palm tree shaded table on the lower terrace of his oceanfront retreat.

David said nothing, reclining uncomfortably in his chair, appearing stiff, as if his back was bothering him.

"Lighten up," Dirk said, nodding at a bottle of bourbon and two glasses with ice cubes floating like clouds of crystal in an amber sea. "You'll feel better about this after you have a drink. C'mon. Humor me. It's a beautiful day."

David's face remained tense as he looked out at the whitecapped waters shimmering beneath the glowing warmth of the sun. "I'll grant you that. Every day's beautiful here. But just for the record, I was rich long before I discovered you brewing cappuccinos at Starbucks. Salud." He smiled thinly and tipped his glass to Dirk, then let the smoky liquid slide down his throat. "God that's good! You know your bourbons. Pappy?"

"Yeah." Dirk poured three fingers for David and three for himself. "Michael sends me a case every year. Look—I didn't know about the heroin until I was in their room. I swear. But it's actually working in my favor. Now the media thinks I'm not only a beast in bed—thanks to your concerned citizen's call about women in the next room over screaming for their lives—but that I'm also addicted to heroin." He paused for a moment to consider the irony of his good fortune, breathing in the warm ocean air.

"You went to jail, Dirk," David pointed out grimly.

"That wasn't part of the plan," Dirk admitted. "But Declan got me out in an hour, and I spent most of that doing cop selfies and signing autographs. And did you happen to turn on your TV last night?"

David gave him a grudging smile. "One of your finer performances. On the steps of the precinct looking suitably contrite. Right up until you parted the sea of paparazzi and sped off in a black, tinted-windowed Escalade. It was very Hollywood of you."

"I couldn't have scripted it any better. They're playing it on every station. *GMA* ran the whole thing this morning."

"But heroin?" David said, shaking his head in frustration. "Jesus Christ! I don't even want to think about—"

"I know. But it wasn't my hotel room—it was *theirs.* And the models—Savannah, Dakota, Eddison or Addison or whatever the fuck her name is—already fessed up to it, and I'm sure they're working something out with the DA. I had no knowledge that there was any heroin in the room. I've already been cleared. *Officially* cleared. Hell—I consented to a drug test at the station. I pissed in a cup. I'm clear."

"But all this—" David began, then looked up and blew out a sigh. He finished half his drink and started over: "All this, all this insanity—and it is insanity, you know! If that heroin was tied to you, not even Declan could save your ass. We're talking prison, Dirk. *Prison!* And not the minimum security country club bullshit for hedge fund guys who forget to pay their taxes. Prison! And for what? Why on God's green earth would you fucking risk everything for a little publicity? Because that's what this is about, right? Publicity?"

"That's the plan."

"Right," David said wearily. He held his glass up to his nose, giving it a deep appreciative sniff. "The plan—and let me know if I'm getting this right—is to garner as much attention as you can. But nothing good. Only the shit that sane people try to avoid." He groaned, then added sarcastically, "Makes perfect sense."

Dirk could almost picture the acid in his agent's stomach spouting up like seawater form a whale's blowhole. "We went over this, David. I need to hit bottom—*rock bottom.*" He drank from his glass, staring off at a yellow lab fetching a piece of driftwood for an elderly woman walking the beach. "The public needs to think I'm out of control. Lost. In a spiral. Charlie Sheen a few years back—but much, much worse."

David smiled, but his eyes were nervous and he was white-knuckling the armrests. "I get the relevance angle here. It's funny—all those times I got on you for not promoting yourself. I think I even accused you of living like an accountant once. But this"—he grimaced and glanced down, shuffling his loafers along the stone tiles—"this is *extreme*. I only wanted you to interview more and do the talk show circuit. Not this. This is… guerrilla marketing. And let's be honest—do you really need this? *You're Dirk Rathman.* No one's more relevant than you. I mean look at you." He waved a hand at Dirk like his appearance offended him. "It's not fair that you look the way you do. You make guys like me look like a different species. And by *different*, I mean uglier, fatter, hairier and just all-around less appealing to the other seven billion people we're sharing the planet with. I don't think it's a coincidence my wife only has sex with me after you stop by the house. And how about your career: Six of the top twenty highest grossing films in the last five years. So this—this *plan* of yours, I just don't—"

"What were they talking about before the cops arrested me?" Dirk interrupted, then drained his glass, holding the whiskey in his mouth for a second or two before swallowing it down. He poured himself another, his eyes on his agent. "Who was generating buzz? Who were the kids talking about at school? Me? Were they talking about me?"

David looked down at his drink guiltily and tilted his glass, making the ice cubes rattle.

Dirk waited until David's eyes had moved back to him. "Do you realize Kim Kardashian has four times as many Twitter followers as me? Can you explain that?"

"Well, you know how it is, Dirk." David coughed into his fist and removed his sunglasses. "She's a shameless media whore." He held them up, checking for prints. "And you're, well, a decent self-respecting person who values his privacy. You've always kept your distance from the… people."

Dirk's jaw tightened. "Let me ask you a question: Do you think I avoid the public because I don't like people or because I can't go anywhere without creating a scene? And if you're having trouble with that one, let me remind you that the paparazzi recently got into a battle royale over my *garbage* and one guy nearly lost a finger. I now have to pay someone to stand guard over my trash to prevent those idiots from cutting each other up with soup can lids."

David put his sunglasses down on the teak table, his nearly bald head bright and beading with sweat. "That was unfortunate. But isn't that why you live like this." He raised his drink to the glittering Mediterranean mansion to their backs, its four levels of retractable glass walls reflecting sun, surf and sand.

"I'm not complaining," Dirk said. "I wouldn't get much sympathy if I did. And I don't deserve it. So I have to live behind security walls in a private guard-gated community. Woe is me." He smiled a self-effacing smile. "That's how most people would live if they had a choice. And some things won't change." He studied David's eyes, pausing for effect. "Even after phase two."

"*Phase two?*" David's expression was hesitant, but amused. "I'm afraid to ask. What's phase two?"

"I'm going to put on a show tomorrow," Dirk said evenly, his face giving no indication as to what *show* might mean.

"Were you going to run this by me?" David asked.

"Sorry." A slightly devious smile creased Dirk's face. "You'll have to buy a ticket like everyone else."

"Just give me a teaser," David said. "Heroin?"

"Not this time."

"Models?"

"Of course."

"Location?"

Dirk laughed. He finished his drink and stood up, then stripped off his shirt and reached down for a large canvass duffel bag next to his chair. "You should stick around for this. I made a few calls of my own. The paparazzi helicopters should be here any minute."

"*Helicopters?*" David's eyes bulged in his red face. He glanced down nervously at the bag. "What do you have in there?"

"Racket and balls," Dirk said, grinning.

"For…?"

"I'm going up to the roof to hit some balls into the ocean. In my thong. Drunk on bourbon."

David gave him a long exasperated look. "Why would you do that?"

"Exactly." Dirk stabbed a finger into the table. "Why would a twenty-five-year-old millionaire movie star get drunk and hit tennis balls off his roof in a thong?"

David laughed reluctantly. "Let me guess. You've lost it? You're spiraling out of control? You've hit rock bottom? You're much, much worse than Charlie Sheen?"

"You're catching on," Dirk said, as he started for the house. Then he stopped and turned to face David. "By the way—I might slip and take a little tumble." He paused, laughing. "But don't worry. It's all part of the plan."

Chapter 6

COPING

Felix set off across campus in a *lucid fog*. That's what he called the state of mind that was neither lucid nor foggy. Too much lucidity and the reality of his life would overwhelm him, spiriting him away into a depthless depression. Too much fog and he couldn't function. But somewhere between lucidity and fogginess was a half-numb, half-lucid state—the *lucid fog*—that allowed him to go through the motions of living without thinking about his life.

As he picked his way along The Yard's billiard table-green grass to avoid the students clogging the path, he noticed an ivy-covered brick building up ahead. He'd been this way before, several times, but he'd never noticed the building. Felix—and everyone else on the football team—had been on campus for two weeks, since the start of 'two-a-days'. Three hours of practice in the morning and three in the afternoon during the hottest month of the year. Six hours each day of team-building torture while his future classmates were enjoying the last few weeks of their summer vacations.

Felix looked around (really *looked*) and saw there were lots of ivy-covered buildings—at least six just on the north side of The Yard. There were also stone archways along the paths. And the buildings were either stone or brick or both. *Stones, arches, and ivy.* Everything Fallon had talked about, but that he hadn't really noticed. He knew it was all there, he'd seen it without seeing it, a side-effect of his half-tranquilized state.

He hung a left at the building with the ivy—which he could now see had snaked its way up to the third floor, strangling large portions of the exterior and the grand entrance columns—and a quick right. Then he headed west along a cobblestone footpath with the sun in his eyes.

Cobblestone.

Fallon had said something about cobblestones too. He glanced down at the pale weathered stones beneath his feet. He'd never really noticed these either—at least he hadn't thought of them as cobblestones. That seemed so George Washington and Thomas Jefferson. If he'd thought about them at all (which he hadn't) they would have been bricks.

What else had he been missing?

And with that simple question to himself, his mind began clicking and coughing and whirring into gear like the engine of an old farm truck taken out of storage after a long winter. This was the problem with being alone. With no one to distract him, his mind, unfettered and allowed to roam, was free to travel down the dark corridors of his consciousness, and in an instant, there was no more fog. Lucidity had returned with a vengeance, cutting through the mental sludge, latching on to the thing at the forefront of his mind: the memories of the fire, the memories that didn't exist.

The doctors couldn't explain the memory loss. They attributed it to head trauma—although they couldn't find anything on the CT scan or X rays to support that theory—smoke inhalation, fortuitous sleep walking, or simply shock. One nurse had whispered in his ear that it was *God's will*— divine intervention. *They didn't know.* And he didn't really care. His parents were gone. That's all that mattered.

A cold blanketing malaise was falling over him. He had to find an escape route, an alternate track for his mind to follow. Looking for a distraction, he twisted his head around, searching the path, but couldn't find anyone that he knew. He wasn't interested in conversation, just someone to hover around. He'd become quite accomplished at hovering. It was amazing how much time you could pass with head nods and a few well-timed monosyllabic responses. It was pathetic, he realized, but it allowed him to avoid the misery of being alone with his troubled thoughts.

But even nods and grunts weren't without their own hazards; if he actually got pulled into the conversation he ran the risk of having a good time. And on the infrequent occasions that had happened, a startlingly realistic image had popped into his head of his parents observing him from above with looks of abject disapproval. It was like he could actually see the disappointed faces of his mom and dad, the hurt and scorn in their tear-filled eyes a painful reminder that having fun (or just not being miserable) was a dishonor to their memories. He was a better son than that. He owed them more than that.

With the late afternoon sun still high in the sky, Felix, despondent but functioning, took the practice field with the rest of the team. About sixty kids in all. Whistles blew and the players lined up quickly for warm-ups, led by Jimmy Clay. Jimmy was the team captain—despite the fact that he was the most violent kid Felix had ever met. Just an average-sized linebacker the year before, Jimmy had somehow packed on forty-five pounds of solid muscle over the summer. He was clearly shooting himself up with steroids—or something else far more potent than protein powder—but the coaches ignored his miraculous weight gain because he was the first pro prospect to put on a Sturgeon uniform since the 1950's.

Two hours into practice, freshman orientation and the walk from Rhodes Hall felt like it had never really happened. The anxiety, the sadness and the pain had all slowly receded, replaced by the smell of freshly-cut grass and the warmth of the early evening sun on his bare arms. *This was nirvana.* Felix wished it would never end. This was the only time he was able to forget about his life, even if for only a few short hours.

More whistles blew and the coaches organized the team in a non-contact scrimmage. They were playing the first game of the season in two days and the coaches seemed optimistic about their chances. But victories were hard to come by, especially in season openers: fourteen straight losses to be exact. The Sturgeons, as it turned out, had always been awful, the runt of the Pacific Northwest Football League—PNFL for short—and the only team to have never won the Rain Cup, the trophy awarded to the league champion.

The coaches conducted the scrimmage at three-quarter speed. The offense executed plays to make sure everyone knew their assignments, and the defense ran to the guy with the ball and put a hand on his chest or back, a tap. Tackling was not permitted. Fifteen plays into this choreographed dress rehearsal, the center snapped the ball to the quarterback, Brant Fisher. Felix cut inside the defensive back lined up across from him and loped unhurriedly toward the middle of the field. Then he raised his hand, signaling Brant to throw him the ball. Brant threw it. But he threw it too high.

Felix took a long stride and jumped off one foot, reaching high into the air. The ball lightly grazed the fingertips of his left hand; he tried to reel it in, to somehow make it stick to his fingers.

There was a loud crunching noise, Felix's head snapped back like his car had been rear-ended on the highway, and the ball sailed away out of sight. For a moment he was flying—backward and facing up—and then his flight through space ended abruptly as he crashed to earth. Felix was stunned. Through his facemask, he could see that the sky was still burning blue. *But why am I looking at the sky?* he thought, disoriented.

"What the hell are you doing, Clay?" a voice hollered above the din of whistles and panicked shouts. Felix knew the voice. It was pure gravel, unmistakable. Coach Bowman—the head coach.

"Huh?" A different voice. This one deeper. Less gravel. Jimmy's.

Someone knelt beside Felix and leaned over him. The orange glow of the sun disappeared behind the man's head. "Don't move!" It was Coach JJ, the trainer. He sounded worried.

"Hey, JJ." Felix wondered if he should be worrying too. He didn't feel any pain. Nothing felt wrong. So why was everybody scrambling around like he was dying?

"Don't move, August!" JJ said anxiously. "Let me get your helmet off."

Felix kept his head still, his peripheral vision picking up the skitterish movements of his teammates gathering around him. They'd taken off their helmets and were whispering in funereal tones.

"That's my starting receiver, you idiot!" Coach Bowman shouted (presumably at Jimmy).

"I thought it was... uh... full contact," Jimmy muttered. He sounded further away than Bowman.

"I think I'm okay," Felix said to JJ.

"Don't move," JJ repeated and unbuckled Felix's chin strap, then gingerly lifted the helmet over his head.

"Holy shit!" someone in the crowd shouted. "Look at the face mask!" Felix saw it. It was pulverized.

"Are you kidding me, Clay!" Coach Bowman reached over and took the damaged helmet from JJ. "You goddamn knew it was no contact. And that was a goddamn helmet-to-helmet hit." He raised it up to eye level, took a few steps in Jimmy's direction, and gave it a disgusted shake. The plastic grill had broken off from the helmet on one side and was swaying limply in the air. "What the hell's a matter with you, son?"

"Sorry coach," Jimmy mumbled. "I was a... playin' the ball. It was an accident. I didn't even see him."

"Try to move your fingers," JJ said to Felix.

Felix did. They moved just fine. Then he tried to sit up, but the trainer put a firm hand on his chest and pushed him back down to the turf. Some of his teammates clapped, apparently relieved that he wasn't paralyzed.

"I'm fine." Felix sat up quickly before JJ could stop him. His ears were ringing a little, but he felt all right.

"You sure?" JJ asked him skeptically, taking out a penlight. He shone it into his left eye, blinding it for a second, and then the right. "Well, your pupils look fine. When were you born?"

"The day I became a Sturgeon," Felix announced, knowing the coaches would like that.

"Good answer, August!" Coach Bowman bellowed, striding up beside him, his large belly straining the fabric of his shirt to its outermost limits. "You sure you're okay, son?"

"Never better," Felix answered confidently.

Coach Bowman smiled down at Felix for a moment, then his eyes found Jimmy (Felix could now see he was standing at the back of the crowd some twenty yards away) and his face set in an angry scowl. "Clay! Get your dumb ass to the track and give me four laps! Do it in under eight or you won't see the field Saturday." Bowman paused and added: "That's enough for today, boys." He blew his whistle in three short blasts. "Hit the showers!"

Brant stepped over to Felix and reached down with his hand as the crowd began to disperse. Felix took it and Brant heaved him up to his feet. "Damn, you're a helluva lot tougher than me," Brant said in a twang. He was from a small town in Texas Felix had never heard of and could never seem to remember.

Felix shrugged and stared down at his hands accusingly. "Sorry. I should've caught it."

Brant laughed. "Seriously? That was a shitty ass throw. I totally hung you out to dry for that roided-up asshole. But don't you worry—his punishment for trying to kill you is four whole laps. You think he's gonna do it in under eight?" He pointed across the field. "Check it out."

Jimmy was on the track. One of his buddies had joined him. Jimmy was laughing. They were both walking.

"What a dick," Felix grumbled, amazed that the coaches were letting him off so easy.

"Yeah, no shit," Brant agreed. "That guy's trouble. And I think he's got it in for you. You better watch your back."

Chapter 7

THE GROUNDSKEEPER

From the window of his third floor office, Bill Stout stood watching the students milling about in The Yard below. He was quite a bit older than the students, old enough, in fact, to be a tenured professor, but he could pass easily for a graduate student if he dressed for the part. He thought of his appearance as 'flexible', and it allowed him to mingle with faculty, alumni, and even students, without appearing out of place.

Bill hadn't always been a 'Bill'. He'd once gone by William. But no one had called him William—outside of his immediate family—since college. The summer before his senior year, he'd worked as an intern at the Green River Psychiatric Hospital. His experiences there had changed him—completely. So he'd thought it best—*fitting*—to retire William along with the life that he'd thought he was going to live. Now he was just Bill, a simple name for complicated times.

He poured himself a cup of tea from a thermos.

The office was large and bright, the south facing window providing a postcard worthy view of the campus and an abundance of natural light. PC had more office space than it knew what to do with (all full-time employees were "taken care of"), but this particular space would still be empty if he hadn't offered a small 'incentive' to his supervisor: $10,000 in exchange for the office (and the job—since he was in no way qualified for his current position) and the promise of $20,000 more at the end of the school year if his supervisor let him "do his own thing."

His only complaint about the office (and it wasn't really a *complaint*) was the shortage of real estate for his books. But PC's newly minted assistant groundskeeper (*lawnmower guy* seemed a better title) had no right to complain about such things because he had no right to an office in the first place. In any event, the problem wasn't the lack of shelving; whatever the upper limit for book toting acceptability might be, Bill had exceeded it: Two full walls of floor-to-ceiling shelves were bursting with books. There were also volumes piled high in front of the shelved books and several teetering towers stacked along the back wall behind a monstrous desk undoubtedly still there because ignoring it was easier than moving an object that weighed more than a truck. In the past seventeen years he'd lived in more places than he cared to recall, but as long as he had his books with him, he never felt completely alone. Even adults are entitled to their security blankets.

When a lovely old lady from HR (her three kids had all graduated with PC degrees, she'd told him proudly) had first brought him here a little over a week ago, the air was heavy with the medicinally sweet smell of lemon Pledge. The desk and an antique walnut table with two matching chairs—which sat beneath the window—had been freshly dusted and polished. And someone had left two brass keys on the table: one for the office door, the other for the desk.

Other than the books, the only personal effects he'd brought with him were some framed maps now displayed on the wall behind the desk. He'd always liked maps. Even as a kid, he'd had a wall-to-wall mural of the Caribbean islands next to his bed. There was something comforting about the constant reminder that the world was much larger than the immediate space that he occupied. That philosophy also applied to books, and it was another reason he surrounded himself with his favorites wherever he went.

He sipped his tea and pulled down the window blinds, then went over to the desk, leaving his teacup on the table. He took out a key from his front pocket, reached down and unlocked the bottom drawer. He spent a few moments pushing aside some papers and folders until he found what he was after.

From the back of the drawer, he retrieved a small brown book. He settled into a comfortable but squeaky roller chair and placed it on the desk. Some parts of the gnarled cover were a slightly darker shade of brown than others and along its bottom edge the leather had begun to peel away from its backing. In the upper-right corner, written in black ink, it said:

The Journal of Eve Ashfield
Ashfield Castle
London England

Ever so gently, he slowly opened the cover and pressed it down until it lay flat against the desk. Just behind the cover was a sheet of crisp notepad paper mottled like a hen's egg, the corners slightly dog-eared. It was swimming in words, words written in black ballpoint ink that had somehow retained most of its original color, though some of the letters had faded to a rich espresso. He called this piece of paper *The Warning*. The name wasn't intended to be clever. It was simply descriptive—that's what it was. After a brief letter from Eve to her sister Elissa, a *warning* filled up most of the page—The Warning—the words that had launched far more ships than Helen of Troy's pretty face.

Bill kept it behind the front cover, right where it was when he'd discovered the journal in Elissa's apartment all those years ago. He'd read it in its entirety on at least a hundred occasions over the years, each time no less exhausting, exhilarating and disorienting than the time before. He knew exactly what it said, but recalling the words from memory and reading them on the page were completely different experiences. And taking into account what he was planning to do shortly, this would be his final opportunity to experience the words that had changed his life forever, the words that he'd first read when he was still 'William'.

He focused his eyes on the piece of paper and began to read:

Elissa, my son came to me this morning, the eve of his 18th birthday, and asked if we believe him to be the Drestian. Had I lied he would have known, so I acknowledged his suspicions. The Warning says that the four signs will reveal the Drestian's identity. We have witnessed all four. There can be no doubt.

He held me in his arms for a long while, then he smiled sadly and said, "I wish there was another way, mother, I really do." There was a strange kindness in his voice, yet nothing will deter him, not even the great love that I know he feels for his family. He intends for his secret to die here with those who have kept it from the world. We have lived in denial of *what was right before us, our love for our son paving the misguided path that will end this night.*

I wish I could have finished this journal long before now, but my son senses such things, and I only dared to prepare The Warning. The rest I will write in haste before he suspects. I do not deserve your forgiveness, yet I pray that you grant it anyway. Goodbye. Eve.

Bill jerked his head up and tore his eyes away from the page, though they were drawn to it like a compass needle to the north. Emotions inundated him—sadness, fear, determination. They were exhilarating, and baffling, and as real as any emotions he'd ever felt. But they weren't his. He sat motionless, breathing slowly until the bizarre sensation of being inside Eve's head had passed. His stomach lurched, forcing bitter bile up through his larynx and into his mouth. He gagged and swallowed it back down. He looked around the office, trying to reorient himself to the present—*to reality*—by focusing on the titles crammed into the shelves next to the desk.

He took a deep breath and glanced down, careful not to let his eyes linger on any of the words long enough to actually read them. The Warning began just below Eve's note to Elissa, the fateful words spoken almost 2,000 years ago. He considered reading it, but then decided against it. His body's reaction to the journal depended on factors he'd never entirely understood, and today felt like one of those days where he couldn't handle The Warning without retching all over the floor—and he had plans to try a new Italian place in the Pearl District.

Leaving The Warning on the desk, he closed the cover and slipped the journal back into the drawer, then locked it with his key. The nausea finally passed. He stared at the speckled paper until he wasn't sure of the time, adrift in decades-old memories. Then, his mouth growing tight, he brought it up slowly, holding it by the top corners with his thumbs and forefingers. The paper fluttered. *Do it!* he told himself. *Do it!* It began to tear and the sound made Bill gasp as if he was in pain. He slapped it down quickly on the desk and ran a callused finger over the sawtooth split, trying to smooth away the wound. He leaned back, slouching, and blew out a frustrated sigh, putting his fingers between his eyebrows as if battling a hangover. He couldn't do it. He could never do it. This wasn't his first attempt.

One day soon, the boy would be here in his office, sitting at his table, reading the journal. That was the plan, a plan that had been formulated long ago. His gaze snapped back to The Warning and he thought about the consequences if the boy saw it: His stomach turned again and a shimmer of dread (and guilt) inched up his throat, causing his teeth to clench. The *plan* didn't include showing him The Warning. He couldn't let that happen. Which was why he needed to shred it, to erase all traces of its existence. But he couldn't do it. *He could never do it...* despite the consequences. This odyssey—*his odyssey*—had all begun with the journal, and he couldn't just tear up The Warning, the most important part, like it was junk mail. And the paper was more than just pulp and chemicals; it was something real and tangible, his only physical connection to Elissa, and he wasn't ready to give that up. Even after all these years there were times when his feelings of love and loss were as confusing and potent as the night she died—*the night she left him*. He would lock The Warning away someplace safe. The boy would never find out about it. Like ships passing in the night.

He stood on legs that felt a little shaky, crossed the office to the window and pulled down on the cord to open the blinds. Another day was slipping away. In a few hours, the sun would begin its descent beyond the cupola-topped buildings to the west. His teacup was on the table. He'd forgotten all about it. He sat down and sipped Earl Grey, wondering what Elissa's son was doing this evening.

Chapter 8

ROOMMATES

Fatassosaurs. There were three: Jonas, Larry and Salty. On the first day of practice Jonas had showed up in a Stegosaurus T-shirt and one of the coaches called him a fatassosaur. The name quickly caught on with the other coaches. And since Jonas was always hanging out with Larry and Salty, the coaches started calling them fatassosaurs too. Now the kids on the team were doing it, but Felix wasn't sure if that was such a good idea. Maybe they carried a little extra pudge around their midsections, like all offensive linemen do, but they weren't fat—they were just *big*. The most menacing-looking trio Felix had ever been around. If he ever found himself in the middle of a brawl he wanted them on his side.

In a lot of ways the fatassosaurs were interchangeable: they were all from Portland and had known each other since pre-school; they were all into ink—they had the same barbwire tattoo coiled around their sunfreckled arms, which were bigger than most kids' legs; and they all had a penchant for wearing T-shirts better suited for pre-pubescent girls. But best of all, they were all perfect candidates for hovering. They spent most of their time giving each other shit, and no one seemed to notice (or maybe they just didn't care) that Felix kept to himself and didn't say much. They were more interested in flexing their biceps than their brains, but being around them and their low-brow banter was distracting, and maybe even a little comforting. It was like eating ice cream out of the carton while watching *Jackass* reruns.

Felix walked behind them, as he usually did. Larry was getting into it with Jonas about something, but Felix wasn't listening. He was content just to be outside. They would be at their dorms shortly—Downey and Satler, where the school assigned every freshman to live during their first year—and there was something waiting for him in Downey (his dorm) that he was dreading. So he soaked up the sunshine and tried to enjoy the moment. It felt awesome; like an extension of football practice, but without the HGH-fueled psychopaths delivering bone-jarring cheap shots. He heard someone—Jonas?—say "Kim" and he knew immediately what they were talking about. He was intimately familiar with the details of the *Kim story*.

Jonas had gone to a party last year and hooked up with a girl he'd never met before—Kim. A few months later, his family had staged a big party for his grandmother's birthday. At the party, Jonas bumped into Kim again only to find out they were distantly related: third cousins twice removed or fourth cousins or something like that. Jonas, stupid drunk one night, made the mistake of telling Larry and Salty about the whole thing.

"So what'd Kim say when she realized she'd had sex with her cousin?" Larry asked Jonas. Felix had heard this exact line at least ten times. Larry was grinning. Nothing made Larry happier than busting Jonas's balls.

"The same thing your mother said," Jonas replied, smiling at what he thought was a witty comeback (the same witty comeback he always used).

"I just love having sex with all my cousins," Salty screeched in a highly disturbing falsetto that gave Felix the chills. Salty had a follow-up to that comedic gem: "That's what we do here in West Virginia."

"Watch your mouth, shitwad!" Larry blasted Salty's shoulder with his forearm, knocking him off the path and into the grass. "That's my mother you're talkin' about."

"Why you hittin' *me*?" Salty complained. "Jonas is the one talkin' shit about your mother."

"I didn't say shit about his mother," Jonas shot back and shoved Salty into Larry, who pushed him right back into Jonas. Felix dropped back a step to avoid the 260-pound human ping pong ball.

Larry grunted. "Nah. You just banged your cousin. You're sick, ya know. How could you do that, you sick freak."

"Incest is best, bitches. Ain't my fault you don't have any bangable cousins." Jonas grinned wide and blew hot air on his fingernails, then buffed them on his massive chest.

Felix felt the edges of his mouth tilting up into a smile, then quickly looked up, expecting to see the disapproving faces of his parents. But there was nothing but clear air and blue sky. For now (at least) he was safe. Up ahead, he saw the brick façade of Downey, and directly across from it, Satler. From a distance, the dorms looked identical, and close up, they still looked identical. The only distinguishing feature between the two all-freshman dorms, tucked away in the northeast corner of campus, was their names: One was named for Bernard Satler, a wealthy alumnus, and the other, for a former dean, Thomas Downey.

Felix skirted around the fatassosaurs to get a better view of the Freshman Yard, a stretch of emerald green grass that separated the dorms. He didn't like what he was seeing: the miniaturized version of The Yard was crawling with people. Little kids were chasing each other across the grass, and older people—parents, he supposed—were walking around aimlessly taking pictures. There was a game of soccer on one side, and on the other, it looked like the students were playing wiffle ball against their parents and younger siblings. He picked up the scent of cooking meat and noticed white smoke drifting up from a line of grills set up at the edge of the lawn over on the Satler side.

When Felix had left the dorm with Allison for freshman orientation it wasn't quite this bad, but it was getting there. The masses had started arriving two days ago, and now every freshman was here, along with some lingering relatives. He just wasn't used to so many people being around. This part of the campus had been practically deserted for the past two weeks; there were days when he didn't even see anyone in Downey. And Downey was really nice, especially since he had the run of the place: It all felt like a posh hotel to Felix. Not that he'd ever stayed at a posh hotel. But now absolute chaos had replaced his fortress of solitude.

When they reached the Freshman Yard, Salty and Jonas left the path and headed toward Satler. "Yo Jonas," Larry called out, as Jonas and Salty strolled right through the middle of the wiffle ball field, getting in the way of a startled-looking little girl trying to run the bases. "If I see your cousin, I'll tell her where she can find you. Oh—I forgot. She's still in high school."

Jonas turned and shouted: "You're such a dick, Larry!" A fifty-something woman with a glove on her hand and a foot on second base flinched and gazed up at Jonas like she was looking at the devil incarnate with her own eyes.

"That's what your cousin told me!" Larry yelled after him and laughed loudly.

Felix smiled, but quickly caught himself and looked up, heart thumping fast. No parents. It seemed the cloud of parental scorn was giving him a temporary reprieve today.

He followed Larry up the steps to Downey, and immediately groaned in frustration. The lobby was worse than the Freshman Yard. It looked like a few hundred people had gathered for a choreographed farewell scene in some cheesy movie. There was lots of hugging, teary-eyed mothers and fathers whose expressions ran the gamut from proud to comatose.

Felix used Larry as a blocker to thread his way through the mob to the staircase adjacent to the elevators, stepping over suitcases and boxes, and dodging students running up and down the stairs like hyperactive children off their meds. They finally made it to the second floor—guys occupied the second and fourth floors, girls the first and third—where Larry told Felix that the Betas (one of the frats) were having a party tonight, then he lumbered off down the hallway.

Felix continued up, taking the stairs two and three at a time, trying to slide past the newcomers without crashing into them. There were tons of people clotting the fourth floor hallway. Most were students, but there was a fair share of parents looking around and unpacking things and just generally trying to act like they didn't feel out of place. The students looked like Felix, only happier and more excited to be there. Some of them said hello. He nodded, and muttered hello back.

When he arrived at his room, he paused, standing at the door, staring at it. This was the moment he'd dreaded. He really liked his room. It sounded lame, but it *was* his private sanctuary, a place where he could be alone and block out the rest of the world and his shitty life. He'd taken it for granted. That chapter was over. Someone else was in there now—*a roommate*—waiting on the other side of the door. Someone he would be sharing the cramped space with for the entire school year.

The air in the hallway suddenly felt heavy. His stomach turned and a spurt of anxiety constricted his throat. He reached out for the knob and realized that his hand had tightened itself into a fist, his fingernails biting into his palm. He blew out a quick breath and relaxed his fingers, curling them around the knob. He cracked open the door and cautiously peered in.

A stranger was lying in Felix's bed, flip flops on, hands clasped behind head, head on pillow. He looked very comfortable.

As Felix stepped into the room, the stranger—*my roommate*, he reminded himself—popped up and smiled at him. He was three or four inches shorter than Felix, but stockier, with dark brown hair and a few days' worth of scruff on his chin.

"Hey, I'm Lucas," he said, still smiling. "You must be Felix. Or at least I hope you're Felix. Cause if you're not, then I'm totally in the wrong room." He started laughing.

Felix smiled back hesitantly, wondering if he'd seen Lucas before somewhere. He looked really familiar. But where was it? Freshman orientation? "Yeah—good to meet you. But um... actually, sorry, but I've been using that one." He pointed apologetically at his bed.

"Oh! Sorry, dude." Lucas smacked his forehead with the heel of his hand. "I needed a little TO from unpacking my shit. I won't bang any chicks on your bed if you don't bang any on mine. Deal?" He laughed. "Sorry, I'm a little out of it. My flight got in late and I didn't get to freshman orientation until that douchey president kid was doin' his, 'once a Sturgeon, forever a Sturgeon' bullshit."

"He is a douche, right?" Felix said.

"No question."

Felix already liked this kid.

"So you've been here a while, right? For football practice?" Lucas took a step back and his eyes appraised him. "Dude, you're *tall*. I bet you're pretty good." If Lucas noticed that Felix was feeling anxious, he wasn't showing it.

"I don't know. I'm okay, I guess." Felix shrugged. "I kinda sucked today though. A steroid freak nearly killed me. I probably have a concussion and don't even know it."

Lucas laughed—a big, hearty, open-mouthed laugh. There was something about it that took Felix by surprise (in a good way). It sounded completely genuine and unselfconscious, the kind of laugh that makes everyone in the room want to laugh right along. Its infectiousness was working its way into Felix, and he felt himself getting pulled in.

"I played football in high school." Lucas struck a Heisman pose. "Back in Excelsior Township, I was a pretty decent running back."

"That's cool. Where's that?"

"Minnesota."

"Wait a minute!" Felix suddenly realized where he'd seen him. "*Lucas* from Minnesota. You're Lucas Mayer. You're Minnesota Mayer! I thought you looked familiar. You're from that reality show, right? What's it called?"

Lucas grinned sheepishly. "*Summer Slumming.*"

"Yeah. That's it. Holy shit! Where was that house? Florida? It was pretty bad, right?"

"Fort Lauderdale," Lucas said, nodding. "It wasn't a house. It was a *shithouse*. A total disaster. Two bedrooms for all ten of us. It sucked. But that was the whole premise of the show. Ten eighteen-year-olds about to go off to college trying to survive the summer in a dump that smells like unwiped ass."

"That's so awesome!" Felix said. "I saw all the episodes—I think. But there weren't very many, were there?"

"Eight. We're still waiting to find out if the network's gonna pick up another season."

Felix had never met a celebrity before—or even seen one in person.

He found himself staring at Lucas, and the first thing that struck him was how much he looked like the kid on TV. Which made perfect sense, of course, because he was the kid on TV. From what he remembered of the show, the girls in the Fort Lauderdale shithouse all loved Lucas, but he kept pissing them off because he was a big time wise ass.

"Hey!" Felix said abruptly. Something had occurred to him. "Didn't you bang whatsherface? In the last episode? The blonde? The hot one."

"Yeah," Lucas admitted, shaking his head like he was embarrassed. "I did. And yeah—she was smoking hot. But doing it on TV was *stupid*. It's hard to explain, but even though you know the cameras are there, sometimes you forget or… maybe it just doesn't register, that on the other side of 'em are like millions of people in their living rooms hoping you make an ass of yourself. And the producers are always in your ear telling you to do something— something crazy or stupid. And it's kinda… addictive, I guess." He dragged a hand over his face and rubbed his eyes. "The show was wild. Don't get me wrong—I loved every minute of it. And I can't even tell you how many chicks I've nailed because I'm on it. But I am *so* happy to be here."

"In Oregon?" Felix asked, surprised.

"Yep."

"It's a long way from Minnesota," Felix said.

"My three older brothers went here. I'm a triple legacy. The admissions office couldn't turn me down."

"Any of 'em still here?"

"No. My brother Bret graduated two years ago, and he was the last— besides me. I have another brother. Tanner. He's a year behind me. He's thinking about making it five Mayers in a row. I don't know if my mom's too happy about that though. She's already freaking out as it is."

Felix puzzled over this for a moment. *"Freaking out?* About what?"

Lucas looked surprised. "Seriously? You're from around here aren't you?"

"Oh," Felix said, finally getting it. "You mean the forest thing."

"Of course I mean the forest thing." Lucas kicked aside a deflated duffel bag, crossed the room and sat down on his bed (just a mattress with no sheets or a pillow). "They just found those two hikers. I heard they were missing limbs and shit. And the guy on the news was saying they haven't found the dude's head." He cringed. "And those three campers—they're still missing, right? The one's from like four months ago. And they were in the *same* forest. Everyone thinks it's connected. My mom definitely does. What's that place called? Andley Forest?"

"Ashfield," Felix corrected, taking a seat on his bed. "It's not too far from here." He knew all about the *forest thing* (everyone in Oregon did), but he'd just been taking it one day at a time. That was the only way he could survive. He felt like he was drowning in a pool of anguish and anxiety and the only way he could get air was to suck it through a straw that seemed to be getting punctured with more holes by the day. His own troubles had been so consuming he really had no idea what was going on in the world. But the murders in Ashfield Forest, the *'Ashfield Forest Mystery'*, the media was calling it, had dominated the headlines, making it impossible for even Felix to ignore.

"You hear anything new?" Lucas asked. "What's the inside scoop? What are the locals saying?"

"Monsters or aliens," Felix said dryly. "That's what the crazies think."

Lucas laughed nervously. "Maybe the crazies are right. It's just… messed up. You couldn't pay me enough to go to that forest. I've seen enough horror movies to know what happens when you go into the woods. Dude—this is depressing. But I've got just the thing." He pushed himself off the mattress, stepped over to the closet next to his bed, and flung open the doors. Felix stood up to see what he was doing. Lucas bent down, reached inside and scooped up a box in both hands which he held above his head for a moment before shouting: "Beer! The number one doctor recommended cure for depression!" He put the box on his bed and after demolishing one end of it, took out two cans and brought one over to Felix.

Lucas pulled back the tab on his can and held it up to Felix who did the same. "Here's to an awesome year. Once a Sturgeon—"

"Forever a Sturgeon," Felix finished, and they clicked their cans together.

Lucas laughed and drank from his can.

Felix took three long swallows and looked around the room. Strangely, even with a roommate, it still felt like a sanctuary. He felt a smile creeping across his face. Then his smile turned into a halting laugh, then finally, he broke into an actual laugh that rivaled Lucas's. He couldn't remember the last time he'd laughed like this. It felt good. It felt really good.

"You know what we're gonna need?" Lucas said, grinning at Felix like they'd been friends for years.

"A fridge," Felix answered quickly. The beer tasted several degrees warmer than room temperature, like it had been sitting in a sun-heated car for a good while.

"Damn right," Lucas agreed. He wiped beer from his chin and belched. "This tastes like piss. Good piss—but still piss."

"Where'd you get this, anyway?"

"Dude, that was my first priority after I found the dorm. There's a little convenience store down the road, and the guy at the counter barely looked at my license."

"Whose license?"

"My brother's. If anyone asks, I'm twenty-six." Lucas smiled and drank from his can.

"I almost forgot." Felix glanced down at his watch. "My friend should be here any minute."

"Cool. Is he on the football team?"

"*She.* Allison. Friend from back home."

"Just a friend?"

Felix nodded. "We hang out a lot, but we've never hooked up or anything."

"Why not? She busted?"

"Not even close," Felix said with a smile. "Probably the hottest girl at my high school."

"You don't have a girlfriend, do you?"

"No." Felix paused. "I dated this girl—Emma—for like three years, then things just... ended right after graduation."

"Why'd you dump her?"

Emma, Felix's girlfriend—*ex-girlfriend*—was the only girl he'd ever been with. They started dating sophomore year and were inseparable all during high school. They did everything together. He'd even told her that he loved her; one star-filled night in the back seat of his Wrangler he'd confessed his unshakeable teenage love to her. And how'd she repay him? Two weeks after graduation she broke up with him. Just like that, three years of movie nights, keggers in the woods, proms and car sex were all discarded like a greasy fast food wrapper. She didn't even call him after the fire. Everyone gets dumped at some point, but the things Emma had told him at the lake—her reasons for breaking up with him—were too embarrassing and too painful to dredge up.

"I... uh... you know, she was getting too serious and all—stage five clinger type," Felix lied, taking a long pull from his can, buying time to come up with something believable. "She was heading off to Seattle for college and I was coming here. I thought I should have my freedom. I didn't wanna be stuck in some dumb long-distance relationship."

"Good for you, dude. Smart move freeing yourself up so you can bang PC chicks."

He bought it, Felix thought, relieved. Lucas went back to the Bud Light box, dug out two more cans and passed one to Felix.

There was a knock at the door. "Felix? Hey, it's me." Then louder, rising above the clamoring buzz of activity out in the hall: "Felix?" A girl's voice—Allison's. Felix took a step toward the door, but it swung open before he could get to it. Allison slipped into the room. Another girl followed. And then another.

"Beer!" Allison exclaimed, noticing the can in Felix's hand. "Nice." She smiled at him. "That better not be the last one!" She turned to the girls and said, "This is Felix," then spun back to Felix and made a fluttery gesture with her hands that made him feel like a contestant on a game show. Back to the girls she went: "This is the guy I was telling you about. The one I went to high school with." Then back to Felix: "This is my roommate Caitlin"— Allison held out her hand toward a girl who was six inches shorter than her, then she pointed at the other girl—"and this is Harper, Caitlin's friend from high school."

"Hey," Felix said to the girls.

"Hey," they said in return.

Lucas stepped up to announce his presence in the room: "And I'm Felix's roommate," he said, handing out beers and getting Felix's attention with a big grin and a quirked eyebrow.

While Lucas passed around the beverages, Felix took the opportunity to check out the new girls. The short one—Caitlin—was cute with honey brown hair streaked with blonde highlights, and a tan so deep and rich it went below the skin, the kind that only comes from spending a long summer at the beach. She wore a pair of enormous diamond studs in her ears and her fingers were wreathed in jewels that sparkled in blue, red, and green. Her watch was understated, but Felix didn't think she bought it at Target. She smelled like money.

The other girl—Harper—was nearly as tall as Allison. Her hair was long, blonde and slightly wavy. It occurred to Felix, quite suddenly, that she was beautiful. He tried not to stare, but the longer he looked at her, the more he realized that she wasn't simply beautiful in a generic kind of way. She was absurdly beautiful, straight from the pages of a *Victoria's Secret* catalogue or the *Sports Illustrated* swimsuit issue. Then, still gaping and unable to take his eyes off her, he quickly changed his mind. She was even hotter than the girls who graced the pages of those publications. She was *impossibly* beautiful; it was like she'd been airbrushed into the room.

Felix felt a warm, awkward flush creep up from his neck to his cheeks and he prayed that no one noticed he was blushing. He was literally light-headed. There wasn't enough air in the room. His mouth was dry, too dry to speak. Luckily for him, Lucas was chatting with the girls about something; he didn't seem nervous at all. The girls laughed. Felix was trying to listen to the conversation, but it was like everyone was speaking in Mandarin.

He knew if he didn't stop staring, Harper was going to think he was a freak. He dragged his eyes away, finally, and glanced around the room, trying to get a handle on himself. They were all standing in a loose circle in the center of the room between beds pushed up against opposite walls. The ceiling was low and the walls were beige-white. Other than one good-sized window overlooking a clump of tall trees that partially concealed a brick building in the distance, the room was done in matching pairs: beds, desks, closets, and little wall mirrors. The arrangement was very practical and utilitarian.

Even after taking inventory of the room, Felix still couldn't focus on what was going on... then Allison saved him. She got his attention with a question about football practice. He sputtered out something about a kid named Jimmy nearly decapitating him.

Everyone laughed.

Felix had apparently, and inadvertently, said something quite funny (he wasn't sure what it was exactly). And when he saw Harper smiling at him it set off another round of shameless staring.

"You wanna hear something funny?" Caitlin said to no one in particular. "You"—she fixed her gaze on Lucas—"look just like that guy on *Summer Slumming*."

Lucas held up one finger and drained his beer. Then he wiped his lips and said, "That's because I *am* that guy on *Summer Slumming*." He bowed deeply as if he was introducing himself to the Queen of England.

"No way!" Allison shouted. "I knew it—but I didn't wanna say anything. They were talking about you downstairs. But everyone thought you were in Satler. I can't believe you're Felix's roommate! This is so cool!"

"I've never known an actual celebrity," Harper said. She sounded excited but not as excited as Allison.

"And you still don't," Lucas remarked with a laugh. "I'm just another reality show idiot."

"Didn't you have sex with that girl?" Caitlin crinkled up her nose in disgust like someone had just thrown a rotting fish into the room. "What was her name? Cheap-bling, or Venus de Sexy, or something ridiculous like that?"

"I did." Lucas dug his free hand into a pocket of his shorts. "And for your information, her name's *Z-Bling.* What'd you think of my performance?"

Everyone laughed.

Everyone except Caitlin. "I'd have given you an F," she said disdainfully.

"*Is that so?*" Lucas feigned surprise. "Well, maybe you can show me what I need to improve on."

Caitlin's eyes bulged from their sockets. Her mouth opened, then closed, then opened again as she looked back and forth from Lucas to Harper as if she was hoping Harper would provide the snappy comeback she was searching her brain for. Finally, she stammered out: "You can't... you can't be serious!"

Lucas smiled at her and laughed. "I'm just jerking your chain, Little C. Come on, drink your beer and relax a little. How are we gonna be friends if you take everything I say so seriously?"

"Don't call me Little C," Caitlin said testily. "I don't like beer. And don't tell me what to do." Harper was laughing in a way that made Felix think she'd seen this from Caitlin many times before.

Lucas grinned at Caitlin's volley, completely nonplussed. "How can you not like beer?"

"I don't know," Caitlin said, annoyed. "Why do I need a reason? I just don't. I like wine."

"Well you might wanna start appreciating it." Lucas smiled. "'Cause I don't think they serve much wine at college parties."

Caitlin frowned as she seemed to consider Lucas's suggestion. Then she held the can up to her lips and took a sip. She quickly brought it back down and made a scrunchy face. "It's bitter."

"The more you drink, the sweeter it gets," Lucas said.

"Okay then," Allison said, watching the exchange between Caitlin and Lucas with a curious expression. "Speaking of serious, what were you guys talking about when we got here? You looked all intense."

Felix didn't want to bring up Emma with Allison in the room. She didn't know all the sordid details, but she knew she broke up with him, and he didn't want everyone knowing (especially Harper) that his high school girlfriend had kicked his sorry ass to the curb.

"Just all the shit goin' on in Ashfield Forest," Felix said. It was the first thing that popped into his head.

"Oh." Caitlin tensed up like a sudden bout of acid reflux had just hit her. "My parents—Harper's too—are concerned about it. But it's not like we're ever going there. That forest is way on the other side of town."

Harper wiped a trace of foam from her upper lip and said quietly, "It's still too close if you ask me. I wish it was on the other side of the world. It's just so depressing."

"Yeah, but not as depressing as the Faceman," Caitlin said in a grim voice, her somber tone darkening the mood like a blanket.

The room went silent, heads nodding in agreement.

"I mean," Caitlin continued, "you can just avoid whatever's going on in the forest. It's simple—you just don't go. Problem solved. But the Faceman... well... he—"

"Finds you, kidnaps you and blows your face off," Harper finished quickly.

More head nodding and nervous grunts of assent.

"If you're an only child, raise your hand," Lucas said, looking around at each of them.

No explanation was necessary; they all knew what that meant.

Caitlin shuddered and slowly raised her hand.

Felix raised his beer above his head. He glanced at Allison, wondering what she was going to do. She was staring at him. Her expression was hard, her eyes cold. He could take a hint. If she didn't want to tell anyone she was adopted (and an only child) that was fine by him. It's not like he would ever volunteer that information anyway. *She had to know that.* He didn't think her eye daggers were really necessary.

"I have a sister," Harper said.

"I have two," Allison said, her fierce stare still on Felix.

"Four brothers," Lucas added. "So I guess that means Felix and Caitlin are going to die this year."

"Hey!" Caitlin screamed at Lucas. "That's not funny. You shouldn't even joke about things like that."

"Okay," Lucas said. "Okay. I'm sorry. I'm just joking. I take it back. Geez. You're awfully sensitive for someone so cute, Little C. Nobody's gonna die this year, okay? Nobody."

Chapter 9

THE BETAS

The frat party started off with the five of them getting lost on the way to the house. Maybe it was because the campus looked different at night or because no one knew their way around (besides Felix, who was walking behind Harper and paying more attention to her ass than where they were going). Or maybe it was the case of beer they'd polished off in two hours. Whatever it was, thirty minutes after leaving the dorm they were right back at the Freshman Yard. Twenty minutes after that, Caitlin took Lucas's phone—the two beers she'd choked down had apparently gone to her head—and took off like a scared rabbit. Lucas chased after her and she fell into a shrub. He got his phone back but she lost a shoe—her *favorite* shoe. A lengthy search yielded nothing, and they were only able to continue on their way after Lucas convinced her that he'd seen an unusually large squirrel scurrying off with it.

Then it got awkward.

It seemed like the entire student body had descended on Greek Row, stately old behemoths clustered along Adams Street on the northwestern corner of campus. While Felix was trying to decide if the houses reminded him of funeral homes or something out of *Gone With The Wind*, a pair of Betas at the door let them all in after taking an unnecessarily long look at the girls. Before Felix had time to get too worked up at the way the Betas were checking out the girls they were inside the house. The inside may have been as stately as the outside, but it was too dark, too crowded, and too loud to get a sense of anything. They made their way to the keg room where a group of Betas swarmed the girls like park pigeons swooping down on bread crumbs scattered on the sidewalk; the Betas brought the girls beers and led them off to the dance floor. Meanwhile, Felix and Lucas got their own beers and led themselves to a darkened corner where they drank and shouted at each other to be heard over music so loud it vibrated the floors and rattled the pictures (horses and boats) on the walls.

Then it got annoying.

Some of the kids at the party didn't look like kids at all. They looked... old. Like adults. And everyone there seemed to know everyone else. And if that wasn't enough to make Felix feel like an outsider, a short Beta with a spiky faux hawk made a point of throwing a shoulder into his chest as he walked by; then he gave Felix a look that left no doubt he was looking for a fight. That happened just as Harper emerged from the dance floor with enough Betas trailing behind her to form a basketball team. Felix watched her break into peals of laughter as one of the Betas (they were all wearing shirts with bright red "Bs" splashed across their chests) leaned in and whispered something in her ear. Felix felt his face getting hot. His stomach started to knot up. Then Harper and her entourage disappeared back into the sea of thrashing bodies. Felix drained the rest of his beer and slipped into line to get another, thinking that this was the worst party ever.

It was about to get a whole lot worse.

Most of the kegs had kicked. It was getting late. Lucas had just told another girl—the fourth tonight—that he wasn't Minnesota Mayer. When Felix gave him a surprised look, Lucas shrugged and said, "If I wanted to bang mediocre chicks I'd have to put 'em on a waiting list." He was laughing, but Felix didn't think it was a joke.

Harper and Caitlin returned to the keg room, heads close together, nodding quickly, mouths working fast. When they were within shouting range, Caitlin gave them a questioning look and said, "She's not with you?"

"Who?" Felix asked. He was already annoyed, and wishing they hadn't come here. When they'd left the dorm, he never thought the night would play out like this. He wasn't expecting to hook up with Harper (of course he'd thought about it—*a lot*), but he didn't think she'd spend the night laughing, dancing and drinking with twenty other guys. What did they have that he didn't? Why didn't she want to hang out with him?

"Allison," Caitlin said.

"We haven't seen her in, I don't know, an hour maybe," Felix replied.

Harper and Caitlin exchanged a glance.

"What's going on?" Felix asked, feeling like Harper and Caitlin were trying to hide something from him. But why would they do that?

"You think she's with *him*?" Harper said to Caitlin.

"I don't know." Caitlin shrugged. "Maybe. But we should look in case..."

"Who's *him*?" Felix shouted at them.

"Come on," Harper said. "I think the rooms are upstairs." She turned and headed down a hallway that led to the front of the house. They all fell in behind her. The place was still overrun with people, but it had thinned out some; Felix could actually see the walls, and he didn't have too much trouble finding the staircase. He also saw someone he knew—a kid on the football team. Felix went up to him and asked if they could have a look upstairs. The kid yawned and went back to his beer.

When they reached the landing, Felix's first thought was how pissed the parents were going to be when they got home. Then he remembered where he was. This wasn't high school. A main hallway ran the length of the house, and it was even more congested than the floor below: wall-to-wall bodies. Everyone had a red plastic cup in hand and some kids had two, probably a strategy employed when the kegs began to run low. A couple to their right was making out, and someone near them was laughing and shouting, "Get a room." As they stood there taking it all in, no one seemed to pay any attention to them.

"Christ!" Lucas said, looking back and forth as if he was about to cross a busy intersection. "If she's in a room, we're never going to find her. Which way you wanna go?"

"Maybe that w—" Harper started to say.

A fat Beta in an orange polo came stumbling out of the nearest room shouting: "You're an asshole, Jeff! I hope that scabby slut makes your dick fall off!" Then he stomped through the hall, but before he could get very far Lucas caught up to him and grabbed his arm to get his attention.

"Hey," Lucas said to him as the Beta freed his arm with a clumsy tug. "We're looking for a girl. Dark hair. Tall. Green shirt—I think. You seen her?"

He laughed and started walking off. Then he stopped and turned back to Lucas. *"I did see her.* See that pretty door?" He pointed off to his left to an area just a short way down the hall. Felix followed his finger and glimpsed strips of red and blue through the shifting crowd. "In there. Why don't you have a look?" He started up with the laughter again as he stumbled away.

Felix found a crease in the crowd and weaved his way to the door. Lucas joined him a few seconds later. It wasn't exactly pretty, but it was painted: a red letter B in the center along with a blue and white shield and two crossed swords beneath it. They looked at each other for a moment, then Lucas shrugged and reached out for the brass knob. He turned it and gave it a push. The door began to swing open. The room was dark, and Felix wondered why Allison would be in a room that—

And that's when everything came crashing down around them.

Felix wasn't sure how it had happened, but he was on the floor, face
down and smothered under bodies. At least three people were on top of
him—he saw a sneaker, a loafer and a large hairy toe sticking out from a flip
flop. He felt hands gripping his ankles, then his legs were wrenched up off
the floor, and he was being dragged away from the door; he looked up just
as it slammed shut. He heard screams. The carpet, rough and smelling of
beer, burned his chin as the door drew further and further away. He pushed
up with his arms, and then more bodies jumped on the pile and he collapsed
flat on his stomach. The screaming grew louder. And mixed in with the
screams was laughter.

"Get off of me, you assholes!" Lucas was shouting. "Get off!" It
sounded like he was on the floor too, and close, though Felix couldn't see
where he was. He had a momentary flashback to earlier in the day of looking
up at a blue sky through the grill of a facemask and wondered what he had
done today to deserve this.

"What the hell's going on?" someone shouted. "What's going on down
there? Pracker! Get up! Get everyone off! Pracker! Hey!"

Felix knew the voice. But from where? He couldn't place it.

The people crushing the air out of Felix began untangling themselves
limb by limb and the load lightened. Then he felt something sharp digging
into his side—a finger?—and he let out a painful shout. He got to his knees
and shrugged the rest of them off. He planted one foot, but before he could
get the other one out from under him, someone pushed him hard in the
chest and he banged up against the wall. Felix glanced over and saw it was
the little punk with the faux hawk. The kid screamed something angry and
incoherent at Felix, then he balled up his hands into fists and brought his
arm back into a punching position. Felix jumped to his feet and raised his
arms to protect his face.

Lucas intervened: He grabbed the kid by the shoulders and threw him
down the hall (he actually caught air), sending him sprawling to the floor.

"Hey!" That same voice again. "Enough! Cut it out! Perry, get your ass
over here!"

Faux hawk punk—*Perry*—scrambled to his feet and was about to
charge at them when a tall blond kid snagged him by the collar and slung
him back into the crowd. Felix saw the blond kid's face—then his jaw
dropped. *It was Grayson Bentley.* And when Felix realized who the girl was
standing beside him, he started choking on carper fibers. *Allison.*

Felix was too stunned to react. Not only had a dozen frat boys
attacked him and Lucas for no reason, but Allison ('best friend' Allison; 'the

only person in the world he trusted' Allison) was practically holding hands with the President of the Student Union. The hall, already a human jungle, was getting even more knotted as kids emerged from their rooms—some only partially dressed—to see what was going on. Someone hit the overhead lights and suddenly the hall seemed as bright as a tanning bed.

Felix stood there with his mouth hanging open, staring stupidly from Allison to Grayson and back again. His eyes met Allison's for a moment and she looked down at the floor, a faint flush creeping over her cheeks.

"What were you doing in there?" Grayson asked them.

Felix didn't know how to respond. *In where?*

Grayson must have seen the confusion on Felix's face because he broke into a big smile.

"What the hell's so funny?" Lucas shouted at Grayson. He was holding onto a button (it looked like a bear had chewed on his shirt) that he glanced down at for a second before tossing it on the floor.

"You're right," Grayson said soberly, walking toward them through the parting crowd, his smile gone. "Breaking into our chapter room isn't a laughing matter. What did you think you were doing?"

Chapter room? Felix didn't even know what that was.

"*Well?*" Grayson demanded when they didn't answer.

"We didn't know it was your chapter room!" Lucas shouted. "Some idiot told us she was in there. We were just looking for *her*." He pointed at Allison, who was still gazing down at her feet.

"Oh." Grayson turned to her, his eyes widening slightly. "Friends of yours?"

"Yeah." Allison quick-stepped over to Felix and took him by the arm. Then she spun around to face Grayson and the mob that had congregated behind him. "I'm sorry, but I've... gotta go."

"Wait a minute," Grayson said in a surprised voice. "This isn't a big deal. The chapter room's supposed to be locked during parties. That was our fault. And for that, I'm very sorry." He turned his attention to Felix and Lucas. "Because of our carelessness, we've put you in a very awkward position."

"*Awkward?*" Lucas yelled. "You just tried to kill us, you ass—" He winced and grabbed at his side, the last word cut short.

Allison had elbowed him in the ribs.

"Please," Grayson said, staring straight at Allison now. "This was *clearly* a misunderstanding. No one got hurt. And the night's still young. Stay. I insist. I have a ninety-seven Brunello you'll absolutely love. When we were in my room didn't you tell me you wanted to learn more about wine? Well... here's your chance."

"Maybe some other time." Allison nudged Felix and Lucas toward the staircase.

Grayson gave Allison a sympathetic smile as if to say *I understand your predicament.* But when she turned away he caught Felix's eye, and his expression changed. He didn't look so sympathetic any more. He looked *angry.* Like Felix had just taken something from him. Something valuable.

Felix wasn't concerned about hurting Grayson's feelings—he just wanted to get the hell out of the Beta house. Felix and Lucas started toward the stairs, pressing through the crowd. A plastic cup hit the wall above Felix's head and beer rained down on them. More cups followed. Through a chorus of jeers and profanities, they covered their heads and plowed their way through the bodies. Someone pushed Felix, knocking him into Lucas, and they stumbled forward, now only a few feet from the end of the landing. And then a large body moved in front of them, blocking their escape route. Felix recognized him from football practice. His name was Pracker—Mark Pracker. Jimmy Clay's buddy—the one who strolled along the track with Jimmy after he got in 'trouble' for the helmet-to-helmet cheapshot.

"You look very familiar," Mark slurred drunkenly, jabbing his finger into Lucas's chest. "Do I know you from somewhere? Like TV or something?"

"Yeah," Lucas answered cheerfully. "I'm Justin Timberlake. Aren't you the kid who threw his panties at me at that concert in Vegas?"

It took some time for Mark's alcohol-sodden brain to process the fact that Lucas had insulted him. As Mark stuttered, *"Panties...?"* Caitlin managed to wedge her way between them and pushed Lucas through another gap in the crowd.

Allison dug her fingernails into Felix's arm and half-dragged him down the stairs. Harper followed right on his heels. They pushed their way through the lobby and out the front double doors and between the embassy-like columns. Without saying a word, they broke into a mad sprint as they crossed the lawn—now littered with red plastic cups—not slowing until they came to a path that wound its way through a grove on the western edge of The Yard.

They finally stopped to catch their breath. In the distance, they could hear shouting and a pounding bass—*th-thump th-thump th-thump*—that seemed to shake the leaves in the branches above. Felix wiped the beer from his face and checked their backs. No one had followed them.

"What the hell were you thinking?" Allison suddenly shouted at Felix. Her cheeks were red, her eyes full of intensity.

"*What?*" Felix hadn't expected that. If anything, he thought she would thank him for rescuing her. "What the hell were *you* thinking? We weren't gonna leave without you. What were you doing with that asshole?"

"He's not an asshole!" Allison's face was nearly purple. Her eyes were on fire. "And what did I tell you? *Huh?* I told you not to piss him off! His dad's the Governor of California. And already... Jesus! *What the fuck's wrong with you?*"

"I don't give a shit who his dad is!" Felix shouted back at her.

"Well you should!" Allison said. "Would it kill you to make things easy on yourself? *Just once?*"

Lucas cleared his throat. "He's definitely an asshole. You heard him. He was talking like he was the President of the United States, not the president of the Student Union." He turned to Allison, his expression serious. "Is his dad *really* the Governor of California?" When she gave him a grudging nod, he looked at Felix and cracked up with laughter. "Dude, that's not good."

Caitlin gaped at Lucas with a look that said *you must be insane.*

Allison narrowed her eyes at Lucas, hands on hips. "How would you know if he's an asshole? You don't even know him." She paused, the anger rolling off of her in seething waves. "I don't even know *you!*"

Lucas didn't appear fazed. "*So?* I've got a ton of experience with assholes. And that dude's definitely an asshole."

Allison fixed her flashing eyes on Felix, all the anger gone from her voice. "Why do you even... what does it matter? I'm not having this conversation." Then she turned and headed in the direction of the dorm. Caitlin chased after her, and then, after a *th-thump* or two, Harper followed. Lucas stayed back with Felix. When the girls were out of sight, Lucas said to him: "Did you notice how he was looking at us?"

Felix nodded. It was impossible to miss.

"That was probably a very dumb thing we just did." He laughed and threw his arm around Felix's shoulder. "It won't be the last. Welcome to college, buddy."

Chapter 10

NO-MAN'S-LAND

An hour before Felix was supposed to meet Lucas and the girls for dinner—he'd showered after his last class and applied an extra layer of deodorant in anticipation of seeing Harper—Allison called and asked him for a favor.

Someone calling herself *Martha* was advertising a pair of cross country skis for thirty-nine dollars on Craigslist. They were brand new, Allison's size, and they were Rossignols—her favorite brand. Martha even lived within walking distance, just a half mile from the football stadium. Allison didn't have a car. Felix did. But his Wrangler had just passed the 230,000 mile mark and it had at least one tire in the grave—it was at the shop (again) getting its transmission repaired. Martha had agreed to hold the skis for her if she picked them up today. It was just too perfect for Allison to pass up; she *had* to have them.

But there was a big black fly in Allison's bowl of chowder.

To the west of campus was "no-man's-land," the most dangerous and crime-ridden neighborhood in all of Portland. Felix hadn't even known about it until he saw an article in a back issue of the student paper—*The Weekly Sturgeon*—he'd read in the common room one day while he was waiting for Larry to come down for football practice. The focus of the article was a student group's attempts to prevent Starbucks from opening a store on 10th Street. The group's concern was that if one corporation gained a foothold a tidal wave of *gentrification* (which they made out to be a very bad thing) would swallow up the entire neighborhood. There was a quote from a Starbucks spokesperson about awaiting word from the zoning board on something called a 'variance'. Felix didn't particularly care—nor have an opinion on the matter—and the zoning issues seemed complicated. But the rest of the story—the background on no-man's-land—was enlightening.

From what Felix could gather, the first three or four blocks weren't terribly dangerous; there were even some PC upper classmen that rented houses there, though the school strongly discouraged it. And then each block grew progressively worse until 22nd Street, which served as the city's Great Wall. It was there that the city had unplugged the whole thing from the power grid and discontinued all city services—no sanitation, no street lights, no running water and no heat. Just block after block of condemned houses awaiting the wrecking ball.

But even that was a problem. The city was embroiled in a dispute with its unionized contractors who refused to tear down anything until they were given assurances that the sites posed no health risks. The city wasn't prepared to give such assurances. So for the past several decades the city had attempted to quarantine everything west of 22nd from the rest of the world. The author described the houses that remained there as 'decrepit little structures that provide shelter for squatters, the homeless, drug dealers and gangs'. When Felix read the article, he'd pictured a post-apocalyptic zombie movie.

And that was just the beginning.

Somewhere beyond the last block of houses—the author didn't say where exactly—was an industrial wasteland of abandoned warehouses, rock quarries and manufacturing facilities that had been fenced off like a penitentiary ever since the company that had owned the property went bankrupt in the seventies. The company had dissolved long ago, but what it left behind—its legacy—wasn't so easily erased: toxins and pollutants contaminated the vast tract of real estate where it operated its businesses, rendering the land 'unusable for the next 300 years'. The author compared it—*it* being the 'environmental catastrophe'—to a dirty bomb (or two) detonating just down the road.

No-man's-land. Not the kind of place Felix wanted to go. Ever.

But twenty minutes after getting off the phone, he was crossing 10th Street—the western boundary that separated the campus from no-man's-land—with Allison.

"How'd I let you talk me into this?" he said to her with a smile.

"You had nothing better to do," Allison replied, smiling back at him. "And it'll be quick. I don't think Martha's making us dinner. But I really appreciate it."

"Like I said, as long as you buy me a pizza we're even. Tonight I'm gonna eat, listen to some music and get some sleep."

"You nervous about tomorrow's game?" she asked.

"Nah. Yeah." He paused. "I guess. Maybe I should be. I don't know. First games always make me a little tense. Everyone says we're gonna suck. That takes the pressure off—weirdly."

She laughed. "But now the team has you, right? Maybe the Sturgeons won't suck as much as everyone thinks."

"Maybe." He didn't mean it. He thought everyone had it right.

They were hurrying along a sidewalk so badly damaged by erosion and tree roots that Felix kept catching his flip flops on the broken, uneven concrete. There was a guy and a girl on the opposite sidewalk walking toward campus and two kids standing by a car and talking—all students. There were also two men sitting on the stoop of a little blue house on the corner. "Townies" they would be called if they strayed east of 10th street. Their clothes, among other things, gave them away: sandals that hadn't been in style in years; jean shorts that had *never* been in style. And their hair—oily and unwashed, and if not technically mullets, damn close. And on their faces, they wore expressions of envy mixed with resentment for the privileged PC students wandering by.

They walked in silence for a spell, enjoying the perfect weather: mid-eighties, the early evening sunlight warm and bright. As they came up on 13th Street Felix was thinking it wasn't as bad as he'd expected. The houses were small and neatly maintained, the front yards mowed short like someone cared about their appearance. Cars filled the driveways, and the yards were being used for extra parking space, but that was the norm when you rent houses to groups of college kids. Felix was wondering if Allison was going to bring up what had happened last night at the Beta house. He'd hinted at it a few times as they'd trooped through campus, but she didn't take the bait. She didn't seem mad at him; she wasn't acting like it anyway.

"You look good," Allison said suddenly. She looked at him and smiled.

"*Huh?*"

"Last night, too. It was nice seeing you have a good time."

He thought she might bring up the freak out, or altercation, or whatever that was—not his state of mind. He started sputtering a reply.

"I know you don't want to talk about it so I'll keep this short. It's okay for you to have a good time. Stop feeling guilty about everything. If you're having fun, that means you're ready to have fun—*and that's okay.* So stop beating yourself up for something that isn't your fault and just roll with it. And get outta your head."

Felix felt himself tense up. After so much time thinking nothing but black thoughts, getting through the night without resorting to the lucid fog seemed like a miracle. Last night was fun (parts of it anyway). And so far today, he was feeling better than he had in a long, long time. So he didn't need anyone, including Allison, ruining it by playing Dr. Freud with his wounded psyche. He knew it was wounded—he just didn't need Allison reminding him of something so abundantly obvious.

"You think Martha's the next Craigslist killer?" she asked.

"So that's why you talked me into this," he said, relieved that she'd changed the subject.

"No," she replied with a light laugh. "Martha sounded normal on the phone. I don't think she's a killer. And I don't think this is all a sinister plot to rob me of my thirty-nine dollars. And if she really wants my cash and my fourteen dollar watch, she's welcome to it."

"She's not getting her thieving hands on your watch while I'm here." He puffed up his chest in an exaggerated display of machismo.

She laughed and the fine lines creasing her forehead disappeared.

"I'm more worried about the Faceman," Felix told her. "We're both solo kids, you know."

Allison understood the implication at once. Her eyebrows knitted together and the lines on her forehead returned. "You talking about last night? Sometimes it's better to keep things to yourself, don't you think? You're all about that. So if you start opening up to strangers, you have my permission to get on my case for being so closed off."

"I didn't mean anything—"

"I know you didn't." She gave him an apologetic smile. Then she wrapped her fingers lightly around his bicep and rested her head on his shoulder for a moment. "Sorry. I didn't mean to be so snappy. But I'm not worried about that ugly ghoul."

"Why not? Didn't you see the news? He killed somebody else. A girl. They found her body in an outhouse this morning. Somewhere down south. Mississippi?"

"Louisiana," she corrected. "And they found her in a shed."

"Same thing. So why aren't you worried?"

"Well, Louisiana's a long way from Portland and the Faceman drives. I don't think he can fly coach."

"Because he can't fit in the seats or because of security?"

"Probably both. And don't forget he doesn't kill more than one person at the same time unless they're related."

"Oh." He nodded thoughtfully. "Yeah, I guess that's right. And we're not related."

"Not that I'm aware of."

They emerged onto 14th Street and Felix's opinion of the neighborhood rapidly began to change.

Halfway down the block, a bare chested man watering the crabgrass in front of his house (a Coors Light cradled in the palm of one hand) stopped what he was doing when he saw them approach. He stared as he took a long pull from the can. Then he shook his head and gave them a look as if to say *you don't belong here. Go home. Go back to your fancy school before someone hurts you…*

Felix felt the weight of the man's eyes on his back as they continued down the street. He looked over his shoulder, but the man had resumed nourishing his weeds. He was facing away, and Felix could see that just above his love-handles he had two perfectly symmetrical patches of thick dark hair shaped like lungs. He thought about cracking a joke, but the deteriorating state of everything around them seemed to affect even his sense of humor, and he let it go after he couldn't come up with anything funny. Each house they passed looked worse than the one before and by the time they reached 15th Street, they were all in some state of decay: weather-beaten; broken gutters; driveways in shambles; peeling paint; chain link fences in back as bowed as the roofs; front lawns that were experiments in what happens when nature is allowed to have its way (no angry men with hair lungs tended the crabgrass here). The cars on the streets and in the driveways were older model sedans and dented pick-up trucks, many with gun racks. Some of the vehicles were in such bad shape Felix couldn't tell if they'd been vandalized. Smashed bottles and trash littered the pot-holed road and the cracked sidewalks. It reminded him of the time he watched the life cycle of a flower on time-lapse video. If this neighborhood was a flower, it would be at the stage where it was losing its petals and turning brown as its short fragile life drained away.

Felix had reached a conclusion: *this place sucked.* It was even worse than he'd imagined. The author of that article in *The Sturgeon Weekly* hadn't quite captured the utter soul-sucking crappiness of this hellhole.

Allison must have been thinking similar thoughts. She moved closer to him, tightening her grip on his arm. "So whadya think Fallon would say about the tree situation here?" She was trying hard to remain upbeat.

Felix had noticed it right away. From 12th Street on there were no trees—just stumps. "I think she'd say there isn't a single tree in no-man's-land they didn't cut down." He forced a smile. Allison was doing the same. "Maybe a beetle problem? Like back home a few years ago."

"Yeah. Maybe."

A souped-up, canary-yellow Mitsubishi Eclipse (huge spoiler, modified muffler, windows tinted black) sped past them. It slowed down at the next intersection (the east end of 15th Street and a cross street not identified by any signs). Felix thought it was going to stop. But then the driver, who was concealed by the tint, floored it, and the car screeched down the street, the rancid smell of burning rubber left in its howling wake.

"Drugs?" Allison shouted over the roar of the engine.

Felix shrugged. That was one possibility. There were others—all bad.

"So what's it like rooming with a celebrity?" Allison asked, her eyes on the car disappearing around the corner. "He seems cool."

"He's awesome. We were just hanging at this coffee place you'd really like—the Caffeine Hut. He actually signed some autographs for these girls who were all over him. I swear this one chick was gonna jump him right there. But he's not at all like, you know, all Hollywood or anything. Most of the time, he just makes fun of himself and the whackos on *Summer Slumming.* How's Caitlin?"

"I love her. She's amazing. I mean, she sincerely cares about making the world a better place. That's what she wants to do with her life. She wants to save the environment, the disenfranchised and anyone who's down on their luck. She's really... amazing."

"Oh." They crossed the intersection where a cloud of blue-white smoke from the Mitsubishi's exhaust still lingered. "That's pretty deep. I'm just hoping to get a job after graduation. And not at the paper mill. So why isn't she rooming with Harper? They're like best friends and all, right? Didn't they grow up together?"

Allison nodded. "Residence life screwed up. They were supposed to be roomies but there was some kinda mixup. Harper's right across the hall and her roommate's weird so it's like she's rooming with us, anyway. She's in our room constantly."

"Oh. How is um... how is she? Harper, I mean." Felix tried to make it sound casual.

"Harper?" Allison's eyes flicked up quickly to his face, and then back down. "She's fine."

"*Fine?*"

"Yeah, she seems... um... nice." Her lips twitched down in a frown. "Harper was, you know, one of the popular kids in high school. Prom queen or homecoming Aphrodite or whatever they call that shit in California."

"So she's *fine* and *nice?*" He couldn't help but laugh at that. "That's what I say about people I don't like."

"That's not what I meant." Allison's lips curved up in a hesitant smile.

No one said anything for a while. They stared bleakly at three houses in a row that had their windows boarded up. The next few houses appeared occupied, though they were somehow worse than the houses that preceded them: Their windows peeked out onto the sidewalk, watching them with their dark hollow eyes. There was a palpable sense of despair about this place. The wind shifted, gusting lightly from west to east, and Felix picked up the vile smell of sewage. Soon it permeated the air.

Allison squinched up her nose and gripped Felix's arm with both hands, giving it a firm squeeze. Her eyes flitted all around. "I'm really glad you're here. I didn't expect it to be *so* bad. Did you see that van turn at the corner?" He had, and it made him think they might be in tomorrow's *Oregonian* as victims of a random drive-by. "Anyway, do you really wanna know about Harper?"

He shrugged like he didn't care one way or the other. He did care, but he was thinking about something else—wishing Allison would change her mind about the skis and they could go back to the dorm. If they turned back now, Lucas (*and* Harper) might still be in the cafeteria.

"Well, according to Caitlin, Harper's got some, well... *serious* guy issues. Even when she was like a freshman in high school, she was dating this older guy. And I guess she was kinda obsessed with him and freaked out when he broke up with her. And the same thing happened with another guy a couple years later. Caitlin said she's a little high strung. You know, high maintenance and... emotional about things. So she exhausts her boyfriends and the relationships end badly. So now, she doesn't trust guys and thinks they're all assholes. Basically, she has trust issues and—hey! I think that's it. The white one." Allison was pointing at something across the street; the dying shell of a squat cottage-style house that looked like a mild autumn gale would flatten and scatter the grimy remains down the desolate street like tumbleweeds in a ghost town. "One eighty-seven, right?"

Felix felt a chill race up his back. "You've gotta be shitting me."

They looked in both directions before crossing the street (not necessary—there were no cars here) and Felix went over to a dinged-up mailbox with a missing front flap to check the peeling reflective numbers on the side. He peered inside just for the hell of it. No mail. "Yeah, one eighty-seven." He turned back to the house. The windows weren't blocked up, but the curtains were drawn. There was no car in the driveway. "This place is a dump. You sure this is the right address?"

"Yep." She waited on the sidewalk, looking all around at the empty street. "She said one eighty-seven sixteenth street. Martha could use a little help with the front yard. You could get lost in there."

"Something did." He pointed at a handlebar with glittery pink tassels rising forlornly above the tall weeds. "Is that a bike? Tricycle, maybe?"

"Shit," Allison whispered. "What's wrong with this place?"

Whatever it was, Felix felt it too, and the sense of apprehension was sitting heavily in his gut and keeping his heart from beating at its ordinary pace. He shook it off and clapped his hands together with more enthusiasm than he actually felt. *This will only take a minute,* he told himself. *Let's just get the skis and get the hell back to campus.*

"Ready to get your forty-dollar skis?" Felix asked with a smile, joining Allison on the sidewalk.

"Thirty-nine dollars," she replied stiffly. "She better have change or I'm gonna kick her ass."

They went up the crumbling concrete walkway and stopped at the door. It was slathered in bright red paint that had run down in streaks and congealed in little glue-like balls at the bottom. Allison raised a fist as if she was about to knock, then she held it there uncertainly for a moment and brought it back down. An apprehensive look passed between them. He felt awkward, like he was going door-to-door selling something to raise money for a school event. Allison pointed at the doorbell. Felix nodded. She gave him a little frown and pushed it. They waited. She pushed it again.

"I don't hear anything." Felix cocked an ear close to the door and listened. "Maybe it doesn't work." He rapped on it with his knuckles. A dog barked in the distance. *Probably a pit bull,* Felix thought grimly, *being trained to eat other pit bulls.* They waited some more. "I don't think anyone lives here." He knocked again. This time harder. The door quaked. "Do you have the number? You should call—"

"Hello?" a woman's voice called out from inside the house.

Felix jumped back. So did Allison.

"Hello. It's Allison." She looked at the door for a moment as if she thought it was going to open. When it didn't, she glanced at Felix and tilted her head, confused. "We spoke on the phone about the skis. Are you Martha?"

"Hello, Allison," the woman said. She had an accent.

Martha sounded younger than Felix had expected. Maybe it was the name. Martha was an old person's name. His grandma used to play bingo at the Elks club with a Martha, and she had to be at least ninety.

"Yes, I'm Martha," the woman continued. "You and your friend can come around back. The skis are on the deck. The gate is unlocked. Do you have the agreed upon payment?"

Allison mouthed the words *agreed upon payment,* shaking her head, perplexed. "*You mean the money?* Yeah, I have thirty-nine dollars. What we talked about."

"Excellent," Martha said. "I'll meet you in back."

"What kind of accent was that?" Felix asked, trailing behind Allison as they high-stepped their way through thick snarls of weeds. "Middle Eastern or something?"

"French... I think."

The latch on the chain link gate had broken off. Allison gave it a nudge and it swung open with a little squawk. They stepped through and started toward the back of the house.

"Hey Allie—how'd she know I was with you, anyway? She said 'you and your friend', right? I didn't see a peephole, did you?"

Allison stared straight ahead, mouth tight, plodding through the vegetation.

Felix's skin was crawling. Something didn't feel right. He swept the backyard with his eyes as they waded through the weeds and blackberry vines that had overrun the property, the prickly barbs nipping at their bare legs. He'd mowed a lot of lawns back home. Thousands. Enough to consider himself an expert on the subject. And this one hadn't been cut in a long time, maybe all summer. The house, the lawn—the whole property—felt unused, abandoned.

"Maybe she saw us through the window?" Allison responded after a while, then pointed off to her right. "Okay, that's a deck"—she tilted her head curiously and frowned—"I think."

At first, Felix didn't see the ravaged, weather-decayed unstained boards roughly configured in the shape of a square. Giant green-tentacled weeds had sprouted up through cracks in the wood, covering it up like an ancient ruin lost to the invading jungle. The deck was accessible through a sliding glass door, but the blinds were drawn, and the windows (just three) were all boarded up. There was nothing on the deck: no skis, or anything else, other than an ant swarm attempting to devour a butterfly drunkenly flapping its half-eaten wings.

"Where are they?" Allison's eyes flitted all around the yard. "You think she's bringing them out? That's what she said, right?"

Felix was trying to come up with a good reason for why Martha had boarded up the windows in back but not in front. He couldn't, and it didn't matter anyway. *He'd seen enough.* He didn't need Peter Parker's spider sense to know something weird was going on. "We should get outta here. I don't think anyone lives here. I don't know what Martha's up to—but I don't like it."

"What about the skis?" Allison snapped, her cheeks flushed. She was annoyed and moving quickly toward angry. "We came all the way out to this shithole. I don't care if she's a crack whore. I'm not leaving without my goddamn skis. Hey Martha!" she called out, starting toward the door in a rush. "Where are the skis? Hey!"

"C'mon, Allie. Let's go."

She ignored him and jumped onto the deck, shouting at Martha to come out.

"Shit." Felix stood there for a moment, wondering what he should do. He sighed, and decided he had to follow after her.

He heard himself groan. Then he couldn't breathe. He felt nothing initially. He simply couldn't breathe. Then the pain arrived: an intolerable seizing pressure that started at his throat and burned all the way up to his scalp. His brain fired off scattered images—a blindfolded hand-tied prisoner falling through a trap door with a noose around his neck; a Mafioso sitting in the passenger seat of a car flailing madly as he was strangled with a piano wire. Felix scratched at his throat. He felt something. It was smooth and thin, like wire or plastic cable. And it was constricting his windpipe, crushing it. He slipped one finger, and then two, under the wire, and managed to suck in a quick shallow breath.

Now that he could breathe again, he realized there was pressure on the tops of his shoulders. And noises behind him—grunting noises. It sounded like a woman. Whoever it was—*Martha?*—wasn't screwing around. She was strong. And she was yanking on the wire, pulling it so hard only the tips of his flip flops were touching the ground.

He slithered a third finger under the wire and took a gasping breath, his heart hammering away in his temples. He reached back with his free hand and stabbed at the space behind his head. His fingers brushed against something hard. He clawed at it and felt something else—a wisp of hair. He curled his fingers around a tendril and squeezed fiercely, digging his fingernails into his palms. Then he pulled on it. The angle was awkward, but he still managed to get a good tug on it. He heard a little yelp—a woman's yelp. Acting on instinct, he took in a deep breath, let go of the wire and twisted his body around, fumbling blindly until he secured another handful of hair in his fist. With both hands clutching Martha's hair in a death grip, he wrenched her head forward, and then, with all his strength, he launched himself toward the weeds, leading with her face, driving it straight into the ground.

She let out a muffled scream.

The cord around his neck loosened.

Felix drew in a heaving breath, then lifted his head and raked his hands through the bramble, clawing and scrabbling to his feet.

So did his assailant.

Martha was facing him. She was tall and lean with long red hair and a jagged scar on her cheek. Her nose was gushing blood. The dark red liquid streamed down her mouth and chin. Her expression was placid, but her eyes were bright and searching. With the back of her left hand, she slowly wiped the blood off her upper lip. From her right hand, a loop of silver wire descended to her knees, standing out vividly against her dark pants. It looked just like the one he'd seen in the mafia flick.

Felix took a step back. Martha took a step forward. Then he remembered Allison. He stole a panicky glance at the deck. She wasn't there. His eyes shifted back to the woman and he found her eyes fixed on his. Her jaw hardened. Her lips were pressed together in a firm line. She took a hard jab-step to his left.

He sidestepped to his right, wondering if Allison had gone inside the house, risking another glance in that direction. The pain in his throat was buried for the moment in an avalanche of adrenaline.

She did it again.

He reacted the same way and shuffled to his right.

The third time she jab-stepped to his left, he knew it had to be some kind of strategy. *But what was she trying to do?* He wasn't going to let her get behind him. Her piano-wire-weapon was useless as long as he kept her in front of him.

She kicked at his left knee, but she was too far away. It had no chance of connecting.

He moved to his right anyway.

Something in his head (intuition? a warning alarm?) was telling him she was setting him up—that she was playing him like a musical instrument. Her eyes were clear and focused. He didn't detect any craziness in those eyes. Or any emotion. She was no crack whore trying to steal his money and Allison's plastic watch. And she moved like an athlete: strong, fluid and graceful. If this was a movie, then this woman would be a professional assassin—a contract killer. His back was now turned to the house and the gate leading to the street.

The woman stopped her jab-stepping and kicking. She stopped circling him like a tiger stalking its prey. She stood motionless. The faintest hint of a smile played at the corners of her mouth. Felix paused, thinking that something was about to happen—something bad. The air felt thick and heavy. The breeze out of the west died out. Then three words flashed through his mind: *She's not alone.* He turned. But it was already too late.

There was a blur of movement, a head of dark hair rushing at him at enormous speed, chin tucked down so that no face was visible. Felix began to raise his arms to protect himself. That was when the impact occurred. The crown of the head crashed into Felix's sternum, knocking him off his feet and driving him backward.

Felix landed on his back, and the ground felt... different. Not as hard as before, almost as though something had cushioned his fall. Then his throat *shrieked.* The air was gone again. The pain had returned. He dug at his throat, trying to wriggle a finger under the wire. But it was pulled tight, slicing into the delicate skin, and the penetrated flesh covered it over, allowing nothing to get beneath it. He felt warmth on his ear and heard the sounds of soft moaning. Just as he realized that the woman was under him—and strangling him with the wire—he saw a pair of black boots rise up from either side of his waist. Then they crossed and laced together, and her long sinewy legs began to squeeze him like an anaconda. He couldn't move. He couldn't breathe. He felt the pressure building behind his eyes. His heart was jackhammering against his rib cage. He continued to claw at his throat. But now he was just flailing. Now it was pointless.

Someone stepped into his field of vision, which was graying at the edges. They knelt down in the weeds and gripped Felix by the wrists, pressing down with their weight, holding down his arms. Felix saw a face—a man's face. A man with dark hair.

Felix struggled, fighting to free his arms, but he couldn't make them work. The man was too powerful. And Felix's strength was seeping away. He looked up at the blue-gray sky and watched a pink-tinted cloud pinwheeling idly toward campus. The man crouched over Felix and stared down at him, blocking out his view of a deepening late summer sky. Felix gazed into eyes devoid of life, and as dark as crude oil.

The man smiled, then let go of his wrists.

Felix didn't have the strength to lift his arms; it was like they were heavier than the weight of the earth. He was completely helpless, too weak to fight back. Too weak to even try. The woman's hot breath whispered across his ear. He felt her heart pounding against his back.

The man swung a leg over his stomach and straddled him. He sat there for a moment, mounting Felix, then reached behind his back and brought out a knife that was long and silver and shaped like a crescent moon.

"Do it!" the woman hissed in Felix's ear. "Kill this monster!"

The man smiled again, then raised the weapon high above his head, clutching it with both hands like an Aztec priest performing a human sacrifice.

Felix stared up at the sharp point of the knife—the knife that was going to pierce his heart. He was about to die. He knew it. He *felt* it. And there was nothing he could do to stop it. *Maybe I'll see mom and dad,* he thought. And then: *I hope Allison got away.* He closed his eyes.

He heard someone scream. It sounded close. *A woman? Allison?* His body felt lighter. Air—*sweet, sweet air*—filled his lungs. Another scream—this one far away. More noises. Loud wrenching noises—earth-shaking noises. The sounds of struggle. Voices. Several voices. Shouting. Then there were footsteps. Footsteps all around him. He felt hands on his face, his neck, all over. The voices were fainter now, growing more distant with each passing second, a thousand miles away.

He opened his eyes. He saw a tunnel, a single beam of bright white light. Slowly, it closed in on itself until there was nothing but a charcoal canvas and then, total darkness.

Chapter 11

BLUE TORO

The paparazzi were gathering en masse outside the restaurant. Dirk had made sure of that. A few anonymously placed calls had started the ball rolling. And by the time he showed up at ten in his gaudiest ride—a yellow Lamborghini—word had spread, and now every celebrity-watcher and opportunistic tourist in the city was waiting for him. As he climbed out of the car, their cameras flashed, and when two models in seven-inch Louboutins emerged from the passenger seat, they went crazy.

A handsome maître d' with impeccable hair and a Spanish accent escorted them through the bar to the dining room, where the white linen table coverings were crisply starched, the silver polished and gleaming, and the candles flickered in crystal dishes. The restaurant—Blue Toro—had become the flavor du jour of the Hollywood establishment ever since its celebrity chef owner had opened it two years ago. The menu was fusion, and so was the ambiance—old Hollywood glamour fusing with modern day adrenaline. A place where normal people couldn't get reservations, and celebrities pulled strings and rank to get the best times and tables. The kind of place where Dirk Rathman wouldn't be caught dead. Normally.

The waiter brought him a bottle of Macallan's 55-year-old single malt and three glasses. His dinner companions were models. And aspiring actresses. Perfect bodies. Perfect faces. Clichés. Just like so many others in this town. But tonight they were props. His props. When you were trying to make a statement, entering a room with a pair of six-foot blonde models wearing ridiculous shoes (and little else) was a good place to start. The women—Iliana and Audrey—loved the attention. Being seen and photographed with one of the most recognizable faces in the world could jump-start their careers. They were using him as much as he was using them. Dirk didn't feel bad for what was about to happen—not for them, anyway.

Dirk sipped his bourbon and looked out at the patrons staring back at him. A few waved, cautiously. He ignored them. They had every reason to stare. Dirk hadn't been out in public like this in years, and many people thought he avoided the spotlight like it was a cancer-causing agent. There was some truth to that. If he did go out—which was rare—he went to venues where he had a connection with the owner; places with private back rooms and private entrances where they whisked him in and out without anyone knowing he'd ever been there. But there was more to their surprised looks than simply spotting a reclusive celebrity having dinner at the trendiest restaurant in town. There was the matter of his arrest two days ago. By now, everyone was aware that the police had busted down a hotel door to find him in bed with two women (along with a mountain of heroin in the room). Then yesterday afternoon, most of the country had watched live coverage of Dirk in a thong hitting tennis balls from the roof of his beachfront mansion. Then they watched as he somersaulted from the roof onto a fortuitously placed awning and into a hedge. Considering all that, Blue Toro was the last place on earth they expected to see him.

The waiter finished taking Dirk's order and Dirk had to assure him that he'd heard him correctly. Twice Dirk had to repeat himself, then finally, he told the skeptical-looking man to hurry along. After finishing his second glass of bourbon, Dirk began drinking straight from the bottle. Iliana and Audrey laughed at his audaciousness, most likely assuming he was one of those celebrities who disregarded etiquette and acted like an ass simply because he could get away with it. Iliana followed suit. She was a wild one. The guests in the dining room cast leery glances at him, murmuring amongst themselves.

And then the entrees appeared.

When the waiter and two helpers arrived at Dirk's table with eight entrees the murmuring grew louder, nearly drowning out the background music. And when the patrons realized that Dirk had ordered the same dish—eight plates of Red Tilefish with the heads still attached—a few gasped in surprise. The blonde on Dirk's right (Iliana) laughed. The blonde on his left (Audrey) made a face and asked him if the fish were still alive.

Dirk closed his eyes to allow the moment to sink in. This was the most important night of his life. It wasn't just his future that hung in the balance. The stakes couldn't be any higher. His new boss had made that very clear to him, and Dirk didn't want to disappoint. He knew he wouldn't be given a second chance. He opened his eyes and drew in a deep breath, then stood up with a water glass in one hand and a butter knife in the other. Once every eye was on him, he tapped the glass with the knife, not stopping until the hum of polite conversation and the clinking of dishes and glasses faded out.

"Ladies and gentlemen," Dirk began. "I hate to interrupt this public display of conspicuous consumption, but I need to say something before I take these two bitches here"—he held out his hands to indicate Iliana and Audrey—"back to my place to hollow out their vaginas." He picked up one of the plates from his table and held it at an angle so that everyone could see the fish; it was grayish-brown and about a foot long. He pinched the forked tail between his thumb and forefinger and let the plate fall to the floor. It shattered. Some of the diners jumped back in their chairs. Dirk slipped a finger down the throat of another fish and hooked it by its gills. Then he stepped over to the nearest table where a couple in their thirties was staring at him, their eyes wide with confusion.

"Are you enjoying your salad, miss?" Dirk asked the woman politely.

A fork loaded with crumbled goat cheese rested in the woman's hand, wavering in front of her mouth. Her other hand caressed the stem of a wine glass. She blinked, her cheeks flushing as red as the wine.

"That salad you're nibbling on," Dirk continued amiably, "costs more than the daily wages of the illegal immigrants washing your dishes in back. And that wine—fine choice by the way—could feed a family of four for a month."

"Oh," she managed to squeak out.

"Punishment is in order," Dirk said, his voice gathering strength. "For your excess, your greed and your sense of entitlement, I have been commanded to punish you."

The man seated across from her started to stand and his napkin tumbled to the floor.

"Wha—" she began to say.

Dirk slapped her across the face with the fish he was holding by the tail, hard. The fish snapped in half, and the part with the head slid greasily down her blouse and nestled in her lap. She screamed. Scales, crisp and smelling faintly of lemon and oregano, clung to her cheek. The man got to his feet, staring dumbfounded. Dirk drew the other fish back steadily, unrushed, and swung it in a tennis style backhand, hitting him between the eyes. This fish was more solid, meatier. The man swiped at his face, falling back into his chair, digging at the fish particles in his eyes. Dirk landed four more smacking blows before the fish was stripped clean of flesh.

The room went deathly quiet. A piano concerto played in the dining room. *Daft Punk* in the bar.

Quickly, but without any urgency in his movements, Dirk strode back to his table and snatched up two more Tilefish. With a discernible purpose in his step and both fish hooked securely through the gills, he approached the table to his left and began pummeling two dapper men who were old enough to be Dirk's grandfathers. Too startled to defend themselves, the men covered their heads and screamed for help. They took a pounding. Dirk didn't end the assault until the cowering men were blanketed with little bits of flesh, bone and scales.

As Dirk turned to retrieve more fish, a man in a dark suit and the maître d' converged on him, walling off his path to the table.

"What the hell do you think you're doing?" Dirk shouted at them as if he was deeply offended. "Do you know who I am?" He paused and then shouted it again, louder: *"Do you know who I am?"*

The men looked like they were afraid to act, which was only natural since protecting customers from drug-crazed celebrities fell far outside the parameters of their job descriptions. Another man in a dark suit rushed over and joined them, but he simply fell into line, appearing even more lost and embarrassed than the others. The three of them stood there side by side, heads down and eyes on their shoes like an auditioning trio nervously awaiting the judge's critique.

"I'm speaking to you!" Dirk screamed at them. When they didn't respond, Dirk scrubbed his hands down the front of the maître d's white shirt, streaking it with fish oil. The maître d' made no move to stop him.

A plump Asian man came hurrying into the room in an awkward waddling trot. He looked around, breathing hard, and his face went pale. "What happened?" he asked the maître d'.

The maître d's eyes skipped from the Asian man to Dirk, then he set his jaw and said nothing. He was probably hoping to get into the 'business' and realized that making enemies with someone like Dirk Rathman would guarantee that would never happen.

The woman with the fish scales clinging to her face pointed a shaking finger at Dirk.

The Asian man's eyes followed the direction of her finger and his eyebrows arched in surprise. He muttered something in Japanese, his eyes moving throughout the room as if he expected one of the patrons to come to his aid. "Mr. Rathman," he said, sounding clumsy and out of breath. "I'm Takamoto. The owner. I'm sorry, but I have to—"

"I'm going to have a seizure," Dirk announced calmly.

"Sorry?" Takamoto stammered.

Dirk hit the floor like a bolt of lightning had struck him. His legs stiffened and his body went rigid. Since he wasn't really seizing, he acted as though his brain was freezing up, picturing bursts of bright orange light flashing behind his eyes. He cradled his head, thrashing like a guppy that had escaped its tank to find life without water much less inviting than it had anticipated. He heard someone shouting for a doctor. But for the most part, the patrons remained calm, serenely watching the spectacle as if this was simply another scene in the evening's entertainment. Dirk wriggled and writhed himself over to his table. The blondes were still in their seats, but now they looked less pleased with themselves.

Dirk reached up and clutched the tablecloth tightly in his hand. Then he gave it a hard tug, sending everything on the table flying through the air: crystal glasses, tableware and the bottle of Macallan's shattered all around him. A plate of Red Tilefish slid across the floor and came to rest at the foot of an anxious-looking man guzzling scotch.

Little pools of bourbon, water, and half-melted ice cubes now studded the floor. Dirk pushed himself up to his feet, making a big show of what a struggle it was, then staggered and stumbled his way out of the dining room and through a hallway and into the bathroom. He reached out wildly for one of the sinks as if he needed it to steady himself. Someone was standing in front of the mirror. Dirk turned to him and screamed: "I'll fucking kill you! Get out! Get out! Get out!"

The man got out, leaving his hand towel on the floor.

Dirk looked at the mirror and smiled. This was actually kind of fun. His face was shiny and slick with sweat. Just faking a seizure was hard work. He splashed cold water on his face. "Anyone in here?" He stepped over to the stalls and checked for feet. None. He went to the door and listened. There were voices. Excited voices. Shouting. He couldn't hear the background music. Someone must have turned it off. He went back to the sinks and ran the water, wetting his hair and spiking it up until it looked wild and out of control. He waited. Timing was everything. The voices outside were growing louder.

"Here goes," he said softly. He placed both hands on the vanity and screamed at his reflection: "He's coming! He's coming! He's coming!" Then he checked his watch and waited. He'd give it ninety seconds.

Ninety seconds later, Dirk came tearing out of the bathroom, yelling like a madman: "He's coming! He's coming! He's coming!" The crowd congregating outside the door turned and ran in terror. He followed the stampede down a long hallway and into the bar where the customers were packed in tight like passengers on a Tokyo subway train. The panicked patrons collided into chairs and tables, knocking them over. Glasses shattered. Liquid sprayed across the floor. Pinned up against the wall, a bald man screamed in pain. A woman was pushed over an upended table and hit her face on the floor. Blood flowed from her forehead. She shrieked. Her friends screamed. More people fell to the floor. They scrambled to get to their feet, crawling frantically to get away. The crowd moved closer to the exit, tripping and pushing one another. Dirk kept screaming: "He's coming! He's coming!" The panic and fear in the air surged. Everyone rushed the exit, fighting to squeeze through the narrow door, trampling anyone still floundering on the floor. Those who made it—including Dirk—streamed out onto the sidewalk like bees escaping the hive.

The sidewalk was overflowing with paparazzi and what appeared to be several busloads of senior citizens (probably shuttled in on a celebrity sightseeing tour). As the frenzied horde escaped from the restaurant, Dirk shouted maniacally, "Terrorists! Terrorists! Run! Run! Run!"

Chaos ensued.

All at once, as if someone had fired a starter's pistol, the crowd scattered in every direction. An elderly man threw his walker at a blue sedan for no apparent reason. Dozens flooded the street, stopping traffic in both directions. The sound of screeching brakes filled the night air. Horns blared. People screamed. Police sirens and fire trucks wailed in the distance.

Dirk weaved his way along the sidewalk through the crowd, blending in with the paparazzi, celebrity-watchers and restaurant patrons, who all lost sight of him as he sprinted across the street to a waiting taxi at the Hotel Anglia. He climbed into the back seat and gave the driver an address. As the car sped away, he looked out the back window and watched the crowd staring around at one another in stunned disbelief.

It all went perfectly. Except for one thing. If only he'd remembered to wash his hands in the bathroom. They smelled like fish.

Chapter 12

PIZZA AND BEERS

Ba-Beep, Ba-Beep, Ba-Beep, Ba-Beep, Ba—

"Roommate violation," Lucas muttered sleepily.

Felix's eyes snapped open. He lay on his side looking at an empty bed—Lucas's bed—on the other side of the room. A blue comforter was gathered up in a loose bunch at the bottom. Tacked to the wall above it were two posters: the logo of the Minnesota Timberwolves and a scenic shot of Eagle Mountain (big trees and a hiking trail). Without moving his head, his eyes rolled up in their sockets until he found Lucas standing by his desk with his pointer finger pressed down on the alarm clock. Behind him, bright mid-morning sunlight was slanting in between the slats of the closed blinds.

"—turning off your roommate's alarm is worse than drinking your roommate's beer," Lucas was saying. "Or banging a chick on your roommate's b—"

"I'm alive." Felix sat up sharply, his hands going to his throat and then his chest.

"Looks that way," Lucas replied glumly as he crossed the room and climbed back into bed.

"How'd I get here?" Felix asked, looking down at himself. Looking down at *his* bed. The bed he'd apparently just slept in.

"Is that a philosophical question or...?"

"No!" Felix said. "I mean, how did I get here? To the room."

"I don't know, dude." Lucas yawned, and rubbed the sleep from his eyes. "I met this chick after dinner at the Student Center and we went back to her room. You were here when I got back. But it was late. Don't you have a game?"

"*A game?*" His thoughts felt disorganized—jumbled.

"Yeah—you know. Football. You chase the guy with the ball and try to kill him. That game."

"I don't understand," Felix said softly. "I don't understand."

"What are you talking about?" Lucas asked, sounding more awake now.

"No-man's-land. Skis. Martha. Allison... *Allison!*" His heart froze in his chest. "Where's Allison?" He threw the blankets back and sprang to his feet.

"Is that a trick question?" Lucas looked confused. "Probably her room. Don't you think?"

Felix was already at the door. He wrenched it open and burst out into the hallway, sprinting for the staircase.

"Dude!" Lucas called after him. "You might wanna put some clothes on!"

Felix flew down the flight of stairs to the third floor, parting a group of girls who screamed and flattened themselves against the wall as he barreled through the hall. When he reached Allison's room, he started pounding on the door. "Allie! Allie!" The girls in the hall whispered and giggled, their eyes clinging to him, but he didn't take notice. "Allison!"

The door opened slowly. Caitlin, wearing Tiffany-blue pajamas, gazed at him groggily. "Felix?" she said, her eyes swollen from sleep. He slipped past her, expecting Allison's bed to be empty, his mouth already choking out the terrifying words: "Where is she?"

But Allison was there, in bed, propped up on an elbow and facing the door, squinting her eyes at Felix. She blinked hard a few times and said in a thick sleep-heavy voice, "Felix? What's going—?"

Felix rushed to Allison's bed and scooped her up in his arms. "Thank God you're okay. Thank God." He'd never experienced relief like this before; it was so intense it hurt like physical pain.

"Hey!" Caitlin shouted at him. "What are you doing to my roommate?"

"Felix?" Allison said, her voice distorting against his chest. "Um... as much as I appreciate the wake-up call, I think you're going to break my ribs." She drew herself back and after looking him over for a moment, began to laugh. "Why are you in your underwear?"

Felix loosened his grip. "I thought you were..." He couldn't finish the sentence. "But you're okay. Right? Right?" He paused for a moment and tried to reassemble the broken thoughts bouncing around madly in his head. "What happened? I thought I was gonna die. The woman with the scar. And the guy—the guy with the knife. They were gonna kill me. What happened? What happened to you? You were on the deck and I looked over and then you were gone and—"

"What the hell are you talking about?" Allison's eyes grew wide. "No one was trying to kill you."

He stared at her for a moment in silence. "Are you joking?"

"*Joking?*" she said. "About…?"

Felix's equilibrium had completely deserted him. He got up from the bed and went over to the window that looked out onto the Freshman Yard. Two kids—Jonas and Salty—were down there throwing a football around. Jonas threw it. Salty dropped it. But how could he be standing in Allison's room watching two fatassosaurs playing catch in the Freshman Yard? Wasn't he at Martha's? Wasn't he fighting for his life? Wasn't he about to die?

"They were trying to kill me," Felix muttered faintly, turning away from the window. The memory sent tremors through his hands, making them shake. Then he shouted: "They were trying to kill me!"

"Who?" Allison asked.

"You don't… you don't know?"

"Know what?"

Felix spoke in a rush: "We went to Martha's house and she told us to go around to the back. The woman came at me with a piano wire. She was strangling me. And then this guy jumped me. He was going to… stab me. And then… and then… I don't know what happened. Everything went… dark."

"Wow!" Caitlin sat down on her bed. She'd slipped into a robe that matched her pajamas. "Sounds like you had a bad dream, big guy. Maybe it—hey!" Her head turned to the door. "Can't you knock?"

"Dorm rules," Lucas replied coolly as he sidled up next to Caitlin on her bed. "An open door means you don't have to knock."

"Get off my bed," Caitlin snapped at him, scowling.

"Relax." Lucas put his arm around her shoulder. "Dorm rule number twenty-three: beds double as sofas. Hey—at least I'm wearing clothes. Check out my roommate." He nodded at Felix and laughed.

Caitlin grabbed Lucas's arm and heaved it over her head. "Dorm rule number one: Don't touch me."

"What am I missing?" Harper asked as she breezed into the room. When she saw Felix (now pacing like an agitated lion) she stopped, stared open-mouthed, blinked and then took a seat next to Caitlin.

"It wasn't a dream!" Felix shouted at Caitlin. "It wasn't. I swear."

"Damn! They grow them big in Coos Bridge." Harper's eyes wandered over Felix's body.

"I don't think that's appropriate," Lucas said with laughter in his voice.

"That's not what I meant!" Harper dropped her head and brought her hands to her lap as if a teacher had scolded her for talking in class. Then her cheeks flushed pink and she turned to Lucas and shouted: "Do you always have your head in the gutter?"

Lucas nodded. "Pretty much."

"Nobody tried to kill you, Felix," Allison said softly, getting up to take a closer look at him.

"The hell they didn't!" Felix's throat hitched and he struggled to keep his voice calm. "The wire thing nearly took my head off." He touched his neck, running his fingers over the skin where the wire had dug in.

"What's he talking about?" Harper whispered to Caitlin, who gave her a confused shrug in return.

Allison tilted up Felix's chin and regarded his throat intently for a long time. "I don't see anything. You're fine. Caitlin's right. It must've been a nightmare."

"That's impossible!"

"Have a look." Allison pointed at the wall mirror next to her closet.

Felix stepped over to it and stared at a reflection of his mouth drifting open as he realized his neck was unmarked. There wasn't a scratch on it—not even a hint of redness. *But that isn't possible,* he thought hollowly. The woman had tried to strangle him—*twice.* The wire had cut into his neck. He'd felt it. *He could still feel it.* The cord tightening around his throat. His lungs screaming for air. The pain. The terrible pain.

"I don't understand," Felix said quietly. "I couldn't have dreamed it. It was too... real."

"So that's what this is all about," Harper said. "I've had some crazy dreams like that. Sometimes I'm so sure they're real that even after I wake up it bothers me. I had a dream once where my old boyfriend cheated on me and I was mad at him for like a week. But then it turned out he really did cheat on me."

"Are you sure that's the point you want to make?" Lucas said to Harper, laughing.

"You're a jerk," she said sourly.

"This was different," Felix muttered, half talking to himself, trying to work out the implications in his frazzled head. "But if... so... if it didn't happen. If they didn't try to kill me. Then what *did* happen? I don't... I don't remember anything. What—"

"I got them," Allison said. "Thirty-nine dollars. As advertised." She flapped a hand at the wall to his back.

"What?" Felix twisted his head around. There were skis—matte black with yellow tips and a big "R" set within a yellow circle—propped up in a corner. "But... how? How'd they get here?"

"You carried them," Allison said simply, a crease appearing between her eyebrows.

"*I what?*" He stared at the skis, feeling confused—and panicked.

"You don't... remember?" Allison asked.

Felix shook his head. "I remember two people trying to kill me in the back yard. A man and a woman. That's it."

"Well, we did go to the back yard," Allison said in a light voice as if she was afraid loud noises might send Felix over the edge. "But Martha was there with the skis. I gave her the money. And we left. She was nice. Said she was moving out today to be with her husband in Denver. Something about a job transfer."

"So nobody... tried to...?"

Allison shook her head.

"Then what happened?" Felix asked, the panic swelling inside him. "After we got them?"

"You were hungry. You wanted pizza. We found a little place on Tenth. You ate a medium all by yourself. And they didn't card us so you drank like three pitchers of beer."

"Dude!" Lucas bellowed and laughed. "That totally explains it. You got wasted drunk and blacked out. And you had some weird hallucinations. That's new. And weird. But maybe the beer was bad... or something. Right?"

A girl passing by stopped outside the door and shouted into the room, "Take it all off!" Then she whistled and moved on.

Felix looked down at himself. He was only wearing boxer briefs. But he didn't care. He felt clouded and heavy, like he was moving in water; he was far too confused for anything to embarrass him.

"Felix!" Another voice from out in the hall. A booming voice. Felix glanced up to see Larry. He was looking down at his watch. "You're gonna be late. Pre-game meal's in ten minutes. See ya there?"

"Uh, yeah." Felix dragged a hand through his hair. He didn't understand what Larry—or anyone else—was talking about. Nobody was making any sense.

"Are you okay?" Harper got up from Caitlin's bed and smiled at him. He noticed for the first time that she only had on a tiny pair of shorts and a tight T-shirt. But not even the vision of Harper's perfect body could penetrate the confusion that had darkened his mind.

"I'm not sure," he said slowly. "That's never happened before. I mean, I've had nightmares. But not like that. It just seems too *real.*"

"But Allison got the skis," Caitlin pointed out. "And you guys had dinner and everything. It was just a dream. What else could it be?"

Allison came over to him and rubbed his arm. "It'll be okay. Now get the hell out of here and go play some football. If you don't score a touchdown I'm gonna be pissed."

Chapter 13

THE GAME

Coach Bowman had gathered the team in the locker room. He was rasping about something, but Felix couldn't focus on the pot-bellied, bull-necked man with the irreparably damaged vocal cords. He figured it was the pre-game speech, although the words didn't mean anything to him. He was completely disconnected from everything around him. His mind was stuck at Martha's house (*Play. Rewind. Play. Rewind. Play...*). But it wasn't like recalling an ordinary memory. It felt like it was still happening to him: the wire cutting into his neck; the pressure of the woman's legs coiling around him, her hot breath whispering across his face; the sense of complete helplessness as he watched the man mounting him; and the stark realization that he couldn't protect himself, that he was weak, that they were going to kill him and that he was going to let them.

He couldn't make it stop. (*Play. Rewind. Play. Rewind. Play...*). He wanted to scream.

But those things didn't even happen. Nobody had tried to kill him. It was just a dream—a very, very vivid dream. And as weird as that was, he couldn't remember what had *really* happened. He didn't remember having pizza and drinking three pitchers of beer with Allison. He didn't remember carrying her skis back to the dorm. *It didn't make any sense.* He was going to go crazy if he couldn't get a handle on what was real and what wasn't. He tried to focus on the words coming out of the coach's mouth, hoping it might yank him back to reality.

"...as a school," Coach Bowman was saying, "we've struggled on the field. We've yet to capture the Rain Cup, and we haven't had many seasons to be proud of. But you should know that playing for PC—and wearing the orange and green—is an honor. I know that you've been told before why we don't play road games. But it's worth repeating. It's because we have Stubbins Stadium. Stubbins Stadium is *ours*. Walter Stubbins didn't just build a stadium. Walter Stubbins built his vision.

"He wanted PC football to be special. And that's why he built an exact replica of Chicago's old Soldier Field right here on our campus. It may be smaller, but it looks just like the greatest stadium ever built. Stubbins Stadium is so special that every school in our league demanded they play here every year. It's a special experience for everyone. And we're damn lucky to have the privilege to play our games here. So when you go out and take that field today, remember you have a wonderful stadium. And give thanks to Walter Stubbins."

Felix followed his teammates out onto the field, thinking that had to be the worst pre-game speech in the history of organized sports. As Brant trotted beside him, he whispered to Felix, laughing: "Do it for Walter Stubbins."

"Hey Brant," Felix said as quietly as he could. "Who are we playing?"

"*Seriously?*" Brant's eyebrows twitched together for a moment. "Bradline. The Cougars. You okay?"

Felix couldn't tell him that he was losing his mind, so he kept his mouth shut. He jogged over to the north side of the field and huddled up with the rest of the team. Someone slapped the top of his helmet and hopped on his back. He spun around to see who it was and got smacked on the helmet again. He didn't know what was going on. Felix had played football his whole life. But this didn't feel like a football game. It had all the trappings of football: coaches barking orders; players shouting at each other, pumping each other up; referees in zebra-patterned shirts; and an off key horn section and overzealous percussionists with *Little Drummer Boy* envy rat-tat-tatting on their snare drums every ten seconds. It all felt totally surreal, more dreamlike than the dream he'd had about almost getting killed in no-man's-land. Somebody pounded on his shoulder pads and yelled in his face like they were going off to war. He couldn't wrap his head around any of it.

He went off by himself and tried to concentrate on something other than scar-faced women and swarthy men with black dead eyes. He found a cottony white cloud hanging high above the goal post on the east side of the field. It didn't seem to be moving. The sun was beating down on the stadium. It was hot. *That's it,* he told himself. *Focus on the weather.* Then he looked up at the stands. The students were already getting rowdy in their section behind the team benches. *I have to get it together. Just stop thinking. It's just a game. I can do this. It's just football.*

It wasn't quite that easy. The first half passed by in a confusing blur of violent collisions, shouting, and whistles. It took everything he had, every bit of concentration, just to run the right plays. The world seemed to be moving in super fast forward. Bodies were zooming in and out of his field of vision so quickly he couldn't keep track of where everyone was. It was like he was stuck in a video game and his settings (and *only* his settings) were set to 'slow and disoriented'.

Before he'd even adjusted to the idea that he was playing in his first college football game, he was back in the locker room. It was halftime. He hadn't realized the horn had sounded. Everyone was angry. Jimmy Clay put a fist into his locker, denting it, and upended the Gatorade table. The seniors screamed at the freshmen. The defense screamed at the offense. Coach Bowman directed his ire at everyone, tantruming for a good while, screaming at the entire team for "playing with their heads up their asses." Felix let it wash over him; he didn't even know the score.

When they went back out onto the field, the first thing Felix did was check the scoreboard. From the halftime hysterics, he expected to be losing by thirty, but they were only down 7-3. He doused his face with ice-cold water from the cooler, trying to shock himself back to reality. The sense of being trapped in some strange limbo diminished by a fraction, but it wasn't until Felix's touchdown catch at the end of the third quarter that things started getting back on track. The catch itself was a minor miracle. He was somewhat conscious of running by the defender and sticking out his arms. Then the ball stuck to his fingers. Touchdown. It all felt entirely accidental, like stumbling upon a hundred dollar bill in the parking lot. But it wasn't the touchdown that did the trick. It was Salty. During the touchdown celebration, Salty became a little too exuberant and clubbed Felix on the helmet, hard. He knocked Felix off his feet, and Felix sat there in the end zone for a full minute seeing stars, an entire galaxy of tiny blinking lights.

Salty's blow cleared his sinuses—and his head. The ground beneath Felix's cleats began to feel firmer, the heat on his neck warmer, the sweat in his nostrils sweeter. Yesterday's events lost their cohesion, the images in his head disaggregating like a jigsaw puzzle still in its box.

The fourth quarter got under way with the Sturgeons in front 10-7. The two teams went back and forth for most of the period with no points to show for it. As the clock ticked down, Felix could feel the crowd's anticipation building. The fans were sensing—daring to believe despite so many years of futility—that the Sturgeons might be able to pull off an upset over the heavily favored visitors. But with time running out, the Cougars drove the length of the field for a touchdown. And just like that, the Sturgeons were trailing 14-10. All the excitement and energy in the stadium broke like a raw egg smashing against a rock.

The Sturgeons took over on offense with just nine seconds left and no timeouts. The outcome seemed certain. Another loss for the Sturgeons. Fifteen in a row on opening day. Brant gathered the offense and called the play, a quick pass to the running back. Felix couldn't believe what he was hearing. The play was good for five yards at most.

"Why don't we just give up?" Felix blurted out, suddenly angry over the play calling equivalent of raising the white flag. "Throw me the ball!"

The huddle went silent. Larry, Salty, Jonas and everyone else looked at Felix like they thought he was crazy. The coaches signaled in the plays and if the players changed them, there would be hell to pay. Everyone knew that.

Brant cocked his head and chuckled. "You can't be serious, August."

"Just throw me the damn ball!"

"Alright," Brant said. "But you better catch it or this'll be the last game we ever play. Give me some time to throw, guys." He broke the huddle.

Brant took the snap from center as Felix sprinted toward the end zone seventy yards away. The offensive line didn't give Brant the time he'd asked for; the Cougars broke through and flushed Brant from the pocket. Brant rolled to his right and heaved the ball just as a Cougar planted his shoulder into his rib cage and slammed him into the grass.

Felix turned his head and caught a glimpse of the ball leaving Brant's hand. Instinctively, he knew that Brant didn't throw it far enough. He stopped and turned back, running toward the line of scrimmage. The ball wobbled and fluttered in the air, then it fell out of the sky at the forty-yard line—right into Felix's hands.

Two Cougars stood between Felix and the goal line. He ran directly at the closest defender, faked a cut to his right, then cut sharply back the other way, leaving him grasping at air. Felix sprinted along the sideline, juking hard to his left and quickly accelerating back to his right. The second defender barely got a hand on his leg as he flew past him.

Felix tore across the turf at full speed. He could see the end zone through his facemask just twenty yards away. He could hear the opponents closing in on him from behind and the roar of the crowd growing louder and louder with each stride. At the four-yard line he dove toward the goal line with the ball in his outstretched hands.

The clock went to 00:00.

He rolled to his feet as the referee raised his arms to signal a touchdown. Stubbins Stadium seemed to go quiet for a moment as if the crowd believed they were witnessing a mass hallucination, and then all at once, pandemonium ensued. Felix stood in the end zone and watched the students scrambling over the railing like a colony of ants descending on a picnic. They swarmed onto the field, hugging the players, the coaches, each other, and anyone else they could find, even the other team.

Transfixed by the scene unfolding before him, Felix made the mistake of not running for cover. Now the horde was coming at him like an invading army. There was nowhere to run. Nowhere to hide. No escape. So he did the only thing he could do. He dropped to the ground and curled up in a ball as the surging mob jumped on him, burying him alive—but he didn't really mind.

The weight crushing down on him didn't feel nearly as immediate as the swirling emotions rising up inside him: he was overjoyed and ecstatic they'd won the game; relieved that he hadn't let his teammates down; and amazed and bewildered at how quickly things could change. Felix's first game felt like someone had pushed him out of an airplane without a parachute and he expected to crash to earth in a bloody Rorschach blotch only to find that he'd landed gracefully on center stage with an audience on its feet applauding his good fortune.

When he finally managed to squirm out from under the pile, they mobbed him again, but at least this time, the students and his teammates let him stay on his feet. He checked the scoreboard, looking over the top of a hundred cell phones taking pictures of the 16-14 final score.

Through all the commotion, Felix heard someone behind him shout: "Hey! Get away from my roommate, you animals!"

He turned to see Lucas, Allison, Harper and Caitlin pushing their way through the crowd. When they reached him, they smothered him in a fierce group hug. Harper lingered the longest, her arms wrapped tightly around his waist. But before he could really enjoy the moment—and he *was* enjoying the moment—his teammates ripped him away and hoisted him off the ground. Then they carried him across the field on their shoulders through a sea of ecstatic adoring fans, a victory procession worthy of a hero.

Chapter 14

THE GROUNDSKEEPER'S OTHER JOB

Bill's new client was hiding something from him. "Michael," he said after a lengthy chat about the lovely mid-September weather, "anyone who saw what you saw would be having difficulties. What you're going through is normal. Perfectly normal."

Michael's watery eyes stared back at him from across the desk. He was sitting in the guest chair, silent and brooding, his hands in his lap, folded, his shoulders rigid as if he was cold.

"Would you like to talk about it?" Bill prompted.

"I'm fine," Michael said curtly and glanced down at his watch. He clearly wasn't *fine*; dark patches smoldered under his eyes. He hadn't been sleeping. Probably not eating well either.

"You don't have to talk to me," Bill said in his pleasant therapist's voice. "But if you do, I can promise you two things. First—you'll feel better. And second—whatever you say within these four walls stays here. I'm not an AshCorp employee. I'm a consultant. I've been doing this for a very long time. Long enough for the folks here to give me a place to hang my hardware." Bill swiveled his chair a quarter turn and cocked his thumb at the wall to his back. Along with a pair of generic water-color prints were framed degrees (bachelor's and master's) and three counselor certifications issued by the state of Oregon. "I take my job very seriously. And I'm very good at it."

Michael studied his hands for a moment, his expression conflicted. Then he rubbed the back of his neck and looked up at Bill. "You won't tell anyone?"

"Not even if I wanted to," Bill replied gravely. "Unless I have a reasonable basis to believe you pose a threat to yourself or someone else, I cannot disclose the contents of our conversation to anyone. I'm here for you, Michael. I'm here to help. Now why don't you talk to me? Tell me about what you saw. Tell me about the bodies."

Michael dug his knuckles into his eye sockets and then pinched the bridge of his nose. "I'm fifty-two. I've got two kids in college and a wife who thinks it's her God given right to drive German cars. I'm going on thirteen years at AshCorp and they pay me like an engineer. But I'm not. I'm not an engineer. And if they cut me loose, I'll be out competing with guys half my age who *are* engineers. I need this job. And the reason they pay me so well is because…" He faltered, his uncertain eyes on Bill.

"They demand and expect your discretion. They've asked you to do things they don't want you talking about." Bill paused, taking in Michael's surprised reaction. "I've been doing this for fifteen years. I'm well versed in AshCorp's ways."

"Yeah." Michael nodded sullenly. "And that's never bothered me. We've cleared miles of forest to build things I've never asked about. Buildings. Tunnels. Generators. Water filtration plants. I don't know what they're used for. And I don't care. As long as they pay me."

"Of course." Bill gave Michael an approving smile as if to say *we all have to pay the mortgage.* "But you're not here because of that. No one's questioning your commitment or your discretion. You're here because your boss informed HR that ever since the incident you've been having *issues.* I think you saw something in the forest. What was it?"

"You know what I saw," Michael said bitterly. "Everyone knows. That's why this is so pointless!" Michael was talking tough, but Bill could see the fear in his eyes.

"Humor me."

Michael blew out a heavy sigh and lifted his eyes to the ceiling as if he was swearing at God for putting him in this position. "Bodies," he said thickly. "Two. I saw two bodies. Last summer. I… I found them."

"Tell me about it," Bill urged.

"There's nothing to tell. They were dead."

"And that's why you can't sleep?" Bill prodded. "Why you're not eating?"

Michael stared down at the floor, wringing his hands.

"I can't help you unless you talk to me. What did you see?"

"Something," Michael said quietly, his eyes moving to the door as if he was thinking about making a run for it. "I saw… something."

"Something?"

Michael shook his head, his face pained.

"Why don't you start from the beginning?" Bill suggested.

"And this won't get out?" Michael asked in a wavering voice. "You sure?"

"This is between me and you," Bill promised. "No one else will know. Now tell me about the day you found the bodies."

Michael let out a long breath and his posture sank, like his bones had grown suddenly weary. "Where I work, it's not like this." He turned his head and lifted his chin to the west-facing window that looked out onto a lawn that had just begun to lighten with the changing seasons. "You have these towers, a pavilion, coffee places, bars and restaurants, a park and a lake. Thirty thousand people come here every day dressed all nice to go to their meetings to talk about pie charts and spreadsheets. But I work out there. In the forest. It's not what people think. If you took your average AshCorp employee and told him to walk a mile into the woods, you'd probably never see him again."

"You could be right," Bill said and meant it. "Now where were you that day?"

Michael put a hand to his face and scrubbed it over his mouth before he spoke: "Quadrant seven. Just like every day for the last three years. Word came down that we needed to clear a few miles of old growth to connect something to something else. I don't know what and I didn't ask. I went out on my ATV to do a terrain check. It got pretty thick so I went on foot. Half a mile in, I see something up ahead in front of this ridge. I think it's maybe an elk so I go all quiet, hoping to see it up close. Maybe even get a picture to show the guys. I come around from the north using the trees as cover expecting to see a nice six-point." He went quiet for a beat. "But there were people there."

"You mean the bodies?"

"No," Michael said, his eyes dropping to his lap, unblinking. "I mean *people*. They were on the ground. Crawling. Moving all funny. Jumping around. Like monkeys or... I don't know. And then they saw me. They were looking right at me. And saying something to each other. Talking. They all stood up. And that's when I saw the bodies. What was left of them anyway. And the people... they um... they weren't *normal*. There was blood. On their faces. Their hands." Michael's face was losing color. "I think they um... I think they were *eating* those people. And their teeth... there was something... something *wrong* with them. They started coming at me. And then I heard someone say 'AshCorp', and they were gone."

"They ran away?"

Michael shook his head and glanced warily at Bill. "Just gone. I ran back to the ATV and got help."

"What do you mean *gone*?"

"I don't know. Just gone." Michael waited a while for Bill to respond, and when he didn't, added bitterly: "You think I'm crazy." He looked sullen again.

"Not at all," Bill said solemnly, his expression warm and understanding. "How many were there? How many did you see?"

"A lot. Eight. Ten. More." Michael's face tightened. "It's not like I stopped to count."

"Just one more question: How would you describe them? Tall? Short? What color was their hair?"

"About as tall as me maybe." Michael put a palm to his forehead and squeezed his eyes shut. "I don't remember anything about... the hair or..." He fell silent.

"Thank you. You did great."

Michael seemed stunned by the compliment. "I did?" he sputtered.

"I know exactly what happened and it's going to put your mind at ease. I've actually reviewed the police report and the file from the medical examiner's office so I can tell you what killed those people—and what you saw that day."

"*You can?*"

"Wolves," Bill told him.

"*Wolves?* Those weren't—"

Bill broke in: "They were wolves, Michael. No one's making any official announcement about it because the re-introduction of wolves into the wild is a very sensitive subject in these parts. But that's what killed them. And that's what you saw."

"But those weren't wolves!" Michael shouted, gesturing angrily with his hands. "I'm telling you, they weren't wolves!"

"You saw wolves," Bill persisted. "What you think you saw was actually your mind playing a trick on you. You see, when you stumbled upon a pack of wolves feeding—*feeding on people*—you went into shock. The sight was too terrible for your mind to process, so it erased those images and created new ones; images less threatening to your psyche. It sounds counter intuitive, but because of the thousands of hours of video images your brain has been exposed to, you've been desensitized to fantastical creatures with big sharp teeth. Your brain actually processes monster-related stimuli in the same way it processes an encounter with a bunny rabbit. And why is that? Because we know monsters don't really exist. They're fake. So like bunnies, they're harmless. Wolves on the other hand..."

"So those were... wolves?" Michael said uncertainly, doubt creeping into his eyes. "Not..."

"You were in shock, Michael. Is it so hard to believe that your mind was playing tricks on you? Trying to protect you?" Bill smiled knowingly. "Or do you honestly believe—*deep down in your gut*—that you saw blood-covered monsters?" With an incredulous quirk of his eyebrow, Bill added wryly, "Monsters that turn... invisible."

"Wolves," Michael said and snorted. "Who would have thought that?" He gave Bill an embarrassed smile and murmured softly, "I saw wolves."

"You saw wolves," Bill repeated, smiling back reassuringly. "Now go home and start taking care of yourself. Get some rest. Get something to eat. You'll feel much better. Trust me. But let's talk next week. Same time. The next time I see you, you'll feel like a new man. I promise."

* * *

Ten minutes later, Bill was steering his Range Rover through a security gate and onto a six lane road—Ashfield Way, the only access point to the AshCorp campus. The woods edged in from the north and south and the tall trees cast long shadows across the asphalt. "Call dad," he said. It took just two rings.

"William?" his dad's harsh voice rasped through the speakers. "Is that you? William?"

"Why do you ask if it's me when you can see my name on your cell? Why can't you just say 'hello' like everyone else?"

"Good afternoon to you too," his dad replied gruffly in a Boston accent that seemed to be thickening with age. "It's been a while. Anything to report?"

"I got confirmation that there's something going on in the seventh quadrant. And that he's protecting it with something very nasty."

"Details?" his dad asked.

"Not much to go on." Bill flew past a Lexus sedan, accelerating to eighty-five. "An appetite for people. Teeth sharp enough to slice through flesh and strong enough to crush bone. Smart. Capacity to communicate. Either very fast or able to go invisible. Nasty."

"Oh my," his dad gasped. "Numbers?"

"No idea."

"Anything else?" his dad prompted.

"No."

A brief silence.

"Are you sure?"

"What are you fishing for?" Bill glanced down skeptically at the monitor.

"Can we discuss the boy?"

"What would you like to discuss?" Bill said, reluctantly, already annoyed with his dad. He turned onto Hermann Boulevard, heading north, the strong afternoon sunlight filtering through the driver's window falling over his arm.

"Can I assume then that you haven't shown him the journal?"

"Correct," Bill answered quickly.

"And you're waiting for what exactly?" His dad's voice was rising. "Time isn't our ally here. Do you intend to let the boy in on our little secret or are you hoping—"

"I'll tell him when he's ready," Bill interrupted.

"When *he's* ready or when *you're* ready?" his dad demanded.

"That's a nice little sound-bite, but it makes no sense. The time isn't right for this. Not yet."

A long silence passed.

"Dad?" Bill checked the monitor, wondering if the signal was lost. "Still there?"

"Do you think it's smart to wait?"

"If I spring it on him now," Bill explained patiently, keeping his voice level, "he won't react well. I know what I'm doing. I know how to control him."

His dad grunted.

"Don't worry," Bill said. "I'll tell him everything soon enough."

"*Everything?*" his dad bellowed, sounding panicked. "You can't show—"

"Sorry. I misspoke." Bill jetted past a Suburban and swerved into the left lane, then flashed his lights at a white Ford Focus until it moved over. "As you and I have discussed on a thousand different occasions over the past seventeen years, he will not be told everything. In fact, I made sure he'll never see Eve's final entry or The Warning."

"You destroyed them?"

"Yes." It wasn't the first time he'd lied to his dad.

"That was wise. If he finds out what this is really all about, he could get a crisis of conscience and do something insipid. We can't have him questioning things or thinking for himself. Teenagers are so predictably and unbearably dramatic."

"Well, fortunately for you," Bill said, holding in a sigh of frustration, "you don't have to handle him. We own the information, remember? He'll think what we want him to think. I'll keep him focused."

Another grunt.

"I've got to get back to PC," Bill muttered, weary of the conversation. "I'm sure there's some shrubberies that need tending to." He hit the END button on the monitor.

Chapter 15

WOODROW'S ROOM

The Caffeine Hut engulfed Felix in a narcotic, aromatic cloud of brewing coffee. He ordered a mug from a student barista and headed toward a stone-manteled fireplace in back.

"I swear!" Allison was saying. She was sitting with her back to the fireplace in a high-backed purple chair with a floral print. Harper's chair, placed right next to Allison's at a cozy angle, was a canary-yellow version of the same design. If the company that made Skittles ever went into the furniture business this would be their showroom.

"You've lost it," Lucas teased. He and Caitlin were sharing an orange sofa across from them.

"What'd Allison lose?" Felix squeezed between Lucas and the armrest. Three on the snubby sofa was tight, but there weren't any empty chairs for him to drag over. The Caffeine Hut was always packed to capacity during the after-dinner hours.

"Hey Felix," Harper said, smiling at him.

"Hey." Harper looked beautiful (as always). Felix let his eyes roam for a moment, then he dragged them away. Over the past three weeks he'd gotten much better at not staring at her. "So what's going on?" he asked, setting his enormous porcelain mug down on a little end table stained with a million cup rings.

"Felix will believe me," Allison said. "I could use a little hometown support here."

"I believe anything she says." Felix sipped his coffee. He yawned mightily (he hadn't been sleeping well lately) and took another sip.

"What about pizza and beers?" Caitlin said, grinning slyly.

"Except for that," Felix replied with a wry smile as Lucas and Harper started laughing. Felix was used to the jokes about Martha and the dark-haired man trying to kill him—not to mention all the grief they were still giving him for running around the dorm in just his briefs. It didn't bother him. It actually made the whole thing seem more ridiculous. More dreamlike.

"So get this," Allison said to Felix. "This morning, my alarm's going off, and I'm in a dead sleep. But it keeps on beeping. And you know it's like the worst noise in the world, right? So I'm thinking—or dreaming—about how much I hate the goddamn clock. And then it stops. So then I finally wake up, and I go to look at the clock and it's off. No bright red numbers. Just blank. So I sit up and look at it, and get this—*it was cracked in half.* Like someone hit it with a hammer. And I was just telling these guys the same thing happened last April. I know the exact date because it was my eighteenth birthday."

"And I was just telling her I went through five alarm clocks last year." Lucas drank from his mug and rested it on his lap. "Anything that beeps at me before ten has a good chance of dying a painful death."

Allison laughed. "Yeah, but still…"

"I can tell you that her clock was in fact broken," Caitlin said. "But I can't tell you how it happened since I had an early class. But I have a theory." She smiled. "Allison can't remember breaking clocks, and Felix can't remember eating pizza, drinking beers, or carrying skis for miles."

"So you think it's like a weird disease that only afflicts Oregonians?" Harper asked Caitlin, her expression playfully severe.

"Watch your step," Lucas warned them. "You Californians are vastly outnumbered here."

"And exactly how many Minnesotans do you think go here?" Caitlin asked. "Just one. Maybe two if I count your ego."

Lucas ran his hand over a flexed bicep. "It's not the quantity, Little C, it's the quality."

"You're completely mental," Caitlin said dully. "What is it with you celebrities, anyway? You and Dirk Rathman should go to couples therapy."

"*Dirk?*" Lucas snorted. "Whatever. I don't even think what he did at that restaurant even really happened. I mean, it happened, I just don't think it *really* happened."

"You think it was staged?" Allison asked.

"Absolutely," Lucas replied. "I bet his agent choreographed the whole thing. It was a publicity stunt. His last movie sucked ass so he pretended to freak out to get some pub. Trust me. I know how these things work."

"Of course you do." Caitlin rolled her eyes dramatically. "Because you and Dirk are totally on the same level. Didn't he beg you to co-star in his next movie? I can just picture the conversation." She held an imaginary phone to her ear. "Hi. Is this Lucas Mayer? *The* Lucas Mayer from the critically acclaimed series *Summer Slumming*? It is? Oh my God! I can't believe

I'm actually talking to Lucas Mayer! This is like a dream come true. Do you mind if I conference in Spielberg? Will you please, please, please be in my next movie? I'll give you anything you want. My private jet? Of course! My house in Hawaii? Of course! Whatever you want! Just please say yes. Please!"

"I never knew uptight vegetarian liberals could be so funny," Lucas quipped. "But you're the one who brought up Dirk. Not me. The only thing I have in common with him is our agent."

"Really?" Felix asked. "You and Dirk have the same agent?" The coffee was working its magic. He loved coming here after dinner (tonight's *dinner* was three protein bars and a jug of Gatorade which he consumed on his way here after a late running practice). The furniture was so ugly Felix thought people with serious drug problems must have designed it. But it was comfortable, and everything about the Caffeine Hut, even the deliberate air of bohemian chicness, was warm and inviting. The only thing he wasn't crazy about was the vintage black-and-white photos plastered on the walls. The monochromes of the campus were cool, but most of the photos were of students (long dead students), and there was something about them that gave him the chills. He tried not to look at them.

"Yep," Lucas answered. "David Litman. I've never actually talked to the guy, but his agency signed me and the whole cast. Fat Johnny P, Fatter Johnny P, Venus de Sexy, Z-Bling, Cleopatra. Everyone."

"Sounds like David Litman's trolling for idiots," Caitlin said dryly.

Lucas shrugged. "Maybe. But he wouldn't have done it if he didn't think we could make him a bunch of money."

"I think it's cool," Harper said.

Caitlin pursed her lips. "I don't get it."

"What's to get?" Lucas said, giving her a look. "You watch it, right? If you have an issue with idiots getting famous and making ridiculous amounts of cash for being stupid, then stop watching."

"She can't." Harper laughed. "She's totally addicted to terrible TV like the rest of us."

"Whatever," Caitlin snorted. She wasn't willing to admit what everyone already knew: She was borderline obsessed with reality TV.

Lucas swallowed down a good portion of what was left in his mug and grinned. Felix recognized this particular expression. It usually meant Lucas was about to screw with somebody, or do something he probably shouldn't—or both.

"Still not impressed, huh?" Lucas said to Caitlin. "Okay, I'll show you something that'll slap the blasé right off your face."

"Is this where I'm supposed to look at you expectantly?" Caitlin asked.

"Yes. Try harder." Lucas placed his mug between his thighs and clapped his hands together to signify, presumably, that he wanted everyone's attention. "First, you need a little background. You've all heard the campus is haunted, right?" He waited for some sign that they knew what he was talking about, but only Allison responded in the affirmative.

"*Haunted?*" Caitlin said. "Did I hear that right?"

"Have you all been living in a cave?" Lucas shook his head like he was dealing with a bunch of imbeciles. "You really didn't know that? Do you know anything at all about the school you attend?" Allison nodded. Everyone else competed for the blankest stare. "Well, you must've noticed the campus is a little weird?"

"Weird like how?" Harper uncrossed her legs and leaned forward in her chair, folding her fingers around her mug.

"For starters," Lucas said, "none of it makes sense. The buildings are all out of proportion. Haven't you noticed? Like Jacobs, Stamford or Madras? I think maybe LaPine too. The top two floors are all closed off. How about Stubbins Stadium? There's maybe three thousand kids here and the stadium holds like a billion people. And the team sucks." He glanced at Felix, giving him a chagrined smile. "Sorry, dude. That last game was tough to watch. And what about the Old Campus? You couldn't have missed that. There's a reason everyone calls it the *dead campus*. It's like it died and was left here to rot."

Caitlin sighed. "I know where the Old Campus is. I just haven't seen it, you know, up close."

"Well, it's gated off," Allison said. "The buildings haven't been used in, I don't know, sixty or seventy years."

"Why don't they do something with them?" Harper asked.

"They're falling apart," Lucas said. "And the school's already got too much space as it is."

"And they can't tear them down even if they wanted to," Allison added. "They're historical landmarks. But they can't be used for anything— not even tours—because the insides are so bad. It's too dangerous."

"And they're haunted," Lucas said. "I'm totally serious. Tyler used to talk about it all the time."

"Am I supposed to know who Tyler is?" Caitlin said with a smirk, then drank from her mug which looked even more oversized in her small hands.

"My oldest brother. Tyler, Dale and Bret—my older brothers—all went here. Tyler told me the frats used to take their pledges to the Old

Campus to haze them. But they stopped because some weird shit started happening. They saw things. You know, ghostly things: women dressed all in white floating through the buildings. Scary shit. And check this out—Tyler lost a bet and had to walk through the Old Campus at night. He said it was the scariest thing he's ever done. That he felt like something was going to kill him."

"Please!" Caitlin let out an exaggerated yawn.

"Then there's the tunnels," Lucas said, giving Caitlin a sharp look.

"The buildings are all connected by tunnels," Allison said, sounding excited. "During World War Two, the administration thought the school might be a target for Japanese bombers, so they built an underground network that connects them all."

Lucas looked at Allison and nodded. "And I've heard some even connect to buildings off campus."

"Seriously?" Harper smiled at Felix like they were privy to some inside joke. He smiled back like he knew what they were in on.

"It's a fact," Allison insisted. "The tunnels exist. They're all locked up and the entrance points are sealed. Nobody'll tell you how to get to them because the school doesn't want anyone going down there."

"Who'd wanna do that?" Felix asked.

"You'd be surprised," Allison replied. "The people who chase ghosts and look for signs of the supernatural are always asking the school for permission to have a look around. The school always tells them no—of course."

Caitlin groaned. "It's not that I don't believe you about the buildings and the tunnels and all that. But there's no such thing as ghosts." She paused, looking at Lucas over the rim of her mug. "Or the supernatural."

"What if I could prove it?" Lucas said to her. If he was joking, he gave no sign of it. The problem with Lucas was he joked around so much that on those rare occasions when he was being serious, nobody believed him.

"Prove what?" Caitlin asked doubtfully. "That there's a ghost on campus?"

"No," Lucas said. "That there are secret rooms on campus."

"Really?" Harper gave him a skeptical look.

Lucas nodded. "But you have to promise you won't tell anyone. Or show anyone. Okay?"

They finished their coffees and agreed to Lucas's terms—even though they all thought he was messing with them. So with Lucas leading the way, they filed out of the bistro and set off along the south side of the Courtyard toward a plaza where all footpaths originated, spinning off in all directions and reconnecting throughout the campus like a spider's web. The moon was bright and up high in a cloudless sky. The days were getting shorter and colder and the leaves were just starting to turn from green to brilliant shades of yellow, orange, and red. Felix dug his hands into the pockets of his worn jeans, wishing he'd put on a sweatshirt. The pathlights glowed softly overhead.

"Where are we going?" Caitlin asked as they approached a Gothic clock tower (marking the halfway point between the Student Center and Woodrow Library) that bore a striking resemblance to the Elizabeth Tower, the keeper of Big Ben. The tallest structure on campus by at least fifty feet, it was sometimes referred to as the Clock Tower or the Campus Phallus, but usually it went by Little Ben.

"The library," Lucas answered.

"Huh?" Caitlin gave Lucas a withering glance. "Um... you do realize we've been to the library before? We go there just about every night. In fact, we were there last night. Even an oversexed reality star like you should be able to remember that."

Lucas smiled at her like she was an annoying but still beloved pet.

They entered the library and headed for the main staircase. It was a busy night. All the reading tables were packed, every chair taken. The first floor's communal tables were popular because you could see who was coming and going; as soon as you walked in, a hundred heads lifted up from books and phones and laptop screens to check you out. They never studied there—the girls hated the distractions (and the ogling). The private rooms on the top two floors were much quieter, and a much better option, if you weren't there for the social scene.

"We're going up." Lucas bounded up the stairs in twos and threes. They all gave each other a look that said *why are we letting him do this to us?* But a moment later, they followed after him. When they reached the third floor, Lucas held up one arm like a pre-school teacher waiting for his students to assemble. The floor was deserted, as it almost always was. On occasion you might find a few students using one of the private rooms, but that was about it; it was a morgue compared to the lower levels.

"Okay, can anyone tell me how many floors are in the library?" Lucas asked.

"Three," Caitlin answered quickly.

"Why do you think that?" Lucas said to her.

"Uh, because that's how many there are," she replied, like she was trying to explain something to a dimwit. "The stairs stop here." She pointed at them. "We're on the third floor. And the elevator only goes up to three."

"Sounds like you've got it all figured out." Lucas broke into a mischievous grin. "Try to keep up." He started off at a trot with everyone in tow, passing rows of carrels and well-lit study tables, then he made his way through a long aisle formed by the tall bookcases. When he reached the end of the aisle, he took a right down a different aisle, and when the complaints from Caitlin and Harper started to rise in volume, he turned left down yet another aisle.

Felix had been here before. Just once. But it was recent. About a week and half ago, he'd been on his way back to the dorm after his Economics class when he saw a kid from his high school. The kid—his name was Travis—saw Felix and started to wave. Then Travis did an abrupt about face and ran off like a field mouse sensing the approach of a low flying hawk. Felix didn't blame him; he figured the kid was just uncomfortable and didn't know what to say to him about his parents. But seeing the look on Travis's face had flipped a switch inside him. Everything—the sadness, the guilt, the confusion, the whole torturous ball of poisonous sorrow—came rushing back, as fresh as the day the ambulance had carried him off to the hospital drugged and strapped down to the gurney like a violent criminal. Felix had found a quiet corner on this floor where he'd put his head down and retreated into his gloom, mourning for a home that no longer existed, trying to ride out the storm. He'd missed two classes—Western Civ and Psychology—and showed up late for football practice, but by dinner, he was stable enough to pretend like he was as sane and well-adjusted as everyone else.

"So what do you have to say about *this*?" Lucas asked as he finally came to a stop. He gestured theatrically, then turned to the side so that everyone could see what was behind him. *This* turned out to be a doorway cordoned off with a black and white laminated sign that read NOT AN EXIT—DO NOT ENTER—STAFF ONLY. The sign looked like it had been printed before any of them were born.

"What's in there?" Caitlin whispered, peering into the doorway.

"Are those stairs?" Allison asked and swiftly hopped over the rope before Lucas could hold her back. She faded into the shadows, then returned a moment later with a smile flashing across her face. "There are stairs in here. But they only go up." She raised a finger toward the ceiling and smiled.

"I thought this was *my* show," Lucas muttered as he stepped over the rope. "Come on." He motioned for them to follow. "But be careful. They took out the bulbs to prevent people like us from noticing this and doing exactly what we're doing right now."

"You sure this is okay?" Felix glanced around to make sure nobody was watching. "What if someone sees us?"

"They won't," Lucas replied. "I'll tell you why in a minute. Come on."

When they were all in the stairwell, they gathered around Lucas in a half circle. The air was cool but dry. It reminded Felix of being in his parents' unfinished basement with the lights turned off, which happened occasionally because the switches tended to short out.

"Isn't it strange that the stairs don't go down?" Caitlin asked in a hushed voice, her eyes wide.

"That's very perceptive of you," Lucas said sarcastically. "*Of course it's strange.* But just wait 'til we get to the top. I'll show you strange. C'mon."

Lucas started up. Felix waited, falling in behind the girls, their stuttering footsteps sounding loud and drum-like. The stairwell was narrow, the ceiling low, the stairs steep. Before long, they reached a landing that connected to another flight of stairs at a right angle, cutting off the light from the third floor as effectively as a vault. Felix bumped into someone in front of him. Whoever it was—he hoped it was Harper—slowed down as if they were waiting for him to catch up.

Felix felt fingers curling around his bare arm. "Who's that?" he asked, keeping his voice low.

"Me." Harper's voice. His pulse raced a few beats faster than before.

"Maybe we should go back," Harper said to him softly. She sounded scared.

"It'll be fine." Felix tried to sound nonchalant. He was curious about where Lucas was leading them, but he was more focused on Harper brushing up against him every time they went up a step together.

Lucas said something that was lost amidst the echoes of scuffling feet and Caitlin huffing about not being able to see anything. There was the sound of a doorknob turning and squeaky hinges in dire need of WD-40. Then the stairwell was suddenly illuminated in a faint yellowish light.

"Here we are," Lucas announced grandly, stepping through the doorway. "Welcome to the fourth floor."

"Just a bunch of bookcases," Caitlin grumbled sourly as if she was trying hard to sound unimpressed.

"On this side, yeah," Lucas responded, his voice slightly defensive. "We are in a library, ya know. This floor's just like the others. We're in the back, so it's just bookcases from one end to the other. On the other side—in the front part—there are study tables and some private rooms."

"It's pretty dark," Felix said as he passed through the doorway with Harper. She'd already let go of his arm and was rejoining Caitlin.

"And dirty," Allison added, running her fingers along a shelf. She wiped the dust off on her jeans. "I guess they don't do much cleaning up here."

Lucas shook his head. "They don't do much of anything up here. Check out the bulbs." They did. Several were out.

"Look at the floors." Harper cringed, pointing at the herringbone patterned hardwoods caked in a dense layer of dust. "They're filthy."

"Like I said, nobody comes up here."

"So what's the story?" Allison asked Lucas. "How come no one knows about this?"

"It's haunted," Lucas said simply.

"Wow!" Allison said, her eyes shining with excitement. "Why? Why's it haunted?"

"That's a very good question," Lucas said slowly. Then very abruptly, and very stiffly, he turned his back and walked briskly away like an English gentleman out for his morning constitutional.

"Hey!" Caitlin called after him in a panicked voice. "Where do you think you're going?"

"I'd keep up if I were you," Lucas said without turning his head. "This place is haunted!"

Caitlin and Harper took off after Lucas while Felix and Allison lagged slightly behind, drifting past bookcases and aisles that seemed to go on for miles. The scale of this floor was somehow different than the others, bigger; even the ceilings looked higher.

Up ahead of everyone, Lucas had stopped in front of a bookshelf. He was staring at it, his head held to the side, at an angle, like he was clearing water from his ears. He started poking at the wood trim and taking out books and putting them back in their slots, seemingly at random.

"What the hell's he up to?" Allison asked as they caught up with Caitlin and Harper.

"No idea," Felix said.

Harper and Caitlin shrugged.

They all stood there for a while watching Lucas doing whatever it was he was doing. Harper hugged her arms across her chest and tapped her foot nervously. Caitlin reached out and traced her fingers along one of the dusty covers and said, "Latin."

"How do you know?" Felix asked.

"Ten years of Catholic school."

"This is it!" Lucas turned around to face everyone, slapping his hands together. A little cloud of yellow tinted dust danced in the space between them.

Harper coughed, annoyed, batting at the iridescent particles.

"Where were we?" Lucas asked. "Oh yes—Allison's question. Well, back in the nineteen forties or fifties, they made the library bigger. This whole floor was added on top of the old library. Anyway, there was this accident with a crane or something, and these four guys working here were killed when everything crashed down on them. Right here on this floor where we're all standing right now four guys were *crushed* to death."

Lucas paused, waiting for a reaction.

"So let me guess," Caitlin said in her I-think-that's-the-most-ridiculous-thing-I've-ever-heard voice. "It's the spirits of these dead guys who are haunting the library?"

"There's more to it than that," Lucas told her. "The four guys were all Indians. You know—Native Americans. Not the dudes from Asia. After it happened, there was this big investigation, and the head Indian guy, the chief or whatever he's called, claimed the four men were working in really shitty conditions because they were Indians and the white dudes working here had it much better."

"That wouldn't surprise me a bit." Caitlin folded her arms, her expression a disapproving scowl.

"PC paid off a bunch of people," Lucas went on. "That's the rumor. You know—important dudes, like judges and Senators. And the Indians got the shaft."

"Of course they did," Caitlin said fiercely. "The rich and powerful always get—"

"Anyway," Lucas interrupted, shaking his head at Caitlin, "the chief of the tribe supposedly cursed this place. I'm not sure why, but someone must've thought that just meant the fourth floor. That's why nobody comes here. Not even the librarians or the cleaning people. Crazy story, huh?"

"Yeah," Harper said listlessly. "Really crazy. Thanks for the super-fun tour. Can we go now?"

"So why are we standing *here*?" Allison asked. "What's up with this"— she pointed in front of her—"wall?"

"*Wall?*" Lucas said with high arching drama in his voice. "Is that what you think this is?" He took a step to his right, then stepped forward and disappeared into the bookshelf.

They stood motionless in the shadowed corner of the library, looking at each other like befuddled spectators trying to unravel the mystery of how the stage magician had retrieved not one, but two bunnies, from his top hat. Felix rocked back on his heels. The girls appeared rooted to the floor. Finally, Felix stepped back and took a closer look at the wall. Every eight feet or so, deeply recessed vertical wood panels about as wide as a person separated the collections into sections, each identified by a numbering system that Felix hadn't figured out yet. Stained espresso—almost black—the panels were several shades darker than the horizontal shelves, the baseboards, and the crown molding. He stared at the panels, wondering why they were so much darker than everything else. And then just like that, he figured it out.

"No way," Felix whispered, stepping toward the panel where Lucas had vanished. He reached out with his hand, and instead of encountering the grainy coolness of wood, he met no resistance at all—*just air*. The panel was missing. In its place was a perfectly concealed opening between two sections of shelving.

"A secret passage," Allison said, her voice rising with excitement. "Cool. You first."

Felix turned sideways and slid into the narrow gap, feeling a light draft on his skin. The scent of aged leather filled his nostrils, reminding him of the old mitt his dad had used when they played catch in the back yard. He shuffled along, arms raised up straight over his head, until his right shoulder bumped up against a wall. Another corridor (an even narrower corridor) faced him and ran parallel to the bookshelf for maybe fifteen or twenty feet. It was dark—but not completely dark—and he could just make out a wall in front of him, which had to be, he thought, where the corridor ended.

"I'm not going in there," Harper complained in a voice that sounded small and far away. "What if there's spiders?"

As Felix came up on the wall—which did appear to be the end of the corridor—he felt the air pressure drop and the currents shifting and swirling around him. There was a doorway to his right. He turned and slipped through it. He heard a noise. He stopped to listen. It sounded like something was rattling. It was nearby but difficult to pinpoint because the light had drained away to near total darkness and the noise seemed to be coming from different, and multiple, directions. Then he detected the movement of something big. A silhouette. Lucas's silhouette.

"One of these damn lamps has gotta work," Lucas muttered. *Click click. Click click.*

Felix took out his cell phone, thinking the flashlight app might help. And that was when—*click click*—the light came on.

"Finally." Lucas blew dust from his fingers.

Felix swiveled his head around, his eyes taking it all in. He couldn't believe what he was seeing. It was like he'd stumbled upon another world. He was in a room, but it wasn't like any room he'd ever seen before. It was big, ornately decorated and everywhere he looked there was *stuff*. High-backed chairs (he counted off ten) surrounded a huge round mahogany table in the center. Scattered across the table were books which had collected a thick layer of dust. Against the wall across from the entrance a pair of wingback chairs faced a tufted leather sofa; a claw-foot marble-topped coffee table rested on a Persian rug between them. Lamps—antiques by the look of them—sat on the floor and on the little tables nestled up against the chairs and the sofa. Distributed around the room were vases and urns of all different sizes (some nearly as tall as Felix), the smaller ones perched on decorative tables with fancily-carved legs. Framed paintings—lots of them—hung from the wainscoted walls, but Felix couldn't make out what they were in the dim light.

"This is so awesome!" Allison stepped into the room, her eyes glinting.

Caitlin and Harper came in right behind her, emerging from the darkened corridor. They didn't look nearly as impressed. Harper, in fact, wore a mixture of fear and revulsion on her face.

"How'd you find out about this?" Felix asked as he continued to stare around the room.

Caitlin sneezed.

"This is the *actual* corner of the library." Lucas smiled proudly. "Tyler found out about it and told me and my other brothers. He went to school with a kid who was the son of a nephew of the guy who was the president of the school when this floor was built. You know, the guy it was named after—President Woodrow. Anyway, this kid told Tyler that Woodrow was obsessed with castles and secret rooms and shit like that. He told him there are other secret rooms somewhere in the library. And also in the other buildings renovated when Woodrow was president.

"My brothers call it Woodrow's Room. So I guess since it's already been named we should call it that. Bret graduated two years ago and he said no one ever came in here except him and a few of his buddies. Which is weird if you think about it because anybody could use it. I mean, there isn't even a door. Anyone could come in if they knew where to look."

"Maybe nobody wants to use it because it's the scariest room in the world." Harper moved closer to Caitlin, clutching her arm. "This whole floor's creepy. Aren't you just a little bit worried about ghosts?"

"*That?*" Lucas waved his hand dismissively. "People have said weird things happen up here. Books falling off shelves. Chairs moving around. Strange noises and shit. But c'mon. Just ask Caitlin. There's no such thing as ghosts, right?"

"I actually agree with you for once," Caitlin said. "But still, it kinda freaks me out. Maybe it's just all the grime. It's disgusting."

"All it needs is some light and a little dusting," Lucas said. "I'm telling you, this is gonna be the coolest room on campus. Trust me."

"Now it's just the creepiest, dirtiest room on campus," Harper said. "I'm going to find a room on the second floor. Who's coming?" She turned and headed out the way they'd come in.

"Wait for me!" Caitlin screeched, scurrying through the doorway.

"You guys suck!" Lucas shouted after them.

They looked from one to the other, then Allison finally said apologetically, "I'd stay. But I can't read in the dark."

Lucas smiled, then he looked around and his face settled into a deep frown. "Lazy ass Bret. Whadya wanna bet he didn't clean this room a single goddamn time while he was here?"

"I don't know," Allison said, brushing her hand across the cover of a book resting on the mahogany table, sending up a dust cloud. "When did you say he graduated?"

"Two years ago."

"No one's been here in a long, long time," she said. "Longer than that maybe."

Lucas went silent for a moment. "He wouldn't lie about that. Bret's lazy as all hell, but he's not afraid of anything."

Allison nodded. "I guess we should go find them before Harper gets eaten by a spider."

Chapter 16

THE NUMBERED ONES

Robby hated his brother. Not all the time. Just most of the time. Like today. Their dad seemed to take enjoyment in telling him that Simon—his younger brother by almost three years—knew how to "take the bull by the horns." The implication, of course, was that Robby didn't. This morning's 'bull' was a black-tailed deer, which they were hunting—hunting in Ashfield Forest.

Robby thought it was a horrendous idea. Simon didn't. So here they were. It didn't matter that Ashfield Forest was AshCorp's private property; that two hikers were killed in Ashfield Forest; or that three others had disappeared in Ashfield Forest without a trace. And it wasn't as if Simon was unaware of these facts. The *Ashfield Forest Mystery* was front page news. Everyone was talking about it and everyone had an opinion. The guys at the car repair shop where Robby worked had plenty of theories. The emissions testing guy, Carlos, thought that a cannibalistic cult had taken up residence in the forest. Robby, on the other hand, along with his boss and the guy who fixed dents, all thought AshCorp was hiding something: quite possibly a rampaging monster which had escaped from the secret lab where AshCorp created it. Simon didn't seem concerned. Their family had hunted in Ashfield Forest long before it was called Ashfield Forest and Simon was going to hunt "wherever he damn well pleased." It was as simple as that.

Just after sunrise, one of the old service roads (with bullet scarred DO NOT ENTER and NO TRESPASSING signs as pocked as the face of the moon posted every quarter mile) had led them deep into the arms of the forest where they'd been picking their way through the ancient woodlands for the past hour. Robby had looked over his shoulder whenever he thought Simon wouldn't catch him to make sure he could see his brother's sunflower yellow Hummer. He'd lost sight of it within minutes. The trees, mostly Douglas firs, got taller and wider, and grew closer together, the further they ventured from the dirt road. They were in an old growth forest—Simon called it a *primeval forest* because he thought it sounded cool and scary—

which meant no one had ever harvested the trees; some had been around for 500 years and stood 300 feet tall. But not every tree was gigantic. Younger Douglas firs grew from the decaying remains of their dead toppled kin, and hemlocks flourished under the shade of their taller cousins.

There weren't any trails so they went where they could—directed by the forest as much as they chose their own paths. Robby knew he would have to rely on Simon to get back to the car. His sense of direction was abysmal, and landmarks never worked for him. A tree was a tree; a winding stream was a winding stream; a rock was a rock. It all looked the same in the woods. The carpet of dense green moss and decomposing logs and branches—which seemed to be everywhere—blanketed everything in uniformity. As a general matter, Robby wasn't afraid of the woods, and he didn't even mind being dependent on his brother to get home—but Ashfield Forest was different. He'd never liked hunting here. Even before it became a *mystery*, he'd always felt like an intruder. Like he didn't belong.

Simon, the natural born leader, stayed ahead of him, the only thing moving against the landscape, going around and between the trees, jumping over logs and brushing aside sword ferns that stretched five feet off the ground. Robby breathed in the clean earthy air and kept his eyes on Simon's back, trudging through the soft squishy soil, trying to stay within ten or fifteen feet of his brother. He loved the smell of the woods, especially early in the morning after a good soaking rain. It was so much better than the poisonous fumes he inhaled at the shop. He hopped over a rock and landed right on a branch. A dry branch. It snapped, breaking the stillness of the early morning calm like a gunshot. As wet as the ground was, he hadn't expected that.

"Oops," he muttered, awaiting the storm.

Simon stopped and turned to face him, his camouflaged attire blending seamlessly into the ferns and moss-shrouded trunks behind him. "Jesus Christ!" he hissed savagely. "What the hell are you doing, numbnuts? Watch where you're going!" He shook his head angrily, then pivoted back around and loped off at a fast clip.

Robby didn't bother to say anything in his own defense. Simon was right. Stomping through the woods like an amateur would scare away every deer from here to Canada. So he set off again, following after Simon in the gray morning light. There wasn't a single cloud visible through the treetops, yet very little light reached the forest floor. The trees were so big they practically blotted out the sky. But every so often, there was a gap where a giant tree had died and fallen to the ground, leaving an opening for the probing sunlight to make its way through the canopy. No clouds today. No birds. No anything. Just clear early October sky.

But something was different today, something was *off*. And it wasn't just the usual Ashfield Forest uneasiness. Robby couldn't put his finger on it, though it had been bothering him since the moment they'd climbed out of the Hummer with their rifles. Simon seemed oblivious to it—whatever *it* was. He just marched along at a blistering pace that Robby could only match by going at an awkward stuttery-stepped half-jog.

Without warning, Simon stopped and held up his arm.

Robby pulled up next to him and looked out at the monotonous canvas in front of them. The forest was quiet and still. There was nothing but... *total silence*. That's what it was. That's what was off. Where were all the forest sounds? What happened to the birds chirping, and the squirrels, voles, rabbits, and other little critters scurrying through the underbrush to get away from them? The forest was silent. *Too silent*.

"Hey Simon," he whispered, glancing sideways.

Simon turned to face his older brother. In his early thirties, Simon was a former high school athlete, and a good one. The girls had always been infatuated with him, and with each passing year, he seemed to get better looking and more fit. He loved to shoot things and he looked the part of the intrepid hunter, just like the guys who graced the covers of *North American Sportsman*, Simon's favorite magazine. At the moment, he just looked annoyed with Robby.

"What?" Simon said irritably, taking off his hat. A fancy downtown salon that charged $60 a visit lovingly tended to his full head of hair. Enzo, the neighborhood barber, buzzed what little hair Robby had remaining for eight bucks and that included the tip.

"Don't you think it's too quiet out here?" Robby said in a low voice. "I can't hear a thing."

Simon scratched his forehead and put the hat back on. "Did you just notice that, genius? Someone musta went through here earlier and spooked all the animals."

"We didn't see any cars on the way in," Robby pointed out.

"True." Simon cocked his head to the side, peering through the low hanging branches of a hemlock draped with strands of spaghetti-like gray-green lichen. "But they could've taken a different road." He pointed off in the distance toward a raised clearing. "C'mon, let's get to the top of that mound over there and have a look around."

Robby had to pump his short legs to keep Simon in sight, and even so, he lost him for a brief and very scary moment as he climbed over a decaying log. Robby skipped around some branches and squeezed between two thick trees instead of going around them for fear of losing Simon again. When he caught up to his brother he was winded, but he felt better. Simon was an asshole, but he knew how to take care of himself. If a monster or a cannibal or some crazy serial killer was out here looking for two more victims he wanted Simon by his side.

The mound didn't afford much of a view. The horizon never seemed to change, though the woods seemed gloomier than before. And colder. Not cold enough to see your breath puffing out like little exhaust clouds. But close. And the forest was still quiet. The silence was eerie, unsettling. Robby's bad feeling was getting stronger, more acute, and he was finding it hard to swallow. He wanted to go back to the Hummer, but if he confessed that to his brother, he'd be risking an avalanche of taunting and ridicule.

"Quiet!" Simon said suddenly.

"I wasn't talking," Robby said, his face furrowed in confusion.

"Shut up! You see that over there?" Simon was pointing at something, his arm held out in front and nearly straight. "Next to the tree with the... the knot... the crooked tree there. Fifty yards straight that way. See it? Ten o'clock. What is that? A bear? That's not a tree, is it?"

"I don't see anything." Robby tried to find ten o'clock, still breathing heavily from his jaunt up the slope.

Simon looked over at him, his mouth tight. "That's three o'clock, you idiot. I said ten o'clock."

Robby knew how to tell time. He was looking at ten o'clock, and there was nothing there. Then he saw it. Or at least he saw something that looked... out of place. "You mean that? That's not a bear—too skinny. Just a tree, I think. Funny shape though. Kinda looks like a person."

"Holy shit!" Simon blurted, flinching back. "It moved!"

Robby didn't see anything move, but a clot of anxiousness suddenly swelled in his stomach. "Are you sure it...?"

"It moved! I'm tellin' you. Give me your binoculars!" Robby slipped the cord over his head and handed them to his brother. "Where'd it go?" Simon muttered as he adjusted the magnification, his head moving back and forth in a sweeping motion. "It was right there." He jabbed a finger in the air. "Dammit Robby! Where'd it go? It couldn't have just disappeared. Were you paying attention?"

Robby was staring intently at a crooked tree, but he wasn't even sure if it was the same tree as before or if they were even looking at the same thing.

There were lots of crooked trees out here. "I dunno. I lost it. I think it was just a tree."

"It moved, dumbass! Trees don't move. Where'd it go?"

"I didn't see anything. Maybe you saw a hunter? Maybe someone in camo?"

"Stop talking and look for it!" Simon ordered harshly.

There was something in Simon's voice that Robby didn't like. He knew his brother got scared just like everyone else, but unlike everyone else, he never let it show. Not even when they were kids. Fear was for girls, Simon would say. *For sissies.* But now, Robby was beginning to wonder if being in Ashfield Forest was worrying Simon more than he was letting on. Maybe he'd just wanted to come out here so that he could tell his buddies about what a brave badass hunter he was. Robby unslung his rifle, tucked the butt tightly against his shoulder, and peered through the scope.

"See anything?" Simon asked him a moment later.

"Trees. Maybe the wind was just blowin' some branches aro—"

"What wind?" Simon said, annoyed. "It was right over—"

Tha-woomp

"What was that?" Robby lowered his rifle, feeling his breath catch in his throat. "You hear that?"

"Yeah." Simon glanced all around, letting the binoculars dangle from the cord around his neck. "What the hell? Sounded like an air gun!"

Tha-woomp.

Tha-woomp.

"There it is again!" Simon said. "Where's it coming from?" He spun in a tight circle, eyes wide with confusion. "What the hell is that?" He shrugged out of the shoulder strap and held his rifle out in front at chest level. "I think it's coming from over that way." He used the barrel to indicate a thick clutch of trees some thirty or forty yards up ahead and to their left. "Let's check it out."

"*What?*" Robby said, surprised. "Let's get the hell outta here. I don't care what it is. C'mon, Simon. People have died out here, ya know."

"Don't be such a little girl," Simon said with a sneering smile. He looked at Robby, and seeing the fear in his eyes, his smile stretched over his handsome face. "What's the matter? You wanna go home and clean your vagina? Don't be such a pussy. Come on." He started off down the slope.

Robby could never say no to Simon. No matter how much he wanted to. He just never had it in him. Even after all these years, to hear his little brother call him a *'girl'* and a *'pussy'* was the absolute worst thing in the world, as emasculating as physical castration. So Robby tagged after him like an obedient Labrador, and when they reached the bottom, they headed for a cluster of three enormous Douglas firs. Centuries ago, the trees had taken root in a straight line, one next to the other, and there had been ample space for the saplings to flourish. But now the trees were prehistorically gigantic and they competed for room, encroaching on each other's territory like skyscrapers constructed too closely together on the same city block.

"Alright," Simon whispered as they approached the trunks, which, Robby noted with apprehension, formed a nearly perfect wall that blocked out everything on the other side. "Whatever I saw was right around here. That deformed tree with the weird knot is there. See?" He motioned off to his left at a little hemlock that had died, probably from some kind of tree disease. "You go around that way and flush it out." He readied his rifle.

"*Me?*" Robby said, his voice scratchy. "Why me?"

"'Cause I'm a better shot than you. Don't be a pussy."

"You gonna shoot it?" Robby asked uncertainly.

"No, I'm gonna invite it over to bang my girlfriend."

"What if it's a person?"

Simon's brow wrinkled in thought as he seemed to consider this possibility. "Okay, hold on a sec. You cover the left, I'll cover the right." He cleared his throat and bellowed: "Hello! If you can hear me, listen up! We have guns and we're not afraid to use 'em. If anyone's back there, come out slowly."

"With your hands up!" Robby added quickly.

"We're not cops, idiot." Simon flicked a disapproving glance at Robby, shaking his head.

In the ethereal quiet of the forest, they waited for what seemed like a very long time. Robby felt small and foolish, and the silence was grating on him, pushing his anxiety buttons. He wished *something* would make a noise. Some birds chirping or a woodpecker chipping away on an old snag would be nice. He'd even settle for a gust of wind.

"Okay," Simon said to him when it was evident that no one was coming out from behind the tree wall. "Go around that way." He nodded to his left. "I'm shooting on sight. I don't care what it is. We gave fair warning. Go!"

Robby gulped down his anxiety and looked at his hands. They were trembling.

"If you see anything, shoot it," Simon said forcefully. "Whatever it is. But don't be a goddamn fucktard and shoot me!"

"Okay." He drew in a deep breath and moved past Simon, gripping the rifle tightly in both hands, squeezing the jitters from his fingers. A sense of dread crept up his throat but a single thought tamped some of it down: *maybe this was his chance to take the bull by the horns.* When his dad found out that he was the one who took the lead maybe he'd stop calling him Gump. He knew it probably wouldn't make much of a difference to his dad, but just the prospect of earning his dad's respect gave him the courage to keep his feet moving forward. With the trunks to his right, he went slowly, careful to keep his boots from getting tangled up in the underbrush or any branches hidden beneath moss and pine needles. When he reached the edge, he paused for a second before circling around the last tree, leading with his head, trying to see if anything was on the other side. He was literally sticking his neck out. His heart was beating so hard it seemed to shake his arms.

But there was no one there: no knife-toting psychopath; no guy in camo; no bear; no cannibal; and no lab-created monster. It was just a small clearing of ferns and some decomposing logs swimming in moss. And beyond that an emerald carpet of vegetation and lots of big trees. More forest. There didn't seem to be an end to it. He turned back and looked for his brother, but the tree wall obscured his view.

"Hey Simon!" he called out, feeling stupid for addressing trees. He didn't like being all alone out here even if he wasn't really all alone. "Nothin' here! I don't see any tracks or anything." He kicked at a fern and checked the ground just to make sure he didn't miss a big pile of steaming bear crap, or anything else that might be obvious. If he missed something like that, and Simon saw it, he would never hear the end of—

A scream ripped through the forest, shattering the silence like a rock skipping across a reflecting pool.

Robby tensed up instantly, the blood in his veins freezing solid, paralyzing him in place. He recognized the voice. It wasn't a spider crawling up your pant leg kind of scream. This was different. This was real. Filled with terror. Robby had never heard his brother scream before—not like that anyway. His heart was pounding fast and he could feel it in his ears. He couldn't breathe. He wanted to run—but not to his brother. He wanted to run as far away as he could from this place. He wanted to get back to the Hummer and tear out of the forest at a hundred miles per hour. But he knew he wouldn't do that (*couldn't* do that); he could never leave his little brother behind. He took one unsteady step forward and then froze again. He felt like his boots were stuck in the ground. His breathing was labored. He wasn't getting enough air. His legs were weak and rubbery.

Another scream.

This time, the sound of Simon's terrified cry rattled Robby out of his stupor like a splash of icy water to the face. He ran in a half crouch, speeding around the wall of trees, holding his rifle at shoulder height, preparing to take aim. He didn't know why Simon was screaming—hazy images of killer bears and mountain lions popped into his head—but he was ready to shoot whatever it might be. He cleared the last tree.

A man was standing in the exact same spot where he'd last seen his brother. His back was turned to Robby, his head bent forward and slightly to the side like he was trying to touch his ear to his shoulder. Dressed entirely in dusty orange, his shirt and pants were too big for his frame, and his shoes (basketball high tops) were different colors: one was chocolate brown, the other, mustard yellow. His hair was dark, short and as wiry as a doll's.

Robby was too stunned to intelligently process what he was seeing. He stared vacantly at the man for a while, thinking odd and dumb thoughts: *Do I know him? What's he doing here? Is he Simon's friend?*

His heart racing, Robby aimed his barrel at the center of the man's back. He swallowed hard and croaked out as loudly as his fear-impaired vocal cords would allow: "Hey!"

The man did nothing.

"You!" Robby tried to shout. His voice was slightly stronger this time, though not nearly as authoritative as he'd hoped. "I'm talking to you, mister!"

No response—again.

Robby's feet felt numb as he forced them to shuffle forward, circling around to get a look at the man's face—to see who he was dealing with. But after a few tentative steps, he saw someone else's face—his brother's. The man was *hugging* Simon. As Robby attempted to make sense of why a strange man in the forest would be hugging his brother, he noticed something else: blood streaming from Simon's nose.

Robby blinked in disbelief, cemented to the spot. Simon was looking up at the sky. His eyes were bulging. And his skin was as white as the walls in Robby's studio apartment above the garage where he worked. The man in the oversized clothes had one hand on the small of Simon's back and the other fastened to the back of his head. His face was buried in the soft hollow of Simon's throat and his jaw was going up and down. Up and down. Like he was chewing on something. Like he was eating.

Robby's rifle went off. He jumped back in surprise as the weapon discharged into the ground, the noise vibrating in his chest. The deafening *ka-krack* echoed throughout the forest. He hadn't intended to pull the trigger; a few inches to the left and he would have blown off his foot. His hands were buzzing from the recoil.

Simon thudded down limply to the forest floor face up, his head coming to rest on an insect ravaged branch, which propped it up like a pillow. Blood spattered across his cheeks and forehead, his eyes glassy and uncomprehending. Robby's eyes slowly drifted down Simon's face and his heart went cold. Then he lost his Cheerios all over his boots. Simon didn't have a mouth or a chin and his neck was shredded. Raggedy strips of bloody flesh protruded grotesquely in every direction. *Sloppy joes,* Robby thought vaguely. *That's what his face looks like.* Blood soaked through his camouflaged jacket from collar to waist.

Methodically, the man turned around, but Robby didn't fully pick up on it. The blood was mesmerizing him. He couldn't take his eyes off his brother's face; it didn't even resemble Simon anymore. Then the movement out of the corner of his eye finally registered in his slow-firing brain and his eyes darted from his brother's mutilated face to the person standing in front of him.

Overcome by shock and fear, Robby felt foggy. He couldn't tell if it was a man or a woman. Its skin was a light sandy color, and its eyes were large and gray. The lips were full and seductive—the lips of a woman. But the jaw was a man's jaw, strong, thick and masculine. Blood coated its mouth and throat like a thick glaze—*Simon's blood.* It was roughly the same height as his brother and built more like a man than a woman: wide shoulders, narrow hips. The man—he decided it must be a man—wasn't moving. He just stared back at him. As Robby was about to pinch his ear to wake himself from this terrible dream, the man opened his mouth and his jaw unhinged like a snake's, his chin dropping all the way down to his sternum. Robby gasped. His mouth was big enough to swallow Robby's head whole and lined with rows of long triangular serrated teeth that simply didn't belong in the mouth of a person.

This can't be happening, Robby thought dimly, staring at the mouth. Things like this don't exist. It wasn't a woman... or a man. It wasn't even human. And then it dawned on him: This is what everyone was talking about. *This* is the answer to the *Ashfield Forest Mystery.* This thing killed all those people. It killed the hikers. It killed the campers. It killed his brother. And it *was* a monster. He'd been right. The guys at the shop were right. Robby's eyes were glued to the bloody teeth. They had to be at least an inch lo—

"Hello," it said in a clear tenor.

"Wha...?"

"Why are you here?" Blood dripped down its chin and onto its shoes.

How can it be talking to me? Monsters don't talk, right?

Tha-woomp.

Tha-woomp.

Two more *things*—Robby didn't know what else to think of them as—had materialized seemingly from nowhere and descended on his brother's body, tearing at it with their teeth. Like animals. Like monsters.

Tha-woomp.

Another thing appeared and joined the others, all viciously diving into Simon's corpse in a feeding frenzy. With a sickening *ripping* sound one of the things tore off Simon's leg at the hip, and then, with the limb locked firmly in its mouth, ran away as if it was a hyena stealing a scrap from a pride of lions. A thing in a red velvet jacket quickly caught up to it and bit into the femur, trying to yank it from the other's mouth. Another thing bit into the foot, tearing the leg off at the knee while the original thief quickly swallowed down Simon's thigh. Meanwhile, the one with the foot in its mouth crouched and sprang into the air, flipping acrobatically and landing high up in a tree, clutching the trunk with its head toward the ground, a bloody boot dangling from its mouth. The others wouldn't give up; two more things jumped onto the trunk ten feet off the ground and slithered effortlessly up the tree. But as soon as they closed in on the one with Simon's boot in its mouth, it vanished—*tha-woomp*—taking its prize with it.

Tha-woomp. Tha-woomp. Tha-woomp. Tha-woomp.

The sound of more things making their arrival in the forest—*were they teleporting?*—resounded all around him. It reminded Robby of air cannons. Like the T-shirt launchers the pretty young girls at the minor league baseball games he went to with his buddy Cal on two-dollar-beer-night used to shoot souvenirs up into the crowd.

The things were savaging what was left of his brother's body like an ant horde swarming a grasshopper. Robby watched as one tore out something—a liver or some other organ—and the others fought over it with growls, shrieks and roars that seemed to cause the forest itself to cower in fear and silence. Another thing ripped off a large piece of flesh and bone from his torso and quickly disappeared with its bounty. It was the worst thing Robby had ever seen. Maybe the worst thing anybody had ever seen. But he couldn't take his eyes off it.

"Look at me," the thing said to Robby.

"Huh?"

"Look at me," it repeated calmly.

He turned his head and looked into its eyes and as he did so, he immediately lost his balance. He managed to keep his feet under him, but he felt dizzy and sick to his stomach.

"Tell me why you're here."

His gut heaved and a wave of nausea rocked him, sending a spurt of stomach acid up his throat.

"Why are you here?" it asked in a steady voice.

"Hunting," Robby replied sluggishly as its eyes held him in their grip. "We're just hunting."

"What are you hunting?"

"Deer. Black-tailed deer."

"Do you have any other reason for being in the forest?"

"We're just hunting. Hunting deer."

"Do you know who I am?"

"No," Robby said.

"I'm Number Twenty-Seven."

Part of Robby's brain was wondering why he was having a conversation with the monster that had just killed his brother. But the rest of his brain was incapable of doing anything besides obeying the thing. It was compelling him to respond, and to respond with the truth. "Can I go now?" Robby asked weakly. The thing only replied with a thin smile, so he added: "Are you going to let me leave?"

Tha-woomp. Tha-woomp.

It laughed. "No one can leave the forest."

Robby saw a flash of color, and before he could react, the thing had knocked him on his back. It moved fast—inhumanly fast. His elbow was shrieking. He'd landed on something hard, and a tingling pain was shooting all the way down to his fingertips. He caught little bursts of movement all around him and then his rifle was ripped out of his hands. He rolled to his stomach and staggered to his feet, searching frantically for his weapon.

There were now three things—*were they all Number Twenty-Seven?*—in front of him. Other than their odd mismatched clothes (one was wearing a puffy ski jacket over a tank top, another wore running shorts with striped knee-high athletic socks, and the third had on overalls with no shirt underneath), they looked identical. He backpedaled away from the wall of trees, keeping his eyes on the things, praying his rifle was in plain sight. He held his breath as he quickly searched all around him. Nothing but moss, ferns, branches, rocks and dirt. *Hopeless.*

He told himself not to panic as he twisted and turned his head in all directions, trying to protect his back—and trying to get some sense of their numbers. There appeared to be at least seven or eight, but they jumped around a lot, and he thought he might be double counting. He was thinking more clearly now, and he no longer felt dizzy. He wanted to make a run for it, but he and Simon had walked for just over an hour before stopping, which put the car at least two miles away. The things were fast—a lot faster than him—and he didn't even know if he could find his way back to the Hummer without getting lost. He didn't stand a chance in hell of getting to the car before they brought him down. So what was left? Yelling for help? He was in the middle of the forest. And all alone. There was only one option left. He unsheathed the eleven-inch Bowie knife from his belt holder and brandished it at the things, watching their faces, expecting them to attack.

They didn't move.

He squatted down in a half-crouch and waved the knife back and forth across his chest just like he'd seen in the movies, just like Schwarzenegger in *Commando*—or was it *Predator*? He wouldn't go down without a fight. He would make his dad proud.

They didn't approach. They simply watched him.

"What are you waiting for?" Robby screamed. "I'm right here! Come on!"

One of the things opened its mouth until it was large enough to swallow a basketball. But it didn't make a move. Neither did the others.

What were they doing? Trying to scare him? Setting him up? Robby glanced over at his brother. The things hadn't left much behind. Simon looked like roadkill after the birds had picked it clean. He couldn't believe that a few ravaged pieces of clothing and a red splotch in a bed of bright green moss was all that was left of his baby brother. It didn't seem possible. Or real.

Tha-woomp.

One of the things disappeared.

Tha-woomp.

Something—a *thing*—was hurtling toward him. It was almost invisibly fast, a purple and orange blur against the backdrop of the forest. He lashed out with his knife and felt it slice across its body. It stopped in its tracks and backed up, snarling and gnashing its wicked-looking teeth. Robby saw with ripe satisfaction that he'd made a four-inch slit in the thing's shirt (a purple and orange striped rugby with a white collar) just above its stomach, revealing a thin patch of beige skin dribbled over with black liquid. His blade hadn't cut deep, but the oily liquid had to be the thing's blood. And that meant he hurt it. And if he hurt it, maybe he could kill it. A whisper of hope rose up in his chest. Maybe he had a chance of getting out of here after all.

Robby's pulse skipped a beat then raced like a hummingbird's. Emboldened, he shouted fiercely, "Come on! Didn't like that, did you? I'll stick you like a pig next time! Come a little closer, you ugly ass monster! Come and get some!"

Tha-woomp.

Tha-woomp.

He felt a stinging pain high up on his back, near the shoulder blade. He tried to stab at whatever was behind him. His arm didn't move. He looked down. A thing had snapped its jaws shut on his wrist. He twisted his head to the left and found himself staring into a pair of dull gray marbles set within puffy white clouds. He'd never seen gray eyes before. Didn't Kelly Clarkson sing some song about gray eyes?

That was hazel eyes, you idiot! His brother's voice. Even in death, he couldn't escape Simon's ridicule. For a moment, the thing's lips parted in a thin smile, then it opened its mouth wide and bit down on the thick cord of muscle that ran from his neck to his shoulder. He could feel its teeth cutting through the flesh, slicing and grinding their way into the bone. But there wasn't much pain, only an intense seizing pressure.

Then the pain came—a sharp searing pain that exploded up his arm. He looked on in horror as it ripped a chunk of flesh from his forearm. It stood up straight and stretched out its neck, swallowing it down in one mighty gulp. Blood, as warm as bath water, gushed from the wound. His hand lost all feeling and the knife slipped out of his fingers, falling into the fronds of a giant fern, disappearing beneath its stalks.

There was a burst of activity in front of him. The thing in the rugby was coming at him, mouth open, baring its horrible teeth. He felt a hand on the back of his neck; the next moment, his head was wrenched back violently and he was looking straight up, his eyes locked on a branch, crooked, black and bare. His throat was completely exposed. In the next instant, a thing—*the one in the rugby?*—sunk its teeth around his Adam's apple, clamping its jaws shut.

Robby tried to scream, and a strangled wheezing gurgle, like water clearing from a snorkel, was all he could manage. He felt tired and weak. He wanted to sleep. His body grew slack and he fell to the ground. He was gazing up at a tiny pocket of sky. Sunshine filtered down greenly through the canopy, making the forest air appear as green as the moss he was laying on.

He could hear the things. They were biting him, tussling over the chunks of flesh they were ripping from his body. They were all over him, on top of him, surrounding him, swarming him, fighting over the scraps. He felt a vague tugging sensation on his shoulder, then he saw a thing standing over him with his arm locked in its jaws, his high school class ring on the middle finger of the hand drooping out of its mouth.

That's my right arm. It's eating my right arm.

A crow flew overhead—the first animal he'd seen in the forest all day. A thing jumped from a nearby tree and snatched the crow out of the air, falling from the sky, clutching the squawking bird in its mouth. Before the thing crashed to the ground it vanished—*tha-woomp.*

Robby couldn't move. He couldn't scream. The sky was turning gray, as gray as the eyes staring down at him. He no longer felt any pain. Only a cold sense of sadness that his dad would never be proud of him.

Chapter 17

THE STALKER

Felix sat on his bed looking down glumly at the Western Civ notes on his lap.

"You sure you don't wanna go?" Lucas asked him. He was buttoning a shirt while checking his hair in the mirror. "Satler's been having some pretty epic parties from what I hear."

Felix sighed. "I can't."

"Because of the game?"

"Yeah. Gotta make sure I'm well rested when we get killed tomorrow." The team they were playing was the current favorite to win the Rain Cup.

"Big mistake," Lucas said with a grin. "I hear there's no cover for supermodels with loose morals."

Felix got up and tossed his notebook on the desk. He wanted to go, but Coach Bowman 'strongly discouraged' the players from partying before game days. Bowman was also strongly inclined to bench kids if he found out they'd been at a party. The girls were all going (it was all they'd talked about at dinner). Harper had even tried to convince him to go in disguise. He went over to the window and looked out through the rain-streaked glass, feeling sorry for himself and thinking it would be just his luck if she ended up meeting some other guy.

Someone was staring up at him. At first, Felix didn't realize what it was because he was standing behind a tree and his head didn't look like a head; it looked more like a bulbous tree wart. But then it occurred to him that the bulbous tree wart had eyes and was sporting a baseball hat.

"Lucas," Felix whispered through clenched teeth. "Someone's down there."

"What?" Lucas said, still fumbling with a button on his sleeve.

Felix shifted his gaze to Lucas and feverishly waved him over. "Come here! Quick! Under that tree." He turned back to the window.

He was gone.

Lucas rushed up beside him. "Where? What tree?" His head moved back and forth. "I don't see anyone."

"Shit! He just... disappeared. He was standing right there." Felix stubbed a finger into the glass. "Next to the big tree there on the other side of that lamppost thing."

Lucas pressed his nose into the window, staring out until his breath fogged up the glass. "You sure?"

"Positive."

"Awesome," Lucas said dryly and turned away from the window. He went over to his closet and took out a pair of shoes, then slumped down on his unmade bed. He sat there for a moment staring at the floor, a look of concern drifting over his face. "I wonder if... if that was..."

"Was what?" Felix took a seat on his desk.

"A while ago—like the first week of class—I thought some dude was following me around. I saw him like three times in three different places."

"Did you get a good look at him?"

Lucas shook his head as he rubbed a smudge off one of his shoes. "He was just some kid. Short. Wearing a hat. I tried to spring a little trap on him at the Student Center but ended up scaring the shit out of these two girls. One was cute though. Heather. She texts me all the time now. She's seriously sweating me. I saw her a couple days ago and she practically dry humped the skin right off my leg."

"The guy out there"—Felix looked toward the window—"had a hat on. You think maybe it was the same kid?"

Lucas shrugged. "Could be some other weird stalker."

"That sucks."

"Yeah, I guess. Not much I can do about it." Lucas stood up and started for the door. "You sure you can't come?"

"Wish I could."

"Alright, dude. Hey—after the game you wanna do some clean-up at Woodrow's? It's been over two weeks and I don't think Caitlin and them are gonna do it for us."

"Sure," Felix said listlessly. "Why not."

"Cool." Lucas stood at the door for a moment with one hand on the knob, then he turned around, his expression troubled. "Don't worry about the party. They're having another one tomorrow. The ones on Saturday are usually more fun, anyway."

"I'm good."

"Okay. Later, dude."

"Later."

After Lucas slipped out into the hallway, Felix picked up his notebook and stretched out on his bed. He tried to concentrate, but the rain was distracting. He set his notes aside and listened to it pounding against the window. It reminded him of home—of sitting in the kitchen with his dad at their little table. Images suddenly crowded into his mind, the psychic partitions holding them back instantly vanishing. He could see his parents' faces. He could hear their voices. His mom was baking another batch of cupcakes. His dad was telling her that she was going to make him fat. Felix was finishing off his second and starting his third because he never gained an ounce no matter how much he ate. And all the while, he could hear the sound of the rain drumming on the roof. The kitchen was warm. A fire crackled in the living room. Chocolate, spices and burning wood filled the air. His mom was bringing him a glass of warm apple juice. His dad was joking that he had to get down on his knees and grovel to get her to bring him anything. Felix felt warmth. He felt loved. He felt like he was part of a family. *His family*.

Now he felt empty and alone. He had no family. His family was dead. He turned toward the wall, covered his head with his pillow and closed his eyes.

Chapter 18

THE GHOST AND ST. ROSE

The glowing red digits on Felix's clock informed him that it was 3:15. Lucas's desk lamp was making an island of light in the darkened room. He didn't remember turning it on. He rubbed his eyes, then looked over at Lucas's bed. Still unmade. But no Lucas. He lay there for a while trying to go back to sleep, but it was an exercise in absurdity. He was wide awake, uncomfortable (he was still wearing his clothes from the day before), and feeling terrible. He'd let the sadness go too far and it had carried him away. Now it was like a physical sickness; it was sticking to him, coating him. If he didn't get it off, it would burn right through his skin and eat at him for days.

His spine popped like dominos when he stood up and stretched. He threw on a hooded sweatshirt and a baseball hat and slipped out of the dorm, emerging into a cool misty drizzle. There wouldn't be another warm day until May—just another thing to be depressed about. No one was hanging out in the Freshman Yard except for a clutch of kids smoking cigarettes under a tree on the north end by Satler, where it looked like the party was still raging. Music was pouring out through open windows on the top two floors. He thought his friends must still be there, and wondered if they were having fun. *Of course they were having fun.* Why wouldn't they be?

I should've gone to the party, he thought miserably, giving himself a swift mental kick to the ass. Now he was missing out on a good time and he still wouldn't get any sleep before the game. Instead, he was about to wander the campus like a loser when he could be... *what?* Hooking up with Harper? Not likely. But he felt like he had a shot. Of course he had no shot at all if he didn't try. He was telling himself that he wasn't at the party because of Coach Bowman's dumb rules. But the rules were just that: dumb. He could get around them; Bowman didn't have a spy network reporting back to him on rule-breakers. So did that mean he *wasn't* trying? But why wouldn't he try? He *wanted* to hook up with Harper. Desperately. Thinking about ravaging her perfect body occupied almost as much time as football practice; it was how he made it through his classes when he grew bored or couldn't focus. But if they did hook up—*big if*—it wouldn't end there. She would want to get to know him. Of course. And it wouldn't take long—maybe five minutes—for Harper to realize he was a total wreck. And once she discovered that she would reject him. Just like Emma had rejected him. He couldn't handle that. Despite how much he liked her. Not even Harper was worth that risk.

With a very melancholy soundtrack playing in his head, he dug his hands into the pockets of his sweatshirt and headed toward The Yard. He turned and walked backward for a spell, letting his feet feel their way along the cobblestones in the soft glow of the pathlights. From a distance, Downey looked peaceful—the rooms were dark, the blinds drawn—a tomb compared to Satler. Everyone in Downey was asleep… or getting lucky. But not Felix. Luck had a strong aversion to him.

He passed by the first few lecture halls on the north side of The Yard without seeing a soul. There was nothing but empty paths and lawns drifted with wet heavy leaves. Alone with his thoughts, he began thinking about the guy he'd caught staring up at his room. *The guy.* It didn't have to be a guy, of course. Girls could be stalkers too. Either way, he couldn't understand why anyone would wait out in the rain just to catch a glimpse of Lucas with his shirt off. So what if he was on TV. What was the point? He just didn't get it.

Voices off to his right made him jump. His eyes flitted up to a sheltering overhang at the entrance of the Culver building where he found the culprits: two kids making out. Felix wasn't alone after all. He watched them for a moment and a puddle of cold water that submerged his sneaker right up to the shoelaces was the reward for his voyeurism.

The Yard looked as desolate as a stretch of farmland. Dew frosted the grass, sparkling beneath the haze. He drew in a deep breath as he rolled the kinks from his neck. He liked the way everything smelled. It was as if the trees and plants were giving off some wonderful floral scent in appreciation of the long drink the elements had bestowed on them. The cold was depressing, though he didn't mind the rain. When you grow up in a town where it's sloppy wet 250 days a year you have one choice: get used to it.

He wasn't sure where he was going. But that was the plan. He didn't care where he ended up. The night air felt good; it was already having a soothing effect. He passed another shadowed lecture hall and found a path that wound its way north as it hugged a dense thicket of sculpted shrubs. It split into two paths to accommodate a specimen tree of some sort, then reconnected on the other side at the edge of an English garden tucked in behind the building. He'd never been this way before. He didn't stop to admire the plantings, though he was sure they were quite lovely. Horticulture wasn't his thing. The mist was thickening, creating a haloing effect with the pathlights. Just past the garden, he came to a clearing where five trees were standing guard like monstrous sentinels—the *Star Trees*. The towering goliaths formed the shape of a five-pointed star, each tree acting as a point. He'd heard some kids talking about it at the dorm, but he didn't know where it was. Until now.

As he neared the southernmost tree, he stopped to have a look around. He tilted his head back, trying to see the tops, but swirling curtains of fog covered them up. The rain lightly spritzed his face like a spray bottle set to mist. It was refreshing. Coming outside had turned out to be a good idea; it was just what he needed. He looked back down and started toward the—

A woman, her back turned to him, stood in the center of the clearing. The sight of her startled him, freezing him in place for a moment. He was sure she wasn't there just a second ago. He kept his eyes on her as he reached out for the tree next to him, feeling the rough bark brush across his fingertips as he slid slowly past it. Her clothes were really odd; it looked like she'd gotten lost on her way home from a costume party—Cinderella came to mind. She was wearing a flowing blue dress that bunched up on the ground all around her. The dress was sleeveless, and her arms, so pale that they shone, hung loosely at her sides. Her hair was dark and long—he couldn't tell if it was brown or black—and it cascaded in lustrous gentle curls to her narrow waist.

"Hey," Felix called out, approaching the woman. "What are you doing out here?" The rain stopped all at once. Of their own accord, his eyes flicked up to the enormous branches of the Star Trees which all met in the center of the clearing, forming a canopy that kept everything beneath them comfortably dry.

She cocked her head and tucked a loose strand of hair behind her ear. Her cheek and the visible part of her jaw were so white it looked like she was wearing stage makeup. If it wasn't 3:30 in the morning, he would have thought she was about to perform at the school theater.

"Hey," he said again. She was close now, no more than ten feet away. Her arms were disturbingly pale, and he wondered if she was standing next to a light he couldn't see. Something had to be making her appear this way. Or was something wrong with her? Was she sick?

"Are you okay?" he asked.

She nodded twice, stiffly.

"Are you hurt?" He took another step. He was close enough to smell her perfume if she was wearing any—she wasn't. Another step. If he reached out he could touch her.

She shook her head. Her shimmering hair—it was dark, but not quite black—swayed elegantly over her shoulders and across her back. His eyes followed the contours of her slender arms down to her fingers, long and delicate, ending in fingernails that were flawless, and somewhat pointy. Her fingers were white. Too white. Bone white. *Vampire!* he thought suddenly, his heart lurching to his throat. An icy fear swept over him as he looked up, expecting to see the face of a monster.

But the person in front of him didn't have fangs. And she wasn't a monster. Far from it. The beautiful woman before him was staring at him, the traces of an inscrutable smile hovering at the edges of her red lips. Her green eyes blazed like smoldering emeralds, roaming over his face, measuring him. She looked older than the girls on campus, but not that much older, and it was hard for Felix to gauge her exact age because his brain had shifted into panic mode like the time he went camping in the fourth grade and discovered he was sharing his sleeping bag with a garter snake.

And then—without warning—she turned and ran.

Felix felt his feet lift off the ground and take flight after her.

He had no idea why he was running after her. He just was. A voice in his head was telling him that running was the right thing to do, but that he should be running in exactly the opposite direction—*back to the dorm.* Ignoring the voice, he ran ahead. The woman's dark hair trailed out behind her as she darted between two of the Star Trees and headed west, already distancing herself from him. He was going faster now, sprinting full bore, passing under hugely thick branches, but still not gaining any ground. It wasn't in Felix's nature to be confident about anything, but he was pretty certain he was the fastest kid on campus. And now a woman dressed like she'd been at the prom was outpacing him, and she was doing it in the strangest way. Her arms weren't even moving; they remained by her sides—and perfectly still—as she ran.

You're chasing after a ghost, you idiot, he told himself as she flew past a stone building with large stained glass windows and an old weathered cross above the entrance. She abruptly changed direction, turning north, and then she disappeared. Felix raced past a noticeboard on the other side of a low wrought iron railing that said ST. ROSE CHAPEL and some other things he couldn't read because the letters were small and his head was bobbing wildly up and down.

He turned the corner and saw a flash of blue vanishing into the ground. At the end of a long bed of withering flowers that bordered the church, he came upon stairs leading down to a heavy oak and iron door. It stood slightly ajar. Left open for him. He didn't hesitate. He scampered down the concrete steps and sprinted through a narrow corridor, searching for the lady in blue. Inside, it was cool, dark and earthy. The ceiling was low, the walls rough stone. Every so often, a bare ceiling bulb provided a pocket of struggling light. His feet slapped against the smooth stone tiles, the only sound he could hear. But where did she go? He slowed down, thinking she must have lost him.

A wisp of blue fabric shot down a hallway to his left. He wasn't sure where she'd come from but now he was closing the gap on her. He turned down the same corridor to find that she was twenty yards ahead, and moving fast—she'd doubled the distance between them in the time it took Felix to mistakenly conclude that he was gaining on her. This corridor was longer—much longer—than the first. It was also angled downward, making him feel like he was going a hundred miles an hour. He was running fast and out of control, almost missing a pair of stairs, just barely avoiding a major wipeout. He kept his feet, using the walls for balance, and barreled ahead.

When the next set of stairs appeared, he was better prepared, and hurdled them without breaking stride. The little voice in his head was back, reminding him that the woman was leading him deep below the ground. Chasing a *vampire* to the center of the earth—to her *lair*—probably wasn't very smart. *But*, the little voice added, *vampires can't tolerate holy ground, right?* So she couldn't be a vampire. So maybe she really was a ghost. *What's the difference, you idiot? You shouldn't be chasing after ghosts either.*

The corridor ended abruptly and the woman blurred away to her right, her dress whipping around the corner. Seconds later, Felix arrived at the wall. Hallways ran in both directions. She was nowhere in sight. He stopped to listen, breathing hard, sweat streaming down his face.

He heard a faint noise coming from the corridor to his left. He took off in that direction, but his wet sneakers lost their grip on the smooth stone floor and he slipped and slammed into a wall, grunting as the ensuing pain from body-checking solid stone shot up his shoulder. He ran on. The noise was getting louder. It sounded like a child banging on a pot with a wooden spoon. The noise was *too* loud, too glaringly obvious in the silence. Was she trying to draw him in? Was this a trap? What the hell was he doing?

He plunged through a doorway, stuttering to a stop before colliding into a long table stacked atop another long table. The woman appeared at the far side of a room filled with chairs and more tables and an assortment of bric a brac. She was moving incredibly fast, a blue streak against the pale walls. And just before she disappeared through another doorway, she glanced over her shoulder. Their eyes met—and then she was gone.

Felix chased after her—even though he had the chills so badly every electrified hair on his body was threatening to ignite—and emerged into a room full of moving boxes and tall metal storage racks packed with candles, dishes, goblets and other small items. He crossed the room, passing through yet another doorway. The voice in his head was screaming at him: *Where the hell are you going?*

The woman breezed through a doorway to his right, her blue dress billowing out behind her. He followed her into a small dark room that smelled of rain and dirt. He skidded to a halting stop and quickly scanned the room, his eyes on high alert for a shock of blue. His breaths were coming fast. There was a noise off to his right. He bolted around a chest-high stack of boxes and came to a wall. And set within the wall... was a door. It was open a crack.

Hand shaking, he reached out for the doorknob before realizing it didn't have one. He paused, confused, then curled his fingers around the edge of the door, feeling the biting coldness of steel. He took a deep breath, and in one motion, flung it open and jumped back.

He was greeted by a blast of cool damp air and a sight he never imagined he would see in a million years. Too stunned to move, he stared straight ahead, standing at the entrance of a tunnel that seemed to go on forever. It wasn't for lack of light that he couldn't see where it ended. Encased in antique-looking metal cages, powerful bulbs (LEDs, or something else like it), brightly illuminated the tunnel.

Not sure why he was doing this—*curiosity? madness?*—he drifted inside. It was wide, twice the width of the corridors to his back, the ceiling high and vaulted. He knew this had to be one of the tunnels Lucas and Allison had been talking about at the Caffeine Hut. He took a few steps, then thought better of it and ran back to the door, checking to make sure it wasn't going to close shut and lock him in. There was no doorknob on this side either, just another keyhole. He closed it and opened it and closed it and opened it. Then he did it all over again for good measure. It seemed safe enough. It couldn't be locked without a key. So as long as no one ventured down here and locked him in he figured he'd be okay to go exploring for a minute.

The air was still, heavy with moisture, and yet there was no sign of water. The floor was hard, dry and flat. The walls were concrete. So were the floors and ceiling. Miles of cold monotonous gray encased everything. Industrial cables, pipes and plastic tubes crisscrossed along the ceiling like veins and arteries. The lights buzzed in the funereal stillness. About twenty feet in, he spotted a glint of something—a reflection?—on the wall up ahead and to his right. It soon became apparent that the ceiling lights were skating across lots of shiny things on the wall, and those shiny things were reflecting back at him. He went over to have a closer look. The *shiny things* turned out to be plaques. Every four or five feet, squarish, postcard-sized plaques were imbedded in the concrete. Most were a bronze color—copper?—and tarnished at the edges.

He examined the closest one, the one at eye level. There was something on it. Some kind of writing? An inscription? He breathed hot air on it and buffed it with his shirtsleeve. Letters began to emerge. R. R-O. *Robert?* It was a name... and dates. It said:

Robert Filton, Jr.
1734-1792

Felix gasped and stumbled back. *This was no ordinary wall.* Below each plaque there was a rectangular impression etched into the concrete like a pencil mark on a piece of paper. He knew what this was. These were storage lockers. Storage lockers for bodies. He was looking at coffins. They were crammed into the wall from top to bottom, and their reach appeared to extend as far as the tunnel itself. An old sepia-toned picture from his Western Civ textbook of the Catacombs in Rome flashed through his mind.

There was a cemetery below campus. And Felix was standing in it.

His skin crawled as a frosty chill slithered into the pit of his stomach, freezing his insides. He backpedaled until he'd pressed himself up against the opposite wall, staring open-mouthed at the bank of coffins. There had to be hundreds of them, maybe even thousands. *Thousands* of dead people down here with him. Nobody knew he was here. Suddenly, he no longer had any interest in finding the woman in the blue dress. He turned and started running flat out toward the door.

It slammed shut.

And then the lights went out.

He froze for a moment as a tingling shiver flashed down his spine. The darkness was complete. Light simply couldn't exist in this subterranean world. Then he reached out until his fingers made contact with the nearest wall. His heart racing, he took a few steps toward the door, skimming his fingers along the wall to keep his feet going in the right direction, feeling its coarse, sandpaper-like surface and the tiny ridges left by trowel blades.

"We've been waiting for you, Felix."

The voice—a woman's voice—was simultaneously coming from nowhere and everywhere.

Felix went cold with fear. He yanked his head around, trying to pinpoint the woman's—*the ghost's*—voice.

"We've been waiting for so many years," she said.

With one hand on the wall and the other out in front of his body, he lurched forward, stumbling toward the door, anticipating at any moment to feel cold dead ghost hands wrapping around him, pulling him down.

His outstretched fingers stubbed painfully into something with a smooth cold surface—*the door.* Frantically, he ran his hands all over it, searching for the doorknob. Then he remembered it didn't have one. He pounded on it, yelling for help.

"Felix."

The voice was right behind him. He felt like she was whispering in his ear, like her lips were brushing against his skin.

He spun around, awaiting the caresses of the ghost's icy fingers on his face. "What do you want?" he shouted, his voice high and wild. He banged on the door with his elbow. Each thump was met by an echo.

"I want you to find your truth," she answered.

"*What?*"

"The choice is yours."

"What choice?" he asked unsteadily, only vaguely aware that he was having a conversation with a ghost.

"The only choice that matters. Welcome, Felix."

Then the lights came back on.

Certain that he was going to be face-to-face with the ghost, he threw up his arms to protect himself.

An interminable moment passed.

He held his breath, and risked a peek between his forearms. He was all alone. It was just him. There was no woman in blue in the tunnel.

With a rush of adrenaline, he turned back to the door and tried to pry it open, but it was flush with the inner wall and his fingers couldn't gain any leverage. He pounded on it. He kicked at it. But the door barely even rattled. When the echoes finally faded and died back to nothing and the silence returned, he attempted something else: He stuck his pinkie in the keyhole and wriggled it around. When all that was left was trying to use his finger as a key, he saw the writing on the wall and gave up. He would have to find another way out.

His legs were jittery and his heart was slamming hard and fast against his sternum as he headed down the tunnel. The ghost's voice—he'd reached a definitive conclusion that she was a ghost—was still ringing in his head: *I want you to find your truth. The choice is yours.* He tried to avoid looking at the wall of coffins to his right. As irrational as it might seem in the safe light of day, at any moment, he half-expected an army of rotting corpses to come crawling out of their caskets. But it was like trying not to rubberneck on the highway at the scene of a twenty-car pile-up—his eyes were just drawn to the plaques. He read some of the names as he moved steadily through the corridor: Louis Multo 1763-1824. Sarah O'Reilly 1754-1813. *Damn*, he thought, awed. *These people have been dead a long time.*

He walked faster, his sneakers scuffling and squishing along on the concrete floor, wishing he hadn't left his cell phone on his desk. When he arrived at another corridor that intersected with the one he was on he felt the tiniest bit of hope, and broke into a jog. The lights started to flicker. He stopped, waiting for the darkness—and the ghost in the blue dress—to return. Then all the lights lit up even brighter than before—*all the lights but one.* On the wall where the two tunnels converged a single bulb continued to flicker. He padded over to it, cautiously, hoping the ghost was trying to show him the way out.

She wasn't.

Below the bulb were three plaques much bigger than the others. He rubbed off a water stain from the one in the center and read the name aloud: "Agatha Pierre-Croix." The moment the syllables left his lips, all the lights in the tunnels dimmed and he felt a cold breath on his cheek.

He jumped back, his head twitching back and forth, waiting. When the ghost didn't appear, he read the names on the plaques next to Agatha's. This time, he read them silently: *Constance Wethersby. Lucinda Stowe.* He noticed that all three women had died the same year. Turning away from the wall, he started down the new tunnel, wondering what was so special about Agatha, Constance and Lucinda, and why they'd all died in 1829.

When he came upon another door (to his left), a trickling sense of hopefulness teased him with warm anticipation. It was squashed a moment later once he realized what he was dealing with. Like the door beneath St. Rose, it was made of steel, it didn't have a doorknob, and only a key could open it it. Out of sheer desperation, he pounded on it, and listened as it boomed and echoed hollowly in the silence, racing up and down the tunnels, swirling like a storm in the stillness. He gave up shortly. It most likely led to a basement deep below another building where no one would be, especially at four in the morning—*if that was the time*. His watch was sharing space with his cell on his desk; he hadn't exactly planned for this.

He tried to work out in his mind which direction he was going as he trudged along through the tunnel. He was probably heading south. But he wasn't entirely sure about that since the ghost woman had mixed him all up in the labyrinth-like corridors beneath the church. The tunnel he was on branched off at forty-five degree angles like a trident. With three tunnels to choose from, he remembered Lucas—or was it Allison?—saying the tunnels connected to every building on campus. And if that was true, and it now appeared that it was, it meant there were miles of tunnels down here. He could walk forever and never find an exit if the only way out was through one of the doors. Because without a key—

I could actually die down here.

The second that thought crossed his mind he told himself to stop being such a wuss. He *would* find a way out. It just might take a while. He took the tunnel to his left and picked up the pace. When he came to a door—this one on his right—he didn't waste much time trying to open it. He just kicked it a few times and yelled "Hello!" until he was sure if by some miracle someone was behind it they would have heard him.

Later—he didn't know how much later because the people who constructed the bomb shelter hadn't thought to hang any clocks on the walls—the tunnel forked, and he took the one to the left. His confidence was sagging, and he was operating on a hunch that he hoped would lead him back to Downey and Satler and the other dorms on the east side of campus; unless, of course, he was even more discombobulated than he felt, in which case, he could be heading due west toward the football stadium and no-man's-land. His sense of direction was good, but this was madness.

Three doors and several forks later, he was starting to lose hope. It all looked very bleak. Everything was tilting against him. Even without the aid of a watch he knew he'd been down here a long while. The solid steel doors were impossible to break down, and according to Lucas and Allison, nobody knew about the tunnels except for the few people who ran the school—and the president and the dean probably didn't spend their weekends sleeping in the basements of hundred-year-old buildings.

I really could die down here, he said to himself, and this time, he didn't think he was acting like such a wuss. But was that really what the ghost was trying to do? Did she lure him into the tunnels so she could watch him slowly lose his mind and starve to death as he searched for a way out? *Don't panic*, he told himself. Being stupid wouldn't help. Freaking out wouldn't help. But he had a damn good reason to freak out. After so much wandering around, the only thing he knew for sure was that the door beneath St. Rose was accessible and the rooms next to it were at least used occasionally. And as much as he didn't want to be anywhere near the cemetery, maybe his best chance of escaping was to head back there and pound on the door and hope someone would happen by. Not a great plan. But better than insanity and starvation. He took one last look around before setting off to retrace his steps, thinking that if he hadn't lost his bearings it would be a miracle.

Something on the ceiling caught his eye. He ran over, stopped beneath it, and stared straight up at a manhole-sized opening carved out of the ceiling; it looked like a giant drill had bored its way through the earth. And then he saw something truly miraculous: sturdy-looking iron staples set within, and running all the way up to the top, of the cylinder—*a ladder.*

He jumped and grabbed hold of the lowest rung, then pulled himself up and started climbing. With only a few rungs left, he lifted his eyes, and what he saw caused the panic in his chest to flare: the ceiling was right over his head and the ladder seemed to run right smack into it—there was no place to go. He'd found a ladder, but it was a ladder to *nowhere*.

Then he lowered his gaze and realized that a small barren room was spread out before him, and that on the far side, attached to the wall, was a second ladder, its rungs descending down through another hole in the ceiling. Pulse racing, he swung his legs over the top of the ladder, scrambled across the concrete space and started to climb. He moved fast, the rusty bars passing beneath him one after the other: *twenty-six, twenty-seven, twenty-eight*, he counted, ticking them off in his head. He paused for a second to check for the ceiling—it was still fifteen or twenty feet above his head—then resumed his climb. *Please don't let this be a dead end. Please.* When he reached the top, he looked over the last rung, hoping to find a big unlocked door with a luminous movie theatre style EXIT sign above it. But it was just another concrete room, this one even smaller than the first. He got to his feet, keeping one arm over his head to make sure he didn't crack it on the low ceiling.

The space was tight, little more than a walk-in closet; it was a damn good thing he wasn't claustrophobic. If he stretched out his arms he could touch two sides with his fingertips, and he had to hunch down to avoid scraping his skull. At least the light was still good. There were two bulbs in the room, both burning bright: One behind the ladder, and the other directly across from it, each protected by the odd metal casings like the others in the tunnels.

But there wasn't a ladder in this room, or a door, or any other kind of opening—just flat, smooth, hard, impenetrable materials. He knew he had to be close to the surface after climbing for so long. There had to be a way out. *This had to lead to something.* The ladders couldn't have been random. *What am I missing?* He stood there for a long while, deep in thought.

When it came to him he felt stupid for not figuring it out sooner: *a secret door.* There had to be a secret door in this room. Just like Woodrow's Room. *But where?* That was the question. Squatting down low, he looked up at the ceiling, then he went over to the wall across from the ladder and starting at the top, placed both hands on it, meticulously working his fingers all the way down to the floor. Then he proceeded to probe the other walls. But there were no levers, no switches and no buttons—nothing that would activate a secret door. *Nothing.* Not a single goddamn thing.

Frustrated and slightly panicked, he knelt down in the center of the room and stared around, focusing on every little bump, groove and ridge on the surface. He wasn't seeing *something* that had to be there. But what? He'd touched, pushed, poked and massaged every square inch of the room. He couldn't have missed anything. *But this has to be the way, and you better figure it out or no one will ever see you again.*

But he *had* missed something, and it hit him like a Jimmy Clay cheap shot. *The bulbs.* He bounced to his feet—and smacked his head on the ceiling because he forgot to duck—and stepped over to the bulb furthest from the ladder. It was near the top of the wall, perfectly centered and extremely bright—he had to squint to look at it. Sweat was gathering on the nape of his neck and rolling down his back. He reached up and lightly touched the metal casing, expecting it to be hot. It was—the first thing he'd been right about all night. He tapped down on it. Nothing happened. He flicked up on it, but that only burned his fingers. Tugging on the sleeve of his sweatshirt, he wrapped it around his hand and nudged the bulb's protective shell to the left.

Something behind the wall made a soft *clicking* sound, like the gears of a grandfather clock before the chime. Then the wall moved, shifting slowly and almost noiselessly from right to left. He stepped back and watched as a narrow, hobbit-sized opening in the bottom right corner of the wall appeared in front of him. It was a safe bet it wouldn't stay open for very long so he hopped over to the little door and crouched down, preparing to step through it. He took one tentative step. Then he stopped.

There were objects dangling in his face... and there was something familiar about them. He reached out and tapped one with his finger. It was soft. It had buttons. Next to it was a thin metal wiry thing hanging from a rod. And next to that was a pair of pants, and next to that, a jacket with a zipper. He squatted down as much as he could, and keeping his head low, duck-walked into the opening, praying that the door wouldn't close and crush him against the wall.

He took a deep breath and shuffled forward with one thought whirling around in his addled brain: *Whose closet is this?*

Chapter 19

ROOM 444

Foot rot. That's what the closet smelled like. It was probably coming from the shoes. Mostly sneakers, but the moldy Limburger stench seemed to be mushrooming up from a pair of topsiders. Guy's shoes. Felix was scooting his way inside a guy's closet, a closet that looked just like Felix's closet in Downey. Same scuffed wood floor, same white painted interior, same size. This was a dorm room. *A guy's dorm room.*

With his butt dragging over the shoe tops and the clothes hanging from the rod brushing against his head, he leaned forward, keeping one hand on the floor for balance, and stuck his face right up against the quarter-inch gap where the doors came together. The room was dark. *Good,* Felix thought hopefully. *Not morning yet.* Whoever lived here was probably sleeping. He pressed his ear against the doors, held his breath and listened. Nothing. Complete silence.

The floor started to vibrate softly and there was a sudden *whirring* noise—the sound of gears in motion. The same sound he'd heard just a moment ago. He knew what it meant: the secret door was about to close. He snatched the hood of his sweatshirt and pulled it around, flattening it against his throat. The *Final Destination* movies had all made their rounds at the August house and he was familiar with death-by-your-own-shirt.

When he was sure that his hood wasn't going to get caught in the door, he twisted his neck around to see what was happening behind him. The door was shifting back into place, slowly draining the light from the closet. He reached out for the topsiders—he couldn't stand the stench any longer and didn't think anyone would miss them if they somehow *disappeared* to the wrong side of the secret door—and a spider crawled out of the shoe and pounced on his finger. The spider was small, and most likely not dangerous to anything bigger than a bug, but Felix reacted like anyone would. He sucked in a jagged breath and took a swipe at it. The spider escaped without injury, but Felix lost his balance and bumped his head against a pair of pants swaying lazily from a sagging hanger. It had a domino effect: The pants swung into a shirt, which tapped another pair of pants, which slapped against three or four empty wire hangers, rattling them like a tambourine.

The portal to the tunnels beneath campus sealed itself shut with an anticlimactic puff, like air blown through a straw. The floor went still. He waited in the darkness. Sweat beaded up on his forehead and slid down his face. His undershirt was sticking to his back. Finally, the hangers stopped dancing. He didn't allow himself a sigh of relief. He may have escaped the tunnels, but he was still trapped—trapped in a closet. And his situation, although perhaps no longer life and death, was still dire. If he didn't get out of here unseen, he was screwed. Best case: the dean would throw him out of school. Worst case: police involvement, maybe even jail time.

So now he needed to escape from something else. A closet. In the dark. And without waking up the kids who lived here. His chances of succeeding seemed dim. But he did have one thing going for him: He didn't know which dorm this was, but for his purposes, it didn't matter. The room layout in every dorm and frat he'd been to was basically the same. Closets were at the foot of the beds on either side of the hallway door. That was pretty much it. Finding the door—even in the dark—should be easy enough. And once he made it that far, the stairs would lead him to safety before anyone saw him (as long as no one was still hanging out in the halls or on their way to the bathroom).

He placed his pointer finger against the door on the right and pressed until he heard the latch click faintly as the magnets (one on the door and one on the frame) separated and the door swung open. He waited a few moments, hoping for silence. Maybe they were out of town? But the sounds of slow, heavy breathing quickly dismembered his hopes. First to Felix's left, then to his right, as if there was an echo in the room.

Okay, Felix said to himself. *Let's do this.*

He stretched one hand outside the closet and planted it firmly on the floor before reaching out with the other hand and doing the same. Then keeping his elbows flexed and his butt low to stay under the hanging clothes, he bear-crawled into the room. His heart pounding fast and hard in his chest, he got up from his crouch, cringing as his rain-soaked sneakers squeaked on the hardwood.

He paused, listening to the heavy—and still uninterrupted—breathing. The room was exactly as he'd pictured it. The closet to his back was on the hallway side of the room. Before him was a window that separated a pair of desks. Felix was standing at the foot of one bed. The other bed was on the far side of the room to his right. His escape hatch, the hallway door, was also to his right, and close, just a few feet away. *Good—so far.*

Then he felt a cold flash of panic and his heart crawled up into his throat. The room wasn't nearly as dark as he would have liked. Alarm clocks on both desks, light seeping in from under the door and through the blinds (loosely shuttered, especially at the bottom where several inches of glowing yellow glass were visible on one side) cast the entire room in softly filtered light. If he woke someone up, would they be able to make out his facial features or would he just appear as a darkened silhouette? He didn't know. And he didn't want to find out. He pulled the hood over his baseball hat.

The kid sprawled out in the bed in front of Felix made a groaning noise and said something. Probably just sleep gibberish. But Felix was tense, and so were his reflexes. He jerked back, and when he did, his arm slapped against the open door. The nudge from his arm started it. Momentum and springback did the rest.

The door banged shut. It was loud. Like a porcelain piggy bank falling from a dresser and smashing on the floor loud. Felix waited motionless, holding his breath. Someone coughed—the kid to his right. He slid his leg out from under the bedding and curled it around the blanket. Felix remained fixed to the spot, frozen, praying that the kid would keep his eyes shut. The room was too damn bright. If the kid opened his eyes, he'd be able to see Felix just as easily as Felix could see him.

A moment passed in silence. The room was calm again. It looked like the kid had gone back to sleep. Felix exhaled silently and took in a long nervous breath. He stood still for another beat and then made up his mind: *Time to go.* Felix made it one step before the kid's eyes popped open. He blinked a few times and then, looking directly at Felix, said sleepily, "Jeremy—what are you doing?"

Felix felt the blood drain from his face.

Seconds ticked by. Felix looked to the door, not sure if he should make a run for it.

"Jeremy," the kid whispered. "Hey!"

Then the other kid—Jeremy—started to stir. He mumbled something and let out a long breezy fart.

The first kid rubbed his eyes with the heels of his hands, then propped himself up on his forearm. Felix could see his eyes shifting back and forth from Felix to his roommate's bed. His mind was probably clouded with sleep, but not so clouded as to think that Jeremy could be in two places at the same time. "Je... Jeremy," he said uncertainly. There was a twinge of fear in his voice. "Jere—"

"Shut up, Andy," Jeremy grunted and rolled onto his side, facing the wall.

"Jeremy!" This time, Andy shouted his roommate's name. Andy was sitting up now, leaning back against his headboard.

Jeremy shot up, startled, his head turning toward Andy.

"Your closet!" Andy pointed at Felix. "Your closet! Your closet!"

When Jeremy's eyes found Felix, he gasped and flinched back so hard he seemed to levitate off his bed.

The time for stealthiness had slipped away. Felix was at the door, yanking it open, and emerging into the hallway. As he slammed the door shut, screams of panic erupted from inside the room. He quickly checked both directions. The hall was empty. The emergency exit door was at one end and close, and the staircase was all the way down at the other end. After taking a swift glance at the room number—444—he sprinted toward the staircase. With just two dorm rooms between Felix and the stairs, the sound of voices—laughing, boisterous voices—rose up from the landing below and crashed down on him like a swinging gate. He slid to a stop, then spun back around and reversed course, tearing down the hall for the emergency exit. In room 444 Jeremy and Andy were now calling for help. With images of prison—communal showers, shivs and large men with a fondness for teenage boys—prompting him to run faster, he rushed to the exit. A sign on the door read ALARM WILL SOUND WHEN OPENED. He'd always wondered if that was true.

The alarm went off with a shrieking, rolling howl the instant he opened the door. He burst out onto the platform and into the sheeting rain. The weather had turned nasty and cold while he was wandering the tunnels. He adjusted his hood and started down the slippery stairs, going fast and reckless. He lost his footing just before the second floor landing and crashed against the railing, nearly cartwheeling over the top. He steadied himself, feeling like someone was blasting him with a fire hose, then went to the other side, the side where there was supposed to be stairs. There were no stairs. But there was something else.

You've got to be kidding me, Felix thought as he stared down at the emergency exit ladder. *Not another goddamn ladder.* He considered jumping. But he had to be at least fifteen feet off the ground. If he landed wrong, he'd be risking a broken ankle. So he settled down onto his stomach and went over the edge backward, searching blindly with his feet, holding on tightly to the bottom of the guard rails. It reminded him of venturing into the deep end of the Coos Bridge public pool when he was five; when he lost contact with the bottom, he'd felt fear—and a serious rush—then the lifeguard had yelled at him to get back to the shallow end.

His feet finally touched down on something solid, and when he felt like his footing was secure, he let go of the railing and latched onto the ladder with both hands. The sirens going off inside the building seemed to be getting louder. Voices were coming at him from all directions. He started down as fast as he dared, thinking he might be in the clear.

A door swung open beneath his feet and kids began streaming out of the dorm. He stopped. The emergency exit ladder was positioned directly above the building's side entrance. If the kids pouring out of the building looked up—even just a little—they couldn't miss him. How would he explain this? What possible reason could he offer for using the emergency exit? The emergency exit for a dorm where he didn't even live. And when Jeremy and Andy told their story, the pieces would all come together and Felix would be toast. Going down was no longer an option. He was trapped—*again*. He glanced up, trying to think. If he couldn't go down maybe he could go up. *The roof.* He could hide out there until everyone went back to bed. He might get pneumonia, but that was better than expulsion, prison and a life in total ruin. He wiped the rain from his eyes and started climbing.

And then the ladder dropped like an elevator in free fall. He held on tight and bent his knees as he braced for impact, expecting it to slam into the ground. But the design of this ladder was a little different. Still five feet off the ground, the ladder's descent came to an abrupt stop, springing Felix into the air like a popcorn kernel heating up to the right temperature. He splashed down on his butt, his momentum carrying him head over heels into a perfectly executed back somersault.

"Hey!" a girl's voice called out to him. She sounded surprised. "Are you okay?"

Felix didn't stick around to chat. He pulled his hat down to the bridge of his nose and took off through the puddled lawn. He knew where he was, but he needed to make sure of it. He circled past the front of the building and found a sheltering tree next to a building that he thought was the medical clinic. He stood there for a while and watched hundreds of students huddling under umbrellas as the RAs shouted at them to get further away from the dorm. He could only imagine what they were saying about the school scheduling a fire drill at this hour—whatever hour *this hour* might be—in this kind of weather. Then he found what he was looking for above the entrance: ASTORIA HALL.

And with that information in hand, he sprinted toward Downey, trying to outrun the rain.

Chapter 20

THE INTERVIEW

AshCorp's interview room was small, and except for a pair of matching chairs facing each other by the wall-to-wall windows, unfurnished. But the view was something to behold. Graham had finished setting up over an hour ago. It didn't take long. He was the camera guy. Setting up the tripod and the boom microphone took all of five minutes, if that. During the week, he was the assistant production manager for the morning news. This was just his *whenever-we-need-you* weekend gig. Management was saving money through 'synergy consolidation'. That's what they were calling it anyway. It just meant low-ranking schmucks like Graham were stuck working two jobs and getting paid for one.

Graham knew he shouldn't be grousing, but he couldn't seem to help himself. All morning, vague complaints thinly disguised as conversation had ben slipping out almost unconsciously, his resentment and dissatisfaction convincing his dark inner thoughts to find their voice. He turned to the woman in the chair and bit down on his lip to keep his tongue from forming words he would certainly regret. Her face was round, her hair short, a full fringe bob with lots of layers and textured bangs hairsprayed into stiff obedience. She wore a conservative black suit and a white blouse, her understated jewelry was minimalistic, classsic. She possessed a rare look: part dignified matriarch, part doting grandmother. It was easy to see why she had been so successful in her career. Her face drew people in, inviting them to share themselves with the world, their dirty laundry, their blackest secrets. *Their side of the story.*

Before he could stop himself, Graham blurted: "Why do they have us come here on the weekend if they're just going to make us wait?" He should have kept his mouth shut. She wasn't just anyone. And she definitely wasn't his doting grandmother. She was Connie Redgrave, the *News Lady,* a moniker she'd earned by anchoring Channel 8's 7:30 news for the past thirty-seven years.

Connie straightened her skirt and looked up from her phone (she was scrolling through her emails), holding his eyes for a long beat before she spoke. "I realize you'd rather be doing something else on a Saturday morning, but I can't help that. I'm here because the president of channel eight asked me to be here. You're here because it's your job. I don't see a distinction between the two. So let's make the best of it." She went back to her phone.

Graham bottled up what he wanted to say and gazed out the window at the endless green of Ashfield Forest. Only a few fractured shafts of light slanted down through a dirty gray sky. His spectacular cloud level perspective of the forest made him feel like he was on the observation deck of a skyscraper. A private treehouse for a billionaire who had run out of ways to spend a bottomless well of inherited wealth. The realization that he was pissing away his weekend (*another* weekend) in a billionaire's treehouse turned the resentment to jealousy, and something much more bitter, not quite hate, but close. Graham and his wife had graduated from Portland College six years ago. She was a teacher. She worked hard, harder than him. They had two kids. Both young: four and one. They'd done everything right. What they were supposed to do. What they were told to do. And between the two of them, they'd piled up $211,000 in student loans. Graham figured at their current pace they'd be debt free and able to put a down payment on a house when they were sixty-one. Just a year younger than Connie Redgrave. And the man Connie was going to interview—the owner of this treehouse—would consider $211,000 (Graham thought of it as his *life's burden*) a typical day's interest on one of his offshore accounts.

Connie's shrewd eyes were on him, sizing him up. "First time here," she asked.

He nodded and rubbed his eyes. He was tired, and he knew the lack of sleep was contributing to his surliness. The baby wasn't much of a sleeper— at least during the night. "A friend of mine works here doing something. I'm not sure what. Or where. He doesn't say much about it. Something involving medical research, I think."

She slipped her phone into a pocketbook next to the chair and stood up, looking at Graham, her expression hard and piercing.

"What is it?" he asked, thinking that something was stuck in his teeth.

"Graham, listen to me very carefully. You need to be mindful of everything you do, and everything you say while we're here, okay?"

"Obviously. It's not my first rodeo."

"Shut up for a second and listen to me. Do not speak unless you're spoken to. I realize you're not a child, but I'm telling you this for your own good. The people you are about to meet should not be underestimated. Show them respect. Keep your mouth shut and you'll be fine. Okay?"

He stood there for a moment, feeling his face getting warm, and wondered if she was joking. Her expression didn't change. Even in heels, her head only came up to his nose, but at the moment, he was the one who felt small. Very small. "Mrs. Redgrave, if I've offe—"

"Listen to me. You're about to meet Lofton Ashfield. I don't know what you've heard about him, but here's all you need to know: He's a powerful man. How powerful?" Connie shook her head, her glossy hair as rigid as a plastic helmet. "I don't know. Nobody does. But I'll tell you a secret: The governor, the police commissioner, and our representatives in Washington won't wipe their asses without asking for his permission."

He nodded, but his eyes were uncertain and questioning.

"I'll do the talking," she continued, and although she smiled, it came out as an order. "If someone asks you a question, you answer it in the least amount of words possible. One word responses are perfect. I know you're bright, but this isn't the time to demonstrate your wit, your intelligence or your loquaciousness. Keep your mouth closed and the camera on. Watch for my signals. If you're not sure what to do, follow my lead."

"Are you trying to make me nervous, Mrs. Redgrave?"

"No. But you should be."

"Excuse us," a voice called into the room.

Graham jumped.

A woman and a man—both younger than Graham—were standing in the doorway, smiling. "Mrs. Redgrave," the woman said cheerfully as they stepped into the room. "Hi. I'm Kayla. We met once before. You probably don't remember me." She giggled shyly. "And you must be Graham Senden." She smiled at Graham, then placed a hand softly on the arm of the man standing next to her. "This is Jalen."

"Nice to meet you," Jalen said with a casual smile.

Kayla was unquestionably pretty. Faceful of freckles and hair that was long and rebellious. Graham barely noticed Jalen. Dark skin. Dark hair. Pretty girl and a big guy. He couldn't control where his eyes were drawn to.

"Lofton wanted us to tell you he will be with you momentarily and that he apologizes for his lateness," Kayla said. Her voice was high, girlish.

Graham gave Connie a look as if to say *these are the people I'm not supposed to underestimate?* They looked like interns. Maybe they were. But would an intern call Lofton Ashfield by his first name?

Two men entered the room, one behind the other. The first man was tall, the other short. The taller man—Graham recognized him as Lofton—nodded at Kayla and she and Jalen went swiftly to the doorway and out into the hall.

"Connie," Lofton said brightly, coming over to her. He was tall and lean with broad, square shoulders that tapered down to a narrow waist. His pale blue eyes seemed to radiate as he smiled at her. Graham knew he was forty (he'd done his research), but his face was ageless—he could pass for twenty-eight or forty-eight. He leaned in gracefully and kissed her on the cheek.

"Mr. Ashfield," Connie said, beaming. "It's so good to see you again. It's been too long. Thank you so much for allowing us to meet with you."

"Connie, please call me Lofton," he said chidingly and gave her a slightly uneven smile. "Haven't we gone through this before?"

"Of course." Connie turned to Graham. "This is Graham Senden."

Graham was suddenly nervous and it took him a moment to find his voice. "It's a pleasure to meet you, Mr. Ashfield." Graham extended his hand, wishing he'd wiped his palm off on his pants.

Lofton smiled and shook it. If he thought it was clammy, it didn't show on his face. "Pleasure to meet you, Graham. And that goes for you too. *Lofton.* Please call me Lofton. I'll consider it an insult if you don't." He turned his head and nodded at the little man standing beside him. "This is Devory Portier."

"It's very nice to see you again, Connie." Devory kept his hands at his sides. "Nice to meet you, Graham." He motioned at the chairs. "I hope this is acceptable. Oh"—he pressed a hand to his chest and shook his head as if chagrined—"I'm afraid Mr. Ashfield only has ten minutes this morning." He bowed stiffly and turned around, then crossed the room to the back wall where he remained standing between paintings depicting the Duomo in Florence.

Ten minutes, Graham thought in disgust. *Typical inconsiderate rich asshole.*

"You obviously know why the station requested an interview," Connie said to Lofton. "But instead of jumping right in, I thought I would ask you a few unrelated questions—background questions. Would you be amenable to that?"

Lofton smiled and settled into a chair. "I think that's a wonderful idea. Shall we begin then?"

Connie sat down in the other chair, crossed her legs and turned her shoulders a few degrees toward Lofton. Graham had taken his position behind the camera and had already turned it on. If he missed something, he would lose his job—*both jobs*. Connie looked up at Graham and gave him a quick nod—the signal that wasn't necessary. Then she stared directly at the camera, smiled and with a practiced, velvety tone said: "This is Connie Redgrave with channel eight news. I'm here today with Lofton Ashfield, the president and CEO of AshCorp. How are you doing Mr. Ashfield?"

"Very well, Connie. Thank you. And please—call me Lofton. I insist."

"Lofton." She smiled, her cheeks going pink, if not quite red, through the studio makeup. "We conducted an online viewer poll this past week. We called it 'what would you ask Lofton Ashfield'. And one question that finished very high in the poll, and one I'm very curious about myself, is this: what was it like to become the CEO of a multinational conglomerate at the age of eighteen? When most people that age are graduating high school, you were already the head of one of the world's largest corporations. How did you handle so much responsibility at such a young age?"

Lofton nodded at Connie, then turned his head to look straight at the camera. "It was certainly an incredible responsibility. A responsibility I never sought. When my parents and grandfather passed away in a terrible tragedy on my eighteenth birthday, I doubted everything. I had doubts about myself. I doubted my ability to lead an organization my grandfather and father had built stone by stone. At first, all my work, all my accomplishments, were to honor the memories of my family. But as time went on, and as AshCorp grew and expanded into new and exciting industries, I gradually became more focused on the future and less on the past. Healing is a long, painful process. But I've always found comfort—and great pride—in knowing that the organization my family built is stronger today than ever before. If they were here with me now, I know they would be very proud of my achievements."

"And now that AshCorp has reached such staggering heights, have you thought about exploring other challenges? Would you consider, for example, running for… public office?"

"How did I know you were going to ask that question?" Lofton said, smiling.

Connie laughed lightly. "Our viewers would never forgive me if I didn't."

"That's really a question only the public can answer." Lofton folded his hands, resting them comfortably on his lap. "You see, the people define the issues that determine who represents them. Today, officials are elected based on their position on issues such as taxes, the economy and social security benefits. I would never minimize the importance of such matters, but I have always been, and will always be, an unapologetic idealist. I believe wholeheartedly that one day society will be free from war and violence, free from disease, free from poverty, and free from corruption.

"One day, the people of this country—the people of all the countries of the world—will wake up and realize that we're capable of so much more. I truly believe one day we'll be committed to sharing the wealth of the world with all of its inhabitants—not just the few who make the rules. And my critics can say what they want about me, but I have faith there will come a time when we'll truly be committed to living in a world where airplanes are not used as weapons that crash into our places of work, where our defenseless children are not gunned down in our schools, and where our citizens are not killed and maimed simply for exercising their right to congregate in public places. One day, we will live without fear. When the people stand up and demand that world—when they demand to live in a world without fear—I will… well, I will gladly do everything in my power to give them what they ask for." Lofton chuckled. "I'm a lone idealist—a lone humanist—in a world of compromisers and cynics. And I promise you, I will never change."

Graham looked up from the camera. He *liked* this guy. He liked him a lot. He felt like Lofton was speaking to him, like they were the only two people in the room. The truth in Lofton's words was irrefutable: *A world without fear.* How incredible would it be to live in a world where he didn't have to worry about some lunatic shooting up his family at work or at the mall or at a parade? Or crumbling under the weight of his *life's burden?* Graham *was* afraid. Afraid of the future. Afraid of everything. But Lofton could take that fear away. Graham *wanted* Lofton's world; he wanted it very badly.

Connie nodded and smiled. "I know that message resonates with millions of people in this country and abroad. But when you speak of a world that is free from war, how do you explain your own company manufacturing the most sophisticated weapons that have ever been developed? While AshCorp's accomplishments in medicine, biotechnology, and alternative energy are all lauded, a recent article in a major publication criticized AshCorp for engineering weapons of war. If you could speak to your critics on that subject what would you say?"

"I genuinely appreciate the opportunity to address this issue," Lofton replied solemnly. "Nothing would give me more pleasure than to permanently shut down my weapons manufacturing division. But unfortunately, not everyone shares my ideals for a world built on peace, prosperity and equality. There will always be those who are unwilling to act for the greater good; individuals who sacrifice their own communities—and humanity's evolution—in the name of impoverished, self-serving philosophies that have no place in our future. Using weapons is not always a sign of weakness. Sometimes it's the only language that's understood by those who are the enemies of everything we should be striving for."

"I... I... see," Connie sputtered out. Then she fell silent. No follow-up question. Her eyes looked distant, her face soft and old, a grandmother lapsing off into a fond memory from the distant past.

"Mrs. Redgrave," Graham hissed as he hit the off switch. "Mrs. Redgrave!"

Connie shook her head groggily and looked up at Graham. She blinked and gave him the *cut* sign.

"Are you okay?" Lofton asked her, concerned. "Would you like a glass of water?"

"No. No, I'm fine. I'm sorry, Mr. Ashfield—*Lofton*. Just a little tired, I think." Her eyes cleared and she straightened up in her chair. She flicked a glance at her watch and then at Devory. Time was running out. "If it's okay, I'll resume with the recent investigations on your property."

"Of course," Lofton said.

Graham had the camera back on before she gave him the nod.

"Thank you, Lofton. As you're obviously aware, two bodies were discovered this past summer in Ashfield Forest. And subsequent to that event, five people have been reported missing, all thought to be in the vicinity of Ashfield Forest at the time of their disappearances. Can you tell us about your involvement in these matters and what you've been able to do to assist the authorities?"

"First, I would like to say my heart goes out to the families and friends of the young couple who died before their time. It's such a terrible tragedy when a life is cut short. And with respect to the five missing individuals, we should not give up hope. The collective hope of the people is a powerful force in times like these." Lofton paused, frowning slightly as if he was reflecting on the meaning of his own words. Then he steepled his fingers, his index fingers touching the underside of his chin. "I have offered my full cooperation to the authorities. They have unfettered access to my lands. From the very beginning, my security personnel have assisted the Portland PD, the state police and local volunteers with the search efforts."

Connie nodded gravely. "But even with your full cooperation, we seem no closer to understanding what may have happened. Do you have any insights?"

"I hate to speculate, Connie. But I will tell you what I have already told the authorities. Ashfield Forest is not an amusement park. It is hundreds of square miles of wilderness—some of the most rugged and densely wooded terrain in North America. It's also home to wild animals such as bears, mountain lions and wolves. The woods can be a dangerous place. So I implore the public to stay out of the forest. Please, for your own safety."

In the back of the room, Devory coughed. Twice. Time was up.

"That's very good advice, Lofton," Connie finished up quickly. "Thank you for your time. It's been a pleasure speaking with you today."

"The pleasure's been mine. Thank you."

Connie raised her eyes to Graham and gave him a smile—half joy, half relief. Graham, on the other hand, felt like he was high, or in love, or both. He didn't want the interview to be over. He wanted Lofton to keep talking. His scalp was tingling, so he ran a hand over it, but it only seemed to spread. Goosebumps slithered up his arms and raced up his back. An idea came to him: Maybe Lofton needed his help? Maybe he had a political action committee or something like that and was looking for volunteers? He took two steps toward Lofton before he felt a hand on his arm.

"We'll take you down to the lobby when you're ready." It was Kayla. Graham hadn't noticed her and Jalen re-entering the room. She was smiling, but there was something in her voice that made him think it was time to go.

Connie was thanking Lofton again for his time. Graham hesitated, and then began to gather up his equipment. Lofton was telling Connie she was a consummate professional. Jalen asked Graham if he needed help with his bags. Devory came over and said something to Connie about approving the copy before it aired. Something about the *usual procedures*. And then Kayla took Graham by the arm again and led him out of the room. Connie was behind him with Jalen as her escort. Kayla was talking to him and smiling and asking him about his wife and if he had kids. He could only manage a wavering smile in return, and before he knew it, they were in an elevator and going down. Lofton, he imagined, was still in his treehouse.

* * *

Lofton stood at the window, looking out, hands in his pockets.

"I think that went well," Devory said.

Lofton didn't respond.

The sound of raindrops drifting against the glass filled the silence.

"Is something troubling you?" Devory asked. "Is it Mr. Rathman?"

"Dirk?" Lofton said. "Dirk has waited his whole life for this, and I've waited a very long time for someone like him to come along. This was the role he was born to play. I have no reservations about his abilities or his commitment."

Devory looked up at Lofton and began to say something, but then appeared to reconsider and stopped himself short.

"It's Jennifer." Lofton glanced down at Devory for a moment. "She was in Prague to have a word with a tester. I haven't heard from her in… too long. Lynch is on his way there now."

Devory frowned deeply. "Do you suspect the Protectors?"

Lofton's eyes became hard and his lips twitched. Devory took a respectful step backward and stared down at the floor.

"I gave Lynch instructions to track them down and to bring them to me," Lofton said coldly. "If he succeeds—and I suspect he won't—they will find out what happens when you *fuck* with me. That girl meant a great deal to me. I would very much like to have a word with the people responsible."

Chapter 21

THE REVOLUTIONARY

Caitlin and Lucas were smiling at each other and it was making Felix nervous. Four hours into the Satler party and Felix was sure they'd finally run out of steam or gotten bored. But this was the calm before the storm. A breather between rounds.

"So why don't you let me buy you a steak?" Lucas asked her. The room they were in was loud (reggae from across the hall was colliding with the techno house blasting from speakers stacked on the desks) and packed. The beer supply had dried up an hour or so ago, but Larry and the other fatassosaurs had saved the night—and ensured hangovers for everyone—with five big jugs of cheap rum and armfuls of Coke.

"*A steak?*" Caitlin said testily, her eyes sharp. "Have you ever been to a slaughterhouse?" She paused, partly for effect, partly because Lucas had been pushing her buttons all night. Felix and Allison laughed. Harper cupped a hand over her mouth, giggling. "It's not funny," Caitlin snapped, giving them all an angry glare.

They laughed harder.

"It's not funny!" Caitlin shouted. "I'm a lifetime member of the League for the Humane Treatment of Animals, and we did a tour of one. I thought I could handle it. But I couldn't. The smell nearly killed me. It's the cruelest, most despicable thing you could ever imagine. Poor helpless animals lining up to have an eight-inch bolt driven into their brains! They're raised in the most horrible conditions, and then they're slaughtered. And you want to know why? So *you*"—she poked a finger into Lucas's chest—"can get fat eating their flesh! And you want to buy me a steak? No thanks. But don't let that stop you. Order two. And I hope you get intestinal worms, diarrhea, heart disease and a double case of *mad cow*!"

Lucas drank from his plastic cup. "You lost me there with the whole humane society tour thing. Was that a yes?"

"I hate you," Caitlin told him.

"C'mon, Little C." Lucas reached out to give her a hug. "You know you love me."

"No," Caitlin replied, crinkling up her nose and swatting his arms away. "I actually hate you."

Felix was laughing so hard he felt weak. He was at a party. He was having an awesome time. Strange. And he was aware of just how strange it was. Earlier today he'd encountered a ghost in a blue dress. And he'd thought the ghost in the blue dress was going to kill him. Then he'd gotten lost in the tunnels beneath campus and thought he was going to die down there. Then he'd been trapped in a dorm closet at Astoria and thought he was going to get caught and tossed out of school. An eventful night. But he hadn't said a word about it to anyone. His friends still seemed to think he was sane even after what had happened—*hadn't happened*—at Martha's house, and then the very-hard-to-explain stripper streak through the dorm that had ensued. So he wasn't going to push his luck with another insane tale—this one about chasing the ghost of Cinderella into the tunnels and through the cemetery beneath St. Rose. He'd considered ways of doing it all afternoon—keeping it to himself was really, really tough—but telling the story without sounding like he needed a room at the psych ward was beyond his abilities.

"Yes!" Lucas shouted gleefully. He was looking down at his cell phone.

"What's up?" Felix asked him.

"Ever hear of Super-Six-Pack-Power-Protein-Plus? S-S-P-P-P-P for short." When everyone shook their heads Lucas continued. "No? Okay—so get this: If I do ten tweets that I got my six-pack from taking S-S-P-P-P-P they'll give me ten thousand bucks."

"What six pack?" Caitlin teased, laughing.

"You want me to show you?" Lucas said to her, one hand tugging up on the front of his shirt.

"God no," Caitlin gasped and made a gagging sound.

"Are you being serious?" Allison's brows knitted together. "Ten thousand for a few tweets?"

Lucas nodded.

"That's some serious cash," Felix said.

"That's twice as much as I made at the Crab Shack waitressing all last summer." Allison tipped her cup back and drained it. "I worked twelve weeks. Double shifts. I busted my ass. Kids threw food at me. Gross old men hit on me all the time. And all you have to do is tweet?"

"I know." Lucas grinned wide. "It's ridiculous. Ever since I got David—that agent dude—I've been endorsing some random products and making pretty good money."

"Dirk's agent?" Felix asked.

"Yeah." Lucas paused for a second thoughtfully. "I'm gonna tell him to tweet it. It's ten grand. What the hell?"

"Your *agent* actually does the tweeting?" Allison asked. She looked disgusted.

"Yeah," Lucas said. "His staff does, anyway. They do that and all my Facebook and Instagram stuff. I don't have to do anything. I just give him the go ahead and his office does all the work. It's awesome. I make money for doing absolutely nothing. One of David's people was telling me last week if *Summer Slumming* gets picked up for another season, I'll be endorsing all kinds of shit. There might even be a book deal. I won't have to write anything. I guess someone ghost writes it for me. And she said something about an advance of some kind. Six figures. How much is that? A lot, right?"

Allison was stunned. "You're going to write a book?"

"Hell no!" Lucas took a long drink from his cup and belched loudly. "Someone's going to write it for me."

"That's completely messed up," Allison complained. "Who'd wanna read a book about you?"

"Hell if I know." Lucas burst out laughing. "I wouldn't! But remember the girl on the other show? What's her name? You know, the short dumb chick with the big hair. Cannoli? She wrote two books."

"Capitalism's so goddamn ridiculous sometimes," Allison muttered, her lips pursed in anger. "If Cannoli had two brain cells the friction would make her head explode. *Two books?* Are you kidding me? Is she even literate? I'd bet my life she couldn't put two coherent sentences together."

Lucas shrugged. "If people want to throw money at me what am I supposed to do? Throw it back at them?"

"So you're not even gonna try the S-S-P-P-P-P?" Caitlin said to him. "Did I leave out a P? How many P's are there again?"

"Why would I do that?"

"You'll endorse a product without even trying it?" Caitlin said incredulously, her eyes boring into Lucas. "That's exactly what's wrong with corporate America. Some company's using slave labor to make this protein powder garbage, and it's using you to sell it to kids who trust you. And you're not even going to try it? That's wrong, Lucas. Wrong."

"Caitlin's right," Allison agreed, still bristling. "If you're going to make money for doing nothing the least you could do is try it. How hard's that?"

"Geez." Lucas threw up his arms and beer slopped out of his cup. "I'm so sorry for making money. My deepest apologies to anyone who's ever been wronged by corporate America. Like that's my responsibility. Anything else you wanna blame me for? How about our dependence on foreign oil? I suppose that's my fault too. Shit! But if you guys feel so strongly about it, I'll try the goddamn powder. Here—look!" He angled his phone so everyone could see the screen while he tapped out the text. When he was done, he read it: "Yes. I'll endorse. Please send sample to me at school." He put the phone back in his pocket. "There. Done. Satisfied?"

Allison grunted. Caitlin made a guttural noise that sounded a lot like a growl.

Without any warning, Jonas bulled his way through the crowd and hoisted Felix onto his shoulder in a fireman's carry. Felix groaned and spilled half his drink on Jonas's shirt. Jonas helicoptered him around for a while and caused a fair amount of destruction in the room before Felix was able to coax him into setting him back down on the floor. Jonas was slurring his words pretty badly, but the lifting and spinning was apparently his way of expressing his appreciation for Felix's touchdown catch that afternoon in typhoon-like conditions (the Sturgeons had beat the Watsforde Planters in a huge upset; the upset of the year so far in the PNFL). But as wasted as Jonas was, Salty was faring much worse; nothing that came out of his mouth resembled any language Felix had ever heard before.

The girls went off to get refills (and to escape Jonas's rampage) with Lucas and a girl that had been following Lucas around all night. Her name was Piper. Petite, with hair the color of copper, her skin was almost as white as the St. Rose Ghost. As Jonas and Salty mumbled something about the game, Felix kept his eyes on Harper. He wasn't alone. Every guy in the room was doing the same thing. Felix was about to go over and say something very witty to her—he'd been rehearsing it in his head while Salty made odd grunting noises mixed in with the occasional roar of laughter—when Jonas suddenly got teary-eyed over a babysitter he still had a crush on.

So Felix finished his drink and reassured Jonas that everything would work out as the three of them stared at a group of nearly naked girls dancing on a bed. Maybe they were warm—the room had become steamy, and the window, although opened, couldn't siphon off the massed body heat—and maybe they were just exhibitionists. Felix didn't care; he was just enjoying the show. He couldn't even taste the rum any more, and he knew it was brimming with the liquid fire because he'd watched Larry pour it. And in spite of the blubbering man-child crying on his shoulder, Felix felt stellar.

"Felix!" Lucas shouted at him from across the room.

Felix's eyes drifted away from the performance on the bed. "What?" he shouted back.

"Whadya say about heading over to the Beta house?" Lucas asked.

"The what?" Felix choked out.

"I know." Lucas crossed the room to him. "It sounds crazy. But Piper here"—he nodded at the little redhead tagging alongside him—"was saying they got something big going on ever there. And you gotta figure they have short memories, right?"

Larry came up from behind Felix and said in a voice so loud Felix jumped in surprise: "C'mon!" His curly blond head towered over everyone. "There's some good guys over there. Just give 'em a chance. We're out of booze, anyway. Salty—the big fat ass—just drank the last of the rum. And this room's starting to stink. I think Salty sharted himself again."

Salty was too wasted to defend himself—or perhaps he really had sharted himself and was trying to keep it under wraps. It would have to remain an eternal mystery because Felix wasn't about to stick his nose up Salty's shorts to find out.

"We'll just go for a while," Lucas suggested. "You know, just see if anything's going on. I mean, what are the chances we get beat up again?"

"Pretty good," Felix said. "I don't... I don't think I'm up for another Beta party. My body can't take it."

"I'm not feeling it," Allison said. "Those guys suck." She sounded drunk.

"Sorry guys," Harper added. "I'm exhausted."

"Fine," Lucas said dejectedly. "You're still in, right?" he said to Caitlin.

Caitlin glanced over at Piper and her brow creased. "I can't let you go off by yourself after what you did the last time you were there. But you better not do anything stupid! You got it?" She slapped Lucas on the arm to make sure he was clear on the matter.

Fifteen minutes later, Felix, Allison and Harper straggled off in the direction of Downey, while Lucas, Caitlin and Piper headed off toward the Beta house with Larry, Jonas and Salty.

"Do you think they'll be all right?" Allison asked as they got off the elevator on the third floor.

"I'm sure they'll be fine." Harper turned to Felix. "What do you think?"

"What's the worst that could happen?" Then he thought about it. The worst that could happen might be pretty bad. "I asked the fatassosaurs to keep an eye on Lucas. Salty and Jonas are completely shitfaced useless, but Larry's keeping it together. I'm sure they'll be all right."

They stopped in the hallway between Allison and Harper's rooms. No one spoke.

"I'm so tired," Allison said after a while, putting her hand over her mouth to cover a hefty yawn. "I'm totally going to sleep in until noon." She looked quizzically at Felix, then at Harper. She stood there in front of her door. Then she yawned again, and unlocked it. "Good night," she said without turning around, and closed the door behind her.

"I'm so glad you made this one," Harper said. "It was so much more fun than last night."

Felix was wondering if everything was all right with Allison. She seemed upset about something. Then he saw Harper's face and forgot all about it. She was smiling at him. He stared at her, not sure what to say, lost in her blue eyes. "Uh... yeah. I had a good time."

"You know," Harper began, then her smile dissolved and she lowered her gaze to the floor.

"What is it?"

"Sometimes when you have a few drinks, everything seems so clear. So obvious." Her eyes lifted up to his face. "Doesn't it?"

"Like...?"

"You know... it's like... when you feel something, and then you think about what you're feeling, and sometimes what you're feeling is just the alcohol—or just a bad idea—but sometimes, what you're feeling just feels... perfect."

"That's what you were thinking about?" Felix asked. They must have been on the same wavelength because he had no trouble understanding her. "At the party?"

She smiled, but it faded quickly. "Yeah. Even when I'm drunk, I analyze everything to death. I just feel like I have to. Because I've... you know... been screwed over a few times."

"Guys?" Felix hazarded.

She nodded. "All these guys I've ever dated were rich, popular, good-looking and supposedly cool." She shook her head bitterly. "But they turned out to be selfish assholes. And after a while, you know, you start to wonder if maybe all guys are just the same. I'm not there yet." She laughed and ran her hands through her hair. "But I realized something tonight. I'm done with assholes. I want to be with a nice guy. You know—somebody who's actually a good person. That's what I'm looking for. That's what I want."

"Okay." It came out a little squeaky.

She stared into his eyes and her lips curled up into a perfect smile. "Has anyone ever told you that your eyes are ridiculously sexy? They're almost like ice. But I don't feel any... coldness."

He stared back, in awe of her beauty, feeling completely over his head as he tried to think of something to say. His tongue felt thick and clumsy, and when he couldn't retrieve the right words, he looked down at the floor. A moment later, he looked up to find that her eyes were nearly closed.

"Hey," he said softly. "You should probably get to bed. You look pretty tired."

"Yeah, I guess I am. Well... um... good night. I had fun tonight." She opened the door to her room. Then she stood there, her back turned to him, and paused like she was waiting for something. Finally she slipped in. After the door closed and he heard the click of the lock, he started up the stairs.

I should've made a move, Felix thought as he reached his floor. *She wanted me to. Didn't she? Didn't she just practically invite me into her room? And what did I do? I stared at my feet like an idiot. What the hell's wrong with me?*

A girl was standing in the hallway in front of his room, leaning back against the wall, facing the door. When she saw him approach, she turned toward him and smiled. He'd never seen her before. And she wasn't the kind of girl you would forget. Tall and skinny with a thick mane of long strawberry blonde hair, she was wearing only a white tank top, yoga shorts and black knee-high riding boots.

"Are you looking for Lucas?" he asked her.

"No," she said. "I'm looking for *you*. Hi Felix."

"*Me?*" he said, surprised to hear his name. "Why?" He checked her out as he walked toward his room. Sick body—no question about that. Interesting outfit too. A little underdressed for a mid-October night, but if she caught cold what did he care?

"Because," she said, undressing him with her dark brown eyes, "you happen to be the hottest guy in the freshman class. Even hotter than your roommate." Her voice was velvety with droplets of smoker's rasp.

"Thanks. I guess. I'm not sure what to do with that."

"You can do me." She flicked out her tongue and left it there, the tip visible for a moment, pressed between her full lips.

"Huh? Oh. Okay." Now he was even more confused. Even if he wasn't drunk—which he most certainly was—this situation would be extremely confusing. "Um... what's your name?" Stupid question, but he felt awkward, and it's all he could come up with.

"Amber." She reached out and touched his chest, tracing her fingers down to his stomach, pausing when she got to the waistband of his jeans. "You're as hard as a rock."

He shivered.

"You like that, don't you?" She lifted her eyebrows provocatively.

"I like your tattoo," he said numbly, not sure why he'd said it. "What is it? A Tiger?"

"Yeah." She turned her wrist over so that her palm faced up. On her inner forearm was a tattoo of a roaring tiger inked from her wrist to the hollow of her arm. Vivid, alternating black and orange stripes made up its body. Its eyes were fire red. Long ivory fangs filled its gaping mouth.

"It's fierce," Felix said, relieved that he was able to distract her. He wasn't sure what was going on. Maybe if he had a few minutes to think, he could sort this out.

"Seen one like it before?" She lowered her eyes to the tattoo. "Do you know what it means?"

He shook his head.

"I'm ERA."

"ERA? Never heard of it."

She leaned into him and whispered in his ear: "It stands for the Evolution Revolution Army. Once you join, you can get the tattoo." She reached around his waist and laced her hands together, wedging her thigh firmly between his legs. "I'm surprised you haven't heard of us." She moved her leg against him, slowly, pressing, releasing, and then pressing again. "The ERA's growing. It's getting bigger and stronger every day." She unclasped her hands and took a step back, her eyes flicking down to his crotch. "Just like you." She smiled, letting the moment, and Felix's uncomfortableness, hang in the air.

"Oh."

"I think you want to invite me into your room now." She said it like she knew he wasn't going to object. She was right.

"Okay," he said vaguely, unlocking the door and nudging it open.

She stepped in front of him, rubbing against him as she entered the room. She sauntered over to the window, placed her hands on the glass, and arched her back. She looked over her shoulder and smiled saucily, staring at him with lusty eyes as she rocked her ass back and forth. "Which bed's yours?" she purred.

He pointed absently while she slinked over to him.

Still pointing, she threw her arms around his neck and pulled his lips against hers, plunging her tongue into his mouth. She tasted like bubble gum, cigarettes and Southern Comfort. She bit down hard on his tongue and grabbed him by his shirt with both hands, bunching it in her fists so that the fabric tightened across his throat. "You can do whatever you want to me! All those nasty things your little girlfriends won't let you do to them."

Her taste was still in his mouth, lingering like motor oil that wouldn't come off in the shower. It was overpowering, disgusting and amazing—all at the same time. She was hot—hot in a slutty way, but still hot. He wanted her in the worst way imaginable. But something wasn't right. His insides were twisting and knotted. *But why?* What was the problem? Maybe it was guilt. But he had no reason to feel guilt. He didn't have a girlfriend for the first time in three years; he was completely unattached. But as he looked at her face, all he could see in his mind's eye was Harper. Harper was perfect and beautiful—and she smelled like vanilla and spring. This trash bag grinding up on him looked like a porn star and smelled like a road weary stripper. This wasn't right.

He gently pushed her away. "Sorry. I can't do this."

"Of course you can *do* this." She tried to pull him against her, but he easily kept her away with his long arms.

"No, I really can't. Sorry. I just... I just need to get my head screwed on straight."

She glanced down at his crotch, her eyes filled with raw sexual energy. "It looks perfectly straight to me."

C'mon. Sorry, but you gotta go." He brushed by her and opened the door, holding it for her.

She crossed the room reluctantly, without urgency, as though she was unwilling to pull up stakes and cede control of the room (and the situation) back to Felix. But Felix was done. He was over this. Over her. Amber. Or whatever the hell her name was.

"You sure?" she said doubtfully. "We could do it on your roommate's bed. Does that turn you on? You like pulling hair?" With a piercing moan she clutched a fistful of hair and yanked her head back.

"You're a freak." He nodded at the doorway.

"Me? A freak?" She gasped, wide-eyed, as if it was the most shocking and salacious accusation she had ever heard. "You have no idea." She stepped into the hallway and turned to look at him. She smiled coyly, running the tip of her finger along her bottom lip. "See you around, Felix August. You won't say *no* next time. They never do."

"Whatever." He pushed the door closed. Then he locked it.

He felt dirty. He changed out of his clothes and lay down on his bed, forcing himself to relax. That was spectacularly weird. A scene from a movie; a movie his parents would never let him watch. He closed his eyes and pictured Harper, trying to block out the images of Amber sizing him up like a sixty-dollar fillet. It wasn't long before he passed out.

A noise in the hallway woke him up. He checked his clock. It was 3:45. His head felt inflated, throbbing, the mezzanine level of what was sure to be a memorable hangover. He gazed blearily across the room at Lucas's empty bed. He wondered for a second in a cloudy half-conscious kind of way if Lucas was all right, then he rolled over and went back to sleep. But not for long.

Chapter 22

THE INTRODUCTION

In the gray light of dawn, Felix trudged across a desolate campus to the Caffeine Hut. Aside from two workers—unfortunate students who must have drawn the short straws to get stuck with the Sunday morning shift—no one was there. The air was thick with the sweet scent of baking goods drifting out from the ovens in back behind the bar with its milk frothers, bean grinders, coffee makers, espresso machines, stainless steel carafes, rows of heavy mugs and tall stacks of little pastry plates.

He ordered a coffee and waited, idly glancing at the old photos on the wall. The early morning light, hazy and subdued, filtered in through the high arched windows, casting a gray pall on the faces of the students in the photos staring back at him. He tried not to look, but their eyes drew him in. He wondered what they would have thought if they'd known that one day, when they were long dead, future generations would be gazing at their faces and thinking about who they were, and how they'd lived. Maybe they did. Maybe they sensed their own mortality. And that was why their faces were smiling, but their eyes were sad and hollow and… suddenly he realized what had been bothering him all this time. Looking at the pictures was like looking at his own reflection in a mirror; in the depths of his own eyes he revealed his pain, his sadness and his guilt, just like in the eyes of the dead people staring back at him, their youth captured in little five by seven images which now hung on the wall of a coffee house.

"Here you go."

Felix shuddered, which made his head hurt more than it already did. He'd had a few too many rums last night. The barista, a cute brunette with a sparkly nose ring, had placed his titanic mug on the counter.

"Thanks." He brought his coffee over to a two-chair table across from the bar. Someone had left a Halloween party flyer behind; it was orange and black with lots of cartoonish drawings of bats, and a skeleton embroiled in a death match with a mummy and a caped Count Dracula—the widow-peaked vampire seemed to have the upper hand in the battle royale.

Just a few weeks until Halloween. This was about the time his mom would start nagging his dad to get the decorations down from the attic. She was practical like that; she knew it usually took him a while to muster up the energy to get the boxes. Halloween wasn't her favorite holiday, but she still decorated the front porch with skeletons, witches, monsters and loads of cobwebs. She didn't want the neighbors to think the Augusts were anti-holiday weirdos. His dad gave her a hard time about it. He said the same thing every year: "We've lived in this neighborhood for forty years, Patricia. The neighbors already know we're weirdos."

Felix pushed the piece of paper aside. He really wished he could sleep. He was exhausted. And now here he was—the Caffeine Hut's first customer of the day—drinking coffee and wondering why he hadn't followed Harper into her room last night. Unless he'd misread the signals, she'd wanted him to. But he'd stood there like a fool, afraid to make a move. There wasn't a guy on the PC campus who wouldn't have accepted the tacit invitation—or at least taken a step to find out if it was an invitation. But Felix's fear controlled him. He wanted her so badly it blurred his vision and screwed with his pulse in ways that made him wonder if he might need medical attention. But he was afraid. Afraid of what would happen if they did hook up. What would the next day look like? Would they start *dating*? Would they be a couple? Boyfriend and girlfriend? How could he be with Harper—or anyone for that matter—when he was living in constant fear of being exposed? All it would take is a single question about his parents and he would shut down. She would want him to open up, to share his feelings with her. But he couldn't. His unwillingness to trust her (which is how she would interpret it) would hurt her deeply. She would question his feelings for her. The accusations would follow. Then the excuses. They would argue. Bitter, creeping resentment would grow between them and divide them. Their relationship would end. Badly. There was no hope for them. Not following her into her room had been the right decision. Why pursue something predestined to fail?

He drank down his coffee without really tasting it.

He hated himself sometimes. Why was his mind always racing in circles? At the crack of dawn on a Sunday morning he shouldn't be at the Caffeine Hut obsessing about Harper. And he shouldn't be torturing himself with his stupid what-would-my-parents-be-doing-if-they-were-still-alive fantasies. It just made him crazy. And sad. If only his brain had an off switch he could—

"Felix?" a voice said. "Excuse me. Felix."

Felix's eyes darted around for the source of it. He found it—found *him*—standing next to his table holding a coffee mug. He was middle-aged, but on the younger side of the spectrum, and tall—maybe even slightly taller than Felix—with dark hair and a nose that looked like it had been broken a few times. Dark stubble covered his face (which held the remnants of a tan) and crept down his neck past the collar of his T-shirt. He was wearing a yellow rain jacket and stained jeans with a rip above one knee. Felix didn't recognize him.

"It's Felix, right?" The man was smiling. "Do you mind if I join you?" He pointed at the empty chair.

"Huh?" Felix was more than just a little out of it, submerged in a deep pool of mental muck. And he wasn't sure where this guy had come from; he hadn't seen anyone come in. Of course, he hadn't been paying attention either.

"Okay," Felix mumbled after a long while, still adrift in his own thoughts. "Do... I... um... do I know..."

"We've never met. I'm Bill Stout. The assistant groundskeeper. I make sure everything on campus looks nice so parents don't feel so bad about paying the ridiculously high tuition." He smiled and settled into the seat across from Felix.

Felix stared down at the table.

"Is that the kona blend you're drinking?" The man nodded at Felix's mug.

Oh God, Felix thought with dismay. He wasn't in the mood to discuss coffee (or anything else). "Uh-huh."

"I'm more of a tea man myself. But I indulge in a cup of coffee every now and again. Good game yesterday. What was the final score?"

"The game?" The guy—did he say his name was Bill?—had a slight accent, but he couldn't place it. He definitely wasn't from around here. "Thirty-five to twenty-one."

"And that was against Watsforde?"

"Uh-huh." Felix glanced around, wondering why Bill was sitting at his table when every table, couch and chair in the place was unoccupied.

"So what's this Rain Cup thing I keep hearing about?" Bill asked casually, like they'd known each other forever.

Felix groaned inwardly. He just wanted to have a cup of coffee in peace. He had a lot on his mind. He wasn't in the mood to talk. Hell—just the thought of having a conversation exhausted him. And chatting with the assistant groundskeeper definitely didn't interest him.

"I'm new here," Bill explained. "I'm not very familiar with PC's traditions."

"Oh." Felix swirled the coffee in his mug, trying to come up with a way to get out of this without appearing like a complete asshole. "If we win our next game we'll win the South Division. And then we'll play the winner of the North for the Rain Cup. It's a trophy."

"I see." Bill smiled. "So the Rain Cup's the PNFL's version of the Lombardi trophy?"

Felix drank from his mug and set it down on the table a little harder than was necessary. If he kept his answers short, he thought, maybe Bill would get the hint and go away. "I guess," he said finally.

"Hmmmm." Bill leaned forward in his chair, regarding him thoughtfully. Felix moved back to maintain the distance between them. It was like they were dancing, with Bill doing the lead.

"You look like you're worried about something," Bill told him.

"*Sorry?*"

"I bet it's midterms. Am I right?"

Felix stared back at him, wondering why on earth the groundskeeper would be talking to him about midterms. He couldn't catch a break. *This was awful.* Felix had been planning to kick back and have two cups of coffee. Maybe three. Not anymore. Now he just wanted to go somewhere else. Somewhere far away from Bill the groundskeeper.

"Look around." Bill flapped a hand at the empty bistro. "On the entire campus, there might be three other students who are conscious. Two haven't gone to bed yet, and the third's got his head in the toilet. You're worrying about midterms."

Felix thought about getting up and leaving. But that would be rude. "Not really," he said tersely. He'd been studying harder than he'd ever studied in his life. He went to the library with Lucas and the girls almost every night, and they stayed for hours. The girls were stone-cold serious about their grades. After all this time, he still couldn't get over how focused they were. He just had to follow their lead: if he studied when they studied, he should be golden—at least in theory.

"Can I offer you some advice?" Bill didn't pause or wait for an answer. "When it comes to taking college exams there are a few tricks you can apply. Never be critical of your professor's opinions. I know you and the other students view your professors as these great fountains of knowledge, but most of them are insecure cowards without an original idea in their heads. They've spent their entire lives hiding behind the work of others in their tenured towers. They're too afraid and too weak to have experienced anything in the real world.

"If they were forced to work a regular nine-to-five job, they'd curl up like babies and cry their eyes out. Don't challenge them. Flatter the egomaniacs whenever you can. Remember you can always appeal to the vanity of the weak-minded. And these people are as fragile as they come. Don't make the mistake of thinking too much. If you regurgitate what they've been telling you in class, you should be fine. It couldn't be any easier."

Felix felt his eyes go wide. Bill didn't talk like a groundskeeper, and Felix had nothing against the profession. From the time he was eleven, he'd been his neighborhood's unofficial lawnmower, mulcher, weed puller and general provider of cheap manual labor. But the way Bill spoke reminded him of his professors; the same people he'd just thoroughly trashed. Finally, against his better judgment, he said, "You got a thing against profs?"

"Something like that."

Felix swirled the dregs, then took long, rushed gulps. Bill was staring at him, watching him closely. He needed to get out of here. Now.

"This wasn't an accident," Bill said to him.

"Huh?" Felix gaped in surprise.

"My being here. It wasn't by chance. And I didn't come here to talk about football. Or midterms."

Felix looked around and wondered if he might need some help. He wasn't the paranoid type, but if this guy had a gun or a knife, he could be in trouble.

"And I'm not a stalker," Bill said with a subtle edge to his voice, taking note of Felix's reaction. "So stop acting like you're on the verge of dialing nine-one-one. I came here to tell you something." He paused. "I came here to tell you that I... knew your mother."

"*You what?*"

"I met your mom a very long time ago."

"*My* mom?" Bill's words struck Felix like a blow to the chin.

"Yes. Patricia August. She was your mom, right?"

Felix nodded, more out of habit than anything else. *Patricia August.* That *was* his mom's name. Just hearing it made his insides contract with pain. His chest tightened and he felt himself slipping into a dark well of depression.

"By the way," Bill said softly. "I'm really sorry about what happened to your mother. And your father—of course. Such a terrible thing."

Bill's condolences turned Felix's pain to hot anger. He looked Bill in the face and said bitterly, "I'm not talking about it." He pushed his chair back from the table and stood up.

"That's not why I'm here," Bill said quickly, holding out his hands for Felix to stay. "Just wait a minute. Your mom gave me something. She wanted me to give it to you when the time was right. I promised her I would."

"She... she what?" Felix stammered out, remaining at the table.

There was a clatter behind them.

Bill glanced over at the counter where a kid wearing a green apron was filling the display case with muffins.

"She what?" Felix said again, gritting his teeth, resisting the impulse to snap his fingers in Bill's face. "Why would she do that?"

"It's a long story."

"Go ahead." Felix sat back down.

Bill stood up from the table. It was like they were on a teeter totter. "I wish I could, but I really have to be on my way. I have a pressing appointment."

"*What?*" Felix's anger was surging. "What is it? What'd she give you?"

"It's hard to explain." Bill's eyes narrowed as he ran a hand over his face. "Let's just say it's a small personal object you should really experience for yourself. I think you'll find it fascinating."

Felix hesitated. Was this guy bullshitting him? If he was bluffing, now was the time to find out. "Then give it to me."

"I'm afraid I don't have it with me," Bill said sympathetically. "It's in storage out of state, but I expect to have it in a few weeks. I'll contact you when I do."

"You've gotta be kidding! Seriously? Then why would you..." he started to say, then let himself trail off.

"Sorry. I'll be in touch soon." Bill took his nearly-full mug over to the bar and set it down on the counter.

"Hey wait!" Felix called after him. "I'll give you my number."

"I've got it," Bill said as the door shut behind him.

Chapter 23

THE UNVEILING

The Gold Digger had recently been voted one of the worst restaurants in Orange County. Dirk Rathman sat in a back booth of the diner staring bemusedly at a ladybug doing laps around the rim of his water glass. The broad-shouldered waitress that brought him his coffee hadn't recognized him. The baseball hat, aviator sunglasses and thick beard seemed an impenetrable disguise.

A man in tan slacks and a pink polo shirt approached Dirk's table. In his mid-forties, he was short and slight with a sunburned face and no hair except for a thin ring that ran from the back of his head to his ears.

"Hello David," Dirk said, glancing up.

"Dirk." David took a seat across from him, letting out a weary groan. "I don't think I'll ever get used to that beard. When do you think you'll be shaving it off?"

"Are you seriously asking me about my facial hair?"

"Of course not." David tapped his fingers nervously on the table. "You know what I'm asking."

"And I think you know why I asked you to come here."

"I thought you were just trying to poison me," David said sourly. He turned around for a moment, wrinkling his nose at a long line of truckers silently shoveling down their lard-laden lunches at the counter. "It doesn't even smell like food in here." He sniffed the air. "It smells like... I can't quite place it. Maybe vinegar, baby shit and taco meat? How's the coffee?"

"Worse than it smells. But probably the safest thing on the menu."

"It'd probably burn a hole in my colon," David said. "So what's the—?"

"First tell me about *Mesmerizer*. Everyone's saying I'm Phillip. Everyone but you."

"Not having a cell makes it a little tricky to have a private conversation with you," David replied. "But I can confirm the rumors. Done deal. And I have the signed contract to prove it. I have no idea what a *Demongel* is. I'll have to ask my daughter about that." He stared at Dirk and a self-satisfied grin fell over his face. "Twenty-two million and a percentage of the gross. We're talking Downey's *Iron Man* money—almost."

"I would have done it for free," Dirk told him.

"Well then it's a damn good thing you have me for an agent. You know it's going to be an absolute monster franchise. Everyone had their hat in the ring. You name 'em: Pine. The Hemsworth brothers. Tatum. Efron. Some moptop from *One Direction*. There'll be at least four movies, and they'll probably stretch it to five—even six. Ten or twelve years before it's done."

Dirk watched a waitress in a grease-stained apron taking an order from a man sitting next to a display case filled with meringue-topped pies that looked like they could double as masonry supplies. "For the next decade, *Mesmerizer* will be jammed down the throats of every teenager and twenty-something in the country." He smiled. "I can't tell you how relieved I am."

"Relieved?" David replied, apparently surprised at Dirk's choice of words. "That you got the part or that your crazy plan actually worked? I'll be the first to admit I had my reservations. But I've gotta hand it to you. You knew what you were doing. You can't turn on the TV or the radio or anything else without hearing about Dirk Rathman. They run that clip all the time of you falling off your house. And the footage at that restaurant is like HD quality. There was so much video taken from so many different angles it looks like Ang Lee directed it. Over ten million mentions on Facebook in the first thirty minutes after the story broke. The kids in my office were very impressed by that. And the speculation's out of control. You've been MIA for seven weeks in case you don't have a calendar wherever it is you're hiding. My office has been denying all the usual rumors: you don't have a drug problem; you don't have an eating disorder; you didn't have a psychotic break; you're not living off the land in the wilderness; you're not suffering from exhaustion; you're not a sex addict; you're not possessed by the devil." He laughed. "If it wasn't for your daily tweets, we'd be buried with death rumors."

"Part of the plan," Dirk said coolly.

"Which reminds me." David leaned forward, placing his elbows on the table. "When I was negotiating *Mesmerizer*, the team there was impressed by your *presence*. It seems that being the center of scandal and controversy makes people very happy these days. And I'm talking about important people here. The empire makers. The guys who lube the gears of the Hollywood machine. The guys whose asses get kissed by Presidents in election years. Your Twitter count is exploding. You left Kim Kardashian's gigantic caboose in your rearview mirror a long time ago. What are you—halfway to Katy Perry now? Taylor Swift?"

"Getting there."

"Well," David said, "without your plan, you don't get the part. I'm sure of that. But there's still one thing I don't understand. Why *negative* publicity? Why do you want everyone to think you're a disaster?"

Dirk sat silently for a moment, a trace of a smile on his face as he looked around to make sure no one was watching. Then he rolled his sleeve back to his elbow and held out his arm, nodding for David to look at it. "Because you can't be saved unless you've fallen," he said slowly, his voice thick with meaning.

David's eyes followed Dirk's prompt. Then he flinched back against his seat, his arms unsticking themselves from the butter and gravy-crusted table. Startled, one hand went to his mouth as he stared down at the tattoo on Dirk's arm; it was a tiger—a snarling tiger—with one heavy paw raised high as if it was about to decapitate its prey, and it stretched across Dirk's forearm from the lower part of his bicep to his wrist. It almost appeared three-dimensional, like it was preparing to jump across the table to take a swipe at him.

"I should've known it was something like this," David said softly, after he'd collected himself. "Some of your tweets are clearly political. But the *ERA?* I know you're a smart guy with a social conscience, but I guess I never thought you'd join something like that. I mean, I know how you feel about the Scientologists."

"This is very different," Dirk said. "And I'm not just joining the ERA. I'm going to be taking on a much more... important role."

"Oh?" David fell silent for a second. He raised an eyebrow at Dirk and said ominously, "How important?"

"*Important.* For now, I need you to keep fanning the flames. When this whole thing is about to burst, I'll need you to arrange a press conference. I'll make an announcement. We'll make it all very official. But until then, you need to keep this quiet. We can't have any leaks. Tell no one. Not even my publicists."

"Of course." David nodded slowly, thoughtfully. "You know—I think the public will like this. The kids love the ERA. It's trending big time with high school and college kids." He paused for a moment, his eyes lowering to the table. "But I'm still not sure what the um... what the end game is here."

"This is it," Dirk said, his voice dropping a register. "And David—*this isn't a game.*"

Chapter 24

BREAKING THE SEAL

The big round table in Woodrow's Room seemed even more massive when it was in use. With ten chairs, and just five people to fill them, all the extra space made them feel small, like they were children crashing the big persons' table at Thanksgiving.

"Did you hear they called off the search for the brothers?" Lucas asked, more interested in talking than studying. "Ashfield Forest strikes again, huh?"

"You're just trying to scare me." Caitlin looked up from her computer. For the first hour, they'd all been whispering to each other as if they were afraid of being found out. But gradually, as they grew more comfortable with the room (it was bright—since Caitlin insisted that every light stay on—and the air didn't seem as musty as before), they began to speak in their normal voices. Except for Caitlin, that is, who was still pitching her voice low.

"I wouldn't have to try," Lucas replied, smiling. Caitlin had agreed to come to Woodrow's Room, but only 'under protest' and on a 'test basis'. If she heard any strange noises or saw anything out of the ordinary, she would leave immediately and had made everyone promise they would leave with her so she wouldn't have to walk the fourth floor by herself.

"Well, they haven't found a thing in almost two weeks," Allison said. "The *Ashfield Forest Mystery* just got more mysterious."

"I still don't think they should give up," Harper said. "So soon, anyway."

Caitlin nodded in agreement.

"What do you think, Felix?" Allison asked. "Felix? Felix!"

"Huh?" Felix was sitting in silence, his forehead propped on one palm, staring idly at the items on the table: notebooks, pens, five laptops, stacks of books, two bottles of water, a Gatorade, three cans of Diet Coke and an empty crumpled bag of kettle cooked barbeque potato chips. His encounter with Bill this morning had been gnawing at him all day. He wanted to tell everyone about it (which compounded the stress he already felt from not being able to tell them about the tunnels and the St. Rose Ghost), but he couldn't without bringing up his parents—and that just wasn't going to happen. So like a looped video, he replayed the conversation with the groundskeeper over and over in his head.

"The *search*," Allison said to him. "They stopped looking. What do you think?"

"Sorry." Felix scrubbed his hands through his hair. "It's awful. But I guess, you know, they wouldn't stop looking if they thought there was any chance they could find them."

"Hey!" Lucas said abruptly, a big grin stretching across his face. "I've got an idea. Anyone up for camping? I hear Ashfield Forest's beautiful this time of year. The fall foliage is supposed to be *spectacular*."

"I like it!" Harper said giddily. "Five college kids on a spur-of-the-moment camping adventure. What could possibly go wrong?" Felix felt himself staring at her, but he didn't fight it too hard. She was wearing a baseball hat and a sweatshirt. She looked amazing. She could wear a burlap sack and still look amazing.

"I think I've seen that movie," Caitlin muttered dryly, a tiny smile touching her lips.

"Why are college kids always so dumb in movies?" Allison was sitting back in her chair with a book in her lap, balanced on her knees. "If this was a movie, we'd all be like, 'awesome idea, Lucas, let's go!' We're *never* going to Ashfield Forest. Like never. Never. Never."

"Never say never." Lucas twirled a pen with his fingers, from thumb to pinkie and back again. He was really quite good at it. Earlier, he'd been balancing a book on his head until Caitlin expressed her annoyance by hitting him in the face with a wadded up piece of paper. "What are you reading, anyway?" he asked curiously, turning to Allison. "That isn't... is that what I think it is? Are you seriously reading that? That bondage shit?" Lucas shook his head in disgust. "I don't even understand why everyone thinks those books are so shocking. Ever hear of the Internet? You want shocking? Go to Google and type in triple an—"

"No." Allison laughed as she held up the paperback so everyone could see the cover: three gorgeous shirtless guys with perfectly sculpted physiques standing in a circle around a beautiful young woman. The girl, wearing a long flowing gown, was on her knees, looking up at the men with a hunted look in her eyes. The men looked like they wanted to have sex with her. Or eat her. Felix wasn't sure which.

"Hey—*Mesmerizer Jolie!*" Harper blurted, wedging a bookmark into her Political Science textbook and snapping it shut. "That's the first one. I think it's my favorite."

"You're reading a book?" Lucas sounded surprised. "Midterms are like a minute away."

Allison shrugged. "I'm all caught up. I'm bored. I wish they'd let me take more classes."

"I'll give you some of mine," Lucas said with a wry look. "If you're so bored, why are you reading a crap book like that?"

Caitlin made a face at him. "You don't even know what it's about. It might be mindless, vapid, brain candy, but it's like an escape, a guilty pleasure. I loved it. And it's like the number one book in the country."

"So what's it about?" Lucas asked.

"I would tell you," Allison said cautiously, "but you're only going to make fun of it."

"I promise I won't." Lucas cracked a grin.

"I don't believe you." Allison paused, smiling. "I'm probably going to regret this. So—I haven't finished it yet. But so far, it's about this girl who's in high school. Her name's Jolie. And there are these three kids who are madly in love with her. But it turns out one's a werewolf, one's a vampire, and the other one—Phillip—he's a Demongel."

"A what?" Lucas asked, confused.

"A Demongel," Harper said. "Half demon, half angel. And the werewolves and the vampires are at war because that's what werewolves and vampires do when they're bored. And the angels are at war against the demons, the werewolves and the vampires. And Phillip's really conflicted because demons and angels are mortal enemies."

"Okay." A smile crept over Lucas's face. "So does the angel part of him get into fights with the demon part? Does he like beat himself up all the time, or what?"

Harper nodded. "Yeah, but it's more emotional battery than physical. He tries to kill himself once in a while, but the angel inside him considers it a sin so he can't actually do it."

"Wow," Lucas said. "That's deep. So why are all those dudes so infatuated with this Jolie chick? Is she hot? She's gotta be, right? Like Kate Upton hot."

"I haven't figured that out yet," Allison said thoughtfully. "She's kind of pathetic in a lot of ways. She's needy, self-absorbed, love-starved and completely dependent on these guys who treat her like a child. And she trips and falls down a lot. I don't know. I think maybe she um... well... she smells nice. But I'm guessing she'll probably end up being a witch, or a fairy, or an alien, or something like that. Or maybe somebody'll bite her and turn her into something scary."

"Interesting." Lucas stroked his chin as though he was deep in thought. "I can tell you—speaking just for me, anyway—that I'm totally into chicks with balance issues that smell like cookie dough. Caitlin"—he turned to her—"if you face-planted once in a while, I might let you take advantage of me when I'm drunk."

"Suck it." Caitlin flipped a page in her textbook without looking up.

Lucas broke out in a roar of hysterical laughter and shouted up at the ceiling, "That's so lame! How can you take that shit seriously, Allison?"

"Yeah?" Allison tossed the book on the table. It slid across the polished surface, almost reaching the center before spinning to a stop after several revolutions. "How can anyone take *you* seriously?"

"I'm not the one reading fairy tale porn," Lucas replied.

Felix slunk down so that the small of his back rested on the edge of the chair. He could see where this was heading.

Allison let out a sharp breath. "And I'm not the one who hooked up with Asher Schimmel's girlfriend!"

"What?" Lucas said. He looked stunned. "How'd you...?" He gave Felix an accusing glance. "Well at least I'm not like Felix over there who hooked up with the girl-with-the-dragon-tattoo!"

"*What?*" Felix sat up abruptly in his chair. "Leave me outta this. I didn't tell Allison anything. And I didn't hook up with that chick! And it's not a dragon. It's a tiger."

"*A tiger tattoo?*" Allison cried out, her eyes wide. "You hooked up with an ERA chick? Are you crazy? Who was it?"

"*You did?*" Harper said to him, a brief grimace tightening her face. "Seriously?"

"No!" Felix felt his hangover coming back. "Her name's Amber. She wanted to hook up. She was all over me and saying some crazy shit. I swear she would've raped me if I didn't boot her ass outta the room."

"She ugly?" Lucas asked, his expression serious.

"No. Trashy—but hot."

"*Hot?*" Lucas flinched like a fork had jabbed him in the eyeball. "So what the hell's wrong with you?"

"Felix has morals," Caitlin said. "You might want to familiarize yourself with the concept."

"Morals?" Lucas hugged his arms across his chest and shivered like the hot water had run out while he was in the shower. "Morals are one thing. Kicking a hot chick out of your room is *insane*."

"I didn't tell anyone about Piper," Felix said solemnly. "I swear."

Lucas pointed a finger at Caitlin. "It was you!"

"She posted it on Facebook, you idiot." Caitlin shook her head as she continued typing on her laptop.

"Oh. Really?" Lucas snorted and laughed. "Damn Facebook. She told me she broke up with Asher last year."

"I told you not to trust her," Caitlin said with a little huff of exasperation.

Lucas shrugged, smiling. "Ah, well. Live and learn."

"You're really taking this to heart, aren't you?" Allison said, her voice thick with sarcasm.

Lucas stared at Allison, his smile fading. "So that's how you wanna play, huh? Okay. Kid gloves are off. I was actually considering keeping this to myself, but not anymore. I have a source who tells me you hooked up with the governor—Grayson Bentley himself."

"*What?*" Felix said. "Grayson?"

Allison picked at the polish on her fingernails, frowning. She was trying to keep her face blank, but she looked like she'd been caught downloading Michael Bolton. "It was just dinner," she admitted, not looking up. "It wasn't a big deal."

"Why would you—?" Felix began.

"Why would I what?" Allison's eyes flashed at Felix. "Go on a date?"

"No," Felix said. "Why would you go on a date with that asshole?"

"*Ohhhhh?*" Allison said, drawing the word out. "And what about Emma? She didn't have any issues? How many years did you waste with that selfish bitch?"

Felix was stunned into silence.

Caitlin squirmed and stood up for a moment to slide a leg between her butt and the seat of her chair. Lucas went back to twirling his pen. Harper leaned back and crossed her legs, observing the exchange.

"Look," Allison said wearily. "For what it's worth—and not that I owe you an explanation—but I agree with you: Grayson's an asshole. And that's it. I'm not talking about it anymore."

"Wait a minute!" Felix said. "Did he do something?"

"No," Allison said calmly. "Simmer down. I can take care of myself. He didn't do anything. I just went out to dinner with him. One time. That was enough. And this was like a month ago, anyway. Okay? So that's it."

"But—"

"You almost hooked up with someone in the ERA," Allison reminded him. "You should be worrying about yourself. They talk like it's a political movement, but I think it's a cult."

"You think so?" Caitlin peered over the screen of her laptop, then clicked it shut. "I agree with their basic platform. I think the government has forgotten it represents the people—*all the people*—and not just the one percenters. And I love how they're so focused on the future. What's their motto?"

"A hundred generations," Allison said.

"That's it!" Caitlin said. "I think it's great they're actually concerned about where we'll be as a society in a hundred generations. The Democrats and Republicans are just focused on getting votes today. They don't care if the air's breathable in a hundred generations. Or about our drinking water, or the fact that we're poisoning ourselves with GMOs, pesticides and chemicals, or that we're over-fishing the oceans. The only fish left glow in the dark because their mercury content's so high. The Democrats and Republicans don't even know what the word *sustainability* means. If we leave it to them, the entire country will be one big toxic no-man's-land. It's about time an organization like the ERA came along."

"I agree with all that," Allison said. "Don't get me wrong. But it still seems like a cult. They're so secretive about everything. And why do they make everyone get the same weird tiger tattoo?"

"Yeah." Caitlin's mouth twitched downward at the corners. "I'm not sure. I wish they wouldn't. I mean, if they didn't, I might even consider joining." She looked slightly dismayed.

Silence followed.

"Anyway," Allison said, breaking a lengthy lull in the conversation. "Back to my fairy tale porn—did you guys hear they're making *Mesmerizer Jolie* into a movie? They're saying Dirk Rathman's going to be Phillip. I saw it on TMZ."

"I know," Caitlin said, her voice shrill with excitement. "He's perfect for that role. I can just picture him as Phillip. I can't wait for it to come out."

"Dirk Rathman is *soooo* goddamn hot," Harper said. Felix felt her eyes on him even before her unusually throaty tone got his attention. She was staring directly at him, her eyes half-closed, dreamy and full of desire. "That man can murder my vagina anytime."

Lucas laughed, burying his face into his folded arms. "That's a classic." He looked up, his face red, and blotted the tears with the heel of his hand. *"Murder my vagina.* I love that one."

Felix stared back bleakly at Harper, but broke off the contest first. He couldn't figure her out. What was the point of that? Was she mad about Amber? Nothing even happened. Only yesterday she was telling him that his eyes were *ridiculously sexy*. And today she wanted Dirk Rathman to murder her vagina. He smothered a heavy sigh by biting down hard on his lower lip—a little too hard. He tasted blood.

The room went silent again. They looked from one to the other, wondering who was going to toss the next grenade.

"Anybody else have something to add?" Caitlin asked, resting her chin on her folded hands, looking around the table. "Any more announcements? Hook ups? Cults? Fairy tale porn? Politics? Anything else?" She paused. "No? Great. Beause I'd like to get a few hours in before dinner." She flipped open her computer and looked down at the screen.

They went back to their textbooks and notes, typed away at their laptops, and Allison resumed her reading of *Mesmerizer Jolie*. The tension faded. But Felix couldn't focus; he couldn't stop thinking about his conversation with Bill.

He sat back in his chair and yawned, gazing at the room.

The first time Lucas had brought them here, all but one of the bulbs was out, and they hadn't been able to see the paintings. But after the game against Watsforde yesterday, he and Lucas had spent two solid hours cleaning, dusting and straightening things out. They'd also changed out the light bulbs—all sixteen of the floor and table lamps in the room (he'd counted them in an OCD moment). And like so many things at PC, Felix found the paintings fascinating—and bizarre.

All were sumptuously framed and all were of President Woodrow striking various poses. There were twenty-nine in all—Felix had also counted the paintings. Several were official-looking portraits he must have sat for when he was serving as president of the school. In one scene, decked out in sportsman's gear complete with hip waders and a hat festooned with fishing flies, he was casting a line into a picturesque river. In another, he was sitting in a tufted wingback chair, smoking an elaborately carved pipe. One huge canvas depicted him reading a book to a group of attentive children in a classroom setting. And in three different paintings, he sat in a lush English garden, appearing relaxed and staring off thoughtfully into the distance as if the future were his to see.

Chapter 25

A BRAVE NEW WORLD

"Three, two, one."

A heavy, immeasurable silence passed.

Gabriela Conseco didn't shudder. She didn't cower. She stared at the face of the man holding the gun at her. That's why he didn't pull the trigger. He didn't like that she wasn't afraid. He didn't like that her unflinching eyes were on his, a defiant smile playing at the edges of her mouth.

"Couldn't do it, could you?" Gabriela said as the man—the Faceman—lowered the muzzle. She had no memory of how she got here, though it wasn't hard to put the pieces together: Cross country practice had just ended and she was standing by her car in the school parking lot fishing for her keys in her backpack. Then she woke up in the desert, lying in the dirt, the Faceman gazing down at her.

A look of amusement flickered over his face, then his thick brows came together over cold dark eyes. "You didn't try. And if you don't try, you're going to fail. And if you fail, I'll have to kill you. And well… I've hit a bit of a losing streak lately, and I'd like to know what you are before I get down to the dirty work. And I absolutely love your name—*Gabriela*. It rolls right off the tongue, doesn't it? I bet all the boys like whispering it in your ear. Would you like me to whisper it in your ear?"

"I'd prefer that you didn't," she said, her eyes filled with revulsion.

"I'm only teasing. That's not my… thing." The Faceman turned to the west where the sun was sitting low on the horizon. He stayed like that for a moment, watching, then he started pacing, the sand beneath his boots crackling under his prodigious weight. "I love the sunsets here," he said, a touch of wistfulness in his voice. "Everyone says Arizona's too hot, but this"—he stopped and lifted a hand toward the mosaic of pinks, purples and reds wreathing the sky—"makes it worth it. And you all have air conditioning and pools so I don't know what you're complaining about anyway. It's lovely, don't you think?"

"Yes." She stared up at him, trying to hold his gaze, but his eyes kept flicking away. The abomination was afraid of her. He could break her in half with his bare hands. But Gabriela could see the darkness inside him—and he could sense it. His demon's face, his monstrous size—everything about him—was revolting, but that was only a reflection of his beastliness. He had no soul. No heart. He was The Beast.

"I don't think I would ever get tired of saying your name," he told her, still staring off at the horizon. "So I'll go through this again, Gabriela. One last time. Because I like you. And I really like your name. I'm normally not inclined to grant second chances. But I very much want you to pass the test. It would be a crying shame if I have to put a bullet into that pretty face of yours." He paused. "But I promise you, this is your final opportunity. Move that rock"—he waved the barrel at a smooth round stone about the size of a tennis ball—"or you die. You get just five seconds. This is crunch time, Gabriela. This is an opportunity to show your mettle. If you pass the test— *hallelujah*—you get to serve a higher power. Are you clear on the ground rules?"

She'd known from the moment of regaining consciousness (feeling cold and numb, her head pounding with pain with each beat of her heart) that she couldn't talk him out of this, so she didn't try. To Gabriela, the devil was more than just a philosophical or theological concept, more than just a word used to describe humanity's wretchedness, what her pastor called the '*Urges*'. The devil was the personification of the Urges—its physical manifestation—and it was standing before her now in the tangible form of the Faceman. But she saw him for who he really was.

"You're the devil," she said plainly, her eyes steady, unafraid. "Your rules mean nothing to me." She glanced down at the rock. He'd been demanding that she "move it with her mind" ever since she awoke. Ridiculous. Only He could do that.

"The devil?" He turned to her, his twisted lips rolling back over his gums in a hideous smile, revealing teeth sharpened like spear tips. The smile quickly fell from his face. "You're smarter than that, Gabriela. I've seen your transcript. I know where you're going to college next year. You've got an Ivy League brain. Put it to use. You must realize the devil is just another name for human nature. We're all the devil. Me. You. Everyone. I just have a little more devil in me than most." He lifted his chin and laughed loudly.

"I'm not afraid of you," she said to him, not seeing the humor. "He has a plan for all of us. I live to serve Him."

"Oh my." The Faceman put a hand to his mouth as if he was

dismayed. "You're one of *those*, aren't you? Now it makes sense. That accounts for your stoic resolve. Your fearlessness. You think this is all just a step along your journey to a better place, don't you? Well, I'll tell you a secret—*this is it*. There's no better place. When you die you don't go to some Shangri-la in the sky to be rejoined with family and friends and dearly loved pets and plants that died because you forgot to water them. The truth, Gabriela, is that when you die—*you die*. It's all over. It's what your life was before you were created in your momma's womb. Does that scare you?"

"You can't tempt me, serpent." In the declining light, Gabriela was suddenly aware that the desert was all around her. She felt its presence. The warm air was heavy with the sweet earthy scent of wet sage and creosote. She breathed it in, letting it infuse her, feeling its beauty and its strength. She smiled. It was somehow fitting that the Faceman would bring her here. To the desert. To the wasteland. A snake testing her faith. It was meant to be.

"Tempt you? I only want you to succeed. *To live.* Don't make a martyr of yourself, Gabriela. There's nothing more than this." He lifted a foot off the ground and stomped it down in a cloud of dust. "There is no other side. No heaven. No hell. Nothing. Trust me. I know."

"You lie with your forked tongue," she told him. "God has a plan for all of us. *He* is in control—not you."

"Is that right?" The Faceman's lips pulled back from his gold teeth. "You think this is God's plan? God wants me to shoot you in the face? God wants you to die out here? You think all this"—he raised his eyes to the pale outline of a quarter moon—"is part of God's grand scheme? If there's a God then he's an evil sonafabitch, don't you think? You said he's in control—in control of everything, correct? Like the plague. Birth defects. Famine. Cancer. Drought. The Holocaust. If God's in control then all those things have to go on *his* résumé. So you may want to reconsider devoting your short precious life to a god who thinks diseases that kill millions and genocide are part of a *plan*." A brief grimace slipped across his face. "Do you really want to die? For him? For nothing?"

"The Lord works in mysterious ways," she said. "We don't get to choose how we're born or how we die. That is in His hands."

"Oh, Gabriela." The Faceman gave her a discouraged shake of his head. "I like you. I do. But you're so misguided. You can choose not to die. Just move the rock."

"I can't," she said firmly. "Only the Lord can perform miracles."

"No, Gabriela." The Faceman frowned down at her. "Your lord's *miracles* are nothing but cheap parlor tricks compared to what I've witnessed.

You're too easily impressed. Burning bushes. Water to wine. Walking on water. Amateur hour, Gabriela. *Amateur hour.* I'm only asking you to move a rock. It can be done. I've seen it. Many times."

"You're the devil."

The Faceman lowered his eyes for a moment and blew out a frustrated sigh through his teeth. "It seems we're at an impasse. You're not the first, you know. I've had to kill others because of their faith in this silly God superstition. But I can see you're a true believer. Nothing I say will convince you that you've been brainwashed by the powers that be to keep you docile and compliant. One day soon that will all come to an end. And the funny thing is, Gabriela, you could've been a big part of it." He sighed and made a clucking noise with his tongue. "Are we ready to begin the test then? Are you prepared for your God's will to be done?"

She nodded. She was calm, content. Her nerves and her heart were steady. She'd always believed that one day God would test her. If this was His plan for her, His test, then she would face it courageously with her faith intact. She didn't shrink away from The Beast; she stood up straight, swept her long dark hair off her shoulders and took a step toward him. The disappointment on his face made her feel stronger, more sure of herself, more sure that He was standing beside her in this, her moment of trial. "I'm ready," she declared.

He raised the gun, one side of his mouth twitching downward. "Move the rock, Gabriela. *Five.*"

"I will not cry," she said evenly.

"*Four.* Come on, Gabriela."

"I will not beg."

"*Three.*"

"Though I walk through the valley of the shadow of death…" Her eyes were clear, her voice strong, and growing louder and more confident with each word.

"*Two.* Scripture's not going to help you, Gabriela. God isn't here. He doesn't exist. If he did, wouldn't he intervene? Wouldn't he protect you? Now move the rock!"

"I will fear no evil." She looked up at him. Their eyes locked. Hers didn't waver.

"*One.* You're disappointing me, Gabriela."

"For thou art with me. Thy rod and thy staff, they comfort me. Thou—"

"*Zero.*" He pulled the trigger.

* * *

The bullet exploded out of the barrel of the .44 and tore through Gabriela's forehead. She thudded to the ground in a mist of blood. The blast echoed across the flatlands like a rolling thunderclap. The Faceman stepped over to her and stared down at her face for a long while, committing it to memory, memorializing it forever in his mind—taking his mental picture. When he was done, he leveled the gun at her face and pulled the trigger five times.

"Stupid, stupid girl," he muttered, shaking his head. "You just died for nothing. For less than nothing." He looked up at the darkening sky as he took a cell phone from his pocket and called a number.

"Yes," the voice on the other end answered.

"Another Wisp," the Faceman said. "What's next?"

"Portland, Oregon," the voice replied. "Lucas Mayer. Goes by a nickname: Minnesota. Student at Portland College. Freshman."

"I'll be there tomorrow."

PART II

"THE RABBIT HOLE"

Chapter 26

MIDTERMS

Felix collapsed on his bed and buried his face in the pillow, pulling both ends over his ears, squeezing his eyes so tightly shut that they hurt. He wanted to erase the world—sound, light, people, everything. He wanted all of it to just go away.

Tiberius 14-37, Caligula 37-41, Claudius 41-54, Nero 54-68... Tiberius 14-37, Caligula 37-41, Claudius 41-54, Nero 54-68—the names and reigns of the early Roman emperors had wedged themselves in his beleaguered mind, cycling over and over like the lyrics of an awful, yet catchy, Ke$Ha song. Felix had just finished his last midterm. His brain hadn't caught on yet. Hence... *Tiberius 14-37, Caligula 37-41, Claudius 41-54, Nero 54-68...*

In the weeks leading up to the exams, he woke up most nights with random facts pounding away like a pulverizing wrecking ball inside his skull. The reigns of the Roman emperors were a favorite of his subconscious. His performance on the midterms was somewhat mixed: Western Civ and Biology went fairly well, Economics not so well, and he hadn't been able to finish the final two questions of his Psychology exam because he'd run out of time.

Midterms were officially behind him now, but there was no overwhelming sense of relief, no weight of the world ascending from his shoulders, no stress melting away like a scoop of lard in a frying pan. Relief was a reward served to those who actually did well on the exams. He didn't qualify for any such honors.

Tiberius 14-37, Caligula 37-41, Claudius 41-54, Nero 54-68... Tiberius 14-37, Caligula 37-41, Claudius 41-54, Nero 54-68...

"Shut the hell up!" Felix screamed into his pillow. He was losing it. His capacity to handle problems (or speed bumps, or hiccups, or anything, really) was stretched invisibly thin, and there was more on his mind than just crashing-and-burning on his midterms. A text he'd receieved from Bill the groundskeeper had twisted his already careening emotional equilibrium another few degrees off kilter. The very instant he'd finished his last exam his phone buzzed in his pocket: *"Felix – It is here. My office. Stamford. 6:30. Bill."*

'It' was here. Whatever *it* meant. His bizarre encounter with the groundskeeper had gradually faded into the background as midterm preparations consumed his time and attention. Bill was full of shit. Felix was certain of that. But, he'd decided, what was the harm in swinging by his office? It would just take a few minutes. If he had nothing from his mom, as Felix expected, he would turn around and come back to the dorm. Easy enough.

But now nothing felt easy; he didn't want to go anywhere. Lying in bed and doing nothing seemed like a very worthwhile objective, an objective he could actually achieve. He needed some sleep. If he could just plunge into a dreamless sleep, he could forget about the satanic tests that had kicked his tired ass all over campus. His brain needed a brief respite from the cluttered mountain of facts, dates, theories, calculations and countless other bits of useless data he couldn't possibly retain in the storage house between his ears for much longer anyway. He was exhausted. And to make things worse, he had a game tomorrow, the biggest game for the Sturgeons in twenty-something years. If they won they would play for the Rain Cup. Hooray! But he was too mentally and physically demolished to even think about a game. He would block it out and deal with it tomorrow. After he got some sleep.

Tiberius 14-37, Caligula 37-41, Claudius 41-54, Nero 54-68... Tiberius 14-37, Caligula 37-41, Claudius 41-54, Nero 54-68...

"Get a grip, Felix!" He dragged himself out of bed and checked his watch. It was already 6:25. Not enough time to eat in the cafeteria. He would have to grab something on his way out. This sucked. He was not in the mood for this. The biggest waste of time ever. Of all the pointless things he'd ever done, this topped them all.

Tiberius 14-37, Caligula 37-41, Claudius...

Chapter 27

THE JOURNAL

In the deepening twilight, Felix gnawed on a protein bar (sweet clumps of sawdust), as he made his way along the footpaths to the Stamford Building. Fallen leaves skittered and rattled across the paths, tumbling over his feet. When he arrived at the front steps he noticed that ash-colored clouds were beginning to drift in from the west. He took one last breath of cool pungent air and slipped inside.

Bill's name wasn't listed in the lobby directory so Felix had to go from office to office checking the nameplates on the doors. After a fair amount of searching he finally found Bill's office on the third floor. Felix stood there for a while, wondering what he was doing and already regretting his decision to come here. A door opened and closed on another floor. Voices, low and serious, floated up from the stairwell. He blew out an anxious sigh and rapped softly on solid wood, hoping Bill wasn't in.

"Hello!" a voice called out immediately from the other side, crushing Felix's hopes. "It's unlocked."

Felix turned the knob and eased the door open. Then he leaned his head in, still holding on to the knob, keeping one foot out in the hall. He found Bill standing behind a desk made out of some kind of dark wood. It was big and sturdy-looking, impressive, presidential even. But it wasn't the desk that caught Felix's eye; it was the books. They were everywhere: The wall facing the door was stuffed with them and they were piled and stacked on the floor wherever they would fit.

"Let me guess," Bill said with a wry smile. "You're thinking I hijacked the office of one of your professors." No groundskeeper uniform this time; he was wearing tan slacks and a dark blue button-down shirt with the sleeves rolled halfway to his elbows. He'd also shaved. He looked like he was about to head off to a business meeting. Or maybe a date.

"Yeah," Felix admitted, wondering why the assistant groundskeeper would have so many books in his office. Then something occurred to him:

why would the assistant groundskeeper even have an office? Felix wasn't sure what he'd expected, but it wasn't this. "What's with the books?"

"Come in. Please."

Felix hesitated for a moment, then decided there was no point in delaying the inevitable. He couldn't turn back now without appearing rude. So he left the door open a crack and stepped in, glancing over at two armchairs in front of the desk, thinking (for some reason) he would sit in one of those chairs and that Bill would stay at the desk.

"I guess you could say I'm an avid reader." Bill came around the desk and stepped past Felix to close the door. While Felix was trying to sort out what was going on, Bill locked the door with the deadbolt, then he went over to the room's only window—beneath it stood a small antique-looking table with a pair of matching chairs—and shut the blinds.

"Well, come on." Bill took a seat at the table. He wasn't looking at Felix. He was looking at something on the table—a book. "I suppose we should do this here. *This* will be the place." His tone was subdued. It reminded Felix of the way people talk in church.

"Do what?" Felix asked.

Bill made a windmilling motion with his hand. "This is what you came for."

A book? Felix thought. Why would his mom have given this guy a book? The only books he remembered her reading were Nicholas Sparks paperbacks and the occasional cookbook. Something didn't feel right about any of this, but despite what his gut was telling him, he approached the table, tentatively.

"Have a seat," Bill said, still staring down at the book. The cover was closed. It was fraying at the edges. It looked old and fragile, like it might disintegrate if the ceiling fan came on.

Felix stopped beside the table.

"Please." Bill nodded at the empty chair. He had a look in his eyes that made Felix feel uneasy. They looked vague, distracted. Void of… something. Felix glanced back at the door to make sure he had a clear path and that a simple turn of the lock would open it—just in case. As he sat down lightly on the very edge of the seat, he rocked the chair out from under the table and angled it so that if he needed to get out quickly he wouldn't bang his legs on anything. Bill seemed oblivious to what he was doing, his eyes unblinking.

"I've been waiting a long time to show you this," Bill said, his eyes returning to Felix. He tapped the book lightly with his forefinger. Twice.

Thump thump. "And I've thought of a hundred different ways to do it. None of them are… ideal. I want you to know that I understand what this will do to you when you read it. How it'll change your life. I wish there was another way—an easier way—but there isn't."

"What are you talking about?" Felix asked, confused. When Bill didn't respond, he pointed at the book. *"This?"*

"Life makes a mockery of our best laid plans, doesn't it? The leaves appear on the trees one day and then change colors and fall off the next. Season after season. Year after year. Over and over and over and over. Before you know it, seventeen years have gone by. When I read this, I was twenty-one. Now here I am. And here you are."

"I don't know what—"

"It's a journal." Bill's eyes moved to the book. "Your aunt's journal. It was given to me by your mother. It was her dying wish that I show it to you."

Felix sat in silence for a moment. Then he said in the most sarcastic voice he could muster: "My *mom* gave you my *aunt's* journal? I got news for you: I don't even have an aunt. My parents were only children."

Bill continued as if he hadn't heard Felix. "Your mom also wanted you to know her name: Elissa. Her name was Elissa."

"Elissa? Who are you talking about?" He wasn't sure if he should attempt to make sense of this or just leave. He threw a glance at the door again. Still a clear path. Same simple deadbolt. "My mom's name is Patricia. I think you got the wrong guy."

Bill shook his head. "There's no easy way to say it. And you have to know this before you read it." He paused. "You were adopted. Your mother's name—your biological mother—was Elissa."

"Okay. Bill… um… no offense or anything, but I'm gonna go now." This guy was clearly crazy. Felix wanted to groan, or yell, or scream— something to demonstrate how stupendously stupid he felt for coming here instead of staying in bed and taking a sixteen-hour nap. "I wasn't adopted. You don't know the first thing about me. And you sure as hell didn't know my mother." He was about to stand up.

"I don't know you?" Bill laughed harshly. "I know everything about you. I know how many miles you have on your Wrangler. I know your forty time from the football camp you attended before your senior year. I know your high school GPA. I know that your parents died in a fire on your eighteenth birthday. But I didn't ask you to come here to tell you things you already know about yourself."

Felix's mouth didn't seem to be working, but his brain was. *Stalker!* he thought, alarmed. *This guy's a stalker. But why... why's he stalking me?* "So you have access to the Internet," he said once he got his tongue to cooperate. "You can get all that from Facebook and a Google search."

"I also know you had your first beer when you were fourteen. When you were two, every time you entered a room, the bulbs burned out. I'm sure you weren't aware of that. And when you were eight, a thirteen-year-old named Nathan used to bully you on your way home from school. Until one day you got really angry and Nathan's appendix and gall bladder both ruptured. And you didn't lay a hand on him."

A little noise slipped out of Felix's mouth, something between a yelp and a gasp. He'd never told anyone about Nathan. Not even his parents. "I think you should just stay away from me, okay?" His voice sounded high and thin. "If I see you again, I'm telling the dean. I'm pretty sure you'll lose your job."

"My job?" Bill snorted. "I have a thing or two going on besides my gardening activities."

Felix looked around the office hesitantly, trying to make sense of how Bill could possibly know about Nathan, but the books and maps didn't provide any answers. It seemed impossible, but Bill had gotten it right. The thing—or *incident* or whatever you wanted to call it—had actually happened. But it was so long ago he'd almost forgotten about it. Besides—it wasn't even his fault that Nathan got hurt. You can't hurt someone by just *wanting* to hurt them. That's what he'd told himself then, and that's what he told himself now whenever he thought about it.

"I understand why you're skeptical." Bill sat back in his chair and folded his arms. "Why would the assistant groundskeeper know you were adopted? Sounds crazy, right? I completely get it—believe me. That's why I need you to read the journal." He flicked a finger toward it. "Once you read it, you'll know I'm telling the truth."

The smart course of action seemed obvious to Felix: he should get the hell out of here. But something about Bill was tweaking his curiosity. The guy was a groundskeeper, but he didn't talk—or act—like someone who dug ditches for a living. And how did Bill know so much about him? And what was he saying about light bulbs burning out?

"Alright," Felix said, ignoring his sensible side. "I'll play along. How'd you meet my mom. My *biological* mom. What's her name again?"

"Elissa. It's not important how we met." Bill's voice was stiff, sharper than before. "Just read the journal. Please."

"I'd really like to know," Felix persisted. "Where'd you meet her?"

"That's not important," Bill said firmly, his expression hard.

"I'd still like to know," Felix responded with equal firmness.

"This is counterproductive," Bill muttered, staring at Felix, but when Felix's gaze didn't wither, he lowered his eyes and sighed. "Fine. When I was in college and just a few years older than you are now, I became disillusioned with school and seriously considered dropping out. A professor of mine talked me into taking an internship at a place called Green River. It's an institution just outside Seattle. An institution for... it's a mental institution. Your mother was a patient there."

"And that's where you met my mom?" Felix exclaimed incredulously. "My mom the mental patient? Is she still in the loony bin?"

Bill dropped his chin and stared down at his lap. "No. She um... she died... just a few... just a few days after we met. You were just a baby at the time." His voice was thick and hitching. He looked up at Felix. "I'm sorry. I really am. I wish that she..." He shook his head and closed his eyes for a moment, then looked away.

A sudden wave of confusion swept over Felix. Was it possible, he asked himself, that Bill wasn't crazy? *Was any of this possible?* There were pictures all over his house and photo albums down in the basement, but he couldn't recall if he'd ever seen a picture of his mom pregnant. He didn't think so, but what did that prove?

"She gave this to me before she passed away." Bill nodded at the journal. "I promised her I'd give it to you. Just read it. Please. It'll all make sense."

Felix reached out for it. Then he hesitated, his hand hovering over the journal like it was a chess board, and he, an indecisive player dithering over his next move. *Bill was screwing with him*, he told himself. He had to be. He *was* crazy. Why else would he be trying to convince him that he was adopted? If he opened the cover, he'd be playing into his sick twisted game. All at once, he was furious—and deeply insulted—that this guy thought he could manipulate him so easily.

Felix snatched his hand away and jumped up from his chair.

"Dammit!" Bill shouted.

Felix was about to tell the groundskeeper to go screw himself when he realized there was a bat in his face. Not a little wooden souvenir bat, but a long heavy-barreled aluminum number with bright black and yellow letters spelling out EASTON. The kind of bat that can crush a skull like an empty beer can.

"What the?" Felix said in disbelief.

"You're not going anywhere," Bill said evenly. He'd gotten to his feet. The guy was quick. Ninja quick. "If you try, you'll be leaving with a rather serious limp."

Felix was frozen with shock. He knew that he should be doing something—threatening to call the police maybe? But his lips were as petrified as the rest of him. He just mumbled, "What the?" again.

Bill's face was a mask. "I've sacrificed everything for this moment. *Everything.* You're going to read the journal. And that's the end of it. I don't want to hurt you." He paused. "But I will if I have to."

"You can't be serious!"

"Don't try me. And in case you're thinking about using your cell"—he tilted his chin to indicate the outline of a phone in Felix's front pocket—"I'll break your goddamn fingers. Now sit your ass down and do as I say." Then he paused again and bellowed: "Sit!"

Felix stayed put, afraid to move. Bill was big, agile, and he looked strong. He was also clearly out of his mind. Felix glanced over at the door and wondered if he could make it. Not a chance. Not before Bill got in a couple of swings anyway. And the window was useless: too small to squeeze through without a lot of body contorting (which would take time), and even if he could manage that, an awkward fall from the third floor would probably shatter most of the bones in his body.

Bill's expression told him that he knew what he was thinking. And so did his actions: He drew the bat back like he was about to swing for the fences.

Felix slumped into his chair, resigned.

Bill remained standing, gripping the bat in his hands like he knew how to handle it. He exhaled slowly, staring down at Felix. "Look—I didn't want to do that. I really didn't. But you gave me no choice. There's too much at stake. You simply don't have the option of not hearing me out, okay?"

"So spit it out!" Felix snapped through his teeth.

"All you have to do is read the journal. That's it. After that, you're free to go. I promise I won't try to stop you."

"Fine." Felix eyed him warily. He had no reason to trust him, but as long as he had the bat, what choice did he have? "Give it to me."

Using his middle finger, Bill slid the journal across the table until it rested in front of Felix.

"You're seriously crazy, you know. A baseball bat? Really? You won't get away with this." Felix had already decided that as soon as he got out of here, he would go straight to campus security. They could deal with this crazy asshole.

"Just turn the cover, Felix. Please. Please."

Felix glanced up at him. The guy was *pleading* with him. He sounded desperate, like he was begging for his life. Why did he want him to read it so badly? And again, Felix thought about his mom, wracking his brain to remember if he'd ever seen a photo of her pregnant.

"As a show of good faith, I'll leave the bat here." Bill placed it on the floor, barrel down, propped up against his chair. "I'm going to make myself a cup of tea. When you're done, we'll talk. Deal?" And then he walked away, crossing the office to his desk.

Felix was all alone at the table.

Now he was really confused. Bill was preoccupied; he was actually pouring himself a cup of tea at his desk. And the bat was his for the taking if he wanted it. He could easily get to it before Bill. It was right in front of him. But he didn't even need it. He could make it to the door before Bill finished filling his cup. He would be out of the building and long gone. There was no way he could catch him. Bill was practically inviting him to take off. Then he looked down at the journal, and all thoughts of escape instantly melted away. It exerted a strange power over him, compelling him to stay. Something inside him wanted to know—*had to know*—what was in it. He didn't know why, but he couldn't just walk away from this. He opened the cover, throwing a quick glance at Bill. Then he placed his forearms on either side of the tattered little book and looked down.

His eyes moved over the lines and swoops and curves, and then the words they formed began to fill his mind. His vision misted and blurred and the world shuddered, rippling suddenly out of focus. There was no Portland College, no Stamford Building. No table. No chair. No crazy man with a bat. Just Felix and the words on the page. But the words were more than just collections of letters sequenced to reflect the thoughts of their owner; they were living things that breathed their meaning inside him, tearing through him like a storm, creating a new reality from the vestiges of the old one. The rhythmic beat of a heart pounded violently in his ears—*th-thump th-thump th-thump*—and as he wondered dully if it was his or the journal's, his consciousness ebbed steadily away until all sense of self was lost and only the words remained.

Elissa, time is short. I have only minutes before Lyndsey comes for this. She will find you. Six months before your 28th birthday, you will immaculately conceive a child—a boy. Do not be scared. You must protect your son at all costs. I love you. You will soon understand why I sent you away.

I will start from the beginning. The Ancients discovered it. Some say the Egyptians were the first, others the Mesopotamians, and still others say it was the peoples who dwelled in the jungles west of the Great River. The knowledge of its discovery has been lost to time. But it was the Druids who adopted it as their God and worshipped it, unlocking its secrets. It was they who named it the SOURCE, the wellspring from which all life flows, the energy that if darkened will extinguish the sun and all life with it. The Druids ritualized the training of those rare individuals born with the gift to draw energy from it to manipulate what most consider the natural order of things. They called them 'Sourcerors' and they were honored above all others. It was the mightiest among them, a man named Myrddin, whose prophecy forever changed the world.

Myrddin's prophecy, known as THE WARNING, is a vision of the future that has been passed down through the ages: It tells us that we have a symbiotic relationship with the Source. It is not just an unalterable wellspring of energy—the Source is like a mirror that absorbs and reflects the state of humankind, constantly changing as we change. In the beginning, the Source was perfect and we were not the base creatures we are today, practically immortal, living without disease or hardship. But with each act of human cruelty, each act of human evil, we damaged ourselves, and in turn, we damaged the Source. It is a cycle that is vicious like no other: as the Source diminishes and darkens, so does human nature, heralding a final tipping point—the SUFFERING TIMES. On that day of judgment, if the Source is not healed, it will die, and none shall be left to witness its passing.

Yet the Source cannot be healed unless we heal ourselves. Our relationship with the source is one of mutual dependency, and as such, the Source can only be repaired through our actions—humankind must first be healed. To restore itself, the Source will deliver the two fated ones. The first will be the DRESTIAN. If he prevails, nations will burn, armies will fall at his feet, and all who refuse to succumb to his rule will be slaughtered like sheep. The Drestian will restore the Source, but at a steep cost: our freedoms will be stripped from us and we shall become his slaves. The second will be a boy born to a woman undefiled—the

BELUS—and only he can defeat the Drestian. If the Belus prevails, then we must restore the Source through our own deeds for the Belus cannot restore the Source on his own. We shall be free. Free to repair what we have damaged and free to destroy what was once perfect. Our fate, and the fate of the world, will be in our own hands.

Centuries passed. The Emperor Constantine learned of The Warning and prepared for the arrival of the fated ones. He sought out all Sourcerors and created a secret society—the Order of Belus, which he organized into five Fortresses, each led by a master Sourceror, its purpose to find the Belus.

But it is not in man's nature to endure consensus for long. A faction within the Order soon emerged that did not share the belief that the Belus was the path to humanity's salvation. This rival group of Sourcerors, calling themselves DRESTIANTES, believed that non-Sourcerors—'WISPS'—were responsible for damaging the Source, and therefore deserving of the punishment and enslavement foretold by The Warning. While the Wisps will be reduced to slavery by the Drestian, the Drestianites believe they will be rewarded for their loyalty and will rule the world alongside him.

Even before the Order split into opposing factions, they were harassed at every turn by the PROTECTORS, a society of assassins who viewed themselves as the guardians of the Source. The Protector's philosophy is simple: Sourcerors damaged the Source by going beyond their intended boundaries to use it for their own selfish needs; if they are allowed to live, they will eventually destroy it, causing all life to come to an end. The only way to guarantee the survival of the Source, therefore, is to kill every last Sourceror, regardless of whether they owe their allegiance to the Belus or the Drestian. From the time of Constantine, the Protectors have kept records of the Sourceror bloodlines and have tirelessly tracked down and killed anyone with a drop of Sourceror blood.

For a thousand years, there was a kind of uneasy balance. The Order searched for the Belus, the Drestianites awaited the Drestian, and both waged war against the Protectors, and sometimes, each other. Then in the year 1250, a Sourceror named Isabella became the master of the First Fortress and everything changed. The leader of the Drestianites convinced her to relinquish her loyalty—to join the Drestianites—and they made a pact: He would abdicate his title to her, and in return, she would sacrifice the entire Order. The pact would forever be known as Isabella's Deceit.

Isabella called a gathering of the five Fortresses to a forest in northern France. It was there that the Drestianites sprung their trap. But before they could finish their ambush, they themselves were ambushed. The Protectors had learned of the gathering and had allied themselves with King Louis IX, who desired the vast treasures the Order was rumored to possess in its Fortresses. The King's archers let loose their arrows, raining down death upon the unsuspecting Sourcerors, the Order and the Drestianites alike. When the last arrow fell, men on horses clad in armor and foot soldiers with long spears and tall shields attacked from all sides.

Nearly every Sourceror was killed in the initial onslaught, yet those who survived unleashed their wrath upon King Louis' army in a manner that will never be forgotten. During the battle, the earth heaved, the heavens thundered, and the forest was leveled. When it was over, the number of dead could not easily be counted. The King's army had been wiped clean from the land. Thousands of Protectors lay dead. And of the Drestianites and the Order of Belus, all but a few left their lives on the field of battle—including

Isabella. It is said that so many lives were lost that day the land itself perished. The rivers ran red and the skies cried tears of blood for a hundred years.

King Louis ransacked the Fortresses and burned the Order's strongholds to the ground. The Order was scattered across Europe, too weak and too disorganized to recruit new Sourcerors. The Protectors intensified their offensive, and like bloodhounds, the assassins tracked down the Sourcerors and murdered them. The fight was over. The Protectors had won. There was only one thing left to do. In order to survive, the last of the Sourcerors went into hiding.

Our family name is Tinshire, Elissa. We were once the most powerful of the Sourceror families. But after Isabella's Deceit, we survived by hiding in the shadows, moving from country to country and from town to town, changing our names, and separating at the first sign that the Protectors had discovered us.

Our numbers dwindled. Many Tinshires did not even know the name Tinshire. But that did not stop the Protectors from killing our young in their cribs. They knew who we were even when we were blind to our own identities. The Tinshires were on the verge of extinction. And then a very strange thing occurred. There were two Tinshire sisters one year apart in age.

The older sister became pregnant and had a girl. Then the younger sister became pregnant with a girl—but she was a virgin. She became pregnant when she was exactly the same age as when her sister had become pregnant. The Tinshires call this phenomenon the CYCLE. The Cycle repeats itself whenever there are two sisters and the older of the two becomes pregnant. We believe the Cycle is the Source's way of preserving the Tinshire bloodline.

Before you could even walk, our father was killed in an accident. When a Tinshire dies in an 'accident', it means the Protectors have found you. You, me and our mother changed our names and moved from Pinder to Evinlock. Five years later, our mother was killed in a car accident. We had no other family. It was just you and me. I had to protect you. So I did what we Tinshires have done since the time of Isabella's Deceit—I sent you away. For you, it was the west coast of America to live with people I trusted. They were not really our aunt and uncle. As I said, you and I are the last of the Tinshires.

I had to do everything in my power to shield you from the Protectors. I had to cut off all ties. I could not call you or write. I hope you understand now that I had no other choice. Sending you away, and being away from you for all this time, has caused me endless pain. It is like a wound that never heals. But I do not regret my decision.

I moved to London. One day, a man approached me and asked if I was 'Eve Tinshire'. I thought he was a Protector. Then I realized who it was. He told me his name was Dietrich Ashfield. The introduction was not necessary. Everyone in England knows of him. He asked me to come to his castle. Curious, I agreed.

He introduced me to his father, Hermann. Then they asked me to 'show them something'. I knew what they meant, but I feigned ignorance. I asked a question of my own. I asked them what they wanted of me. Then they answered. I had showed them 'something' without them even knowing. Our mother called it PERSUASION. The Source touches Sourcerors in different ways.

Hermann and Dietrich had come into the possession of a manuscript (no time to explain how) called Constantine's Manifesto which contains The Warning and a history of the Order. Hermann and Dietrich believed the Suffering Times were upon us and the Drestian's arrival imminent. They were searching for Sourcerors to rebuild the Order. I was the first, and unfortunately, the last—they found no others. From the very day of my arrival, they insisted I stay in the castle where they could protect me. If I had just left, then none of this would have happened.

That is where I live to this day—happily for many years. I will not lie to you: At first, I felt like a princess in her castle. And having sent you to live with strangers in a strange country, I felt terrible that I was so happy. It was so unfair. There were so many times I thought about asking Dietrich to bring you home. But something inside me—a voice I always imagined was our mother's—warned me against it.

Dietrich and I fell in love. It seems strange, that I, a virtual vagabond, would fall in love with the heir to the Ashfield Empire. But it happened. And it was real. Then I became pregnant. Dietrich insisted we marry. He wanted me to know his love was true. Proof was not necessary, but I accepted and became Eve Ashfield.

My pregnancy was utter torment. Dietrich, however, was thrilled. He wanted to be a father. But I knew he and Hermann hoped my child would be another Sourceror—one who might perhaps re-establish the Order. I could not blame them. They thought they had their secrets. But the one keeping secrets was me: They did not know about the Cycle. They did not know about you. And they did not know you were destined to conceive a child in twenty-one years. And if I were to have a son, you would have a son. A son born without a father—the Belus.

What would that mean for my son? I kept asking myself. If your son was destined to be the Belus, then wouldn't my son be the Drestian? But how could the Drestian come from me? From my body? I knew I had choices. I could have ended the pregnancy. But I chose not to. I had the baby. A boy. We named him Lofton.

That seems so long ago—so many years have passed. Now you are 24—you will be pregnant in just 3 years. And in all this time, I have never told the Ashfields about you or the Cycle—and I never will.

From the very beginning it was obvious that Lofton was a powerful Sourceror. At six months, he exploded a jar of pureed peas to express his distaste. As a toddler, whenever he was near mechanical equipment it would turn on and off on its own. At five, he could manipulate his toys to chase his grandfather around the castle. I watched for the signs he might be the Drestian. But there were none—at first. In the years that followed, Lofton was at times good-natured and innocent, the furthest thing from what I imagined the

Drestian would be. And then there were times when I questioned what he was. Out in the courtyard one day, he created fire and unleashed it on a horse, turning the poor animal into ash in seconds.

Lofton has done other cruel things over the years, like with the horse, but I know it gives him no pleasure. But I also know he has no aversion to doing it. He will do anything as long as it serves a purpose.

You should always be wary of the Protectors even though Dietrich and Hermann believe they have disbanded. With the Sourcerors either dead or unaware of what they are, the Protectors' mission has been accomplished. Even so, I worried about Lofton like any mother would. At 13, Lofton began sneaking out of the castle at night. To do what, I cannot say. I admonished him and reminded him of the dangers, but he just smiled and said, "Really, mother. You honestly believe that I have anything to fear from someone who thinks a knife and a garrote are weapons?"

It was about that time I suspected he was the Drestian. He sensed it and began concealing things from me—his abilities. I tried to persuade him to talk to me, but he knew what I was doing. His mind was closed to me. It always has been to an extent. He may be my son, but

"Felix! Felix! Felix!"

The voice sounded like it was calling to him from the other side of the ocean.

"Felix! Come on now. Felix! Wake up. That's it. You're doing fine. Just stay where you are. Here, have some soda. The caffeine will help. Come on now, snap out of it."

Felix found himself staring down at a mottled piece of paper with writing on it. The page was full. The ink was good. A ballpoint. No blots. The last word on it, he noticed, was "but." He realized he was sitting in a chair. There was a table in front of him. He blinked. Everything went dark and then flashed white. The piece of paper, he knew, connected to other pieces of paper and all together, they formed a book—a journal. His aunt's journal. A silver can with looping black and red script intruded on the space between his face and the journal. A Diet Coke can. The can looked small because the hand holding it was big, the fingers long and thick. Felix turned his head to the right and saw a face. He focused on the nose. It looked like a boxer's nose.

"Here," the man said, looking at him anxiously. "Just have a drink. I know this is hard."

Felix made no effort to take the can. He didn't move. The man's name came to him: Bill. The room was out of focus, distorted. His peripheral vision was graying around the edges. The world was bending in strange ways. He felt nauseous. His stomach heaved. He dropped his head between his knees and threw up on the floor. He didn't care. He wiped his mouth. It came away smelling like a protein bar.

"Don't worry about that," Bill said, standing up straight and sliding back a few feet. "That's fine. Just have a drink." He held the can out to Felix. "You'll feel better."

Felix wanted to leave. He just wasn't sure if his legs were working; he couldn't feel them. His stomach churned. His head throbbed. The room was tilting and spinning. It was making him sick. He threw up again. Less volume this time, but the smell was even worse.

Bill watched him as the seconds (minutes? hours?) ticked by.

Felix strained the limits of his voice to choke out two words: "What happened?"

"You read the journal." Bill pointed at it. "Remember? The journal."

Felix stared at it numbly. "I don't understand." His voice sounded weak, distant.

Bill set the can down on the table, reaching over Felix's shoulder to stay clear of the mess on the floor. "Of course you don't. Your aunt's journal is cursed. That's how I think of it anyway. Did you feel like you were experiencing someone else's emotions? Well—that's because you were. Your dead aunt's. When you read the journal you feel what your Aunt Eve was feeling. You're drawn into her emotions. You can't escape from them. That's why it's so extraordinarily difficult to stop reading once you've started. I've also learned the hard way there are physical consequences: disorientation, nausea, headaches and confusion. Basically, what you're..."

The words passed over him like a gust of wind. Some time passed. How much, Felix would never know.

"...allows you to tap into the feelings of another person who was writing in another time. The experience creates a kind of disconnect, or sensory overload that confuses your central nervous system. We're obviously not designed to feel someone else's emotions. That's just my theory, anyway. There's no way to validate it because a book like this has never existed."

He couldn't focus on what Bill was saying. He didn't even try. He just needed his legs to work. More time passed.

"...and despite what everyone thinks about him, he's actually the Drestain. You know who Lofton Ashfield is, don't you?"

Felix didn't answer.

"Felix?"

Felix's brain felt like a garbage disposal had chewed it up. Words and phrases were spinning around like a cyclone in his head: *Drestian, Belus, Elissa, Drestianites, Protectors, Tiberius 14-37, Caligula 37-41, Claudius...*

"Felix?"

No response.

"You're the Belus," Bill told him. "Do you understand? You're not just a Sourceror. *You* are the Belus."

"I don't believe you." Felix couldn't listen to this any more. He stood abruptly and his prickly half-numb legs buckled for a moment. "This thing's a crock of shit. It's stupid." He swiped at the journal, lost his balance and missed by at least a foot.

"It'll take you some time to recover," Bill said reassuringly. "You were reading for a long time. Just stick around. You'll feel better. We'll talk. Okay?"

"Whatever." The walls were closing in around him, suffocating him. He felt like he was going to burst out of his skin if he didn't get out of the room. He took a few tentative steps toward the door. His body seemed thick, wooden.

"Felix, don't leave." Bill sounded anxious now. "You're in no condition to be on your own. You could hurt yourself."

"I don't care," he said, half aware that he was badly slurring the words. "I have a game tomorrow. A football game. Maybe we'll be in the Rain Cup. Win. We've gotta win."

"I'll go with you." Bill started toward him.

"Get away from me!" Felix shouted, waving him off. He flung the door open and limped heavily out of the office.

Bill didn't try to stop him.

Chapter 28

HEADBUTTS AND FOOTSTEPS

The stairs of the Stamford Building seemed to be swimming in cooking grease. Felix slipped and stumbled, but somehow stuck the dismount, planting his feet on the smooth flat stones of a path. He went left and started walking without considering where it might lead him. It was dark. Darker than most nights. Heavy clouds. No moonlight. Only the pathlights glowing softly overhead lit the way to wherever the path was taking him. The ground felt like it was moving in waves beneath his feet. He fell to his knees and got back up, drifting along until he couldn't stay upright any longer, catching himself against a statue of a Greek god wearing a fig leaf over his private parts. He started up again, his inner ear spinning like a roulette wheel, reminding him of the time he went deep sea fishing with his dad and was slammed so badly with motion sickness he actually contemplated going overboard to get off the boat.

His stomach heaved. He doubled over and retched on the ground. Not much came out. He'd already left his meager dinner on the floor in Bill's office. He placed his hand against a thicket of shrubs to hold himself up, but the stiff branches gave way and he fell through, getting raked in the process. He retched again.

"Yuck!" a girl's voice cried out up ahead.

The sound dug into Felix's brain. He wiped his mouth and pushed his way through the hedge, then ducked under a small spreading maple to get to a path that led him away from the offended girl. His head was pounding, splintering with pain. It hurt in a way that a couple of Advil couldn't fix.

So I'm the Belus, Felix thought sluggishly, half-conscious that he was laughing out loud. Two kids strolling toward him (smiling, hand-in-hand) gave him a weird look and a wide berth. *The Belus?* What did that even mean? It wasn't even a real word. *Adopted?* How could he be adopted? He couldn't be—right? Bill was full of shit. What was wrong with that guy? His parents were dead. Wasn't that bad enough? Why would he tell him that he was adopted? That his birth mother was dead? That his mom and dad weren't even his real parents? Why would he lie?

I wasn't adopted.

But what if everything Bill said was true? What about the journal? How do you explain that? He'd read it and experienced whatever the hell that was—*his aunt's emotions.* Bill couldn't make that up. That wasn't a party trick. He'd *felt* that. But there had to be an explanation. Drugs? It must have been drugs. Maybe something on the paper? *Isn't that how you get high on LSD?* Maybe he was tripping? That must be it. That asshole had drugged him.

But what if he wasn't high? Then what? But the journal was crazy; nothing in it could possibly be true. *Could it?* There's no such thing as the Source or Sourcerors. No such thing as the Drestian, or the Belus, or cursed journals. And people aren't immaculately conceived. Bullshit! It was all bullshit! *The Cycle?* What the hell's that? Just the drugs talking—that's all. He caught his foot on something and nearly fell. The earth kept bucking and shifting under his feet. He couldn't feel his legs. They'd gone numb again. His vision was going in and out of focus, graying and clouding over, then, in intermittent bursts, lighting up like it was midday. He tripped again and fell against a low branch that clipped the very top of his ear. It stung.

Felix kept his head down, eating up chunks of winding path, kicking his way through drifts of brittle leaves, paying no attention to where he was going. A foul rotten taste filled his mouth: Partially digested protein bar and stomach acid. His gut was knotting and cramping up with sharp rolling spasms. His throat burned. He wanted to curl up in a bed of leaves and sleep off the pain. He'd never felt so sick. Or so confused. Maybe he was dreaming? But it didn't feel like a dream. So it had to be drugs. Some kind of—

Thud!

White light flashed behind his eyes and he stumbled backward, reeling, and fell on his ass. He put his hand to his howling head. Something had struck him in the forehead, dead-center. His eyes watering, he heaved himself up off the hard ground, searching for the culprit. He found it. All metal, it was thick and square at the base and long, thin and curved at the neck: a lamppost.

As he blinked fiercely to clear out the air raid sirens going off in his head, he noticed the darkened outline of an enormous familiar-looking structure in the distance. He knew where he was: the parking lot next to the football stadium. If he hadn't headbutted the lamppost, he might have wandered right off campus and into no-man's-land. *How the hell did I get here?*

he wondered. Nothing like this had ever happened to him before, not even during the dismal days of the lucid fog.

The parking lot was empty. He was all alone. A gusting wind suddenly picked up, biting through his clothes. The smell of rain was in the air. Stuttering moonlight shone briefly through a rift in the clouds. He watched a paper cup rolling end over end across the asphalt. All was silent except for the sound of the wind and the leaves rustling across the pavement. He stood there for a long while listening to the wind, watching the leaves.

The rain started to fall. At first it was a sprinkle, a drifting drizzle. Then the sprinkle became a gushing, driving Willamette Valley rainstorm that soaked him to the skin in seconds. He looked up at the starless sky and said weakly, "I'm Felix," hoping it would somehow calm the bizarre collection of disconnected thoughts pounding away inside his aching skull.

No you're not, a voice in his head answered in reply.

"I am," Felix said.

No. You're the Belus.

"I'm Felix."

You don't know what you are. You don't even know your real name.

"I'm Felix!"

The voice in his head laughed.

He crumpled to the ground and screamed at the pavement, the last of his strength rushing out of him. He felt like he was crumbling. He got on his hands and knees and rocked himself back and forth, letting the rain wash over him, its icy fingers running down his back, forcing him back to life. The rain was cold. It was *real.* Something he could feel and understand. There was no doubting its existence or what it meant. It was just water. It made things wet. Slowly, the pain and the sickness (but not the confusion) began to fade.

Then he heard—or thought he heard—*something.* Behind him. A whisper of movement. A bare vibration. A stirring in the darkness. Whatever it was, it jolted him into alertness. He staggered to his feet and cleared the rain from his eyes. He heard it again. This time it was off to his left. Darkness had clamped down on the world as he lay on the ground and he wondered how it could have happened so suddenly. His was the only island of light left in the lot. The others had gone out, blanketed in heavy sheets of rain and a thick mist that had descended without warning. The yellow halo cast from above shaded abruptly into blackness; he stared into it, and for a moment, he thought he heard—*imagined?*—footsteps. Another sound—the same sound. Other side. To his right. He jerked his head around. Nothing but the night (and whatever was lurking there, protected in its shadowy embrace).

"Hello?" Felix called out hoarsely, his voice cracking, small. He rotated himself in tight circles and whipped his head around trying to see everything all at once. "Hello?"

As the pain and the nausea dimmed, another sensation—*a feeling? A premonition?*—rose up from the pit of his stomach: *something very bad was about to happen.* He'd felt it before. At Martha's house just before two people had tried to kill him. But that was a dream, he reminded himself. Nobody had tried to kill him—that was all in his head. But this felt like a dream too. Maybe he was dreaming? But what if he wasn't? He didn't know if he was dreaming or not. He was losing his mind. That's what it was. Bill hadn't drugged him. He was just going crazy.

Run! a voice in Felix's head shouted.

"What?" he said, confused by the warning ringing in his mind.

Run! Now!

Felix bolted flat out across the parking lot, the raindrops pelting his face, stinging his eyes, nearly blinding him. There were sounds behind him—the sound of footsteps. This time he was certain of it. They were close. Someone was chasing him. *The woman?* What if it was the woman with the scar on her face? What if she was real? What if she was back to finish what she started?

But that was just a dream.

Then why are you hearing footsteps? Why is she chasing you?

He flew past the practice fields and as the end of the parking lot drew near, the sound of feet striking wet pavement grew louder, coming from everywhere. How many were after him? He thought back to the man with the knife. He remembered his eyes as clearly as if they were staring back at him through the rain: black, flat, cruel. *Was he here? With the woman?* Felix's ears were telling him that whoever was behind him was gaining on him. He wanted to look back, but he was afraid it would slow him down—and afraid of what he might see. His legs were pumping machine-like as he raced past dorms, gardens, a clump of sad leafless trees and then a row of brick buildings. He could see the western edge of The Yard. His legs were on fire, but he broke through the barrier, pushing himself through the pain.

The paths were deserted, but he didn't have time to think about where everyone had gone. His lungs were burning. He cut through the rain, tearing past a sea of swirling mist hanging low over The Yard. A haunted air had enveloped the campus: the mist was working its way up from the ground, weaving its way through the branches, arches and columns and up the faces of the buildings, reaching up to the dormers and gables and roofs, cloaking everything in a preternatural shroud of dream-like whiteness.

He kept going. He forced his legs to churn faster and faster. Almost there. The Freshman Yard came into view. Then his dorm. When he reached Downey, he bounded up the front stairs and threw himself through an open door, slipping on the floor and sprawling head first across the foyer.

He lay there next to the elevators coughing and huffing, trying to catch his breath. *I'm safe,* he said to himself, relieved. *Safe. I made it.* He heard voices, loud, high and excited—drunk voices. He glanced over. Two girls stood in the lobby staring down at him like he was a visitor from an alien planet.

Felix dragged himself to his feet, hands on his knees, breathing hard. Rivulets of rainwater dribbled onto the floor. His clothes were wringing wet, clinging to his body as he plodded up the stairs, leaving little puddles of water on the dark runner with each squishing step. The girls were laughing. The higher he climbed, the louder their laughter sounded; the strange auditory effect was disorienting. There was almost no activity in the hallways and not a soul on the fourth floor. The dorm was strangely quiet, especially for a Friday night. And he wondered, for a moment, what time it was. He opened the door to his room and groped around for a while to find the light switch before flipping it on.

A shriek came from Lucas's bed.

What the hell? Felix thought dimly, too tired to jump. Too tired to react in any way. *Now what?* He saw flashes of twined white skin disappearing beneath a dark comforter snatched up from the foot of the bed. The pillow was on the floor. A tousle of red hair poked out from the top and a girl's face slowly appeared as she brushed her hair to the side, revealing porcelain skin. *Piper.* Large frightened eyes stared aghast at Felix.

"Dude." Lucas's head popped up next to Piper's, his hair bedraggled. "Dude... um... I didn't know where you were. You mind if I use the room a little longer?" Piper retreated back under the blankets. "Could you maybe hang out downstairs or something? I think I only need like five or six more minutes." He paused thoughtfully. "Maybe a little longer. I'm kinda drunk."

Felix backed out of the room, pulled the door shut and started for the stairs.

"Dude, can you turn out the light?" he heard Lucas's distant voice shout from the other side of the wall to his right. Audible, but still more distant: "Piper's a little shy. Duuude!"

A moment later, without knowing how it had happened, he arrived at a place he knew well: third floor hall, Harper's room to his right, Allison's to his left. He gazed blearily at a rain-streaked window at the far end of the corridor; it was glowing faintly orange from the outside lights that illuminated it.

He closed his eyes for a moment and felt himself swoon. He was drained. His mind was in a state of disarray, total free fall. He doubted his own sanity. He needed to talk to someone, to be with someone. He couldn't handle being alone with his own thoughts—his own craziness. He was an inch away from collapsing in an exhausted heap in the middle of the empty hallway.

He turned to his left and knocked on the door as softly as he could. There were rustling sounds behind the door after a half minute of silence, then it opened a crack.

"Who is it?" a girl's voice said.

"It's me," he said weakly. "Felix."

"*Felix?*" The door swung open. Allison stood in the doorway wearing a pair of light blue shorts and a gray PC T-shirt, her jaw dropping at the sight of him. Her hair was tied back in a slightly unruly bunch.

"Oh my God! What the hell? What happened to you?" She took him by the elbow and tugged him into the room, closing the door behind him. "You're soaking wet." She covered up a yawn with the back of her hand. "What were you doing outside? It's pouring." She went to her closet and dug through a laundry basket until she found a towel. She tossed it to him. "Sorry, I didn't have time to do laundry. Midterms." She glanced down at his feet and frowned. "Take your shoes off. Caitlin's gonna have a shitfit conniption."

He heel-stepped out of his sneakers, then toweled off his head.

"Where's Caitlin?" he asked, seeing that she wasn't in her bed.

"Her parents are in town for her dad's birthday. She's staying with them at The Four Seasons. She'd totally freak if she saw the mess you're making. What's going on? Where were you?"

"I think I'm losin' it, Allie." He went quiet for a second. "I don't know."

"How can you not know where you were?" She looked perplexed. "Just tell me what happened."

"I... uh... I was being chased."

"*Chased?* By who?"

"I don't know. I didn't... um... actually see anyone." He knew that sounded ridiculous. "I was over by the stadium. I heard something. Footsteps, I think. Yeah. I'm pretty sure. And then they chased me."

She placed her hands on her hips and her brow creased. "Take your clothes off. Caitlin's back tomorrow and you know she's a neat freak."

"Wha—?"

"Now! C'mon. We went to the lake together like a thousand times. I've seen you in shorts. Get a grip."

He pulled the sweatshirt over his head and unzipped his jeans. The rain had glued them to his legs and he had to practically pry them off. He dried himself with the towel. Sort of. He was too spent and bewildered to care about being wet (or having nothing on but his boxer briefs).

"That's better." Allison looked him over. "Now tell me what this is all about. You're not making any sense. You're not drunk, are you? Were you out partying with the fatassosaurs?"

"Uh-uh." He slumped down on Caitlin's bed. "I think I've lost it. I mean, seriously lost it."

Allison sat beside him. "What were you doing at the stadium? That's like the least safe place on campus, you know. No-man's-land's right there."

"I was um… I was… uh… just walking. Thinking."

"At three-thirty in the morning?" She gave him a skeptical look. "In a storm?"

He sat silently, shaking his head.

"C'mon, Felix. What's going on? Talk to me."

He wasn't trying to be evasive. He was just so confused about what had happened he didn't know what to say. How could he explain something he didn't understand himself?

"Felix!" she nearly shouted, after the silence had dragged on. Her eyes flared, demanding an explanation.

"I met this guy a while ago," he began, the words tumbling out slowly, awkwardly. "His name's Bill. He's a groundskeeper, an assistant groundskeeper, actually. He works here. At the school. I saw him earlier tonight. I went to his office and he told me that… that…" He hesitated.

"What'd he tell you? C'mon."

"That I was adopted." He stared straight ahead, too embarrassed to look her in the face.

"*What?*"

"Yeah. I know. I must be crazy."

"The *assistant groundskeeper* told you that you were adopted?"

Felix nodded, wishing he hadn't said anything.

"Why would he do that? How could this guy—*Bill?*—possibly know something like that? Besides, you weren't adopted."

"I know."

"So why would he—?"

"He thinks that... um... I don't know. Look, I mean, it makes no sense. He... uh... showed me something. It's not like anything that um..."

"What was it?"

"It's nothing." He'd already said too much. Now he was just making an ass of himself. "The guy's full of shit. He just freaked me out. I think I just kinda lost it. Maybe I'm just imagining things. I don't know. I'm just so damn tired."

Allison placed her hand on the back of his neck and he let his head settle onto her shoulder. "It'll be okay," she said softly, running her fingers through his wet hair. "You just need some sleep. You look exhausted. And you have a big game in a few hours."

"Yeah," Felix said, not really hearing her. "The journal couldn't have been real. I just imagined it."

"What journal?" She pulled back a little, making his ear bounce up and down on the bony part of her shoulder.

"Nothing. I'm just... tired. Just losing my goddamn mind." He closed his eyes and sank to his side, his head pressing into Caitlin's soft goose-down pillow. It smelled like feathers and fruity shampoo.

The mattress shifted under him as Allison got up from the bed and padded across the room in her bare feet. A moment later, he felt the comforting weight of a quilted blanket spreading over him.

"You haven't lost your mind," he heard Allison say from a million miles away. Then she leaned down and placed a light kiss on his cheek. *Soft lips,* he thought, before losing himself in the tunneling darkness.

Chapter 29

VALIDATION

Pain. So much pain. Everything hurt. *Air.* Felix needed air. It felt like every molecule of oxygen had been crushed out of his lungs. He caught a faint whiff of something acrid. *Burning rubber?* He heard sounds. The faraway sounds of… a voice. Someone was calling to him—calling his name.

He lay on a hard surface. On his back. The floor? *What the hell am I doing on the floor?* His eyelids fluttered, but they were heavy, sealed shut, and his attempts to get them unstuck were unsuccessful.

"Felix! Wake up! C'mon! Please. Wake up!"

He felt hands on his chest, shaking him, and he was conscious of not having a shirt on. He drew in a deep breath of sweet, sweet air. Better. Images came rushing back to him in torrents. Bill. He remembered being in Bill's office. The journal—he remembered that too. He also remembered the parking lot next to Stubbins, and the rain, and then someone chasing him back to the dorm.

The voice was still saying his name, shouting at him. A girl's voice. He tried to open his eyes. The world went white, then dark, and then white again, like he was on a train going through a series of tunnels on a sunny day. Light was filtering in through a window, listless and gray. Morning. He saw the girl's face hovering over him. Pretty, dark hair, green eyes. *Allison.* She was on her knees, looking down at him, her hands on his bare chest. *Allison's room. That's where I am.* He remembered going up the stairs and finding Lucas hooking up with Piper—that's why he'd come down here. But why was he lying on the floor? Didn't he crash on Caitlin's bed?

"Allie," he groaned. "What's goin' on?"

"Good question." She got to her feet, her eyes dancing around the room.

He sat up and noticed he was also missing his pants. He was about to ask her where she'd put his clothes when he realized the room was destroyed: Half of the room—Caitlin's side—had been torched. The desk was gone. And aside from a few pieces of the metal frame (warped into odd curvey shapes) so was the bed. The wall and ceiling, charred and blistered from the heat, bubbled up like little volcanoes where the paint had melted. The floor looked like the catch basin of a charcoal grill after the embers die out. Some of the floorboards had completely burned away and disintegrated, leaving miniature fjords in the blackened landscape. Everything was smothered in ash. There had obviously been a fire. But nothing was smoldering. There was no smoke. It looked as though someone had extinguished it days ago.

Felix jumped up, pointing numbly. "Fire. Fire." Then it occurred to him that he should be checking to see if Allison was hurt. She seemed fine. Then he checked himself. No burns. Nothing unusual besides the fact that the back of his head was roaring with pain and he was in Allison's room wearing only his underwear—again. He had also apparently slept through a fire.

"Fire. Fire," he kept mumbling.

Allison glanced at him absently and nodded. She was pacing, her eyes filled with panic, like a hunted animal. Her movements were erratic and quick-twitched, almost bird-like. She stopped next to a pile of ash and knelt down, poking at it delicately with her finger. "It's not even hot." She stood and turned to Felix. "Weird. Do you remember anything?"

"Why didn't the fire alarm go off?" He rubbed the back of his head. "What happened? Are you okay?"

"I don't know." Allison blew the ash off her finger, sending a puff of fine dry dust into the air like a warm breath in the winter cold.

"You don't know?"

She was taking fast irregular breaths, hugging her arms over her midsection. He didn't like the way she was looking at him. He took a step toward her and she stepped back, trembling. The color had drained from her face.

"Allie?" he asked, wondering what the hell was going on.

Her eyes misted, the tears welling up like water behind a failing dam.

"What happened?"

She shook her head sharply. "Sorry. I think I might be in shock."

"*Shock?* Why?"

She stared at him, her wide eyes searching and... *scared?*

"Should we call someone?" Felix rolled his shoulders to unkink his neck.

"No!" she shouted. "Don't do that!"

"Allie—?"

"I saw it. I saw it." Allison was breathing like she'd just returned from one of her pre-dawn runs.

"Saw what?"

She watched him, her jaw set in stiff resolve, then tears spilled from her eyes. He'd never seen her cry before, not like this anyway. *What was happening?* He reached out for her. For a second, he thought she was going to pull away, and then she collapsed into him, sobbing into his chest. He held her, waiting for an explanation, but she seemed content to bathe him in warm saline.

Finally, she stepped back and looked up at him.

"Can you please tell me what happened?" Felix said to her.

"I'm either crazy or everything just got really interesting."

He waited.

She looked over at Caitlin's side of the room, clearing her eyes with the back of her hand. "Okay. It really happened. *That* really happened." She jabbed a finger toward the spot where Caitlin's bed had once stood. "So I'm not crazy."

"*What* really happened?" His stomach tightened as the anxiousness started to flare. "What happened? Can you just tell me what the hell happened? How'd I get—?"

"You're not gonna believe this."

"Allie!"

"Okay. Okay. It's just... I don't know... what I... okay." She paused, her cheeks wet with tears. "Here goes. And I swear on my life it's true."

He cocked his head and said warily, "Okay." Something told him this was going to be a doozy. His heart was fluttering somewhere in his throat, making it difficult to breathe.

"You were floating above the bed and everything around you was exploding and turning to ash." She planted her hands on her hips and looked at him fiercely, challenging him not to believe her.

Felix stumbled back a step and choked on his own spit. He cleared his throat. "*Floating?*"

"Yeah."

"And then what happened?" He couldn't keep his voice level.

"That's it. While you were hanging out by the ceiling, the bed and the desk and everything else was just kind of catching fire and melting. And everything—pieces of all this shit and all this gray stuff—was flying around you. Then the room got really hot, and I thought the whole thing was going up in flames. And then I screamed. It must've woken you up. Everything just hit the floor. And then you hit the floor. You were way up there. It must've hurt. You hit it pretty hard."

In his half-stunned state, his near nakedness suddenly concerned him more than the apparent fact that he could float and melt dorm furniture. "Where are my clothes?"

"Huh? Oh. Closet." She pointed at it.

He went over to the closet and snatched up his sweatshirt (still sopping wet), then pulled it over his head. It was uncomfortably cold, but he didn't notice because his mind was fixating on the bomb that had just gone off in his head: *The journal!* It wasn't that everything he'd read had suddenly come flooding back into his awareness. It was already there, inside him. He knew that he'd read it. But now the words on the pages had context. Now they actually meant something—they actually felt real. The reality of his situation had chiseled its way down into his consciousness until it struck a nerve center of actual understanding. Now he got it. He knew what it meant. And that left him shell-shocked. Totally floored.

"It's all true," he said in a whisper, an icy fear crystallizing in his brain.

"What's true?" she asked cautiously.

"The whole thing." He heaved his jeans over his legs and zipped them up.

"Sorry?"

"It's all true." Felix stared bleakly at the room, unable to grasp how he could have done this. *But he did.* He *knew* that he did.

"What?"

"The whole goddamn thing is true. I can't believe this. I can't believe this is happening. Oh my God. It's all true. The whole thing. Everything he told me. Shit! What am I gonna do now? What am I gonna do? What do I do? What do I—"

"What are you talking about?" A thin flush of color had crept back over Allison's face. Not much, but she was less pale than Piper. "What's all true?" she demanded.

"You'd never believe me."

"Are you fucking kidding me?" she shouted. "Seriously? After what I just saw! I'll believe *anything* you tell me. Anything!"

He ran his hands over his face and felt a small knot in the center of his forehead. He winced at the memory of colliding with the lamppost, and at the pain shooting through his head. He wandered over to the window. The sun was up, but still low in the sky, dull and coppery. The Freshman Yard was currently the exclusive play area for a pair of squirrels chasing each other around a big oak tree.

"Felix...?"

"Okay." He turned away from the window and hesitated, unsure of what—or how much—he should tell her. But why shouldn't he tell her everything? There was no one he trusted more than Allison. He trusted her with his life. Besides, he thought, glancing at the drifts of ash that were once Caitlin's bed, the truth was probably less ridiculous than any lie he could possibly spin.

"Well?" she said impatiently.

"So I told you about Bill, right?"

She nodded. "The groundskeeper."

"So a while back, he told me he had something from my mom. So I went to his office last night to see what it was. It was a journal. But it wasn't from my mom. Not... you know... uh... Patricia. The journal was from my real mom. It was my real mom's sister's journal. She'd sent it to my mom, then my mom gave it to Bill. That's why he had it. I guess that he... uh... before she died he promised her he'd show it to me."

"You said something about a journal last night. So you... you really were adopted? Seriously? And your mom... your real mom... she's... dead?"

"Yeah."

"I'm sorry." Allison's eyes filled with tears.

"It's not like I knew her." Felix was struck by her reaction. He didn't know what to think. His *real* mom. How could he have a real mom? Should he be sad? But how could he feel sad—or feel anything—for someone he couldn't remember? Someone who died so long ago?

"I know, but still..." She wiped the corners of her eyes. "So what's it say? The journal. You read it?"

"Yeah. That's what made me crazy last night. I think it's why I thought I was being chased. Anyway, it's... cursed."

"*Cursed?*"

"Yep. I swear."

"Cursed how?"

"It's beyond weird. You feel my aunt's emotions when you read it. It's like getting on a roller coaster that won't let you off. I pretty much puked up my guts all over campus."

"So what's in it?" she asked eagerly. "What'd it say?"

Felix spoke rapidly: "'Elissa, time is short. I have only minutes before Lyndsey comes for this. She will find you. Six months before your twenty—'"

"How are you doing that?" she interrupted, looking at him as if he had suddenly started speaking in fluent German. "It's like you're reading it."

He was more surprised than Allison. "I have no idea. I just… I just know what it says. I mean, I *know* the whole thing. I think I could tell you the whole journal word-for-word. It's like it's burned into my brain or something."

"Weird. So who's Elissa?"

"Oh. Sorry." He paused. "My mom." He dropped his head and studied his toes. "It sounds so strange to say that. *My mom.*"

"Got it. Okay. Keep going."

Felix recited the journal from the beginning. Allison listened in rapt silence, hanging on his every word, exhibiting nearly every possible facial expression, biting her tongue every ten seconds or so. When he reached the part where Eve decided to keep her baby, she couldn't restrain herself any longer.

"*Lofton?*" she shouted, causing him to pause. "Lofton Ashfield? *The* Lofton Ashfield? No Way! Say that part again."

"'I had the baby. A boy. We named him Lofton.'" Felix was still amazed—and impressed with himself—that he knew the journal by heart. He didn't even have to go back to the start. He could stop and pick it up from any point in the story.

"Wow! Unreal! Lofton Ashfield's the Drestian. And you're the Belus!"

Felix didn't know what to say so he just shrugged. "I'm not done yet."

"Sorry. I couldn't help it. This is unbelievable! Lofton Ashfield's like the most powerful guy in the state. Maybe the entire country. Probably the most popular too. But he's really the Drestian? Crazy! And you're the Belus? You? Felix August? You're the Belus? This is totally unreal. I can't believe this. Do you realize how cool this is?"

"*Cool?*"

"Are you kidding? You'll probably think I'm crazy, but after I read the last *Harry Potter* book, you know what I did? I cried. I literally cried for like two whole days. The adventure was over. Harry had won. Voldemort was dead. And Harry was all grown up. The boy wizard. The boy who saved the entire wizarding world was some middle-aged guy. He had kids, and a wife, and a pot belly. He wasn't searching for horcruxes. He was shuffling folders at some stupid normal job and gossiping at the water cooler about whether some intern was having an affair with her loser boss. The magic was dead. Harry was like everyone else in this boring world. But now we get to live our own adventure. Don't you see?" She was meandering around the room in little circles and figure eights as though she had to keep moving to bottle up her excitement. "The fate of the world is at stake, and only *you* can save it! I knew there had to be more to life than mindless paper pushing jobs. I didn't think it'd be this. But..." Allison gave him an embarrased smile. "Sorry. I guess I got carried away."

How could she be so amped? he wondered. He wasn't amped at all. More than anything, he was floundering in some higher realm of confusion that he hadn't known existed. And the small part of him that wasn't confused was just flat-out scared. And if there was any emotional machinery not saturated with confusion and fear, a drowning layer of doubt submerged it. He still wasn't sure what to believe. Despite the proof—the room was staring him in the face—he doubted. Strongly doubted.

"I don't know," he said. "I'm not sure if they got the right kid for this job. How can *I* be the Belus?"

"It's fate," she said confidently, like she actually knew what she was talking about. "And I think it's incredible! Sorry. Okay. I'll stop. Tell me the rest."

Felix waded back in right where he'd left off, and when he was finally finished, Allison blurted out: "That's it? That's it?"

"Yeah," he replied, confused.

"Mid-sentence? It ends mid-sentence?"

Felix nodded slowly.

"Why?" She gave him a long curious look. "What happened?"

He shrugged and said vaguely, "Bill didn't say anything. Or maybe he did and I don't remember."

Her troubled expression faded and she smiled at him, her eyes burning with excitement. "You realize this is the most amazing story ever! Do you have any idea what'll happen if we tell people about this?"

"They'll think we're insane," Felix said flatly. "Then I think Lofton—*the Drestian*—will kill us. That's part of the adventure you're forgetting."

"Oh. Yeah. Well... yeah, I suppose you're right. But there's no adventure without a little danger, right?"

"I still can't believe this is happening," Felix said. "We're from some little dive town on the coast. Things like this aren't supposed to happen to people like us."

"Says who? And I think it's cool." She paused, her eyes fixing on his in a measuring stare. "So how do you plan on saving the world from dictatorship and enslavement?"

Felix stared back at her and blinked, wondering if she was being serious. Her face gave nothing away. Then she broke out in a big smile and started laughing. He joined in. The notion of Felix saving the world was inherently ridiculous, and when you said it out loud, it was even more ridiculous. It was funny, hilarious even. The punch line of a joke, a comedian's closing flourish, the grand finale. How could you not laugh? The whole thing was a monumental lark; at any second, someone was almost certainly going to pop into the room to tell them this was just an elaborate hoax. Or maybe it was all a mistake. Maybe the cosmic forces—whoever was responsible for that Source thing—had screwed up. Maybe they had the wrong kid. *Sorry Felix, there was a clerical error. We meant to pick a sophomore at Ohio State. Wrong school. Wrong year. Wrong kid. Oops. Sorry.*

"I guess I should probably tell Bill about this," Felix said.

"This guy Bill. He's a *groundskeeper?* Are you sure that's all he is?"

"I don't know anything about him."

"Alright. Well, we need to figure out what to do about this." She cocked her thumb at Caitlin's side of the room. "She's gonna stroke out when she sees this. And you have a game, you know?"

"Shit!" He'd totally forgotten about it. "What time is it? It's an early kickoff."

She checked the clock next to her bed. "Seven thirty."

"I'm already late for pre-game breakfast! I gotta go." He started toward the door.

"Hold on!" She snared his arm before he could get past her. "Here's what you're going to do first." Allison had snapped back into let's-get-shit-done mode. "Go to your room. I'm sure Lucas is still sleeping. Then—oh! You didn't say anything to him last night, did you?"

"No. He was hooking up with Piper so I came down here."

"Piper?" She rolled her eyes. "He's such a slut."

"I was actually heading down to the common room to crash on a couch, but then I got to your floor, and I guess that I... I just wanted to talk to you."

She smiled and quickly turned her head to look at something on her desk that had suddenly captured her interest. Her cheeks had gone pink. "Alright, Belus." She went over to the window. "Go to your room, get your stuff and get outta here. I'll give you ten minutes then I'm pulling the alarm. They'll have to evacuate the building. When the firemen get here, they'll find this disaster." She pointed off to her right. "I'll tell them I woke up smelling smoke, jumped out of bed and pulled the alarm. It's kind of strange it died on its own, but I'm not the expert on fires. Hey, are you gonna tell anybody else about this?"

"No." He shook his head emphatically. "I'm still trying to wrap my mind around it."

"I agree."

"Yeah, so don't tell—"

"I won't say a word," Allison promised. "You can trust me."

"I know. Give me a few minutes to get my shit together."

*   *   *

Lucas, to Felix's immense relief, was all alone and sleeping soundly. Felix grabbed his things and slipped back out of the room. Lucas didn't stir. When the fire alarm sounded, Felix had just reached The Yard. Wailing and screeching, rising and falling in waves, it rolled across campus. And then just as he entered Ferguson Hall, he could hear the fire trucks howling to a stop on 1st Street.

Chapter 30

TIMETABLES

"Hello, Dad," Bill said into his phone. He was standing at the table in his office, looking out the window at The Yard below.

"Hello, William. I haven't heard from you in a while. How have you been?"

"Living the dream as an assistant groundskeeper. The other day, I was mowing the lawn and some smartass kid yelled, 'you missed a spot'. That's a good one. These kids are funny. The next kid who does that is going to get circumcised with my hedge clippers."

"You sound tired. I hope that's not discouragement I hear in your voice."

"*Me?* Discouraged? I'm an eternal optimist. You know that. I didn't get much sleep last night. That's all." Bill rubbed a hand over his chin, pausing for dramatic effect as the moment seemed to call for it. "I met with Felix last night."

"And…?"

"He read the journal."

A short pause. Bill thought he heard his dad let out a single relieved breath.

"And so it begins."

"Yeah," Bill replied. "After all this time."

"How did you convince him to do it?"

Bill glanced at the baseball bat propped up against a stack of books in the corner. "I asked him politely."

"Sure you did," his dad said skeptically. "I know you, William. Sometimes you're the proverbial bull in a china shop. It's that temper of yours. If you'd learn to control it, you might make things easier on yourself."

"I'll try to remember that," Bill muttered softly.

"So how did he react?"

"Exactly as we had anticipated," Bill answered.

"Refused to believe a word?"

"Of course not. But he'll be back. Soon. Once it starts to sink in, he'll want to know what it all means."

"I hope he doesn't wait too long." There was a note of anxiousness in his dad's voice.

No one spoke.

His dad was waiting for a response.

It never came. This was about a timetable, and that was a conversation Bill was determined to avoid. The situation was too fluid for that, and besides, he had a plan.

"So tell me," his dad said after a while, "what's he look like in person these days? Does he still look like Lofton?"

"The similarity's hard to miss. Felix is a little bigger, but they could be father and son."

"And what's the boy... like?"

"*Like?* He's an eighteen-year-old kid." Bill put the phone on speaker and set it on the table, taking a seat. "He seems conflicted about something. But what teenager doesn't? He's probably got himself worked up about girls. Not to mention midterms, football, and of course, his parents. He's a small-town kid. You know that. You know everything about him. I'd describe him as a simple, unsophisticated kid. But he's not dumb. He's actually quite smart, smarter than he realizes. And he won't always be simple."

A phlegmy cough rattled through the phone as Bill's dad worked out something in his throat. "It's the simple-minded that make me nervous. They cannot even grasp that there are things beyond their understanding. And that makes them *dangerous*. That makes them confident controlling the lives of others. Hitler and Stalin were such men. Simple-minded monsters."

"He's not Hitler." Bill stared at the phone and shook his head. "Jesus, Dad. He's eighteen. And he's on our side, remember?"

"Hitler was once eighteen," his dad barked in his gravelly voice. "And the boy has the potential to make Hitler look like Mother Theresa."

An uncomfortable silence followed.

Bill gazed out the window and sighed, watching two students out for an early morning jog cut across The Yard through a light mist that was beginning to lift. The grass was wet, though it had stopped raining a few hours ago, and the sky was mostly clear.

"Do you think he has any idea of what he's capable of?" his dad asked, finally breaking the quiet.

"No. None whatsoever."

"All that power," his dad growled softly, like a contented lion. "The power of the universe flows in that boy's veins, and he doesn't even know it. Can you imagine what it must be like to wield that kind of energy?"

"No. But I intend to bring it out of him."

"And when do you anticipate that happening?"

"I'll start training him when I think he's ready," Bill said adamantly, aware that his tone alone wouldn't cause his dad to drop the subject. But it was worth a try.

"But we don't have the luxury of time! If you don't start training he won't—"

"He's not ready! This isn't something you can force. And *you're* telling me that *I'm* the bull in a china shop? I'm dealing with an eighteen-year-old kid who's been through a lot. He's got enough teenage angst to supply the rest of the school. If I push too hard, or too soon, he'll break. He's like an unloaded gun at this point and you're telling me to fill him with bullets. So don't you think we should know where he's aiming before I show him how to pull the trigger? I have a good read on this kid. I've been doing my homework since he was in diapers. I know what I'm doing."

"Of course you do, William," his dad said in an overly pleasant voice. "Fine. That's fine. Train the boy when *he's* ready. By all means, let the boy dictate the schedule. That makes perfect sense."

"I'll call you later," Bill said, ignoring his dad's sarcasm. "I have a game to attend. If the Sturgeons win, we'll play for the Rain Cup."

"The rain what?"

"That's right. Gotta go." He ended the call, amused by his dad's consternation.

Chapter 31

RAIN CUP ON THE HORIZON

Felix caught the ball on the Sturgeons' eighteen-yard line, dodged a defender, stiff-armed another to the facemask and darted out of bounds at the thirty-five. The whistle blew. The crowd cheered anxiously. He glanced up at the clock—eight seconds left. He flipped the ball to the official and jogged back to the huddle.

He still couldn't believe he was playing in a football game. The past twenty-four hours hadn't exactly been a typical day: he finished his midterms; a groundskeeper threatened to break his fingers with a bat; he found out he was adopted; he read a cursed journal; he imagined people chasing him (people who wanted to kill him); he defied gravity and set fire to Caitlin's bed (in his sleep); and if he understood the journal correctly, he was not only immaculately conceived, he was the only person capable of preventing the Drestian (aka Lofton Ashfield) from enslaving the world.

During pregame warm-ups, he'd been mostly catatonic and went through the motions of getting ready for the game, relying on habit and muscle memory to conceal his state of mind from the coaches. And this wasn't just any game: The only thing standing between the Sturgeons and a shot at playing for the Rain Cup was the Milford Lava Bears. The game was huge—the most important game anyone in attendance could remember. But Milford presented a gigantic obstacle. And as the game wore on—in front of the largest crowd in school history—it was clear they were simply the better team: bigger, stronger and faster at nearly every position.

Yet the scrappy Sturgeons had gone after them full throttle, putting everything they had into every play. His teammates' determination and desire was contagious, and by the mid-point of the first quarter, Felix had stopped thinking about the journal and whatever it was that had happened in Allison's room. It wasn't as hard as he'd thought it would be. It was all so bizarre, and so surreal, it wasn't much different than trying to shake the lingering effects of a bad dream.

The only distraction he hadn't been able to block out was Bill's voice in his head telling him that he was adopted. He wasn't sure why, but he thought it was probably because he could actually grasp the concept. Adoption was almost normal—at least compared to finding out that he was the Belus (among other things). So between plays his mind had drifted; he wondered why his parents had never told him, and if they ever planned to. He'd never know. It was their secret—a secret they took with them to their graves.

And now, with just eight seconds left, the Sturgeons were down by four points. They'd outhustled and outworked Milford the entire game. But it looked like talent was going to win out over heart and effort. Brant huddled the offense and took a knee. He looked up at his teammates and said with a smile, "Helluva game guys. Whadya say? We got one play left. Nothin' to lose. I'm throwin' it to August. Felix, you catch it and run. Déjà vu, baby." He broke the huddle.

Felix lined up on the left side of the formation in the slot position. At "two" the center snapped the ball to Brant. Felix pushed aside the defender and Brant delivered the ball to him in full stride. He tucked it tightly under his arm and took off down the middle of the field, leaving Lava Bears in his wake. He jumped over a diving defender at the forty-yard line. Another player slammed a shoulder into Felix's thigh but bounced off without slowing him down. At the fifty, he cut back sharply to his right, split two defenders, and making it to the sideline, turned on the jets.

At least half the players on Milford had the angle on Felix—he had no chance of reaching the end zone (or so it appeared). But the yard markers beneath his feet flew by: 40... 30... 20. The entire defense was in pursuit. He could hear their cleats striking the ground, churning up the soggy turf. He could hear their panting breath as they thundered down on him, diving at him in turns, swiping at his legs. The sounds triggered a primordial fear deep down in his consciousness—and a recent memory, a memory that couldn't be suppressed no matter how focused he was on staying in the moment. *They're back*, he thought, the panic surging inside him. *They're trying to get me. Trying to kill me.*

Felix barreled ahead, tearing past the ten-yard line, his legs a blur. The crowd roared in anticipation. The end zone was right in front of him (4... 3... 2...). He reached out for the goal line.

Something blindsided Felix, crashing into him, sending him flying through the air and out of bounds. He jumped to his feet—and for reasons unknown to him, raised his right arm up to his shoulder, fingers extended—

prepared to protect himself against the dark-haired man and the woman with the scar. But the only people around him were wearing two-tone uniforms, helmets and shoulder pads. He wasn't being attacked in no-man's-land—or *dreaming* about being attacked in no-man's-land. And he wasn't being chased—or imagining being chased—across campus in the rain and mist. He was playing football. *Snap out of it*, he told himself. *Snap out of it!* He stared at the referee, waiting for him to hoist up his arms to signal a touchdown.

He didn't. Instead, he looked Felix straight in the eye and said: "Out at the one. Out of bounds at the one. Game over." Then he turned and ran off.

Felix stared at the man's diminishing back in disbelief. He felt his jaw drop. His mouthpiece tumbled out of his mouth and landed on the grass between his feet. The ref was wrong—he had to be. He must have misheard him. It had to be a mistake. He looked up at the scoreboard. It read 00:00. He spun around and around trying to find someone to tell him that the game wasn't really over. It couldn't be over.

But it was. The Lava Bears were already celebrating on the field.

Felix collapsed on his butt, elbows on knees, head down. He sat there on the wet grass, alone, drained. The stadium was silent, the crowd stunned.

"Felix. Hey, buddy. Felix. C'mon, man. Get up."

He recognized Larry's voice. But he didn't move. He didn't have it in him.

"C'mon, August." A different voice—Salty's. "Keep your chin up. That was the most awesome play I've ever seen. C'mon."

Felix looked up. Larry, Salty, Jonas and Brant were all there, helmets off. And behind them were the rest of his teammates. Larry and Salty reached down and hauled him up by his grass-stained jersey. Then they moved across the field toward the tunnel beneath the east side stands like a herd of depressed lumbering animals. Felix kept his head down, letting the fatassosaurs lead him away.

In the locker room, Felix sat on a bench to strip off his gear. He shrugged out of his shoulder pads and banged them against his locker in frustration. How could the season be over? So much for winning the Rain Cup this year. So much for making PC football history. With everything else going on in his life, he knew that a game shouldn't matter. He shouldn't care. *But he did.* He didn't understand how it had ended so wrong. How did they knock him out of bounds inches—*inches*—away from scoring the winning touchdown? Why did he let that happen? Why didn't he run faster? Why didn't he score? He blew the game. He blew the whole season. He blew it for everyone—the whole team. It was all his—

His gut contracted so violently a seizing grunt burst through his teeth, causing all eyes in the room to turn to him. He ran to the bathroom, launched himself into a stall and threw up his pre-game breakfast of oatmeal, toast and apple juice in three shaking heaves. After his stomach had settled, he got up off his knees and wiped the tears from his eyes, then opened the door.

Jimmy Clay was blocking the doorway, feet planted wide, an expression of pure hatred on his scarlet face. Before Felix could react, Jimmy punched him in the stomach with every ounce of his steroid-enhanced strength, burying his fist up to his wrist. Felix's feet lifted off the floor. The air escaped him all at once. Unable to catch his breath, his legs reduced to jelly, Felix felt himself falling backward. And then two iron hands, like vises, gripped his arms and pulled him forward. The pain was excruciating. He felt like he would never be able to breathe again. Like his lungs had been permanently deflated.

Jimmy's face—an acne-riddled mask of sheer fury—was pressed into his own. His foul breath was so rancid Felix could taste it. "You lost the game for me, you little bitch!" Jimmy whispered in a low menacing snarl. "There's gonna be pro scouts at the Rain Cup. And now they won't see me play. You fuck with my career again and I'll cut off your balls!" Jimmy hacked up an enormous mouthful of phlegm and spat in his face. Felix felt the warm sticky mess dripping down his mouth and chin, and he couldn't do anything to stop it. He couldn't breathe. He couldn't move his arms. He was helpless.

Jimmy released him and slammed a forearm into Felix's chest. It was like getting hit with a sledgehammer. He tripped over the toilet and fell over backward, banging his head against the wall. He heard footsteps, Jimmy walking away. He lay there on the piss-spattered floor for a long while, wiping the putrid phlegm from his face, gasping for air.

When he finally felt like he wasn't going to die, he struggled to his feet and opened the stall door a few inches, half-expecting Jimmy to be there waiting for him. He wasn't. Felix limped over to the row of sinks and washed his face in scalding water, using up an entire dispenser of coarse pink soap. Then he showered, changed and left the building without saying a word to anyone.

Chapter 32

ANSWERS

"Tough break," Bill said to Felix. "Good game though. Best game all year." He sipped his tea and leaned back in his chair. He continued to watch him for a while, then finally placed his cup on the table and sighed. "So are you going to say something or should I grab a book to pass the time?"

Felix was seething. His blood boiled, infused with rage. He'd beelined it for Bill's office right after he fled the stadium, prepared to assault him with a thousand questions. But each time he opened his mouth, the thought of Jimmy made his mind cloud over and his tongue clot. He stared out the window at a quartet of robins zipping over The Yard, landing on the roof of Rhodes Hall. He usually liked birds just fine (who didn't?), but at the moment he felt nothing but hatred for the feathery devils that carpet bombed his Wrangler nearly every day.

"They say it's a game of inches," Bill offered.

"It's not that," Felix said, breaking his silence. "It's just this guy on the team. He's such an asshole. I'd like to rip his head off."

"Hey!" Bill shouted with a jab of his finger. "Hey! Don't even say that. Don't even *think* it! You think little Nathan's gall bladder exploded all on its own?"

Felix jerked back in his chair, his fingers curling around the armrests. The suddenness of Bill's outburst was startling. Felix watched as Bill's expression changed from pleasant to angry—the veins bulging in his neck were a dead giveaway—to neutral in a span of about three seconds.

"Fine," Felix said. "I won't rip his head off. But I'd like to take your bat to his ugly face."

"That's more like it." Bill smiled approvingly. "As long as his organs remain intact and you don't kill him you can borrow it. Just bring it back when you're done. I use it once in a while on cheeky teenagers." He looked down at his teacup. "I forgot to ask. Would you like some tea?"

"No thanks."

"So now that you're talking, what would you like to talk about? I'm sure you have a few things on your mind."

Felix forced a smile, thinking that was a candidate for understatement of the year. He tried to gather his thoughts. He fixed his eyes on a pocket of sunlight falling across a bookshelf to Bill's back as he argued with himself on where to begin. "So... um... last night... I uh... I melted my friend's room."

"You what?"

"Yeah. While I slept. I guess I kinda flew around and burned everything up."

"Flew?"

"More like levitated. I guess I was way up above the bed. Kinda floating there."

Bill sipped his tea calmly. "And there was a fire?"

"Sort of. I guess it was like a fire. But different. It's hard to explain. When Allison woke me up, it was already out."

"This was in Downey?" Bill's face was a mask. From his reaction, Felix thought, levitating and fire starting must be everyday occurrences. This guy was unpredictable. He'd gone ballistic over a harmless off-the-cuff remark about killing Jimmy. Meanwhile, flying and spontaneous combustion only warranted a thoughtful frown and increased tea consumption.

"Yeah," Felix answered.

"Allison Jasner?"

"Uh-huh."

"I didn't hear anything about a dorm going up in smoke. I assume she's okay?"

"She's fine." Felix ran his hand up and down the back of his head. It took him a moment to realize that something was different: the bump was gone. He rechecked. Couldn't find it. His fingers went to his forehead. No bump there either (and no pain). They were there this morning. Weren't they? Could they have healed? That fast? No. He didn't think so, anyway. So what did that mean? Did he imagine them? Were they even there in the first place?

"Where was her roommate?" Bill asked. "That's Caitlin, isn't it? Caitlin DuPont?"

It took Felix a moment to process the question because he was still trying to make sense of his unscathed skull. Then there was an abrupt shifting of gears as he tried to make sense of Bill's unsettling level of knowledge. "Yeah," he said finally. "Out with her parents doing something."

He didn't know Bill. Before today, he'd met him exactly twice. He knew nothing about him. But Bill—*Complete Stranger Bill*—seemed to know everything about him. He felt like his life had been hacked.

"Okay." Bill stroked his chin. "So Allison's the only one who witnessed what happened?"

"Yeah." Felix felt his shoulders tense up. Bill's questions were making him anxious. It was like taking a pop quiz he hadn't prepared for; being unconscious for the whole *event* put him at a slight disadvantage if Bill was hoping for a detailed account. And now that he couldn't find the lump on the back of his head, he wasn't so sure it had even really happened. He wondered if Allison had somehow imagined it. Or maybe she'd dreamed it. It was starting to feel a lot like no-man's-land all over again. All this I'm-not-sure-what's-real-and-what's-not bullshit was going to send him over the edge.

"And what did you tell her?" Bill stared at him, his eyes narrowing.

Felix waited for a second before answering. "Everything." He knew Bill wouldn't like that.

"*Why?*" Bill shouted. "You just jeopardized your life and put your friend in danger. This isn't a children's story! Just because we're the good guys doesn't mean we're going to win! In the real world, the bad guys win all the time. You need to think through—"

"What was I supposed to do?" Felix interrupted, his own temper rising. "She *saw* me. How would you explain that?"

"Fair point." Bill was already calm again. "You're right. Do you trust her?"

Felix nodded. "You must've told someone about the journal before."

"Never," Bill replied without hesitation, shaking his head. "It's not the kind of thing you can share unless you want to die unexpectedly. You look tired."

"I could use some sleep. And some food. Nothing's staying down lately."

"Tell me about it." Bill lowered his gaze to the floor next to Felix's chair. "Do you want me to order you something? A pizza? On me."

"I'm good." Felix picked at a callus on his palm, wondering if he should ask the question that had been gnawing at him. "So I was thinking about... what was she... like? My mom. You knew her, right?"

"I thought you might ask about her." Bill studied his teacup for a moment, his expression softening. "She was... well, she made quite an impression on me. I'll never forget her. She was beautiful. She was sad. And she was sick. Very sick. I didn't get to know her very well, but I can tell you one thing for certain: She loved you very much. When we met, she had no business being alive. Yet she willed herself to live. She held on until she knew that one day you'd find out who you are. She made me promise that I would tell you. And then she... passed on." He paused, and a shadow seemed to cross over his face as he looked toward the window. After a while, his attention returned to Felix but there was a troubled vagueness in his eyes. "And in case you're wondering, I see a lot of her in you."

Felix looked down at his lap. He felt something. But what? Sadness? Anger? Loss? He didn't know. He couldn't even think of her as his mom. It was just too weird. He already had a mom—and she was dead. And this new mom, she was dead too. Two moms. Both dead. Looking for a distraction, his eyes settled on a small army of kids out on the lawn fighting over a bright orange Frisbee in the warm afternoon sunshine.

"Fate was pretty shitty to her." Bill's voice was bitter. "She deserved better."

Felix didn't want to dwell on her. "Hey—so I was thinking: If I'm the only one who can defeat this Drestian guy, you gotta figure we're not gonna be friends. He'll wanna kill me, right? And I love how the journal describes him: 'Nations will burn, armies will fall at his feet, and all who refuse to succumb to his rule will be slaughtered like sheep'. That's pretty dramatic shit." He laughed to himself, thinking the exhaustion must be making him high. Why else would he be joking about something that amounted to a death sentence?

"How did you do that?" Bill placed his elbows on the table, arching an eyebrow. "That was verbatim."

"I could tell you the whole journal if I wanted. Every word."

"Interesting." Bill steepled his fingers. "And to answer your question... yes. Sorry. That's a helluva way to start your college career, isn't it?" He gave Felix a curious look and added: "But you seem to be handling it remarkably well."

Felix shrugged as if to say *what do you want me to do?* He was so wiped out from the events of the past day that he felt flat, almost incapable of emotion. Maybe he should be running around screaming like a lunatic. Maybe that's what most people would do. But he was just too tired to react like most people. And besides the fatigue, there was another factor at work: *skepticism.* His doubt was acting as a powerful sedative, dulling the sharp edges of his confusion and fear.

"Well, the good news is he doesn't know you exist," Bill told him.

"Lofton never knew about your mom, the Cycle, or the journal. But just to be safe, I erased your mom's life. There are no records for her. It's like she never was. I also erased your birth and adoption records. Your parents couldn't have proved you were adopted even if they'd wanted to."

"How'd you do all that?"

"A lot of well-spent money and knowing the right people. I covered all the bases. Lofton doesn't know you're his cousin. He doesn't know you're the Belus. You're safe. I've made sure of that."

"Then why's he in Portland? I thought he was British. What the hell's he doing here? That can't be a coincidence, right?"

Bill glanced at the window. "It is a coincidence."

"Seriously?"

"Seriously."

"But—"

"If Lofton knew you were here, you'd be dead," Bill told him in a firm voice. "Can we agree on that? You're obviously still alive. So he must not know you're here. Therefore, Lofton's presence in our fair city of roses is purely a coincidence."

"Oh." Bill's logic seemed flawless. Then again, Felix's brain was slogging along like his first car, a '99 Pontiac Bonneville that only made it a month before the engine seized up and died on him.

"But you don't need to worry about Lofton just yet," Bill said amiably. "You're not ready for that. And you won't be for a while. You look a little pale. You sure you don't want me to order you something? Chinese food? How about some juice? Your blood sugar's probably low."

"Nah. I'm gonna grab a burger." Felix pushed his chair out from the table and started to stand. He had more questions—a lot more—but a crushing wave of fatigue had risen up and crashed down on him.

"Okay." Bill dropped his eyes to the table, then brushed aside some imaginary dust. "I'll let you go. But before bed tonight, can you do me a favor? Try to relax, okay? If you melt another dorm room, people will start talking. Stick around for a minute and I'll show you a few things I find helpful when I feel like I'm about to lose it. It works." A flicker of a smile passed over his face. "Sometimes."

Chapter 33

SECRETS

It was just after eight o'clock. Downey's fourth floor was calm. Felix nodded at a guy whose name might be Aaron or Adam—or maybe it was Steve?—and stopped in front of his room. After gorging himself at the McDonald's on 1st Street—three double cheeseburgers, two large orders of fries and a large chocolate shake—he'd crashed on the couch in Woodrow's Room. The leather was soft and the windowless room was as quiet and dark as a cave. If some Native American ghosts had an issue with him being there, he figured it was worth the risk.

By now, he figured, Lucas and the girls had to be out partying and celebrating the end of midterms. He didn't want to party. He didn't want to hang out with anyone or do anything. He just wanted to hibernate in his bed for a few days and see what the world looked like when he woke up—it couldn't make any less sense than it did now. Then a terrible thought occurred to him and he paused, his hand on the doorknob: What if Lucas was hooking up with Piper or some other random chick? But it was too early in the night for that—he hoped. He opened the door.

The room erupted in an explosion of sound and light.

Felix was still a little groggy from his five hour nap. He stood there trying to work out what was going on. Allison, Caitlin, Lucas and Harper were all sitting on the floor, shouting raucously and clapping their hands. His first thought: *this isn't my birthday.* His second thought: *what the hell did they do to my room?* Colorful, shimmering streamers and ribbons, and garlands made up of glittered dots, slithered across the window and closets and hung from the ceiling like psychedelic hippie-inspired stalactites; green and orange helium balloons floated around in bunches, skirting along the ceiling, stalling at the corners; life-sized wall decals of NFLers—Tom Brady, Clay Matthews, J.J. Watt and Peyton Manning—plastered the walls (Brady and Manning were posed somewhat unconventionally, suggestive of acts you would never see on a football field); and in the back of the room, a wall-to-wall banner spelled out FOOTBALL HERO in huge silvery light-reflecting letters. Glittering streamers taped to the light fixture swayed in the wake of the balloon generated currents, casting the room in sparkly color-shifting light like a disco ball; one moment everything was blue, the next pink, the next orange.

"Felix!" Lucas shouted, springing to his feet, nearly tripping over a pair of cardboard boxes on the floor beside him. He crumpled up a grease splotched paper bag with a Taco Bell logo on it and tossed it in a waste basket by his closet. He came up to Felix with a big grin on his face, his arms held out wide.

Felix knew what was coming. "Really?" He smiled despite himself.

Lucas wrapped him up in a bear hug and pinned his arms to his sides, spinning him in a half-circle so that his back was to the girls. "Bring it in tight everyone!" Lucas ordered. "Group hug for our football hero!"

They converged on him. There were so many arms and bodies on Felix he felt like one of those unfortunate victims on *When Animals Attack*. The top of someone's head—Caitlin's?—was burrowing up his armpit. He started laughing. He couldn't help it. "Okay! Okay! I got it. You're mushing me. Get the hell off me, you freaks!"

Someone's lips pressed against his ear. It tickled. "You okay?" Allison's voice.

He nodded quickly and shouted: "We lost, you idiots! Get away from me!"

"That whole team thing's vastly overrated." Lucas let him go. "If those other Sturgeon dudes were half as good as you, you'd have won by fifty points."

"What do you think of the decorations?" Harper asked.

Felix looked at her and literally forgot what she'd just asked him. She was smiling. She was also wearing clothes that hugged every inch of her magnificent body, which had the effect of immediately improving his mood (and lifting his grogginess).

"They're great," he said vaguely. Then he came to his senses. "No they're not. This is crap for a kid's party. Where'd you get this shit?"

Everyone laughed.

"Caitlin and I went to a party store right after the game," Lucas explained. "And we may or may not have used your car without your permission. By the way, I think the Wrangler could die like any minute. It's not sounding so good. Could be terminal. Anyway, have a seat. C'mon. We got your chair ready for you." He pointed at five pillows arranged in a circle on the floor.

"What's in the boxes?" Felix asked, bending over to read the shipping labels.

"I'll get to that." Lucas sank into a pillow butt-first. "Take your seats!"

Felix hacked his way through the silky streamers and garlands and sat cross-legged on a pillow.

"Did you hear what happened to our room?" Caitlin asked Felix, sitting down next to him Japanese-style.

His head held down, Felix looked up through his eyebrows and saw Allison twitch, an almost imperceptible shake of her head. He felt a twinge of guilt as he said, "Uh-uh."

"There was a fire," Caitlin said excitedly. "I wasn't there. But oh my God." She looked at Allison. "Thank God you're okay." She put her hand over her heart, on the verge of tears.

"It wasn't really as scary as you might think." Allison's eyes moved to Felix. "I woke up smelling smoke, but the fire was already out."

"So you're okay?" Felix hoped he was showing the right amount of concern. His acting skills sucked.

Allison smiled and her eyes lit up like sparklers. "Never better." Then her smile faded and her forehead crinkled up with worry lines. "But I could kill Dr. Borakslovic. I hate that bitch."

"Who's that?" Felix asked. "Isn't she the skinny—"

"The dean," Allison said sourly. "At freshman orientation, remember that ugly hag who looked like she was going to tongue kiss Grayson? Her."

"Oh yeah," Felix said. "What'd she do?"

"She wanted to move us to Satler," Caitlin told him. "And she was insinuating that it was cigarettes. And since I wasn't there…"

"I could kill her!" Allison shouted. "And that's *after* the fire department came and said it was caused by faulty electrical wiring. And I don't smoke! If I did, I'd take a cigarette and burn out her eyes."

"But it all worked out." Caitlin gave Allison an alarmed look. "The school's paying for all the stuff that got damaged. *And* we got a room here."

"But it's on the first floor," Harper said, puckering her lower lip. "We're not neighbors anymore. I'm so sad."

What would it be like to kiss Harper? Felix wondered, staring at her mouth. That same thought had crossed his mind maybe fifty thousand times since he'd first met her.

Lucas clapped his hands together to get everyone's attention. It worked. Heads swiveled. "Are you done yet? You guys have been talkin' about the goddamn fire all day."

"Nobody said you had to hang out with us," Caitlin said hotly.

"You know you'd be lost without me, Little C. Ready?"

The girls nodded.

"For what?" Felix asked.

"I'm getting to that," Lucas said. "Okay. As you all know, most of our low-brow classmates are out getting wasted drunk right now at the frats and dorms. And while they're drinking nasty, watered-down, skunky beer out of unwashed recycled plastic cups, we're going to get wasted drunk like a bunch of fancy high society types."

Felix glanced at the boxes and wondered what was in them. Beer?

"Caitlin, if you will." Lucas made a grand sweeping gesture at the smaller of the two boxes, like a game show host revealing the hidden prize. "Please open it, my lovely assistant."

"I'm not your assistant," Caitlin said primly. Then she smiled. "But I am lovely." She pulled it toward her and started tugging futilely on a long piece of tape stuck to the top. She grunted. "I need scissors."

Lucas whispered to her: "It's already open. Just pass one to everybody."

"Oh. Duh." She spread apart the top flaps and reached in, coming out with a crystal wine glass in her hand.

"Ooooh!" Harper said admiringly, her eyes growing wide. "That's so pretty."

"It looks expensive," Allison said.

Caitlin held it up close to her face, appraising it. "It is. This stuff's really nice. Where'd you get this?"

"Are *you* directing this little fiesta?" Lucas said to her. "Just pass them out and limit the questions."

Caitlin sniffed and handed out the glasses.

Lucas flipped open the flaps of the larger box and pressed them down tightly against the sides.

"I know what's in there!" Caitlin leaned into Lucas, trying to peer over his arm.

Lucas removed a single piece of thick cream-colored stationery from the box and turned to her. "You're a genius. My money's on you for summa."

Caitlin raised her arm like she was going to backhand him.

"I like it rough." He waved the paper in Caitlin's face. "Do you mind? This is a note from David. My agent."

"Cool," Harper said excitedly. "What's it say?"

Lucas looked down at it. "Congratulations on Sota. I hope you like—"

"What's Sota?" Caitlin interrupted.

"I should've skipped that part," Lucas muttered. "Shit. You won't give up, will you?"

Caitlin shook her head.

"Fine. *Sota* is short for Minnesota. You know, it's the Sota in Minnesota."

"And…?" Harper said, prompting him to elaborate.

"It's a *cologne*." Lucas sounded like he was deeply embarrassed, but Felix couldn't tell if he was joking about the cologne, or if he was being serious about the cologne and feigning embarrassment, or if he was serious about the cologne and actually embarrassed. Lucas was a tough kid to read sometimes.

"Sota the cologne?" Caitlin said, clearly confused. Then her eyes got really big. "Shut up! Shut up! You've got to be kidding. *You* have your own cologne? That's ridiculous!"

"Seriously?" Felix said.

Lucas started laughing. "You wanna hear the tag line?" He paused to clear his throat. "'Experience the mystery and lifestyle of Minnesota.'"

"The *mystery* of Minnesota?" Harper said, laughing.

"And *lifestyle*," Lucas wailed. "Don't forget the lifestyle!" He fell on his back, laughing like a maniac.

And then everyone joined in. Felix had never known anyone whose laughter was so wonderfully contagious. And in spite of his current state, and to his surprise, he laughed like everyone else. Allison was watching him closely, smiling at him, apparently pleased that he was outwardly functioning like his normal self.

"Can I finish now?" Lucas rolled back onto his pillow and sat up, then picked the note up from off the floor and began reading again: "Okay—so congratulations on Sota. Blah, blah, blah. I hope you like wine. Blah, blah, blah. I encourage you to drink at least one bottle and do something newsworthily stupid. Blah, blah, blah. Enjoy. David. That's it." He reached his hand into the box and started taking out bottles, handing two to Harper, two to Caitlin and keeping one for himself. "Pass them around," he directed. "One per person. You heard the guy."

When Allison got hers, she ran her finger over the top. "Is there a corkscrew?"

"Three." Lucas tossed her one. "David thought of everything. He's like a miracle worker."

"My parents drink this sometimes." Caitlin turned her bottle over in her hands, eyeing the label like a sommelier. "This is like a two-hundred-dollar bottle of wine, you know. And there's twelve in there."

"You're kidding." Allison uncorked her bottle with a resounding *pop* and then handed her opener to Felix. Their eyes met. She looked concerned for a second. Then she smiled. Felix wondered if she was expecting him to do something. He gave her a little smile and shrugged, trying to let her know, that all things considered, he was doing all right.

"Why so surprised?" Lucas said. "This is how Minnesota rolls. This is what's called experiencing the mystery and lifestyle of Minnesota."

Allison threw her cork at Lucas and it bounced off his forehead. "And that's what I call throwing a cork at Minnesota's head," she said proudly.

"Nice shot, Allison," Caitlin said. "You're such a dork, Lucas."

Lucas just grinned.

"What in the world are you doing?" Harper asked Felix with an appalled look on her face. "You're not supposed to kill it."

Felix had already gouged his finger with the corkscrew and was thoroughly destroying the cork. "I've never opened a bottle of wine before. I'm from Coos Bridge, remember? We drink cheap beer in the woods."

"Need help?" Harper reached out for the bottle.

"I got it." Allison snatched it away from Felix. "Someone has to represent our town or everyone will think we were raised in caves." Harper shrank back to her pillow as Allison uncorked the bottle and handed it back to him.

Lucas clapped his hands and rubbed them together in anticipation, looking all around. "We're going to play a game. If anyone doesn't want to participate, you can leave and go find some new friends. We'll do this in stages. Stage one is drinking a glass of fancy wine. So pour yourself a big glass."

Everyone did.

"Now chug it," Lucas commanded.

"Chug it?" Harper sounded surprised. "I thought we were being fancy high society types?"

Lucas shook his head. "The wine's fancy. We're not. We're in college. Chug it." He lifted his glass to his mouth and started gulping it down.

Felix took a sip. It was smooth, rich and smoky—nothing at all like the wine he'd had with his parents occasionally at dinner. He took a bigger drink. Everybody was drinking, and drinking fast. He took two big gulps and swallowed it down. It was really good. When he finished, he rested the crystal glass on his lap and wiped his mouth. Only Caitlin had any left. He watched as she tilted her glass and quickly drained the last little bit.

"I didn't know wine could taste like that," Felix said.

Everyone was smiling. And because of the way the streamers were shifting around and brushing against the ceiling light, their teeth all appeared green.

"Pour another glass," Lucas said. "It's stage two. Time to play the game."

"This is so much fun!" Caitlin filled her glass with the dark red liquid. "What's the game?"

Lucas filled his own glass. "I call it the secret game. It's all about sharing your deepest, darkest, most intimate secrets."

"Like what?" Allison gave Felix an apprehensive glance.

"Could be anything," Lucas explained. "But if it's not deep, dark, or intimate, you get a *fail*. And if you fail, you have to do it again."

Caitlin frowned. "But who decides what—?"

"I decide," Lucas said bluntly. "I'm the judge. I'll be fair, but you can't argue my decisions. If you don't agree with the rules, you know where the door is. Everyone in?"

No one objected.

"This is gonna be so awesome!" Lucas grinned wide. "But I'll fail your asses if your secrets suck. And you can't leave the room until you get a pass."

"I live here." Felix laughed. He wasn't unaware of the fact that he was commenting on the taste of the wine—and enjoying the wine—and laughing and joking around like nothing out of the ordinary had recently happened. But what was he supposed to do? Go back to Woodrow's Room and hide for the rest of the semester?

"That threat wasn't meant so much for you." Lucas smiled.

Allison took a huge gulp of wine. "So who's going first?"

"I'm the judge," Lucas said slowly, sitting up straight. He held out his hand, palm turned up, like a statue of a Roman senator delivering some grand speech. "I make the rules." He paused. "The lucky bastard who gets to start us off is... drum roll please... Lucas Mayer. Me. I'll go."

"This better be good," Caitlin told him.

"I do everything good," Lucas replied.

"I think you mean *well*," Caitlin corrected.

"Step off, Little C." Lucas brought his glass up to his nose and gave it a big sniff before swallowing down another mouthful. "Well here goes.

Whose idea was this, anyway?" He laughed. "What was I thinking? Okay. So then. Well—"

"Get on with it," Allison heckled. "C'mon!"

Lucas cupped his glass in both hands and stared straight ahead. A string of personalized balloons (FELIX was scrawled out in glittery gold letters) suddenly dropped from the ceiling and he swatted them away. "I was held back in the first grade," he said, looking at their faces. "I had to take it twice. And I got special-ed all through high school."

After a long silence, Caitlin said, "Why?"

"I'm dyslexic." Lucas turned to face her.

"Is that the reading thing?" Felix asked.

Lucas nodded. "For me, yeah. So in first grade, I didn't have trouble with anything else. You know math or coloring or whatever you do when you're six. But I couldn't read or spell for shit. My teacher didn't catch on for almost the whole year, and I think my parents were in denial. But then the school got involved and wouldn't let me go to the next grade. My parents had me tested and they figured out I have dyslexia."

"That must've been really tough," Harper said.

"It was embarrassing," Lucas replied thoughtfully. "The word just sounds so bad: *Dyslexia*. It sounds like some awful STD or something. But it really just means I have a little trouble with reading and writing."

"Then you got help?" Allison asked.

"Uh-huh. Once everyone knew what the problem was, it wasn't a big deal. I met with a specialist a few times a month through high school. It's really not an issue now. It just takes me a little longer to read and write. It doesn't help on tests. That's for sure."

"You told your profs, didn't you?" Caitlin said.

Lucas shook his head sharply. "Hell no."

"Why not?" Caitlin said, surprised. "They'd give you extra time. I think they have to. I think it's a law or school policy or something."

Lucas filled his glass and then Caitlin's. "I didn't tell my profs, and I'm not going to. I don't want special treatment. I don't have a disability. If I can't do something as good—*as well*—as everyone else, it's on me to improve. I don't want to play by a different set of rules."

"I can't believe how much I respect you right now." Caitlin shook her head in wonderment. "What's wrong with me? I hope I'm not getting sick."

Lucas smiled at her. "I wouldn't get used to it."

"Here's to Lucas." Allison raised her glass in a toast. "If anyone deserves to have their own cologne, it's him. Cheers." They touched glasses and drank.

Lucas did a little bow. "Okay, okay, if everyone's done basking in my greatness, I'll give myself a pass. Next up is our own football hero. A dude who's so fast you have to wonder if he's gonna take flight... Felix August."

"My turn?" Felix tensed up like a cat getting ready to pounce. "Okay. Let's see..." *What can I tell them? How about, I'm the Belus. If I don't defeat the Drestian, all of you and the rest of the world will either be dead or his slaves. And the Drestian, in case you're wondering, is Lofton Ashfield. You know, the richest man in the world. No. How about, hey guys, I was immaculately conceived. That would go over well. The St. Rose Ghost? The cemetery below campus? Or how about, I actually have no idea if I'm sane or not. Nah. I could tell them about...* "I got one."

"Okay," Lucas said eagerly. "Let's hear it."

Felix gulped down half his glass. "So after the game, I was in the bathroom. And then... um... Jimmy Clay—you know who he is, right?"

"The huge steroid freak," Lucas said.

"Yeah. So out of nowhere he jumps me and hits me in the stomach."

Caitlin nodded hesitantly.

"And then what...?" Harper asked.

"It hurt like hell!" Felix shouted.

Lucas shook his head disapprovingly. "Am I gonna have to explain the rules to you again? Your secret has to be deep, dark or intimate. Jimmy's done that to like fifty kids in the last week. He's an animal. They should put him in a cage. But so what?"

"Really?" Felix said. *No pass?* But Jimmy attacked him and threw him in a pool of piss. It was humiliating and disgusting. "You're not gonna..."

"Sorry, dude," Lucas said. "Fail. Fail. Fail. I think you should drink the rest of your bottle while you think about the consequences of your actions." He smiled. "Okay. Next up, hailing from the same town as the kid whose secret really, really sucked is... Allison Jasner!"

"Yay!" Caitlin cheered, clapping one hand against her crystal.

Allison looked around the room nervously. "Wow. This is harder than I thought it'd be. Okay then. Whew. Well, do you guys remember when we first met? Our first night. We were right here in this room talking about the Faceman. Remember?"

"You don't look anything like the Faceman," Lucas told her. "So if you're trying to confess to the murders, don't bother."

"Is it because I have a nose and both ears?" Allison smiled anxiously. "We were talking about who was an only child. And I... I lied. I told you guys I have two sisters. I don't. I mean, I have two sisters. But they're not my real sisters. I was adopted." She looked first right then left to make sure everyone was listening. They were. No one was going to miss this. "My parents died in a car crash when I was six. CPS took me because I didn't have any other family. I was shipped around a lot. Lots of different schools. Lots of group homes. Lots of different people. And then the Jasners adopted me when I was fourteen. So I'm a… I'm a foster kid."

"No shit," Lucas said in a low voice.

"I can't even imagine how terrible that must've been." Caitlin dabbed at her tears. "I had no idea. You were such a little girl. I'm so sorry."

"It's nobody's fault, and there's nothing to be sorry about." All nervousness was gone from Allison's voice now. "I was never treated badly. There were a few places that, well… they treated me fine, but let's just say I didn't feel much love. But the Jasners are great. I love my mom and dad. My sisters are pretty awful, but I'm just glad to be where I'm at. It could've been much worse." She smiled and added: "And that's that."

"Pass!" Lucas looked up from the bottle he'd just uncorked. "No brainer. Definite pass." He poured himself a little and then topped off Harper. "Okay, here we go again with this year's déjà vu entrant, Felix August. Remember: deep, dark or intimate. Make me proud."

"Okay. This one's good."

Allison gave him a look.

"So you guys know that in high school I dated the same girl for like the last three years?"

"Emma?" Lucas said.

"Uh-huh." Felix looked down at his hands. "So I told everyone—or at least Lucas anyway—that I broke up with her. But the truth is, she um… she broke up with me." He looked up.

No one was impressed.

"Felix, Felix, Felix," Lucas said softly, shaking his head.

"Wait!" Felix raised a hand in protest. "It gets better. Well, worse, actually. I never told anyone *why* she dumped me. I don't even think Allison knows and she's sort of friends with her. So a few weeks after graduation, we were at this party at the lake. Emma had a few wine coolers in her, and she came up to me and said she wanted to talk. She had this look on her face. She was so… sure of herself. So confident. She told me that… that I was like everyone else in that shitty little hick town. That I was going to flunk out of college and be back watching football games on Friday nights with my loser friends talking about the glory days. She said she was going to do something with her life. She was going to be somebody. She had to leave me behind because I was going to drag her down. If she stayed with me, she'd end up living in a trailer eating Cheetos and drinking beer at the bowling alley. She said I was one step removed from white trash. And I guess that um… I guess maybe I believed her."

"Oh my God!" Harper burst out. "That's terrible. What a bitch!"

Allison emptied her glass and reached for her bottle. "The next time I see her, I'm going to tear her lungs out. And just so you know, I'll never talk to her again. I haven't even heard from her since last summer. And she was always about the big city. She's in Seattle now, and she thinks she's all cool. She always talked about living in New York or London. That's just how she is." She held up her empty bottle. "Hey Sota. Can you get me another one of these? This stuff's delicious."

Lucas filled Felix's glass and then handed the bottle to Allison. "Sometimes losing something is the best thing that can ever happen to you." He clanked his glass against Felix's and took a long drink. "And I'll give Allison a hand if she needs help removing that bitch's lungs."

"Don't get me wrong. I've been over her for a long time." Felix glanced at Harper, hoping she might be smiling, but her glass was to her lips and he couldn't see her face. "But getting dumped is kinda embarrassing. Especially when they do it like that."

"I wouldn't know." Lucas grinned. "Okay, so this time, I'm giving Felix a… pass! Next up, we have, okay, let's see, looks like I'm down to the two California chicks. I'm gonna go with… Caitlin DuPont. You're up, Little C."

"It's a good thing I'm drunk. This is hard. Geesh." Caitlin took a deep breath. "Okay. So my secret isn't dark, and it isn't intimate, but it is deep. Wait—maybe it is intimate! Oh, I don't know. Whatever. You better give me a pass!" She made a face at Lucas to make sure he knew she was being serious. "Okay. Here goes. I'm a… I'm a virgin."

The room went silent.

Felix spoke first. "Wow. Really?"

"Good for you," Allison said.

"Thanks." Caitlin was looking at Lucas like she expected him to make a wiseass remark. Felix was definitely expecting Lucas to make a wiseass remark. How could he pass up on an opportunity like this?

"Go on," Lucas said without even a hint of a smile, all business. "You're gonna need to do more than that to get a pass."

Caitlin groaned. "Fine. So what do you want to know? I can tell you…" She hesitated. "Okay, so I'll tell you why I'm a virgin."

"I think we know why," Lucas quipped.

"That's not what I meant, dummy. So anyway, I decided a few years ago that I wouldn't have sex until I'm married. And it's not because of religious reasons or anything like that. I'm Catholic. But so is Harper. And she's not a virgin."

"*Caitlin!*" Harper shrieked. "Hey!"

"I'm sorry." Caitlin ducked her head apologetically. "I didn't mean it like that. That came out all wrong."

Harper laughed. "I'm just kidding, dear. It's okay."

"What I was trying to say," Caitlin went on, "is that I won't have sex until I'm married because my virginity is a gift. I can only give it away once. It's special. And the person who receives it should be the man I spend the rest of my life with. I know that makes me seem old-fashioned. But, well, that's just how I feel."

"That's how I feel, too," Lucas deadpanned. "I'm saving my special little gift for the woman I marry."

"I take back everything I said about how much I respect you!" Caitlin snapped, scowling.

"That hurts," Lucas said, clearing imaginary tears from his eyes. "But seriously. Why don't you marry me, Little C? I'll cherish your special little gift. I'll cradle it and treasure it and—"

"I hate you!" Caitlin jumped up from her pillow and threw herself on top of him. Lucas rolled onto his side, laughing hysterically. "I seriously hate you so much!" Caitlin squealed. "Why can't you be normal like everyone else?" When she finally got up, she fixed her hair and stumbled back to her pillow, embarrassed, but trying not to show it. Then she glared at Lucas. "I better get a pass!"

Lucas sat up, still giggling like a little boy. "Yes, my lovely little treasure keeper, you passed. Okay, who's next? Harper, right? Harper Connolly, you're next. Who needs wine?"

Caitlin and Felix raised their glasses. Felix was drinking it like water. Not only was the wine the best thing he'd ever tasted, the alcohol was numbing his mind, mellowing him out, calming his nerves. There hadn't been nearly enough time to assimilate everything that had happened to him, to think it all through, and now he felt less pressure, less necessity, to make sense of it all. The wine was exactly what he needed.

Lucas uncorked two bottles, passed them around, and said to Harper, "Make it good."

"Give me some of that." Harper reached for Caitlin's bottle, filled her glass and took a big drink. "So my secret is a secret, because, well, I don't tell people about it. I know that sounds brilliant." She laughed nervously. "And I haven't told anyone because it makes me seem shallow and superficial, and like I'm not such a good person."

That got everyone's attention.

"So anyway, you know how sometimes we talk about the thing that scares us the most? People say stuff like drowning, or clowns, or spiders, or shit like that, right? Well, the thing that scares me the most is growing old. Just the idea of growing old freaks me out. I honestly can't even really understand or… um… how do I say this? I can't imagine myself being old. You know, like, I can't picture someone asking me how old I am, and me saying, 'I'm thirty'. And it's not the part about dying that scares me. But for some reason, when I think of being older, I have this feeling I'm in somebody else's body. I just feel like, and I know this sounds weird, but I feel like I was always meant to be young." She looked right at Felix and smiled.

He smiled back.

"That probably means I have some kind of major psychological issues," Harper went on. "I guess I'll have to deal with that later. I mean, I do understand I won't be eighteen forever. I'm not crazy or anything. I guess I'm just a little vain. Maybe I'm just a stupid girl. I like girl power anthems, and shoes, and handbags and *Sex and the City*. And I can't imagine not liking those things. In fact, I can't even remember a time when I didn't like those things. It's like I was born at fifteen. But now… now I'm afraid if I'm fifty and I haven't changed, I'll be kind of pathetic. I don't know. I am what I am. Sorry. I hope you guys still like me."

"Are you kidding?" Lucas said. "Weren't you listening? I'm illiterate. Nobody wanted Allison. Felix got dumped because he's white trash. And there isn't a single guy in the whole world who'll have sex with Caitlin. You're just the Kardashian of the group. Every group needs one of those."

Harper smiled.

"And you passed," Lucas told her. "More wine anyone? I'm making a new rule: no one leaves until the room's dry. Bottoms up!"

Chapter 34

WHAT THE CAT DRAGGED IN

Caitlin dropped her tray on the table noisily and stuffed a cherry tomato in her mouth before sitting down. She chewed it up and swallowed, and without looking up, popped in another one.

"What's up with her?" Felix asked Harper. He nearly had to shout to be heard. The cafeteria was packed. When it was raining, like now, the kids living in Downey tended to stay in for dinner, and stay longer than usual; given the number of rainy days so far this semester, some were already well on their way to packing on the dreaded 'freshman fifteen'.

Felix was feeling fairly stable—for the moment. His stability levels were constantly in flux, a fact that had shadowed his day-to-day since the night Bill had showed him the journal. Despite what the calendar said, the past two weeks had felt like one endless night. Sometimes he fared pretty well, getting through the days like a normal college kid, and other times he couldn't rein in his wandering, questioning mind and it challenged his sanity at every turn. He tried to put his thoughts on lockdown, to stay in the present, but it was an arduous task. Conversations, in particular, were a slippery beast. There were times—entire days on occasion—when the only way he could keep up was to ask everyone to repeat themselves. He'd said "huh?" and "what?" so often, he wondered if his friends thought he might be suffering from hearing loss. Allison, of course, knew what was going on, and where his head really was.

He watched her across the table casually cutting up fingerling potatoes and a side of string beans. He was envious. Allison was a rock, an actor extraordinaire; Felix's incineration of her room didn't seem to affect her behavior at all. Must be nice, he thought enviously, to be able to compartmentalize like that.

Caitlin was in a dour mood. She was turning her fork over and over and staring at her food like it had just called her a Republican.

"She got a B on her Political Science midterm," Harper said by way of explanation.

"Oh." Felix didn't see the connection.

Lucas swallowed a mouthful of chicken cutlet. "So what are you so pissed about?"

"What am I pissed about?" Caitlin shouted, snapping out of her stupor. "I killed that exam! I'm pretty sure that… that… maybe the prof made a mistake. Maybe she gave me the wrong grade."

"Did you get it back?" Allison asked her. "You could check."

"I already did." Looking discouraged, Caitlin ate another tomato. "But I still think she screwed it up somehow. Maybe the stupid TA graded it. He looks like *The Kid With The Hood* anyway."

Felix blinked. *The Kid With The Hood.* That's what everyone was calling the dorm invader. How would Caitlin react if she knew that she was sharing a salt shaker with *The Kid With The Hood?* Probably not very well. He'd first noticed the posters on the community boards inside the Student Center about a month ago and now they were all over campus. The posters were an artist's rendering of a man's face, a man wearing a hood, and below the face was a caption that read: Please Contact Campus Security If You See This Man. Everyone knew that the guy on the poster had broken into a dorm room in Astoria Hall—room 444—but the posters had become a campus-wide joke and were frequently the subject of clever satirization in *The Weekly Sturgeon*, which implicated the school's administrators and professors, including President Taylor and Dr. Borakslovic, in the mysterious dorm room invasion. The sketch was so bad—the hood concealed everything but the mouth and chin—it could have been just about anyone between the ages of fifteen and a 110.

Lucas grinned at Caitlin. "It's awesome that you're finally taking out your anger on those vegetables 'cause you know it's totally their fault you didn't get an A." He cut up some chicken and added: "You know what your problem is?"

"Oh do tell," Caitlin sighed wearily.

"Expectations. You'd be much more at peace with yourself if you didn't aim so high. I've always said the key to success is low expectations. I'm full of wise sayings like that if you take the time to get to know me."

"I don't like you," Caitlin said sourly, forking a cucumber slice.

"Getting a B's pretty good," Felix offered.

"No shit," Lucas agreed. "I got one B, two C's and an A, and you don't see me acting all homicidal at my dinner."

"That's exactly what I got," Felix replied. He'd hoped to do better, but he could live with being in the chunkiest part of the bell curve.

"What'd you get the A in?" Allison asked him.

"Psychology."

Allison looked surprised. "I thought you said you bombed that one. Isn't that Professor Malone's class? He's supposed to be a tough grader. I know a girl in your class who's super smart and she got a B minus."

"Sucks for her." Felix shrugged. "I thought I did okay on it. I didn't think he'd give me an A, but I'm not gonna ask him about it. How'd you do?"

Allison grinned sheepishly. "Okay."

Caitlin looked up from her plate. "All A's. Congrats."

"Good job," Harper said.

"Thanks."

"Speaking of straight A wonder children," Lucas said, chewing on a french fry, "did you all hear about the girl in Arizona? Gabriela something? They just found her body in the desert."

Everyone nodded. It had been all over the news.

"I guess that puts things in perspective," Caitlin muttered guiltily. "I'm all upset about a dumb test, and this girl in Arizona—Gabriela Conseco—was shot in the face six times by the Faceman. And she was such an amazing girl. Did you read about her? Four point student. Captain of the volleyball team. She built houses for the homeless in Nicaragua during the summers. And they said she'd gotten into Yale."

Allison put her fork down and said grimly, "She was only seventeen, just a year younger than us. All that potential. And in an instant, a goddamn serial killer took it all away. I wish they'd catch that bastard."

"It's terrible," Felix said in a low voice. "I can't imagine what it'd be like if the Faceman was pointing his gun at you. Talk about a nightmare."

"It blows," Lucas said. "When they catch him, they should shoot *him* in the face six times. Let the punishment fit the crime."

"That's the last thing they should do." Caitlin shook her head vigorously. "The government shouldn't be permitted to kill anyone. He should be locked up for the rest of his life. I think if the government did something about all the guns out there Gabriela might still be alive."

"You've gotta be kidding!" Lucas exclaimed. "He deserves to die! And banning guns wouldn't prevent that psycho from killing people. You're nuts if you think that..."

Felix glanced around the cafeteria to see if Lucas's shouting had caused heads to turn, but no one was paying any attention to them. No one could hear them. The room wasn't designed with acoustics in mind, so the roaring background din of a few hundred boisterous students—laughter, loud conversations, cutlery scraping against porcelain, and the *clankety-clanking* of kids stacking and setting aside dishes and glasses at the clean-up stations—went bouncing and reverberating off the wall panels instead of the wall panels absorbing the collection of sounds.

"Come on you two," Harper said mildly. "If I'd known you were going to get into the merits of capital punishment and tighter gun control laws, I'd have eaten in my room."

"Totally agree with that." Felix smiled at her.

Harper returned the smile, holding it a second longer than he was comfortable with. She still made him nervous sometimes.

"You're right," Lucas said brightly. "I can convince her of the error of her liberal ways later."

"I *really* don't like you," Caitlin grumbled. "Seriously."

"You know you love me. Oh—I almost forgot! I wanted to show you guys something." Lucas reached under the table, fumbled around in his backpack for a moment, and with a "ta-da" came away with a cylindrical container with a blue and white label which he held up for everyone to see.

"What the hell's that?" Felix asked, as Lucas placed it next to his plate.

Allison read the label out loud: "Super-Six-Pack-Power-Protein-Plus. Hey! It's that S-S-P-P-P-P stuff!"

"I just got it today." Lucas was grinning like he was up to something. "I thought we could all try it out. You know, see if you guys like it."

"Cool!" Harper said.

"And if we like it," Allison said to him, squinting hard to read the label, "you'll agree to endorse it?"

Lucas looked at her like she'd lost her mind. "And *you* got straight A's? Talk about grade inflation. I'm already endorsing it."

"*What?*" Caitlin said, surprised. "I thought—"

"I agreed to *try* it. I never said I had to like it. Money's in the bank."

Caitlin plucked up her fork. From the look on her face, and the way she was holding it, she was seriously thinking about skewering Lucas's hand—or some other body part.

"Well, I think it's cool he's at least trying it," Felix said to Caitlin, hoping to defuse the situation before they launched into round 322 of their year-long bickering session. "And I'm sure it'll be good. It's just protein powder. How bad could it be?"

"Exactly!" Lucas said. "See! Felix knows what's up. Allison has a four point, but we got common sense." He popped off the plastic cover and peeled away the aluminum liner beneath it. He leaned forward and submerged his nose into the container, giving it a sniff. Then he jerked his head back like he'd been blasted in the eyes with pepper spray and pushed it away, nearly knocking it over.

"Oh God!" Lucas gasped, making a face like he'd walked in on his parents having sex. "That smells... a... a little *funky*. Whadya think?" He retrieved it, holding it up so Felix could get a whiff.

"Ewwwwww!" Felix covered his nose, and yanked his face away from the container. It was absolutely rancid, a mixture of sour milk and foot fungus. "Cat piss! I mean, seriously. My grandma had this old cat with a kidney problem that pissed all over the house. And that"—he pointed at the S-S-P-P-P-P—"smells just like her house."

Caitlin crossed her arms, looking smug and self-satisfied. "I hope your cologne smells just like it. Then everyone can experience the *mystery and lifestyle* of smelling like cat urine. Not that you'd care. Drink up, wise old sage."

"Kinda serves you right," Allison said, laughing. "Maybe next time, you'll actually try the product. Now you're the face of protein powder that smells like piss."

Lucas put the cover back on the container and slipped it into his backpack. "Ah well." He shrugged. "Live and learn, right? Wow, that stuff's disgusting. I'd love to try it just to shut you guys up, but I'm pretty sure I'd toss my cookies."

"Please don't," Caitlin told him, her expression serious. "I'm not interested in substituting my vinaigrette for your vomit."

"Anyone else not in the mood to go to the library?" Harper sank back in her chair and looked around the table. "Wanna watch a movie in my room? My weirdo roommate's out again with her weirdo boyfriend."

"Sounds good," Lucas said. "I don't need an excuse not to study."

"I'm in," Caitlin said.

Allison nodded. "Sure."

Shit, Felix thought, staring down helplessly at his half-eaten plate of pasta, trying to decide what to tell her. He knew that he should have concocted something in advance, but he hadn't had a minute to himself all day. And now that he was on the spot, his mind was drawing a blank.

"Felix?" Harper said expectantly. "We can even watch some mindless Dirk Rathman action flick if you want. You in?"

Felix smiled in an attempt to conceal his consternation. "I can't," he muttered.

"Sorry?" Harper said, tilting her head in surprise. "Why not? You have something better to do?"

"I... I uh... I need to study. I'm really behind in Psychology. Malone gave the class like a hundred pages to read, and I haven't even started." That made no sense whatsoever. *Stupid.*

Harper's face flushed, her jaw tightened. "You can't be serious. Finals are like a month away, and Malone just gave you an A. You're killing that class."

Felix didn't know what to say. He shifted around uncomfortably in his chair, started to mumble something, and ended up looking down at his plate.

"I don't get it," Harper said, the anger in her voice apparent to everyone at the table. "Why would you go to the library when the rest of us are—"

"Hey!" Allison snapped, her eyes flashing. "Why are you jumping down his throat? He wants to freakin' study. Cut him some slack!"

"Chill out!" Harper snapped back. "I didn't jump down his throat."

Felix sat there silently, embarrassed. No one spoke for a good minute.

"Well go study!" Harper shouted at him. Now she was really fired up. "You have pages to read, don't you?"

Without making eye contact with anyone, Felix gathered his things and got up from the table. He made his way out of the cafeteria, berating himself for not having prepared a better excuse. Just when he reached the lobby, he heard Allison calling his name.

"What's going on?" she whispered, once she'd caught up to him. "You're not really studying, are you?"

Felix looked around to make sure nobody could hear them. A few students were playing pool and watching TV in the common room, but no one within earshot. "I'm meeting Bill at midnight at some old building in the Old Campus."

"The *dead campus?*" Allison's eyes grew large. "Why?"

"He wants me to start training."

"Training?" She paused. "Oh. You mean—"

"To use the Source," he said, as quietly as he could.

Allison's eyes lit up. "Really? What are you gonna do?"

He shook his head. "Guess I'll find out."

She smiled. "I'm jammed up all day tomorrow, but swing by my room before dinner, okay?"

"Hey, Allie, do you think Harper is... you think... she seems pretty mad. You think she's all right? I'm such a shitty liar."

Allison shrugged, still smiling. "That was pretty bad. Don't worry. She's just a little moody. She'll get over it. Probably already has."

Chapter 35

THE DEAD CAMPUS

On a cold late autumn night, Felix slogged his way toward the Old Campus, holding his umbrella out in front like a shield, trying to stay dry, which wasn't an easy thing to do because the rain was falling in relentless sheets, hitting him sideways. He'd killed time at the Caffeine Hut studying (unsuccessfully), drinking coffee (until his hands began to tremor), fretting over Harper (she'd overreacted but he didn't blame her), and kicking himself for being such an idiot (his mom used to say she could tell when he was lying even before he opened his mouth—his body language gave him away).

The conditions weren't exactly ideal for a midnight stroll. He followed a desolate path past the Student Center and the buildings beyond it to the west, through a grove of firs and a little garden full of stones, grass and statues, and over a creek—the Mill Stream—that drew its waters from a natural spring. Then he saw it: Tucked behind stone fortifications like a medieval fortress, the pitched rooflines of six enormous buildings came into view—the Old Campus. Although the architecture was similar to the rest of the campus, the Old Campus buildings, adorned with towers, spires, roofs, sub-roofs, chimneys, peaks and gables, had been finished with more of an artistic flourish.

He leaned into a stiff headwind, frequently peeking over the umbrella to see where he was in relation to the stone walls (and to make sure he didn't smash his face into another lamppost). Each time he stole a glance, the buildings drew nearer until finally he reached the eastern wall and began searching for the entrance. On his trips to the stadium, the gate had seemed prominent enough, and he was sure he knew where it was. But he'd never looked for it in a rainstorm in the dead of night. Eventually he found it, but not before going in the wrong direction and having to double back.

He dug his free hand deeper into the pocket of his jacket and slipped through the unlatched iron gate, then headed toward the center of the Old Campus along a dismally-lit brick walkway. The antique light posts may have been cutting edge in the nineteenth century, but now they were dreadfully inadequate, illuminating just pockets of the meandering path and the patchy threadbare grass next to it. The buildings remained in the shadows, the darkened husks standing guard like ominous, malevolent sphinxes.

The wind was ferocious, thrashing his umbrella, straining his grip on the curved handle. Low-hanging branches stretched across the path, slithering like the tentacles of a giant sea monster. Buildings on either side— front doors padlocked, warning signs nailed to the doors cautioning people to stay out—watched him hurrying along, looming in pools of eerie wind- shifting shadows. The buildings reminded him of tombstones; their windows, black soulless eyes.

The Old Campus had never inspired much thought or curiosity for Felix. It just sat there. He'd seen it from a distance a hundred times, and from that vantage point, despite the odd calmness of the place—only birds seemed to go there—it somehow blended right in, just another part of campus, no different than the dorms or lecture halls. But inside the walls everything looked different. This was not PC. It was as if the rusting iron gate was a threshold that transported unwary visitors through space and time to a different place, a place with no connection at all to PC. Felix felt like an intruder, like his presence was stirring up bitter, resentful feelings. He remembered Lucas talking about how scared his brother had been when he came through here after losing a bet—how he felt like something wanted to kill him. The story seemed funny at the time. But now Felix could relate. Being here was unnerving. Right out of a slasher movie. Maybe this was where the St. Rose Ghost lurked when she wasn't haunting the Star Trees and luring kids into the tunnels beneath the chapel. He glanced over his shoulder to see if she was trailing after him. The possibility of it didn't seem so foolish. Not at all.

He tried not to think about her glowing green eyes, or the thousands of bodies buried in the secret cemetery. This wasn't the best place to dwell on ghosts and hidden graves. But her voice was inside his head, and he could hear it as clearly as if she was whispering the words in his ear: *I want you to find your truth. The choice is yours.* It made his skin crawl, though he still had no idea what it meant. Assuming, of course, that he hadn't imagined it.

He made it to the center building without encountering the St. Rose Ghost, or anyone else, living or dead, and for the first time, he noticed the quiet stillness. It was as though the high walls encircling the Old Campus had somehow magically insulated it from the sounds of the modern world. *Why couldn't Bill have chosen someplace else to do this?* he wondered. *Even the tunnels would be better than—*

"Felix," a voice hissed from behind.

He gasped and spun around.

"It's me." Bill emerged from the darkness, his face shrouded in shadows from the umbrella he was holding.

"You scared the shit outta me!" Felix said, his voice shaky.

"Sorry. Nobody comes around here, especially at night. But we can't be too careful. Come on, follow me."

Bill led him past the front entrance—chiseled into the stone façade above the padlocked double doors were the words INVERNESS HALL—and around to the side of the building where they stopped at a door badly in need of a new coat of paint. Bill quickly inserted a key into the keyhole, unlocking the door with a loud *click*.

Felix flinched at the sound.

"It's okay," Bill assured him. "Get in." Bill pushed the door open a crack and held it for him, locking it behind them once they were in.

It was even darker inside. The air was cool and musty. Felix's eyes strained to make out his surroundings. The ancient building was as dark as a tomb. It was like being submerged in a tarpit, a sea of oil. But as he stood there waiting for his eyes to start working, to adjust to the gloom, he became aware that a tiny amount of pale yellow light was filtering through the dirty windowpanes. He was standing in a long narrow hallway with doors on either side. He shook his umbrella dry and stowed it away in his backpack.

In a low voice, Bill said, "This way."

Felix felt somewhat conscious of being alone with Bill, a virtual stranger, in a dead campus building, but that was far less concerning than what they were presently doing. If campus security showed up, Lucas would have their dorm room all to himself; the administration likely frowned upon breaking into buildings, and he was willing to bet his life that it constituted a violation of the Student Code of Conduct, even though he, and every student who'd ever attended PC, had never read it.

They proceeded slowly down the hallway, the old wooden floors creaking loudly with each step. Something scurried along the floor up ahead, making scratching noises. Felix wasn't rat-phobic, but he would definitely flip out (and maybe jump out a window) if he felt claws scampering up his leg. The hallway ended, opening up to a large circular room with a magnificent antebellum-style imperial staircase.

"We're in the lobby," Bill whispered. "We're going up to the library. Be careful where you step. This is the oldest building on campus. Some of the stairs have seen better days."

"Okay," Felix whispered back as they started up. "How many floors are there?"

"Four," Bill said over his shoulder. "All these old buildings are nearly identical. We're going to the top."

"Why's it so cold in here?" He buried his hands in his jacket pockets, his wet sneakers rasping on the worn wooden steps.

"The heat's turned off. It's not much warmer in here than it is outside."

"I noticed." Felix snagged his foot on the lip of one of the stairs and had to catch himself on the railing.

"Careful," Bill said.

The stairs crackled and groaned as they made their way up in the darkness. Some part of Felix's brain was in a masochistic mood, amusing itself by torturing the rest of his brain with thoughts of what it would feel like to fall through a staircase. He tried to block out the images of flesh-piercing compound fractures and bleeding to death in the cellar of a thousand-year-old building, instead focusing on Bill's feet, trying to step where he stepped. The faint light coming in through the windows grew weaker the higher they climbed, gradually fading out altogether. When they reached the fourth floor landing, Bill stopped, and Felix promptly bumped into his backside.

"Sorry," Felix said. It was completely and absolutely dark, as dark as the tunnel beneath St. Rose when the lights went out. He couldn't see Bill, but he could hear him; it sounded like he was slowly dragging his rubber galoshes across the floor in a circle, trying to reorient himself in the inky darkness.

"Hey," Felix whispered. "I can't see shit."

"No kidding. It's a little better in the library. Grab the back of my jacket and stay tight."

Felix took a handful of Bill's pea coat and shuffled along behind as Bill led him down what Felix imagined could only be a hallway. Just after he stepped on the back of Bill's shoes for the third time, a pocket of gray light appeared up ahead and to his right.

"This is it," Bill said a moment later as he stepped through the opening with Felix in tow. There was just enough light for Felix to see that it was a room. A really big room. The pungent smell of dank decaying leather filled the air. Across from the doorway were windows—lots of windows. He wanted to see where he was—he'd gotten completely discombobulated stumbling his way up the staircase—so he let go of Bill's jacket and crossed the room, careful to avoid a table and several chairs in his way. The windows looked out onto another Old Campus building to the north which obstructed everything but a strip of parking lot adjacent to Stubbins Stadium—the same spot where he'd headbutted a lamppost and lost his mind for a spell.

"We need to do something about that. Give me a hand." Bill was no longer whispering. And he was making noises. Strange noises. Grunting?

Felix turned away from the windows to search for him. It took a moment to locate him because he was hidden behind a very large object that he was apparently trying to push across the floor. It must have been heavy because he wasn't having much success.

"What are you doing?" Felix's voice sounded small in the vast room.

"What does it look like? Damn. This thing's heavy." Bill stood up straight and clapped the dust off his hands. Felix could now see that the *thing* was a bookcase—a big bookcase. "But this'll be perfect," Bill said. "Perfect height. There are eight windows and more than enough of these. I don't know why I didn't think of this before. If you help, it should be relatively easy to slide them over there." He looked toward the windows. "As long as the floor doesn't collapse, that is."

"Seriously?" Felix glanced down warily at the floor and lifted a foot, as if that would actually make him lighter.

"I'm joking," Bill said with a little chuckle. "This building's built like an old battleship. C'mon. Roll up your sleeves and let's get to work."

There was nothing *relatively easy* about moving a twelve-foot solid wood bookcase. The racket they were making worried Felix at first, but after a while, he didn't care. He just wanted to be done with it without slipping a disk in his back. As soon as they blocked out the last window, he sat down on a table to catch his breath.

"Good." Bill went over to the doorway, wiping sweat from his forehead. "There are two entrances to this room and both face the hallway. Any light that escapes won't be visible to anyone who happens to be passing by Inverness from any direction. We've taken care of the windows, so without—"

"I can't see a goddamn thing," Felix complained, breathing fast.

"I was about to say, without any further ado, let there be light."

And just like that, there was sudden illumination from above. Huge ornate Victorian chandeliers stretched across the length of the room, suspended high overhead from a vaulted ceiling detailed with beautiful old-world millwork. Paneled with thick polished wood, the dark dusty walls were repositories for books which sat atop shelves mounted on corbels carved to resemble grapes, leaves, lions and angels. Scattered throughout in random groupings were tables, desks, chairs and bookcases (like the ones now covering up the windows). The room had been left in a permanent state of confused disarray. It was like half of its contents had been evacuated during a Japanese air raid, and the rest, forgotten.

"Quite a room, don't you think?" Bill said proudly.

"It's actually pretty cool." Felix's breath steamed in the cold air. "So this is the old library, huh?" It reminded him a lot of Woodrow's Room.

"It was for over a hundred years. The building was mothballed a long time ago, and it's too costly to reconfigure, which is too bad, because they don't build 'em like this anymore. On the other hand, I've been scouting locations since I arrived in Portland, and this room's perfect."

Felix had lost track of time moving the bookcases; he didn't know if it was one or three. He wanted to check his watch, but he knew Bill wouldn't like that. "What's up with the lights?"

Bill looked up wearily at the chandeliers and cursed, a look of disappointment creasing his face for a moment. "I actually replaced all the damn bulbs less than a week ago. They keep going out. I suppose it's the antiquated electrical system. I'm just glad the school didn't turn that off when it disconnected the heat and water."

"Hey," Felix said. "Where'd you get the key, anyway? The key to the building?"

"I'm the assistant groundskeeper, remember? I have the keys to every building on campus. I have access to everything. You think I took this job because I like cleaning dog shit off The Yard?" He smiled at Felix. "Now if you don't have any more questions, I think we should start. It's late as it is, and I'm sure you'd like to get a little sleep tonight."

"Sure. Let's do it." Felix paused and gave him a questioning look. "What are we doing?"

"Follow me." Bill wedged his way between a pair of lion-pawed desks, through a loose semicircle of high-backed chairs with curved armrests, and around an upside down table, its legs sticking up like a four-poster bed. He stopped in front of a large rectangular reading table in the center of the room. On top was a stack of books several feet high. "I want you to stand over there." He motioned at a spot a few feet behind the table.

Felix went around to the other side. He looked at the pile of books and then at Bill, who was watching him closely. "Now what?" he asked uncertainly.

"Move them onto the floor without touching them," Bill instructed.

"*What?*"

"Move the books."

"How do I do that?"

"The same way you destroyed Allison's room."

"I was sleeping," Felix replied flatly. "I don't know how I did that. I just did."

"That's exactly it. *You just did.* That's all there is to it. If you want to do it—you can do it."

"You make it sound easy."

Bill lifted his eyes to the ceiling and laughed. "It's like anything else. It'll be easy once you know what you're doing. You're the Belus. You just need to learn how to unlock the Source. That's it."

"That's still not very helpful," Felix sighed.

Bill started pacing, his footsteps echoing in the huge space. "It's not necessary to be in a heightened emotional state in order to use the Source, but when your emotions are running high, for example, when you're extremely upset or angry, it leaks out of you. That's what happened with little Nathan and explains why he's now getting along with fewer organs than the rest of us. It also happened at your dorm."

"So are you saying I can unlock this Source thing by getting really pissed off?"

Bill stopped and turned to face him. "Probably. But I don't want you to make a habit of this. I think we should just try this approach until you get the hang of it, okay? Now I'm going to say some things that'll make you very angry. I want you to understand right now that I'm only doing this to help you. I don't mean any of it. I don't want you to lose control. I want you to focus on the books. I want you to move the books. That's it. And above all else, *do not get angry at me.* Please. Understand?"

Felix nodded, fixing his eyes on the books. And despite the chill in the room, and his wet clothes—he could almost hear his mom's voice telling him to change out of them before he caught cold—he started to sweat.

"Ready?" Bill said. It appeared he might be sweating too.

Felix swallowed hard. "Bring it."

"Why are you here?" Bill demanded.

"Huh?" Felix shifted his gaze to Bill.

"Dammit!" Bill shouted angrily. "Just answer the goddamn question! Don't look at me!"

Felix nodded, startled, returning his attention to the books. "Sorry."

"Why'd you come to PC? Did you think coming to this glorified prep school would make you smarter? Did you think a place that pretends to be a snooty, upper crust English boarding school would give you a clever accent?"

"I like—"

"It's pathetic! The school's trying to be something it's not. Little Ben? Seriously? This is Oregon. Not England. Not Oxford. Not Cambridge. And you're just a dumb kid from a small town who fell for it. This isn't going to change who you are or where you come from."

Coos Bridge? Is he making fun of my hometown? Is that where he was going with this? *Please.* This wasn't going to make him angry.

"Why don't you have a girlfriend?" Bill said to him.

"What?" Felix heard himself say.

"Why don't you have a girlfriend?"

"Because… because Emma dumped me. I haven't—"

"Why'd she dump you?"

"Why?" Bill was clueless if he thought this was going to piss him off.

"You know the answer!" Bill shouted. "Why'd she dump you?"

"She said… she said I wasn't like her."

"Is that what she said? *Bullshit!* She said you're not good enough for her. Didn't she? Didn't she? Didn't she?" Each time Bill said 'didn't she?' his voice grew louder, higher and angrier.

"Yes!" Sweat trickled down his forehead. His face was hot. Now Bill was starting to irritate him.

"She knew you would never amount to anything. She knew you were going to be a failure. She thought you'd flunk out of college. Didn't she? Didn't she?"

"Yes!"

"She thought you'd end up in the mill, didn't she?"

"Yes!" His limbs were growing warm.

"She's right!" Bill screamed.

"What?"

"You're too goddamn stupid to understand that Emma was right!"

"What? What are you talking about? No she—"

"You're not good enough for her! You never were! You never will be!"

"Shut up!"

"She dumped you like garbage!" Bill screamed, spittle spewing from his mouth.

"Shut up!" His stomach felt strange. His legs were shaking.

"She knew she could do better than you!"

"Shut up!" Now it was working; he wanted to jump over the table and plant his fist in Bill's face.

"Emma cheated on you! She liked cheating on you. It turned her on. You were *nothing* to her! You were just a pet. A goddamn fluffy kitten. Pretty with no substance. You hear that? No substance! None! Somebody to keep around until something better came along. And that's what you deserve. Because you're nothing! And you never will be! You're a loser! *You're white trash! White. Trash.* "

The table began to vibrate. Then it shook. The legs lifted off the floor and bounced up and down, banging against the wood like a barn door in a windstorm. The books shifted around. The ones at the top of the stack slid off their perch, landing on the table with light *thudding* sounds.

"Focus!" Bill screamed at him. "The Books! Make them move! Make them move!"

Felix felt like everything had suddenly snapped into slow motion. He gritted his teeth and whispered to himself: "Move. Move. Get. Off. The. Table. Now."

Every book on the table rocketed across the room and smashed into the wall. The echo cracked and rippled, finally fading away into the dusty recesses of the library.

"What are you feeling?" Bill shouted. He was in front of Felix now, his fingers pressing into Felix's shoulders. "What do you feel? Focus on what you're feeling. Talk to me! What do you feel?"

Felix's breath felt tight in his throat. His whole body was shaking. He didn't know if he was in shock, or what, but he felt *weird*. It was like he was watching somebody else from above. Maybe it was what people call an out-of-body-experience. He'd just made thirty books *fly* across the room. People can't do stuff like that, right? How did he do that? And then it dawned on him as suddenly as if the ceiling had crashed down on his head.

"It's all true," he whispered softly. *The journal. Allison's room. I'm the Belus. Lofton Ashfield's the Drestian. My parents weren't my real parents. My real mom died in a mental hospital. This isn't a hoax. I'm not being punked. It's all true. It's really true. Damn.*

"What are you feeling?" Bill demanded, giving him a shake. "C'mon! Focus for me."

Felix still had an urge to punch him in the face. "Warm and cold. I feel... uh... I feel... my legs and arms are a little tingly. And there's something in my gut. Here." He placed a hand on his stomach.

"What is it? What do you feel?"

"I don't know. It's weird. Heavy. I guess. It feels kinda heavy."

"This is very important," Bill said slowly, emphasizing each word. "Listen to me carefully. Focus on what you're feeling now. Focus very hard. You need to recapture it, okay? This is how you'll feel when you use the Source. Can you remember this? Can you make yourself feel this way?"

"I just did that, didn't I?" A smile spread across Felix's face. "I just did that with my *mind*. Unbelievable!"

"Don't be so impressed with yourself," Bill chided. "You're the Belus. That was child's play." He turned and took off across the room to where the books lay on the floor in a heaping pile. "I didn't mean any of that, by the way! Emma's just a stupid kid. And my apologies to PC, although I do think the clock tower belongs in a theme park." He scooped up an armful of books and ran back to the table. "You're not a loser. And you're the furthest thing from white trash than anyone I've ever met." He dropped them on the table, sending up little puffs of white dust into the chilly air. Then he went to work hastily constructing a leaning-tower-of-Pisa-like structure.

"You can do better than Emma," Bill went on. "And you will." Bill's voice sounded higher than normal. He was excited, but trying to hide it.

"It's okay." Felix didn't feel warm anymore—or cold—and he wasn't angry at Bill. His arms and legs were no longer tingling. He ran his hand over his stomach. The heavy sensation was gone. "I'm over her. I totally don't give a shit anymore." He recalled the *secret game* he'd played with his friends a few weeks ago. "But for some weird reason she keeps coming up."

Bill wasn't listening. He was straightening up the tower. "I want you to do that again." He stepped back from the table. "Just like before. Close your eyes and visualize what you felt when you moved the books. When you recapture that feeling, open your eyes and move them. Got it?"

"Okay." Felix cracked his knuckles and rolled his shoulders, steeling himself, breathing out firmly. He stared at the books in the half light of the library and then closed his eyes. He'd used visualization techniques in high school. His basketball coach thought it would improve his jump shot. This was basically the same thing. He breathed in through his nose. The books were giving off a hint of dampness.

So my arms were tingling, he thought. *Tingle. Start tingling.* He concentrated on his arms. They began to feel warm. A moment later, his fingers, then his hands, began to tingle. The warm prickling sensation spread up his arms and through his torso. It worked its way down his legs to his sneakers. *Now my gut. Heavy. Heavy. Heavy. Make it feel heavy.* Something shifted and tightened in his midsection. It was an odd sensation. It wasn't like eating too much and it wasn't like doing a hundred crunches: this was completely different.

He opened his eyes.

"Do it!" Bill commanded.

Felix raised his right hand to shoulder height. He didn't know why he raised his hand; it was almost like his arm had a life of its own.

"Do it!"

The books exploded off the table, blistering across the room and slamming into the wall like a flock of directionally challenged birds mistaking a window for open air. The sharp corner of one hardbound pierced the wood paneling like a dart.

"Wow!" Bill whistled appreciatively. "That had some velocity."

Felix lowered his hand, laughing. "That was awesome!"

It looked like Bill was about to say something to put a lid on Felix's excitement, but then thought better of it. "Yeah—that was pretty awesome. How do you feel?"

"Fine." He looked down at himself. Everything had already returned to normal. Nothing was tingly, heavy, warm or cold—except for his feet which were beginning to feel a little numb because of his wet shoes.

"Excellent. I want you to try one more thing before we call it a night." Bill reached down under the table and picked up a single book. It was a Russian title with a long name Felix didn't recognize. "Let's work on your control. Above all else, at this stage, that has to be your goal. It's absolutely critical. Okay?"

"So what am I doing?" Felix asked. He was eager to try it again, to see what he could do.

"Show me some subtlety." Bill gently placed the book in the center of the table.

Felix raised his right hand and went through the same visualization steps as before. One corner of the book came off the table an inch or two, then it flipped over. It struggled, kicking like a turtle stuck on its back. It jumped up a foot, hovered for a second and then shot toward the ceiling as though guided by an invisible hand. He tried to control it, but it was resisting him, wobbling around like a drunken pigeon. He wanted it to go up, and immediately it dropped several feet like an airplane encountering clear-air turbulence.

"Dammit!" Felix shouted, as the book, its pages fluttering, shot across the room away from him. He directed every ounce of energy at the book and finally caused it to stop just as it kissed the wall. Then he pulled it back, reeling it in like a fish caught on a hook.

"I'm gonna send it over to you." He glanced over at Bill to see where he was. The book floated past Felix, making its way toward Bill. It was directly over the table now. He felt like he could do this. He was getting the knack. He could control it. He guided it closer to Bill. *Slow and gentle*, he said to himself. It actually listened to him, gliding smoothly through the air. *Slow and gentle. Slow and gentle. Slow and—*

Ka-ploof.

The book exploded in a cloud of confetti that hung in the air for a moment before wafting down lazily to the table and the floor all around it.

"*What the?*" Felix said, stunned. "What happened?"

Bill was laughing. He picked up a handful of paper and tossed it overhead like a New Year's Eve reveler. "That looked like a pillow getting in the way of a shotgun."

"I didn't try to do that. I don't even know how I did it."

"Don't be discouraged." Bill came over to him. "It's going to take some time before you get the feel for this. You should focus on the bigger picture. Think about what you just accomplished. There's only one other person in the entire world who can do what you just did."

He thought for a moment and said, "Lofton?"

Bill nodded, brushing aside some paper from the table. "Would you mind bringing Allison by my office sometime? I'd like to meet her."

"Uh… sure." He paused, watching Bill, but his expression showed nothing. "Why?" he asked.

"Nothing in particular." Bill started toward the doorway. Felix followed. "I just want to talk to her. But it may have to wait a while. I won't be around much for the next week or two. There are some things I need to take care of. As soon as I free up I'll text you."

Bill turned off the lights and they carefully made their way back down the hallway and the warped stairs, slipping out of the building the way they came. In a pounding rain, they left the Old Campus in opposite directions.

Chapter 36

BIRTHDAY WISHES

Mia saw the crater in the road a split second too late. The front left tire of the Volkswagen Jetta sank into the rain-filled pothole and splashed muddy water onto the windshield. She cringed. German engineers had designed her car for paved roads, not roads like these. The suspension made a frightful grinding noise, causing her passenger to shout out: "What the hell was that?"

"Sorry, Ethan," she said meekly, glancing over at him. He was wearing a thick knitted ski hat that was pulled down to his eyebrows. Beneath the hat was a blindfold. He couldn't see a thing. She'd made sure of that.

"Where the hell are we?" He sounded like he was about to fly off the handle.

"Almost there," she said.

"Almost *where?*"

"You'll find out when we get there." She let off the accelerator and swerved to avoid another hole. "Is it my birthday or yours?"

Ethan's lips tightened for a moment, then he frowned. "Yours, dear."

"So would this be my birthday wish or your birthday wish?"

"Yours, dear," he said obediently.

"Thank you, Ethan," she said in her customer-service-rep-reading-from-a-script-voice (because she knew it annoyed him). "And thank you for your cooperation."

He groaned and folded his arms across his chest.

The rubber blades on the windshield wipers squeaked as they began to gain traction and catch against the drying glass. It had poured through the night, but when they left their apartment in northeast Portland in the small hours of the morning it had eased to an intermittent drizzle. Now the rain had finally stopped. And that was a good thing, because they were about to go for a walk in the woods.

Mia had been dating Ethan for almost four years and they'd shared an apartment for the last two. They worked for the same company—that was where they'd met—and they were both accountants. But their mutual attraction had very little to do with crunching numbers or auditing financial statements.

Their friends liked to call them 'the crazy people with the boring jobs'. Ethan, clever man that he was, just referred to their lifestyle as *mullet living*. They were all business up front: predictable, conservative, white collar jobs. But in the back, on their own time, they were adrenaline junkies who fed their addiction with any activity where screwing up meant instantaneous death: cliff jumping, free climbing, sky diving and bungee jumping out of helicopters were some of their favorites.

When Mia analyzed their relationship, which she was doing quite a lot of these days since her parents were pressuring her to get married before she turned thirty (she'd actually called her dad an asshole the last time he told her it was "time to cut bait or fish"), she thought that a single event had defined it. She believed most couples could say that if they gave it a little consideration. And for Mia and Ethan, that event had occurred three years ago.

Just before Mia's twenty-sixth birthday, Ethan had asked her if she had a birthday wish. After only a moment's thought, she told him that she'd always wanted to hangglide along the northern California coastline. So on the night of her birthday, over a candlelight dinner at her favorite Turkish restaurant, he gave her a card that read: 'Your wish has been granted. Your bags are packed'.

The trip to California was amazing. She had the time of her life. Ethan organized the whole thing, even down to the tiniest details, and catered to her every need. It was fun, exciting, and spontaneous, like something right out of a movie.

And that's how the birthday wish tradition had begun.

Mia had absolutely and wholeheartedly loved the idea at first. It was romantic. It was thoughtful. Romance and thoughtfulness—two qualities she'd never experienced in a guy before. It was perfect. And it made her feel like Ethan really loved her and wanted to make her happy.

But now as they sped along the rutted, nearly washed-out forest service road in Mia's not-all-terrain vehicle, she had very different feelings about the tradition—*mixed feelings*—and was beginning to wonder if she was taking things a little too far. She quickly dismissed that notion, tightening her fingers on the steering wheel. Even if she was getting a little carried away, it wasn't her fault—it was Ethan's. Although if Ethan knew what she was planning to do to him in a few minutes, he would place the blame squarely on an old lady who died before he had a chance to meet her.

When Mia was eight, her Serbian grandmother—Nana Vujicic—had read her palm after much pleading. Nana was different. And Mia sensed it. But it wasn't really a secret. She scared the shit out of all the kids in Mia's neighborhood and even Mia's mom called her a 'mad gypsy'. Nana just had a way about her that put people on edge; when she looked at you it was like she was seeing through you, inside you. And she had a tendency of saying the craziest things, but there was always truth in her words. In the old days, Mia imagined a pitchfork-carrying mob would have burned Nana at the stake for practicing witchcraft. On that day so many years ago, Nana had held Mia's hand for a very long time, then she pulled it close to her weathered face and muttered something in Serbian, tracing her knotted forefinger along the lines of her palm. Finally, Nana let go of her hand and said in her heavily accented English: "You have much life in you, Mia. Much spirit. But I see sharks in your future. I'm sorry, dear."

On the spot, Mia vowed she would never so much as dip her toe in the ocean. And she'd stuck to that promise. It wasn't out of paranoia or superstition that she stayed out of the water—she'd felt the *truth* in her Nana's warning deep down in her bones, and saw no point in making it a self-fulfilling prophecy.

And then six months ago, just prior to Ethan's last birthday, while watching reruns of *Sons of Anarchy* in bed, he'd presented her with his birthday wish: scuba diving in Washington's Puget Sound. Mia had an epic meltdown. She fought with him continuously for a solid month. She tried to talk him out of it. She tried everything. Desperate, she told him she would arrange to parachute off the Eiffel Tower. She was willing to spend time in a Parisian jail if it meant avoiding the ocean. But Ethan wasn't interested in doing anything else and he wouldn't back down. He cajoled her. He begged her. He promised her nothing would happen, that he would take care of her. He told her scuba diving was safer than crossing a street in downtown Portland. Ethan could be very convincing when he wanted to be. And in the end, he wore her down and she caved.

Mia and Ethan had spent less than an hour in the ocean. Nothing terrible happened. They saw lots of pretty fish. They didn't see a single shark. But it was the worst hour of her life. She'd never been so scared or so certain that a dumb animal (a *fish* for Christ's sake!) was going to eat her. When the dive master and her assistant pulled Mia back onto the boat she was shocked to still be alive. And all the way back to the harbor she whispered numbly to herself over and over: "Nana was wrong. Nana was wrong."

Mia braked the car, fishtailing through the muck for a ways before finally coming to a stop. They'd only been on the dirt road a few minutes. She checked the odometer: exactly half a mile from Dobbs Highway. But no other cars. Or people. Not even at the campground they'd just passed; the picnic benches and campfire sites were empty. Not surprising. It was too late in the year for camping and the Portland weather had been predictably wet and awful for the past month. She looked all around and smiled as the anticipation bubbled up inside her. Finally, it was time. This was called payback. Payback on an epic scale. She'd waited months for this, and she planned to enjoy every wonderful minute of it.

"All right, sugar lips," she said sweetly, putting the car in park and cutting the engine. "Get out."

"We better not be where I think we are," Ethan groused. "If I smell trees, I won't be happy."

"You'll find out soon enough." Mia clapped her hands. "Out. C'mon. Chop chop." She climbed out of the car and went around to the passenger side, her feet squishing into the mud up to her ankles. She opened the door for him.

"Did you forget that I can't see?" Ethan didn't make any attempt to get out, sitting in his seat like a recalcitrant teenager.

"Did you forget how to use your legs?" Mia looked down at him, shaking her head. "Take my hand, darling."

He unbuckled his seatbelt, then he just sat there, stewing.

She grabbed his hand and placed it on her wrist, then pulled him out of the car and kicked the door shut, leaving a mud print of her shoe under the window. "Ready?"

"Ready for what?" Ethan said darkly. His chin dropped like he was looking down at his feet. "This doesn't feel like a sidewalk."

"Just hold onto my arm and remember whose birthday it is."

Ethan groaned.

She led him around some seedlings and ferns creeping onto the edge of the road, and then, in the cold and bitter morning air, they set off into the forest. She followed a thin serpentine ribbon of path that was fairly easy to navigate, even with Ethan clutching her arm and dragging his feet like he'd recently had a stroke. Before long, the woods were all around them, closing in on them. The sky darkened. She smiled, her excitement growing with each step. The trees got bigger, the ferns denser. The trail vanished. The ground was soft and dewy, soggy in places. Thick branches and massive logs covered the forest floor like landmines on a battlefield. Ethan stumbled often, but rarely spoke, and then only to complain.

"Watch your feet, Ethan," Mia warned. "Got one right in front." She skipped around a mossy rock as smooth and round as a riverbed stone. He tripped on it and she had to reach around his waist to keep him from falling.

"Shit!" Mia shouted, annoyed. "When'd you become such a goddamn klutz?" She looked over her shoulder to check for the car. It was now just a sliver of cobalt blue in the distance. "I told you to watch your feet."

"How come I think I'm gonna be pissed when I take off this blindfold?"

"When'd I tell you to start thinking?" Mia snapped at him. "Just keep walking, lover. And stop complaining. You're bothering me." They plodded along in silence for a spell. Turning, she looked for the car. She couldn't see it. *Perfect.* She stopped. They hadn't walked long. Ten minutes at most. Without giving Ethan any warning, she shrugged off his hand and silently slinked away from him. Then she stood there, studying his face (the parts she could see anyway), taking it all in like a spectator at a much-anticipated sporting event.

"Hey!" Ethan said anxiously, his breath puffing out white in the cold. "Mia! Hey! Where'd you go?" He held his hands out in front of his body like a sleepwalker, searching for her.

"I'm right here." She watched him, smiling.

He grabbed at his hat.

"*Not yet!*" she shrieked. "Not until I say so! This is *my* wish."

He unclenched his hand, reluctantly, and his arm returned to his side.

"Where do you think you are?" she asked.

"I don't know," he shot back bitterly. "Some psychotic woman blindfolded me." Then he pointed at her. "But we better not be in the goddamn woods!"

"What do you have against the woods, anyway?" she asked casually.

"You know I hate the woods!"

"But why?"

"Why do I need a reason? I just do. Can I take this thing off now?" He reached up to his head again.

"No!" Mia tried to sound angry and thought she was doing a convincing job of it.

Ethan was starting to get scared. She could hear it in his voice. She didn't want him to freak out or go into hysterics, but she intended to teach him a lesson. "Remember what you did to me on your last birthday?" she said, her voice pleasant. "Do you remember that, darling?"

"*What?*" He paused for a few beats, giving his head a dismayed shake.

"You mean the scuba thing? Seriously? C'mon, Mia. You planning to hold that against me forever? I thought you'd like it. Once you got in the water and got into it, I thought you'd really like it. I swear. I thought I was doing you a favor."

"Is that so?" she said icily. *"A favor?* You're such an asshole. You knew what my Nana told me, but you just disregarded it."

"About the *sharks?* C'mon! She was a crazy old lady. No disrespect to her, of course. Rest in peace and all that. But palm reading? She was a superstitious circus fr—"

"Maybe she was a little eccentric," she admitted. "But do you have any idea how terrified I was? Do you?"

"Well, yeah, I do know," he replied thickly. "You won't shut the hell up about it. I told you I'm sorry like a million freaking times. I just thought it'd be fun. If I knew Serbians held grudges forever, I'd have never done it." Ethan was shifting his weight from one foot to the other, squirming like a toddler trying not to pee in his big-boy pants.

"I was thinking about forgiving you." She knew that what she was doing was probably cruel, but she was enjoying it too much to stop. And he deserved it. "But then I thought, maybe it'd be good for you if you got a taste of your own medicine. Then you'd finally understand what it was like for me to be in the open water like that." She raised her arms and looked up to the canopy. "I think this will make us closer as a couple. You know, make our undying love for each other even more undying."

"You're outta your mind," he murmured under his breath, his jaw flexing with tension. "I'm taking this thing off."

"No you're not," she said forcefully. "Not until you hear the kicker."

"The *kicker?*"

"Yes, my tall, dark and handsome prince—the kicker. Not only are you in the woods, you, my love, are presently enjoying my esteemed company in the heart of... *Ashfield Forest.*"

Ethan froze. No more shifting of his feet. No more squirming. His hands moved to his face, slowly, mechanically. He peeled away the hat and the blindfold, holding them for a moment before letting them drop to the ground. His eyes were huge, mouth open, face pale.

Mia didn't laugh. But she wanted to. After so much planning, this was exactly the reaction she'd hoped for. It was exactly what Ethan deserved.

"Are you crazy?" Ethan whispered. *"Ashfield Forest? Ashfield Forest?* Where's the car!" He started spinning in circles, first clockwise, then counterclockwise, then back the other way. He tripped over something and caught himself against a twisted tree branch. "We gotta get outta here!"

Mia started to laugh. She couldn't control herself any longer.

"What's so funny? Where's the car?"

She laughed harder.

"Mia, goddammit! This isn't funny. You know what's been happening out here! Where's the fucking car?"

He was really panicking now. His voice was breaking. He was about to lose it. Time to put an end to this before he ran off into the woods and got himself lost. "Ethan! Hey! Look at me, darling. I was lying. This isn't Ashfield Forest. That's not where we are." She stepped toward him, cutting through a thick patch of ferns that came up to her waist. "C'mon, relax. It's okay."

"What?" he said, his frightened eyes darting all around. "We're... we're not? This isn't..."

"No," she said, laughing. "Ashfield's on the other side of Dobbs Highway. This is a state park, you idiot."

"Really?" Ethan was shaking, his breaths coming fast and shallow. "It's not... we're not..."

"We're in a park," she repeated slowly. "And the car's like a minute away. It's just over there." She cocked her thumb behind her.

He started to say something, then hesitated, and lifted his eyes to the towering trees surrounding them. "But we're still in the goddamn woods, Mia. I hate the woods. You know that."

She continued to watch him, more amused than ever. Her brave, adventure-hungry, I-stare-death-in-the-face-and-laugh boyfriend was acting like a frightened child trying to come to terms with the bogeyman under his bed. It was hysterical. She laughed so hard her stomach started to hurt.

"Mia!"

"Well I needed to teach you a lesson," she said, wiping tears from the corners of her eyes.

"Can we go? Please?" Ethan glanced up at the treetops then turned his head to check behind him. "I seriously don't want to be here."

"I don't know what you're so worried about. It's nice in the woods. It's peaceful. Quiet. What could possibly happen out here?" Mia was trying to scare him—again. She couldn't seem to help herself. "It's nice with no one around to disturb you. I feel like I can really think out here. Maybe we should do this more often."

"Mia! The car!" His fear was turning to anger.

"You're such a baby. Did you learn your lesson?"

"*What?*" Ethan said, sounding perplexed.

"Just be a good boy and nod your head and I'll show you where the car is."

"Mia!"

"Nod your head!" she demanded.

"You're crazy!"

"Not nice, dear. Nod your head and say, 'I deserve this and I'll never make my wonderful girlfriend get in the ocean again.'"

He gave her a resigned (and most likely insincere) smile. "Fine." He bobbed his head up and down in a spot on imitation of a bobble head. "I was nodding in case you missed it."

"Don't be a smartass."

"I deserve this and I'll never make my *fantastic* girlfriend get in the ocean again."

"*Wonderful* girlfriend," she said, delighting in the correction.

"Wonderful," he repeated with a sigh. "The car?"

"Was that so hard? I'll even let you drive." Mia glanced down for a second to unzip the jacket pocket where she'd put her keys. She found them, then she looked up.

Ethan was gone.

She stepped back, startled, hugging herself against a sudden gust of cold wind. "Ethan!" she called out uncertainly, her head moving all around. "Not funny, lover! Ethan!"

No response. The low gray clouds had moved off to the east, yet in the dark of the forest the rain continued unabated, drizzling down coldly, heavily, from the branches above.

Something stirred in the forest, a whisper of movement across the face of the ancient woodlands.

A chill raced up her back as she searched for it, but the forest went suddenly quiet again, serenity reigning under the brooding calm of the canopy; all she could hear was her own breathing and her feet lifting and falling among roots wrestling for dominance beneath the rain packed groundcover. She stood still, listening for the sound, her heart thumping fast in her temples. The air felt thin. Her lungs worked harder, quickening to compensate for the tightness in her chest.

She heard it again and her gaze jerked toward a giant fir; at its base it was wider than the Jetta. A branch snapped and the rustling grew louder, more frantic, like something big was struggling to make its way through the underbrush.

A voice cried out from behind the tree. She flinched back, her muscles tense and alert. Then she heard her name, followed by moaning, and then her name again. Almost instantly, Mia felt herself relax. Her breathing calmed. It was just Ethan. He was trying to scare her—but it wasn't going to work. Now she was annoyed. She couldn't believe he was trying to turn the tables on her birthday wish. *Her* birthday wish.

She took a few steps toward the tree and shouted angrily, "Ethan! This isn't funny, butthead! Joke's gonna be on you! Guess which one of us doesn't know where the car is?" A thick layer of bright green moss shrouded the trunk like frosting on a St. Patrick's Day cake. She reached the tree and stuck a finger into the moss. It was soft and spongy. She peeled off a chunk and played with it. It was strangely tactile, like a stress ball.

More moaning. Louder and more anguished this time.

"Gimme a break! That's some performance you got goin' on back there. You going for an Oscar, dear? Should I call the Academy and conference them in?" She kept close to the trunk and began circling around to the other side, her anger rising by the second, making her face hot.

"I'm gonna make your life so miserable! You know that thing you like so much they call 'sex'? Ain't none comin' your way for a long, long time, buddy. You're gonna be having a real close relationship with your hand, you prick. If you think this is spooking me, it's not. I'll leave without you." The other side came into view. "It's gonna be a long walk home if—"

A pack of dogs was eating something. *What was it? A deer?* She stared at the dogs, watching with morbid fascination as they buried their heads deep into the innards of the bloody disemboweled animal. Then one of the dogs stood—it stood on two legs. It was wearing pants and a shirt. It put something in its mouth. It had hands. Fingers. And then it was no longer there. It just disappeared. There was a *pop*—like the uncorking of a champagne bottle—and then it was gone.

Mia's brain wasn't processing what her eyes were seeing. Her brain was trying to tell her that dogs don't walk on two legs, that dogs don't wear pants and shirts. She looked down at the deer. It was bathed in blood. Another one of the strange two-legged dogs stood up and moved to the side.

The deer had a face—*a human face.* And the face looked like... Ethan's.

She screamed. The little pieces of moss slipped from her fingers.

"Hello," a voice said. "Hello. Miss? Good morning."

She tugged her eyes away from Ethan's ghostly blood-spattered face and searched for the voice. Just off to her right, she saw someone approaching her. She couldn't tell at first if it was a man or a woman, but the hair was short and the clothes couldn't be purchased in the women's department at Nordstrom. Concluding that it must be a man—and not a woman or bi-pedal dog—she noticed his unusual attire: a mixture of nineteenth century English dandy and modern-day street beggar. He was wearing shoddy paint-splotched overalls, a paisley ascot, double-breasted blazer and a feathered fedora. The man stopped in front of her.

She could hear sounds coming from where Ethan lay on the ground. Terrible sounds. Feeding sounds. She looked down at him again. The dogs? The men? Whatever they were, were all over him.

"Look at me," the man demanded in a quiet voice.

She obeyed reflexively, without a thought. His lips were enviably full and puffy and it made her think of an actress whose name she couldn't recall. Then she saw his eyes and everything went suddenly haywire. There was something strange about them: large and the color of rain clouds, as she stared into them, she began to feel queasy and unbalanced. Wobbling on her feet, she tried to look away, but it was like an invisible but unbreakable bond had tethered their eyes together.

"Can I show you something?" he asked politely.

She nodded, mesmerized, still gazing into his hypnotic eyes.

He opened his mouth, and she looked on in horror as his jaw descended to the lapel of his navy-blue jacket. Petrified, she stared into the cavernous mouth, her heart pounding hard in her throat, the sound filling her ears. What she saw there—rows of triangular serrated daggers—were the teeth of a shark.

He snapped his mouth shut and smiled. "Does that frighten you?"

"Yes." She sounded like a robot, and she knew it. It was like listening to someone else's voice. "Are you a shark?" Mia was terrified, but it was as if her fear had been de-linked from the fight-or-flight control center of her brain. She couldn't act on her fear; she could only stand there and wait for whatever was about to happen.

"No. I'm Number Two." He laughed. It wasn't an unpleasant sound.

Another one appeared out of nowhere, a stringy piece of denim-covered flesh dangling from the corner of its bloody mouth.

"Get back!" Number Two snarled at the other, enraged. "She's mine! Know your place, Number Forty-Six."

The other one (Number Forty-Six) growled defiantly but backed up a step. "She's not yours! We shouldn't even be here. We're outside the quadrants. What if *he* learns of this?"

Mia barely understood their conversation. *Forty-Six? Is that what he said?*

"We'll leave no trace of them behind," Number Two responded, his eyes moving away from Mia. "He will never know."

The moment his eyes released her she was less groggy, and some degree of lucidity came back to her. Her eyes searched for Ethan in the gray light of the forest, but he wasn't there. The shredded fabric of the coat she'd given him for Christmas last year and one bloody shoe was all that remained of her boyfriend.

Number Two took her firmly by the chin, pressing his cold fingers into her skin, and twisted her head around. Once again, she was looking into his slate-gray eyes, feeling weak and pliable, like her mind was no longer hers to control.

"That's better." Number Two's voice was tranquil, comforting. "What do you have in your hand?"

"Car keys."

"Give them to me."

She did.

"Are you going to hurt me?" she asked timidly.

"Yes." He smiled, his lips curving up into sharp peaks at the corners like a crescent moon tilted on its side. "I'm going to eat you."

Tears welled up in her eyes.

"Tell me why you're here?"

"It's my birthday." She felt numb, paralyzed. Why couldn't she run? Why was she answering his questions? What was happening? "It's my birthday wish."

Number Two removed his hand from her face and laughed as a host of others approached from all sides. "Your birthday wish?"

"I wanted to scare my boyfriend. That's why we're here." She wanted to run, but she was fossilized, lost in the swirling storm clouds staring back at her.

"Do you think he's scared now?"

She nodded. The tears rolled down her cheeks.

He opened his mouth and cocked his head like he was going to kiss her.

Mia knew what was coming next and there was nothing she could do to prevent it. *Nana was right*, she thought, horrified, staring into the mouth of the shark. *Nana was right. Nana was—*

Chapter 37

THE REPORT

"How did it go last night?" the voice rasped through the tiny speaker in Bill's phone.

Bill sat at the table in his kitchen, a creased and yellowed Forest Service map spread out in front of him. Some of the logging trails were highlighted in orange. He set aside the marker and looked down at the phone. "Well. It went well. It was... incredible. If that's the right word. To witness it, to actually see—*to feel*—the Source in use is indescribable. The air was just filled with something. Energy, electricity—I don't know. It was like the atmosphere was crackling with power, like..." He left it at that as there were no words to describe it.

"A veil had been lifted and the true nature of the universe had revealed itself to you for the first time. I..." His dad hesitated. "I'm envious. I wish I could have been there to see it for myself. What did the boy do exactly?"

"I had him move some objects," Bill replied, surprised at his dad's poetic foray. "He didn't have any trouble with it. For a first try, I'd say it went exceptionally well. That is, until I asked him to manipulate a single book and he vaporized it."

His dad chuckled. "I'm sure you'll be working on fixing that tonight."

Bill hesitated before he said, "Not tonight."

"*No?* Why not? Why aren't you pressing? We can't send him into the forest until he knows what he's doing. There isn't much time."

"It's not that simple."

"Delaying his training doesn't make it any less complicated."

"How many times are we going to have this conversation?" Bill said wearily. "I need to take things slowly with Felix. He doesn't have an off button just yet, and I'm afraid if he has too much power, and not enough control, things could become, well, problematic."

"*Problematic?*" His dad paused. "What happened? I know that tone, son."

Bill sighed silently and looked out at the back yard through French doors. For the first time in a long while, it wasn't raining. Morning sunlight streamed into the kitchen through the doors and a large window above the farmhouse sink. He liked the kitchen. And the house. He'd purchased it fully furnished just two weeks before the start of classes. It was nice. And close to campus.

"He fell asleep at a friend's the night I showed him the journal," Bill explained. "His friend awoke to find him hovering close to the ceiling and burning up the room. But no one was hurt. No one suspects anything, except for his friend. And she—according to Felix—can be trusted." He waited for the eruption he knew was coming. The grandfather clock in the living room *tick-tocked* melodiously, ushering in the bomb about to detonate.

But to his surprise, his dad said simply, "Isn't that precisely why you need to accelerate the boy's training?"

Bill said nothing, thinking his dad might have a point.

"William?"

"Perhaps," Bill muttered, unwilling to acknowledge that his dad could be right.

"Perhaps?" his dad growled incredulously.

"I know what I'm doing! Would it kill you to have a little faith in me? I'm so goddamn sick of arguing about this!"

"Watch your temper, son!" his dad roared. "Remember who you're speaking to. You have an obligation to see this through before—"

"Are we seriously discussing this again? For nearly twenty years that's all I've heard from you. A constant mantra about my obligation to humanity. Ever since I met that damn woman at Green River that's been my fate. I accept that. I do. But I don't need you reminding me that I'm the only person capable of molding an eighteen-year-old kid into a goddamn savior!"

"Enough with the self-pity! It doesn't suit you. You're a Stout. Act like it. We both know what's at stake."

"Don't tell me what's at stake!" Bill screamed at the phone. "I've dedicated my entire life to this. Look at where I'm at! What do I have? Do I have a wife? Do I have kids? Do I have friends? Do I have any life at all? *Don't you dare tell me what's at stake!"* Shaking with anger, he grabbed the phone and cocked his arm back into a throwing position. Then he stopped. *Don't let him get to you,* he said to himself. *Relax. It's not worth it.* He closed his eyes and concentrated on his breathing. *In. Out.* He so badly wanted to hurl his phone (and his dad) through the glass doors. He breathed. *In. Out.* He opened his eyes and placed the phone next to an empty teacup.

"You'll have to forgive me for reminding you on occasion that it's only the fate of the world that's at stake," his dad said gruffly after a long silence had passed. "In any event, if you're not planning to continue the boy's training in the immediate future, what are your plans?"

Bill looked at the fridge, and then at the clock above the sink. 10:15. Too early for a beer. "Ashfield Forest. As soon as the sun sets. I may be there for a few days this time."

"Hunting?"

"Searching. Lofton must be keeping his toys somewhere."

"Okay. Be careful, William. Those *toys* are not something you want to encounter without the boy along for the ride. But I trust in the meantime you're taking precautions."

"I've only been unprepared once in my life and I'll never let that happen again."

"Well, I should hope not," his dad replied, sounding confused. "Call me when you get back."

"I will." Bill hit the END button, picked up the marker, and returned to the map. Then he went to the fridge to get a beer. It was after noon somewhere.

Chapter 38

DEMONSTRATION

"You in there?" Felix rapped on Allison's door, idly watching a group of girls laughing their way down the hall toward the cafeteria. "It's me."

The door flung open and Felix flinched back in surprise. "Get in here! What took you so long?" Allison snatched the sleeve of his shirt and yanked him into the room, kicking the door shut with a *bang*.

"What's with the manhandling?" Felix said, smiling at her.

"I've been dying to talk to you all day. Caitlin just went to the caf. I told her I'd meet her in a few minutes. We have to be quick."

Felix straightened his shirt. He'd only been to Allison and Caitlin's first-floor room a couple of times since the 'relocation under duress' as Allison called it. They'd replaced everything lost in the fire so their new room looked just like the old one: same framed family photos; same wall art; same little area rug with the southwestern motif; same complete lack of typical college-dorm-room-messiness.

The faint grayness of artificial light leaked through the edges and between the slats of the closed blinds. It was already dark out. The sun had set a few hours ago. The abbreviated daylight hours and interminably overcast rainy November skies made it seem like the sun was vacationing on the other side of the equator and only interested in making the occasional cameo up north. The kids who'd come from sunnier climates were just beginning to understand what they'd signed up for.

"So what happened?" Allison asked excitedly. "What'd you do? What was it like?" She was literally jumping up and down. Her long hair, pulled back in a ponytail, bounced all around her shoulders.

"I made some books fly across the room," Felix said casually, like he was telling her she should bring an umbrella for later because it had started to rain again. "It was in this monster room. The old library. Inverness. It's huge."

"*Really?* They flew? How'd you do it?"

He thought back to Bill screaming at him, telling him that Emma dumped him because he was a loser. That he would never amount to anything. It still stung even though he knew that Bill had only been trying to get him to tap into the Source. "I just can."

Allison's expression informed him that his explanation was sadly inadequate. He thought for a minute, struggling to come up with an analogy. "It's sort of like swimming. When you jump in you just kinda know you're not gonna sink, right? You don't know why you can swim, you just know how to move your body in the water. I don't know." He wasn't sure if that helped or not.

"Alright, well just show me." Her eyes were dancing with anticipation. "Please. Please. Pleeeeease."

"I thought Caitlin was waiting for you," Felix teased. "Lucas is probably there by now. We should get going or we'll miss their first tiff of the night." He looked down at his watch, toying with her.

"Come on," she pleaded, giving him a nudge to the shoulder.

She was so excited. So happy. There were no worry lines on her forehead. He loved seeing her like this. All of her prickliness and intensity, all of her rough edges, had smoothed over. She was softer, more girlish, more... something. *How could he say no?*

"Okay." He searched the room for a suitable object, something smallish no one would miss too much if he accidentally killed it. He trained his eyes on a chair. Right size—and it belonged to the school. It wouldn't be mourned after if something tragic happened to it. And something tragic could very well happen to it; he didn't have a ton of confidence in his Source-wielding abilities. He raised his right hand toward it. Almost immediately, the tingly pins and needles flooded his body and a lead weight settled in his gut.

The chair bounced around and then rumbled slowly and unsteadily away from the desk. Felix wanted to make the chair slide elegantly across the floor to the center of the room where Allison could take a seat, and he could do something cool at the end, like say, "Voila," or take a bow, or something grandiose like that. He glanced at Allison. She was beaming, holding her hands together like she was in prayer.

The chair snagged itself on the rug.

He tried to make it go up, to go over the edge, but it wasn't easy. He concentrated. The front legs jerked up off the floor, fell back down, then popped back up, making the chair look like a rodeo bronco trying to buck its rider. He focused harder on lifting it off the floor and it popped up a few feet, dropped back to the floor with a thud, jumped up again, and then with a loud *crack*, all four legs splintered and snapped off from the bottom of the seat. The shattered legs, along with the rest of the chair, fell to the floor. So much for the grandiose finale, he thought, disappointed.

"Oops." Felix went over to have a look at it; it was mangled. "It's hard to control. I was trying that with a book and—"

Allison embraced him fiercely, throwing her arms around his waist, pressing her face into his shoulder. She was trembling, saying something, but he couldn't catch the words.

"Allie?" He took a step back, surprised, his arms at his sides.

She hugged him tightly, like she was afraid to let go.

"You okay?" He held her, conscious of her body, the firmness of her legs. The way she smelled. Something clean and sweet but not perfumey. He didn't know if she was laughing or crying.

"Sorry." She tilted her head back to look up at him. Her eyes were dry. "It's just... it's just so, I don't know... it's just so *awesome*! I can't believe this. I can't explain it. But I just love that you can do that." She looked down at the chair. "I love what it means. Everything's so different now. So exciting. I feel like there's a point to all this. Nothing's meaningless anymore." She smiled. "And you are officially the most interesting guy in the world!"

"Nah." He smiled back shyly. "It's still that old bearded guy with the cool accent. Whose chair is that, anyway?"

"Caitlin's."

"*Really?* Shit. I keep trashing her stuff."

They started laughing.

"What the—?" a voice said.

Harper stood in the doorway, one hand on the doorknob, the other covering her mouth. She looked absolutely stunned, frozen in place, as she watched Felix and Allison locked in an embrace and laughing like they were enjoying their first dance as husband and wife.

Felix clumsily let go of Allison and stepped back numbly, digging his hands into his pockets, staring stupidly at his feet. He felt like his mom had just walked in on him making out with Emma.

"Have you seen Caitlin?" Harper asked, her voice cold and stiff.

"She's in the caf," Allison said lightly. Unlike Felix, she wasn't acting like the cops had caught her drinking beer out of a paper bag in the park.

Harper noticed the chair and did a double take.

"Felix was just helping me with it," Allison said preemptively.

"Looks like he was helping you with *something*." Harper's eyes narrowed suspiciously. "What happened?"

"I was trying to get something out of my closet," Allison said pleasantly, smiling. "Piece of advice: don't stand on the chairs. They're pretty flimsy."

"How's he going to fix that?" Harper asked dubiously, her gaze trained on Allison. Felix felt like he was no longer in the room.

"He's not," Allison replied. "We decided that it's unfixable."

"Are you eating?" Felix asked Harper, hoping he sounded less guilty than he felt.

"Yeah." Harper didn't look at him—she just turned and stalked out of the room, disappearing down the hallway.

Great, Felix thought miserably. *Now she's even more pissed at me.* He shook his head in disgust and headed for the hall. Allison followed, stealing a glance at the chair on the way out, smiling. The last thing she seemed concerned about was whether Harper was mad at him.

Chapter 39

HEAVEN'S ON FIRE

The world was hazy, cloaked in shadows. Felix was lying on his back, looking up. He was on a bed and in a room—that much he could tell. For no good reason, he had the curious sensation that he'd been here before. He tried to get a better look, but he couldn't turn his head. He tried to move his arms, then his legs. They wouldn't budge; it was like he was glued to the mattress.

The shadows were getting darker. The room grew warmer. Sweat slid down his face as the temperature rose rapidly. The area around him began to glow a deep reddish color. The bed started to move, vibrating and rattling in short staccato bursts. Then it heaved violently like a boat caught out at sea in a raging storm. The red cloud spread outward, expanding, stretching out to the edges of his peripheral vision. And then it all stopped. The bed was still. The temperature dropped. The room was peaceful and silent.

What just happened? Felix wondered. *Where the hell am I?* Before he could even begin to unpeel the first of the infinite layers of his confusion, a roaring tornado consumed the room. The winds were ferocious. Objects were whirling through the maroon-tinted mist, crashing into the walls and exploding into flames; burning fragments fell onto the bed and all around the room. He struggled against his invisible chains. But it was no use. He was stuck to the bed like an insect snared on a strip of flypaper.

The blanket caught fire and the flames danced across the foot of the bed. He tried to scream, but he couldn't find his voice. His heart was racing. Sweat dripped from his body, soaking the sheets. The carpet ignited. The fire spread across the floor, climbing up the walls and covering the ceiling as if the heavens were aflame. Thick smoke billowed all around him, stinging his eyes. The fire ate through the blanket and crept steadily up to his legs, and then his stomach, and then his chest, inching closer to his face. He watched in horror. He tried to scream but all that came out was a shrill, hollow whistling sound. The heat was unbearable. The air scorched his lungs. The hot flames lapped at his face like a thirsty demon. He felt his cheeks and forehead blistering. Something warm and gelatinous oozed from the bursting pustules. His hair caught fire, crackling. His skin melted away, devoured by the scorching heat, and now the flesh beneath it was charring like a side of beef on a grill. The scent of meat filled the room. Even through the agonizing pain, Felix's tortured mind understood that it was the smell of his own cooking flesh.

He screamed. He screamed again. And again. And again.

"Felix! Felix! Wake up! Holy shit! Wake up!"

His eyes snapped open. Lucas was standing over him—screaming. It took Felix a moment to realize that Lucas wasn't screaming. The voice he was hearing was his own. *I'm in the dorm*, Felix thought, intensely relieved that he wasn't burning to death. It was a dream. Just a dream. And then he panicked, every nerve in his body firing at once. He felt a thin sheen of sweat coating his body as he swung his legs off the mattress and staggered out of bed, looking frantically around the room.

"You okay?" Felix shouted at Lucas, fearing he might have gone nuclear again in his sleep. "Everything all right?" He threw himself on the floor and checked under his bed. Then he jumped up and wrenched open the closet doors.

"Take it easy, dude." Lucas withdrew a few steps, watching Felix curiously from the center of the room, smearing his eyes blearily with the heels of his hands. Lucas, wearing only green and orange PC boxers with a smiling sturgeon on his butt, looked very confused, and very tired. "It's just another dream. Third one this week, dude. You think you're done scaring the shit out of me?"

Deeply relieved that this wasn't a sequel, Felix slumped down on his bed and took a deep breath. He didn't need Lucas to keep track of how many times he'd had this dream: Each time it scared the hell out of him, each time it was exactly the same, and each time it was horrifyingly unforgettable.

"Sorry," Felix said contritely. Most of his panic had melted away, but not enough to calm his racing heart. "Shit. Sorry about waking you up."

"It's okay." Lucas flipped the light switch and returned to his bed. "You remember anything?"

Felix considered his options as he stared up at the darkened ceiling, but his answer was never in doubt. He would lie, just like he had every time before. "No."

"Too bad," Lucas said. "G'night, dude."

"G'night."

Chapter 40

WOLVES

"You look like hell," Allison said to Felix as they walked along a path on the north side of The Yard.

"Thanks." He zipped up his jacket until the puffy down-filled collar covered his chin. It was bitingly cold, the coldest day of the year so far. The chill gnawed at his ears and the tip of his nose. "I didn't get much sleep. I keep having these really weird dreams."

She gave him a searching look, her breaths escaping in little clouds into the frigid air. "You okay?"

"I guess." Felix wasn't sure if he was okay or not. The dreams were really getting to him, bleeding into his waking life, but he didn't know what to do about it. Ten o'clock classes had ended and the eleven o'clocks were about to start. The path and the steps to the lecture halls were clotted with students and drifted with clumps of fallen leaves.

"So where's Bill's office?" she asked, as they skirted around a group of students hanging out in front of the Siegler Building. "Did you say it was in Stamford?"

"Yeah."

"Did he say... um... did he say why he wants to see me?"

"Not really. I haven't even talked to him in like a week and a half. Not since I saw him at Inverness."

"Oh. So what'd he do, text you?"

"Uh-huh."

They walked in silence the rest of the way, both staring at the ground. When they arrived at Bill's office (they'd taken the stairs to stay warm) they found that the door had been left open for them. Felix shrugged out of his jacket. The comforting warmth of Stamford's central heat had felt great at first, but now he was starting to sweat. He poked his head into the room and said, "Bill?"

Bill was sitting at his desk with his laptop open in front of him, eyes focused on the screen. He looked up, startled. "Oh—hey Felix." He snapped the monitor shut. "Come in. Is Allison with you?"

"Hi!" Allison stepped around Felix and entered the office.

Bill got up from his chair and leaned over his desk to shake her hand. "Nice to meet you, Allison. Please have a seat." He motioned at the two guest chairs. "It's a cold one out there, isn't it? The weather guy says the high will only be forty today. Either of you like a cup of tea?"

Felix shook his head and dropped his backpack on the floor, then sank heavily into the chair, sliding down until the small of his back rested on the edge of the seat. He folded his coat in half and held it on his lap.

"No thanks." Allison slipped out of her jacket and took a seat in the other chair, her eyes roaming around the room. Then she looked at Bill and said simply, "You don't look like a groundskeeper." Felix agreed. Bill was dressed like an investment banker on business casual day: tan slacks, leather loafers and a blue button-down shirt. Felix had seen him like this before so he wasn't surprised.

Bill smiled at Allison. "I'm trying to encourage my colleagues to take fashion more seriously."

Allison laughed.

Bill settled back into his chair, then he looked at Felix and his eyebrows nearly came together over his nose. "You look a little chalky. You sick?"

"Just tired. Nightmares keep waking me up."

"Nightmares? About what?"

"Burning to death."

"*Burning to death?*" Bill's eyes went wide for a moment. "Are you doing your relaxation techniques?"

"Sometimes. They don't seem to be working."

"Have you—"

"Sorry." Allison held up her arm and nodded at her watch apologetically. "Not to be rude, but we actually have to meet our friends in a few minutes. Can we hurry this up?"

"Of course," Bill said. "This won't take long. So you're probably wondering why I wanted to meet you."

Allison nodded, her face placid.

"It's pretty simple really. The three of us know something the rest of the world is blind to. We know about The Warning. We know that Lofton Ashfield is the Drestian. We know that Felix is the Belus. And we also know that the world isn't what it seems. If Lofton has put things in motion—and he has—you'll start to look for the signs. You'll see them everywhere once you know what to look for: the liberal politician with an unerringly consistent voting record who suddenly becomes an advocate for press censorship and the criminalization of public assemblies; senators from neighboring states forming alliances irrespective of political party; and most telling, the government's inaction—*deliberate inaction*—to combat violence and poverty and to provide basic services to its citizens, which is clearly by design. The more incompetent, self-interested and corrupt the government appears, the easier it will be for Lofton to offer the people an alternative. *His* alternative. Living in this world—the real world—won't be easy for you. You could feel isolated. You may doubt yourself. You may even feel like you've lost your mind. So I just wanted to make sure you're okay."

"I'm fine with all that," Allison said lightly, shrugging. "I really am. I always thought—always hoped—that there was something more to all this. Something below the surface more important than all the trivial crap everyone's so obsessed about."

"Good," Bill said. "That's good. I appreciate that perspective. But if you ever need to talk with someone, I'll make myself available. Make sure you get my number from Felix. If you have any questions or anything, you can—"

"I do have a question," she interrupted, causing Bill to raise an eyebrow. "Why would anyone follow Lofton?"

"Good question," Bill said with a nod of his head. "According to The Warning, the Drestian *will* fix the Source, but the Belus"—his eyes went pointedly to Felix who was studying the maps on the wall behind Bill's desk—"can only fix the Source with help from all of us—from humankind."

"But Lofton will also make everyone his slaves," Allison pointed out.

"That's right," Bill agreed. "It's a classic example of competing political philosophies. If you follow Lofton, you're giving away your freedom and your self-determination, but you gain certainty and security— *and* the survival of the Source. If you follow Felix, you believe that freedom is something that cannot be given or traded away. You believe freedom is a critical component of our makeup, and that without it, there is no point to our lives, regardless of the consequences—*and there are consequences*. Because if Felix and the rest of us—humankind that is—fail, the Source will fail. To put it simply, those who would follow Lofton have no faith that we can solve our own problems so they would hand over control—and their freedom—to a single man who will solve our problems for us. And those who would follow Felix believe we should have the right to decide our own fate, the right to fight for our own destiny, and that servitude to one man's will, one man's rule, can never be tolerated even if it means the end of the universe."

"That's what I thought," Allison said.

Felix glanced at her, thinking she was joking, but she looked serious.

Bill leaned back in his chair and smiled at her. "Well I'm glad we've reached the same conclusion."

Allison looked down at the floor and crossed one boot over the other. Then she lifted her gaze and said, "I have another question."

"Shoot."

"Why is Lofton killing people in Ashfield Forest?"

"Sorry?" Bill said, surprised.

"The *Ashfield Forest Mystery*," Allison said. "Isn't it obvious? He's the Drestian. It's his forest. He must be responsible."

"Lofton's not killing anyone," Bill said fervently, shaking his head. "At least not in Ashfield Forest."

"Bullshit!" Felix blurted and sat up straight. "Allison's right! I can't believe I didn't see the connection. That can't be a coin—"

"Coincidence? It is—believe it or not. I happen to know what's going on, and I can tell you." Bill paused, watching them. "But you have to promise to keep this between us." He waited until they nodded their assent. "Wolves," he announced.

"*Wolves?*" they said in unison.

"Three domesticated packs were released into the wild over the past two years. Sometime last year, they came together to form a super-pack. The zoologists working with the governor's office believe that because the wolves were raised in captivity, they don't fear people, as they should, but instead view them as a source of food. As we speak, every wolf expert and big game hunter on the west coast is in Ashfield Forest attempting to locate the pack. And when they find them, they'll kill them."

"How come we haven't been hearing about this super-pack on the news?" Allison asked skeptically.

"Politics," Bill said with loathing in his voice, his mouth twisting into a frown. "The governor approved the re-introduction of wolves despite the protests of farmers and the lobbyists who represent them. If this were to become public, the governor would be wading through a shitstorm with an election year coming up. Lofton's doing the governor a favor. He'll keep it quiet and allow access to his forest in exchange for whatever he may need from the governor down the road."

"How do you know all this?" Felix asked.

"I know some people," Bill replied cryptically.

Allison stood up and turned to Felix. "We're late."

Felix grabbed his backpack and got to his feet, yawning.

"You look like shit," Bill said to him.

"I feel like shit."

"Well pull it together," Bill urged, giving Felix a smile. "I'll be seeing you tonight. Twelve sharp. Don't be late."

Felix groaned.

"Nice meeting you, Allison."

"You too," she said on her way out, her coat tucked under her arm. "See you around."

Chapter 41

STALKING STALKERS

The grass was wet and half frozen, crunching under their feet as they made their way through The Yard. The sun had crept higher in a white sky while they were in Bill's office.

"He's younger than I thought he'd be," Allison said to Felix.

"I think he's thirty-eight or thirty-nine. That's pretty old."

"That is pretty old," she agreed. "He's lying, you know."

"*Lying?* About what?"

"I don't know."

"So how do you know he's lying?"

Allison started to say something, but nothing intelligible came out, and she fell into silence. He watched her, waiting for a response. The lawn ended. The southeast corner of the library was visible off in the distance and Little Ben's enormous clock face poked its head above Garner Hall. He was getting restless. Maybe it was the lack of sleep. "Allie? What the hell?"

"Sorry," she said with an irritated shake of her head. "I don't know why I know. I just do."

"Like an intuition thing," he hazarded.

"No. This is different. It's like a... I don't know. It's just a feeling, I guess." She clamped her jaw, staring down silently at the ground.

Felix knew she was smoldering beneath her stony expression. He'd seen this before; impatient by nature, if Allison couldn't immediately wrap her head around something she became frustrated with herself. He decided not to push her.

"Hey Felix!" a girl's voice rang out from the path up ahead.

He didn't recognize the voice, but he recognized the body it was attached to: Amber. Her long skinny legs reached right up to her mound of wavy strawberry blonde hair. She sauntered right over to him and he had to pull up to avoid running into her.

"Hey," Felix said hesitantly, wishing he'd noticed her earlier so that he could have taken evasive action.

"How's it going?" Amber said. She was wearing sheer black leggings and a tight cleavage-revealing sweater. No coat. She was either immune or oblivious to the weather.

"Good." He glanced furtively at Allison. "Good. It's all good." He took a step back, trying to reclaim his personal bubble.

"It looks good." Amber smiled and moved closer. She was practically on top of him. Her sultry brown eyes were eating him up, making him feel awkward. She bit down softly on her lip. "So who are you doing these days?"

"*Who?*"

Amber smiled at his confusion. "There's a party tonight at Astoria. Common room on the second floor. There'll be lots of beer. And anything else you might wanna get your hands on. *Including me.*" She drew out the last two words in a lusty breath, more moan than speech. Then she smiled suggestively and ran her hands over her ass, which he couldn't help but notice (and stare at) because it was phenomenal.

Felix coughed nervously, trying not to look at Allison. He could feel her eyes burning into him. "Yeah, sure. I'll try to make it."

"Your friend can come too if she wants," Amber offered like an afterthought, her eyes remaining fixed on Felix.

Allison jumped in, apparently not appreciating the bystander treatment. "I have a name—Allison. Thanks, but I think I have plans."

"That's too bad," Amber replied with practiced insincerity. "Hope to see you there, big guy." She took her time looking him up and down, then licked her lips and walked away.

They started up again.

"That's the ERA chick, isn't it?" Allison said when Amber was out of earshot.

"Yeah."

"I think she might like you." She laughed.

He grinned crookedly. "She scares me."

"You know she's a trophy hunter," Allison told him.

"A what?"

"She bags guys."

Felix considered this as they put the library and Little Ben behind them. Beyond the Courtyard and past a stretch of perfectly spaced trees stood the Student Center, which was attracting droves of students swaddled in heavy coats.

"You mean, she like mounts their heads on the wall?" he asked.

Allison nodded. "That's the word on the street, anyway. She's just a year ahead of us but the list of guys she's slept with is long and illustrious."

"Really? Who's on it?"

"Just the most popular and hottest guys on campus. I don't know any names, but it's supposedly a veritable who's who at PC."

"Seriously?" Felix said, recalling his steamy encounter with Amber after the Satler party. "Why would she do that?"

"Who knows? Low self-esteem. Daddy issues. Maybe she just likes hooking up with hot guys. Got me."

"And she's ERA," Felix added. "She's got a lot going on. I saw a guy with a tiger tattoo the other day. In Western Civ. He must be ERA, right?"

"I'm sure he is. Two girls in my English class have them on their feet. They wear flip flops even on days like this. Showing off their tats, I guess."

"I thought it had to be on your arm," Felix said.

Allison shook her head. "I think most are, but it's not a requirement or anything. Some of them—oh shit!" She looked startled, then her eyes darted all around like she wanted to make a run for it. "Shoot me. Not him."

"Not who?"

Allison didn't have to answer. Grayson Bentley was coming directly at them, smiling. He was always smiling. It was like he was so pleased with himself he couldn't help but be happy.

"Oh God," Felix muttered.

Grayson waved and said cheerfully, "Hello."

"Hey," Allison replied dully. "We're actually on our way to—"

"I haven't seen you around the house in a while," Grayson said to Allison, stopping them in the middle of the path. "You either." He nodded at Felix with the same degree of dismissive rudeness as if Felix was a busboy at Friendly's asking permission to clear off his table.

"I've been busy," Allison told him.

"I can see that." Grayson regarded Felix like he had the Ebola virus.

"See ya." Felix tried to step around him. He couldn't take this guy, not even in limited doses. He hated the way he seemed to own every situation. It was like he was never uncomfortable. He figured Grayson had been told how great he was from the day he was born, and that message was now part of his fabric—he didn't just think he was better than everyone else, he *knew* he was better than everyone else. Unfortunately, his résumé backed up his lofty opinion of himself.

"Hold on a sec." Grayson leaned in confidentially to get Felix's attention. "I was thinking about you the other day. I know this kid who lives in Astoria. His name's Jeremy. Real smart, but socially, he's a train wreck. Total disaster. I'm sure you know the type. Anyway, he's desperate to join my frat. Thinks it'll get him laid." He laughed loudly, his breath steaming thick in the cold. "We had a few beers at the house—probably his first ever. You know how some kids are, you give 'em a drink or two and they won't shut the hell up. He wouldn't stop talking. The kid really opened up like I was his priest or something."

Felix was starting to sweat.

"Do you know who my dad is?" Grayson asked.

"Never met him," Felix said.

Grayson ignored Felix's comment. "One thing my dad taught me is the value of information. He says it's the most valuable commodity in the world. The people who control the flow of information, control the world. And that's a fact."

"I'm sure your dad's right," Allison said. "We gotta go."

"So Jeremy," Grayson continued, forging ahead, "is the kid whose room was broken into by *The Kid With The Hood*. He told me some very interesting things. He said he got a good look at him. He said that he's tall and moves real quick. Like an athlete. Maybe a football player. You wouldn't know anyone like that would you?"

"Yeah, it was me," Felix said, trying to crack a big sarcastic grin. "I break into dorm rooms and steal underwear when I've got nothing going on."

Grayson laughed and clapped him on the shoulder like they were best buddies. Felix breathed a little easier.

"Is there a point to this?" Allison asked.

"I'm just busting his chops," Grayson said to Allison. "Jeremy will probably be the next Mark Zuckerberg, but I wouldn't let him in the Beta house if he was the last pledge on earth. The guy's pure chick repellent. With enough losers like him in the frat, you reach a critical mass, a tipping point, and before you know it, your house is crawling with dorks running around dressed like hobbits and wizards and watching *Star Wars* wearing Darth Vader masks." He laughed and waved at some kids passing by.

"Nice seeing you." Allison used the kids as a diversion to step off the path and make her way past him. Felix followed and they headed for the Student Center.

"Maybe I'll see you at the house sometime?" Grayson called after them.

Allison waved without turning around and said in a soft voice, "Not likely, asshole." Felix kept his hands in his coat pockets. "What the hell's going on today?" she burst out a moment later. "Who's next? What is this? The skank and asshole parade? What do you think that was about?"

"No idea." Felix was working out in his mind whether any part of what Grayson had said could be true and whether he should start avoiding Jeremy (not that he saw him around much—twice, actually, and both times at a distance).

"Why would he insinuate that you're *The Kid With The Hood*?" Allison asked.

"Because your ex-boyfriend's an asshole."

"*Ex-boyfriend?*" She laughed and shoved him off the path into a giant rhododendron. "I'll hurt you if—hey! What are they doing?"

"Who?"

"Them," she said, pointing.

Felix followed the line of her finger and spotted Lucas, Caitlin and Harper across from the Student Center huddled together stiffly against the chill, heads down, standing in the shadow of an enormous leafless tree. Their breaths were puffing out white in the icy air, mingling for a moment and then disappearing.

"What the hell are they up to?" Felix said to her. "We're supposed to meet at the Caffeine Hut, right?"

"Yeah." Allison sped up.

"What's up, guys?" Felix called out when he and Allison were within shouting distance. They looked like they were checking out each other's shoes… then Felix noticed the cell phone. Lucas was holding it down by his waist and Caitlin and Harper were regarding it intently. Only Lucas glanced up at the sound of Felix's voice (it appeared he was muttering obscenities under his breath), his eyes shifting nervously.

"What are you doing out here?" Allison asked them. "It's freezing."

"Get over here," Lucas said through his teeth. "Just pretend like you're checking out my phone." Their collars were turned up around their ears, their cheeks well-rouged from the cold.

"Huh?" Felix said, puzzled. "Why?"

"Just do it," Lucas ordered.

They wedged themselves between Harper and Caitlin, and Allison asked in a low voice, "What are we doing?"

"Hi guys," Caitlin whispered, keeping her eyes on the phone. "Good question. I just got here. What are we doing?" She glanced up at Lucas.

"You're watching a viral video on YouTube," Lucas said. "It's awesome. It's the Michigan lacrosse team lip syncing *Love Me Baby* in their locker room."

"What?" Felix looked down at the phone. The screen was black. "What the hell's—"

"Just *pretend* like you're watching the video," Lucas said, his voice strained and tense. "If the lacrosse team lip syncing doesn't do it for you, pretend you're watching a little kid hitting his dad in the nuts with a golf club. I could watch those groin shot vids all day long."

"Have you all lost your minds?" Allison said, taking a short step back. "I'm gonna go get a cup of hot coffee. Let me know when you regain your sanity."

"I'm being followed," Lucas said tersely.

Felix was getting better at recognizing when Lucas wasn't screwing around. Now was one of those times.

"There's this kid who's been after me since the start of school." Lucas looked over at Felix. "The kid I told you about way back when. I've seen him like five or six times. I thought I had him cornered a couple times, but he got away. Is he still there?"

Harper looked up from the phone. Felix watched her deep blue eyes moving back and forth as she scanned the outside of the Student Center. A moment later she nodded. "Yeah. He's doing a terrible job of hiding behind one of the columns. Third from the left on the library side. He's on his cell."

Felix started to turn his head to see what she was looking at but Lucas stopped him by hissing, "Don't! You're gonna spook him. Look at the phone."

Felix ducked like a turtle hiding in its shell. "Sorry. What's he look like?"

"Short, curly haired little shit," Lucas said. "He's got a PC hat on."

"He's also wearing a green PC jacket," Harper chipped in, frowning. "Very tacky. It looks like he's getting his fashion advice from the student bookstore."

"I see him." Allison stared over Felix's shoulder. "He's facing this way. He's definitely checking us out."

"That little shit." Lucas started off toward the Student Center. "I'm gonna kill him."

"Hold on." Felix snagged Lucas's arm, stopping him before he could get very far. "Let's go to the stadium. Nobody'll be there. Let's make him come to us."

Lucas chewed on the side of his thumbnail, fuming. "Yeah," he said after a while. "Yeah. Yeah. I like that. No one will see us pummeling the shit out of the little bastard if we do it there."

"Oh, stop," Caitlin sighed, shaking her head. "You're not going to pummel anybody."

Without a word, Lucas turned and trooped off in the direction of Stubbins Stadium. They all fell in behind and no one argued, but Caitlin made her reluctance known with her groans and sighs and other little noises.

"Don't turn around unless I tell you to," Lucas said once they'd distanced themselves from the bustle outside the Student Center. "This kid's like some kind of genetically engineered super spy. Every time I think I have him, he slips right through my fingers."

Allison laughed. "Yeah, he looks exactly like Jason Bourne. I think even Caitlin could take him."

"Hey!" Caitlin said, eyes wide and mouth open, offended. "I'm tougher than I look."

They passed the Caffeine Hut, trying to conduct themselves like they didn't know someone was following them and failing miserably in their attempts at having a normal conversation. After Lucas offered up a couple of gems like: "Do you think I could get Miley Cyrus to send me a picture of her lady parts?" and, "Who do you think would win in a fight, a lion or a shark?" Caitlin called him an idiot. Before they could start fighting again, which seemed inevitable, Allison distracted them by changing the subject to the ERA. It worked for a while. Everyone agreed there were at least one or two kids with tiger tattoos in all their classes. After that, the conversation stalled.

A few minutes later, with Ferguson Hall now behind them and the Bryant Center in sight, Lucas broke the silence: "Okay, let's see if the little punk is still tailing us. Can you do a little pirouette or something?" he said to Caitlin.

"*A what?*" Caitlin said.

"I don't know what you call it," Lucas said impatiently. "Just do a little girly twirly ice dancing ballerina thingamajigger. You know. You're a chick."

"You're a jerk," Caitlin replied.

"I'll do it," Allison told him. She spun around and whispered dramatically, "If Hannah Montana sent you a pic of her lady parts, I think I'd lose all faith in humanity. And I'm going with the shark." Then she did two pirouettes and put her arm around Lucas's shoulder. "Brace yourself: Bourne's still there. Fifty yards behind us. Just crossed the Mill Stream. Looks like he's on his phone."

"Nice!" Lucas said. "See. Allison knew what I meant."

"You're an idiot," Caitlin said flatly.

There was shouting in the distance, followed by whistles, then a smattering of boisterous cheering and hand clapping. Applause. They rounded a bend in the path and the practice fields just east of the stadium appeared up ahead. All three fields were teeming with people.

"Soccer tournament," Harper said.

"Shit!" Lucas howled in disgust. "Stupid intramurals. This isn't gonna work."

Felix had an idea. "C'mon." He changed direction, quickening his pace. "This way."

"These boots have heels," Harper protested, struggling to keep up. "And in case you didn't notice, I'm wearing a skirt."

Felix did notice. It was impossible not to notice Harper, especially when she wore a mid-thigh skirt and black knee-high boots with pointy toes and three-inch heels. But today was the first time since she'd walked in on Allison hugging him that she wasn't treating him like he was an axe murderer. She was even kind of talking to him in a roundabout way—even though they didn't look at each other when they spoke—so he didn't want her to catch him staring at her. He thought it might break the positive momentum.

"Where are we going?" Lucas asked, catching up to Felix.

"You'll see," Felix said, thinking he might as well have a little fun with this. He led them along a path that ran parallel to the stone wall on the north side of the Old Campus. The path doglegged right. A short distance later they came to the east gate.

As soon as Caitlin understood what Felix was contemplating, she said with white-faced horror, "We're not actually going in there, are we?" She pointed at the gate like it was the entrance to hell.

"Isn't it locked?" Lucas asked.

"No," Felix said quickly—too quickly. That wasn't something he would know unless he'd been here before. He tried to cover up his mistake. "I don't see a lock, anyway."

It was a swinging gravity gate, but the locking mechanism had broken off and no one had bothered to replace it. A bracket shaped like a flower had once held the latch arm in place—eight half-ovals set in a circle to resemble petals. The gate had been painted with layer upon layer of black paint, but not since the latch had broken off, and now the iron beneath it was rusting orange. The little flower looked bright and deliberate, like some artistic soul had stenciled it on to ornament the entry point.

Felix gave it a push, putting his weight into it. Paint and rust had thickened and sludged the rods, pins, cylinders and other working parts. It groaned like an old arthritic man getting up off the sofa after a tryptophan-rich holiday feast. He stole a quick glance over his shoulder as he crossed into the Old Campus, catching a glimpse of a green jacket.

"He's still there," Felix said quietly. "Stay close." He led them onto the same brick walkway he'd taken the night he met Bill at Inverness. Light trickled down bleakly through the low overhanging branches of massive oaks. The sky darkened. It was almost midday outside the walls. Twilight inside. Or so it felt.

"This place is seriously creepy," Caitlin whispered, tagging along after Felix. "I don't think we're supposed to be here. Won't we get in trouble if someone sees us?"

"We'll be fine," Felix assured her as they crept along in a tight mass. The Old Campus looked different during the day. At night, it was like the Disneyland of haunted houses. But now, it looked less like the site of a horror movie set in Victorian Transylvania and more like an abandoned asylum. The buildings were crumbling from decades of benign neglect: grimed over with bird droppings and a forest of creeping vines, too browned and brittle to be alive, too stubborn and entrenched to be dead; bottom-floor windows broken, jagged and spidery, the work of pranksters and vandals; and rooflines that sagged where they should have soared, slate tiles lost to weather and time. The trees looked different here too, like an ugly subspecies of the well-tended beauties that graced the campus, their branches curled and twisted in sharp, awkward angles as if they were in pain.

"It's kinda cool," Allison said, her eyes flitting in every direction with something approaching wonderment, like a tourist enjoying a boat ride down the Amazon. "Where are we going?"

"At the end of this one"—Felix pointed at the chained and padlocked doors of the building to their right—"we're gonna go around the corner and hide. We'll jump him when he walks by us."

"Awesome!" Lucas said.

Caitlin shook her head at Lucas with scowling disapproval. "You seriously need sensitivity training."

"I don't even know what that is," Lucas said.

"Exactly."

"Exactly what? You need uptightness training, and meat-eating training, and lameness training, and—"

"Shut up!" Harper stage-whispered.

Felix stepped off the path and jogged over to the side entry stairs where he motioned for everyone to join him. A moment later, they came struggling up the rain-eroded knoll and gathered around him.

"Okay," Felix said, looking at each of them. "When he walks by, I'll tackle him."

"*Tackle?*" Caitlin said in surprise, her eyes fearful. "What if you hurt him? Maybe he's just some dumb kid who's incomprehensibly infatuated with Lucas and just wants his autograph."

"Caitlin's right," Allison whispered. "You're not Jimmy Clay. You can't just go around tackling people."

"Sure he can," Lucas said angrily. "He's not a *person.* He's a *stalker.* Whose side are you on?"

"Maybe they're right," Felix said to him. "I'll just... uh... restrain him."

"Whatever," Lucas grunted. "Let's just get the little shit so I can find out why he's following me around."

They waited in a pool of deep unmoving shadows. There was no wind, yet it felt colder now, like the ground was leaching the warmth from their bodies. They blew hot air on their fingers and bounced on the balls of their feet to stay warm. Nobody spoke. Felix readied himself with one hand on the hard turf like a sprinter preparing for the starter's pistol to go off. A minute passed. And then another. He was about to give up when a PC hat appeared in front of them. Before the kid knew what had hit him, Felix fastened his grip on the front of his jacket. Scrawny and short—his head barely came up to Felix's chest—he screamed like a child and made a comically weak attempt to kick Felix in the shin.

"Stop!" Felix shouted at him. "Quit kicking!" It wasn't hard to restrain him (no harder than controlling a child throwing a tantrum). But Felix was trying not to hurt him, which made it a bit more challenging.

Lucas jumped to Felix's side and shouted in his face: "Why the hell are you following me?"

"Help!" the kid screamed, eyes bulging in fear, his head twisting and thrashing madly. "Let me go! Help!" He made a weak swipe at Felix. When that didn't work, he used his fingernails, raking them across the top of Felix's hands.

"Ouch!" Felix let go of his jacket and the kid lost his balance, tumbling onto the grass, his hat spinning off his head.

"Shit!" Felix shouted. Long traces of blood lined the back of his left hand. "You little shit!"

The kid fumbled around for his hat, then used a thick-trunked oak to push himself awkwardly off the ground. The grass was frosted with dew and it left wet patches on his knees and belly. He had a mountain of curly brown hair that made his head look huge and wildly out of proportion to his frail jellyfish body.

"Who are you?" Lucas screamed. He looked like he was dangerously close to following through on his threat to pummel him. Not unwarranted, Felix thought, given the circumstances, but it was strange to see him so angry.

"Quinn Traynor," the kid muttered, unzipping his jacket. "My name's Quinn Traynor." A camera with a long telephoto attachment dangled from a strap around his neck. He turned it over in his hands. "Shit!" He stamped his foot on the ground. "The lens is cracked. Do you have any idea how much this is going to cost me?" The kid—Quinn—was actually mad at them, but his appearance made it hard to take him seriously. Anger didn't really suit him; his outburst was more pathetic than threatening.

"You little punk ass bitch!" Lucas balled up his right hand into a fist. "So that's what you're doing! I should shove that thing up your ass!"

"Easy, Lucas," Caitlin said, sidling up next to him and taking him by the arm.

"Why don't you tell us what's going on," Allison said calmly.

Quinn glanced around for a moment as though he was thinking about making a dash for it, then he grimaced and sighed deeply. "I guess the jig is up. I mean look at me!" He tapped the Sturgeon logo on the front of his satiny jacket. "I look ridiculous! I'm not even a student."

"You're not?" Harper said, her eyes growing large with surprise. "Well then you definitely look ridiculous dressed like that."

"So what are you doing here?" Felix asked.

Quinn pointed a stubby finger at Lucas. "Him. I'm a photographer. And a reporter. I work for *Hollywood Reality Bites*."

"The tabloid?" Caitlin asked.

Quinn nodded.

"So you're a paparazzi dirtbag?" Lucas said, seething.

"*Paparazzo* dirtbag," Quinn corrected, putting his hat back on. "My editor assigned me to you. And my assignment is to get a photo of you doing drugs, getting in a fight or hooking up with some dirty little ho-bag. I've been following you for three months and I've gotten zilch. Not a single photo I can sell."

"Good," Lucas said.

"*Good?*" Quinn let out an exasperated huff. "Do you have any idea what it's like out there in the real world? Do you think I want to do this? I graduated from *Dartmouth*. Now I'm pretending to be a student so I can get a picture of you. And you're not cooperating. You go to the library a lot. When you hook up with chicks—and I know that you do—you do it discreetly. And your friends are pure vanilla. You're the least interesting reality star in the world. I wish I'd been assigned to Cleopatra. Just the other day she got wasted and broke into someone's apartment and passed out. The cat was bothering her so she threw it out the window."

"It wasn't her cat." Caitlin cupped a hand over her mouth to stifle a laugh. She glanced around, embarrassed. "Sorry. I read about that the other day." Then she added quickly: "And the cat was fine. In case you're wondering."

"Cry me a river, douche bag," Lucas said to Quinn.

Quinn's eyes went to his broken camera. "Yeah. Right. *I'm* the douche bag. Now I have less than nothing. No photo. No camera. And my cover's blown." Then a smug smile crossed his boyish face. "But I do have one card left to play."

"What are you talking about?" Lucas asked. "What card?"

"Well, you just assaulted me and damaged my property," Quinn said quickly. "If I make a phone call, I'm sure my editor would be more than happy to bring a lawsuit against you on my behalf."

"Is that right?" Allison said, raising an eyebrow at him. "I'm sure the dean would like to meet you. We'll invite the cops. You're not a student so that means you're trespassing. I don't think you're cut out for jail. Your cell mate's gonna love making you his little bitch."

"But that still doesn't justify your vicious assault," Quinn responded like an experienced litigator. "You had no right to attack me and cause such grievous physical harm. My editor would seriously love nothing more than to sue you. All of you. It's like free publicity for the paper. They live for that kind of shit."

"*Attack you?*" Lucas yelled. "You can't be serious! You fell 'cause you have some kind of weird old man's body. Nobody did anything to you."

"I don't really see it that way," Quinn said coolly and brushed at a grass stain on his knee, wincing like his leg was shattered beyond repair. "I guess that'll come down to who the jury believes." Then he smiled slyly and said, "Or... we could make a deal."

"A deal?" Lucas said skeptically.

"I still have my cell." Quinn held it up like a detective showing his badge to an eyewitness. "If you let me take a few pictures with this"—he nodded at the phone—"I'll agree not to sue."

"Pictures of what?" Felix asked.

"Him"—Quinn tilted his cell at Lucas—"kissing someone."

"*Kissing?*" Lucas said.

"Yeah," Quinn replied. "You know, that thing people do with their lips and tongues."

Harper made a gagging noise.

"Who?" Lucas asked, ignoring Quinn's sarcastic tone. "Who would I kiss?"

"Doesn't matter to me." Quinn gestured disinterestedly at the girls. "They'll all do. I've gotta hand it to you, Lucas Mayer. Your friends are all hot."

Lucas turned to the girls. "What do you guys think?"

"He's a disgusting asshole but he kind of has a point," Allison said. "Do you really want a tabloid suing you? And it's just a kiss. No big deal."

Lucas looked at Felix for confirmation.

"Why not?" Felix said. "Do it and be done with this jackass."

"Okay, asshole," Lucas said to Quinn. "It's a deal. But you have to promise that this is where it ends. I don't want to see you again! Ever!"

"Oh, you won't," Quinn replied confidently. "I can't escape from this disgusting college utopia fast enough. So if we have an understanding, then by all means, please get started."

Lucas looked at the girls. "Well? So, um, well... who wants to experience the lifestyle and mystery of Minnesota?"

"I'll do it," Caitlin said, and stepped forward before anyone else could answer, leaving Harper and Allison rooted in place, stunned. "*What?*" Caitlin said to them, glancing over her shoulder. "I have kissed guys before."

"Good," Quinn said. "You're a little short, but you'll do. Now just come over this way and—"

"Not my face!" Caitlin shouted. "My face better not be in your crappy paper. Just the back of my head. Got it?"

"Fine," Quinn said. "No problem. Testy little thing, aren't you?"

Lucas smiled at her. "Thanks Little C."

"Don't mention it."

Lucas placed his hands on her tiny waist and glanced over at Quinn who was positioning himself so that only the back of Caitlin's head would appear in the photo.

"Is this okay?" Lucas asked him.

Quinn held up his cell phone like a painter trying to get a sense of his subject's scale. "You're good. Whenever you're ready."

Caitlin smiled shyly.

"Are you prepared to experience the lifestyle and—"

"Just shut up and kiss me."

They kissed. Their lips only touched for a second. Then they kissed again. This time the kiss lasted just a little longer than the first. Lucas's head flinched back and he raised his eyebrows, looking like he'd opened a birthday card from the great aunt who sent him a crumpled five dollar bill every year to find that this year he was the recipient of ten crisp hundred dollar notes. Caitlin smiled and wrapped her arms gently around his neck. Her eyes closed, and then they kissed. They really kissed. Finally, she pulled herself away and tapped him on the chest.

"You owe me one, Minnesota."

Felix felt his jaw drop. Harper and Allison were both smiling like bridal bouquets had just landed in their outstretched arms.

"That should do." Quinn grinned, scrolling through the photos on his phone with his index finger. "It was nice meeting you all, but I sincerely hope I never see any of you ever again."

"Where you going?" Felix asked him.

"L.A." Quinn raised his phone above his head and shook it triumphantly. "Got my ticket right here, bitches!"

Chapter 42

THE GARROTE

Instructions. Bill was giving Felix instructions—telling him to do something. But what? Felix stood in front of one of the aircraft carrier length reading tables in the old library. It was late. Well past midnight. This was his second trip to the Old Campus today. Behind the table, pushed up against the wall, were metal gym lockers, wooden doors lined up like portals to nowhere, and filing cabinets stacked on top of each other three and four high. On the floor was an odd assortment of alarm clocks and locks. Bill had been busy.

"Do it," Bill ordered.

"Okay." Felix didn't know what Bill wanted him to do, though it probably involved one of the locks on the table. He was flailing in deep space, completely out of it.

Felix only had one class on Thursday afternoons: Western Civ. With ten minutes left, his professor had grown bored with the Carolingians and went off on a tangent about an ancient Roman sect that called themselves the Nocturnists. The Nocturnists believed that our perception of reality—life—was really just a dream. Felix filtered out most of it. He'd heard this drivel before. It was mindless crap. Getting high and philosophizing about *what if this is all just a dream, dude?* was a favorite pastime of every pothead on campus. When the professor mentioned that the Nocturnists were known to consume huge amounts of mushrooms with hallucinogenic properties, everyone had a good laugh. Then she finished up her impromptu lecture with a line from a familiar song: *Merrily, merrily, merrily, merrily, life is but a dream.* Something clicked. His heart rate quickened, racing uncontrollably. The walls closed in on him like a monstrous trash compactor. As surreptitiously as possible, he did a Google search on his phone. He found what he was looking for at once. It was right there. One word. The meaning of a single word had succeeded in irreparably shaking the foundations of his strange new life. That's all it took. The truth was there. It had been there all along.

"Felix? Hey! Did you hear me?"

"Yeah." He blinked and rattled his head. He took a deep breath. The room was gloomier this time. More bulbs had died. The air was glacial and permeated with the scent of damp musty leather.

"You okay?" Bill came over to get a better look at Felix's face. Bill was dressed like he was planning a home invasion: black pea coat, black boots, black hat and black gloves.

"Just tired," Felix sighed. "Long day."

"You sure?"

Felix nodded.

"So get to it."

"Sorry. I wasn't—"

"I noticed." Bill clapped his hands together and a puff of dust burst from his gloves, glimmering in the gray light. "The small lock. Start with that. Come on. I need you to rally."

"What am I...?"

"Shit." Bill waved the dust away, giving Felix a sharp look. "Break it. Don't move it. Got it?"

"Right." Felix stared at the lock, waiting for the heavy feeling in his stomach to make an appearance. When it did, he raised his hand, which was pink and stiff with cold. The lock scooted across the rutted surface in fits and starts, like a toy car with a missing wheel or two. It settled itself and took off on a straight path, gaining speed as it neared the end. Then it exploded in a fiery tempest, spraying the wall with needle-sharp metal fragments.

Felix jumped back and fell to his knees, ducking for cover. Bill didn't move.

"Not bad." Bill stepped over to the table and examined the jagged black hole on top. The lock had disintegrated. "But if you'd been listening, you would've heard me tell you not to move it."

Not bad? Felix thought that was way better than not bad. He couldn't believe he'd just done that. He pushed himself up to his feet, numb from the cold. "Seriously? I just blew the shit out of it! On the first try!"

Bill turned to face him. "You beat up a little lock. What are you looking for? A pat on the back?"

Felix's startled expression was met with silence.

"I just thought... that it was pretty good that I—"

"You're not getting the big picture!" Bill shouted at him. "You're not some pathetic character in a movie. You're not some kid learning how to wax on and wax off. You don't need tights or a wand or a utility belt!" He was gesturing wildly, his face contorted in a sudden fury. "You blew up a Walmart trinket! Hooray!"

Felix was stunned. What happened? What did he do wrong? "What the hell?" he muttered, staring off sullenly at the table. "I did what you asked."

"I'm sorry." Bill squeezed the bridge of his nose between his forefinger and thumb and exhaled slowly. "That wasn't fair. I apologize. Shit. It's just that... time isn't on our side, Felix. In the very near future, I'm going to ask you to do something you can't even imagine. And if you're not prepared then..." He shook his head, hesitating. "Look, there are things out there that... well... I just want you to be ready. I don't want anything to happen to you."

"I get it." Felix tugged on his ski hat, pulling it down over his ears. He felt more alert now. Bill's outburst had jolted the lethargy right out of him. "You don't have to freak out on me though. I don't want anything to happen to me either. What's next?"

Felix spent the next hour destroying things with assembly-line efficiency: Bill pointed at objects—alarm clocks, locks, doors, old office furniture—and Felix blew them to smithereens. After a while, the room began to look like a junkyard. The lockers and filing cabinets (twisted and unrecognizable), and pieces of metal, wood, plastic, and even some stiff strands of wire, were scattered across the floor and embedded in the walls and ceiling.

"Had enough?" Bill asked, coming up beside him.

"Yeah." He was exhausted. He wanted to go to bed. A memory cracked through his fatigue and he managed a light laugh. "When I was little, I used to make these buildings and skyscrapers—whole towns—out of Legos. Then I'd wreck 'em."

Bill smiled. "Well I've got one more thing for you to wreck. Then we'll call it a night. I want you to work on your control."

"That didn't go too well last time," Felix said in a tired voice.

"It's all about focus." Bill reached into his jacket pocket and came away with a shiny chrome-plated combination lock. He placed it on the table. "Explode it, but contain the damage. I don't want to see any pieces flying around or any shrapnel in my ass. Okay?"

It had to be really late. Felix was on the verge of falling asleep on his feet. He wanted to tell Bill to explode it himself, but he didn't want him going ballistic again. He took a deep breath and stared at the lock. Blowing it up would be easy. But blowing it up while trying to control the collateral damage was impossible; it was like adjusting the volume on a TV to go up and down at the same time—you had to pick one, right?

He concentrated on the lock. It quivered. And then it did something completely unexpected: with an audible *wha-whuff* it burst into flames. It burned and crackled, the fire laying low, covering the lock in a suffocating layer of deep red flames. Then it changed from blood red to white and a pillar of fire shot up like a geyser, reaching for the ceiling.

Felix just stood there, staring at it, more incredulous than panicked. This wasn't possible. He had to be seeing things. But the fire was real enough. It was hot. Intensely hot. Waves of heat were pouring from the swirling column, distorting the air around it.

"Bill!" He stepped away, shielding his face from the heat.

Bill was already in motion. He'd grabbed a ratty-looking blanket from the far corner of the room and was sprinting toward the fire. He hurdled a chair and threw the blanket, spreading it out like he was making a bed. His aim wasn't very good. One corner just nicked the tall column of flames, and with a thundering roar, the blanket instantly ignited in a fireball. One second later, it had turned to ash. Smoke billowed up in choking clouds.

Bill jumped back. "I can't put it out! You have to do it!"

"How?" Felix coughed and gagged.

"Just do it!" Bill screamed. "Now!"

The fire was spreading, pooling across the tabletop, creeping down the legs and onto the floor, devouring the wood. Felix's lungs were filling with smoke. They burned. He lifted his hand to the table and turned his mind toward extinguishing the flames, wishing them away. "Stop! Stop!" he heard himself say.

To his surprise, it actually worked. The towering pillar went flat and the flames shrank, receding from the edges of the table, withering like they were watching a film clip of the last thirty seconds run in reverse. And then, just as suddenly as it had started, the fire was gone. He lowered his hand, icy sweat trickling down his pale face. Relief swept over him.

"What the hell was that?" Felix coughed out, feeling stunned, disoriented. The room was white with smoke.

Bill was covering his mouth with his upturned collar. He stepped over to the table and pulled off his gloves, holding his hands just above the lock (the loop had melted and merged into the body of the lock and now it looked like a silver divotless golf ball) like he was warming them at a campfire. He gave it a brisk pat then plucked it up and brought it to Felix.

"It's not even warm." Bill held it out for Felix to inspect. "It's like it never caught fire. Here, touch it."

Felix poked it with his finger. It was cool, but not quite cold. "Just like Allison's room."

"Do you think you could do that again?"

Felix didn't pause to think about it. He concentrated, recreating what he'd felt just a moment before. He closed his eyes and imagined the sensation, stretching out his arm, palm facing up. He opened his eyes. Flames erupted from his outstretched hand. He felt the heat. But it didn't burn. It didn't hurt. He watched the column of flames (just like the one that had nearly set the library ablaze), making it go higher, then lower. He smiled. He couldn't help it. *I can control fire.* It was undoubtedly the most amazing thing he'd ever seen. But he didn't let out a barbaric battle cry. He didn't go into shock. All things considered, he stayed surprisingly calm. This was off-the-charts strange. Completely mind-blowing. No doubt about that. But this was just another drop in his bucket of supernatural weirdness. Just a few weeks ago, he didn't know that he could make books fly with his mind or turn a metal gym locker into abstract art simply because he wanted to. The weird and the fantastic were quickly becoming as mundane as having coffee at the Caffeine Hut and studying in Woodrow's Room. He was getting used to it. So now he could make fire shoot from his hands. Add it to the list.

He wanted the fire to go out. In his head, he uttered the word "Stop," and the flames listened. The fire disappeared, closing in on itself in the thick gloom of the library like it was never there. He looked at Bill, expecting him to be amazed or impressed or awe-struck—or all of the above.

Bill just looked pissed.

"See what you can do when you actually focus! If you burn Inverness to the ground where will you train? Do you have any idea what I went through to secure this building? Just to set up this room? You come here like you have someplace better to be, and then you act surprised when you screw things up. This isn't a goddamn game! You can't half-ass this, Felix! Why the hell aren't you taking this seriously? What you did was piss poor and grossly irresponsible. Get your head on…"

Bill was losing his shit again. Felix couldn't take it. Not now. He slumped to the floor, letting his head loll between his knees, jamming his palms into his eye sockets. The wide plank floorboards creaked under his weight. He was too tapped out to worry about the floor giving way. He almost welcomed it if it meant he wouldn't have to listen to Bill.

"Hey," Bill said after a while. His voice was softer now. "What's going on? I wouldn't be so tough on you if I thought you couldn't handle it. Something's been bothering you all night. I can see that. Talk to me."

The floorboards popped and groaned.

"C'mon. Talk to me. What's on your mind?"

Felix sighed heavily and removed his hat, stuffing it into a jacket pocket. Steam floated off his sweating hair-matted head, drifting up and mingling with the smoke that had nowhere else to go; they couldn't crack the windows with the bookcases blocking them. Bill had taken a seat on the floor across from him, staring at him, his expression almost tender.

"My Western Civ prof was talking about dreams, and it got me thinking about my dream," Felix began, his voice gritty with smoke. "She said something about life being a dream. And then this line from the journal came back to me. It was like in my head, and I couldn't stop thinking about it. You know—the one where Lofton's mom is worried about him leaving the castle. You know what I'm talking about?"

Bill nodded.

"So it goes like this," Felix said, reciting the journal from memory. "Lofton says, 'Really mother. You honestly believe that I have anything to fear from someone who thinks a knife and a garrote are weapons'. That's exactly what it says."

"I'm familiar with it."

"It's that one word that's messing with me. I mean, I thought it was real. Then I thought it was a dream. Now I think maybe I was right the first time, and it really was real. Now I'm flipping out because I don't know what to think. One goddamn word."

Bill tilted his head questioningly. "What word?"

"*Garrote.* When I read the journal, I didn't know what a garrote was. I thought it was a sword or something."

Bill shook his head. "It's a wire assassins use to strangle their victims. It's a weapon used by the Protectors."

"I know what it is now. I looked it up. That's the problem."

"I don't know what you're getting at. What's the problem?"

"It was in my dream," Felix tried to explain. "The garrote. The garrote was in my dream."

"You dreamed about a garrote?" Bill said, confused. "I thought you were dreaming about a fire?"

"I am. This was a different dream."

Bill gasped softly and coughed, as if his breath had caught in his throat. He focused his gaze on Felix and said gravely, "Tell me the rest."

One of the bulbs in the chandelier directly above them went out with a loud *clap*, startling Felix. He rocked himself to his feet and went over to the table, brushing his fingers along the scorched remains.

"Felix?" Bill prompted.

"Sorry. So this was back when school just started. Right before the first football game. Me and Allison went to this lady's house in no-man's-land to buy some skis. She asked us to go around back. The skis weren't there. Then two people tried to kill me. There was a woman. She had a garrote. That wire thing. I was fighting with her and then this guy tackled me. The woman got the garrote around my neck, and then the guy pulled out a knife. It was long." An image of the knife swam up in his mind and his eyes misted. "Long and curved. He was going to stab me. Right in the chest." He placed a hand over his heart. "That's the last thing I remember. I woke up in my bed."

Bill's face went dark. "What happened to Allison?"

"Nothing. The next day I told her about it and she looked at me like I was crazy. She said it was a dream and laughed it off. My friends all laughed. They still give me shit about it. She bought the skis. I saw them. Still has 'em. She said we just went out and had some food. We drank a lot of beer. So of course I thought it was just a dream. But now that I know what a garrote is, it just seems…"

"Why didn't you tell me about this?" Bill exclaimed, springing to his feet. He clenched both hands, veins bulged in his neck.

"I didn't even know you! I hadn't read the journal. And I didn't know what the hell a garrote is. What kind of word is that, anyway? And Allison told me it was a dream. Everyone told me it was a dream."

"It wasn't a dream!"

Bill had just confirmed what he'd strongly suspected. But for some reason, it didn't lift the cloud of confusion. He ran his hands over his face. He was just so tired. Every day was more confusing and exhausting than the last.

Bill started pacing. "I can't believe this is happening. I can't believe I'm even saying this. *The Protectors*. You and Allison had an encounter with the Protectors. That's the only rational explanation."

"But then who—"

"Who saved you?" Bill said. "A Sourceror, obviously."

"I thought they were gone. The Protectors wiped them out."

"No. The *Order* was wiped out. The Protectors can't prevent Sourcerors from being born. They're probably born every day for all we know."

"So the Protectors… they… they tried to *kill* me? That woman. And that man. They were Protectors? And they really tried to kill me?"

Bill nodded. "You just described their weapons."

"And a Sourceror saved me? So that means… that means there must be other Sourcerors out there, right? Other people on… *on our side?*"

"It seems so."

"Is it the Order?" Felix asked. "Is the Order back? Are they following me around?"

"I don't know. I don't know what's going on. I honestly don't know."

"But why… why would Allison lie to me? Does that… does that mean that…?"

"I don't think she's lying. She actually believes you weren't attacked. Remember what your aunt said about *persuasion?*"

Felix nodded. "'The Source touches Sourcerors in different ways,'" he recited from the journal.

"Right. Your aunt persuaded her husband and father-in-law to talk. And your mom, she… she persuaded me to look for the journal in her apartment, and to…" Bill stopped pacing and looked down at the floor, rubbing his eyes fiercely with the back of his hands. Then he shook his head and shuddered. "The person who saved you must've been a Sourceror with the power of persuasion, and that person persuaded Allison to believe you weren't attacked. But like your mom and aunt, their power isn't limitless. Remember how your aunt couldn't persuade Lofton to tell her what he was thinking?"

"So Allison was brainwashed to think that nothing happened?" Felix was struggling to work out the implications in his frazzled mind. "That we just ate pizza and drank beer?"

"Yes. But you're too strong. You're just like Lofton. You can't be persuaded. Your memories can't be manipulated. That's why you remember what actually happened." Bill dug his hands into his jacket pockets and stared at the floor with an uncharacteristically dull expression. His eyes were distant, vacant, as if he wasn't entirely present.

Felix waited a full minute. "Bill?"

"Sorry." Bill put his hand to his face and looked up at Felix. "This is what your pseudo-intellectual professors would refer to as a paradigm shift. My world just changed in an instant. I'm sure you can relate." He chuckled humorlessly. "I thought I was all alone in this for so many long years. But now I know I'm not. *We're* not. Don't you see? This changes everything. The war never ended. The Protectors and the Sourcerors are still out there waging a battle that started two thousand years ago." He pointed at Felix. "And in the center of this whole thing is you."

"So what do I do now?" Felix felt oddly calm. One good thing about sleep deprivation was its numbing effects. At least he could count on that. "They know who I am, right?"

Bill shook his head. "Only we know you're the Belus. But the Protectors seem to have discovered that you're a Sourceror. And to them, it doesn't matter. They're sworn to kill all Sourcerors."

"So they'll come after me again, won't they?"

"I'm surprised they haven't already. That's another reason you need to be more focused on your training. They'll be back. And if you can't protect yourself they'll kill you."

"Great," Felix said sarcastically. "My life just keeps getting better and better."

Bill smiled. "So how do you like college so far?"

If he wasn't so tired he would have laughed. "Love it. Let's get outta here. I'm wiped out."

Chapter 43

QUINN

Quinn Traynor uploaded the last of the pictures from his cell phone onto his laptop. The quality wasn't great, but there were people in the paper's creative studio that could clean it up. He was sitting in his kitchen at a found-on-the-side-of-the-road folding table. He'd shimmed up one leg with a copy of *The Weekly Sturgeon* (he thought of it as graffiti with punctuation) to keep the top level, but if he rested his arm on it or placed too much weight on the edges, the legs would buckle, causing the whole thing to collapse. He'd learned that the hard way. The first time it tipped over, his computer had slid off and the monitor shattered on the floor. He wasn't having much luck with electronics lately.

It wasn't just the table that belonged in a landfill. The entire house did. He hated it. The smothering ambiance of general decrepitude tugged at his insides—and his pride. Living in a boarded-up two bedroom mold pit in no-man's-land wasn't what he'd envisioned when he chose a career in journalism. The assignment coordinator at *Hollywood Reality Bites* had insisted that in order to 'maintain his cover' he had to avoid communal living, and that included any apartment buildings near the Portland College campus. And with a miserly pittance of a rental stipend, it was either this foreclosed dump on 17th Street that he was renting from the bank or a refrigerator box under the bridge.

At least the electricity was working for the moment. Without it, he would lose the heat—a tragic but not unlikely occurrence on a bitterly cold night like tonight. The electricity had gone out so many times since he'd moved in last August it felt like he had a personal relationship with Trish and Nevaeh, two of the call-center reps who worked for the power company.

He went through the pictures (fourteen in all) of Lucas Mayer kissing Caitlin. She was pretty, but the pictures weren't exactly ideal. He would have preferred a photo of Lucas making out with the hot blonde in the short skirt—or even better, Lucas having a threesome with the hot blonde and the tall dark-haired chick. Now that would be *ideal*. But back to reality: the photos he'd actually taken weren't worth very much—$300 for the best shot. If he created a story around it, however, spun it into something tawdry or illicit, the price would climb exponentially. Instead of kissing a college freshman, maybe Lucas was kissing a *high school* freshman. A fifteen-year-old. Now that would be worth something ($3,000-$4,000). His editor wouldn't care enough not to believe him—*Hollywood Reality Bites* wasn't known for vigorous fact-checking or third party corroboration—so his only risk was Lucas coming forward to challenge the story. But then his friend would find herself in the anonymity-stripping glare of the media's spotlight, and Caitlin seemed like the shy prudish type, not one to own up to tongue fencing with a reality star. Lucas, predictable jaw-thrusting-chest-thumping meathead that he appeared to be, would do the chivalrous thing and stay quiet to protect his friend's innocence (and anonymity). And the story would run unimpeded. He smiled to himself. Sometimes, even Quinn was impressed by his own cleverness, his ability to see things steps ahead of everyone else.

But none of that really mattered, anyway. He'd finally acquired his photo. He was done with his assignment. The extra money would be nice, but he just wanted out of this dump. This lowest circle of Dante's hell. The ceilings sagged. The walls were streaked and splotched with water stains. He was beginning to feel sick. Sick all the time. Probably from the mold. It was in the walls. The ceiling. Everywhere. It darkened the lathing and showed through the cracked decaying plaster. But thanks to the photos on his computer this would be his last night in hell (morning actually; it was already 2:30, but he was too excited to sleep). He'd already booked his plane ticket. At eleven o'clock he would be on a flight to L.A.

Quinn wasn't exactly proud of what he was doing with his life, though he'd come to terms with it. The paper paid him a base salary of $30,000 and 'bonuses' for photos it published in print or on its website. When he first started working there after graduating from Dartmouth, he'd spent two months chasing down a story involving the Russian center for the Lakers, Arvidas Karielinko. 'Arvi', as he was known to everyone, was born in Chechnya, and Quinn, through countless hours of painstaking research and several nights hiding out in the shrubs across the street from Arvi's mansion (during which he fancied himself an actual investigative reporter) discovered that Arvi had ties to Muslim extremists. After two weeks of sixteen-hour days at his computer, he produced a Pulitzer-worthy article—at least in his mind—which he proudly submitted to his editor, expecting praise, money, promotions and the more discerning women in the office to instantly fall in love with his brilliant mind.

His editor's response after reading it: "What the fuck are you doing, you fucking idiot? You think you're working for the *Wall Street Journal?* Get rid of this shit and go help Nicole. She's working on something hot."

The *hot* story Nicole was working on had turned out to be an exposé on why no one had recently seen the reality TV personality Cassie Studebaker in high heels. Nicole had a source who claimed that Cassie, who had regularly worn five-inch stilettos while she was eight months pregnant, couldn't wear heels anymore because she had bunions. So Quinn had spent the better part of a week examining digitally enlarged photos of Cassie Studebaker's feet to determine if she had any bony enlargements near her big toes.

Quinn never discovered any bunions, but he did discover that Cassie Studebaker had the brain capacity of a zoo monkey. He also discovered she was hauling in forty million dollars a year. Quinn, on the other hand, was a Rhodes Scholar semi-finalist with a 184 IQ, and his career path had led him to inspecting some idiot celebrity's feet for toe bumps. Quinn's parents had brought him up to believe that America was the great meritocracy, a country that rewarded intellect and cleverness with wealth and status—and maybe even fame. But no. It was all an insidious lie. The symbolism of the bunion hunt hadn't escaped him, and it heightened his disgust for a society that worshipped vapid narcissists like Cassie, while leaving geniuses like him to live insignificant, meaningless lives.

After that, Quinn decided he would never again feel guilty about invading a celebrity's privacy for financial gain. It was just like the situation with Lucas Mayer. *Summer Slumming* was being renewed—he knew a guy who knew a guy who was a grip for the production company. And the word from this grip was that each cast member would be making $75,000 an episode. It was infuriating. The 'Summer Slummers' as his paper sometimes called them, were relative nobodies, a million levels removed from the pantheon of the Hollywood elite, and they were set to make more in just one episode than Quinn had ever made in an entire year.

He scrolled down the screen, comparing the pictures. "Guess this is the one," he said with a sigh. Lucas's eyes were slightly bulging in the photo, making it look like he'd been caught in the act of doing something highly suspect. The girl he was kissing—Caitlin—was short enough to pass for someone much younger. He even had a headline in mind, something blunt and without irony or wit, something your *Average Joe* and *Average Jane* could latch on to without worrying about taxing their middle-of-the-road brains too much: *Minnesota Mayer Caught Kissing Fifteen-Year-Old.*

"I'm actually partial to the one just above it," a voice said. "It's much more intimate. More romantic."

Quinn froze. The voice—a deep, rumbling voice—came from behind him. Slowly, he swiveled his chair around.

The man standing in his kitchen was at least a foot taller than Arvi Karielinko. And much thicker. He looked out of place, like an adult playing in a child's toy house.

Quinn screamed, his insides turning to water.

The man was holding a bottle of beer in his hand. The bottle looked tiny, like one of those single-shot bottles of booze Quinn was planning to get loaded on during his flight. He smiled and took a swig. His teeth were gold. And pointy.

Quinn screamed again.

"Do that again, and I'll dig your eyes out with my thumbs." The man's voice was pleasant, devoid of malice.

Quinn sucked in his breath, trying not to make a sound. The face looking back at him was bizarre and terrifying; everything was out of order, confused, like someone had played a cruel joke on Mr. Potato Head by putting the parts in all the wrong places. The man was unmistakable. Quinn screamed. He couldn't help it. Terror gripped his brain.

He took another drink from the bottle. "Thanks for the beer. And by the way, another scream out of you, and I'm afraid I'll have to kill you. Comprendes?"

Quinn nodded. He felt his mouth hanging open; the muscles and tendons that held everything together had gone slack. He felt some other muscles going slack. *Please don't pee,* he said to himself. *Please.* He didn't have to restrain the urge to run. He couldn't run. It was physically impossible. His muscles had frozen solid in fear. And he was afraid if he stood up, his bladder would relax and he would pee himself. He couldn't let that happen. Not again. Not after what had happened so many years ago as a still immature thirteen-year-old too embarrassed to use the group shower after gym class. The older boys had seized the opportunity, taking his towel from him, leaving him fully exposed. The kids laughed. So did the teacher. He'd stood there in front of everyone, living a waking nightmare. And then the inescapability of the situation engulfed him in hot shame and he'd wet himself. There was no recovery from that. The kids were cruel. Relentless. He'd transferred to a different school, but the sense of humiliation couldn't be left behind.

"Beautiful. I assume you know who I am?"

Quinn took a deep breath, forcing himself to think. He was intimately familiar with the Faceman: His cross-country rampage had fascinated him and he'd followed the story from the beginning, reading everything he could find on the subject. Now he needed to use that knowledge to his advantage. Quinn didn't lack self-awareness: He was the proverbial ninety-eight pound weakling on the beach getting sand kicked in his face. He had no illusions about taking on anyone in a physical confrontation unless suicide was the goal. But even if Quinn was the biggest baddest dude around, it wouldn't matter; the Faceman was gigantic, like some kick ass axe-wielding god-of-war character from a video game.

But you're a genius. You are a genius. Quinn repeated the words to himself, realizing, oddly, that he was uniquely equipped for this. Physical gifts were not called for here. Inflated, beach-ready biceps and pecs wouldn't count for anything against the Faceman. But what Quinn possessed—a dazzling intellect—was the one thing the Faceman couldn't match. In some ways, this was like a surreal and nightmarish extension of the potholed road he'd been traveling on for as long as he could remember; Quinn's life had been defined by cleft-chinned jocks looking right through him, like their senses couldn't recognize a fellow male with so little testosterone, and pretty glossy-lipped girls regarding him with embarrassment and horror if he struck up a conversation or tried to buy them a drink (*Oh God! I hope no one sees this loser talking to me.*).

But you're a genius.

Those were the words where he found comfort, the words that reminded him he was better than them. His brain—the part of us that meant something, that separated us from less evolved forms of life—ran circles and loop de loops around theirs. His brain was responsible for perfect scores on the ACT and the SAT. His brain had gotten him into Dartmouth. He knew things—*understood* things—that the dumb beautiful people could never understand because they were too busy being beautiful—and dumb.

You're a genius.

His intellect was his ticket out of here, his survival card. If anyone could outwit a dumb psychopath—*the Faceman had to be dumb, right?*—it was Quinn Traynor. He just had to stay cool and control his fear—because fear, he knew from reading a lot of sci fi, was the *mind killer.*

"You're Nick Blair," Quinn said, keeping his voice almost steady. "The Faceman."

"Bingo! And you're Quinn Traynor, intrepid photographer and occasional writer for *Hollywood Reality Bites*. It's nice to meet you."

Quinn didn't know how to respond. He just nodded.

"Do you know what I do for a living?" the Faceman asked.

"No." It never occurred to Quinn that the Faceman made a living.

"I kill people."

Quinn swallowed hard, his eyes growing wide with horror. "Look, um, Mr. Faceman, I think I know what's going on here."

"You do?"

"Yeah. I know you served in the military. I know you were some kind of superstar special forces guy, am I correct?"

"You are," the Faceman replied kindly, a hideous grin stretching across his face. "Go on."

"Okay." Quinn paused, wiping his palms on his pants, heart thumping fast. "So when you were in the military serving our country overseas, you were protecting all of us, but you went through some terrible experiences people like me can't even imagine, right? But then when you came back to America no one understood what you went through over there. No one understood the dangers you faced and how you'd kept all of us safe from terrorists. Instead, your fellow Americans yelled at you, cursed at you, called you names like *baby killer*. And then you couldn't even get a job. Over there, you're operating million dollar machines, but here, you couldn't even find a job washing dishes. Am I right?"

The Faceman nodded, a grave expression crossing his face. Then he slapped his thigh and burst out laughing. "Are you doing *First Blood*? Is that Colonel Trautman's speech to Rambo? I love it. That's classic. And I love Rambo. I'm a huge fan of the Slyster, but you should know that me and Rambo don't have much in common. You see, Rambo only killed people when his back was to the wall. I kill people when they disappoint me. When they fail. When they turn out to be Wisps."

A surge of icy fear slithered up Quinn's spine, but he forced himself to stay calm. "What's a... am I a...?"

"A Wisp?" the Faceman said. "It means you're normal, Quinn. I know you think you're special, but believe me, you're not. Which is why I'm going to kill you."

"Wait, wait, wait." Quinn held up his hands, begging him to keep away from him. "Please. Please don't kill me. Just listen to me." Quinn sat there thinking fast. The Faceman was clearly too deranged for rational discourse. *But everyone needs something,* he thought. He simply had to find out what the Faceman needed and negotiate that in exchange for his life. "I'll give you anything you want. Anything. Just don't kill me."

The Faceman's lips peeled back from his teeth in a smile and he gazed down on him with dark, impassive eyes. "So now it's on to *Plan B*, is it? I can see you're a brave one. But I'll take you up on your offer. There is something I want from you."

"What? What is it?" *This was his chance.* "Anything you want. Just tell me what it is. It's yours."

The Faceman seemed to enjoy watching Quinn grovel like a junkie looking for a fix. "I want information."

"*Information?* Okay. Sure. Sure. What do you—"

"One thing you learn in the military is that when you follow a target, you have to make sure you're not somebody else's target. I've been watching you, Quinn. I know you've been trailing a Portland College student. The one in the photo there." He pointed at the monitor. "His name's Lucas Mayer, correct?"

"Yes." Quinn was trembling like a stray dog caught out in the rain. His stomach felt loose and weak. *Don't pee yourself. Please. Don't let him see that.*

"Who has Lucas been in contact with?"

"Lots of people," Quinn croaked. His mouth was dry and his quivering lips struggled to form words. *Fear is the mind killer,* he reminded himself. He had to stay cool and let his brain work its magic. "He's a college student. He sees hundreds of people every day."

"Who are his *main* contacts, Quinn. Give me names. And tell me what you know about them."

"Okay. And if I do…" He hesitated. "Then you'll let me go?"

"Of course."

"You… you promise?"

"Sure."

The only way out of the house was through the front door, and the only way to access the door was from the hallway the Faceman was blocking (*literally* blocking, his impossibly wide shoulders brushed up against both walls). There was another door, a sliding glass door in the adjacent living room that led to a back yard that looked like a war zone, but it was boarded up from the outside. Quinn was abundantly aware that there was no possibility of escape; the only way he was going to extricate himself from this situation was to convince the Faceman to let him go. But if anyone could do it, it was him.

Because you are a genius. You are a genius.

"Okay, well, he mainly hangs out with his roommate and three girls. All freshmen. His roommate's Felix August. He's a football player. Tall, serious kid who kind of keeps to himself. The girls are Caitlin DuPont, Allison Jasner and Harper Connolly. Harper and Allison are both extremely attractive. All the guys are in love with Harper. If Brooklyn Decker had a younger hotter sister, it'd be her. Allison's a little standoffish. She's got a bit of an attitude. Caitlin's the bleeding-heart liberal of the group. She'd join a committee to save just about anything if she thought it was endangered."

"Have you ever noticed anyone else?" the Faceman asked. "Or anything out of the ordinary? Maybe someone hanging around Lucas who doesn't seem to belong."

"Um… well." Quinn's breath was coming fast and thin. He felt lightheaded. He took a deep breath and glanced down at the crud-spattered linoleum floor, praying it wasn't puddled in piss. It wasn't. *Deep breath,* he told himself. *You're a genius. You can do this.* "I've seen the same three or four guys following Harper around. If she gets a cup of coffee or checks her mail, they're usually there. Watching her. I think they're just infatuated with her but who knows these days. And I have noticed this other guy, an older guy, a few times. He's probably in his thirties or forties. I think he's a professor. He's black. Has a beard."

"Professor Malone?" the Faceman asked. "The Psychology professor?"

"I don't know his name."

The Faceman smiled down at Quinn as he finished his beer. "Eleven eleven seventeenth street, correct?"

"Sorry? Eleven eleven seven—"

"Your address," the Faceman interrupted. "It has a nice ring to it. Eleven eleven seventeenth street. Eleven eleven. Eleven eleven."

"Yeah," Quinn mumbled weakly. "I guess it does."

"Is the rent paid up?"

"*The rent?* Yes. Through the end of the year."

"Perfect." The Faceman glanced around the kitchen. A sheet of plywood blacked out the lone window above the sink. "This is just what I need."

"Can I go now?" Quinn's voice was faltering. "I gave you what you wanted. The information. That's what you wanted, right? You said you'd let me go. You promised."

"What did you give me?" the Faceman said slowly. "That's not information. That's common knowledge. You gave me nothing. You told me about the people Lucas spends ninety-nine percent of his time with. And you call yourself a reporter?" He laughed, his teeth glimmering under the overhead fluorescents.

"Please," Quinn begged. "I have a sister. She's only sixteen. She looks up to me. I'm supposed to teach her how to drive. And my mom—she's sick. She needs me. Please. Let me go. I promise I won't tell anyone I saw you. I swear. Please."

"You have a fine basement." The Faceman put his empty beer bottle on the counter. "Did you know that? Have you been down to the basement?"

"No."

"I know you haven't. Do you know why I know?"

Quinn shook his head.

"Because I've been living in your basement for the past three weeks."

"Oh my God! Oh my God!" Quinn felt like he was going to hyperventilate. The thought of the Faceman living in his house caused him to chill over like ice crystals had formed all over his skin. He choked back the tears but not before a few big drops leaked from the corners of his eyes and rolled down his pudgy cheeks. His plan wasn't working. And he didn't have a Plan C.

"Crying like a little girl, I see," the Faceman mocked, laughing. "Your basement isn't finished, but there's lots of space. There's even a nice long work bench down there. You didn't have any tools so I brought some of my own after I moved in. I've always been a huge fan of saws. It's amazing what you can do with a good saw. You may not know this, but a properly sharpened saw will go clean through flesh and bone like room temperature table butter." He smiled and locked eyes with Quinn. "It won't take me long to saw you up into snack-sized pieces. I'll be carrying you out of here in a duffel bag."

"Oh my God!" Quinn wailed in terror.

"And there's this remarkably well maintained furnace at the old paper plant just a few blocks from here. I'm a fan of your neighborhood, Quinn. I even like the name. No-man's-land. Has a nice ring to it, doesn't it? So this furnace at the plant gets just hot enough to turn bone to ash. I tried it out the other day on one of your neighbors. She was old and had a limp. I think I did her a favor by putting her out of her misery. Anyway, I'm happy to say that the furnace exceeded even my demanding expectations. When I'm done with you, it'll be like you never existed. After all, you didn't leave much of a mark during your life, did you? Too bad, 'cause you only get one."

Quinn screamed.

The Faceman folded his arms and the veins popped out under his skin like garden hoses. "You know what really pisses me off about you, Quinn?"

His lips rolled back over his teeth like a wolf about to take a bite out of its prey. "It isn't the screaming. I mean, that's tiresome, but I realize I have that effect on people. I'm not exactly new to the business of killing. What pisses me off is that you have no survival instincts. You just sit there. You haven't even thought about trying to fight or escape. You haven't even moved. I killed a rat in your basement the other day. I grabbed its throat and squeezed the life right out of it. And do you know what that filthy rodent did before it died? It bit me. A rat bit me. A rat has more fight in it than you. A rat has more will to live than you. You don't deserve to live."

"Please. Please. No. No. Please. I don't—"

"Shut up. Relax. I'm not going to shoot you in the face."

"You're not?" Quinn said hopefully. He was shaking so hard his voice warbled.

"No. I find that shooting people doesn't satisfy all my needs. It lacks a certain *personal* touch I crave. For someone like you, I prefer to use my hands." He grinned. "And a nice sharp saw."

"Help me!" Quinn shouted, twisting around in his chair. He knew that no one could hear him. The surrounding houses were abandoned and the drug dealers and prostitutes who sometimes conducted their business out on his street weren't the type to call 911 if they heard someone yelling for help—but he screamed anyway. "Please! Someone! Someone help me! No. No. No. Oh God! Nononono."

The Faceman was on top of Quinn in an instant, gripping him by the back of his chicken neck with one meaty hand and lifting him out of his chair. The bones in his neck made soft cracking sounds under the crushing force of the Faceman's fingers. He flailed helplessly, his feet swinging above the floor.

"We're going to play a little game." The Faceman smiled and drew Quinn in close, bringing his face right up to his own. The Faceman's colorless eyes were the size of billiard balls, the fragment of nose that remained was bigger than Quinn's fist, and his mouth could swallow an apple in a single bite. He didn't look human. The Faceman's smile widened and he whispered: "It's called *how much pain can you endure before you die?*"

Quinn screamed. And then he felt a rush of warmth travel down his legs.

The Faceman carried Quinn across the room and jerked open a door just off the kitchen—the door to the basement. Quinn swung his arms and kicked frantically like a drowning swimmer trying to find solid ground. He felt warm liquid dribbling down his feet, pattering on the floor. He'd never

342 | FELIX CHRONICLES: FRESHMEN

felt weaker or more helpless (or more ashamed). He was at the mercy of the Faceman, and Quinn knew that mercy wasn't a concept he subscribed to.

"Let me introduce you to the basement," the Faceman said, hurling Quinn through the doorway into the darkness below. Quinn felt the cold damp air rushing over him, then he crashed against the stairs, thudding down hard, tha-thumping to a jarring stop at the bottom. Something *crunched*. He heard it before he felt the sharp flashing pain in his wrist. He screamed, but even to his own ears, it sounded fainter than before, more like anguished, defeated moans than cries for help. The room smelled dank, like black spores and rotting wood.

Quinn heard the snap of a stiff switch and the lights came on. He was lying on his stomach, his face pressed against hard gray concrete. He couldn't move. He was in too much pain and too scared to even try, so he just lay there, sobbing. He heard the heavy *thud, thud, thud* of the Faceman's footsteps coming down the staircase, tolling like the bell of a grand European cathedral, heralding Quinn's departure from this world.

"Don't worry, Quinn Traynor," the Faceman called down the stairs, laughing. "In five or six hours, this will all be over."

Chapter 44

SMOKE AND LIES

The light from the hallway leaked into the room and took aim at Lucas. He appeared to be sleeping. But now a diagonal strip of yellow light was slapping him across the face. Felix slipped in and eased the door back, clicking it shut. He waited. No movement. He crept across the darkened room and stripped down to his boxers, leaving his clothes in a pile next to his bed. He was still thawing out from the suddenness of emerging from the brutal cold into the warmth of the dorm. His nose and chin burned and itched, his cheeks felt chafed and prickly. He pulled back the cover and crawled in. His head hit the pillow. The crisp sheets were pleasantly cool for a second, then they enveloped him in soft warmth as the heavy comforter settled slowly over him, capturing the heat from his own body. It felt wonderful. He hesitated before closing his eyes, daring to hope that tonight might be the night his mind would give him a reprieve from the dream that haunted his sleep. *Please. Cut me some slack.*

"Hey." A voice from the other side of the room. Lucas.

Felix wanted to ignore him. Maybe pretend like he was asleep? Not realistic. He'd just climbed into bed and Lucas knew that he wasn't narcoleptic.

"Sorry," Felix said. His voice was scratchy. He cleared his throat. "Did I wake you up?"

"It's okay. It's like three, ya know. The girls stopped by before. Around eleven. They wanted to hang out. They asked where you were."

"What'd you tell 'em?"

"I said I didn't know." Lucas yawned.

Silence for a beat. Would Lucas ask the question?

"So where were you, anyway?" Lucas asked sleepily.

There it was.

"You're not out banging some heinous chick you're too embarrassed to tell me about, are you?"

"No." Felix smiled into the dark, looking up at the ceiling. "I got over my heinous-chick-fetish last year. I was just out for a walk." What else could he tell him?

"*A walk?*" The deep skepticism in Lucas's voice carried easily across the room. "It's cold enough to freeze pee midstream, dude."

"I just needed to clear my head."

"Right," Lucas said softly. He sniffed. Then he sniffed again. "Hey—is that smoke?"

Shit! Felix thought, alarmed. *I must smell like I was rolling around in a bonfire.* He hadn't planned for Lucas waking up; he hadn't even considered it. And it didn't occur to him that the scent of the old library—currently smoke—would hitch a ride on his clothes and travel back with him. After fleeing the Old Campus—he literally ran, fearing the winter-like chill might make the St. Rose Ghost lonely for warm-blooded teenage boys—his only concern was making it to the dorm without the Protectors killing him. He didn't think they would come after him on campus, but he had no basis to support that theory. It was just an assumption. Maybe he was wrong. Maybe they didn't play by any rules.

"I swear I can smell something." Lucas sounded calm, like he was just making an observation. That was good, because Felix didn't need him panicking and jumping out of bed. If he did that and ambled over to Felix's side, he stood a better than even chance of figuring out that his clothes were the source.

"It's gotta be from outside," Felix replied, thinking it would be disingenuous to deny that the room smelled like smoke. "Someone's got a fire going, I guess."

"I hope it's not Allison's room."

"No shit."

"You think you're gonna have that nightmare again?" Lucas asked. "Like last night?"

"I don't know." As exhausted as Felix was, he was afraid to close his eyes. The prospect of being burned alive was deeply depressing.

"It'd be cool if you'd give me a heads-up. I could like mentally prepare myself for what's coming."

"Sorry," Felix said. "I feel, you know I… I wish I didn't have them. Sorry."

"I'm just busting your balls, dude."

"Oh."

The room went silent again.

"Hey," Lucas said suddenly. "You know um… if you wanna talk about something, well, I'm a pretty decent listener. For a dude, I mean. I won't listen for like an hour or anything. I'm not a chick. But if you keep it short, I'll probably stay awake."

Gray moonlight probed through cracks in the drawn blinds. A strip of light slashed horizontally across Felix's knees. He lifted up his right hand and watched it playing across his fingertips. What would Lucas say if he shot fire from his hand? What would he say if he raised the wastebasket off the floor and crumpled it? Or exploded it? He could tell Lucas some things—show him some things—that would blow his mind. A part of him wanted to. Keeping secrets, especially colossal ones like his, was physically draining. But he knew he couldn't tell him. No good could come of it.

Felix changed the subject. "So what's up with Caitlin?"

"*Caitlin?*" Lucas coughed. "Nothing. Why?"

"I don't know. You guys like, you know, kissed or whatever."

"Yeah, so?" Lucas said defensively, then paused. "I don't know. I don't think I'm her kinda guy. And you know, Caitlin's like, a really good girl. She's not like other, you know, she's a cool chick. She deserves someone… better than me."

Felix didn't know what to say to that.

"Thanks for helping out with that midget stalker asshole." This time Lucas changed the subject. "I hope that little shit didn't hurt you too bad."

Felix laughed. "I think I'll survive."

"'Night, dude," Lucas said. "Sweet dreams."

"Sure."

Chapter 45

THE GHOST IN THE PICTURE

Felix stood in front of the Caffeine Hut, the aroma of brewing coffee drifting out through little cracks and fissures around the door. Harper wanted to meet him. She'd sent him a text during his Economics class: *I want to see you. Hut in 15?* He was already late, yet he didn't go in. He was trying to sketch out a plan in his head, but he couldn't tamp down the nervousness inching up his throat. Harper hadn't made eye contact with him in three weeks so he thought he should have a plan. A script. Something to fall back on if she was in a mood, or if awkward silences overwhelmed him. But planning and scripting were best left for times when you weren't falling apart like the stitching on the Prada knockoff wallet his mom had brought back with her from her trip to New York City two summers ago.

Final exams were looming and Felix's nerves were fraying like an old rope. A maddeningly persistent anxiousness was gripping him, making him jumpy and tired at the same time. The latter was mainly due to the nightmares that woke him up almost every night. And on those rare nights when he didn't have the burning-to-death-in-agonizing-pain dream, he still couldn't sleep because of the fear and the dreaded expectation that he would wake up screaming. So with everything else going on in his life—including the recent discovery that a 2,000-year-old secret society had targeted him for assasination—he found it a little ironic that he worried about tests as much as ever.

But in a strange way, it made perfect sense: The crazier his life became, the tighter he held on to the things from his old life. Worrying about exams like everyone else meant he could be just like everyone else. It was the same reason losing a football game bothered him so much he threw up in a toilet. Football and exams were trivial, even irrelevant, when compared to The Warning. He knew that. But caring about football games and stressing over tests made him feel normal—and he liked feeling normal. He wasn't ready to give that up.

Felix found Harper sitting in a purple lounge chair in a back corner next to a roaring fire. She waved at him. He swallowed back his nerves and made his way through the yard sale furniture. There were lots of harried-looking students in full-blown finals mode poring over notes, staring at computer screens, tapping on keyboards. Late morning sunlight from the arched windows filled the room; everything looked a few shades lighter than it did after nightfall, when he usually came in for coffee.

"Hey," she said brightly. She was holding a mug in each hand. "I already got you a cup. I hope it's not cold."

Good sign. She wasn't in a surly mood. This wasn't a setup. She didn't arrange this to berate him or to pick a fight. Felix shrugged out of his jacket and sat down in a sun-faded blue and orange club chair with overstuffed armrests and a high back. The chair was placed at an angle to Harper's so that they weren't directly facing each other.

"Thanks." She handed him the mug. He sniffed the steam out of habit. There was none. He took a sip. It was tepid. He acted like it wasn't. "It's good."

"Espresso roast," she said, rolling a long strand of hair between her fingers. "I know you like the strong stuff."

He took another sip and stared at a log crackling in the fireplace. He couldn't bring himself to look at her. He could see her long legs out of the corner of one eye. Sheathed in denim. Black boots. Her shirt was dark and a jacket was draped over the back of her chair. The awkwardness was mutual. She shifted in her chair, drinking from her mug. For a while, they both let the occasional cracks of burning wood mingling with the soft hum of conversations from the other tables fill the void.

"Best seat in the house, huh?" Felix said. It was better than commenting on the unseasonably warm weather.

"I love looking at the fire," Harper said, nodding at it. "There's just something about the way the flames dance. I hope that doesn't make me a pyro."

"Yeah, it's nice." He kept his eyes on the fire.

"So… um… have you seen Lucas?" Harper said, clearly searching for something to talk about. "He has my English notes. I let him borrow them but I need 'em back."

"Not since last night." Felix fidgeted with his mug. "He didn't come back to the room. Didn't he leave Woodrow's before us?"

"Yeah. He said his dyslexia was kicking in and he couldn't study anymore." Harper smiled impishly. "You think he met someone special?"

Felix laughed. "Did you text him?"

"Twice." She checked the phone on her lap. "No word back."

"Shit! That reminds me." Felix glanced at his watch. "I got a text from my Biology TA yesterday. I totally forgot. I'm supposed to meet her in ten minutes. I'm dying in that class. Sorry."

"That's okay. I guess it's that time of year. We're all getting slammed. Caitlin and Allison are supposed to be here at eleven, anyway. We might go to Woodrow's Room later, but I don't know. It's still a little creepy if you ask me. Allison's okay with it, but if you guys aren't there, I think I hear noises sometimes."

"That's just the dead Indians scalping kids. Nothing to worry about."

Harper laughed. It was a nice laugh. Full. Genuine. And a little flirty.

He meant to steal a quick glance at her, but once his eyes flitted to her face they locked on tight. He stared. She was beautiful. Disarmingly beautiful. He couldn't take his eyes off her.

"I know I'm a bitch," Harper said shyly. "That's why I wanted to talk to you. I'm sorry. My sister tells me that all the time. I used to fight with her about it and tell her she was too nice for her own good. But she's right. And sometimes, I just don't realize when I'm acting that way."

"About…?"

"You know." She sipped her coffee. "That movie thing was just so idiotic. You didn't feel like watching a movie and I reacted like you poisoned my dog."

"It's okay."

"No, it's not okay. And I know you and Allison are just friends. But I saw you guys, you know… and… I… I don't know." She stared down at her hands, looking embarrassed.

"We're tight," Felix told her. "We go way back."

"I know." The edges of Harper's mouth dipped lower, but she quickly recovered. "I'd be lying if I said I wasn't a little envious of how well she knows you. And don't get me wrong. I love her. I think she's great. But is she a little… *intense?* Maybe it's different with you, but sometimes she seems like she's—and I know this isn't a bad thing—but she seems so *driven.* And I wonder if it's because she's a foster kid and feels like she has something to prove."

"That's just how she is. Maybe I'm used to it."

"Anyway." Harper looked at the fire and her face tensed. "I know it's got nothing to do with a movie or Allison." She turned to him, chewing on her lip. "I know about your… your parents. We all do. Allison told us."

"Oh." It always startled Felix whenever anyone brought up his parents, although he knew that was stupid. It was like finding himself surprised every time he caught some random guy staring at Harper, just like the rangy-looking kid in the plaid chair by the window pretending to read an organic chemistry textbook. "Yeah, well, I guess, um, I figured she did. No one ever asked about them and I could tell you were all avoiding it."

Harper nodded. "You know that night when you and Lucas opened the Betas' chapter room? Well, when you were getting a beer, Allison told us. Then she said she hadn't seen you smile in like months, and if anyone said anything and ruined your mood, she'd sneak into our rooms and slit our fucking throats."

"Seriously?" Felix said, his head jerking back against the chair.

"No joke. Exact words. 'I'll slit your fucking throats.'"

Felix laughed. "Maybe she is a little intense."

Harper waded right back in. "I can't imagine what it'd be like to lose your mom and dad. I'm sure there's times when you just want to be by yourself. Or be with people you know—and trust. I'm sorry about how I've been lately. I just wanted you to know that."

"It's okay. Really." He balanced the mug on his thigh, the coffee churning sourly in his gut.

She smiled nervously. He knew she wasn't going to drop this. Her smile was perfect. Her body was perfect. Her eyes were bluer than any blue he could imagine. She was the hottest girl he'd ever known. But he still didn't want to talk about his parents.

"Do you want to talk about it?" she asked gently.

He didn't. But what choice did he have? He watched two girls carrying coffees and a saucer stacked with brownies and biscotti over from the bar. They settled into a yellow loveseat with black piping and flamingo pink seat cushions. Probably the ugliest couch in all of America.

"It's tough," he said after a long pause. He scratched the back of his head, his eyes moving all around the room. "Some days are better than others. I miss them. I miss them a lot."

She leaned forward and reached across the armrests, putting her hand on his, lightly caressing his fingers. A little tickling whisper scurried up his back. She looked at him, her face full of tenderness and concern, and said, "Tell me about it."

This is what happens when you open up, he thought bleakly. *Everyone wants to dig deeper, to know everything. To dig until they get at the core. Well, here we go:* "You wanna know what the hardest thing is? It's when I'm having fun. When I'm hanging out with you guys and we're just having a good time. A part of my mind is like, why the hell are you doing this? How can you be partying with your friends when your parents just died? I feel like... I feel like I'm betraying their memory. That if they could look down on me, they'd be thinking I don't even care. They just died and I'm out partying. What kind of a shitty son am I? How could I do that to them? That's, um, yeah... that's the hardest part. I just miss them. I can't believe they're really gone. Sometimes I look at my phone and I see my number, you know, for home. I think about calling. And I think someone will answer. My mom will just pick up and say 'hello' and tell me to study hard and we'll talk about whatever. And my dad will get on and ask me if I've kissed any girls. He always said dumb stuff like that." He went quiet for a moment. "But no one's there. No one's answering."

Harper was choking back tears. Unsuccessfully. He watched as she smeared them around her cheeks. Felix wasn't the kind of person who derived pleasure or validation from other people's sympathy. Making people cry just made him feel guilty. It made him feel like shit.

"I know how this is going to sound, but you know your parents would want you to be happy," Harper said, sniffing. "They wouldn't want you feeling sorry for yourself. You know that, right?"

"I guess." Felix had had enough. He lifted his shoulders and let them drop. He could only think about this for so long before the sadness consumed him and sent him into a death spiral. Harper must have sensed it.

"So what are you doing for Christmas?" she asked, her voice a little too high with forced cheer. "I can't believe it's coming up. Do you have any grandparents or anyone to spend it with?"

Felix shook his head, staring into his mug, swirling the coffee around in a circle. "When my parents had me they were both pretty old. By the time I got to high school, I lost my last grandparent. My mom's mom. She lived not too far from us up the coast. Cancer. I'm the last of the Augusts, I guess. But we used to have Christmas dinner at our house. We didn't have any relatives other than my grandma. But my mom and dad had a lot of friends who'd come over. It just sort of became a tradition. My mom would cook all day, and my dad and I would go out in the woods and chop down a little tree. They loved Christmas."

She smiled sadly, clearing her eyes quickly with the back of her hand. "That sounds nice. So what are you going to do this year?"

"I haven't really thought about it." Complete lie. He'd thought about it a ton. "I'll figure something out." In case his dishonesty had etched itself all across his face, he masked it by taking a drink from his mug.

"You really deserve to be happy. I hope you know that. You're a great guy. You really are." He felt Harper's gaze and their eyes met, like two people at a party checking each other out at the same time. He fought the temptation to look away. And won.

She smiled, playing with her hair. "Now we just need to figure out what makes you happy."

"That's a tough question." He returned her smile, feeling the heat rushing into his face. "What do you think makes me happy?" That was bold. But it felt right. And it was time to make a move.

Her eyebrows twitched up for a second. "I think I can come up with a thing or two. When's your last final?"

"Monday. I'll be like the first one done."

"Mine's on Tuesday, and I'm not flying home until Saturday. That gives me like four whole days to do whatever I want."

"Really?" He swallowed hard. The handle of the mug suddenly felt slick, like it was going to slip right out of his fingers.

She crossed her legs and sank back in her chair, a smile spreading over her face. "Maybe we can hang out when I'm done?"

He nodded, his heart pumping fast, resonating in his temples. *This was happening. This was really happening.*

"Just the two of us?" she asked hopefully, holding him in her stare. "Maybe we can ditch the wolf pack for a while."

"Sounds good." His heart seemed to be skipping every third beat. *Stay cool,* he said to himself. *You don't want her to think you're desperate—or too eager.* "I'd like that." *Good.* His voice only had a small hitch in it.

"Me too."

He checked his watch. "Shit. I'm late. I really gotta go. I'll see ya later?" *The meeting with his TA maybe wasn't such a bad break after all,* he thought. If he stayed, she might start asking about his parents again and if he reacted badly she could change her mind about ditching the wolf pack. Better to leave on a high note.

"You can count on it." Her cell phone rang. She looked down at the screen. "It's Caitlin." She smiled and gave him a fluttery finger wave. "Hey," she said into the phone, scooting her chair around, squaring herself to the fireplace.

Felix grabbed his coat and headed toward the exit. He couldn't stop grinning. Harper had officially announced that she was into him; there was no doubt about it. He felt high with insane happiness. He wanted to jump on a table and proclaim to the world that Harper Connolly was into him. He wanted everyone to know. Harper could have any guy on campus and she'd chosen *him*. Everything seemed brighter and sunnier than the muddled half-light he'd been living in. Everything seemed better. He felt like singing (something he only did alone in his Jeep), and dancing (although he wasn't drunk or on his way to becoming drunk), and ripping off his shirt and running through campus like he'd scored a goal in a World Cup match. They could think he was crazy. He didn't care. He didn't care what anyone thought. Because Harper Connolly was into him. And that's all that mattered. The world wasn't such a bad place. In fact, it was awesome and beautiful and full of hope and endless possibilities. Not even his fear and his sadness could weigh him down. No weight on earth was great enough to tether him to the floor. He felt light on his feet. He wasn't walking—he was floating. He felt lighter than air. He felt like he could take flight and soar up into the clouds. Life was good. Better than good. Fantastic. *Perfect!*

He passed along the wall of sepia-toned photos, randomly glancing at them. He normally avoided the pictures because the eyes skeeved him out. But he was too elated for anything to darken his mood, even pictures of kids who were now worm food. Just before the coffee bar, something in one of the photos jumped out at him, pulling him back like he'd been lassoed. He stopped and searched for it among the hundreds of photos jostling for space; all were black-and-whites, even the handful taken in the last few years. He found it three photos over from the end of the bar: A five-by-seven in a simple black frame.

He leaned in close, leading with his nose, studying every detail. In the picture, three women were standing side by side with a stone building in the background. Above their heads, he could read the words INVERNESS HALL—the words that had caught his eye. The women wore dark ankle-length dresses and their hair was pulled back in tight face-stretching buns. They looked like they'd just gotten off the Mayflower. Then he noticed their faces and his jaw dropped.

Felix knew the woman in the center. He'd met her. It was the St. Rose Ghost.

"You look like you just saw a ghost." A girl's voice at his side.

"Huh?" Felix flicked a sideways glance at her. She was one of the students who worked behind the bar. He'd ordered a few hundred coffees from her since the start of school but their conversations hadn't evolved past "thanks" and "you're welcome." She wore glasses—the black-rimmed kind that make you look a little naughty—and not that he'd given it much thought, but she was friendly, and there was something about her face that was guileless and likeable. He didn't know her name, and at the moment, he was too stunned to think about asking.

"That's the founder's photo." She nodded at the picture. "That's what you're looking at, right? It's not really a photo, you know. It's actually a print of a painting from around 1820. The real one's in color and it's in Dean Borakslovic's office behind glass. Photography hadn't been invented yet."

"The founder's photo?" he said hesitantly, staring at the face of the woman—the ghost—he'd met at the Star Trees. There was no question in his mind, not a single shred of doubt, that it was her. His skin was crawling almost as much as when she'd looked at him with her strangely iridescent eyes.

"Uh-huh. This is the only known picture of the three founders of Portland College. It's kind of famous in its own way, I suppose. None of them ever sat for official portraits or anything like that. The one on the left is Lucinda Stowe"—she pointed at her—"the one on the right is Constance Wethersby, and in the center's—"

"Agatha."

"Yeah." She sounded impressed. "Very good. How'd you know that?"

"Lucky guess."

"Agatha Pierre-Croix was the first president of PC and she was best friends with Constance and Lucinda. They weren't originally from around here. They were all east coasters who met at Harvard. No one really knows why they came to Oregon or why they decided to start a college in Portland. I only know so much about them because we have to learn the history of PC to be in my sorority."

"Oh." Now he had absolute proof, absolute certainty, that he'd seen a ghost. Not that he'd ever really doubted it. And now that he knew for sure, and even though it was a little freaky, it was sort of a relief: confirmation he hadn't been imagining things. Confirmation he wasn't crazy.

"Do you wanna know something really weird?" she whispered, looking over at the bar to make sure there weren't any customers in line.

Felix shrugged. It couldn't possibly be any weirder than what Agatha Pierre-Croix was doing these days.

"They all died in eighteen twenty—"

"Nine," he finished the sentence for her. When he was down in the tunnels standing in front of their coffins, he remembered thinking how strange it was that they'd all died in the same year.

"Yeah," she said, surprised. Then she nodded solemnly. "But I bet you don't know how they died?"

He shook his head and glanced at the back of the bistro. Harper was still talking on her phone, laughing about something. The kid with the organic chemistry text had changed tables, taking a chair closer to Harper but behind her where she couldn't see him.

The girl moved in closer to Felix, her shoulder touching his arm. They stared at the photo together like it held some kind of mystical power. "Well," she said in a soft whisper, "officially they died in a gas leak at the chapel. You know—the church on campus? St. Rose. Them and four other people. If you buy any books on the history of this place, they'll say seven people, including the founders, died from carbon monoxide poisoning. But that's not what really happened."

"So what happened?"

"They were witches."

"What?"

She nodded. "That's the story, anyway. Our own Portland College was founded by three witches. *Can you believe it?* And they ran a coven right here on campus and held meetings at St. Rose in some secret room. There's supposed to be secret rooms all over campus, but no one I know has ever found one. And a friend of mine spends all her free time hunting. I look too. When I have time. Anyway, one night in 1829, a group of religious fanatics stormed the church during a meeting of the coven and killed them all. But they didn't just kill them. They cut out their hearts."

"Cut out their hearts?" Felix's eyes started to water as an image of a dark-haired man preparing to drive a curved blade into his chest gripped his mind. There was only one group he knew of that made a habit of cutting out hearts.

"Uh-huh. Cut the hearts right out and took 'em with them. Sounds just like a horror movie, right? Can you imagine what people would've thought if they knew the school was founded by witches who had their hearts removed by religious nutjobs? That sounds like satanic rituals and other weirdness, right? So of course the school couldn't let anyone know what really happened to the founders. So it was all covered up. Lots of things get covered up here."

"How do you know all this?" he asked.

"It's just the truth. I mean, I guess it's not exactly common knowledge. But it's the truth. There are so many stories about this place. Maybe not all of them are true. But this one is. One thing about our lovely little campus, there's more to it than meets the eye."

"Yeah." She was right about that.

"You're Felix, right?" Her eyes turned up to his.

"Uh-huh."

"I'm Sophia. I watched you play football. You're good. Nice to officially meet you. You're friends with Minnesota, aren't you?"

He nodded.

"You guys are like our best customers." Sophia looked over at the line, now four deep. The only other person working behind the bar was frowning at her with a hateful stare. "I better start dispensing caffeine," she grumbled. "Kaleb's gonna blow a gasket. See ya."

"Yeah. Thanks for the history lesson."

"No problem," Sophia said over her shoulder as she went to resume her barista duties.

Felix's cell phone beeped. He took one last lingering glance at the face of Agatha Pierre-Croix before dragging it from his pocket. He looked down at the screen.

It was a text from Lucas. It said: "in trouble. 11-11 17th st. hurry."

Chapter 46

TRAPS AND BRICKS

Felix stared at the text from Lucas. 11-11 17th Street was right in the heart of no-man's-land. He headed west, staying off the paths, skirting the crowds.

He texted back: "nml? joke?"

Lucas's next text came just a second later, like he'd set his phone to auto-reply: "yes-nml. no joke. serious trouble. hurry. pls."

Felix picked up his pace.

He called Lucas's number. It went straight to voicemail: "This is Lucas. Leave a message after the beep. *Beeeep.*"

Lucas was a funny guy, but he wasn't into practical jokes; it wasn't his thing. Felix hadn't seen Lucas since last night. Neither had Harper.

He started running.

17th Street was exactly as he'd pictured it. Most of the houses on the block were boarded up, and the few that weren't should have been. Two lots had been bulldozed, but city hall must have forgotten to tell anyone to clear away the debris. The street was deserted. He hadn't seen anyone since 14th. Not a bad thing considering the quality of the characters that voluntarily frequented this part of town. There was only one car parked on the block— a wood-paneled station wagon with no hubcaps. Probably stolen. Taken for a joyride and then dumped here, a wasteland the Portland PD had given up on years ago. The sky had suddenly gone gray, hanging low and stagnant as if the shroud of chemical contamination hovering over no-man's-land like a dense and poisonous fog was drawing the gathering clouds to it.

He rested for a second, hands on knees, chest heaving, getting his wind back. He hopped off the dangerously neglected sidewalk, his feet crunching over broken glass as he crossed the street. The house with the address of 11-11 17th Street was a single-story ranch that looked like its occupants had fled in the dark of night before the cops, bounty hunters or rival gangs could capture or kill them. The house was a lurid shade of orange, but so much paint had peeled away that an older color, the color beneath it—blue—was now more prominent. There were three windows in front. All boarded up. The storm door had fallen off and was propped up against the main door at a forty-five degree angle like it was holding it up (or keeping something from getting out). The low-sloped roof was falling in on itself; the roofing material had been installed from long rolls cut into strips and then glued down. Some strips were missing, presumably blown away. The rest had lost their grip, curling up at the seams, bunching, rolling and sliding off the edges, dangling like dreadlocks. The gutters had pulled away from the frame, frozen in freefall stasis, dipping close to the tall foliage on the ground. Patches of brownish-green moss clung to large swaths of the exterior, and like Martha's house—which was right around the corner—the little lawn next to the front walkway was a jungle of weeds and garbage. The chain link fence—matted with trash and battered and sagging like a car had driven over it—must have enclosed the back yard at one time, but not any more. In places it was lying flat and covered over entirely with weeds snaking their way through the metal coils, thriving like adaptable fish making use of a sunken ship as though it were a coral reef.

Felix had two choices: do nothing and go back to campus, or have a look inside. Not a dizzying array of options, but not knowing Lucas's whereabouts confounded his decision. If Lucas was in the house, he was definitely in trouble. He was certain of that. But what if Felix went charging in and Lucas wasn't there? Or what if instead of finding Lucas, he found the Protectors lying in wait with their garrotes and knives? They'd laid a trap for him in no-man's-land once before. Maybe they were unimaginative one-trick ponies trying the same hand again? But he had the texts from Lucas. So he must be in the house. Right? But maybe somebody had stolen his phone. Maybe it was just Lucas's phone in there. Not Lucas. So then who was using it? Maybe some tweeker took it. Maybe there were a hundred squatting meth heads inside who wouldn't react very well if he crashed their meth party. Maybe—but not likely. The Protectors—the trap setters—were the obvious odds-on favorite. But even if it was a trap it wouldn't change the fact that the Protectors were using Lucas as bait. Which meant his life was in grave danger. Which meant Felix couldn't go back to campus. Not until he had a look inside. Doing nothing didn't seem like such a viable option anymore.

So Felix went up to the front door, moved the storm door aside and started thumping on it. "Lucas! Lucas! Are you in there! Hey! Open up!" He pounded feverishly on the door. "Lucas!" He raised his arm back behind his head and brought his fist down as hard as he could.

The door suddenly swung open and Felix's hand found nothing but air.

He lurched forward, losing his balance, his arm still out in front of his body. A shape appeared. It wasn't silhouetted in the doorway. It *filled* the doorway. Something gripped Felix's outstretched arm and the back of his head. Something incredibly strong. His own forward momentum caused him to stumble over the doorjamb, carrying him a step inside the house. Then whatever had hold of him yanked him in the rest of the way and flung him to the floor. He barrel-rolled two or three times then crashed against a hard vertical surface, face down, head jammed up against one wall, legs bent by another, knees tucked into his chest. The door slammed shut behind him. He scrambled to his hands and knees, brought one foot out from under him and pushed off with his—

Felix was snatched off the floor like a cat by its scruff. The entry hall was cramped and dim. He couldn't see anyone. He tried to turn his head, and a sudden biting pressure on his throat cut the movement short. Reaching behind his head, he grasped for whatever was crushing his neck. He felt something. But it didn't make any sense. It felt like fingers. A hand? But that was impossible. It was too big. A hand couldn't simultaneously hold him up in the air by the back of his neck and crush his windpipe in the front. No hand was that big. Or that strong. It was a machine, he thought vaguely, overcome by confusion. He was caught in the clutches of some kind of hydraulic machine.

Whatever had hold of him shook him like a lion trying to snap the neck of a gazelle. He felt himself being wrenched backward, his head brushing and bumping against the ceiling. He stopped abruptly, his feet dangling a foot above the floor. Then it propelled him toward the wall face-first. He didn't have time to cover up. He felt something give way—the plaster?—as his face smashed against the wall. He heard a loud *cracking* sound. But it wasn't the wall that gave way and cracked; it was the bones and cartilage in his nose. He felt hot liquid pouring out of his nostrils.

Disoriented, his eyes were thrown out of focus, clouding and haloing at the edges. As it pulled him away from the wall, he caught a glimpse of blood—a swirly smear of dark red on primer gray—and then it tossed him through the air like a child's toy. He sailed down a narrow hallway, the walls blurring by, bounced on the floor and skidded into a table. One of the legs snapped off and the tabletop fell on him. He pushed it away and scrabbled around on the slippery tile, finally getting to his feet. He looked up.

Something was standing in front of him. It wasn't a machine. It was a man. But not just any man. He was two heads taller than Felix and twice as wide. His twisted and contorted face was a Cubist nightmare, like the subject of one of Picasso's stranger paintings. His mouth was set halfway between a ghoulish smile and a snarl, his teeth gold and polished and shaped like spikes. His nose was missing a nostril; what remained was an amorphous glob of flesh. One ear was gone. The other was hard and balled up like a chunk of dried cauliflower.

Felix felt his mouth working silently, trying to articulate words that his brain wasn't capable of formulating. He took a numb, clumsy step backward, but there was nowhere to go. His back was brushing up against a wall. He had a hard time believing, *really believing*, what was happening, what he was seeing. How could he be standing in an abandoned house in no-man's-land looking at the Faceman? *The Faceman*. The last person in the world he expected to see. His brain started spewing up random disconnected images of the Faceman that he'd seen on TV and the Internet, comparing them to the giant towering over him. Then it occurred to him that this situation was really, really bad; he'd come here to find Lucas, and instead, he found the Faceman. A hundred meth addicts, or even the Protectors, would have been preferable to this.

"I assume you know who I am?" the Faceman said conversationally. The veins in his rippling forearms were as thick as ropes. "I apologize for my lack of hospitality. But I've found with athletic types it's best I set a certain tone. I think it prevents, shall we say, misunderstandings."

Felix used the sleeve of his jacket to wipe the blood from his face. The air was cool with an undercurrent of something nasty. Maybe garbage. Maybe something else. Something much worse. They were in the kitchen in the rear of the house. The light was dull and artificially yellow, dreary but adequate. A tiny sane part of him told him to be quiet. To do as he was told. He ignored it.

"Where's Lucas?" Felix shouted, standing up straight.

"Ahhh, so you're a feisty one, eh? That's good. But we'll need to establish some ground rules if we're going to get along."

"*Where's Lucas?*" Beads of blood shot from Felix's mouth, spattering the checkered linoleum floor.

The Faceman frowned but only one side of his mouth turned down. The other was fixed in a perpetual rebel yell. He reached behind his waist and came away with a silver handgun. He wheeled it around and pointed it at Felix's face. It shimmered beneath the fluorescent tube lights on the ceiling. The Faceman stood at the entrance to the hallway just inside the kitchen, but with his arm extended, the tip of the muzzle was close enough for Felix to sniff if he leaned forward on his toes. The Faceman's wingspan was tremendous. He could easily dunk without jumping.

"Rule number one: I ask the questions. Understood?"

Felix's eyes were trained on the gun. It was huge. The Faceman's index finger was resting against the trigger. One little twitch and a steel bullet would smash into his forehead and wreck his brain.

"Where's Lucas?"

The Faceman shook his head, his expression disappointed but slightly amused, a patient teacher dealing with a gifted but headstrong student. "I see that following rules may be a problem for you. Every so often, I get a kid like you. Off with you. Go! Now!" He motioned with the gun toward the room off the kitchen.

Felix started toward the living room, slowly. Blood was flowing into his mouth and dripping down his chin, falling into the grimy loops of a forest green shag carpet. His eyes danced all around, taking inventory. The living room was ten feet across and narrow. Thousands of flicked cigarette ashes speckled the threadbare carpet, like flies on vomit. Sections of it had been torn off the floor for no reason Felix could think of. A sofa sat against the wall facing the outer wall. Many years ago, it might have blended in reasonably well at the Caffeine Hut. Now it was mostly demolished and crusted over with things he didn't want to think about. Foam, stained yellow by time and smoke, bulged from long gashes in the upholstery. He stopped at the far end in front of a mint green wall. There were no pictures. Just holes. Some looked like people had made them. Fists. Heads maybe. Others looked like the work of mice. The Faceman stepped forward until he straddled the line between the kitchen and the living room, still pointing the gun at Felix.

"If you say *Lucas* just one more time, I'll put a bullet in your head. Is that a concept you understand?"

Felix said nothing. He wasn't scared. It could have been shock or concern for Lucas that dulled his fear. But he knew it was something else.

"Please respond verbally. I tend to perceive silence as insubordination." The Faceman spoke like he was giving instructions to a child. He waited for Felix to answer.

"Okay," Felix said.

"Good. Let's start over. Do you know who I am?"

"The Faceman."

"Correct. Do you know what I do for a living?"

"You shoot kids in the face." Felix searched the room with his eyes. No sign of Lucas: no jacket, no backpack, no phone. *Good.* He breathed out a silent sigh of relief.

The Faceman laughed. "That's true. But that's only part of my job."

Felix shook his head, trying to clear out the cobwebs. His ears were ringing and blood still flowed freely from his shattered nose. His face felt heavy from the swelling and throbbed with pain. But he was thinking clearly and his peripheral vision was back to normal. He wondered, briefly, why he didn't have a concussion.

"I serve the highest power in the universe," the Faceman proclaimed.

Felix started for a moment. Then he stared at him, thinking the Faceman was a cliché. Just another psycho who believed some higher power—God—wanted him to kill people. He could have guessed that.

"But if you pass the test and demonstrate you're not a Wisp," the Faceman went on, "you'll have the honor of serving him."

Wisp?

A line from the journal snapped into Felix's head with limitless clarity, like a blast from a foghorn on a still morning: *This rival group of Sourcerors, calling themselves Drestianites, believed that non-Sourcerors—Wisps—were responsible for damaging the Source...*

"Who's *him?*" Felix asked.

"The one who's going to set everything right." The Faceman let the gun fall to his side. "And all you need to do is pass the test. If you're special, you'll join him. You'll serve him with the others."

The others?

"What test?" Felix asked.

"It's simple. See that brick?" The Faceman pointed at a sliding glass door boarded up from the outside, preventing any light from brightening the room. On the floor beside the door was a brick, badly weathered and whitened with striations in a marble pattern.

Felix nodded, and then remembered the insubordination threat. "Yes," he answered.

"Make it move. If you're special, you can move it."

"What? The brick? What do you mean?" This was starting to feel a lot like his first trip to Inverness.

"Move the brick with your mind," the Faceman instructed. "If you can do it, you pass the test. Only Sourcerors can pass the test."

Sourcerors? He's testing for Sourcerors?

"What if I can't?"

He raised the gun, leveling it at Felix. His face darkened. "You die."

"How many have passed the test?" Felix asked.

The Faceman regarded him curiously for a moment. "Twelve."

"How many have failed?"

The Faceman took one gigantic stride toward him, cocking his head questioningly. "You're very inquisitive." He ran a hand over his chin, as if he was considering something. "Eighty-five."

Eighty-five?

Felix couldn't even comprehend that number. So much life. Lost. Taken. By one man. "You've killed eighty-five people?" he managed to choke out.

"*People?* Oh dear me no. I've killed eighty-five *teenagers.* All Wisps. Of course. I've killed many others. More than I can remember. I used to keep a list somewhere." His lips peeled back over his teeth in a smile as he patted down the pockets of his hunting vest. "But I think I must've misplaced it."

"Are there others like you?" Felix was pushing it, but he had to know. "Other testers?"

"Of course!" the Faceman growled. The smile was gone. "No more questions! Move the brick or you'll die where you stand. If you want to be number eighty-six, then by all means, please ask another question."

Felix didn't hesitate. "Where's Lucas?"

Felix's brazen defiance seemed to stun the Faceman. Then he bared his teeth and raised the barrel, aiming it directly at Felix's face. "You're not very bright, are you? But you don't seem... scared. You haven't screamed once, or even begged for your life. You remind me of someone I recently had the pleasure of meeting. Her name was Gabriela. Great name. Terribly deluded. I hope you're not thinking God is going to strike me down."

"These people," Felix said, pressing on. "What'd you call them? Sourcerors? You have another name for them?" Asking the question was risky, but he wanted to remove all doubt. He had to be sure. And he didn't think the Faceman would pull the trigger until he administered the test.

"You are an annoying little punk. I'm beginning to hope you don't pass. Another name?" The Faceman paused. "He calls them his Drestianites. One more question out of you and—"

"I can move it," Felix said quickly. "I can move the brick. I think I'm a... I'm one of those Sourceror people. So you don't wanna shoot me. I can serve him, right? I can be a Drestianite. So tell me what happened to Lucas."

The Faceman's wide brow furrowed with deep horizontal lines. He nodded slow and unsure once, twice and then a third time. Finally, he took the gun off Felix's face. "So you want to know what happened to Lucas Mayer?"

"Yes." Felix already knew the answer. Or at least he thought he knew the answer. Lucas had never been here. The Faceman had just used his phone to lure Felix into the house. The Faceman wanted to test Felix. Not Lucas. Lucas was fine. He was probably in their room right now looking for his phone. *But what if he was wrong?* What if he'd missed something? Misread what was going on here? Fear clamped down on him. Sweat started to trickle down his neck. His heart hammered in his temples.

"As you wish." The Faceman dipped his head for a moment, giving him a bow. "Late last night, your friend left the library and went out for a walk, probably in search of one of his late-night trysts. I executed what the authorities like to refer to as"—he made quotation marks with his fingers—"an *abduction*. I brought Lucas here. He stood right where you're standing now. No. He was actually two feet to your right." He motioned with the barrel, two quick shakes to his left. "I asked him to move the brick." He nodded at it. "I'm afraid Lucas wasn't special. He wasn't a Sourceror. He failed." He paused, smiling, his dark eyes glittering with cruel pleasure. "So I shot him in the face. And then I shot him in the face again. And then I shot him in the face again, again and again. You get the picture."

Felix went numb. His nose no longer hurt. He didn't feel any pain. His heart thundered in his chest, charged currents raced over his skin, the blood roared in his ears like a derailing locomotive.

"I hope this isn't upsetting you," the Faceman said mockingly. He grinned his livid, malicious grin. "You wanted to know what happened to your roommate, right? Well, so after I blew his face off, I took his body down to the basement. I used a saw—two saws actually—and a knife to make your friend more *portable*. I stuffed his arms, his legs, his torso and his head into a bag which I took to an abandoned factory not far from here. There's a furnace there I used to dispose of the body. It's one of my favorite techniques. There's really nothing left of your friend. Maybe a few scoops of ash. Ashes to ashes, right? And so concluded the short happy life of Minnesota Mayer. *Minnesota Mayer.* It has a nice ring to it, doesn't it? I've always liked alliterative names. Minnesota Mayer. Minnesota Mayer." His smile widened, reveling in the anguish he was causing Felix.

Felix locked eyes with him. He'd come here for only one reason—to find Lucas. Encountering the Faceman hadn't changed that. If he'd found Lucas alive and well (or if Lucas had never been here) Felix would have probably tried to escape. Or so he imagined. But escaping was now the furthest thing from his mind. Every cell in Felix's body was screaming for vengeance. He wanted to kill the Faceman. He wanted to see him lying in a pool of blood.

"Now move the goddamn brick!" the Faceman bellowed, and the walls seemed to vibrate. "I'm going to count down from ten. If you haven't moved it by zero, I'm putting a bullet in your head."

"You want me to move the brick?" Felix said softly.

"Ten, nine, eight..."

"You want me to move it?" Felix said, this time a little louder.

"Seven, six, five, four..."

"You want me to move it?" Felix screamed.

"Three, two, one..."

Felix pointed at the brick and shouted: "Move!" He didn't see the brick fly across the room—it went too fast for his eyes to trace—but he saw the Faceman's features erupt in a cloud of blood, bone and teeth. The brick found its mark, smashing into the center of his face, crushing his mouth and severing his jaw, destroying everything below his nose.

Slowly, understanding dawned in the Faceman's eyes and they grew large. The impact had caused his arm to fall alongside his leg, the muzzle pointing at the floor. He looked down at the gun, the enormous muscles in his shoulder straining as he attempted to raise it against the weight of some unseen force, his eyes clouding with dark confusion. The veins swelled in his trembling forearm as the barrel began to rise, the deadly cylinder drawing Felix into its sights. The Faceman's arm suddenly straightened out hard and rigid and locked down tight next to his body, the muzzle, once again, aimed at the floor. A red line, no wider than a pen mark, formed around his wrist, and it started to bleed. The line became wider and the blood began to flow more steadily, the wound expanding and deepening, revealing bones and ligaments. His trigger finger twitched and the gun fired into the filthy shag, shaking the floor and rattling the little house like a sonic boom. His hand bent back grotesquely, the remaining flesh and bone snapped, and his hand, still clutching the gun, dropped to the floor. Blood fountained from the stump.

The Faceman glowered down at Felix, his eyes full of hate and fury, and charged him like an enraged bull, his chin dangling by strands of dripping flesh. He took one stride that covered half the distance between them before Felix knocked him sideways with the sofa. The Faceman stumbled, fighting to regain his balance, swiping at it wildly, batting it away. Blood poured from his arm, showering the dingy hovel of a room.

Like a pendulum, Felix drew the sofa back and slammed it into the Faceman, pinning him against the sliding glass door, bludgeoning him with his makeshift battering ram. Stuffing spilled onto the floor from wide rips in the fabric. The glass shattered. The Faceman tried to stay on his feet, but the sofa pounded into him with the force of a speeding car and he plunged through the door. The rotting plywood detached from the house and collapsed under his weight, sending him sprawling out into the back yard, the jagged glass encircling the frame slicing deep into his flesh. He struggled to his feet and headed south, limping to the back of the property, a heavy trail of blood following after him.

He was trying to get away.

Felix waved his hand and the outer wall crumbled and burst into the yard like a wrecking ball had swept through, clearing a path for him. He stepped through the opening, glancing at the brick on the kitchen floor.

The Faceman looked over his shoulder at Felix and quickened his pace. There was no longer any cruelty or hubris in his eyes. There was only fear. The hunter, the apex predator, had now become the hunted. He turned his head and started to run. He didn't make it very far. Felix's aim was pure. The brick entered the back of the Faceman's head and exited through his face. The Faceman took one more stumbling step before collapsing in the bramble. He landed sideways lying on one shoulder, his chest turned up to the sky.

Felix ran over to the body. Was he dead? He nudged him with his foot. He didn't move. Felix would have checked to see if he was breathing but there was nothing to check—he didn't have a face. He was allowing himself one brief but very firm sigh of relief when it occurred to him that he'd never seen a dead person before. The Faceman was dead. Very dead. No question about that. His face looked like a neighbor's Halloween pumpkin he and his friends had smashed with baseball bats in junior high. Blood (and other stuff) was puddling around his head. It was disgusting. But it didn't bother Felix. Not in the slightest. Being in the presence of a dead man—a man dead because of him—gave him no pause. And it wasn't that he lacked the capacity to feel; he wasn't blank or numb or bereft of emotion like a stunned survivor of a plane crash. Felix was saturated with feeling, dripping with it. But the only emotion he felt was rage. Bloodlust. He wanted to kill the Faceman. Again. If it was possible, he'd resurrect him so he could smash in his face and watch him die. One death wasn't enough. He felt so much anger that—*Lucas!*

Leaving the body in the thorny weeds, he turned and rushed back to the living room through an opening that would have been no less immense if falling space debris had struck the house. After a quick, frantic search, he found a door in the kitchen that led down to a basement. He fumbled for the light switch and flipped it on. He jumped down the stairs. There weren't many. The ceiling was low, with exposed two-by-fours and hanging sixty-watt bulbs. The cold damp space was empty except for a foldaway cot and a worn duffel bag with a camouflage print. There was a workbench on one side that ran the length of the wall. Tools were on it: two saws and a long serrated hunting knife. *I used a saw—two saws actually—and a knife to make your friend more portable.* The wood all along the surface of the bench was stained a deep purplish color like it had been soaking in the wine Lucas's agent had sent. Felix went over to the bench, picked up a saw, and examined the blade. Crusty red stuff—blood?—coated the metal, and even the wooden handle. It gave off a terrible odor, the odor of death. Then he saw the hairs stuck between the ridges of the teeth. Human hair. Brown hair.

Felix's heart sank. But he didn't scream. He just whispered, "No." He said it only once. What more was there to say? He sat on the floor and buried his head in his hands, staring at the concrete. It didn't feel real. Maybe it made no sense—especially with so much evidence inundating his senses—but he didn't feel like Lucas was dead. Lucas couldn't be dead. He couldn't be. It wasn't possible. Felix took a deep breath, exhaled slowly and pushed himself up to his feet. A sickly sweet slightly metallic smell permeated the air. Was it blood? It had to be. Then a thought began to chisel its way through his calcifying sadness and misery, breaking it up, allowing an alternate possibility to emerge: What if the Faceman was lying? Maybe the blood on the saw was someone else's? Maybe it wasn't Lucas's?

Buoyed by the smallest shred of hope, Felix flew up the stairs, ran out the front door and sprinted toward campus. At 12th Street, he fished his cell phone from his pocket and tapped the screen.

Allison answered. "Hey, Felix. What's up? We're studying at the Caffeine Hut if you wanna—"

"He killed Lucas!" Felix shouted into the phone, panting.

"What?"

"Have you seen him? Have you seen Lucas?"

She didn't repond.

"Have you seen Lucas?" Felix screamed.

"No," Allison said tentatively.

"Are Harper and Caitlin there?"

"Yeah."

"Ask them! Ask them!"

Felix heard Allison ask the question and Harper and Caitlin say "No" in the background. He tore past a flatbed truck idling at a stop sign and crossed 10th Street without looking in either direction. Tires squealed on pavement. Horns sounded, long, irate.

"They said they haven't—"

"I heard! Go to Woodrow's Room and see if he's there!"

"He's not," Allison told him. "We were just there. Harper got spooked so we left."

"Meet me at the dorm!" He slipped the phone back in his pocket. The parking lots next to Stubbins Stadium were already behind him. The main part of the campus came rushing up. He stayed off the paths to avoid barreling into anyone, bombing along the fringes of The Yard, passing one building after another—Cutler, Stamford, Siegler, Jacobs—eliciting lots of shocked looks and a few startled screams. On the eastern edge of The Yard, he saw Allison. She was standing on the grass looking in his direction, waiting. When she spotted him, she came running toward him.

"Your face?" she shouted, sliding to a halt, arms out like a surfer riding a wave. Her face went pale. Their paths crossed for an instant and then Felix blew by her.

"Hey! Your face?" Allison shouted after him. She sounded like she was twenty or thirty yards back. Felix didn't answer. He didn't understand what she was saying. He just kept running.

Allison chased after him. "Wait! Wait! What happened?"

Felix slowed, letting her catch up. "I think he killed him!"

"*What?*"

There was no time to talk. No time to explain.

Allison matched him pace for pace. They raced past the Freshman Yard and cut through Downey's lobby, dodging a group of students waiting for the elevators, then up the four flights to Felix's room. He turned the knob. It was locked. He took the key from his pocket with fumbling fingers, stabbing futilely at the keyhole before finally finding it. The lock sprung back. Felix held his breath. He turned the knob and pushed the door open.

Lucas was lounging on his bed, listening to music on his earphones, looking down at an issue of *Maxim* spread across his lap. His head was bobbing up and down, his lips moving, mouthing the words to some song.

"Thank God!" Felix dove on top of Lucas like he was recreating his Bradline College touchdown leap and gripped him in a ferocious hug. Overwhelmed by an avalanche of elation and relief, he closed his eyes and squeezed Lucas's shoulders. *He's alive. He's alive. He's alive.*

"*What the?*" Lucas yelped in a startled half squeal, like a boy in the throes of puberty, scared at first, and then quickly transitioning to complete bewilderment when he realized it was Felix who was mauling him. He pushed him away, then gasped audibly at the sight of Felix's face. "Whoa! What the hell happened to you, dude?" Then he looked down at his shirt. "You bled on me! What the hell? I like this shirt."

Felix sat next to Lucas, breathing heavily, staring at him, relieved, surprised and overjoyed that he was alive. Lucas stared back at him with an expression of poorly concealed revulsion.

"Thank God," Felix panted. "I thought you were dead. Thank God. Thank God."

"*Dead?* What are you talking about? Dude, your face is a mess."

"Felix," Allison said, warning him with a firm shake of her head.

"There he is," Caitlin said, as she stepped into the room with Harper. "Hey Lucas. These guys"—she pointed at Allison—"were starting to worry us."

"Oh my God!" Harper exclaimed when she saw Felix. "What happened to you?"

Caitlin looked over at him and promptly let loose an operatic shriek.

Felix stood up, absently running a hand over his face. There were layers of scabrous caked-on blood, like a thick veneer of char on a piece of bread left in the toaster too long. He'd forgotten all about his nose. He knew that he must look like a disaster. He glanced down at himself. The disaster wasn't just confined to his face. The front of his jacket, his jeans, even his sneakers, were streaked and spotted with bloodstains. *Shit.* Harper was staring at him, waiting for a response. He mumbled a few incoherent words, gibberish, trying to come up with something.

"It's huge!" Caitlin squawked. "It's gotta be broken. You should go to the emergency room."

"I'm fine," Felix said and tried to give them an embarrassed *I'm-sorry-for-making-you-worry* smile. "It's nothing."

Lucas got up from his bed and came over to him. "That's definitely broken. Let's get you to the hospital. C'mon."

"I'm fine," Felix protested. "Seriously. It's not as bad as it looks."

"What happened?" Harper asked, worried.

"Yeah," Lucas said. "Why'd you think I was dead?"

"*Dead?*" Caitlin echoed, bulging her eyes at Lucas. "Who's dead?"

"I went for a walk and this homeless guy attacked me." Felix was thinking quickly. "He was pretty big and I didn't see him coming. He um… he hit me with a tennis racket. And then he said something about Lucas. He said something about having your phone. I don't know." He thought that wasn't such a horrendous lie. "Maybe I was just all woozy after the guy hit me."

"My phone's right there." Lucas pointed at his bed, eyeing Felix cautiously. The phone was on his pillow.

"Your poor nose!" Harper looked deeply sympathetic. "Are you sure you don't want to go to the hospital?"

"Yeah," Felix said. "I'm good. I just need to clean up a little bit."

"Good idea." Allison urged him toward the door with her eyes. "I'll give you a hand."

Felix grabbed a towel from his closet and stepped out into the hallway with Allison. She shut the door behind them and they started down the hall, keeping their voices pitched low. "What the hell happened?" she asked him.

"I... I killed the Faceman."

"You what?"

"Yeah. He was a tester. He tested kids to see if they were Sourcerors. I think he was building an army for Lofton. You know, the Drestianites."

"The Drestianites?" She stopped, too stunned to walk. "Seriously? Like from the journal?"

Felix nodded, taking her by the elbow to help her along. "The Faceman said if I passed the test I could serve *him*."

"That's insane. So does that mean...?" Allison's eyes grew wide. "Do you think Lofton knows? Does he know who you are?"

"I don't know." Felix hadn't had time to think about any of that. "I um... I killed him pretty quick." It felt so strange to say that, to say that he'd killed someone. "And he didn't know I'm... you know... different. That's why he was testing me to begin with. I didn't like give him any time to tell Lofton I passed his test or anything."

"Are you sure he's dead?" Allison asked.

"Yeah." He felt his nose. It hurt, but the pain wasn't as bad as before. "I should tell Bill."

"No!" she snapped suddenly. "I don't trust him."

Her reaction surprised him, but he was too tired to argue with her. He was totally drained. "Okay." They'd arrived at the men's room. "Can you tell the guys I'm fine and I'll be back in a minute? And can you ask Lucas to bring me some clothes?"

"Sure."

He turned to go into the bathroom.

"Felix," she whispered after him.

"Yeah."

"You okay?"

He paused, unsure of the right answer. "I think so."

"Um... hey... good job. I mean, that guy was a total psychopath. He deserved to die."

They stood there for a moment in silence.

"He killed eighty-five kids," Felix said, his voice hoarse with exhaustion. "He told me that."

"Jesus," she said softly. "That fucking monster. At least there won't be an eighty-six."

Felix looked down at the floor and said wearily, "There are others. He wasn't the only one."

Chapter 47

BREAKING NEWS

Lucas sat in a chair across from Allison with his tray piled high with carnivore-appropriate food. Allison had been playing with her dinner, waiting to see if Felix was going to show. She'd wanted to stop by his room, or call him, to see how he was holding up, but he was throwing off a vibe like he wanted to be alone. Killing the Faceman had rattled him to the bone, and instead of talking to her about it, he'd gone back to his old habit of retreating into his gloom and suffering alone like a penitent monk.

Harper looked up when she saw Lucas. "Felix coming?"

"No. He's in our room resting his nose. Says he's not hungry."

That answers that question, Allison thought, disappointed.

"Is he okay?" Harper asked anxiously.

"His face is wrecked, but he still won't let anyone look at it." Lucas glanced around the cafeteria. Most of the tables were empty. "Where is everyone?"

"Watching the news." Caitlin sniffed. "Didn't you notice there's like a million people in the common room?"

"I guess," Lucas said with a shrug. "This is crazy. The most notorious mass murderer in American history was found dead just down the street. Crazy. Absolutely crazy. My mom won't stop calling. Says she wants me to transfer to a nice safe school back home."

Allison grunted, watching everyone carefully, looking for signs that one of them was drawing a connection between the Faceman's death and Felix's broken nose. The link was tenuous at best, yet Allison had been running at a heightened state of alertness ever since the story broke a few hours ago.

Caitlin sniffed again. Her nose was painfully red from a cold. "Anything new? All the stations are running the same story on a loop. 'Faceman found dead in Portland, Oregon. Details to follow. How's the weekend weather looking, Jim?' I'm going to be saying that in my sleep."

Lucas was staring at his food, not touching it. "So you don't know?"

"Know what?" Allison asked, suddenly nervous. She bit down on the side of her lip.

"You're not gonna believe this. Hold on." Lucas took his phone from his pocket, tapped the screen, scrolled down and tapped it again. "Okay. Here it is. So this is from the Associated Press. According to this, the story was posted"—he checked his watch—"twenty minutes ago."

"What's it say?" Harper asked, annoyed that Lucas was taking so long. She hadn't touched her food either. No one seemed very hungry.

Lucas started reading: "'The Portland police department has confirmed that the body discovered this afternoon in west Portland near the campus of Portland College is that of Nick Blair, better known by his moniker, the Faceman, a suspect in the murder of at least sixty people. The cause of Blair's death is not known at this time. Blair's body was found in an area of Portland known as no-man's-land at a private residence leased to Quinn Traynor, an employee of *Hollywood Reality Bites*, a celebrity news and gossip publication headquartered in Los Angeles, California. Mr. Traynor was reportedly in Portland on assignment.'"

"*Quinn Traynor?*" Caitlin said, eyes wide. "Isn't that the guy who—"

"Yeah," Lucas interrupted. "My stalker. The guy we posed for a few weeks back. That might explain why our picture never ran in his paper."

A shimmer of panic squirmed around in Allison's gut and her feet began jittering under the table. The connection between Felix and the Faceman just got a whole lot less tenuous. She had to talk to Felix, but she couldn't just get up and leave the table without raising suspicions.

Caitlin flushed crimson, staring at her bottle of water. If anyone brought up *The Kiss*—its official title—she blushed and looked like she was going to die from embarrassment. Normally, Allison would have had a good laugh at Caitlin's expense. But not today.

"That's where the Faceman died?" Harper asked. "At that guy's house? At Quinn's house?"

"Yeah, but it gets better." Lucas looked down at his phone and started reading again: "'According to sources, Mr. Traynor's parents reported him missing ten days ago after he missed his flight to Los Angeles and could not be reached. The Portland police department would not confirm such reports, but did confirm that Mr. Traynor's whereabouts are currently not known. Mr. Traynor, twenty-seven years old, is a graduate of Dartmouth College, and a resident of Los Angeles. Anyone with information regarding Mr. Traynor's whereabouts should contact the Portland police department immediately.'"

"Oh my God!" Harper said in a voice loud enough to snare the attention of the students at the next table over. "Should we, I don't know, call the police... or... something?"

"And tell them what?" Allison demanded. She realized she was nail drumming on her tray and stopped herself. She didn't like where this was going.

Harper looked around the table, clearly determined to draw Caitlin and Lucas to her side. "I don't know. But if he went missing ten days ago, then maybe we were the last people to see him. Isn't that something the police might want to know?"

"I don't see how that's relevant," Allison said firmly. Probably too firmly.

Harper cocked her head back and exhaled upward, fluttering a long strand of hair that had dipped beneath her eyebrow. She narrowed her eyes at Allison for a second, then went back to picking at her salad. Lucas put his phone away. He still hadn't eaten anything.

"So Traynor was following me around for months," Lucas said distantly, almost like he was talking to himself. "Then on maybe the same day we have our little rendezvous with him at the dead campus, he disappears. Then the Faceman gets killed at Traynor's house." He stared down at his plate, deep in thought.

"What is it?" Caitlin asked him. "What's wrong?"

Allison felt a surge of panic. She didn't think anyone could possibly piece together what had actually happened to the Faceman, but the connection to the photographer had changed everything, and the look on Lucas's face was causing her to second-guess herself.

"I know what happened." Lucas stood up.

Allison blinked.

"What are you talking about?" Harper said, still red-faced from her exchange with Allison. "You mean to that Quinn guy?"

Lucas snatched an apple from Caitlin's tray and a bag of chips from Allison's. "I gotta go." And just like that, he headed out of the cafeteria at a jog.

Allison started to stand, then caught herself and quickly sat back down before anyone took notice. She knew where Lucas was going. But there was nothing she could do about it. Hopefully he was on the wrong track, and if he wasn't, it was up to Felix to convince him otherwise.

"What are we supposed to do with this?" Caitlin frowned in disgust, shaking her head at the mound of meat on Lucas's plate. "What a waste." Then her face brightened. "I just had an amazing idea—you think I could start a program to donate uneaten food to the hungry?"

Chapter 48

SLEUTH

I killed a man, Felix thought darkly. *I killed a man and I feel absolutely nothing. I. Killed. A. Man.* The words sounded so strange. So surreal.

I killed a man. I killed a man.

He skipped the song he was listening to on his phone—*Fall Out Boy's* "My Songs Know What You Did In The Dark" seemed appropriate, and not in a good way. He hoped the next one would do a better job of calming his nerves. "Death Valley" was, improbably, worse. He lay on his bed, trying to relax, trying to make sense of what he was feeling. Only his desk lamp was on. The blinds were shut. But his cocoon of soft light and thundering guitars wasn't helping.

I killed a man. I killed a man.

He had to kill the Faceman. He didn't have a choice. He knew all that. But he didn't just kill him—he'd wanted to kill him. Killing someone and wanting to kill someone are different things, right? *Intent's important. Isn't it?* But there was more to it than that; he'd wanted to make him suffer. But if anyone deserved to suffer, if anyone deserved to die a terrible death, it was the Faceman. But still...

I killed a man. I killed a man.

Felix didn't feel guilt. He didn't feel regret or remorse. He felt nothing. And this wasn't the first time he'd experienced a complete absence of emotion. He'd felt the same dark void, the same sense of emotional nothingness when he learned that his real mom had died in a mental hospital. Even now, he didn't feel any sadness or loss or anything else when he thought about her. Shouldn't he be feeling something? Was something wrong with him? He touched the screen, skipping to the next song.

I killed a man. I killed a man.

Out of the corner of his eye, he saw the door swing open and Lucas step into the room. He closed it behind him and flipped on the light. Then he turned and lobbed over an apple underhanded. Felix reached up and snatched it out of the air with one hand.

Lucas's expression changed all at once. "What happened to your face?" he gasped.

His cocoon shattered, Felix plucked the buds from his ears, squinting against the bright overhead lights. "Huh?"

"Your face!" Lucas was pointing at him with a look of disbelief.

"Tennis racket. Remember?"

"Look in the mirror, dude."

"Why?"

"Just do it."

Felix set the phone aside and went over to the wall mirror next to his closet. He looked at his reflection. His face was completely healed: no swelling, no gash across the bridge, no redness anywhere, and no dark circles under his eyes. He was shocked. He blinked. Nothing changed. Still perfectly uninjured. Still the same nose he'd been looking at his whole life. He couldn't believe it. But he couldn't let Lucas know that he was surprised. He quickly pulled himself together and went stone-faced. *This was completely mind-bending.* He was stunned, just as stunned as Lucas—or at least as stunned as Lucas appeared to be with his eyes going wide and his jaw slack. Then Felix had a strange realization: This wasn't the first occasion that he'd recovered from an injury in startlingly little time. He recalled the lump on his forehead from colliding with a lamppost; the contusion on the back of his head the night he firebombed Allison's room; the bruised solar plexus from Jimmy Clay's ferocious blow to his stomach; the irrigation ditches Quinn Traynor's fingernails had left on his hand; and sundry bumps and bruises and twisted ankles from playing football. None had left a mark or lingered for more than a day.

"How the hell...?" Lucas came over to get a better look at him.

"Funny, right?" Felix said lightly, smiling. He ran a finger over his nose. "It looked a lot worse than it actually was. After I got all the blood and everything off, it wasn't that bad. And then I iced it for a while. I guess that took care of the swelling."

Lucas shook his head, staring at him.

"It was just a bloody nose," Felix told him. "No biggie."

"It was broken, dude," Lucas insisted, regaining his voice. "I've seen a broken nose before and yours was broken. My brother broke his in high school and he had raccoon eyes for like a month."

Felix fell onto his bed, leaning against the wall, his legs out straight and hanging off the edge of the mattress. "I was trying to tell you guys I was fine, but you didn't wanna believe me."

Lucas still looked unconvinced. But he was wavering.

"What else could it be?" Felix said as he picked up his phone.

Lucas said nothing. If he was thinking about offering an alternate explanation he didn't show any sign of it. "Did you hear where they found the Faceman?"

Felix nodded. All afternoon, he'd been obsessively refreshing his "Faceman found dead" Internet search. When he saw the article that Quinn Traynor had rented the house in no-man's-land, he'd nearly choked on a protein bar.

"Crazy, huh?" Lucas sat down on his desk, tearing open a small bag of kettle-cooked potato chips. A Nerf football rolled off the desk, tumbling across the floor until a pile of gym clothes and a rain coat stopped its progress. Lucas didn't even notice. He looked serious, focused. "It's funny how Traynor goes missing the same day we see him. Don't you think that's kind of a strange coincidence?"

Felix shrugged. "I guess."

"So I was thinking about it. I have a theory. Wanna hear it?"

"A theory about what?" Felix asked distractedly, fiddling with his phone.

"About what happened to the Faceman."

"He died," Felix said with a mouthful of apple, attempting to look relaxed. He swallowed. "Everyone knows what happened to him. It's all over the Internet."

Lucas was studying him carefully, skeptically. "So I have this crazy idea. I was trying to figure out if there was some kind of connection between the Faceman, Traynor, and all of us." He aimed his gaze at Felix and added: "I know what it is."

Felix twisted his mouth and gave his head a shake as if to say *I have no idea where you're going with this.*

"The Faceman killed teenagers," Lucas continued, undeterred. "He didn't kill older people. And Quinn Traynor was like twenty-seven. He was old."

"So?"

"Traynor followed me—followed us—around for a long time, right? And 'cause of his age, I don't think the Faceman was after him. I think he was after one of us. Probably you, Caitlin or Allison. You guys are only children."

"*What?*" Felix exclaimed, doing his best to sound surprised. "Get outta here!" He'd been thinking about the connection as well and had drawn the exact same conclusion.

Lucas plowed on. "So this is what happened: The Faceman's following us, and he notices we're being followed by someone else. Traynor. So the Faceman goes to Traynor's house to find out what he's doing. And then he kills him. He went missing ten days ago, right? That dude's a goner. No way they're finding him alive. And then the Faceman somehow convinces you that I'm at Traynor's house. So you go there. That's how your face gets busted up. He tells you I'm dead, that he killed me. And then you kill him." He raised his hand, pointing a finger at Felix. "*You* killed the Faceman."

"You think *I* killed the Faceman?" Felix burst out, making a face like Lucas was spewing the most ridiculous nonsensical bullshit ever spewed in the history of humankind. Then to add insult to injury, he started laughing hysterically.

"Yeah," Lucas said defensively. "I do."

Felix laughed even harder. "You think I killed the Faceman? You're crazy. How could I have done that? That guy's a monster. He was like eight feet tall."

"I don't know." Lucas tossed the bag of chips on his desk and folded his arms. "But a homeless dude goin' all Rafael Nadal on your face is... weird."

Still laughing, hugging his midsection, Felix said, "You think that's weirder than me killing the Faceman? C'mon! The girls are gonna love this. Where are they? I gotta tell 'em." He tapped on the screen of his cell phone like he was making a call.

Lucas frowned, and ever so slowly, bit by bit, the first indication of doubt began to creep across his face. "But there was that thing with Traynor at the Old Campus. And you thought I was dead. And now the Faceman's dead. And then your nose. And you were... you know... and..." He gave Felix a chagrined smile. "Shit. Maybe I'm losin' it. You keep waking me up, ya know. This is exactly what happens when I don't get enough sleep." He let out a heavy snorting sigh. "Sorry. Some theory, huh? I'm not doing drugs. I swear."

Felix wiped the tears from his eyes. "I won't tell anyone. Not even the girls. So where were you last night, anyway?" He was overwhelmingly relieved that Lucas believed him. He was also overwhelmingly feeling like shit for lying to him. But he didn't have a choice. There was no other way.

"I met this chick at the library on my way out. Jessica Cherry."

"*Jessica Cherry?* Stripper?"

Lucas laughed. "No. Nice stripper name though, right? She's a junior. Lives off campus. Hot. Clingy. I made a run for it when she was in the bathroom."

"The girls still in the caf?" Felix asked.

"Probably."

"Wanna get 'em and go to Woodrow's? I've got two finals a week from Friday." He yawned. "We should hit the Hut first. I could use some coffee."

"You could use some sleep, dude," Lucas suggested. "Have you thought about maybe talking to somebody about those dreams? You know, you could maybe, um... talk to someone... at the counseling center?"

"Not a bad idea," Felix agreed. "Maybe after finals."

Chapter 49

THE PRESSER

Felix sank into a sofa in Downey's common room, letting his backpack fall to the floor between his knees. His last final, Biology, had concluded just twenty minutes ago—his first semester of college was officially in the books.

Heading into finals, his goal had been modest: pass (and maybe improve on his midterm grades). But the nightmares hadn't cooperated, only intensifying over the past week and a half. As he sat for the exams, absolutely fried and barely coherent enough to focus for more than a few minutes at a time, his brain was more impermeable rock than absorbent sponge. How was he supposed to retain anything he'd learned, and put it down on paper, when the smell of his own cooking flesh was fresh in his nostrils?

He stared numbly at the TV, still wearing his winter coat (he was too tired to take it off and couldn't remember if he'd buttoned or zipped it). He blinked from the bright light streaming in from the tall windows peeking out onto the Freshman Yard. The sunshine wasn't a mid-December illusion, though it did mask the nearly freezing conditions outside. And according to the weather report he was half-watching, it looked like a nasty winter storm was moving in late tonight; the computer simulations showed the clouds— dark portentous shades of red—covering the entire western half of the state.

There were quite a few kids in the common room, but Felix didn't look around to see if he knew anyone. He didn't want to get caught up in some mindless idle chitchat. He was wiped out. Body-slammed. His eyes burned like someone had used them to put out their cigarettes.

Felix felt the sofa shudder as someone sat next to him.

"Did it start yet?" A girl's voice.

Felix didn't answer.

"Twelve, right?" the girl asked him. She sounded excited.

"Huh?" Dimly, he glanced to his right. It was Caitlin. Now he remembered why he was here, and why he hadn't gone straight to his room.

He wondered, vaguely, how long he'd been sitting here. It must have been a while, because now the air was heavy with pungent, unfamiliar spices—Indian food?—drifting out from the cafeteria. And the room was filling up fast. Kids were now crammed into the sofas and chairs, sitting on the coffee tables and floor and standing along the wall in the back of the room. And it had gotten really loud. Everyone was talking a few decibels higher than normal, like they were all at a club trying to hear each other over the pounding music.

"The press conference." Caitlin looked at Felix as though she was wondering if he had a pulse. "It starts at twelve, right?" Caitlin checked her watch as Allison squeezed onto the sofa between Caitlin and a guy wearing a knitted scarf looped loosely around his neck. Scarf guy frowned at Allison, annoyed that he had no choice but to scoot over.

"I can't wait to hear what he says," Allison said. "This should be pure gold. Instant classic."

"Wazzup?" a voice said from behind the sofa. Felix recognized it. He turned his head and said, "Hey Lucas." Harper was standing next to him.

"Hey," Harper said, putting her hand on Felix's shoulder for just a second, more of a tap really, a quick meaningless gesture.

"Hey." Felix hadn't had any alone time with Harper since they'd met at the Caffeine Hut and made plans to get together after finals. He was starting to wonder if everything they'd talked about over lukewarm coffees wasn't going to pan out; maybe it was like getting wasted and hooking up, then waking up the next day and pretending that nothing had happened. Probably. So much for Harper being into him.

"Can somebody turn that up?" Lucas shouted. "Who's got the remote?"

"Me," said a plump-faced girl squeezed into a skinny high-backed armchair with two other kids. The girl wasn't blessed in the beauty department. Her short blonde hair looked like a Supercuts trainee had hacked it up on her first day at work. She smiled at Lucas and turned up the volume. Lucas smiled back and she blushed.

"What time is it?" Harper asked.

A freckly, red-haired kid sitting next to Felix—he hadn't even noticed him until now—looked up at Harper and mumbled shyly, "News over press after con... con... conference. Eleven fif... fifty-seven." Felix felt sorry for the hapless kid. Harper had a way of making guys babble incoherently.

The local news was just finishing up. The volume was still too low for Felix to catch everything the pretty newscaster with the glow-in-the-dark teeth was talking about, but it had something to do with a community center. The color patterns on the TV blinked in and out for a moment and then the scene changed from the studio to a ribbon-cutting ceremony where a group of finely dressed men in dark overcoats and colorful scarves stood laughing in front of a sparkling new building. A caption at the bottom read: Lofton Ashfield Donates $35 Million To Youth Center—Set to Open December 19.

"That's a lot of cash," Lucas said. "Thirty-five mil. Geez."

"Not for him," Harper replied. "He keeps that in his change drawer."

Felix watched as Lofton, with a small mob of local dignitaries surrounding him, snipped the shiny red ribbon with cartoonishly oversized scissors.

"Weird!" Caitlin said, looking back and forth between Felix and the TV. "Lofton Ashfield looks just like you."

Felix snorted.

Lofton was speaking into a reporter's microphone, saying something about the importance of giving youth every opportunity to achieve their potential.

And if they don't show any potential, Felix thought, *then you just have one of your testers shoot them in the face.*

"He does kinda look like you, dude," Lucas agreed.

"You think?" Felix tried to make a joke of it: "Maybe we're related."

"How cool would that be?" Caitlin said with a sideways glance at him.

"Pretty cool," Felix replied thickly.

On the ninety-inch TV screen, Lofton was shaking hands with the mayor, a senator, the chief of police, and some other people acting like they were quite important; all of them were beaming at Lofton like he'd just handed them winning Powerball tickets.

It wasn't the shared resemblance, though obvious, that bothered Felix. When he studied images of Lofton—there were thousands online—what rankled him was that his perception, his takeaway, was the same as everyone else's: Lofton was a pillar of the community, a billionaire titan of industry with a philanthropic streak and a penchant for frequenting the city's finest restaurants with twenty-something models. The guy was Bruce Wayne, but richer and less reclusive.

But he was more than that—much more than that. Lofton had everyone fooled. And no one could see it. *Not even Felix.* And that's what bothered him. Shouldn't he sense something? In the presence of the Faceman, Felix had felt his pure primordial hate and malice, his desire to kill for the thrill of it, for the sheer pleasure of taking another's life. Yet the Faceman was just an insect compared to Lofton, a dutiful worker bee carrying out his appointed tasks. Lofton had everyone—the politicians and business leaders on TV, the kids in the common room—completely enthralled. But Felix wasn't like everyone else. So shouldn't he be able to see through his sheep's clothing? See him for who he really was? Beneath Lofton's tanned, smiling countenance, shouldn't he be able to perceive the face of evil? Shouldn't there be some hint of his true identity? Perhaps a certain look in his eye, or a bearing, maybe an expression that would betray his true nature. But Lofton evidenced none of these characteristics. For a man destined to slaughter and enslave (*nations will burn, armies will fall at his feet, and all who refuse to succumb to his rule will be slaughtered like sheep*), he personified respectability and authority. Lofton didn't come across as evil; he came across as remarkable, enviable and charismatic.

The cameras switched over to a different location, abruptly cutting short Felix's troubling thoughts: Two men sat behind a table covered in a rich royal blue cloth embroidered along the fringes like a tapestry with a gold crown insignia in the center. The men appeared to have evolved from completely different gene pools. One was tall and handsome, the lucky recipient of striking the genetic lottery. The other was blessed, presumably, with less surface oriented traits. He was small with an unfortunately premature horseshoe shaped head of hair. But they did have one thing in common: each had a microphone and a glass filled with water.

"Here we go!" somebody yelled excitedly from the back of the room. "Turn it up!"

The homely girl with the remote maxed out the volume, scowling at whoever had yelled at her.

The small man on the TV began to speak. The ambient noise drowned him out.

"Shut up!" somebody on the cafeteria side of the room shouted, a guy with a deep voice.

"You shut up!" a girl shouted back, standing just off the foyer.

"Quiet!" a third person—a guy who sounded like Bennett, the second floor RA—screamed a little hysterically, like he was losing it. "Both of you shut up!"

"...and I would like to begin," the small man was saying, "by letting the members of the press know that Dirk will not be answering any questions today."

"That's David," Lucas said in a low voice. "My agent."

"Thanks for the wine," Caitlin said softly, giggling.

"Dirk will make a statement," David continued. "At the conclusion of the statement, if you have any questions, please direct them to me. So at this time, I would like to welcome Dirk Rathman." David clapped enthusiastically, nodding at the press, inviting them to join in.

There was a smattering of applause at the press conference and some sporadic shouts, whistling and catcalls in the common room.

Dirk smiled and pulled the microphone closer to him.

"That man's absolutely delicious," a girl standing behind Felix said. He couldn't tell who it was and didn't bother to find out. Every girl at PC seemed obsessed with him.

The anticipation in Downey's common room was electric. When word of Dirk's press conference was leaked a week ago, it had caused an immediate uproar in the media. The story was so big it even supplanted the shocking news of a British royal spotted purchasing a pack of gum and a bottle of water at a discount pharmacy, inciting talk, and surprise among many, that the royals apparently chew gum and consume liquids just like everyone else. For the past week, the tabloids and celebrity news programs had been featuring an endless supply of opinions on a media event that was expected to double the ratings of the Diane Sawyer interview of Bruce Jenner's transgender announcement.

"In early September of this year," Dirk began, "I had an epiphany. Unfortunately, my epiphany resulted in some property damage at one of my favorite restaurants. And of course, an even more unfortunate occurrence involving... fish."

There was laughter among the reporters.

"I'm happy to say I made amends with Mr. Takamoto, the owner of Blue Toro. He's even invited me back."

More laughter.

"I know many of you are wondering what happened to me. I've read some of the stories out there, and while many are entertaining, I can assure you none of them are true. I was not in rehab. I was not abducted by aliens."

A few chuckles.

"The truth is, even after so much career success, my life felt empty. It felt meaningless. I spent my life hiding. I hid from my responsibilities as an American and as a citizen of this world. I now realize there can be no true meaning in our lives if we don't participate in something that's greater than ourselves."

He took a sip of water from his crystal glass. "So after my epiphany at

Blue Toro, I made a vow. I made a vow to myself, and I made a vow to everyone who joins my cause. Today, I am introducing myself to all of you for the first time, not as Dirk Rathman the actor, but as Dirk Rathman the chief spokesperson of the Evolution Revolution Army."

Dirk slid his chair back from the table, rolled up his sleeve and raised his arm above his head, revealing a glorious, brightly-inked tiger tattoo coiled around his forearm like a snake. The cameras zoomed in on the tiger's ruby eyes, curved ivory fangs and flashing hard-edged black and orange stripes.

There was a lot of gasping and oohing and aahing—at the press conference and in the common room.

"Get outta here!" Lucas said.

"You've got to be kidding me." Allison put her hands to her mouth in surprise.

"I can't say I'm shocked by your response," Dirk said, once his agent had restored order with the press corps. "I imagine you weren't expecting that. But if you're asking yourselves why I decided to join the ERA, and why I decided to humbly accept my position within the movement, just look at the world around us. We're literally killing ourselves so a few rich men can get richer. As a society, we're capable of so much more. But our leaders and our politicians are afraid, they're afraid to do what's right. They're focused on the *here*. They're focused on the *now*. And look at where that has brought us.

"We now live in a world where our children die from disease and from obscene acts of violence—both of which are preventable—while a handful of billionaires dictate public policy without a shred of concern for the families who have lost so much and continue to lose so much, every day. These greedy self-serving individuals do not care about your welfare or the welfare of our children. They care only about themselves and the thickness of their wallets. The policies these individuals—*these criminals*—have forced upon our society are literally killing us, all of us."

Dirk was pointing into the camera, moving his hand up and down like he was wielding a hammer. "The air we breathe is poisoned. The food we eat is poisoned. The water we drink is poisoned. And our streets, our homes, our shopping centers, our places of work and our schools are all poisoned by an abhorrent lawlessness that could be instantly eradicated with common sense measures that reflect a shared ideal of a better, safer world. A world without fear. Think about that, ladies and gentlemen: *a world without fear.*

"The world we live in today is not sustainable, my friends. Things must change. And they will. I promise you. The government cannot continue to represent only the interests of a few. The time has come to make the changes, the tough changes, that future generations will look back on and say, *that's when it all began*. That's when the world woke up and demanded a better way."

Dirk smiled. "And just one more thing. I also want everyone to know that I'm ecstatic to be playing the role of Phillip in the first installment of *Mesmerizer Jolie*. I understand from my agent that we'll be holding a separate press conference in the coming weeks. Thank you." Once again, he raised his tattooed arm high above his head. But this time, he made a fist, and shouted: "A hundred generations!"

"*A hundred generations!*" echoed a chorus of voices in the common room.

The hair on Felix's neck stood up. He jumped to his feet and looked around. Several arms were reaching toward the ceiling, hands balled into fists, bare forearms covered with blazing streaks of black, orange, white and red. The other students moved cautiously away from those saluting the ERA's new chief spokesperson, forming little islands around them.

Felix did a quick head count before the ERA members lowered their arms and the voids filled with curious students. Felix couldn't believe what he was seeing; there were seven in Downey alone. Then he noticed a familiar face. Make that eight.

Amber stood off to one side, alone. She saw him looking at her. She smiled. Then she cupped a breast and blew him a kiss.

Chapter 50

THE ELF TREE

Knocking. Someone was knocking on his door. The infernal sound was grating, abruptly pulling Felix toward consciousness. He was dreaming. He knew it was a dream. It was one of those rare dreams that ignore the supposedly impenetrable barrier that separates the dream world from reality. He didn't want to leave the dream. He was with his dad. It was Christmas day. They were in the woods, trudging through deep powdery snow, searching for the perfect tree.

Knock. Knock. Knock.

Stay in the dream, he told himself. His dad laughed and pointed at a short, fat, bushy tree. He told his dad it was a nice tree if you were a midget. "It's an elf tree," his dad replied with an easy smile. "It's Christmas, Felix. Be nice to the midgets."

Felix giggled like he used to when he was a kid, when life was carefree and uncomplicated. When his dad was alive.

Knock. Knock.

His dad's features were becoming fuzzy, distorted. *Stay in the dream.* His dad said something. His lips moved but Felix couldn't hear the words. His dad was losing substance, blending into an ever brightening background. "Don't go!" Felix shouted, frantic. "Dad! Don't leave! Dad! Dad!" Then his dad was gone. And so was the dream. He recreated the scene in his memory, determined to hold on to the peaceful feeling of being with his dad on Christmas, but it too was fading, slipping away.

Knock-Knock. Knock-Knock-Knock.

He opened his eyes. He was no longer in the pristine winter woods with his dad. He was lying on his side, looking at a room that he and Lucas hadn't cleaned in months. The slivers of wood floor still visible beneath the bedlam were speckled with balls of lint, tiny fragments of crushed leaves, and whatever else they'd tracked in, probably just plain old dirt.

"Felix?" a girl's voice called out from the hallway.

"Yeah," he muttered groggily, wishing he could go back to his dream, the first non-burning-to-death dream he'd had in weeks. "Just a sec."

"Felix?" More knocking. "Felix? You in there?"

"Yeah. Hold on." He got up and unkinked his neck. He'd fallen asleep in an awkward position with his clothes still on. The blinds were open. It was dark outside, but not in the room. The ceiling light and both desk lamps were burning bright. He couldn't recall leaving them on. He kicked aside a pile of laundry and crossed the room, extremely annoyed that the interloper on the other side of the door had cut short his time with his dad. He opened it.

It was Harper. She was smiling.

He was no longer annoyed.

"You have major bed-head," she said and quickly slipped past him, stepping through the chaos of clothes, backpacks, shoes and umbrellas, finally stopping when she found a clear spot near his desk. "So what are you doing?" She turned to face him. "Besides napping."

Felix closed the door, smoothing down his hair. "I guess I fell asleep."

"You're so lucky to be done with finals."

"Sure." He didn't feel lucky. His finals had been a disaster. He retraced her path through the clutter, hands in pockets, eyes on the floor.

"So what are you doing?" She brushed aside a wavy strand of hair that had fallen over her chin.

"I was slee—"

"No," she said with a little laugh. Then she stared at him and a strange look fell over her face, a look he couldn't decipher—a look he'd never seen before. His pulse quickened. He could feel it throbbing in his throat. "What are you doing right now?" she asked, moving into him and wrapping her arms around his waist. He breathed in her intoxicating scent. Emboldened—maybe he was still half asleep?—he reached around her and pulled her in closer, his hands wandering down her slender back. She tilted her head to the side and lifted her chin, inviting him to kiss her. He did. Her lips were soft. She opened her mouth and let him in.

Am I still dreaming? Felix thought with dawning wonder, hoping desperately that he wasn't.

His hands went lower, heart pounding ferociously. He wondered if she could feel it through his shirt. She moved against him, moaning softly. He wanted her. He *needed* her.

"I've been wanting to do that all year," she purred.

"Me too," Felix said, his breath coming out in little shudders. "Why... why now?"

Harper laughed as if she found the question funny. "When I saw you downstairs for Dirk's presser, you looked a little sad and I just wanted to make sure you're still on the same page with me. You know, what we talked about before, at the Hut." She raised an eyebrow at him and bit down flirtatiously on her bottom lip. "We are on the same page, right?"

"Same page. Same sentence." They kissed. Felix's hands went everywhere all at once. It didn't seem possible, but her body was even more perfect than he'd imagined.

"*Oh shit!*" he suddenly burst out, pulling back. He looked down at his watch. He was late. He closed his eyes for a moment and said a silent curse to whoever was responsible for ruining the most amazing experience of his life. When he was done cursing, he started thinking. Now he had to come up with something credible to tell Harper because he definitely couldn't tell her that he had a crucially important meeting scheduled with PC's assistant groundskeeper. After three weeks of texting ("help! dream's killing me!" was typical), Bill had finally and reluctantly agreed to "see what I can do to help."

"I'm late," Felix muttered weakly. "It's five forty." Even weaker.

"Late for what?" She pressed her hips against his. He hesitated and drew away for a second, then pressed back. Time to grow up. He knew she could feel him. He was glad. And then he hesitated again, thinking about the dream: *the bed, the flames, the pain.*

"I have... a... a meeting with... the guy who..." He could scarcely think. He was a terrible liar to begin with, and now the most distracting girl on the planet was in his arms, drowning his brain in hormones. Maybe he could postpone his meeting with Bill? Call him and do it another time? But Bill's schedule was unpredictable; he didn't exactly maintain regular office hours. Felix hadn't even seen him since his last trip to Inverness, the trip that almost ended with the Old Campus losing a building. And for whatever reason, he believed that Bill was the only person who could exorcise him of the nightmares ruining his life—the only person who could salvage what remained of his sanity.

She kissed him in a way that made him think that Emma had no idea what she was doing. "Instead of doing this," she said, her lips curling up in a seductive smile, "you'd rather meet with...?"

"Um... my... my parents' lawyer. He's in town. It's got something to do with the insurance or something. I'm supposed to meet him downtown at five." That was pretty good, he thought, all things considered.

"Oh." Her eyebrows tugged in. "Well... that does sound important." She moved back a little. "And we can do this"—she leaned into him, *melting with him*, just like the lyrics from the *Modern English* song he used to listen to in high school when he only dreamed about making out with a girl like this—"later."

"Sorry." Felix had never uttered an apology filled with more sincerity.

"It's okay. I actually wanna hit the library for a few hours, anyway. My last final's tomorrow morning. Tuesday at noon, I'll be the happiest girl alive. When do you think you'll be done?"

"I don't know. Maybe around seven?"

"Perfect. I think everyone's pulling an all-nighter in Woodrow's. If you want, you can come by my room when you get back. My roommate's out. We can pick this up." She touched her lips to his, finishing with a feathery flick of her tongue. "And when we're *finished*"—her flirty smile let him know exactly what she meant—"we can get some dinner somewhere."

He nodded. There was nothing he needed to say. This was perfect. If a dream had ever come true, it was this.

"And then after dinner," she went on, smiling her gorgeous smile, "we can go back to my room, and do it *again*. And maybe even *again*—if you're up to it."

He had to have her. He had to have her now. Bill would understand if he didn't show up for their meeting. It was just a dream, after all. It wasn't that bad. It wouldn't kill him. He kissed her and let his hands roam. Her lips moved to his ear.

"Felix," she whispered. "You better go."

"I know." He didn't stop. He couldn't stop.

"Felix…"

"Okay." He dragged himself away from her even though it was the last thing in the world he wanted to do. He looked into her beautiful blue eyes and she smiled.

"We've got all night," Harper told him. "All week. My flight's not until Saturday, remember?"

"Okay. I've got this under control." He laughed because he most certainly did not have it under control.

"Crazy about Dirk, don't you think?" Harper said abruptly. "I never thought he cared enough to do something like join the ERA, let alone become the grand dragon or whatever he's calling himself."

"Huh?" Felix wasn't sure what she was talking about.

Harper laughed at the confused expression on his face. "I'm just trying to make you think about something besides what I'm going to let you do to me tonight. You better get going. My room. Seven o'clock."

She kissed him lightly on the lips. "I miss you already."

Chapter 51

THE ROOM

"You're late," Bill said gruffly from his chair under the window. He paused, observing Felix with a steady, scrutinizing gaze. "What are you so pleased about?"

Felix could only shrug. It was entirely possible that a perma-grin was affixed to his face, but he couldn't help it. He slipped out of his puffy winter jacket and tossed it, along with his umbrella, in the corner, then sat down across from Bill. He'd managed to stay dry on his trek from the dorm, but a winter rainstorm hung in the air. The heavens were about to open up.

Felix sank back and looked out the window at the hundreds of soft glowing orbs dotting the buildings on the other side of The Yard. Beneath each orb, he pictured tables crowded with frazzled, heavily caffeinated students hunkering down for the rest of the night, noses deep into books, eyes glued to computer screens. The wonderful scent of Harper on his shirt cast his attention in a different direction, the way her body felt next to his, the little sounds she made when he touched her. He smiled at the memory.

"Would you like some tea?" Bill asked, his eyes narrowing. "I have a nice peppermint you might like. It's excellent this time of year."

"I'm good."

A clock tolled on the south side of campus, six pounding chimes that swept between the stone buildings and over the lawns and gardens and through the trees, reverberating across the face of the Stamford Building and right up into the office where they sat at the table. Little Ben was conspiring against Felix.

"I think I counted six," Bill said dryly. "If you were on time, I believe there would have been five."

"I know. I'm late. What can I say? Sorry. I was… busy."

Bill ran a hand over his face and leaned back in his chair, as though he was attempting to divine the reason for Felix's good mood from some subtle expression or involuntary gesture. "A girl?" he hazarded.

Felix tried to keep a poker face, but he was just too damn happy: one corner of his mouth lifted in a smile.

"Allison?" Bill asked.

Felix shook his head, surprised that he thought it would be her.

"Harper?"

Felix shrugged.

"Good for you. She looks a lot like this girl I knew in college, a USC cheerleader who—"

"Alright, alright. I got it. Sorry, it's just a little weird talking about girls with..." Felix trailed off awkwardly.

Bill laughed lightly. "I forgot. Anyone over thirty couldn't possibly know anything about girls."

"Let's get going!" Felix checked his watch impatiently. "I've got things to do. Hurry up and fix me. C'mon."

"You're the one who's late," Bill pointed out. "All right then, I don't want you to miss out on your *things*. So here's what we're going to do. I'll induce a state of deep relaxation. It's a little like hypnosis, but you won't be susceptible to suggestion or anything like that. You'll always be in control. Once you're relaxed, I'll ask you questions about your dream. You told me you're in a room, right?"

Felix nodded.

"But you can't see very clearly because the room is hazy?"

He nodded again.

"I'm hoping that once you're relaxed, the details of the dream will become clearer."

"Then what?" Felix asked, confused. "What's the point of that?"

"I think what's happening is your mind is making a big deal out of nothing. In this dream of yours, you're in a room and you can't see what's around you. Your conscious mind isn't coping very well with the unknown. It wants to know what's lurking in the shadows. And the only way to get a peek is to dream."

"So my mind's hitting the rewind button and bringing the dream back?" Felix said, finally understanding where Bill was going. "Is that what you mean?"

"Exactly. Once your conscious mind knows what's hiding in this dream room of yours, there'll be no need to have another look. The dream should just go away like any other dream."

"So you're gonna break the rewind button?" Felix asked.

"Smash it if we can," Bill said, smiling. "I'm almost certain you're dreaming about Allison's room. I think there's still some small part of your mind that's trying to comprehend exactly what you did that night."

"So how's this deep relaxation thing work?"

"You'll be sort of half-sleeping," Bill explained, folding his hands and resting them on his lap. "You ever have a dream where you know you're dreaming?"

"An elf tree," Felix replied with a grin.

"A what?"

"Never mind."

"Anyway," Bill continued, giving him a look, "half-sleeping may feel a little strange to you. But don't worry. When I clap my hands *twice*, you'll come right out of it. Got it?"

"Twice. Sure. Okay." Felix rubbed his hands on his jeans, wiping off the sweat that had gathered in the creases of his palms. He was nervous, but excited.

"Okay, then. Let's do this." Bill shuffled his chair over so that they were facing each other, their knees nearly touching. "Make yourself comfortable. Close your eyes."

Felix leaned back and let his eyelids drop. The room was silent except for the patter of rain against the window. The silence lengthened.

"Relax and breathe slowly and deeply," Bill said, breaking the stillness.

Felix took three long breaths and let the air out as slowly as he could manage.

"That's it," Bill said, his voice low, soothing. "Breathe deeply and relax. Let everything go. Try to empty your mind. Now open your eyes."

He did.

A tarnished coin attached to a silver chain dangled in his face, spinning clockwise, and then when it had spent the force of its movement, it sprung back and spun in the opposite direction.

"Keep your eyes on the coin," Bill intoned. "Relax and breathe. Focus on your breathing. In and out. In and out. Nice and easy. That's it. Now follow the coin with just your eyes. Keep your head still." With a slight turn of his wrist, Bill began to rock the coin back and forth in a smooth, steady, undulating arc.

Felix followed its graceful motion with his eyes. There was something strangely magnetic about it; he wasn't sure if he could take his eyes away from it even if he wanted to.

"Watch the coin and listen to my voice. Can you hear me?"

"Yes." To Felix's surprise, his voice sounded flat, almost a monotone.

"I want you to return to the place in your dream. I want you to return to the room where you saw the fire. Can you do that?"

"Yes."

Felix was standing in a room, a room that looked nothing like Bill's office. He looked all around, wondering if he was dreaming. If he was, he was sharing it with Bill because Bill was right beside him, still holding the silver chain in his hand. The floor was heaped with clothes. Posters—concerts and sports—covered the room's dark blue walls. Thumbtacked to the back of the door was a Seattle Seahawks cheerleader calendar. A blond wood Ikea desk sat near the wall in one corner beneath a window that looked out onto a road with streetlamps some distance off and houses shadowed save for their porch lights. Scattered across the desktop were books, an iPod, stacks of CDs, a laptop and an orange cereal bowl with melted ice cream at the bottom. A clip-on desk lamp with a stretchy flexible neck was radiating down directly onto the varnished wood, amplifying the bulb's wattage, illuminating the room with streaky diamond-patterned white light.

In the closet next to the door, shirts hung from a sagging wooden rod, and carelessly stacked bundles of pants and sweatshirts leaned against each other on a shelf mounted above it. On the closet floor, shoes, more piles of clothes and several shoeboxes competed for space with baseball bats, a basketball, footballs, a lacrosse stick, baseball gloves and a pair of heavy dumbbells. A bed stood under a window hidden behind cream-colored curtains. There was someone in it. He appeared to be sleeping. His hair was thick and sandy blond and his arms were at his sides resting loosely above the covers.

An icy shock of recognition coursed through Felix. He knew where he was. *But it wasn't possible.* That room no longer existed. "Holy shit!" he stammered, baffled. "This is my room. That's... that's me!" He pointed hesitantly at the bed. "What the hell? What happened? This is *my* bedroom!" He stared at himself lying in bed. "What the hell's going on? This isn't the room from my dream. This is *my* room."

Bill was just as surprised. He stood stock still, stroking his chin, assessing the room. "Hold on," he said, his voice rising a notch. "Just keep it together."

Felix crossed the room—his feet lifted, his knees bent, and his legs extended forward like he was walking, but it felt different, like he was half-floating and half-treading water. The floor wasn't exactly supporting his weight, and he wasn't sinking through it either. He reached out for a *Coldplay* poster and his hand passed cleanly through it—and the wall—all the way up to his wrist. But that's where it stopped. He couldn't force it in any deeper. He kicked at a T-shirt lying on the floor and his foot didn't disturb it.

"Weird," Felix said, his head swimming in confusion. "It's like we're ghosts. But this... this isn't the right room. What are we doing here?"

Bill didn't say anything. He was staring at the door with an odd look in his eyes, as if he was expecting something to happen.

"What's going on?" Felix demanded. "Bill! Hey! What is this?"

"I'm not sure," Bill said thoughtfully, turning to face him. "We're not really in your bedroom. We're still in my office." He glanced down at the chain in his hand. "I think we're actually in a memory. And in this particular memory"—he gestured at the bed—"you were sleeping."

"How can we be in a memory?"

"When you read your aunt's journal, you felt what she was feeling, right?"

Felix nodded, staring at himself sleeping in bed.

"And why is that?" Bill asked.

"Because it's cursed," Felix said quickly. "That's what you told me."

"Right. And because it's cursed, whoever reads it feels your aunt's emotions, what she felt when she was writing in the journal. And now, we're... *inside* your memory." Bill paused, scratching his chin. His voice sounded different, like he was thinking out loud. "But we're not just experiencing your emotions. We're actually *experiencing* the memory. We're seeing what happened. But why would that be? Why... why would—"

Almost immediately, the pieces of the puzzle shifted into place for Felix. "The memory's cursed," he said.

A frightened expression crossed Bill's face. Then very abruptly, he struck his hands together in a single sharp clap and drew them apart—

"Stop!" Felix shouted, pointing at Bill. "We're not going anywhere! Why's this memory cursed? What's going to happen?"

"Felix," Bill said softly. He'd gone slightly pale. "You don't want to see this. Let's go. There's nothing you can learn from this."

"We're staying!" Felix told him sternly. "Don't clap your hands! Promise me!"

Bill clapped them together twice in rapid succession.

But nothing happened.

Bill looked confused. Then he frowned and shook his head. "That only works if you want it to work. You're in control. Please, let's go. Trust me. Let me get us out of here. You don't want to see this."

Felix looked around, ignoring Bill. Here he was, standing in his old room, seeing all his things exactly as he remembered them. He had to be here for a reason, and he wasn't going to leave until he knew what it was. He went over to his desk and found the iPod that was lost in the fire. He'd bought a new one a few months ago, just before midterms, but the old one was a present from his mom and she'd had it monogramed on the back.

"Felix!" Bill shouted, breaking his reverie. "Something's happening."

The sleeping Felix—his past self—was moving. His arms were twitching a little. Then the movements gradually grew more pronounced. He flipped up the blankets and they fell in a tangled heap at the foot of the bed. Drenched in sweat, he was wearing only a pair of dark gray boxers; the perspiration soaked into the sheets around him, forming an outline of his body.

"Please," Bill pleaded, moving toward him. "Let's get out of here. You don't want to see this."

Felix stayed put. *He had to see this.*

Everything near the sleeping Felix began to glow a deep shade of red, lighting up the room. His body spasmed as if he was having a seizure. Then he instantly grew calm. He lay there for a while, hushed and sedate. Seconds passed. He levitated off the bed, ascending slowly, incrementally, until he was close enough to touch the ceiling. And then he went quiet again, perfectly still, suspended horizontally as if he was lying on an invisible mattress. The bed bounced up and down violently, the metal legs slamming down so hard on the carpeted floor the light fixture on the ceiling shattered. The red light began to expand, edging outward, spreading languidly and inexorably across the room like a cloud, enveloping everything in its blood red embrace.

Chaos ensued: a scorching wind blistered through the room with a deafening roar. Books, CDs, clothes, dishes and shoes lifted into the air and hovered for a moment before taking direct aim at the sleeping Felix like iron filings to a magnet. Larger objects soon followed in their wake: the Swedish-made desk and its matching chair; the shelf in the closet; and the pair of dumbbells, which smashed into a mural of the Cascade Mountains next to the bed, leaving two gaping holes.

And then the flying objects burst into flames.

Lit up like kerosene torches, books, magazines, and hundreds of DVDs, began zigzagging crazily, crashing into walls, spitting out puffs of blazing ash and splintered plastic. Burning fragments whistled like arrows and fell to the floor, igniting the carpet and the curtains behind the headboard. The fire spread quickly. Smoke filled the room. And yet the sleeping Felix remained undisturbed.

"*Felix!*" a man's panic-stricken voice shouted from outside the room. "Felix! Open the door! Felix! Open the door now!" The doorknob rattled.

"Felix!" a woman's voice cried out. "Felix! Oh my God! I smell smoke! Felix, please open the door!" She sounded terrified. There was a resounding thump on the other side of the door; the molding and wood trim around the hinges made a creaking noise. "Come on!" screamed the woman. "Break it down! There's a fire! Break it down! Use your shoulder!"

"I'm trying, Patricia!" the man shouted back. "I'm trying!" The door shook, but scarcely moved inside its frame. "Felix! Come on, son! Felix!"

"My parents!" Felix shouted at Bill. "Mom! Dad! You're alive!" He ran to the door, reaching for it, and his hand went right through the doorknob like it was mist. He tried to shimmy his way to the other side, to pass through it, but it was as though the memory had made him a prisoner and the room was his cell.

A constellation of flaming debris was gathering around the sleeping Felix, circling him slowly as the swirling cloud surrounding his body began to pulsate like a pumping heart. Each ear-shattering beat released an explosive shock wave of energy, flaring like the sun.

The room was quickly becoming an inferno.

And for the first time, Felix realized what was happening: this room—*his bedroom*—was the room from his dream. But it was more than just a dream. It was a memory. A memory of the night he turned eighteen. A memory of the night his parents had died. At some cognitive level, Felix now understood that he wasn't really in his bedroom. He knew that he was inside the memory. And in the memory, his body had no substance. He was just a shadow. But he had to do something. He turned away from the door and jumped through the fiery rubble encircling the sleeping Felix, screaming at him—*screaming at himself*—to wake up. It had no effect. He was perfectly at peace, his face an emotionless mask.

"Get outta here!" Felix yelled at his parents, running back to the door. "Get outta here! Run! Get mom outta the house! Run!"

"Felix!" his dad shouted back, as if he had heard him. "Open the door! I can't get it open! Please, son! Wake up!"

"Dad! Run! Run!" Felix screamed until his vocal cords ached. Until it felt like his throat would split open. He looked over his shoulder at Bill, who was standing in the center of the room, watching him, tears flowing freely down his face.

"Bill!" Felix called out to him, his voice frantic and filled with desperation. "Help me! Do something! Oh God! Help me! Help me!"

"Come on, Felix!" his mom screamed in terror. "Open the door! Wake up! Please! Wake up! Open the—"

Fire and sound consumed Felix, a simmering gaseous ball of molten orange flames he could see and hear, but not feel. The room shook and rippled, surging upward as if it was resting on the mouth of an erupting volcano. Something passed through him—fluttering pages from a book?—followed by floorboards, pieces of glass, two-by-fours and chunks of drywall. Overhead the sparkling night sky stretched away endlessly.

Where'd the roof go? Felix wondered faintly as he watched the bedroom walls exploding out into the driveway and the street in front. The frame of the house shifted, twisting, grinding and finally snapping. The floor collapsed, crashing on top of the kitchen below.

Felix looked for the door through the smoke and fire. It was no longer there. The hallway outside his bedroom where his parents had been only seconds before was also gone. The top floor of the house had been obliterated. He stared in disbelief at the empty space where his parents had stood, where they had begged him to open the door. Now there was nothing. They were gone. In an instant, their voices had been silenced, silenced forever.

The sleeping Felix tilted, almost machine-like, until he was perpendicular to the ground far below, then he drifted across the bedroom and out into what was once the hallway. The flaming ruins orbiting his body continued to pulsate with bright crimson energy, burning and destroying everything in their path, shooting off in all directions, annihilating all that they touched. He descended slowly, majestically, down the collapsing shell of a staircase to the lower level of the house where he came to a stop, his feet hovering just above the floor.

Numbly, Felix trailed closely behind, tethered to his past self. He didn't have a choice. It was as if the memory was forcing itself on him, imposing its cruel will, making him watch until the very end. The remains of the second floor came crashing down, sending up clouds of powdery white dust and smoke that spiraled into the warm summer air in enormous plumes.

The walls twisted and bent, the wood splintering, bulging and crackling against the unnatural torque. The earth shuddered. Massive flaming sections of the house—walls, floors, entire rooms—rocketed into the night sky, circling overhead like burning airplanes in a holding pattern. And then with a sound that was eerily similar to a Fourth of July fireworks display, they all exploded into innumerable scorched fragments, tiny and feather-light, that blanketed the heavens, darkening the stars. The wreckage wafted down slowly, peacefully, like snowflakes on a windless night, forming little piles all across the property.

The sleeping Felix glided through the smoke-filled carcass of the house, crossing the living room and into the back yard where small fires were breaking out in the lawn and flower beds. He hovered above the grass, his back to the smoldering foundation of the house. And then the red cloud around his body faded all at once, like a lamp when the power cord is ripped from the wall. He fell to the ground and his face slammed into the lawn. He lay there motionless, blood trickling from his nose and from a corner of his mouth.

Felix looked down at the sleeping Felix—at himself. He could hear Bill's footsteps behind him and the sound of sirens far off in the distance.

Bill looked at Felix with trepidation.

"It was me!" Felix cried out. "It was me! It was me! It was—"

Bill clapped twice.

Chapter 52

INTO DARKNESS

Made of silver, the coin was blackened, dull and scratched on its surface. Felix was reclining in an armchair, watching the coin swinging back and forth in his face; he was in Bill's office in exactly the same position, doing exactly what he'd been doing before a cursed memory had taken him into its vortex. He fell forward, collapsing to the floor, screaming in agony. He felt hands on his back. Bill was saying something in a low voice, but the words held no meaning.

Felix shrugged Bill away and stood up, then tripped over something— *a stack of books? an umbrella?*—and braced himself against a book-lined wall. As he stumbled toward the door, he heard the thumping sounds of heavy volumes falling from a shelf and Bill's voice growing louder.

He flung open the door and ran to the stairwell, careening down the stairs without holding on to the banister, crashing into walls, falling, descending each flight faster and more recklessly than the one before until he reached the lobby. He burst through the main doors, staggered down the front steps and lost his footing on the wet slippery surface, sprawling to the footpath bordering The Yard.

Felix pushed himself off the puddled ground and ran headlong into a cold rainy December night. Everything inside him had shattered. He was broken. He felt only pain—an all-encompassing anguish that burned like acid, extinguishing everything in the world but the images of what he'd done to his parents. He needed to get away, to go someplace where he could escape from the memory. He had to hide from it. Bury it. Submerge it in the deepest ocean trench, a place without light and life, a place where he could vanish, lose consciousness and erase the memory forever.

Felix wanted to die.

Chapter 53

CONFESSION

"Dad, it's me," Bill said tiredly. "I know it's late." His cell phone was on the table with the speaker turned on. His forehead was hot. He felt like he was running a fever. The jacket he'd been wearing earlier was now lying crumpled on the floor. He'd untucked his shirt and rolled up the sleeves to his elbows. His hair, already disheveled, spiked up into wayward clumps as he raked a hand along the top of his head.

"It's not that late, but I am in bed," his dad croaked in a voice that sounded even raspier than usual. Bill had woken him up, but his dad wouldn't acknowledge that because he thought it a sign of weakness that he required sleep. "I don't want to disturb your mother. Give me a minute. I'll go to the library."

Bill sat at the table and waited, unmoving, staring trance-like at his haggard reflection in the window. The same thing he'd been doing since Felix ran out of his office two hours ago.

"Okay, William," his dad said after several minutes had passed. "I assume you wouldn't be calling at this ungodly hour if it wasn't something about the boy."

"We have an issue."

"An issue?" His dad was suddenly alert.

Bill described Felix's cursed memory, sticking to the facts, recounting every detail. When he was done, he checked his watch. Twenty minutes had gone by.

"That's not an *issue*," his dad bellowed. "I would characterize it as a full-blown catastrophe! How could you allow this to happen?"

Bill had predicted this. Before hitting the call button on his phone, he knew that his dad would blame him. The last time they spoke, Bill had told him about Felix and Allison's run in with the Protectors in no-man's-land. The 'implications' hadn't even surprised his dad all that much—the mobilization of the Protectors (which they'd thought were dormant) and the possible restoration of the Order—but he lambasted Bill for a full hour for nearly getting Felix killed, for failing to protect him. The prospect of being blamed for something beyond his control was so irritating he'd spent much of the past two hours debating whether he should even make the call; in the end, he'd decided it was just too important to withhold.

"I didn't *allow* anything to happen," Bill said stiffly through his teeth. He breathed in through his nose and out through his mouth, trying to remain calm.

"No? Then pray tell where the boy may be."

"I'm sure he's at his grandmother's place." Bill kept his voice steady only with tremendous effort. "He has nowhere else to go."

"His grandmother's place?" His dad paused for a beat. "Oh. The cottage in that little coastal town near Washington?"

"Yes. Cove Rock."

"Well then goddammit, if you know where he is, why aren't you in your car?"

"Do you really think he'll want to see me right now after what just happened? He's as likely to kill me as he is to talk."

His dad didn't have an immediate response to that. He cleared his throat with a phlegmy, grinding half cough—like a chainsaw on the first pull of the cord—that required Bill to expend every last ounce of restraint not to end the call. This was how his dad bought time when he didn't know the answer to something. It was just one of his annoying habits.

Bill sat in silence, leaning back in his chair, staring at the phone, waiting for his dad to speak.

"I'm sure you're right," his dad said after a long while. "So what's your plan?"

"I'll have Allison get him."

"Another teenager?" his dad replied with contempt in his voice. "Is that a good idea?"

"Do you have a better one? She's the only one who knows what Felix is. And he trusts her. He trusts her more than anyone. Nobody else can bring him back."

"When will you tell her?" his dad asked.

"I think Felix is going to need some time by himself. I'll give him two or three days, then I'll talk to Allison."

"I'd give him four."

"Fine." Bill sighed soundlessly at his dad's incorrigible contrarianism, another of his charming traits. "Four days it is then. I'll wait until Friday."

"And William, one other thing before I go back to bed: We can't lose this war because of your ill-conceived therapy session. Bring the boy back. Let me know when you do."

Chapter 54

MISSING

"Have you seen him?" Harper burst out as soon as Allison sat down at the table.

Allison had gone out for an early run and studied through breakfast. The time had slipped away from her and now she was late for lunch. Harper, Lucas and Caitlin must have arrived much earlier because they didn't have a lot left on their plates. Allison's stomach was rumbling and the turkey sandwich on her tray was making her mouth water. Starvation felt like a distinct possibility. "Who?" she asked, removing the toothpicks from the top slice of bread.

The cafeteria was busier than usual, the air full of manic conversation and the clatter of knives and forks on sturdy bulk-purchased tableware. The rain had finally stopped and pale sunshine poured in through the tall windows, bathing the table in warm streaming light.

"Felix," Harper answered.

"Uh-uh." Allison shook her head and took the sandwich in both hands, sizing it up for the first bite. She was too focused on her lunch to notice the concern in Harper's voice, but she felt Harper's eyes following her movements so she glanced sideways at her, mouth open, and saw the expression Harper was wearing on her face. She nearly dropped the sandwich.

"What do you mean have I *seen* him?" Allison said to Harper, her stomach turning.

"He wasn't in our room when we got back from Woodrow's," Lucas somehow managed to garble out while chewing on a mouthful of cheeseburger.

"Where is he?" Allison asked.

"We don't know," Harper said bluntly. "That's why I asked you."

"Oh." No longer hungry, Allison placed the sandwich on her plate. "But we didn't get back until like four in the morning, right?"

Lucas yawned and nodded. He was tired. They all were. Sleep reservoirs were severely depleted, drying up from the sweltering pressure of finals week.

"I haven't seen him since Dirk's press conference," Allison said.

"Same," Lucas mumbled. Then he set about demolishing the rest of his burger and fries.

"So um… who saw him last?" Allison felt a spurt of anxiousness creeping up her throat, but tried not to show it.

"Me," Harper said. "I think. Right before I met up with you guys at Woodrow's. That was around what? Six?"

Caitlin nodded, picking at some sliced carrots and apples she'd segregated to one side of her plate.

Allison turned to Harper. "Did he say anything to you? Was he going somewhere?"

"He told me he had to meet with his parents' attorney. Something about their insurance. He was going downtown."

"*Insurance?*" Allison said, her voice rising in surprise. "That was all settled months ago. Back before school started."

Harper's face flushed and her teeth clenched, then she looked down at her plate.

"Maybe he just went home?" Caitlin suggested, watching Harper from across the table with a look of concern. "He finished his finals yesterday, didn't he?"

"He doesn't have a home," Lucas reminded her. "But I think he's still on campus. All his shit's still in our room. Clothes. Bathroom stuff. You can say what you want about dudes and questionable hygiene, but we never travel without a toothbrush."

"Anyone text him?" Allison asked, as calmly as possible.

Harper nodded, still staring at her plate.

"And you didn't hear anything?"

"Obviously not," Harper said sharply, looking up to meet Allison's gaze. "If I had, we wouldn't be having this conversation."

"Text me if you hear from him." Allison stood.

"Where are you going?" Caitlin asked, her eyes moving from Allison to her uneaten sandwich. "Why so worried? He probably just went out partying with his football buddies and passed out somewhere."

"Probably," Allison said lightly, and forced a smile as she picked up her tray and backed away from the table. "I'm just going to have a look around. Let me know if you see him."

404 | FELIX CHRONICLES: FRESHMEN

Allison set off across campus, trying not to panic. Her friends probably thought she was overreacting. But her friends were oblivious. Only Allison (and Bill) knew that Felix was in constant danger. The Protectors and the Faceman had already tried to kill him (even though Allison still couldn't remember what had really happened in 'Martha's' back yard). The Faceman was six feet under. But Felix had told her that the Protectors were still out there, just waiting for an opportunity.

Allison checked Felix's usual haunts—the Caffeine Hut, Woodrow's Room, the Bryant Center and Satler (the fatassosaurs hadn't seen him in a few days)—then she went to his secret places, the places she'd followed him to when he wanted to be alone and thought no one was watching him: the little room on the top floor of the Madras Building that looked out onto the stadium and no-man's-land; the chapel just past the Star Trees—St. Rose— which gave her the chills the moment she stepped inside; the garden to the west of the Student Center hidden behind evergreens and stacked-stone walls and trellises covered in crawling vines where the pathways made their way through clipped grass lawns and beds of finely crushed rock and under ornate archways, all connecting to the center, to a bronze statue of Sacagawea, and the world went silent and still except for the sound of rushing water from the nearby Mill Stream.

Finding Felix on campus was a long shot—probably impossible—if he didn't want to be found. There were too many places to search, too many places for Felix to hide. And Felix was more familiar with the campus than anyone she knew; not even the Old Campus was off limits to him. So Allison decided on a different approach, something she probably should have done from the beginning: she started looking for his Jeep. She checked the main parking lot, the overflow lots next to the football stadium, and the side streets Felix sometimes used if a spot opened up near the dorm. No Jeep anywhere. After hours of walking, her feet were beginning to hurt. But at least she'd learned something: No Jeep meant Felix had left campus. But why would he leave without telling anyone where he was going or what he was doing? Why would he leave without taking anything with him? And why did he tell Harper he was meeting with his parents' lawyer? Why would he lie to her? What was he really doing last night? None of it added up. None of it made sense.

She tried to convince herself that there were other plausible explanations, but she kept coming back to the only conclusion that fit the facts: Something had clearly happened to Felix. Something was wrong. Allison had hit a dead end and she couldn't do anything more on her own.

She knew that there was one person who might have some answers but she was wary of asking for his help. Turning to him for guidance would establish a precedent (and not a good one) and she didn't want to be in a position of needing to rely on someone she had no confidence in. But Allison was at a loss and out of ideas. So against her better judgment, she sent a text to Bill.

* * *

The next day, early Wednesday morning, she received a text in reply: "Felix is fine. Details to follow. Trust me."

The text only assuaged some of her fears. Allison didn't trust Bill. And she didn't trust that they shared the same definition of 'fine'. She texted him again, inquiring about the 'details'.

Silence followed.

So Allison went about her day as best she could. She took two finals (crushed them) and prepared for her remaining exams. She also checked Bill's office—locked door, lights off, bundle of mail on the floor. She searched for Felix (same places, same result) even though she was certain he wasn't on campus.

Around her friends she acted as though she wasn't concerned, but with every passing hour she grew more anxious. Despite her efforts, it soon began to show. And her concern was spreading like a virus. Lucas behaved like a different person: pensive, reserved and thoughtful. Allison found the transformation strange and disturbing. Harper was moodier than usual, snapping at anyone who crossed her path with only the slightest pretense of provocation; no one was immune, not even Caitlin.

* * *

On Thursday, Allison received another text from Bill: "Details coming soon. Please be patient." She wasn't feeling very patient. But Bill wasn't giving her much of a choice.

By this point, no one had seen or heard from Felix in three days. He hadn't responded to any texts or answered his phone and there was no other way to contact him. Harper was of the firm opinion that something bad had happened to him. She kept bringing up teenage depression, red flags and warning signs. Lucas thought Felix just wanted to be alone, that he was holed up somewhere "decompressing." Caitlin was on the fence; she wasn't sure what to think.

And then Lucas did something monumentally stupid: He told Caitlin and Harper about Felix's nightmares. He thought it would convince them that Felix was just feeling solitary—that he was simply looking for a change of scenery to escape from the awful dreams tormenting his sleep. It didn't have the intended effect. Harper flew off the handle, accusing Lucas of concealing important information. And Caitlin started siding with her. Now they both believed that Felix was in serious trouble. Allison tried to stay neutral—she just needed to buy some time until Bill provided her with the 'details'. Late that night, Harper, Lucas and Caitlin came to an important decision. If they didn't hear from Felix the next day, they would call the police.

* * *

Friday morning, Allison awoke before sunrise and left the dorm while Caitlin was still in bed. Exhausted after finishing her last final the day before, she was in dire need of sleep, but she didn't want to see Caitlin (or anyone else). She had a strong feeling that her friends wouldn't actually call the Portland PD until they talked to her. It wasn't that they needed her permission, but she thought they would want her in the room when they made the call. Because once that call was placed, jaded men and women would scrutinize their 'bad feelings' and 'speculation' and either dismiss them as overimaginative teenagers with too much time on their hands or escalate their concerns to the scary world of reports, statements, and interviews at the precinct. Everything would get real in a hurry.

Allison waited to hear from Bill, killing time, ignoring the calls and texts from Caitlin and Lucas, wondering what the 'details' might be. For dinner, she snuck a sandwich into the library and ate it in Woodrow's Room. At just after nine o'clock while flipping through a magazine, she received the long awaited text: "He's in Cove Rock. Come to my office. I'll give you my car keys."

She rushed out of the library and called Caitlin to find out where everyone was. They were all in Lucas's room, and a hot second away from calling the police to report Felix missing. They would have done it already, but they couldn't decide on who should make the call. Allison told them to stay put and not to do anything until she got there.

As soon as Allison stepped into the room, a sinking feeling crept over her. The space was depressing, and even with the light on, it seemed dark. With all of Felix's belongings still there, it reminded her of a highway shrine. "I know where he is," she announced, not mincing words.

They all stood up, gathering around her.

"Is he okay?" Harper asked anxiously.

"I think so," Allison replied, careful with her words. "He's at the coast."

"Did you talk to him?" Lucas asked.

"Yeah," she lied. "But just for a minute. He just said he's okay and not to worry." She made it sound convincing.

"What happened to him?" Harper asked. Her eyes were slightly puffy. "Why'd he leave?"

"I'm not exactly sure," Allison answered truthfully. "I just think with everything going on, it was just too... just too much for him. Maybe he couldn't handle it all." That was her best guess. And she couldn't tell them anything more than that.

Harper turned her back to Allison and went over to the window.

"I better get going," Allison told them. "I'll let you know when I see him."

"Should we go with you?" Lucas asked her.

Allison shook her head. "I just think he wants to, you know, just keep away from... everything."

Allison started for the door.

"How are you getting there?" Caitlin asked.

"Huh?" Allison hadn't expected that. "I'm borrowing a car from... Bill."

"Who's Bill?" Lucas asked.

"Just a guy I know. I've gotta go."

Chapter 55

COVE ROCK

Cove Rock was dead. Bill's Range Rover sped through the deserted town in a steady downpour. It was just after midnight and Allison was fighting off sleep, catching herself, for the third time, drifting off. She drove hunched forward over the steering wheel, stereo blasting, singing along to the music, talking to herself and doing whatever else she could think of to stay awake. She'd set the cabin temperature at fifty-six degrees. She would have opened the windows to let the chilly air in, but feared she might drown (and ruin the plush interior of the nicest car she'd ever been in).

The heartache she felt for Felix had kept her awake for the first half hour of the trip. For the next thirty minutes, her seething fury stoked her, keeping her alert: She would never forgive Bill for waiting four days to tell her about the cursed memory, to tell her that Felix had witnessed himself killing his parents. But not even her anger could ward off the enchantress of sleep. The all-nighters studying for finals had taken their toll. She'd never needed a cup of coffee so badly.

The shops and restaurants were all closed for the night. The streets were quiet and empty. This was what Cove Rock was like in December. Tourist season had ended months ago. As she passed the last shop on the main strip—'Harry's Hardware & Supplies'—she looked toward the bay, trying to catch a glimpse of the town symbol and namesake, the object that attracted visitors from near and far: a monolithic pillar of stone jutting 250 feet above the cold Pacific waters like the finger of an ancient god of the ocean. But nothing was illuminated beyond the streetlamps and the security lights ringing the store fronts.

The rain started coming down in torrents. The wipers couldn't keep up. Allison considered pulling over to wait out the worst of it, but the forecasters were predicting that the storm wouldn't dissipate until morning. And she was close. So she pushed on despite the limited visibility and her throbbing head. A mile past Harry's, on the fringes of the town limits, she arrived at a weather-beaten stop sign missing a 'P'. She remembered it from the last time she was here.

She turned left—toward the ocean—down an unpaved road with DEAD END signs posted on both sides of the narrow lane. Keeping the speed just above an idle, the Range Rover churned its way along the uneven, potholed surface, locking into the established ruts. Water splashed. Gravel crunched and popped under the tires. There were no streetlights here. Set back from the road behind low fences and hedges, the silhouettes of small gray houses stood out. None had their porch lights on.

At the end of the cul-de-sac parked in the driveway of a plain Cape Cod was a Wrangler with big tires and a dark top. She pulled up next to the Jeep and turned off the car. She hesitated, thinking about what she could possibly say to Felix. Nothing really came to mind. With the stereo off, the battering din of the rain grew a few notches, rattling the car and the inside of her skull, making it hard to think. The glass quickly fogged up with moisture. She climbed out. The rain hit her like a fist. The winds carried the salty scent of the ocean and a faint trace of wood smoke from a chimney. She headed for the front door and promptly stepped into a deep puddle of freezing water.

"Shit!" She lifted up her foot in a flamingo pose, struggling to remain balanced as a raging wind blew her back against the car. Before she could find drier ground, the automatic timer expired and the headlights clicked off. She was swimming in darkness, barely able to see the pavement beneath her feet. The rain ran down her forehead and into her eyes. She wondered if having bushier eyebrows might be helpful at a time like this (the sort of thought that comes to you when you're exhausted and desperate).

She hadn't thought to bring an umbrella in her rush to leave campus. Not that it would do much good. The winds would chew it up and spit it out in no time at all. The clouds swirled overhead, hanging low. She heard a clanking noise in the distance.

Once her eyes adjusted to the bleakness, she made her way up the short, slightly inclined driveway, leaning into a fierce headwind, the rain slapping her face. A sliver of soft yellow light seeped through a window next to the front door. She wiped the water from her eyes and stepped off the rain-puddled concrete, slogging her way through the front yard. Squeezing through a clump of foundation hedges, she pressed her nose right up against the rain-streaked glass, squinting hard, trying to see into the house. A light was on somewhere in one of the back rooms. She stood there for a while watching, but there was no movement inside.

Before she could make her way to the door she heard it again. Metal against metal—*clankety-clank clankety-clank*—then it died back to nothing. It sounded like it was coming from the back yard, but she couldn't be sure. The rain was doing weird things to the world, dampening and distorting sounds, causing almost as much havoc with her hearing as her vision. She set off to inspect the noise, to see what it was, not sure if she was simply curious or if she was chasing some gut instinct. She reached the edge of the house. She took one more step—

A gust of wind knocked her down, stealing her breath away. Without the buffer of the little Cape, the winds roaring inland from off the ocean were powerful enough to overturn a box truck. It took Allison a moment to realize she was no longer upright, that she was gazing up at the sky. Dark clouds covered most of the stars, but pockets of dim twinkling lights slid in and out of view. The moon was full or close to it. She didn't stop to admire it for long. The rain was coming down hard and fast in enormous droplets, pricking and burning her face like the pecking of an ice pick. The ground was hard, wet and cold. The smell of the ocean filled her nostrils, intense and overwhelming, so strong she felt as though she'd been plunged into the sea itself.

Clankety-clank.

The sound was closer now, clearer.

She rolled onto her stomach and pushed herself to her feet, crouching down low to stay balanced. A gust hit her like a freight train. She lost her footing and slipped. Her legs shot out from under her and she crashed to the ground, her face buried in an icy puddle. She scrabbled around helplessly on the grass like it was wet ice, unable to gain any traction, sprawling out like a newborn fawn learning to walk. Trying to stay calm, she slowed down her movements, taking her time, steadying herself. She made it to a sitting position and transitioned to her hands and knees. Then digging the toes of her boots into the unforgiving turf, she started to bear-crawl toward the ocean until she finally reached ground that felt a little less slippery. She stood up straight, bracing herself against the wind, looking around for the source of the sound.

She found it: a flagpole. A flagless flagpole. A stretch of chain links connecting the pull cord to the base had come undone and was whipping about, banging against the metal pole.

But there was something else.

Someone was standing at the edge of the yard. He faced the ocean that loomed up in the distance, his bare skin glowing white under the dim haze leaking through the clouds. He was wearing only a pair of gym shorts, dark-colored and baggy, that rippled in the wind.

It was Felix.

Allison struggled toward him, resisting the desire to call out. He probably wouldn't be able to hear her though the rain and the wind anyway. But that wasn't the reason she remained quiet. Her concern was something else entirely: she didn't want to startle him.

Felix was standing on a ledge at the top of a cliff.

Allison couldn't remember where the drop-off points were. *Drop-off points*. That's what Felix's parent had called them. The yard wasn't landscaped with children in mind; it didn't end at a white picket fence. Or any fence at all. For the most part, it simply melded into the horizon (the ocean), a gentle slope that merged into a trail that crisscrossed the face of the cliff, leading to the beach down below. But there were parts of the yard where there was no gentle slope, just ledges with a straight-edged drop of ten feet or more before a flat piece of land—the trail—would catch you. If you were really unlucky and happened to stumble down in just the wrong spot, the narrow trail wouldn't intervene at all; your descent wouldn't end until you crashed into the rocks at the bottom of the cliff.

She shuffled forward on the slick grass, slowly, mindfully. It was hard enough to see with what little moonlight managed to wriggle its way through the shifting clouds. But when the cloud cover clamped down overhead the world went black. The darkness was confusing and deceptive, blending the ground the sky and the ocean into a single contiguous backdrop. Each step was a leap of faith.

She stopped. She was close now. Felix was just a few feet away, balanced precariously at the edge of one of the drop-off points, with only the blended darkness of the ocean and the sky in the background. There was nothing in front of him but cold swirling air. He was staring out at the ocean, his eyes open but unblinking. His face and his body were stark white, deathly pale. The rain engulfed him, the wind whistled over him. But somehow, he remained statue-still, unaffected, as though the night sky was clear and calm and the rushing winds a tickling breeze.

"Felix," she said softly—too softly. She raised her voice, straining so that he could hear her over the roar of the ocean winds. Rain dribbled into her mouth—it tasted salty—as she called out his name.

The chain clattered against the flagpole.

Felix didn't move.

She shouted his name again. Nothing in response.

The rain tore through Allison's clothes, drenching her to the skin. For a moment, she was conscious of everything around her, overly conscious, hyper-aware of every detail. It flooded her senses, overstimulating her, clogging her bandwidth. She felt the vastness of the ocean and the smothering force of the elements. The darkness weighed down on her. She felt small and vulnerable.

She took a second to find her center, to collect herself. Then she reached out and touched Felix's bare arm, expecting it to be as frosty as the bitingly cold night. She gasped and pulled her hand back when her fingertips felt skin as warm as the cup of coffee she'd longed for during the drive. She shouted his name again. No response. No acknowledgment at all. He was lost in his own world.

Felix didn't appear to be freezing. But Allison was. Her ears and cheeks were starting to go numb. Her fingers felt stiff and heavy. She needed to get inside. She took hold of his arm with both hands and tugged him backward, pulling him away from the cliff and toward the house. At first, she felt resistance, not conscious resistance, but it was there all the same. Then his body loosened and she dragged and nudged him across the yard to the side door, his bare feet shuffling unsteadily alongside hers. Soft light filtered out through a frosted glass window in its center. She expected to find it locked, but the knob moved easily when she turned it. The door swung open. She shoved Felix inside and then followed behind, the blowing rain howling in after them. She pushed the door shut, fighting winds unwilling to give up so easily on their newfound foothold.

The space she found herself in was narrow and multi-purpose: a mudroom that doubled as a laundry room. On one side there was a washer and dryer with shelving above full of neatly stacked towels and containers of detergent and fabric softener. On the other side, a pair of wicker laundry baskets sat on the floor. A varnished captain's wheel hung on the wall between them, the top pegs used for hanging coats and hats. A cascading motif of canary yellow flowers with faded green stalks and leaves papered over the walls.

Allison stood there for a moment, breathing hard, shivering, and dripping water onto a beige runner that foot traffic had stained dark down the middle. She stared at Felix. His size surprised her. He was wider in the shoulders and thicker through the chest and arms than she remembered. He didn't look like the kid she used to hang out with at the lake. His skin was disturbingly white. It didn't seem possible that blood could flow beneath skin that appeared so frozen. But when she touched him, he felt warm. His

R.T. LOWE | **413**

face was a mask. His eyes were distant, vacant, and paler than she remembered, like blue ice. If he knew that Allison was there, he gave no sign of it. There was no spark of recognition on his face. Nothing to indicate he was aware of his environment or where he was. She shouted his name several times. Nothing. Nothing was registering.

She quickly formulated a plan. She didn't know if it was one of those things people only do on TV—like reading a book and drinking wine by candlelight in a bubble bath—but she was about to find out.

She slapped him in the face, hard. Felix didn't flinch. Didn't react.

She did it again, even harder this time. The next time she slapped him, the sound echoed in the little room. The left side of Felix's face was strawberry red. But still no reaction. No expression. He didn't feel anything. Oblivious to the pain.

"Sorry Felix," Allison muttered under her breath.

She staggered her feet with her right foot set back slightly behind her left, a half step at most. She balled her hand into a tight fist, her knuckles going white. She rotated her shoulders a quarter turn clockwise and pulled her arm back like she was drawing an arrow in a bow. Then she brought her arm forward in a crisp straight line, generating power and speed from her hips and legs, driving her fist straight into Felix's face.

Chapter 56

GRANDMA'S HOUSE

Lightning crackled and flashed behind Felix's eyes. He heard his parents' voices. They were calling out to him, begging him to open the door. The door shuddered. His dad cried out. His mom screamed. Everything went hot, orange and confusing.

Then it all blinked out, fading into nothingness as a stinging sensation passed over his face and warm liquid filled his mouth. The pain and the rich metallic taste of blood tugged at his memory, dredging up new images. He was on his back, dazed, looking up at an azure sky through the facemask of his football helmet. The sky vanished, turning into an office with book-lined walls; he was sitting in a chair staring down at the mottled pages of a cursed journal. Now he stood in a parking lot rubbing his forehead, a sharp splintering pain creeping up to the crown of his head; a lamppost stared back at him impassively, the football stadium looming in the distance. Then the blacktop beneath his feet became the grainy coolness of a wooden floor, the night sky the ceiling of a dorm room, smooth, white and unbroken except for the face of a girl—Allison—hovering over him, shouting his name, shaking him by the shoulders. The scene shifted. He was viewing a wall from an odd perspective, an unnatural height, like he was standing on a stepladder; the wall was gray, ugly and stained with a splash of blood that looked as if it had been smeared on in a single swirling brushstroke. His feet thrashed out, searching for solid ground as the hand of a giant crushed his neck.

And then, once again, the images faded away.

Familiar sounds reached out to him, thawing the ice, chipping away at his defenses: water rushing through pipes; a storm door rattling in its frame; a furnace whirring and hissing from some subterranean lair; plantings, rustling outside, bending with the wind, scraping against a house; rain drumming on the roof, tapping on the windows. A cornucopia of sounds. Familiar sounds. He knew where he was.

Felix blinked hard.

He saw green eyes, soft and sad. Hair that was dark, wet and matted. Cheeks smudged with mud. A chin speckled with blades of grass browned like straw. *Allison's face.* She was talking to him, saying his name, drawing him out of himself, luring him into the world.

Yet there was a part of Felix, a quorum perhaps, that resisted. It didn't want to come out. It wanted to remain frozen, to stay numb. If it relinquished its icy grip and allowed him to break free of the protective shell, there would be repercussions. He would have to feel. He would have to open his eyes to the dark truth hiding just beyond the reach of his conscious self, the catalyst for what he had become.

But Allison was crying, and as he watched each tear well up in her fierce green eyes and slide down her face, something inside him—*his resistance*—started to melt. She stood there, drenched, sobbing like a little girl. Then she fell into him, holding onto him, burying her face in his chest.

The fog was lifting.

"I thought you were dead," Allison said through her sobs. She was *here*, Felix realized. Here with him. Speaking to him. And he understood she was here—understood what her words meant.

Awareness crashed down on him like a waterfall. Now he was exposed, naked, at the mercy of his memory. It went to work at once, stripping away the vestiges of his psychic armor, digging into his flesh, boring into his raw nerves, tearing him open and leaving him with the knowledge of a terrible, singular reality: *It wasn't a dream.* What he'd done to his parents wasn't a nightmare. They were dead. And he had killed them. The ache was in his bones, in his chest and in his throat, heavy and hot. The guilt twisted itself around his heart, forming a hard knot that squeezed with each beat, stealing the air from his lungs.

Allison stepped back and looked up at him tentatively. She was shivering. Her teeth chattered. She tried to speak but her voice caught in her throat.

"Can you hear me?" she asked after a moment, her eyes tear-soaked.

Felix nodded weakly. His throat was dry. His mouth burned. He ran his tongue over his teeth and felt splits and cracks all along the soft tissue of his gum line. He didn't think to wonder what had happened.

"I'm so sorry. I'm so sorry." Allison reached out for him again, holding him and running her trembling fingers over his back. "Can you talk?"

Felix couldn't remember the last time he talked. He couldn't remember much of anything. He had no recollection of coming to Cove Rock or any idea of how long he'd been here.

"Just say something." Allison shivered, soaking the rug beneath her.

"Something," Felix murmured. His voice sounded ragged and hoarse.

A sad smile tugged at Allison's lips. "I'm just glad you're okay." She hesitated, her lip quivering. "I'm so sorry about... about your parents. I spoke to Bill. He told me everything."

Felix didn't answer. There were no words.

"I know what happened," she sobbed, her eyes filling with tears.

Felix let the roar of the storm sweeping over the house fill the silence between them. After a long pause, he said stiffly, "You know what happened?"

She nodded, the tears mixing with the rainwater and running down her face like rivulets on glass.

"You shouldn't be here," Felix said slowly. There was a hollow resonance to his voice. He turned and stepped away, leaving Allison alone as he went down the hall to the living room, stopping in front of an undraped picture window. His reflection stared back at him and he quickly looked away, unable to meet his own gaze. In the window, he saw Allison approaching from behind. She'd taken off her jacket and boots and was drying her hair with a towel. She came up beside him.

"I would've been here sooner if Bill hadn't..." Her expression hardened as she wrapped the towel around her shoulders like a shawl.

"You should go," Felix told her.

"I'm not going anywhere."

"You shouldn't be around me. Just go. Please."

Allison stared back stubbornly at his reflection, defiant, unmoving.

The rain slammed into the window in wind-swept sheets. The room was bright and warm but drafty in the way old houses tend to be.

"I could... hurt you. Don't you understand? There's something"—Felix looked down helplessly at his hands—"something wrong with me."

"It wasn't your fault," Allison said. "You didn't—"

Felix cut her off. *"Didn't what?* Didn't kill them? I saw it with my own eyes. Don't you get it? I killed my parents. I'm a monster."

"It wasn't your fault," she said again, softly, biting back tears.

"Tell that to my parents!" Felix snapped.

"You were sleeping."

"So what?" Felix said, a sudden anger coiling inside him. "That won't bring them back."

"I know," Allison said, and the sadness in her voice only made him angrier. "But it wasn't your fault."

"Then whose fault was it?"

"It was nobody's fault."

"Bullshit!"

"But you—"

"I don't care!" Felix shouted, his eyes bulging. "You can't change what I did! You can't change what happened! You can't change what I am!"

"Some adventure, huh?" Allison said abruptly.

"What?" he said, confused.

"Do you remember when you told me about the journal? Remember how excited I was?" Allison shook her head, smiling humorlessly. "I thought we were embarking on some great adventure, just like in the books. You were going to save the world, and I was going to be your faithful sidekick. I was such an idiot."

Felix watched her reflection in the glass, his anger fading.

"I didn't realize it until the drive here," she went on. "I was thinking about it in the car. The kids in those stories don't feel like they're on some epic adventure. It's just cool and exciting if you're not doing it. If you're living it, like we are, it sucks. Now look at us. Your parents are dead. You killed them in your sleep. That's a really shitty adventure story."

Felix swallowed down a mouthful of blood and grimaced at the taste.

"But none of that matters," Allison continued. "You didn't want this. You didn't ask for any of this. I get that. But you don't have a choice. You need to understand that the world needs you."

"You can't be serious!" Felix shouted bitterly through his teeth. "The world? The world needs me? I don't give a shit about the world. What has the world done for me?"

"What about your parents?" Allison countered.

"What about them?" Felix said with a chill in his voice.

"They didn't do anything for you? You don't give a shit about them?"

"That's the dumbest thing—"

"Is it?" Allison said, her voice rising. She took a deep breath, her shoulders stiffening as she exhaled slowly. "What do you think they'd want you to do?" She paused, watching him. "Well...?"

"That's not fair," Felix answered in a flat voice.

"I know it's not—but it's got nothing to do with fair." Allison took his hand in hers and smiled forlornly at his reflection. "I'm sorry about all this— and I know you don't want to hear that right now. And I know you don't

418 | FELIX CHRONICLES: FRESHMEN

want to hear that the world needs you. But it does. And I don't know if it makes a difference to you or not, but me and Lucas and Caitlin and Harper, we're all part of this crazy world too." She lowered her eyes for a moment and a thoughtful look passed over her tired face. "And you know, I um… I feel like something really bad is coming my way. Maybe it'll happen to me. Maybe someone else. I don't know. I don't know what it is, but I just feel, I feel this incredible… sadness. I get these feelings a lot lately. And I just, I just know that only you can make things right."

"I just want to be normal," Felix said miserably. "I don't want to be the… whatever the fuck it is I am."

"I know." Allison let go of his hand and sniffed the air, then she made a face. The house smelled a little wet. "I love what you've done to the place."

Allison had been to the house a few times during high school and always gave him a hard time about the questionable décor. His grandma hadn't updated the interior in ages and most of the furnishings had belonged to her. The living room was a fair representation of the house as a whole. Dark brown carpet. Dark paneled walls. A series of four tourist-quality seascape prints, one for each wall. A plaid sofa pushed up against one wall. A matching pair of upholstered chairs with floral prints across from an old console TV. Next to that a tarnished brass floor lamp with a dusty ruffled shade. Tchotchkes—seashells, crystal animals, ceramic dolls, tiny replicas of the Liberty Bell and the Empire State Building, and an assortment of other vacation souvenirs—displayed on every available horizontal surface.

"Yeah," Felix sighed. "It's pretty bad. But you know my parents were planning to fix it up. My dad was retiring next year. They wanted to spend their summers here. They liked the beach. They loved this place. They had plans. Lots of plans. Not anymore."

"I think you told me that." Her voice sounded distant and she was gazing down at the floor. She fidgeted with the frayed edges of the towel dangling over her shoulders, lifted her eyes to his, and said cautiously, "When I talked to Bill, he said something, something you should probably know. We talked about your mom—your real mom. You don't know why she died, do you?"

He stared back at her, feeling a sudden coldness whisper up his spine.

"Your mom hadn't heard from her sister in something like twenty years. And then one day the journal just showed up in her mailbox. Of course she couldn't have known it was cursed. So she was in this trance—or whatever happens to you when you read it—and her friend came into her apartment. Her best friend. The journal triggered something inside your mom but she didn't know that it was happening. She didn't realize what she was doing to her friend. One minute she's in a trance reading a journal from her long-lost sister, and the next, she's awake and watching her friend fall off a fifteenth-floor balcony. Your mom killed her best friend. But it wasn't your mom's fault."

"So wha—"

"But she still felt responsible," Allison persisted. "She never forgave herself. *Don't you get it?* She wasn't even sick! But the guilt ate at her like a cancer. And in the end, it killed her."

"Why are you telling me this?" His mom was dead. Did it really matter what killed her?

"Because it's the same thing that happened to you," Allison said bluntly. "And you can't let the guilt kill you like it did your mom."

"You don't understand," he said wearily. "You don't understand what it's like to have this…" He couldn't convey the pain he felt—the suffocating anguish that made him want to dive into the ocean and never come up for air. Words were cheap and inadequate. All he could do was shake his head.

"Maybe I don't," Allison admitted. "But I know you're going to want to punish yourself. I know you, Felix. I know how you are. I know it won't be easy. But you're not alone in this. You might think you are. But you're not. You can't give up. *You can't.*"

She started to cry.

"I don't know what I'm supposed to do." Felix watched the tears slide down her cheeks and hung his head guiltily. He didn't know how he could go on living with the knowledge of what he'd done. How could he go back to his old life like nothing had even happened? "I feel like I deserve to… I don't know… I deserve to die, or go to hell or…"

Allison wiped her eyes with a muddy shirtsleeve, leaving behind more dark smudges on her face. "This really, really sucks, and I'm really sorry. This is just so unfair and so shitty. But you have to fight this. You can't give up. You can't give up on yourself. And you can't give up on me. I won't let you." She looked at him sharply, eyes flaring. "And I will kick your ass if I have to! But you will not quit on me!"

He watched her, wordless, amazed by her fire, her spirit.

"Felix! Do you hear me?"

He nodded.

"Promise me!" she said, brushing away her tears. "Promise me you won't give up."

Felix didn't know if he could commit to anything right now, let alone something like that, but Allison needed to hear the words from his mouth, and her eyes locked on his, demanding an answer.

"I promise," he said in a soft voice

"Good. And I promise to always have your back. Oh—I almost forgot." She took her phone from the back pocket of her jeans and started tapping on the screen with her thumbs. "I need to let everyone know you're okay. They're worried, you know. They were like a minute away from calling the police." After finishing the text, she put the phone away.

He yawned.

"When was the last time you got any sleep?" she asked.

"High school."

"I believe you. You look like shit."

"Thanks."

"You grow the absolute worst facial hair." She cracked a smile. "Please shave in the morning. I can't be seen with you looking like this. I have my reputation to protect."

He smiled for her. That was the best way to end the conversation. He'd talked enough for one night. The fatigue was pressing down on him, growing heavier by the minute.

"So where are you, um, sleeping?" She turned to look around the room.

"Here." He pointed at the sofa. "It's a pull out. I like this room. You can hear the ocean."

Allison rubbed her eyes tiredly. "What bedroom should I use?"

"Whichever. They're all the same." For the first time, he realized that Allison was completely exhausted.

She glanced down at herself, frowning. "I didn't bring any clothes with me."

"I should have something from last summer in the bedroom. The one on the left." He motioned with his hand toward the hall. "Check the dresser. T-shirts and shorts, I think. Maybe some sweatshirts. Throw your clothes in the washer if you want. It's kinda old, but better than nothing."

"Okay. Well, I guess, um, I'll go to bed. You okay?"

He shrugged.

She turned and walked out of the room, apparently satisfied with the noncommittal gesture.

He unfurled the foldable mattress from the worn-out sofa and grabbed a pair of blankets and a pillow from the closet. There was a little pile of clothes, apparently worn, on the floor. He sifted through them until he found a pair of boxers. He stripped out of his shorts and put on the boxers, leaving the shorts on top of the pile. He used one of the blankets to dry off—he wasn't sure why he was so wet, but from Allison's appearance, he surmised they'd been outside—and tossed it on the rest of the clothes. The sounds of running water from a faucet in the hallway bathroom and the washing machine grinding and coughing into life echoed throughout the house.

"Hey, Allie!" he called out, sitting down on the bed, dragging a hand through damp, limp hair.

"Yeah?" she called back, by the sound of it, from the bedroom that faced the driveway.

"Good night."

"Good night, Felix."

He turned off the lights and lay down on the thin mattress, shimmying over to one side until he found a spot that didn't have a steel bar running up his back. The mattress springs creaked and twanged under his weight. He stared at the peaked ceiling. Every little detail—the slightly darker patch where someone had used touch-up paint, the Tiffany-style light fixture with vividly-colored grapes, pears, apples and peaches, the cobweb in the corner that shuddered from some mysterious draft too subtle to feel—was somehow etched into his memory. It seemed he'd been sleeping here for more than a few nights. He wondered what day it was.

He heard light footsteps padding across the floor. A rush of cool air swept over him as the cover lifted up for a second, then he felt Allison climbing into the bed.

"Close your eyes," she whispered, pulling the fleece blanket over them, wrapping her arms around him. "You need to sleep. Just close your eyes."

He lay there, feeling the softness of her bare legs against his, the warmth of her body. He turned to his side, his back to Allison, and curled up against her, letting her cradle him in her arms.

"Thanks for coming for me," he said into the darkness.

"There's nothing I wouldn't do for you, Felix."

"I just wish… I wish I could let go of *this*." He placed a clenched hand over his heart. "I'm just so… so full of all this toxic shit. I feel like, I don't know, like a bottle someone keeps shaking up. And it… it needs to… it has to open. Someone's gotta open it. God, I swear I'm gonna… I don't know… I'm gonna lose it. I'm gonna explode if I can't get all this shit outta me. I'm gonna blow up. Someone's gotta—"

"*You* need to open the bottle," Allison whispered softly, her arms tightening around him, her warm breath on his cheek. "You need to let it out."

"I can't. I don't know how. I…"

"Let it out."

"I can't." His eyes felt hot.

"Don't be afraid, Felix. Just let it out."

He didn't want to cry. He had no right to cry. Crying was self-pity. And self-pity was acceptance. And he would never accept what he'd done. But he felt a sudden surge of emotion pulsing through him. He fought it. Tears wouldn't heal the hole in his soul. Or numb the hurt. Or give comfort. But the grief in his bones and in his heart fought back, seeking to escape. He had to contain it before it broke through. There was no salvation in letting it out. No relief. Only more clarity. More pain. But he couldn't stop it. It was too late for that. He didn't have the strength. His throat clenched. And then all the anguish and guilt flourishing inside him, malignant and glacial, came pouring out in a heaving rush; the last of his remaining defenses were melting away.

"I killed them, Allie." Saying the words didn't cleanse the poison raging inside him or dull the pain, yet they came nonetheless, spilling out from his trembling lips. "I killed them. I killed my mom and dad. What did I do? What did I do? I'm so sorry. I'm so sorry. I'm so sorry…"

And then he cried.

He cried long into the night. And finally, when there were no tears left, he closed his eyes and slept.

* * *

Allison held him. And when Felix had shed his last tear, and she knew that he was sleeping, she let herself drift off.

Chapter 57

FAREWELLS AND SUSPICIONS

Lucas dragged his suitcase into Caitlin's room and closed the door behind him. He left the suitcase by the door and tossed a large green duffel bag and a backpack next to it. He yawned, holding the back of his hand against his mouth. The blinds were drawn and one of the bulbs in the ceiling light was out. The atmosphere in the room was somber and subdued, as depressing as the gloom and mist hanging over the campus.

"I hate early flights," he announced.

Caitlin and Harper nodded blearily in agreement.

"Did you get Allison's text?" Caitlin asked from her desk where she sat organizing some papers.

"Yeah." He crossed the room and took a seat on Allison's chair.

"What'd it say again?" Harper rubbed the sleep from her eyes. She was sitting on Caitlin's bed with one suitcase between her knees and another nestled against the footboard.

Lucas took his phone from his pocket and tapped the screen a few times. "Let's see. Oh—here it is: 'Seeing you in your full glory is proof that there is a God. I miss you. Why don't you call me?' Sorry. Wrong one." He scrolled down. "Okay, this is it: 'I'm unworthy of your love but I beg you: let me be your sex slave. I need you. I have to have you. Why don't you call me?' Oops. Sorry. That's not it either."

"Lucas!" Caitlin shouted, glowering at him. "This is serious."

"That's your problem, Little C," Lucas replied casually, keeping his eyes on the phone. "Haven't you learned anything from me? You take everything way too seriously." He scrolled down some more, murmuring to himself. "Uh, here it is. It says, 'He's fine. I have him.'"

"She can keep him," Harper said acidly.

"What's up with you?" Lucas put his phone away, casting a curious glance at Harper.

"Nothing," Harper answered stiffly. "Just guys doin' what guys do best. Why should I be surprised?"

"Huh?" Lucas said.

Caitlin got his attention with a frantic head shake, bulging her eyes warningly at him, drawing her hand back and forth across her neck—the universal sign for 'kill whatever it is you're about to say'.

Lucas stared at her, bewildered.

Harper seemed oblivious to their pathetic attempts at silent communication. "I'm so over all this," she said softly. "I need some serious *me* time. I'm just so sick of this happening every goddamn time I... shit. Whatever. Maybe I just won't come back next semester."

"Someone's being dramatic," Lucas replied with a grin. "And I'm the actor."

"You're not an actor," Caitlin told him as she looked over her itinerary. "Daniel Day-Lewis is an actor. Denzel Washington is an actor. You're just an idiot pretending to be even more idiotic than you really are."

Lucas laughed at her. "That's seriously hurtful. And you know I was shooting for an Emmy this year." He turned to Harper. "I don't think Felix is just any guy, by the way."

"What are you talking about?" Harper said testily. "There's nothing going on between me and—"

"That's not what I mean," Lucas broke in. "I think there's something going on with *him*. Something really strange."

"Like what?" Caitlin folded the itinerary in half and stuffed it into a checkerboard-patterned Louis Vuitton wallet.

There was a burst of shouting out in the hallway. Most of the dorm's residents were clearing out today. The mass exodus was creating chaos on every floor, move-in day flipped on its head, like a series of digital photos scrolled through in reverse order. Lucas looked over at the door, stroking the whiskers in the goatee he'd been growing, mainly because Caitlin despised it. With a thoughtful expression on his face, he stood up and started pacing around the room. Harper and Caitlin watched him from their seats, appearing both puzzled and bored.

"You guys remember when Felix woke up thinking Allison was dead or kidnapped, or whatever it was?" Lucas began. "He ran around the dorm naked and crashed your room. Remember that?"

"At what point do you think we suffered brain damage?" Caitlin said. "Of course we remember. But he wasn't naked. He had his underwear on. You're such an exaggerator."

"Pizza and beers," Harper added. "That was the thing with the skis at that woman's house in no-man's-land, right? But he just went out with Allison and drank too much and had a bad dream."

"Sure he did," Lucas said, his voice clotting with skepticism. "Then there was the fire in your old room"—he nodded at Caitlin—"the night you were out. Felix wasn't in my room that night. I was hooking up with some supermodel. I forgot which one. There's been so many."

"You mean *Piper*?" Caitlin said with an eye roll and a theatrical frown. "I didn't know they were signing up little albinos to be supermodels."

Lucas grinned at Caitlin as if she was the most amusing person in the world before continuing. "Felix said he slept on a couch in the common room. But who knows? Maybe he was in Allison's room. It's possible, right?"

Harper frowned, staring down vacantly at her fingernails.

Lucas reached over Caitlin's shoulder and snatched up a pen from her desk. "And if he was in Allison's room, maybe he had something to do with the fire."

"You think Felix is a pyro?" Caitlin asked incredulously, reaching back for the pen, but Lucas was on the move again. "You're such an idiot."

Lucas rolled the pen over one finger and under the next, twirling it from thumb to pinkie and back again. "Maybe I am. But wait until I'm done before you write me off as an idiot."

"Whatever makes you feel better about yourself," Caitlin said curtly.

"Then there's the nightmares," Lucas pressed on, ignoring Caitlin's barbs. "The only good thing about Felix's disappearing act is that I actually got some sleep this week."

"Yeah, but the dreams have gotta have something to do with his parents," Harper said, scooting her suitcase back and forth across the floor in front of her. When no one responded, she looked over at Caitlin, waiting for her confirmation.

"Makes sense," Caitlin said with a little shrug.

"I don't think so." Lucas gave them an adamant shake of his head as he stepped toward the door. "He won't talk about his parents with me. But that's not what's goin' on."

"I don't know," Harper said. "I talked to him about his parents once and it made him really uncomfortable. He's got some serious issues with the whole thing."

"Of course he does," Caitlin replied. "Who wouldn't? It's tragic. I feel so bad for him."

"But that's not it," Lucas insisted. "I'm telling you, it's got nothing to do with his parents. And get this—he's also been out a few times late at night and he won't say what he's doing. We'd all get back from the library at eleven or whatever and then he'd leave the dorm. He'd come back around two or three. And one time, he smelled like smoke."

"Maybe he smokes?" Caitlin quipped.

"No he doesn't." Lucas made a face at Caitlin that left no doubt he thought she was being a moron. "And it wasn't cigarette smoke. It was like smoke from a fire—an *actual* fire. And with the fire in your old room"—he pointed the pen at Caitlin—"who knows? Right?"

Harper fiddled with the nametag on her suitcase, wrinkling her forehead. "That's kinda weird."

"There's more." Lucas checked his hair in the wall mirror next to Allison's closet. "You have to admit it's strange that he just left school without saying a word to anyone. He didn't take anything with him either. It was like he was running from something."

Caitlin nodded slowly. "That's true."

"And even weirder"—he tossed the pen in the air; it flipped end over end, reached its zenith, stopped, then fell, landing softly in his fingers—"is what I think happened to the Faceman."

"*The Faceman?*" Harper said, her eyes snapping wide in surprise.

"Yeah. Don't you remember?" Lucas crossed the room again and sat on the edge of Allison's desk, resting his feet on her chair. "On the day the Faceman was killed, Felix thought *I* was dead. He thought somebody had killed me. He was running around all crazy. And when he saw I was alive, he gave me a pretty serious bro-hug. And he bled all over me, remember?"

"The homeless guy hit him in the nose," Caitlin said.

"Sure," Lucas snorted. "A random homeless guy attacked him with a tennis racket and told him I was dead. *That couldn't have happened.* That just can't be true, right? Don't you think that's bullshit? It's gotta be."

"It doesn't really add up when you put it like that," Harper said thoughtfully. "Especially when he thought Allison was dead at the start of the year. Why does he keep thinking everyone's dying?"

"Good question." Lucas nodded at Harper. "I called him out on it too. I told him I thought he killed the Faceman, and that the Faceman broke his nose."

"That's absurd!" Caitlin snickered. Then she paused, her eyebrows knitting together. "So um… what'd he say?"

"He laughed at me and made a joke of it. Said I was crazy. But you know what's really crazy? Am I the only one who thinks it's odd that his nose healed in like four hours?"

"I don't know." Harper got up from Caitlin's bed and stretched. Her clothes were form-fitting and stretchy—travel attire—and she was wearing her favorite pair of brown boots; one of them was sagging a little so she bent over and pulled up on it, tugging it back into place. "He said it was just a bloody nose."

"*Seriously?*" Lucas said. "And you believe that? You saw it. It was huge and all busted up."

"It did look pretty bad," Caitlin agreed.

"So what are you saying?" Harper asked with skeptical shake of her head. "Felix has a magic nose? Felix killed the Faceman? Please. How could he have killed the Faceman? The pictures I saw online were disgusting. The Faceman's head was all... gross." She made a squinchy face and shivered.

Lucas slid off the desk and settled into the chair. "I don't know what's going on with Felix. But it's *something*. And it's something big. And you know what we're going to do next semester?"

Harper and Caitlin looked at him blankly.

"You guys can't be that dense." Lucas let out a heavy sigh and rolled his eyes. "We're gonna find out."

"Oh," Harper muttered.

"Whatever you say," Caitlin said, her voice going high with feigned enthusiasm. "When we get back, we'll uncover the great conspiracy behind Felix the serial-killer-slaying-boy-with-the-magic-nose. Now can I write you off as an idiot?"

"I don't know," Harper said to Caitlin, apparently reconsidering Lucas's suspicions. "Maybe he's right. Maybe he's on to something." She turned to Lucas, pulling on her ponytail. "Do you think... um... you think Allison's... *involved?*"

"No question," Lucas said quickly.

Caitlin glanced over at the clock beside her bed. "We should get going. The cab's probably here."

"Wait a sec!" Harper shouted suddenly. "Shit! I totally forgot to sign up for English next semester."

"*You what?*" Caitlin said.

"Dammit!" Harper checked her watch. "Professor Weems makes you meet with her in person if you're going to take her class. I really like her and she's the easiest grader in the department. She said she'd keep office hours until noon today. I gotta go talk to her."

"We have a flight in two hours," Caitlin reminded her, sounding tense.

"I'll be there." Harper picked up the leather coat draped across the top of her suitcase. "I've got the number for the taxi company. You guys go ahead and I'll meet you there. It'll just take me a few minutes."

"We'll wait for you," Caitlin offered.

"The taxi's already here," Harper said. "And Lucas has an earlier flight."

Caitlin frowned. "Okay, but you better not be late. You know I don't like to fly by myself."

"I'll be there." Harper slipped into her jacket and started toward the door, pulling her suitcases behind her. Then she stopped and turned around. "I almost forgot. I guess this is it, Lucas. I can't believe the semester's over. It went by so fast."

"We'll be back before you know it," Lucas replied lightly. "But if you feel like you're missing me during the break, all you have to do is check out my website. There's a picture of me with my shirt off looking awesome and ripped and drinking some ice cold Super-Six-Pack-Power-Protein-Plus."

"You're drinking that cat piss on your website?" Harper said, smiling.

"It's actually just water, but don't tell anyone."

"Why do I have to share a taxi with this animal?" Caitlin said, sighing at him. "Do you have any idea how much I'm looking forward to not seeing you for a whole month?"

Chapter 58

WE MEET AGAIN

"How can you still be hungry?" Allison said to Felix as they entered the 7-Eleven on Cove Rock's main commercial strip. "You just ate a six-egg omelet and a pig plate."

"It wasn't a *pig plate*. It was the pound-o-pork-platter. And I think I may have gone without food for almost a week. So cut me some slack."

"Can you grab me a water?" Allison asked as she sidled over to the magazine racks next to the registers.

Felix made his way to the snacks aisle and perused the shelves, trying to decide if he was in the mood for sweet or salty. He wasn't in any hurry. They'd gotten up just after sunrise and had breakfast at his favorite Cove Rock diner. It was still early. Bill would get his swanky SUV back before noon.

Felix had actually managed to get some sleep last night (dreamless sleep) and other than his bottomless appetite there didn't seem to be anything wrong with him—physically at least. But as soon as he woke up, the promise he'd made to Allison started weighing on him and a new emotion—regret—crawled into his gut, nesting like a territorial animal. Allison would never understand the darkness eating away at his insides. For the rest of his life, every single day would be an endless battle to lock away the memory of killing his parents to the depths of his consciousness, to some place deep below the surface. And like a poisonous snake hiding in the cool shade of a rock, it would lay there in silence, lurking, waiting for the opportunity to slither out from under to torment his mind and threaten his sanity.

Even if he somehow found the strength to cope with the insatiable guilt, he could never forget the terrible images or erase them from his mind. Allison wanted him to save the world from Lofton. But Felix didn't know if he could save himself. At least in that regard, for the first time, he now felt a connection with his real mom. He understood what it was like for her to live with the knowledge of killing her friend. He understood how she must have longed to escape those feelings. He didn't blame her for deciding that death was the only real escape; he could relate. Yes—he'd made a promise to Allison. He would keep that promise. But only for today. He couldn't promise her next month, next week or even tomorrow. Today was the best he could do.

As Felix checked out the dizzying selection of artery cloggers, a woman with short blonde hair passed by his aisle, shooting him a discreet sideways glance. She breezed by so swiftly he nearly missed her. Going with salty, Felix reached for a jar of honey roasted peanuts. Then he froze, stopping in mid-motion.

The blonde woman had a sawtooth scar on her cheek.

He blinked, and a memory—a picture—formed in his mind, an image of a woman with blood flowing from her nose. It ran down her face in sheets, yet she appeared unconcerned, her eyes focused and calculating. And on her cheek—her right cheek—was a scar shaped like a high voltage warning.

No way, Felix thought, shaking the memory from his head. That couldn't have been, could it? He plucked the jar from the shelf and ambled down the aisle, trying to appear relaxed, pretending to look for chips. He took a moment to steady his breathing, then stole a glance at the security mirror in the corner, high up on the wall near the ceiling.

The woman had stopped in the juice section of the beverages aisle. She was tall with broad shoulders and long slender arms. Felix watched as she took a small container of orange juice from a refrigerator and held it up to her face like she was skeptical of the expiration date. She lifted her chin, her eyes flitting up to the security mirror.

Felix glanced away just in time and began feverishly studying a bag of Fritos corn chips on the shelf in front of him, resisting an overwhelming urge to look up at the mirror. The scar looked similar to one he'd seen before. But the woman who bore it, the woman at Martha's house, had long red hair. Of course you can cut hair. And dye it. He needed to get a better look at the scar to be sure, to dispel any doubts. His heart beating fast, he sucked in a deep breath and raised his eyes to the mirror.

She was gone.

Felix was stunned into stillness, but only for a moment. He grabbed a snack-sized bag of barbecue chips and headed for the beverages aisle, treading cautiously while still trying to act like he was just loading up on junk food for a road trip. When he reached the aisle, he turned, pulling up for an instant in surprise.

He wasn't alone.

Near the far end of the aisle, a man and a woman, deep in conversation, were at the self-serve coffee bar. Both were well-dressed, tall and solidly built. Felix could see the man's face, but the woman's back was turned to him. He tried to listen to their conversation, but the refrigerators were emitting a low humming sound and some kids a few aisles over were arguing about something and making a terrible racket; all he caught was one word: "sugar." The man filled a paper cup with coffee, then lifted his eyes to peek over the woman's shoulder.

Felix turned his head before the man's eyes could lock on his. He kept walking and glanced up at the security mirror behind them. He located the woman with the scar; she was in the aisle he'd just vacated—the snacks aisle—and a man with dusty brown skin and midnight-black hair had joined her. Felix gasped inwardly. Even from the slightly distorted image in the oval mirror, he could tell that the man was put together like a tank.

He swallowed hard, a trickle of warm sweat slaloming down his back. He tucked the chips under the same arm that held the peanuts, and without looking, fumbled around for two bottles of water. Using his foot to close the refrigerator door, he started toward the registers, passing by the coffee bar, getting as close as he could to the couple without alerting them that he was trying to listen in on their conversation.

But they'd gone quiet. The man was staring stupidly into his cup and the woman seemed to be under the spell of a packet of artificial sweetener she was holding in her fingers. Then from her lips came the word "sugar." She said it quite clearly, and not in response to anything the man had said to her.

What is that, some kind of code word? Felix wondered as his eyes flickered down the snacks aisle. The man with the black hair was on the move, approaching the back of the store. The woman was still there, studying the list of ingredients on a Snickers bar like it included the meaning of life. This time, Felix got a good look at the right side of her face. There was no doubt about it. His pulse quickened.

The scar was the same.

He walked faster, but not so fast as to draw attention to himself. Allison was right where he'd left her. "Hey!" he whispered over her shoulder.

"Yeah," she said distractedly, holding out an issue of *Us Weekly* in front of her. "Got my water?"

"*Allie,*" he hissed through his teeth.

"Can you believe this?" She kept her eyes on the magazine. "It's an article about Dirk Rathman. It says that since his little press conference, the ERA's gotten five hundred thousand new members. Most are high school and college kids and twenty-somethings. They're saying some parents are pissed because of the tiger tattoo thing, but the ERA's relaxing its rules. So now kids can get the fake ones and—"

"Allison!" He nudged her with his elbow.

"What?" She twisted her neck to look at him, annoyed at the unprovoked jostling.

"Don't," he warned.

"Don't what?"

"Don't look at me," he said without moving his lips. "Keep reading."

"Okay," she said warily, dropping her eyes. "What's going on?"

"Remember those people at Martha's?" He looked up at the security mirror behind the registers. The two people at the coffee bar hadn't moved and the woman with the scar was in the same aisle, but now she was idling toward the chips section. He couldn't find the shorter man. He'd disappeared.

Allison nodded hesitantly. Her shoulders tensed up.

"They're here."

"Here?" she said, her eyes shifting, apprehension creeping into her voice.

"Yes. Here. As in, here in this store." Felix checked the mirror again.

"Okay." She bit down on her lip for a moment. "What do you want me to do?"

"Just be cool," he whispered. "Just give me that and keep your eyes on me. Don't look around. I'm watching them."

Allison handed him the magazine and they stepped over to the closest register. A sullen, pimply-faced high schooler bagged the items and Felix paid in cash.

"Let's go," he said, taking the plastic bag from the clerk.

The automatic doors *whooshed* open as Felix led Allison out of the store past an entry sidewalk littered with gum wrappers and peanut husks. They swiftly made their way through the parking lot to the Range Rover.

"How many?" Allison asked as soon as they climbed into the car.

"Four. I think." He stared at the entrance, squinting into the morning sunlight reflecting brightly off the glass store front. "Two men and two women. I'm not sure about the two getting coffee. They were acting weird. Kept saying 'sugar'. They definitely aren't locals. I guess they could be tourists. Maybe from Europe or something; their clothes are a little tight. The other two were at Martha's."

"You sure?"

"Positive. The woman with the red hair's in there, the one with the scar on her face. She's blonde now, but it's definitely her. The guy with the black hair is in there too. The last time I saw him, he was trying to gut me." Reflexively, his hand went to his chest.

"What are we gonna do?"

"Sit here until they leave."

"To see if they're all together?" she asked a short pause later, her brow creasing.

He nodded. He had to know how many were after him.

They didn't have to wait long. All four emerged from the store at the same time like a scene from a movie: Dark clothes, hard expressions, unhurried movements so graceful a soundtrack must have been playing in the background as they crossed the lot and slipped silently into a black Mercedes SUV parked at an adjacent Exxon.

"I guess you have your answer." Allison watched them through the windshield.

"Yeah. I guess I do." She was right. Question answered. There were four. Now what?

"Who do they think they are anyway, the Cullens?" A smile played on the edges of Allison's lips.

Felix snickered.

"Sorry." Allison laughed. "I think I'm spending too much time with Lucas." Her expression turned suddenly serious. "They're Protectors, aren't they?"

Protectors.

The word alone caused Felix to shudder as though the marrow in his bones was frosting over, chilling him to the core.

He nodded.

"What's your plan?"

"I don't have one."

"Oh."

"How about we just get the hell outta here?" Felix pushed the ignition button and shifted into drive, wheeling out of the parking lot and onto Main Street.

"Are they following us?" Allison asked a moment later.

Felix checked the rearview mirror just as a black Mercedes sped out of the gas station. "Yeah. They're comin' up behind us."

Felix was driving fast and recklessly, nearly brushing the bumper of a white Subaru station wagon with a back window half covered in family stickers—a mom, a dad, two boys, four girls, two dogs, three cats and something that could have been a bird or a hamster. Main Street was a two-lane road—one on each side—and the double yellow stripes down the center were an unambiguous indication that the local cops frowned upon passing. Felix saw an opening and gunned it. The SUV accelerated past the Subaru like a rocket, hurling them against their seats. They made it with room to spare, but a man driving a gray minivan in the oncoming lane gave him the finger. So did the driver of the Subaru, a middle-aged woman, most likely the mom in the sticker family.

"You know we can't go to the police," Allison said, turning to look behind them.

"No shit. I wasn't going to. I just didn't... I don't... I don't know where... *shit!* I told you I don't have a plan." He didn't know where he was going; he was just driving, trying to put as much space between themselves and the Protectors as possible.

"They're just going to keep coming after you, you know. They tried to kill you before. Now they're back. You can't keep running."

He glanced over at her. "Are you saying what I think you're saying?"

Allison bit her lip in thought for a moment before answering. "Let's make a stand." Her voice was strong, flowing with confidence. "Let's fight."

"*Really?*" Felix said, startled. "They'll try to *kill* us. These people aren't screwing around. I don't want you to get hurt."

"I can take care of myself. And I have you." She smiled at him. "I know you'd never let anything happen to me."

He was breathing a little faster now. "I don't know. I don't know." His palms were sweating. He gripped the leather cover on the steering wheel, clenching and unclenching his hands. He checked the mirror. The black Mercedes was two cars back and trying to pass the car in front of it. This didn't seem real. It was like a car chase on TV, something he should be watching in the comfort of Downey's common room; something Vin Diesel should be doing, not him.

"There's four of 'em," Felix said, talking for his own benefit more than Allison's. "These aren't regular people. The Protectors are assassins. They kill Sourcerors. That's all they do. That's what they're trained to do. I don't know if I can do this."

"You can do it," she said earnestly, watching him. "It's time to let these assholes know that if they're going to mess with you they better bring a goddamn army." There was steel in her voice.

Felix could almost feel Allison's energy, her resolve. Goose bumps bristled up and down his arms. He thought he might try to run through a brick wall if she pointed him in the right direction. And he couldn't help but think that maybe she was right; he couldn't run forever, after all.

"Well," Felix began, "we... we need to go somewhere, somewhere that's not out in the open. We can't let them surround us."

"I agree. So what's the plan?"

Felix wracked his brain, trying to come up with something. Then it hit him—from where, he had no idea.

"I got it!" He slapped the wheel. "Cliff Walk."

"*Cliff Walk?*" Allison said. "Isn't that place closed?"

"Yeah. You're gonna think I'm crazy, but I have an idea."

Chapter 59

THE CLIFF WALK

The Range Rover wheeled around the bend. Up ahead, two wooden roadblocks, each painted with alternating red and white diagonal stripes, blocked the road. There was no way around them. Felix floored it. Just when the words CLIFF WALK—CLOSED TO THE PUBLIC came into view, the SUV barreled through the blockade, leaving behind a trail of kindling.

"That's gonna leave a mark." Felix glanced up at the rearview mirror. "This is a sweet car, too. Probably ran Bill at least a hundred thousand."

"A hundred thousand *dollars*?" Allison looked out the back window. "You sure he's just a groundskeeper?"

He shrugged.

"I haven't seen them since the last turn." She sounded worried. "We didn't lose them, did we?"

"They're coming." He was sure of that. He glanced down at the speedometer. They were doing sixty-two. When they'd turned onto Cliff Walk Road a mile back, he'd noticed a pair of signs cautioning drivers to keep their speed under fifteen.

Felix sped the car around a tight corner, the tires hugging the road. He let off the gas until they were through the turn, then he pressed the accelerator to the floor. The dense, unbroken woods edging the road were a brown-green blur. "Should be almost there."

"I've only been here once." Allison checked behind them again. "I think it was the year they closed it. When was that? Like our freshman year of high school?"

"Sophomore year," Felix said. He stared ahead, trying to concentrate, only vaguely remembering the road. He hadn't been here in years.

The Cliff Walk—just a few miles north of Cove Rock—was a mile-long path along the edge of a 700-foot sheer cliff overlooking the Pacific Ocean. Before the earthquake, a thick plexiglass barrier had prevented careless tourists from getting too close to the edge of one of the highest sea cliffs in the world. But now the barrier, along with large sections of the walkway, was under water, having fallen into the ocean during the cataclysmic natural disaster that had caused fires and flooding from Canada to Mexico.

Felix tapped the brakes and veered sharply into an empty parking lot. The tires screeched as he stomped on the accelerator, steering the car toward a small clapboard structure at the west end of the lot. It came up on them in a hurry. He slammed on the brakes a little too late: The car skidded to a stop, but not before it bumped into a faded sign warning visitors not to stray from the designated walkway.

Felix exhaled sharply.

They couldn't have announced their presence at the park more conspicuously; anyone coming into the lot couldn't possibly miss Bill's Range Rover. *Okay*, he thought. *So far so good.* He opened his door and shouted "Let's go!" but it wasn't necessary—Allison's door was slamming shut before he could get the words out. They spilled out of the car and raced across the beaten blacktop toward the tottering little building that up close looked like a converted storage shed. A sign above a window blocked up with a sheet of particle board read TICKET KIOSK.

It was warmer than yesterday, but still cold, and the day was beginning to deteriorate. The air was bitter. Clouds ringed the horizon, thin and high, moving in fast like a tightening noose.

On the other side of the kiosk were tourist information signs with colorful photos of the Cliff Walk and facts about the volcanic activity that had formed the cliffs millions of years ago and a picnic area where families once ate peanut butter and jelly sandwiches and salt water taffy while admiring the majestic ocean views. They tore past the benches and tables and hurdled a rusty anchor chain strung between two weathered posts. The Cliff Walk's nautical-themed entrance was a little campy, but fitting, considering the park's location.

"I guess we don't need a ticket!" Allison shouted as they ran along the rock path worn smooth by weather and time and the shoes of innumerable visitors. The ground was wet from yesterday's torrential downpour, the puddles rippling in the wind.

Felix remembered coming here with his parents in the seventh grade. The wind had gusted so violently that day he was afraid it would lift him up and blow him right off the cliff. He remembered being scared, and his mom telling him he was safe—that the Cliff Walk was the safest place in the world.

He pounded ahead, keeping his eyes on the path, feet hammering on stone. Allison matched his every pace. On one side of the walkway there was nothing but open air and a 700-foot drop to the shallow waters and gray rocks below; the path simply disappeared. On the other side, signs reading KEEP OFF THE EMBANKMENT were staked into the ground at the base of a steep but scalable slope

The path was mostly intact for the first fifty or sixty yards, then it narrowed and widened at varying intervals in a zigzagging pattern. They clung to the foot of the embankment as the path shrank to sidewalk-like proportions. They didn't slow down. Felix could hear Allison's footsteps behind him. With only a bare strip of rock between them and the ocean directly below, Felix felt like he was running on air, keenly aware that death was literally just inches away. All it would take is one slippery rock, or a simple misstep, and that would be the end of their adventure.

The sound of tires squealing on pavement pierced a hole through the howling winds.

"That's gotta be them!" Felix shouted and the wind seemed to blow the words right back in his face. The path opened up. Not much, but enough to lessen the sensation that he was balancing on a tightrope. "They're in the parking lot."

"Where are we going?"

"I'll know it when I see it."

He kept running until they came to a long stretch of path that expanded to about the width of a two-lane road. He slowed to a jog, and Allison caught up with him. This was what he was looking for. He stopped.

"This should work," he panted, wiping the sweat from his face.

Allison placed her hands on her hips, her eyes flitting all around as she breathed in the salty ocean air. "Here? Why here?" Her breath puffed out white and trailed instantly away.

"We need to get to the top." He pointed at the slope. They'd talked about his plan in the car, but only for a minute, and he hadn't gone into any level of detail because it wasn't terribly complex. "But I want to see this first." He tilted his head toward the ocean.

Allison nodded, the relentless winds whipping her long hair across her face. Felix turned to her as she took in a deep breath and let it out slowly. A single deep breath—the only indication that she'd just sprinted flat-out for five minutes. He stared at her, suddenly feeling closer to her than he'd ever felt before. Then he noticed something.

"You have freckles on your nose," he told her.

"Did we just meet?" Allison laughed, a faint blush creeping into her cheeks.

Felix smiled back at her.

They stood there and grinned at each other, feeling the soft slanted sun rays on their faces, listening to the wind, the birds, and the rainwater from yesterday's storm trickling along some unseen channels heading to lower ground. Felix felt no sense of finality. If this was the end, if they were going to *lose* (his mind, out of habit and past experience, continued framing everything as though it was a game), then wouldn't he be feeling *something*? A dark sense of forewarning? Some sort of premonition?

Felix reached out with his hand and she held out hers, the fabric of her jacket snapping in the wind. He took her hand, and together, they walked over to the edge and peered straight down. The face of the cliff was almost perfectly flat. They didn't need a sign to warn them that falling off the Cliff Walk meant certain death; there was no safety net, nothing to grab onto on the way down other than an occasional passing seagull.

The ocean was calm for the moment, no sounds of rushing water or crashing waves. The color of brushed nickel, the water was foamy and studded with whitecaps that appeared no bigger than drops of rain. Enormous salt-bleached driftwood trees sprinkled the tide line; they looked tiny, like twigs a bird might make use of to fabricate a nest. Felix watched the waves gently rolling across the vertical rock columns that poked their heads above the surface of the water near the base of the cliff. As the waves receded from the shoreline, seafoam surrounded the rock formations—the fluffy white stuff always reminded Felix of whip cream.

"Wow!" Allison took a step back, wide-eyed. "Good thing I don't have vertigo. I don't remember it being this high."

"This is crazy," Felix muttered, pulling her away from the edge. He stopped for a second, checking to see if there was any activity on the path, then they ran to the other side, ignoring the KEEP OFF THE EMBANKMENT sign, and started climbing. Time and the elements had taken their toll on the slope: the surface was as smooth as an agate. It was also slippery from yesterday's rain. They scaled it quickly, dropping to all fours to get up the last few feet.

When the ground finally leveled, they stood and looked off at the forest spread out before them, growing thick and wild in the distance, merging with the mountains looming above the coastline. Nearer to the embankment, a field of tall spreading ferns flourished unchecked among clusters of evergreens and stumps wreathed in moss. The park's employees must have been waging a war against the advancing woods; the casualties now reposed next to the stumps where they had fallen, limbless and cut into shorter lengths to be carried away.

Lying on the ground next to one of the stumps off to his left Felix noticed a section of tree with ends of equal girth, taller than Felix and as thick as a telephone pole. A chainsaw had cleanly shorn off its branches. The log wasn't unique. There were others just like it littered across the field, but for some reason, this particular log gave him an idea. He pointed, silently willing the log to come to him. It advanced through the underbrush, creating its own path through the ferns which bent low and sprang back once it had passed as if bowing respectfully at the strange sight. He let it drop next to him and it crashed down on the rocks, settling in among them.

Allison's eyes lit up. "How do you do that?"

"I don't know." He really didn't.

"What's it for?"

"Backup plan."

She gave him a questioning look.

"C'mon, they should be here any minute." He scampered up to the top of one of the larger rocks to get a better view of the path.

No one was there. No movement. Nothing out of the ordinary.

He jumped off the rock and flattened out on his belly, inching toward the edge of the embankment in an army crawl. "How's this?" He looked up at Allison. "Can they see me?"

Allison ran around to the south side—the side the Protectors would be approaching from. She shook her head. "You're good there. Those rocks"—she jerked her thumb at the bare outcropping Felix was concealing himself behind—"hide everything but your head."

"Okay. Good. Get over here."

She settled down on her stomach and wriggled her way forward until she lay down next to him on the cold, damp rocks. "So this is your brilliant plan, huh?" She nudged him with her elbow, smiling sarcastically.

Felix smiled back. "I hope it works."

"Sometimes simple plans are the best plans. As soon as they walk by, you'll..."

"Push them off the cliff," he answered simply. *Sounds easy.* But was there an even easier plan? A better plan? He glanced down at his palm and thought about Inverness, and the lock. And the fire that sprang from his hand with a thought. But he'd only used fire—intentionally—that one time. Could he do it again? Could he control it? Or would it explode out of him like a tempest and incinerate everything—including Allison. He calmed his thoughts for a moment, and keeping his gaze leveled on his palm, tried to create a flame. Nothing happened. He let out a discouraged breath and focused harder, forcing the dull heavy sensation to take root deep in his gut. He felt it, finally, but no flame appeared. He choked down an angry outburst to hide his frustration from Allison (and to avoid alerting the Protectors to their location). He knew why it wasn't working; he was holding back, afraid the single tower of flame might turn out to be a wall of fire as long as the Cliff Walk itself. He was too unsure of himself, and too distracted, to use fire. His original plan—*the simple plan*—would have to work. It worked on the Faceman. It would work on the Protectors. He hoped.

Allison craned her neck to see the path, her expression troubled. "Felix, um… hey… if this thing goes sideways, can you do something for me?"

He kept quiet, thinking he wouldn't like what she was going to say.

The corners of her mouth dipped lower. "Promise me you won't give up."

"It's not gonna go sideways," he said earnestly, shaking his head. "And I won't let anything happen to you."

She placed her hand on his, squeezing it like she was trying to steal his warmth. "You promise?"

"I promise." His voice sounded small and empty in the echo-less space.

They waited in silence.

He stared at the path, wondering if he could make good on that promise or if it was just another hollow commitment. The minutes ticked by. "What's taking 'em so damn long?" he grumbled.

Allison spoke in a rush, as though she'd been preparing a response in her head. "No way they missed the car. They had to know where we were going. You plastered the roadblocks. They must've seen that. And there's nowhere to go around here but the Cliff Walk. I mean, the road ends at the parking lot entrance, right? And didn't we just hear their car? That had to be them."

He nodded. His stomach felt tight, cramping up like he hadn't taken in enough fluids during a hot mid-August two-a-day session. He forced himself to breathe deeply and some of the tightness eased up.

"They don't use guns, right?" she asked with forced liveliness.

"Nope." He kept his eyes on the path. "Knives and garrotes."

"Old school assassins, huh?"

Felix nodded, trying to stay calm, to control his breathing like Bill had taught him. He checked his watch. Then he checked it again. His eyes scoured the path below and the tree line above, but the horizon didn't change. There was no sound except for the wind whistling over the rocks and hissing through the evergreens, stirring their stiff limbs.

They waited. The shadows cast by the late morning sun grew longer, stretching out over the wet ground. The wind bit through the thin material of Felix's jacket and the sweatshirt beneath it, blowing all the warmth from his body. The sun seemed to be moving slower than normal, sticking to the same point in a sky that was turning misty and gray. The clouds were advancing, beating back the sun, draining the light from the sky.

"Where the hell are they?" Felix muttered. His anxiety was starting to get the better of him, his nerves coiled like barbwire. An intense sinking sensation was taking hold of him, making him feel slightly nauseated. The pound-o-pork platter was churning in his stomach. His tongue felt heavy and alien, like an old piece of carpet.

"Be patient." Allison tightened the grip on his hand. It was meant to reassure him. It didn't.

Felix took his eyes off the path to steal a peek at her. Her face was rigid, her brow furrowed over her searching gaze. And then he saw it—a flicker of doubt fell over her face as if she'd just realized that what they were doing was foolishly amateurish, half-baked and dangerous.

This wasn't a good idea, he thought mournfully. His plan wasn't *simple.* His plan was just *stupid.* What did he know about fighting? Nothing. And this wasn't a game. This wasn't going to be a harmless football practice skirmish where coaches blow whistles and someone steps in to break it up. This was going to be a fight to the death. How did he let Allison talk him into this? The temptation to climb up on the tallest rock he could find and look down at least some length of the path was almost irresis—

Snap.

It came from behind them. The unmistakable sound of wood—Felix imagined a branch on the ground or a low hanging tree limb—yielding to heavy pressure, straining past the breaking point.

Felix and Allison twisted their heads around in unison to see that all four Protectors had smashed through the nearest grouping of trees. It was like they had risen out of the earth, and now they were moving swiftly over the rough terrain, gliding as though their feet weren't even touching the ground.

The panic Felix felt was instant, jolting through him. His heart hammered hard and high up in his chest, banging so loudly in his ears he could barely hear. He let go of Allison's hand and jumped to his feet; she did the same. The Protectors' breath made small white clouds in the air as they bore down on them. There was nowhere to run. They were sitting ducks. Felix's plan had only succeeded in boxing them in: forest on one side, ocean on the other, Protectors to their backs and rough jumbles of rock up ahead. He should have known they wouldn't fall for his trap—it was far too obvious. The Protectors weren't idiots; they'd stayed off the path and outflanked them, using the forest for cover. Now they would be all over them in seconds.

The Protectors in the lead—the woman with the scar on her cheek and the man from the coffee bar—drew their knives back, readying themselves for the kill.

As if he was dreaming, Felix felt himself raise his arm and point at the ground in front of the Protectors. Then he *lifted* a thin layer of the earth's crust into the air. Everything near the surface—rocks, branches, dirt, wood chips, and tough prickly bramble—exploded upwards and whipped around like a cyclone, battering the Protectors as they advanced toward them. One of the larger rocks struck the man from the coffee bar on the head and he lost his balance, stumbling back and nearly falling.

The newly blonde scar-faced woman—Felix thought of her as *Scar*—glared at the man scornfully and shouted: "Parni, wake up!"

The man—*Parni*—shook his head in pain, swiping at the blood that gushed down the side of his face from a deep wound just above his temple. Scar motioned with her hand and she and Parni bolted toward the trees. Felix *blocked* them, using the rocks and earth to push them back, closing them in with his mobile wall.

"Felix!" Allison hissed in his ear.

Felix saw them.

The dark-haired man and the other woman had darted forward, attempting to skirt around the cloud of debris. Felix cast a portion of the barrier at them in sharp cyclonic bursts, forcing them to cover up and move back. Scar and Parni had altered their course, charging fast, parallel to the tree line; the barrier shadowed them, stinging them like a swarm of bees protecting their hive, leaving behind bloody marks on their unprotected hands and faces. Scar motioned at Parni and they stopped. Suddenly, they split off from one another, Parni probing the center while Scar drew back and bolted for the trees. Felix reined her in, throwing up mounds of sticks and dirt at her face. Scar retreated several paces, then turned and came around to join the others, shouting something that Felix couldn't make out.

Scar watched Felix through a curtain of debris that now stretched twenty feet across as the others dropped back and fell in behind her. She stood there a step or two ahead of the others, her face showing nothing. Scar was assessing. The others looked at her, waiting for instructions. The man with the dark hair growled at Scar. His face was red and cords bulged on his thick neck. Scar stared at him for a moment and he quieted, dropping his eyes to the ground submissively.

"Now what?" Felix said to Allison.

She didn't answer.

Scar raised her arm and slowly extended her index finger, directing it at Felix, her eyes still on him. Slowly, her arm shifted to her left until she was pointing at Allison. Scar turned her head a twitch and said, "Parni." He stepped up beside her, his cheek and jaw steaming with blood.

"Parni," Scar said evenly, her eyes now fixed on Allison, "please go kill that bitch for me."

Parni nodded. Then he ran straight for the barrier and jumped, hands on the crown of his head, elbows aimed out in front to guard his face. The wood chips and small jagged rocks shredded his clothes and nipped at him, cutting through to his skin. But he made it to the other side. He picked up speed, making a line for Allison and Felix at a full sprint.

Felix conjured up another wall, throwing it at Parni. He hurled himself through it without breaking stride. Parni was closing in on them. Felix erected another partition, but Parni was already crashing through it. Now he was on them, standing just a few feet away.

Allison gasped. But she didn't try to run.

Felix was stunned by his size. He was tall—taller than Felix—with mounds of thickly packed muscle that tensed and rippled beneath his dark turtleneck. He'd seemed smaller at the convenience store when he was holding a paper cup filled with cheap coffee.

Parni went straight for Allison, as quick as an explosion, his knife held at his side. Felix tried to shield Allison with his earthen wall, but Parni was too close. He raised his curved dagger. In a sudden moment of panic, Felix realized that Parni was about to stab Allison in the throat.

And then Allison kicked Parni savagely in the crotch.

Parni grunted and doubled over.

Allison didn't stop there. She swung an elbow that caught Parni just above the eye, snapping his head back. She followed up the elbow with a left hook that landed on his jaw, sending up a spray of blood from his mouth. She tried to land another left hook, but Parni blocked it with his arm and drove his shoulder into her chest.

Allison fell straight back with Parni on top. She dug her foot into his stomach and kicked up. He flipped over her, but he'd grabbed onto her coat and she tumbled right along with him, rolling down the embankment, somersaulting all the way to the path below.

Felix watched in terror as they toppled down the slope.

Allison sprung to her feet and moved slowly backward, distancing herself from Parni, being careful not to step off the end of the path. As Felix watched Allison backpedaling, he completely lost his focus—he'd forgotten all about his terrestrial defenses. And now there was no barrier between Felix and the three assassins.

Scar and the man with the black hair were silently stalking him like wolves. Scar was now behind him and the man was off to Felix's left, slipping between a pair of saplings, moving closer. The other woman—the woman from the coffee bar—stood directly in front of Felix, facing him. She was tall and lean, just like Scar, who Felix had decided was clearly the person in charge. Her long chestnut hair was pulled back in a ponytail. Her blue eyes were bright, lively. She was quite pretty. She was also holding two knives, one in each hand, and obviously determined to end Felix's life on this blustery December morning.

"Bianca, kill this abomination," Scar ordered. Her voice was empty of emotion, though her dark eyes were filled with disgust.

"My pleasure, Tripoli," Bianca replied, grinning eagerly.

Now Scar had a new name: Tripoli. *Parni, Bianca and Tripoli,* Felix thought. *Weird names. Funny, the things you think about when people are trying to kill you.*

Bianca's eyes narrowed into thin lines as she began to work the crescent moon-shaped knives around her body with the artistry of a ballerina. A blur of shining white metal, the sharp blades reflected the sunlight like polished mirrors. Her movements were fluid and effortless; the knives were like extensions of her body, moving through space, appearing and vanishing all at once like flickering candlelight.

Felix blinked a little and swallowed down his adrenaline rush. He'd never seen anything like this before. The way she manipulated the knives was mesmerizing. It was like being a spectator at a magic show.

"Kill him!" Tripoli commanded.

Bianca rushed at Felix.

Felix waved his hand.

Bianca turned the knives on herself and plunged both blades into her neck all the way up to the handles. She stood there, eyes wide with confusion, choking on the blood that frothed from her open mouth. Dead on her feet, staring at Felix with sightless eyes, she fell sideways and slid down the embankment.

Take that, bitch! Felix thought triumphantly, glancing down to see that Allison and Parni were circling each other, both dangerously close to the cliff's edge. With a finger twitch, Felix broke off a bowling ball-sized rock from the outcropping and sent it shooting at Tripoli's midsection.

Tripoli jumped high in the air—the rock flew harmlessly beneath her—landed on her hands, sprung forward onto her feet and flipped over Felix's head.

A flashing pain flared above his shoulder blade. He spun around.

Tripoli was standing with her back to the embankment, her knife red with blood—Felix's blood. And in her other hand, she was holding something else—a garrote. A hint of a smile played across her lips.

The heavy ache in his back let Felix know that the knife had cut deep. That made him angry. He flicked his finger, determined to blow Tripoli a thousand feet out to sea.

She jumped.

He *knocked* her backward, but only clipped her feet, and she avoided the brunt of the force. She flipped head-over-heels like a high diver and soared over the slope in a graceful arc, touching down on the walkway a stone's throw from Allison and Parni.

The man with the black hair came at Felix like an enraged barbarian. Felix wheeled around instinctively, lifting his arms to protect his face. The man slashed downward with his knife and then across his body, grunting with each tremendous effort; he wasn't just trying to kill Felix, he was trying to cut him in half. Felix jumped back, the blade whistling past his face. The man was slashing left, slashing right, snarling and swinging the knife like a club. It was like dodging a running chain saw. Felix jumped back to avoid the berserker's knife, but he jumped back a little too far. His feet landed on a steeply-angled section of the slope. He tried to dig his toes in, but his sneakers couldn't get any traction on the smooth rain-polished rocks. He started to fall backward, his arms making tight little circles in the air as he fought to stay on his feet.

The man pounced on Felix with the agility of a spider and attempted to drive the knife into his chest.

Felix *caught* the man's knife arm, immobilizing it, but now with the man's weight pressing down on him, he couldn't keep his balance. Felix fell on his back and slid down the embankment with the man on top, leading with his head, which bumped and banged along the rocks all the way down.

When Felix finally came to a sudden stop at the bottom of the slope, he was lying on his back, looking straight up, groggy and in pain. The man was straddling Felix's chest, mounting him, just like at Martha's house. He gazed down at Felix with his dull black eyes, his mouth set in a contemptuous sneer. His lips were swollen and blackened and blood streamed from cuts above an eyebrow and the bridge of his nose. He raised his arms high above his head, holding the dagger with both hands, preparing to stab Felix in the chest, seconds away from cutting out his heart. Just within Felix's line of sight, he saw Tripoli striding toward him from the ocean-side of the path.

"*Get off!*" Felix shouted furiously.

The man flew straight up into the air.

Felix rolled over and got up. The man landed lightly on his feet in one graceful and soundless movement.

Allie, Felix thought, panicked, shooting a glance in the direction of where he'd last seen her. She was still there, still fighting with Parni along the edge of the cliff. Parni lashed a kick at her head. Allison ducked and swung her leg around, sweeping Parni's support leg out from under him. He landed on his back, just inches from descending into oblivion. Allison stood there with her arms at her sides, staring down at him with a quizzical expression as if surprised that she'd knocked him down. Her windblown hair was loose and wild, whipping around her head. Parni grunted angrily and popped back up to his feet.

The dark-haired man screamed and swung his knife wildly at Felix, going for his throat. Felix *stopped* his arm and pushed him back several feet. Felix's eyes, of their own accord, kept flicking to Allison, but the man had already recovered and was on the attack again. Felix stepped swiftly away from the embankment. Tripoli was closer now, hurrying toward him with her garrote and knife in hand. Felix didn't know how long Allison could hold out against Parni, but whenever his attention strayed from the threat in front of him, he nearly got himself killed. Before he could help Allison, he had to help himself.

He focused on the man for a fraction of a second and *pushed* him in front of Tripoli, causing her to run right up his back. The man didn't seem surprised that invisible bonds were controlling his body, but he did look angry; he bared his teeth like a rabid dog and yelled. Tripoli didn't so much as stumble, but when she tried to step around him, Felix slid the man like a chess piece across the smooth stones, obstructing her, blocking her path. Tripoli swiped at the man's shoulders, fighting to get by him. Felix shifted the man a little to the right. Then a little more. Then a little more. *There.*

Their backs were now turned to the embankment, their faces to the ocean. Felix lifted his eyes for a fleeting moment to a little spot at the top of the slope.

His backup plan.

The log glided down the embankment, spinning horizontally like a boomerang, a subtle, almost noiseless undercurrent in the background of the roaring wind. Felix positioned the massive section of tree directly behind the man and Tripoli. Then he *swung* it like a baseball bat.

At the last possible moment, Tripoli seemed to sense that something was approaching and dropped flat on the ground.

The man never saw it coming.

The log smashed against the side of his head, splattering bone, flesh and gray matter across the path and out into the ocean. His headless body crumpled to the ground. He didn't even twitch.

The log kept twirling. Felix swung it at Tripoli.

She ducked and jumped lithely toward him.

He brought the log in closer, and swung it at her again, harder this time.

She hit the ground, lying flat.

Felix realized his mistake a second too late.

Like an oncoming freight train, the log slammed against Felix's shoulder with a sickening *crunch*, sending him flying through the air. He crashed down hard, bounced, and then skidded toward the edge of the cliff. With very little room between him and the end of the walkway, he came to a skittering stop. His shoulder—his entire body—was on fire. He couldn't move his arm. It had to be broken; it hurt too much for it not to be.

"Felix!" he heard Allison cry out through the ringing in his ears. And then there was a scream—Allison's?—followed by a *thudding* sound. He used his good arm to get to his knees, pushing himself away from the edge, his mouth filled with the coppery taste of blood. He lifted his head to look up at—

He couldn't breathe. It was like all the oxygen in the world had instantly vanished. He clawed at his throat. He felt something—a cord. *The garrote.* Felix's eyes flitted up, catching a blurry glimpse of the bottom half of Tripoli's face. She yanked violently on the garrote with a ferocious animalistic strength that belied her slender frame. "This time, you die!" she howled. "Die, you devil!" And with a primal victory roar, she pulled Felix onto his back, wrapped her long legs around his waist and squeezed.

Felix's heart was pounding in his rib cage like a jackhammer. His eyes were bulging. His lips were turning blue. If he didn't get the wire off, he'd be dead in thirty seconds. But even through the organ-splintering pain and the specter of death so close he could almost feel its icy breath on his skin, one thought was spinning its way through his mind: *Not. This. Time.*

Tripoli's fingers started to fracture. Both index fingers and her thumbs bent back and cracked sickeningly. Another finger broke, the crisp *pop* of the bone sounding like a firecracker in Felix's ears. And then another. But still, she stubbornly held onto the garrote, tightening the wire around his neck. His eyes rolled back in his head and all light blinked out. In its place, there was only pain, an incomprehensible pain.

Then Tripoli's fingers began to bleed.

The middle finger on her left hand snapped off, ripping away at the knuckle. Blood squirted into the air and Felix felt its warmth speckling across his face like summer rain. The ring finger next to it twisted around until only a thin piece of skin held it in place. The skin tore and her finger dropped into a puddle with a splashing *plop*. She screamed and then finally let go of the garrote.

Felix sucked in a breath of sweet ocean air and flung himself to one side in a swift roll, getting to a knee.

Tripoli was already on her feet as Felix raised his hand toward her. Blood poured from her severed fingers and pooled on the path. She took a running leap toward him. In mid-stride she stopped, abruptly, like someone had hit the pause button on a TV. And then, with an expression of total bewilderment, she looked on as her arms rose above her head and the garrote coiled itself around her neck. Holding onto the garrote with both hands, she lifted herself off the ground. Her feet kicked. Her face turned purple. Her eyes bulged.

Felix stood up, still trying to catch his breath, a red rage taking hold of him. "How does that feel, you fucking bitch!"

Allison screamed.

Parni was grabbing her by the back of the head with one hand and taking chopping iron-fisted shots at her face with the other. Allison deflected most of the blows with her raised forearms, but some were getting through. At some level, Felix was conscious that Allison was embroiled in a life and death fight with Parni. Yet he couldn't draw his attention away from Tripoli. The rage that had bloomed inside him was complete, incoherent. He was going to make her *suffer*—make her feel exactly what he'd felt. He flicked a finger and the wire tightened on her throat. The squiggly veins under her eyes swelled green, close to bursting. He smiled with satisfaction.

Allison elbowed Parni in the stomach, then connected with a wicked uppercut to the chin. A tooth flew from Parni's mouth, landing on the path not far from the dark-haired man's headless body. Parni let go of her hair and stumbled, balancing himself with one hand on the ground. He gave his head a quick shake, stood up in a crouch, hands in a fighting position. Then he froze. His body went rigid and a look of sheer panic passed over his features like a shadow. Allison backed up a step and watched as Parni's head tilted loosely to the side, twitching violently. His fingers bent stiffly and his elbows dug into his sides. He clawed at the air, mouth open, eyes going in different directions. The blow to Parni's face had damaged something beneath the skin that Allison couldn't see. He was having a seizure. He was vulnerable.

Allison came up off her feet in a sudden pounce, bringing her arm forward from the side, a looping punch with enough force to break the bones in Parni's face, enough force to put him to sleep for a very long time.

Parni shot forward, lunging in close and dropping low to avoid her fist, then he exploded upward with his knee, driving it powerfully into Allison's stomach. Still in midair, Allison's body wrapped around Parni's leg, sagging forward until her face and feet were close to touching. They both hit the ground at the same time. Parni on legs that were as steady as the look in his eyes. Allison stumbled dizzily, awkwardly, falling toward the ocean. She brought up both arms and clutched at her midsection, white-faced, gasping for air, wheezing. Her back to the ocean, unsteady, she rocked back and forth on her heels, dazed.

Parni measured her with his cool assassin's eyes, sizing her up, his lips pressed together into a tight line. Allison drew herself up and squared her shoulders, head held high, standing tall, as if she knew what was coming and realized that all she had left to preserve was her pride.

Parni rotated on the ball of his left foot, spinning himself clockwise, uncorking his right leg around his body in an explosive roundhouse kick which ended with his leg fully extended and his foot planted in the center of Allison's chest. The force of the blow lifted Allison off her feet, driving her backward. As she sailed past the end of the cliff, she frantically reached out with her hands, trying to grab hold of the rocks in front of her. Her green eyes grew large with fear... and something else. As he watched helplessly from down the path, Felix would always remember the look in Allison's eyes: the sudden realization that the path was beyond her reach—the realization that she was going to fall 700 feet to her death.

And then she was gone.

The last thing Felix saw was Allison's long dark hair spilling out in waves, rising in the air around her face as if she was floating in water.

Felix stared stupidly, his jaw dropping in shock.

That didn't just happen! No! No! No! No!

Parni stepped back from the edge. Then very deliberately, he turned to face Felix, his mouth curling up into a smug smile, the lines on his face showing white through a slick of blood.

Felix screamed something. He felt his mouth working, but the words meant nothing.

Tripoli made a guttural, strangling sound. Her feet were still kicking, trying to reach the rocky sanctuary just beneath her toes. She grasped frenetically at the wire around her neck. Unthinkingly, numbly, Felix raised a finger and she crashed into the embankment.

Parni was running at Felix now, flying along the walkway, slashing viciously at the space before him with his knife. He let out a roar and his lips rolled back over his teeth to the gum lines. Through the dark haze clouding his mind, Felix pointed at Parni and Parni lurched to a sudden stop. Then he *lifted* him up until his feet lost contact with the ground. Parni's expression changed. The anger was still there, but the smugness was gone. And in his eyes there was something new... the seeds of fear.

Felix stood there, unmoving, head swimming, trying to make sense of what had just happened. He glanced over at where Allison had been just a few seconds before. There was nothing but gray sky.

Parni screamed furiously at Felix in a language that didn't sound like English.

Detached and dissociated from the world around him, Felix dragged his eyes away from the cliff's edge and stared up at the face of the man who had just killed his best friend. The desire to end his life was overwhelming— and he had every intention of giving in to it. But he wasn't going to just kill him. He was going to *hurt* him. He was going to make him suffer. Allison was dead. There was no need to hold anything back now.

Parni went up in flames as if his body had been soaked in jet fuel, every square inch of him consumed in white-hot fire. He screamed and writhed in agony, twisting and flailing his limbs. Gradually, as the thickening clouds continued to settle in overhead, his screams began to dwindle, becoming lost to winds that had grown increasingly frigid. Felix extinguished the flames. He walked over to Parni and looked up at him, studying his bloodied, charred form like it was an insect that had just stung him.

"How did that feel?" Felix said coldly. "You like that?"

Parni's lips moved noiselessly, his red eyes searching for Felix. When Parni found him, he began to speak in a halting whisper: "Pu... pu... please..."

Felix didn't know if he was begging for mercy or begging for a quick death. He didn't care. He set Parni on fire again, the flames engulfing him like a blanket. Parni's wretched screams floated up to the clouds pressing down on the Cliff Walk, and as his cries began to wane, Felix let the fire go out. Parni's ravaged body scarcely looked human. Felix had spared nothing. Even Parni's lips had burned away, melted by the flames. But his chest still rose and fell; he was still breathing. *Good*, Felix thought sadistically, lighting him up like a torch, yearning to hear his tortured screams. But this time he didn't scream. His head simply fell forward and he went limp.

"I'm not done with you yet!" Felix raged, increasing the intensity of the fire, the wind whipping the flames around him. "I'll tell you when you can die!" But the man was dead. Well past dead. His flesh was turning to powder, the stiff gusts breaking over the path scattering the ashes across the walkway and up the embankment.

Felix didn't feel less anger. He didn't feel less pain. There was no catharsis borne from avenging Allison's death. Felix's world had just ended. He had a limitless reservoir of rage to take out on the man—a rage that had yet to be sated.

But Parni was beyond his reach. There was nothing more Felix could do to him. He gazed on him for a moment with vile contempt in his eyes. Then he waved his hand, sending Parni's flaming remains spiraling off the cliff into the icy waters far below.

Everything was silent and still.

The battle was over.

Felix looked all around, eyes wild and horrified, as if he had just arrived and the carnage he was observing was the work of another. In the center of the walkway, a body with no head was lying at an odd angle in a pool of blood. Crumpled at the base of the slope was the broken figure of Tripoli. And next to her, Bianca lay on her back with two knife handles sticking out from her throat, the blades buried up to the shafts. He had killed the Protectors.

But where's Allison? Didn't you promise to protect her?

He had killed them all. He had won.

Did you? Then where is she?

It wasn't supposed to happen like this. She can't be gone. She must be here. She must. His eyes roamed up and down the path, over the grim scene spread out before him.

She's dead, Felix! Dead! You'll never see her again! You promised to protect her! You promised!

This was all wrong. How could she be dead? How could that be? He quieted the voices in his head, listening to the winds singing their haunting songs as they rushed over the cliff. He looked out at the ocean for a long while, feeling numb, like everything inside him had shut down and gone dark. He'd just let his best friend die. Just like his mom—his real mom—had let her best friend fall to her death. All these years later, the family curse had come full circle. *How could this have happened? How could I be like someone I never knew?*

Felix sank to his knees, burying his face in his hands. *It wasn't possible. She couldn't really be dead. How could I let this happen?* He lifted his face to the heavens and screamed in anguish.

A solitary seagull returned his grief-filled cries, mocking him as the finality of Allison's death seized his consciousness, tearing at his soul, drowning him in a depthless sea of misery. This was more than he could bear. He'd already lost so much. Suffered so much. He didn't have the capacity for this. Not this. Anything but this. He couldn't take it.

"Felix," he said, his voice hoarse, cracking. "Why? Why? Why…?"

"Felix."

He paused, his eyes moving everywhere all at once. *Was that an echo? The voices in his head?*

"Felix."

There it was again. Felix stood up, ears trained, listening for his name.

"Felix!"

He definitely heard it that time.

"Felix! Help!"

It was coming from the ocean. He jumped to his feet, ran helter-skelter and dove, throwing himself head first, sliding toward the end of the walkway, picking up speed as the end of the world loomed up. He was going fast. Too fast. He was going to fly right off the path. One side of his body snagged on something, turning him sideways. His right hand reached out and clawed at the stones, slowing his momentum as he started slipping off the path. With only the cold Pacific air supporting the left side of his body, he dug his fingers into the rocks, grinding to a stop. He swung his dangling leg back onto the path, and still on his stomach, his head hanging over the side, he peered down.

Twenty feet below, Allison was holding onto a rock—a tiny little bulge in the cliff no larger than a dinner plate—with just her fingertips. The cliff angled slightly inward toward the walkway, leaving no footholds, and her legs were swaying from side to side like a falling leaf.

"Hurry!" she screamed up at Felix with desperation in her eyes.

"You're alive!" he shouted down at her, not realizing that he was smiling. He couldn't believe it. *Allison was alive. She was actually alive.* He stared at her with a huge grin on his face, too amazed and relieved to think about helping her.

"Not much longer if you don't do something!"

"Sorry," he muttered, getting to a squatting position, urgently searching for something to bring her up to the path. He saw the log. Not ideal, but he thought it just might work.

"Lift me up!" she screamed. "I'm slipping."

"I'll break your arms!" Felix screamed back.

"I don't care! Break them!"

"Wait a sec!" He looked hard at the log and focused his energy, willing it to cross the path to him (not easy given his muddled state), then he lowered it down the face of the cliff vertically, like it used to stand in the soil before the park employees sliced through it with their chain saws, forcing it to a stop when it was next to her. He tried to keep the log from bobbing into her, but the wind was fearsome and balancing it properly was futile.

Allison glanced at it, winced, and blurted out: "You've got to be kidding!"

"Grab it!"

The wind was whipping wildly, swinging her back and forth. One hand slipped off the rock as a sudden gale jerked her to one side. For a few terrifying seconds, her body was nearly parallel to the dark waters below, yet somehow she kept her grip with only one hand. Then she clutched onto the rock with both hands when the buffeting winds swung her in the opposite direction, slamming her into the log.

"There's no branches!" Allison shouted, looking at the log. "Nothing to hold onto!"

"Just get your arms around it!"

"This is the best you can do?" she shouted angrily.

He thought for a moment before shouting back: "I don't see a rope up here! Just grab it! Trust me!"

She muttered something that was lost in the wind as she released one hand and turned her body toward the log.

He inched it closer to her, steadying it, keeping it as still as possible.

She let go of the rock with her other hand and reached out for it, extending both arms.

Felix held his breath. Everything seemed to be moving in slow motion.

Allison's fingers scraped into the bark and bit hard, pulling the log into her chest. The log banged against the cliff and she let out a startled shout as one hand came free. She grasped at it, unable to lace her fingers together, dropping suddenly, her nails raking down through its soft rotting shell, peeling off bark as she went. She adjusted her grip, clamping her forearms to slow her descent, hugging her body against it. Her fall temporarily stalled, she blew out a steaming breath and looked up at Felix. Then she raised one leg, and then the other, curling both around the log, squeezing it between her thighs.

"You okay?" Felix shouted down at her.

"Fantastic! *What do you think?* Bring me up!"

He pushed himself to his feet and concentrated on making the log ascend up the face of the cliff swiftly but without jarring Allison or unhinging her fragile grip. "Thank you. Thank you. Thank you," he whispered elatedly to himself as the top of the log rose above the path. He started to breathe a little easier, expecting to have the log, and Allison, on firmer ground any second.

A searing pain exploded in the back of his leg and he hit the ground hard, landing on the same shoulder the swinging log had crushed just a moment ago. He grabbed at his leg and felt something. A foreign object. Something strange was protruding out of his right calf. He ran his fingers over it, and after a few stunned moments, concluded that it was the hilt of a knife. He lay there, confused, wondering what on earth he was doing on the ground with a knife in his leg. Then a pair of fists, dripping blood, and a long wire intruded on his field of vision, passing over his face and blocking out the sky. He swatted the bloody hands away and jumped to his feet, his right leg immediately howling in pain.

Tripoli was down on the path in front of him, propping herself up on her elbows. Her blonde hair was streaked red. Blood ringed her throat and ran down her face from ugly gashes on her cheeks and forehead. Her hands were a bloody mess. Her legs were bent, broken and useless, drenched in blood from hip to ankle.

He grimaced with fury and reached down to pull the knife from his—

"*Allie!*" Felix shouted in terror, suddenly realizing Allison was in a free fall.

He waved a finger at Tripoli, flinging her against the embankment; she stuck to it for a moment, then slid down to the bottom slowly in a twisted heap.

His blood racing, Felix turned to the ocean, raised both arms and screamed at the top of his lungs: *"Uuuuuuppppppppp!"*

He stepped back from the edge and waited, too afraid to look down.

In the distance, something came into view—but it wasn't Allison. A rock, long and jagged along its edges, crested the plane of the walkway and continued skyward. Another pillar of stone appeared next to the first, and then another. Soon, an armada of broken sea stacks obscured the skyline. Some were small and unremarkable—except for their altitude—others big (the size of motorcycles and cars), and three magnificent columns of rock, trailing streams of rushing water from huge crevices in their surface, were as large as school buses.

He stared out at the rocks, waiting with a sense of complete helplessness. He couldn't lose Allison. *Not again.* He waited. Time passed like a frozen eternity in purgatory. Then he saw it, the cleanly severed end of a tree rising slowly above the edge of the walkway. His stomach lurched. His heart stopped in his chest. He resisted the temptation to bring it up faster as he watched it ascend inch by inch for some immeasurable period of time.

And then there was a face, a face reddened by the elements pressed tightly against the rough bark. Allison was clinging to the very bottom of the log, her eyes closed and her legs swinging in the open air.

With a sudden rush of glorious, exhilarating relief, Felix brought the log onto the path. When Allison was just a few feet above him, she opened her eyes and let go, dropping into his arms. He caught her, but lost his footing in the process and tripped, and together they tumbled to the ground.

"Thank you," she breathed in his ear, panting softly. "Thanks for bringing me back."

The words she'd said to him yesterday came to his mind, and he repeated them to her. "There's nothing I wouldn't do for you, Allie." He held her tightly, crushing her to him, smothering her; she didn't seem to mind.

She lay there in his arms for a long while as they looked up at the swirling rain-heavy clouds like two fortunate but exhausted castaways tossed ashore on some distant uncharted island. Finally, she pushed herself up and gazed out at the strange rock formations hovering hundreds of feet above the water.

"Hey, you might wanna drop those things. If anyone saw this…" She shook her head in awe.

He smiled and let them fall. A crackling charge coursed through the air a moment later when they impacted the shoreline. The ground trembled and shook, not unlike the day the earthquake had struck and forever transformed the idyllic nature walk.

"I hope the rest of this thing doesn't collapse," Allison said softly as the tremors began to subside. Then she looked down at Felix and raised her eyebrows in surprise. "You have a knife in your leg."

"Oh. I forgot." Felix grinned raggedly at the absurdity of forgetting such a thing. "That's why you took that little log ride." He reached down and pulled it out. Blood trickled down his leg like sap from a tree. "Owwww! Shit! That hurts!" He held it up close to his face and watched the blood slide languidly down the blade to his fingers. With an angry grunt, he threw it off the cliff.

"You two devils are very sweet," a voice croaked.

Felix turned to see that Tripoli was smiling at them, on her back, her mouth filled with blood (and very few teeth).

"You've gotta be shitting me," Felix murmered. He heaved himself to his feet and limped painfully over to Tripoli. Her body was wrecked and he wondered for a moment how she could still be alive. "Why are you doing this?" he shouted down at her. "Why are you trying to kill me?"

He felt a hand on his shoulder. Allison's. Her face was grim, determined.

Tripoli laughed and blood bubbles formed at the corners of her mouth. "You're not... you're not... even... the one."

"*What?*" Felix said, confused. "What do you mean? What are you talking about?"

"I'll... tell." Tripoli's eyes closed, then fluttered open. Her breathing sounded gurgly, as though her lungs were filling with blood.

Felix got on his knees and shook her roughly. "Tell me!"

"*Felix...*" Allison warned, holding out a cautioning hand.

"Here... closer... I tell."

He bowed his head, placing his ear next to her mouth. "Tell—"

Tripoli's arm flinched.

Felix didn't have time to react. A hot, stinging pain just beneath his rib cage was followed by dull, thick pressure. It hurt. A lot. He screamed in agony, his fearful eyes glancing down. Tripoli had stuck him with a knife. She'd shoved it in deep; he couldn't see the blade, only the glinting steel handle sticking out from his jacket. He screamed again. Then he reacted in a burst of fury: He *broke* her arm in two, snapping it with a satisfying crack. The splintery edged bone cut through her shirt just below her elbow.

Tripoli laughed gleefully, too far gone to feel pain. Her limbs went slack and her laughter caught in her throat mid-cackle, then her eyes glossed over and her head lolled to the side as if her final wish was to look out at the ocean one last time.

Felix fell onto his back and curled up on his side, hugging his arms across his stomach, fearing that if he didn't, his guts would spill out all over the path.

"Felix!" Allison shrieked with panic, jumping beside him, hands on him. "Oh my God! Oh my God! Felix!"

His stomach was raging with molten pain. Blood pumped from the wound, spreading over his hands and arms. "How bad is it?" he asked.

Allison ripped open his jacket and gasped. "It's in there a few inches." Her voice was shaky. "It's a puncture wound. She didn't hara-kiri you or anything, but you're bleeding pretty bad."

Some of the pain had already subsided. Felix grabbed the knife by the handle and yanked it out furiously. "That bitch! *I hate that fucking woman!*"

"Are you okay?" Allison looked at him uncertainly, wiping the corners of her eyes. "I thought…"

"I'm great." He struggled to his feet, wincing, and tossed the knife on the ground next to Tripoli.

Allison stood up and took a step back, giving Felix a curious look. "You're *covered* in blood, in case you're wondering."

"I don't think all of it's mine," he replied, using his sleeve to wipe off his face. He eyed her for a moment. "You don't look much better."

"Really?" she said, feigning dismay. She held up her arms and looked herself over. Dirt and pitch smudged one side of her face. A lock of wet hair was plastered to her cheek—wet with what Felix didn't want to think about considering the various substances residing on the log. Her clothes were stained with blood. Her hair was matted with it. "Just bumps and bruises," she said casually. "Maybe a few scratches." She turned her hands, bringing her fingers up close to her face. "Damn nails! I just had a manicure."

Felix snorted.

She circled him, looking him over slowly with a steady, studious gaze.

"What are you doing?" he asked, looking at her skeptically.

She smiled. "How many times did you get stabbed?"

It was such a ridiculous question he found himself laughing. "I lost count. Ouch. Oh." He clutched at his stomach, keeling over in pain. "It hurts to laugh. Ouch. Don't make me laugh. Ahhh…"

Allison started laughing.

Drunk with exhaustion and relief, they laughed all the way back to the car.

Chapter 60

THE TRUNK

The adrenaline rush passed quickly. Nothing seemed very funny anymore. They were back at the parking lot searching Bill's car for a first aid kit. Felix was staring inside the trunk, empty of not only a white box with a red cross but empty of everything, which probably should have made him wonder why he continued to stare at it. But something about it didn't look right. Above the headrests he could see the back of Allison's head; she was in the passenger seat.

"Anything?" Felix called out to her.

"No." She snapped the glove box shut. "You?"

"Nope."

"I don't need it anyway," she muttered. Felix could hear the irritation in her voice and he knew where it was coming from. He didn't agree with her self-diagnosis—*"nicks and scrapes,"* she insisted—and thought an actual doctor should take a look at her injuries. Of course a trip to the ER was out of the question because of the annoying proclivity of those in the medical profession to ask meddling questions. So that left the first aid kit. Allison was being predictably stubborn about not needing it and kept reminding him that "while we're wasting time looking for it, what do you think will happen if someone shows up here and sees us in the parking lot and associates the two kids with the Range Rover with the three corpses on the Cliff Walk."

He was starting to think she had a point.

Allison hopped out of the car and climbed into the back seat. A fat drop of rain landed on Felix's nose while Allison plunged her hand into the plastic bag from 7-Eleven, flipping aside a magazine (the one with Dirk Rathman and his new tattoo featured on the cover), a bag of chips and a jar of peanuts. She sighed loudly so that Felix could hear her consternation, then opened a bottle of water and took a long drink. The raindrops drummed heavy on the roof of the car and left dark spots on the asphalt where they landed. Felix thought the weather was about to get really nasty.

And then, as if the weather gods wanted to make light of his meteorological prognostications, the sun emerged from behind a bank of clouds, bathing the parking lot in a cool, steely winter glow.

"Nada?" Felix asked.

"Nada."

"You're not even looking," Felix complained. "What about under the seats?"

"I'm not the one who got stabbed like forty million times." She gave him a harsh look and scooted across the seat, letting her legs hang out of the car.

"Can you toss me one of those?" Felix tilted up his chin at the bottle of Poland Spring in Allison's hand. He was thirsty enough to lap up the puddles studding the lot.

Allison slipped out of the car and came around back, handing him a bottle.

Felix drank half of it in four long swallows, watching Allison as he did. The wind tugged at her hair, blowing strands of it across her face, but not so many as to conceal the blood spatters on her cheeks and brow, her swollen lips or the nasty red welts next to her left ear and on her forehead.

Allison suddenly flipped up his sweatshirt and splashed water on his bare stomach.

He jumped back in surprise, flinching from the cold. "Why'd you do that?"

"Just to confirm something," she said thoughtfully, using his shirt and the sleeve of her own to dry him off. "Let me look." She yanked up on the front of his shirt again, raising it up to his chest.

Now he understood what she was doing.

"It doesn't hurt, does it?" Allison said quietly. Her gaze fixed on his eyes for a moment before moving back to his stomach.

He shook his head. He'd never felt better. Strange, considering the knife wound to his gut—just one of *several* knife wounds—had bled so much that his shirt and jeans looked like they'd been used to sop up the floor of a slaughterhouse. After Allison cleaned off most of the blood, already crusty and more blackish in color than red, and the skin was once again visible, they couldn't find the wound; it had healed completely.

Allison's forehead wrinkled in confusion for a half-second and then smoothed over, her lips twitching up in a smile. "That's pretty cool." She ran a lone finger over his stomach. "Not even a scar."

"Just like my nose," Felix replied, recalling how surprised he'd been when he looked in his dorm room mirror and realized his broken nose from tangling with the Faceman had fixed itself in just a few hours. But this time, the healing process was faster, significantly faster. Tripoli had stabbed him in the gut fifteen minutes ago at most. His, whatever you wanted to call them, *abilities, powers*—words like that sounded corny and comic bookish to him, evoking images of capes and masks—seemed to be escalating. He wondered for a moment where it would all end and shivered.

"Just like your nose," Allison repeated. Then she added with a groan: "Must be nice. I hurt everywhere."

A thought occurred to him as he stared at the trunk and he blurted, "Where's the spare tire?" There were five latches on the floor: One in each corner and one centered in the front. He tugged on the corner latches. Nothing happened. Then he slid his fingers over the latch in front. It felt like the 'on off' switch from the old printer he'd had in high school. He pressed down on one side of it—the raised side—and the floor flipped open like the mouth of a giant clam, revealing a false floor.

"Holy shit!" Felix shouted. On TV, false floors were primarily used to hide drugs, guns, money, and the occasional dead body. Life was imitating art: Bill's concealed the biggest gun in the world.

Allison's mouth formed a big letter O and her eyes bulged. "Did you know that Bill drives around with a cannon in his car?" She pointed at it, startled. "What the hell is that thing?"

"I don't know anything about it," he said softly, staring at it. The polished barrel was black and as thick as Felix's wrist. "Damn. This thing's huge. I think it's a military shotgun. Lucas and I play this computer game sometimes—that's the gun we use. It's an automatic, I think. I'm pretty sure Bill's not supposed to have it unless he's like a cop or special agent or something."

"He's not just a groundskeeper, is he?" Allison didn't get a response from Felix—there were only so many head shakes and shrugs in his arsenal—so she continued to look down at it suspiciously, standing back from the trunk as if she was afraid the gun might go off all on its own.

"We better hide this," Felix said, thinking that one of these days he really needed to get together with Bill and ask him some questions; he knew almost nothing about the guy. He pressed down on the floor panel, trying to muscle it back into place, but it only gave way in front, bending down slightly.

"Here." Allison stepped up to the car and nudged him aside with her hip. "You're going to break it. I bet you need to press this." She pushed down on the other end of the switch with her thumb—the raised side—and sure enough, the floor panel silently closed. No more cannon.

A long silence followed as Felix considered what to do with the gun, finally deciding the best place for it was right where it was. "I guess we should go." He slammed the trunk shut and started for the driver's side door.

"What about our clothes?" Allison said, sounding troubled. "If a cop pulls us over for speeding we're screwed."

Felix stopped and turned back to her with a grin on his face. "How do you feel about unwashed gym clothes?"

"My favorite." She smiled, then abruptly squinched up her face in pain, putting her hand to her mouth. She glanced down at the blood on her fingertips and added wistfully, "Is that all you brought?"

"We're lucky I even have 'em. I was planning to do a load of laundry at the dorm before I head back."

Her expression stiff with skepticism, Felix led Allison around to the back seat where she watched him dig through his grandma's floral print duffel bag until he found shorts and hooded sweatshirts for them both, hers orange and green, his blue and gray. He set his aside and lobbed hers over his shoulder. Allison snagged them with one hand, using the other to affect an exaggerated pose: a dramatic pinching of her nose between her thumb and forefinger.

And then they took off their clothes.

Allison's undergarments had survived the fight unscathed. Felix's hadn't—his underwear was soaked through with blood—and he didn't have a spare pair in the bag so he was forced to keep them on. They smiled at each other, though not out of nervousness or insecurity; after what they'd just endured, stripping down to their pale goose-bumped skin seemed both trivial and the most natural thing in the world. Allison shivered as the shifting winter winds tore across the parking lot.

Felix should have probably realized it earlier, but once he did, it came as a shock, like a punch to the face: He felt the cold, but *he* wasn't cold. He watched Allison's breath puffing out in little trailing clouds. It was like he could see her body heat dissolving away as the winds nipped at her exposed skin. He knew the bitter coastal air was just a few digits north of refrigerator temperature. But he felt... comfortable.

He must have had a strange expression on his face because Allison narrowed her eyes at him. "Let me guess—you're not cold."

Felix shook his head apologetically.

"You suck." Allison laughed as she pulled the extra-large hoodie over her head. The sweatshirt bagged on her and hung down straight to the hem of her shorts. She pushed back the puddles of fabric on her sleeves. "Okay. Ready." She started for the passenger side, walking with a mild limp.

He hid the clothes they'd had on—now little more than blood-stained rags—at the bottom of the bag, covering them up with the rest of his laundry. He slid the bag onto the floor and stuffed it under the seat, then closed the door. As he turned to head toward the front of the car his eyes were drawn to the black Mercedes SUV parked just two spaces away. He swallowed convulsively. He'd been trying not to look but now that it had him in its grip, he hesitated, and his eyes roamed over it. Tripoli, Parni, Bianca and the now headless man whose name he didn't know, had left the engine running. The streaming clouds of idling exhaust chuffing out from the dual exhaust pipes rose up but only as high as the bumper before the scouring gales carried them away. The cocky bastards had expected a quick kill and a quick escape.

But it wasn't the Protectors' arrogance that bothered Felix. Just a little while ago, four people—*people,* he reminded himself—had climbed out of that car. A lot of things about the world and his life confused him. But there was one thing he knew for certain: Those four people wouldn't be climbing back into the car. They wouldn't be driving out of here. That reality, the absolute finality of that fact, was terrifying. Four people—four *actual* living, breathing people who had *existed* just an hour ago—no longer existed. They were no longer living and breathing. They were gone. Gone because of him.

The sound of overstressed tires on pavement sent shock waves running through Felix's body. His eyes snapped away from the Mercedes and he looked to the mouth of the parking lot. What he saw made his stomach clench.

A silver sedan was speeding toward them.

Felix stepped away from Bill's car and glanced over at Allison. She nodded at him. She didn't have to say a word because her expression told him everything he needed to know: They were thinking the same thing. Her thoughts mirrored his.

Felix raised a hand toward the sedan, staring ahead blackly. His jaw hardened. A burst of adrenaline pulsed through his veins. Whoever was in the car—the fifth Protector late for the party?—was going to deeply regret coming to the Cliff Walk.

Felix had been stabbed enough for one day.

The sedan skidded to a screeching stop, writhing plumes of blue smoke rising up from the asphalt beneath the tires. The car puffed out exhaust which wafted for only a moment before whipping away in the winds. Then the engine cut out. The driver's door swung open as sheets of sunlight shone down through a swirling veil of cloud cover. Felix stared at the windshield, squinting against the glare, but all he could make out was that the visor was in the down position. He couldn't see the driver's face.

A foot emerged from the car—a dark brown riding boot—followed by another. The driver—a woman, Felix concluded quickly, based on the boots—stood up. Above the door her head appeared; long wavy blonde hair whipped around her face in the wind, covering it up almost completely. Felix still couldn't see her face. Yet there was something familiar about her. He didn't know what it was—the color of her hair? the shape of her head?—but he felt his throat tighten. She turned and started running toward him, her hair falling back from her forehead, dancing on her shoulders. When he saw her face he nearly passed out on his feet.

It was Harper.

Chapter 61

THE UNEXPECTED VISITOR

Felix felt his mouth fall open in astonishment as he watched Harper running toward him. A smile stretched across her face, her cheeks turning instantly pink from the chill. As Harper drew near, she hesitated, some of the newfound color draining from her face. Felix exchanged an uneasy glance with Allison while Harper looked at them suspiciously, no doubt puzzling over what they were doing at the Cliff Walk parking lot in the freezing cold wearing only shorts and sweatshirts. The three of them looked from one to the other, waiting for someone to say something. It was hard to decide who looked the most surprised.

The silence dragged on, weighing heavier with every second.

"Hey Harper," Felix finally muttered, awkwardly, sinking his hands deep into the pockets of his sweatshirt.

And then, to his surprise, Harper ran right up to him and threw her arms around him, hugging him tightly, squeezing him like she was afraid someone was going to rip him from her arms. "Thank God you're okay."

"I'm fine," he murmured.

"Hey." Allison came around the front of Bill's car, giving Felix a questioning look.

"I was so worried about you," Harper said to Felix. "I've been looking for you all morning."

Felix couldn't believe Harper was here—actually here, at the Cliff Walk, in his arms, right this very second. A thousand different things were going through his head all at once, choking off whatever synapses are responsible for speech and higher thought. His few non-oxygen-deprived brain cells were trying to come up with a plausible explanation as to why he and Allison were hanging out at the Cliff Walk with a Range Rover and a Mercedes at their personal disposal—not to mention why their faces were spattered with blood and grime.

Harper took a step back, giving Felix's eyes the space they needed to settle on the familiar features of her face: her gorgeous blue eyes, her broad shapely mouth, and the little spots on her cheeks where dimples formed when she laughed. She looked up at him, smiling shyly. "So do you want to tell me what happened to you guys?"

"Whose car is that?" Allison broke in, pointing at the sedan, a newer model Nissan Altima with Washington plates.

"Fallon's friend." Harper's eyes stayed on Felix. "I have to get it back to her today 'cause she's going back to Olympia tomorrow. I can't even tell you how worried I've been. The same goes for Caitlin and Lucas. You shouldn't have just left without saying anything."

"I know. It's just that..." There was no way to explain to her what had happened in Bill's office, and even if he could, he knew that he didn't want to, so he let the sentence trail off in the wind.

"I didn't know you were so close to our RD," Allison said, her voice guarded. "You've talked to Fallon like three times all year."

"We're not." Harper paused. "But no one's around the dorm but her and some of her friends."

"How'd you find us?" Allison asked.

"Your text." Harper's eyebrows pulled together. "You told us you were in Cove Rock so I went to Felix's grandma's house—thank God for the Internet—but no one was there. It's a good thing it's a small town 'cause I was about to head back to Portland, but I saw you guys driving this"—she looked over at the Range Rover—"when I was getting gas on Main Street. I followed you, but I got caught behind some cars and couldn't see where you'd turned off. I kept going for like another thirty minutes. I knew you must've gotten off the main road somewhere, so I hung a U-ey and went down a few roads looking for you. And then I drove down Cliff Walk Road and saw Felix's car in the parking lot." She smiled brightly at Felix. "And now here I am."

He smiled back, but it felt strained, like he was posing for a school photo.

"*Felix's car?*" Allison said, confused.

Harper tilted her head as though she didn't understand the question. "Yeah," she said after a moment of hesitation, nodding at the Range Rover. "Felix's car."

"You think *that's* Felix's car?" Allison asked with a faint, skeptical laugh. "You're joking, right?"

"Of course I'm joking." Abruptly, Harper started to giggle.

Felix laughed along, although he didn't really get the joke—maybe he was just too fried for humor.

Allison wasn't laughing. She crossed her arms, watching Harper with wary eyes. "So tell me about Felix's car."

"What do you mean?" Harper's tone was defensive.

"What kind of car is it? What's it look like?"

"What's she talking about?" Harper said to Felix, shaking her head and rolling her eyes as if to say *Allison's losing it.*

"C'mon, Harper," Allison persisted. "Simple question. What kind of car does Felix drive?" A sharp edge had crept into her voice.

"It's a car!" Harper snapped through tight lips, throwing up her arms. "Who cares? I don't remember."

"How can you not remember?" Allison said doubtfully. "You've been in it."

"Hey," Felix interjected. "I'm not taking it personally. My car's kinda forgettable. It's not a big deal."

"Forgettable?" Allison shouted over the wind as she uncrossed her arms. "Are you being serious? Your car's a disaster—but definitely not forgettable."

"Whatever." Harper smiled, but it didn't reach up to her eyes.

Allison and Harper stared silently at each other. The air felt tense, and heavier than the cold mist moving in over the shoreline.

With a cock of her head, as if something had suddenly occurred to her, Allison took out her cell from the pocket of her oversized hoodie, tapped the screen and regarded it with a serious expression. Then her eyes grew large and the fine worry lines vanished from her forehead. She looked up from the phone. "So how'd you know we were in Cove Rock?" she said to Harper.

"Your text," Harper said curtly, her expression turning hard. "You already asked me that. What's your deal, anyway?"

"You mean the text where I said, 'He's fine. I got him'. Where'd I say anything about Cove Rock?"

"What are you even talking about?" Harper's voice was edging higher. "If you didn't tell me you were in Cove Rock, then how the hell did I know to come here?"

"Good question!" Allison held out her phone with a quick thrust—arm straight, elbow locked—so that Harper could see the screen. "Read it! Where's it say Cove Rock? C'mon! Read it!"

Harper swatted the phone from Allison's hand. It hit the ground and skipped across the pavement, stopping under the engine block of Bill's car.

A weighty silence descended on the Cliff Walk.

"What the hell?" Allison yelled in surprise. "What are you—"

Without warning—not so much as a word or a twitch—Harper kicked Allison in the side of the head, sending her reeling against the hood of the Range Rover.

Felix was absolutely stunned. He'd seen a lot of crazy things recently—things sane people would simply never believe—but this was right near the apex of that sky-scraping pile of strangeness. He was still trying to figure out why Harper thought he owned a Range Rover and whether or not she'd ever seen his Wrangler (it had been at the repair shop for most of the semester), and the dispute over the text was lost on him because he didn't know what Allison had sent. But now his text and car-related confusion faded into the background as he watched Allison steadying herself against Bill's car, placing a stunned hand over the red blotch on her face where Harper had just unleashed some kind of karate kick he never imagined she was capable of—Harper was into shoes, expensive pocketbooks and romantic comedies. Not martial arts.

Allison pushed herself away from the car, bristling with anger, and went after her. Felix knew he had to do something before things got really out of control. "Hey!" he shouted sharply, reaching out for Harper. "Stop! Both of you!"

The palm of her hand flashed out at him, striking him in the chest. His eyes involuntarily closed for a moment, and when they opened, he found himself reclining on his butt ten feet from where Harper was standing. He sucked in a wheezing breath of cold air, feeling as though his sternum had been grafted onto his spine, like the two were now part of the same skeletal architecture. Harper—all 110 pounds of her—had hit him harder than he'd ever been hit in his life, Jimmy Clay included. After a few more painful breaths, he concluded that his lungs hadn't collapsed, but he was struggling to reorient himself to the strange fact that Harper could punch like a battering ram.

While Felix was trying to chase the clouds from his mind, and trying to breathe, Allison was throwing a hard, seriously-intentioned punch at Harper's face—which she deftly blocked. Harper countered with her own left hook that Allison ducked under. Harper followed that up by exploding on Allison with a flurry of punches and kicks. Allison covered up, using her arms and shins to block the blows. Harper snapped off a kick at Allison's lower leg. Allison jumped and landed a crushing blow to Harper's head, knocking her sideways. Felix expected Harper to be down for the count. But she didn't even wobble; she just allowed the momentum of the punch to carry her over into a cartwheel, then she bounced back up to her feet.

Harper stepped back and acknowledged Allison for a moment with an appraising eye and an approving nod of her head. Then she smiled, placing her hand along the contours of her cheek. "You've got some skills, girl—unlike your boyfriend over there." She jabbed a thumb disparagingly at Felix who was still on his butt, watching the fight like a dumbfounded spectator, stunned into immobility at the sight of Allison and Harper throwing themselves at each other like experienced MMA fighters.

"They say everyone has their own methods," Harper began, glancing back and forth from Allison to Felix. "But if you're going to test someone, why not have a little fun doing it?" She drew her hands behind her waist and clasped them together as if she was about to start pacing. But she didn't—she stayed put, her eyes on Allison. "I've been wanting to do this for a while now. So it's not like I haven't given it any thought." She paused, then broke out into a big smile. "You guys ready to have some fun?" When she brought her hands forward, they were no longer empty.

Felix's first impression was that she was holding an electrical cord in each hand. They were black, coated in rubber, rolled up just like electrical cords get rolled up and stored away when they're not in use, and otherwise very cord-like in every way. Of course that didn't make any sense. Why would Harper be walking around with electrical cords? And where would she be hiding them? In her jacket?

The electrical cords—which was exactly what they turned out to be—uncoiled themselves all on their own, extending out until they reached well past Allison on either side of her, framing her in. And then the air crackled like the gun in Bill's trunk had fired off two rounds.

Felix jumped at the sound—so much so that his butt actually lifted off the blacktop.

Allison was rapidly backpedaling away from Harper, sliding toward the sedan. The electrical cords followed after her, cutting through the air in looping circles, coiling and lashing out like vipers. Like whips. But much longer than whips—nearly twice the length of Fallon's Nissan.

Felix gawked. Then he blinked hard to make sure he wasn't hallucinating. A moment later when his eyes continued to confirm that Harper was in fact wielding a pair of electrical cords, he sprang to his feet and tried to tell her to stop. When he couldn't get his voice to project any sound, he cleared it and tried again.

"Harper, stop." It sounded weak. *Whiny.* Harper heard him but it only made her laugh as she stalked after Allison.

"Come on girlfriend," Harper said sweetly, ignoring Felix, trailing behind the hissing cords.

Allison stole a darting glance at Felix and said, "A little help, please!" The car was to her back. She was almost out of space.

"What's *he* gonna do?" Harper said with a chuckle, and stopped.

"Just calm down," Felix managed to say, moving closer. "I don't want to hurt you."

At that, Harper burst out in a hearty roar of laughter, her eyes briefly moving to Felix before her punishing stare returned to Allison. "Why don't you come closer, Allison? Aren't we friends? I thought we were like BFFs?" One of the cords raised itself up and snapped down inches from Allison's face, rippling the air and sweeping the hair back from her forehead.

Allison jumped back until she was pressing up against the car. Trapped. *"Felix...?"*

"Please, stop," Felix pleaded as the cords swung in circles and loops above Allison's head, slicing through the damp air. "Let's talk."

Harper rolled her eyes at him. "Would you just shut the hell up!"

Felix was close enough now to get a good look at Harper's hands. Any lingering doubts lingered no more: Harper wasn't moving her hands. She just held on to the ends as though she was gripping a pair of pencils in a child's fist-grip. But the cords were moving—which didn't make sense, of course. Unless—

A cord was whistling directly for his face. He jerked his head back and threw himself to the ground. When he lifted his head, he realized Harper had set them up. She wasn't going after him. She wasn't taking him seriously—that much was clear. Her target all along had been Allison.

Both cords had wrapped themselves around Allison's arms, beginning at the elbows and winding their way up to her wrists like lethal vines. The taut cables were stretching her arms out straight and unbending, pulling them away from her body and over her head at forty-five degree angles. From the look on Allison's face, Felix could tell she was trying to break free, though the cords didn't bend or sag.

"That was too easy." Harper puckered her lips in disappointment. "I'd really hate to have to fail you both." She nodded solemnly at Allison. "I thought you, at least, had a shot. But if I have to, I will. After all, I did take an oath. And if you're not Sourcerors that's not really my fault, now is it? Not all of us can be Drestianites."

Drestianites?

The possibility that Harper could actually be a Sourceror—a Drestianite!—had no more than crossed Felix's mind when Allison went airborne. The cords around Allison's arms jerked her feet off the pavement and pulled her toward Harper, who was rearing her head back. As soon as Allison's elevation dropped and her toes skidded along the surface, Harper snapped her head forward and smashed her forehead into Allison's face.

Allison stumbled backward, her eyes went white, and for an instant, her mouth fell open and her head slumped to one side as if she'd lost consciousness. She blinked woozily as blood poured from her mouth. Harper looked amused, like she was watching a sitcom in the common room before dinner. Then she started taunting her. "Ooooh. That looks like it hurt, Allie. Nice move though, don't you think?" She raised her arms and addressed the heavens: "And yes, ladies and gentlemen, *that* just happened! *Boo-yah!*"

Felix sprang into action without thinking about what he was going to do. Harper saw him coming out of the corner of her eye. She turned her head slowly and stared him down, smiling. "Take another step and I'll tear her arms off!"

Felix froze, afraid to move; it didn't seem like an idle threat, especially after watching her toss Allison around like she was weightless. He thought for a moment, but couldn't come up with anything that wouldn't end in broken bones. He was confident that he could break Harper's arms just like he'd broken Tripoli's—*but that would involve breaking Harper's arms*—and there had to be a way to resolve this without crippling Harper. But where did that leave him? He couldn't do nothing. And he obviously couldn't let Harper dismember Allison. So he stood there watching, hoping a better plan would present itself to him—and soon.

And then Allison made a move of her own.

Gripping an electrical cord in each hand, Allison tugged hard and yanked Harper off balance, causing her to lurch forward. Before Harper knew what was happening, Allison slammed her forehead into her face. Harper teetered, looking bewildered, and sank to her butt, blood trickling from her nose. The cord coiled around Allison's left arm shriveled up and thumped to the ground beside her.

The beginnings of a plan came to Felix's mind: If he moved fast he could restrain Harper with her own cord. That way he wouldn't have to break her arms or hurt her. They could even talk; he could find out who she really was and why she was here—maybe there was a sensible explanation for all this. He sprinted for her, keeping his eyes on the cord still looped around Allison's right arm.

The world was upside down. No—not the world—*Felix* was upside down. Upside down and suspended high above the parking lot as though he was a bungee jumper after the descent waiting for the operator to lower him to the surface. His arms hung straight, fingers pointing down. A black cord had coiled itself around his left leg from knee to ankle. He raised his upper body until it was parallel to the ground and forced his fingers under the cord, which was on tighter than a blood pressure sleeve. Then he felt a fierce tug at the ankle, and suddenly, he was heading back to earth, and fast.

Out of instinct, Felix covered up his head as the pavement rose up and greeted him in a cold hard embrace. Scorching pain consumed his whole body. In his line of sight (ground level lying on his belly) were two SUVs and the ticket kiosk in the background. He wondered where Harper was for just a moment before realizing he was facing the wrong way.

Like a jungle snare latching onto a careless animal, Harper snatched him up into the air. He heard Allison shouting his name. He searched for her, but he was swinging back and forth with his eyes pointing down at the asphalt ten feet below. Just as he glimpsed a blurred fragment of Allison—it looked like she was still wobbly, and only the cord was keeping her on her feet—Harper rag-dolled him against the crumbling asphalt, crushing the air out of his lungs.

"Had enough?" Harper looked over at him, giving her head a disappointing shake, unmoved by the fresh blood that spattered his bare legs. She hoisted him back up off the ground and said in a pleasant voice: "I should probably just put you out of your misery since you're no use to us."

Felix caught a glimpse of her face just before his own face smashed into one of the dull yellow parking lines painted in evenly spaced rows across the rain-spotted pavement. She was laughing with her mouth wide open, like a tantruming child gleefully taking out her anger on her most expensive toy to get a reaction from her parents. Through the fog of confusion, he wondered how she could do this to him, and how she could be *enjoying* it.

And then Allison—once again—took matters into her own hands.

Fighting through the cord that Harper was using to shackle her, Allison lunged at Harper and landed a ferocious overhand to the face. Followed by two more: *whack, whack.* The sound of bony knuckles on soft facial tissue split through the misty, moisture-heavy wind currents. The last of Allison's blows opened up a deep gash beneath Harper's left eye.

The choking pressure on Felix's lower leg cut out all at once as the long cable slithered its way back to where Harper stood, returning to the source like a retractable vacuum cord. He dropped out of the sky, tucking his chin to his breastbone at the last second to avoid landing on his head.

When he hit the pavement, something in his back crunched and a shooting pain traveled in waves all the way down to his toes. He forced himself to his stomach, the wind crushed out of him, and watched as Harper put a hand to her face, feeling for the cut and wiping the blood that dribbled down her flushed cheek. For a moment, she examined the blood on her fingers with a look of confusion that slipped into surprise. Then her jaw hardened and she exhaled sharply through her teeth, her eyes burning with fury.

Harper released the cord from Allison's arm.

Allison didn't use the opportunity to flee. Instead, she went on the offensive, kicking viciously at Harper's face. Harper sank low and Allison's boot whistled over her head. Before Allison could pull her foot back, Harper twined a cord around her ankle and yanked her off the ground. Allison flipped head over feet and dangled upside down, throwing punches at the air.

Harper cocked her head and studied Allison—now face to face with her—and a terrifying calmness fell over her eyes. Then the other cord (lying in a loose bundle on the ground next to her) rose up and moved through the air like a probing snake toward Allison's neck.

In a burst of recognition, Felix connected the dull look in Harper's eyes and the cord's destination. What was about to unfold was as certain to him as if he'd already witnessed it. He *knew* that Harper was going to kill Allison. He *knew* that she was going to rip her head clean from her shoulders.

"Stop!" Felix jumped to his feet and pointed at Harper. Now he had to do something—regardless of the risks. He focused his thoughts on the electrical cords, but controlling them was harder than he'd anticipated. It wasn't like manipulating a book or a log or even a sea stack. He felt *resistance*. Like the things themselves didn't want him to control them. He knew he could use more power—*just push harder*—but Harper still had one cord wound around Allison's leg. If he pushed the wrong way or pushed too forcefully, Allison could lose her foot. But pushing gently had an odd effect: given the resistance he was encountering, the substance of the objects, which he *felt* in his mind, began to slip away. It was like trying to control a shadow without manipulating the thing casting it.

So Felix pushed harder.

The cord in Harper's right hand began to thrash wildly like an unattended fire hose. Harper stared at it with a startled look in her eyes. As Felix gained control of it, the whipsawing diminished, until finally, he stopped it in place.

Slowly, carefully, Felix *unwound* the cord looped around Allison's ankle. Harper looked furious, staring with homicidal rage at Allison, thinking that she was the one controlling the cords like a hacker remotely accessing a computer. When Felix finally peeled away the last bit of cord, Allison dropped straight down, head first. She twisted her body and pulled her knees into her chest, striking the pavement with her hands and shins. Then she popped up and hastily backed away from Harper, hurrying to Felix's side, giving him a look he interpreted as *it's about time!*

Harper stared at the cords, then at Felix. Her eyes widened and her face grew dark. She understood what had happened—and who was responsible. "What are you doing?" she screamed at Felix, her eyes bulging with anger.

"Stop and I'll let you go!" Felix shouted at her.

But Harper wouldn't stop. She stubbornly resisted him, refusing to give up control of the weapons. Her arms, extended and held out in front as though she was holding a steering wheel, trembled. Under Felix's control, the cords were long, straight and as rigid as javelins. Harper's legs shook and her knees buckled. She stumbled in the direction of the Nissan, all the while yelling angrily at Felix, cursing at him.

"Just drop those goddamn things!" Felix stepped toward Harper, his face tightening. "We can work this out. Let's talk. You don't have to do this."

"No!" Harper screamed. "This isn't possible! Stop it! Let me go!"

"Harper!" For the first time since Felix saw the car speeding into the lot, he felt *real* anger. And then he felt something else. From the deepest part of his being, an enormous burst of energy erupted and lashed out at the objects in Harper's hands. The part of him that released it had no concern for the consequences. It only wanted to strike Harper down, to teach her a lesson.

The cords surged with electricity, crackling and lighting up like comets entering the atmosphere. The earth rumbled, swelling and receding in thunderous waves. Harper moved her arms out to her sides and widened her base, attempting to stay balanced. Her eyes found Felix and her lips parted as if she was about to say something. And then she was hauled off her feet and sent hurtling across the parking lot like a mosquito straying too close to a ceiling fan. She collided against the driver's side of Fallon's sedan, and for a moment, everything seemed frozen in time. With her hands raised high overhead, the cords went limp, falling behind her where they slapped down on the car, thumping across the hood. Then it began: The car rocked on deflating tires. The hood popped open and slammed into the windshield, snapping off at the brackets and careening off toward the kiosk. Orange and white sparks burst into the sky from the engine and tailpipe. The windows shattered. The tires flattened, sinking in on themselves. The rims crumpled. The cabin lit up bright for a moment. And then—*wha-wuff*—the car exploded in a roaring fireball.

Jaggedy-edged car parts rocketed in every direction. Allison crouched down low and covered her head, but nothing disturbed her or Felix or the space around them. A shroud of black smoke enveloped the parking lot. The air smelled of gasoline and burning rubber. The word 'shield' hadn't flashed across Felix's mind, yet he'd created one, unconsciously, and it was working perfectly, deflecting the flaming debris and preventing the heat of the conflagration from getting through. He took a step toward the car, trying to control the fear swelling inside him. He felt Allison's hand on his arm. He knew that Harper was on the wrong side of the shield. Unprotected. He had to get to her. But he was blind. Beyond the dark swirling veil he couldn't see a thing.

He took another step.

"Not yet," Allison said softly, gently pulling him back.

So they waited.

The frigid winds shifted and changed direction, blowing the dense smoke toward the mountains. Through the haze, the burning wreckage came into view, the winds pulling the flames high into the gray sky. Harper appeared—at first he felt relief, then terror. She looked waifish, a ghostly soldier limping awkwardly toward them, struggling to get to the next trench.

With a thought, Felix dropped the invisible barrier. The temperature spiked instantly, and he heard Allison say "shit" in surprise. Through the huge curls of thick smoke, he saw Harper, still stumbling forward, clutching at her chest. He waded into the field of destruction with Allison beside him. The heat rolled over them, warping the air around them. They covered their faces and picked their way through the smoldering landscape. The acrid smoke limited their visibility to whatever the mercurial winds allowed. Harper stopped moving, hunched over next to a tire set aflame. With thousand-degree air burning down their windpipes, they converged on Harper from opposite sides and dragged her away, retracing their path through the blistered blacktop. Harper made no attempt to support her own weight.

When the air no longer seared their lungs and they had distanced themselves from the worst of the fire and the mechanical carnage, Felix nodded at Allison and they eased Harper onto her back in a sleeping position. His eyes suddenly felt like they were on fire. He dug his knuckles into his sockets, pressing back the stinging smoke.

A startled scream escaped from Allison's lips.

His eyes snapped open, taking a moment to clear, and when they refocused, they fixed on Harper. A metal rod, grooved and cleaved off at the top like the point of a dagger, protruded from the center of Harper's chest. He sucked in a gasping breath and fell to his knees, reaching out for the object. And that was when he realized that Harper's neck was wrecked. It wasn't a cut. It was a divot.

Allison gagged.

Felix stared at the blood—*the life*—pumping out of the horrible wound in steady, predictable bursts. Feeling numb, he jammed his closed hand against Harper's neck, trying to stanch the bleeding. But it was no use. The wound was too deep. No amount of pressure was going to help. "Harper!" he screamed, panicked, a shattering rush of emotion pulsing through him. "I'm sorry. Oh my God. What did I do? What did I do?" The words came out heavy, catching in his throat.

Allison knelt down beside him and took Harper's hand.

"I'm so sorry," Felix whispered hoarsely. The hysteria bubbled up in his chest. His throat was ragged and rusty with smoke and misery. He stared down at the girl who literally took his breath away the first time he saw her—the girl who put his heart into arrhythmia every time she looked at him. He thought (in those infrequent moments when he was brave enough to admit it to himself) that she might be the one—the love of his life, the girl he would spend forever with. And now that girl and all of his perfectly foolish teenage dreams were dying on the cold winter ground in front of him.

Harper tried to speak, but only coughed up blood. The rain, which had settled into a steady, quiet drizzle, suddenly broke, and sunlight filtered in through ribbons of fast-moving clouds, falling over her body.

"Why?" Allison said with thick despair, tears rolling down her cheeks. "Harper, why'd you do this?"

Harper's body shook. Her breathing was wet and rattling. Blood streamed from the corners of her mouth.

Felix was watching Harper die, watching the life drain out of her—and there was nothing he could do to stop it. He felt completely powerless. Helpless.

And then something very strange happened.

Harper's body trembled uncontrollably for a moment. Then her black leggings were no longer black leggings; they were jeans, dark blue but faded in a striped pattern down her thighs. Her black leather jacket with the tab collar and quilting on the shoulders vanished and reappeared as a gray down-filled winter coat. The brown leather riding boots with the buckled straps around the calf and ankle became wheat-colored Timberland work boots. The new clothes were bigger than the old clothes. And the legs, arms and feet that resided within the new clothes appeared to be bulging and lengthening, filling up the jeans, winter coat and Timberlands until they fit properly. So it wasn't just the clothes that had grown. *Harper* had grown. Substantially. Harper's face—the face Felix had fallen in love with on that first night in his dorm room—was also changing. Before Felix's eyes, the clouds of blonde hair withered away, shriveling up into coarser stuff that was now short and just a few shades removed from what most people would consider midnight black. Harper's straight perky nose flattened out and broadened until it was nearly as wide as her mouth. Her lips lost their fullness, becoming straight lines, their prominence diminishing as her chin and jaw grew thicker and wider. The chin grew a dusting of the same coarse black hair—*whiskers*. And finally, her eyes—her beautiful eyes—went from deep blue to coffee-brown, from large and roundish to small and slightly droopy at the corners. It was like watching a girl morphing into a werewolf. Only he wasn't looking at a werewolf. He was looking at a guy. *A guy.*

Harper—the most beautiful girl he'd ever known—had turned into a guy.

Felix struggled to his feet, his hand dripping blood onto the pavement.

"I'm not Harper," the guy croaked. The voice had also changed. Now it was a medium tenor. Everything seemed to have changed—except for his age. He was young, no older than Felix and Allison.

"*What the?*" Allison murmured, stunned. She let go of *his* hand.

Felix was speechless. He didn't know what was going on. *What happened to Harper? Is this Harper? Is Harper really a guy?*

"Where's Harper?" Allison shouted at him. She had already collected her wits as Felix stared down in total bewilderment, his eyes locking onto the goatee, trying to comprehend how Harper could have grown facial hair.

"The airport," he answered softly. "That's where I touched her."

"*Touched her?*" Allison flinched. "What do you mean? Did you hurt her?"

"No. That's how I do it." He coughed up more blood, his face contorting in pain. "That's how I adopt the way people look. I have to touch them."

"Harper's alive?" Felix's voice was high and desperate. A flicker of hope—and understanding—was rising inside him, working its way through the diamond-hard substrate of confusion coating his brain.

He nodded and put a hand on the steel bar, curling his fingers around it.

"So you're *not* Harper?" Felix asked tentatively, as the strange reality of what was happening dawned on him. *This guy wasn't Harper*—Harper wasn't bleeding out in front of him. Some guy—some random guy with a goatee—was bleeding out in front of him. "Who are you then?"

"Riley."

"Who sent you?" Allison asked suddenly. "Did Lofton send you?"

"*Lofton?*" Riley said with surprise in his voice, creasing his forehead. "Lofton would kill me if he knew what I was doing. I just wanted to... to impress... Lynch. I screwed something up and I..." He drifted. "Nobody knows what I'm doing. I'm so stupid." His eyes closed and tears leaked down the sides of his face.

"Who's Lynch?" Felix asked.

Riley didn't respond.

"Who's Lynch?" Felix repeated, shouting this time.

Riley struggled against the weight of his eyelids. "I saw your names on the list. That's all. I thought I'd test you. I guess I got carried away. Stupid. I'm always so... stupid."

"What list?" Allison asked.

"The list," Riley said quietly, his voice barely audible, the shifting winds drowning him out. "You're all on it. Your friends. Lots of other people too."

"What's it for?" Felix asked anxiously. "Are you looking for Drestianites?"

Riley stared vacantly at Felix. "No one's ever done that to me before. Not even Lynch. Or the others. How'd you do that?"

"What's Lofton doing?" Felix screamed, restraining a sudden urge to beat the answers out of him. "What's he doing with the list?" He stepped back a ways to stay clear of the ever-expanding pool of blood forming around Riley's neck.

"He's looking for someone," Riley said weakly. "I just wanted to go on an adventure." He coughed. "Like in the movies. Prove I could do something important."

"Who's he looking for?" Felix shouted.

"I don't want to die." Riley sounded scared. Tears welled up in his frightened eyes and slid down his face, leaving trails in the sooty film of smoke residue on his cheeks. "It hurts. It hurts so much. I don't wanna die. Not like this."

"Who's he looking for?" Felix shouted again.

"I don't wanna…" Riley began, and then his eyes dimmed and went still, half-open and looking up at the sky in an empty death stare.

"Hey!" Straddling the blood on the ground, Felix grabbed his coat and gave him a rough shake. *"Hey!* Who's he looking for? *Hey!"*

"He's gone!" Allison got up and tugged on Felix's arm. "C'mon! Someone's gonna see all this smoke. The fire department will be here soon."

Felix gazed down at Riley, slowly shaking his head in wonder. He couldn't believe that just a moment ago, Riley had been Harper—or at least, Riley had *looked* just like Harper. It was still mystifying. "What do we do with him?"

"Leave him," Allison replied as she headed for the Range Rover. "Let's get the hell outta here!" She retrieved her phone from under the car before climbing into the passenger seat.

Felix followed after her and slipped in behind the steering wheel, slamming the door shut. "What do we do about this?" He stabbed a finger at himself, then at Allison. He was bloodied from his face to his feet. She didn't look much better; her lips were split open, one eye had swollen nearly shut and dried blood crusted the lower half of her face.

"We'll have to find a rest stop on the way."

Felix started the car and floored it, pulling out of the parking lot and leaving the Cliff Walk behind.

Chapter 62

THE DRIVE

"I didn't just kill Harper, right?" Felix asked with fear in his voice as the Range Rover rolled over what was left of the roadblocks. Any clarity or relief he'd felt just a moment ago was already gone, replaced with endless avenues of confusion.

"I don't think so." Allison was tapping on her phone, using her thumbs.

"Should we call her?"

"Already ahead of you. But I'm not sure she'd want to talk to either of us right now." She placed the phone on her lap. "I just texted Caitlin. She should be home by now."

"Why wouldn't she want to talk to me?" Felix asked after a moment's reflection, confused. "What'd I do?"

"Did you tell her something about your parents' attorney? That you had to meet with him?"

"Yeah. The night I... went to Bill's."

"Well"—she shivered and cranked up the cabin temperature—"I might've told her you didn't have any reason to see him."

"*What?* Why'd you do that?"

"I wasn't worried about Harper catching you in a lie. I'd just found out that no one knew where you were and I was scared shitless. It just... slipped out."

"Great," he muttered sarcastically.

Just as they turned onto a country two-lane—and before Felix had time to dwell on the revelation that Harper was mad at him—Allison's phone beeped.

"It's Caitlin," she said, looking down at the screen.

"*And...?*" He was nervous. He knew he shouldn't be, but he needed confirmation—he needed proof of life.

"She says, 'Flight was fine. At home. Harper's staying for dinner.

Already bored to death. Miss school so much—even that idiot Lucas. Call me later.'"

"Harper's staying for dinner?"

"That's what it says."

"So she's there?" he said hopefully. "At Caitlin's?"

Allison nodded.

Felix breathed a double sigh of relief. The first for Harper. She was alive. He hadn't killed her. Good thing—*very good thing.* He reserved the second for himself: Now he could stop worrying about the possibility that Riley had catfished him on a supernatural level.

"Crazy though, huh?" Allison was leaning forward in her chair to check out her eye in the visor mirror. It wasn't getting any better. She needed ice. "What'd that kid say? He *adopts* the way people look? Just what the world needs—Sourcerors who can take the appearance of anyone they want. That's scary on so many different levels."

"No shit," he agreed. It was actually terrifying. Too terrifying to contemplate at the moment. Felix swerved the car around the remains of a dead animal in the middle of their lane—maybe a deer?—that looked like every scavenger in the state had snacked on it. "That list Riley was talking about—you think the Faceman had one too? He knew about me and Lucas. Must be the same list, right? But why are we all on it? You think it's random?"

"No idea." Allison snapped the plastic cover over the mirror and flipped the visor back in place. "We're going to have to tell them, you know."

Felix had been thinking the same thing. "Tell them what though?"

"Everything," she answered simply.

"Bill's not gonna like that."

"Screw Bill! What do you think would happen if one of Lofton's minions kidnaps Caitlin and tells her to move a brick with her mind?"

"Nothing good." He imagined Caitlin cowering in the shadow of the Faceman, a brick on the floor between them. It made him shiver almost as much as Allison—even though he was starting to feel a little warm. "I can't let that happen. I'm just not sure how I can…" Felix left the rest unsaid, the sentence without a conclusion, not wanting to verbalize something so obvious: Lucas was in Minnesota; Harper and Caitlin were in California; Allison would be spending the break in Coos Bridge. How was he supposed to protect everybody—even assuming he could—when they were spread out across half the damn country?

Allison seemed to sense what he was worrying about. "We'll figure something out," she assured him. "We just need a plan. And we need to be smart."

"Yeah," Felix snorted. His planning skills needed some sharpening. The only thing he was planning for now was how to get cleaned up before they got back to school. The gritty surface of the parking lot had scraped away most of the skin on his hands and everything from the knees down. It didn't hurt, but the intense itching sensation was annoying. He thought if he could scrape the blood off it might help. "I'll pull over if I see a rest area. We need to change out of these clothes."

She nodded, looking out the window. She opened her mouth in a huge yawn and said, "More sweaty gym shorts?"

He grunted. He didn't think Allison was going to like the available options in the duffel bag.

* * *

Thirty miles down the road, Allison looked over at him and cleared her throat. "What are you thinking about?"

He shook his head and shrugged tiredly. He could still hear the roar of the wind in his ears. The inside of the car smelled like the ocean. And blood. He'd been driving in the slow lane along Highway 30, trying not to draw the attention of any state troopers. He felt her eyes on him but kept his on the road, staring straight ahead at nothing.

"Felix…?"

"I'm just wiped out. You wanna listen to a different station?" He hit the preset button a few times until he found a satellite channel playing an *Imagine Dragons* song he knew Allison liked.

"C'mon," she said, her eyebrows drawn in. "What's on your mind?"

He turned off the windshield wipers. The drizzle had thickened into a soft pattering rain, then went back to being a drizzle. But now that he thought about it, he hadn't seen a drop in a while. "I don't know. I guess, it's just that, back there, at the Cliff Walk… it's… nothing."

"Felix!"

"I just killed five people, Allie. Five!" He held up five fingers in case the word *five* didn't do justice to the enormity of the number when the subject was *how many people have you killed today?* "And that one big guy…" He hesitated. He couldn't tell Allison that he'd tortured Parni to death. If he hadn't died on him before he was done (whatever *done* might mean), he could still be out on the Cliff Walk listening to his blood-curdling screams. And liking it. "I... *burned* him alive."

"He nearly landed on me on the way down," Allison said. "When'd you start doing... *that?*"

"Doing what?"

"Controlling fire." Her voice sounded cautious.

"I don't know. A month ago, I guess. But I never used it to, you know..."

A frown hovered on the edges of Allison's lips, then her face went blank. "So you can just burn things? With your... just your mind?"

He nodded, but didn't elaborate. Neither of them spoke for a long time. He glanced at her, but couldn't make sense of her expression.

"But you thought he killed me, right?" Allison finally said. "You must've been pissed. I'd be pissed if I thought someone had killed you. I don't know what I would do."

For a moment, Felix relived the terrible pain that had ripped through him when he thought Allison had died and a deep ache spread from his chest, tightening his throat. "But there's... there's more."

"*More?*"

"The Faceman. I killed him too—remember. And Riley. And I killed... my... my parents." He took his eyes off the road and looked at her, blinking back the tears, fighting them off. "I've killed *eight* people since last summer. That can't be a good thing."

She nodded, and stared out her window in silence.

Three miles later, and still no response, he turned his head toward her. Her expression hadn't changed. Still unreadable. "I thought you'd try to cheer me up," he told her.

"Sorry," she said a little absentmindedly. She tried to smile but it turned into a wince. "I was just thinking that... this is only the beginning." She looked down at her hands, brow creasing, while Felix fidgeted with the steering wheel, waiting for her to continue. When she did, she sounded calm, almost sleepy.

"What happened to your parents wasn't your fault," Allison went on. "You know that. But you killed the Faceman, the Protectors and that Riley kid—*who was a Drestianite, by the way*—because you didn't have a choice. They were trying to kill you. If you hadn't killed them, you'd be dead. And so would I. You understand that, right?"

"I don't want to kill anyone," Felix said quietly.

Allison smiled, but the effort just made her wince again. She dragged a finger over a bottom lip that would probably need a few stitches. "I'm glad it bothers you. I'd be a little worried if killing people didn't prick your conscience. Especially with what... what you can do. I mean, you can do some pretty incredible shit. But I think it's just going to get worse. There's going to be *more*: more Protectors, more Facemen, more Drestianites, more whatever the hell's out there. And if you don't kill them..."

"They'll kill me. I know. I get it. But it still sucks."

Her shoulders lifted and fell in a stiff shrug. Then she made a fist, running her fingers over her bruised knuckles.

"When'd you become such a badass, anyway?" Felix asked, forcing a grin. "You were kicking the shit out of Riley and that huge Parni guy."

Allison's voice was still calm, but her eyes were dark and focused. "When I was fighting with Parni—and Riley—it was like I was watching myself from above. I was punching, kicking and dodging punches, and doing all these things, and I don't even know how I was doing it." She unclenched her hand.

"You ever take boxing, or an MMA class, or anything like that before?"

Allison shook her head, then took a fistful of hair with one hand, and with the other rolled the tips between her fingers as though she was checking for split ends. "Maybe it's a Croix thing."

That gave Felix a jolt. "A what thing?"

"Croix. My real name. The name I was born with, anyway. C-R-O—"

"I-X," he finished quickly. A strip of skin that ran right down the center of his back began to crawl. "C-R-O-I-X. Croix?"

"Yeah," she said, watching him.

"Seriously?"

"Yeah. So? Why?"

"I never knew that," Felix said.

"Why would you? I don't think I ever told you. So what?"

"You ever hear of Agatha Pierre-Croix?"

"Agatha Pierre-Croix?" Allison repeated softly, her eyes narrowing in thought. "You mean PC's founder?"

"Uh-huh." Something told him it wasn't a coincidence.

"What?" Allison gave him a sharp look. "You think she's a distant relative or something? I don't think the name's *that* uncommon."

What do I think? I think she's a ghost who lives in the tunnels beneath St. Rose, he'd started to say, but caught himself. For now, he just shrugged and said nothing. The silence lengthened. Allison watched him, her eyes keen and questioning. They rode through a valley of blanketing ground fog that made the road disappear like a magic trick. Felix stared out at the swirling dragon's breath, too tired to talk and too tired to think. He would tell Allison about the ghost of Agatha, the tunnels and the cemetery beneath campus, room 444 at Astoria, and that he was *The Kid With The Hood*—she would probably think that last part was hysterical—but not right now. That was a long story, and he was too exhausted to get into it. Later.

"Do you—" She broke off, paused for a second, then gave her head an adamant shake. "Where's your phone?" She thrust out her hand. "I want to talk to Bill."

Felix reached into the pocket of his baggy gym shorts (once a shade of pale blue, now dark red), brought out his cell, unlocked it, and handed it to her. She tapped, scrolled, tapped twice more, then placed it in a cup holder between the seats when she was done.

Bill answered on the second ring. "Hello?" The phone was on speaker. "Felix? Hello?" He sounded anxious.

"Yeah," Felix said. "Hey Bill." An oncoming car with lights on top sped toward them, closing the distance a little too quickly. Sweat was trickling down his sides—but that was because Allison had set the temperature to seventy-eight degrees. He eased down on the brake, even though he was already going a needle tick under the speed limit, but it was only a service truck from the Department of Fish and Wildlife.

"It's really good to hear your voice," Bill said, the relief in his voice thick. "Are you okay? Is Allison with you?"

"I'm here," she said.

"Hi, Allison. I thought you guys might already be here."

Felix glanced over at Allison, but she just looked back at him bleakly—his cue to explain why they were running late. "Yeah, we had a little... *incident* with the Protectors." Then Felix added: "And a Sourceror."

There was silence.

"You there?" Felix's eyes flitted down to the phone.

"Was the Sourceror with the Order?" Bill asked hesitantly.

"No," Felix replied.

Bill spoke in a rush: "Grab your passports and meet me at PDX. I have a safe house in—"

"Lofton doesn't know," Allison interrupted. "The kid was acting on his own."

Another pause. This one longer.

"How can you be sure of that?" Bill asked.

"He told us," Allison answered.

"But how—" Bill began.

"He was telling the truth." Allison ran a finger over her swollen eye and grimaced in pain, her lips pulling back over her teeth.

Felix believed her. Maybe it was the unwavering certainty in her voice. Maybe it was something else. Whatever it was, Bill seemed to believe her too.

"Okay. Okay. So what happened? Are you guys okay? What happened to the Protectors? And the Sourceror?"

"We're fine." Felix's knuckles tightened on the wheel, going white. "The kid um... um... I... the Protectors... they um... I didn't have a choice so—"

"Felix took care of them," Allison answered for him. Bill started to say something, and she blurted out: "We need to talk to you. Your office in forty-five." She tapped the screen, ending the call.

Felix glanced over at her, surprised. "What's up?"

Allison ignored him. She had her phone back out and was pecking at it with her index finger, searching for something.

The ground fog had returned. Reluctantly, Felix focused on the road, throwing sideways glances at her as she manipulated the display.

"...have you thought about exploring other challenges?" came a woman's voice from the phone. A plucky broadcaster's voice.

"Who's that?" Felix asked.

"I think I know what Bill's been lying about," Allison said distantly, preoccupied.

"What?"

A man's voice: "...in public places. One day we will live without fear. When the people..."

"Is that Lofton—?" Felix started.

"Yes," Allison said, aiming a hand at him: Be quiet.

A woman's voice: "...all thought to be in the vicinity of Ashfield Forest at the time of their..."

"Is that—?"

"Yes," Allison said, then she shushed him.

Lofton's voice: "...hundreds of square miles of wilderness. Some of the most rugged and densely wooded terrain in North America. It's also home to wild animals such as bears, mountain lions and wolves. The woods can..."

Allison tapped the phone, her jaw clenched. "Wolves. Did you hear that? He said wolves."

"So?" Felix said. Then it hit him. "You mean—?"

"That lying motherfucker."

Chapter 63

THE TEN-HEADED BEAST

The peppering began as soon as Felix and Allison entered Bill's office: "Where did you first see the Protectors? Cove Rock? How many were there? Did the Drestianite tell you anything? Any idea how they found you? Did anyone see what happened?"

"Why don't you tell us about Ashfield Forest?" Allison countered.

Felix went over to the window without a word and looked out. He didn't want to get into it with Bill. But he wasn't going to stop Allison. It was raining again, and the sky, dark and foreboding, reflected his mood. The Yard was deserted. Other than a scattering of lonely stragglers still packing up or waiting for rides, everyone had gone home; the entire campus had assumed the same general air of ghostliness as the Old Campus.

"Sorry?" Bill looked startled as he sat at his desk with his laptop open in front of him.

"Ashfield Forest," she repeated, slowly articulating each syllable. "Why don't you tell Felix the truth? And if you say 'wolves', I'm going to slap your face off. You told us Lofton was protecting the governor because the governor had allowed the reintroduction of wolves. You said Lofton was keeping it quiet. So why would Lofton tell Connie Redgrave on national TV that there are wolves in Ashfield Forest? Does that strike you as somewhat inconsistent?"

Bill measured her for a moment, then sighed and shifted his gaze to Felix. "It's not that simple."

"Just tell him the truth!" Allison shouted. "Why's that so hard?"

"I was hoping to do this at a later date," Bill said with dismay in his voice. He looked over Allison's shoulder toward the window for a moment, then half-snorted and shook his head as though the irony of some private joke was amusing him. He reached down with one hand and pulled open a desk drawer, and after a bit of shuffling, he came away with a sheet of paper, yellowed and rolled up like architectural plans. He got up from his chair and carried it across the office, then spread it out on the table beneath the window where Felix was standing.

Felix could see right away that it was a map of some kind. At the top, and centered, was the word WILDERNESS. Diagonal green lines filled up most of the map. But there were other colors. A fair amount of blue: a teardrop shape with the words CLEAR LAKE next to it stood out near one corner, with two smaller teardrops (unnamed) opposite it, and squiggly lines (some long, some short) that could only be rivers. There were portions shaded-in with browns (both light and dark), and heavy green lines that framed in large tracts of land within their boundaries. There were two prominent black lines too long and too straight to be anything other than roads, and several smaller lines (black but fading to gray) that wound their way here and there without any obvious start or end points. Most of the smaller lines had been highlighted with an orange marker. There were a few big numbers, which made Felix think they were elevations. And ten Roman numerals: I through X. I, II, III, IV and V were stamped, and evenly spaced, across the bottom, and VI, VII, VIII, IX and X were imprinted at the top directly above I through V.

Allison joined Felix and Bill at the table, squeezing herself between them. "Where is this? What's that?" She pointed at four red circles (one with an X through it) that Felix had just noticed. Bill didn't react when he saw her knuckles: pink, puffy and capped with bloody open wounds that hadn't had time to scab over.

"What you're looking at," Bill explained, using his cell phone to anchor down one side that kept curling up, "is a map of Ashfield Forest. It's actually an old forest service map I've been updating for a very long time. The forest is divided into ten quadrants, which is an old state bureau of land management designation. Anyway, each quadrant is forty square miles. What you're pointing at"—he nodded at Allison—"are facilities where something I've been searching for may be… hiding. I recently crossed out one site—the one with the X—because I concluded they're not there. But these three circles here, here and here"—he drummed on the map with his forefinger—"are all possibilities."

"What's that have to do with the people getting ki—" Allison started to say.

"I'm getting to that." Bill shifted the map a quarter turn clockwise. "Now these blue dots"—there were two—"represent the location of the bodies found last summer. And these dots"—there were seven, also blue—"represent the last known locations of the people still missing."

"They're all grouped together," Felix noted, examining the dots as he tried to make sense of their relationship to everything else on the map. In some ways, it was easier to read than a standard roadmap, but the scale was confusing, and there was no legend to use for guidance.

"Except for these two," Bill pointed out, using the knuckle of his little finger to rap on the blue dots a few map inches removed from the others. "This is Dobbs Highway." With a quick vertical stroke of his finger, he traced the path of one of the bold black lines—this one tracked all the way across the map's length from west to east. "It separates Ashfield Forest from this land over here"—he flipped a thumb sideways to indicate north—"which is still owned by the state. This is where Mia Vujicic told her friends she was taking her boyfriend Ethan Powers for some sort of birthday surprise hike in the woods. Mia and Ethan haven't been seen since."

"They've been on the news a lot." Allison leaned forward over the map, practically obscuring Felix's view of it with the back of her head. "I've seen missing person posters all over town with their pictures."

Bill nodded. "So aside from them, there's an obvious cluster in the seventh and eighth quadrants which I think is still significant despite the one anomalous event."

Allison shook her head sharply, then turned to look up at Bill. "All these dots and circles are really pretty, but why don't you tell Felix—"

"Do you need some ice for your face?" Bill interrupted. "I have some Advil if you need it. You have a lot of swelling. You should take something."

"No," she said, annoyed. "I'm fine." She wasn't fine. Her eye had swollen completely shut, and besides the pain (she'd told Felix in the car that her whole face was throbbing and aching badly), she was having problems with her depth perception and it was making her dizzy. When they'd come up the stairs to Bill's office, they had to stop at the second-floor landing because she felt like she was going to throw up.

Bill sniffed the air. "What's that smell? Do you guys smell something?"

"It's our clothes," Felix admitted, too tired to care about the stench. They'd given up on the idea of cleaning up at a rest stop when they realized they looked like participants in a chainsaw massacre. Instead, they came across a country creek—as winding and bucolic as a Thomas Kinkade painting—not far from the highway. They cleaned up in the icy waters, washing off the battle detritus, the blood, dirt, and some spongy stuff Felix found stuck to his hair that he was forced to acknowledge had once resided inside the dark-haired man's skull. When they finished their impromptu nature baths, they'd changed into clothes even ranker than the ones they'd put on at the Cliff Walk parking lot. Felix had ended up ditching his old clothes, unsalvageable as they were, under a mound of pine needles in a grove next to the creek.

"Why are you stalling?" Allison demanded. "We stink. We get it. Now tell us what's happening in the forest."

Bill pressed his fingers to his temples and let out a heaving sigh. Then he gave Allison a long, exasperated look. "It's not wolves. And all those people"—he swept his hand over the map—"they're not *missing*. They're dead. And their bodies will never be found."

"I knew it!" Allison looked at Bill as if to say *I would very much like for you to drop dead right now.* "I knew you were lying about something."

Felix shook his head and gazed out the window. What little light remained—gray, cold and depressing—was already dimming as dusk descended on the campus. The sun would soon be setting beyond Ferguson Hall and Stubbins Stadium. He hated the short winter days. "So what is it?" he asked wearily.

"I did it for your own good, Felix," Bill said earnestly. "I was going to tell you at a better time. Please try to understand. You've been through so much this year. I just didn't think it was fair to tell you about the... things... that are... well..."

"What is it?" Felix asked sharply. "The what?"

Bill tucked his hands into his armpits and looked at them steadily, his expression hardening. "I don't know everything we need to know, but what I do know is this: They eat what they kill. They're vicious. They're strong. Fast—invisibly fast. They're smart. They're pack hunters. They're not animals but they're not human either. I don't know their numbers. I believe Lofton created them. And we need to stop them before he uses them for whatever he's planning."

Felix turned away from the window, his anger rising up to his throat. "You lied to me! I asked you straight up. *And you lied.*"

"I thought it was the right thing to do."

"Brilliant," Allison said with disgust. "How the hell could you do this to him? He trusts you!"

"And what do you mean *stop them*?" Felix asked, his voice calm. His anger had no legs. He was too tapped out to sustain any emotion.

"That's what I've been searching for." Bill turned and went to his desk, the floorboards creaking under his feet. He sat down on the edge, his back brushing up against a green-shaded banker's lamp, and pointed toward the map. "That's what those red circles there are all about."

Allison nearly stubbed her nose into the map, tilting her head so that her working eye was directly over Roman numerals VII and VIII. "What are you talking about? The buildings?"

"Yes. I have a theory. I believe Lofton keeps them somewhere, at least during the night. If we're talking about significant numbers—and I think we are—then the building they would require must be significant in size. If we can locate where they shelter, we can take care of them—*all of them*—in a single surgical strike."

"So you need to go into the forest?" Felix's eyes shifted to the map.

"*We* need to go into the forest," Bill corrected. "And soon. I don't know what Lofton has in mind, but given the frequency of the attacks and the fact that the last two were killed outside Ashfield Forest, I think we need to act quickly."

"How quickly?" Felix asked reluctantly, unsure if he was prepared for the answer.

"Spring." Then Bill paused for a second and added: "At the latest."

"*Spring?*" Felix choked out. He stared blankly at the window without really seeing anything beyond it as the meaning of that word settled in, working its way into his exhausted brain.

"Well this is just fantastic!" Allison snapped at Bill. "It's not enough to send Felix into Lofton's forest. You were planning to do it without telling him that there are monsters out there eating people."

"You haven't been listening to a word I've said!" Bill snapped back, his face reddening in anger. His expression sank for a moment and his eyes dropped slowly to the floor, embarrassed. He slipped his hands into the pockets of his heather gray slacks, then took them out and crossed his arms uncomfortably. He moved a few paces toward them, his gaze directed at Allison. "I was going to tell Felix," he said in a low voice, "but not until after the break. It wasn't something I wanted to burden him with just yet." Then he turned to Felix and said softly, "I really am sorry about not being completely truthful with you. But you must know I only have your best interests in mind."

"Brilliant." Allison's eyes shone with fury. "You're seriously unbelievable."

Felix wasn't sure what to do with any of this. He'd just had an all-out battle with four Protectors—and *killed* them. If that wasn't awful enough, he'd also killed Harper. Or at least, he thought he'd killed Harper until Riley changed back into a guy. And for a few horrifying moments, he thought Allison had died. And now Bill was telling him that in the very near future, he would have to go into Ashfield Forest to kill monsters.

How much more of this can I take? Felix looked around the room, trying to clear his head. Everything was coming at him in waves. It was like a ten-headed mythological beast that couldn't be killed—every time he lopped off one of its heads, two more just sprang up to take its place. An object in the corner captured his attention: His winter jacket was draped across the back of a chair. He'd left it the last time he was here—the night he watched himself kill his parents. The images of that night flashed through his mind, and he felt the dread and the sorrow stirring inside him. He felt hot. The air was thick... and smoky. Sweat began to roll down the back of his neck. He was out of breath. He needed to get some air.

"You okay?" Bill asked him, seeing the consternation on his face.

Breathe, Felix told himself. *Breathe.* He stood silent, looking down at his feet, determined to pull himself together. When he raised his head, he managed a nod, and tried to be convincing about it. But from the skeptical look on Bill's face, he gathered that he wasn't very successful.

Bill smiled sympathetically at Felix. Then he turned to Allison and said accusingly, "See? This is obviously too much for him right now. Which is why it would've been better to discuss this after the break."

"*Sure!*" Allison replied with bitter sarcasm. "Let's just conceal the truth until it's more convenient for *you.* That makes perfect sense. It makes as much sense as throwing Felix into the woods with a bunch of monsters."

Bill was working his jaw, gritting his teeth. Then he closed his eyes for a moment and exhaled slowly through his nose. Felix recognized it as one of the relaxation techniques he had taught him after he set Allison's room on fire.

"I can't believe you kept this from him!" Allison persisted, her face flushing so much Felix worried that her nose and lips were going to start bleeding again. "And you"—she whirled on Felix—"I can't believe you're so calm. You should be pissed at him!"

"I'm too tired to be pissed," Felix muttered after a moment's reflection. "I wish he hadn't lied, but I understand why he did. If he'd told me about this earlier, I don't know if I could've handled it. It's not like he's trying to kill me." He glanced at Bill doubtfully. "Right?"

"I promised Elissa—*your mother*—on her deathbed that I would look after you. I didn't make that promise lightly." Bill's face seemed to age before them, his voice husky, raw. "I knew what... I knew... I understood that making that promise would result in certain... consequences. And I accepted them. All of them. And as much as I want to keep you safe, we're going to have to take some calculated risks. But believe me, I'm doing everything in my power to prepare you and protect you. Felix, your life is more important than anything in this world. If you die, we're all as good as dead. You're the Belus, after all."

"I'm the Belus," Felix repeated vaguely. "That reminds me. One of the Protectors told me that I'm not the one. What'd she mean?"

"I don't know," Bill said too quickly, shaking his head. *"You're not the one?* I have no idea what that means."

"You're lying!" Allison pointed an accusing finger at Bill. "That's a lie. You confess to one lie and then you lie about something else!"

"I assure you I am not lying," Bill said solemnly, placing a hand over his heart.

"Then why would she say that to me?" Felix asked.

"It doesn't mean anything," Bill told him. *"The one?* The one *what?* Sounds like gibberish to me. It could be a... tactic of some kind. Psychological warfare. The Protectors might be trying to get inside your head. Maybe they're trying to make you doubt yourself." He shrugged. "That's the only explanation I can think of."

Allison checked her watch. "That's about all the psycho-babble crap I can take for one day. My mom's going to be here soon." She started for the hallway and looked back at Felix. "You coming?"

"Yeah. Oh—hey Bill, you mind if I borrow your car during the break? I didn't think mine could make it here and back so we just took yours."

"Sure," Bill replied absently, as if he hadn't been listening. "I've got a spare."

Felix moved toward the door.

"So you won't be going together, then?" Bill asked.

There was a hitch in Bill's voice that gave Felix pause; it sounded like he was implying something. Felix stopped next to Allison in the doorway. "I'm going back to Cove Rock," he said.

"And you're going home?" Bill said to Allison.

She nodded.

"I don't think that's a good idea." Bill stepped closer. Felix could see that his eyes were rimmed red. It looked like he hadn't been getting much sleep. "The Protectors have tried to kill you twice—*both of you*—and they'll try again. And even if Lofton isn't aware that one of his Drestianites paid you a visit, the fact that you killed him complicates matters exponentially." He regarded Allison thoughtfully. "I think you should spend the winter break with Felix. You'll be far safer if you're with him."

She laughed derisively. "I don't think my parents will go for that."

"Would your parents rather you be alive and with Felix or dead and living at home?" Bill's expression was grave. So was his tone. He wasn't offering up a suggestion.

The office went quiet.

"He's got a point," Felix said to Allison. "If they come after you when I'm in Cove Rock, what'll you do? If something happened to you"—he dropped his gaze to the floor—"I... I don't... I don't know what I'd..." He looked up and stared into the one eye that was still visible. "I can't do this without you, Allie. I need you."

She bit down on her lip, her face twisting in pain, and forced her wounded eye to open. Then she stared back at him. Her dazzling green eyes, so full of passion and tenacity, softened all at once. "Oh geez." She smiled hesitantly, her lips actually twitching up at the corners. And this time, she didn't wince. "You're probably right. Shit. I can't wait to have that conversation with my parents."

Bill cleared his throat to get their attention. "If either of you need anything—anything at all—call me. Get some rest. You're going to be very busy next semester. I expect it to be quite... eventful. And be careful. The world's a hazardous place for the two of you. There are powerful forces out there that want you dead. They're all dangerous—*extremely* dangerous."

With one foot out the door, Felix turned to Bill, a crooked smile slowly creeping across his face. "So am I."

END OF BOOK ONE

Made in the USA
Middletown, DE
26 June 2016